W9-ASH-916

The
Beverly Lewis
Amish Romance
COLLECTION

Books by Beverly Lewis

The Proving • *The Ebb Tide* • *The Wish*
The Atonement • *The Photograph*
The Love Letters • *The River*

HOME TO HICKORY HOLLOW

The Fiddler • *The Bridesmaid* • *The Guardian*
The Secret Keeper • *The Last Bride*

THE ROSE TRILOGY

The Thorn • *The Judgment* • *The Mercy*

ABRAM'S DAUGHTERS

The Covenant • *The Betrayal* • *The Sacrifice*
The Prodigal • *The Revelation*

THE HERITAGE OF LANCASTER COUNTY

The Shunning • *The Confession* • *The Reckoning*

ANNIE'S PEOPLE

The Preacher's Daughter • *The Englisher* • *The Brethren*

THE COURTSHIP OF NELLIE FISHER

The Parting • *The Forbidden* • *The Longing*

SEASONS OF GRACE

The Secret • *The Missing* • *The Telling*

The Postcard • *The Crossroad*

The Redemption of Sarah Cain
Sanctuary (with David Lewis) • *Child of Mine* (with David Lewis)
The Sunroom • *October Song*

Amish Prayers
The Beverly Lewis Amish Heritage Cookbook

www.beverlylewis.com

The
Beverly Lewis
Amish Romance
COLLECTION

BEVERLY
LEWIS

The Bridesmaid
The Secret Keeper
The Photograph

BETHANYHOUSE

a division of Baker Publishing Group
Minneapolis, Minnesota

© 2012, 2013, 2015 by Beverly M. Lewis, Inc.

Previously published in three separate volumes:
  The Bridesmaid © 2012
  The Secret Keeper © 2013
  The Photograph © 2015

Published by Bethany House Publishers
11400 Hampshire Avenue South
Bloomington, Minnesota 55438
www.bethanyhouse.com

Bethany House Publishers is a division of
Baker Publishing Group, Grand Rapids, Michigan

Printed in the United States of America

All rights reserved. No part of this publication may be reproduced, stored in a retrieval system, or transmitted in any form or by any means—for example, electronic, photocopy, recording—without the prior written permission of the publisher. The only exception is brief quotations in printed reviews.

ISBN 978-0-7642-3164-3

Library of Congress Control Number: 2017942069

The poem quoted in chapter 18 of *The Secret Keeper* can be found in its entirety under "Morning Thoughts" in the June 1859 copy of *The Friend of Youth and Child's Magazine.*

Scripture quotations are from the King James Version of the Bible.

This story is a work of fiction. With the exception of recognized historical figures and events, all characters and events are the product of the author's imagination. Any resemblance to any person, living or dead, is purely coincidental.

Cover design by Eric Walljasper

17 18 19 20 21 22 23   7 6 5 4 3 2 1

Contents

The
Bridesmaid

Prologue

*T*HREE *times a bridesmaid, never a bride."*

That's just what my younger sister said about me—in front of our engaged cousins, no less—most of them planning to marry come Amish wedding season. A mere five months away.

Seventeen-year-old Cora Jane's words echoed in my head . . . and rippled through my heart. *Jah*, she was as superstitious as many of us in Hickory Hollow, but to be so glib about announcing it?

There I was, sitting on the sand at Virginia Beach, surrounded by oodles of *Englischers*—families with little children, young couples, and singles like me. All had come for the sunset. Some were celebrating more than others, relaxing on their portable beach chairs with cans of soft drinks.

Meanwhile, my younger Witmer cousins, Malinda, Ruthann, and Lena—first cousins to each other—and my fair-haired sister Cora Jane were up yonder on the boardwalk, laughing and eating cotton candy. Sighing, I recalled Cousin Malinda earlier today, looking mighty excited when she asked me to be in her wedding. We had been packing sandwiches with Cora Jane and the others for a picnic lunch when Malinda leaned over to ask me, her face pink from more than the June sun. If I was to agree, it would be the third time I'd be a *Newesitzer*—side sitter, or attendant in a wedding.

"It just ain't schmaert, Joanna," Cora Jane warned, her big blue eyes flashing. "You're already twenty-four, ya know!"

And still a Maidel. I shrugged away the wretched thought. Drawing a

9

long breath, I tried to relax on the beach, alone with my writing notebook . . . away from Cousin Malinda and other relatives who'd come to attend tomorrow's funeral for my great-uncle Amos Kurtz. We'd traveled in large vans to honor the eighty-eight-year-old deacon, who was revered in Hickory Hollow and the Shipshewana, Indiana, church district where he later lived. As a result, many Amish had come to pay last respects and to offer comfort to his elderly widow. Years ago Amos and Martha had retired here in Virginia, joining a growing community of other aging Amish near the ocean they loved.

My thoughts returned to Cousin Malinda's upcoming wedding—and her kindly request. Although I'd once yearned for a beau and marriage, I'd given up on love. And I wished I'd never confided in Cora Jane about any of that. I rejected her pity—and anyone else's, for that matter. Goodness knows, I've dished out enough of that on myself!

Opening my notebook to the end of the last scene in my current story, I pushed my bare feet into the warm sand, still wearing my green dress and matching cape apron. My white organdy *Kapp* was safely in the hotel room—no sense in getting it unnecessarily soiled. Even so, as I sat fretting and looking ever so Plain amongst all the folk in skimpy bathing suits and shorts, I knew I must be a peculiar spectacle. The years of wearing Amish attire at market and elsewhere outside the confines of the community had led me to accept the fact there would always be curious stares.

But soaking up the ocean spray and salty scent was worth any amount of attention. Oh, the wonderful-*gut* feeling of the sea breeze against my hair, still up in a tight bun. How I longed to let it down . . . let the wind blow through it. Still, I didn't want to add to the misconceptions far too many Englischers already had about us, some even from novels they'd read.

My pen poised, I played my favorite what-if game as I began to write. The squeal of a sea gull caught my attention as the sun fell, faster now it seemed, behind me, over my shoulders, its gleaming rays fanning out to the clouds high above. I leaned back and stared at the evolving light show above me, letting my mind wander as I watched beachcombers and shell collectors. Certainly I hadn't meant to be rude, ignoring Malinda's request.

Yet, dare I accept?

Out of the corner of my eye, I noticed a tall Amish fellow walking barefoot in the foamy surf, snapping pictures every few seconds. A curious sight, to be sure! His black pant legs were rolled up, and he was minus his straw hat. His light brown hair fell below his ears, longer than that of the young men in the Hickory Hollow church district back home. I could scarcely pry my gaze from him.

"What's he doin' here?" I whispered, observing his amble through the gentle breakers, his handsome face aglow with a rosy cast.

Then, surprisingly, he glanced over at me.

"Hullo there." He smiled in the fading golden light.

I almost looked around to make sure his greeting was meant for me. "Hullo," I managed to reply, quickly closing my notebook.

As the sky dimmed, he moved away from the water and walked right toward me. "Mind if I join ya?"

"*Nee*, not at all."

He sat down beside me, pointing to a black ship on the horizon.

"*Jah*, awful perty." I felt too shy to say more.

We sat, not speaking, amidst the smell of popcorn and sea air while beams of red, pink, and gold sprayed the sky from the west.

"No wonder people thought the earth was flat, back before Columbus," he said quietly.

I nodded. "Sure looks that way from here."

"Ever see anything like this?"

"My first visit to the ocean," I admitted. "So, no."

He turned slowly, unexpectedly. "I'm Eben Troyer, from Indiana." His smile was disarming.

"Joanna Kurtz . . . from Hickory Hollow."

"Ah, Pennsylvania, where some of my cousins grew up. But I've never been there—unique name for a town, *jah*?"

We talked further, and I soon learned that soft-spoken Eben had come here for his deacon's funeral. I could hardly wait to say that it was the same service my family and I had come to attend.

"Well, how's that for a coincidence?" he said, his features growing faint in the twilight.

He showed me his camera, saying he took mostly pictures of landscapes and animals, same as our bishop, John Beiler, allowed. "Rarely pictures of people," he remarked . . . although the way Eben brought it up, he almost sounded like he wanted to take *my* picture.

His attention flabbergasted me, but it was ever so pleasing. No one had ever sought me out like this. For sure and for certain, my family and every last one of my girl cousins had written me off as destined to be an *alt Maidel*.

"How long are ya here for?" he asked, his smile warming my heart anew.

"Three days, counting today."

Then Eben surprised me again, asking if I'd like to walk with him to the fishing pier down yonder. I agreed, and he politely offered his hand as I got up from my sandy perch. Oh, glory be, we must've walked for miles into the night. So far and so long we got ourselves plumb lost trying to find our way back.

··· ➤ ➤ ···

Following the funeral the next day, Eben and I hurried again to the beach. There, we waded into the ocean up to our knees—in our clothes, of all silly things. And later, after the sun and wind dried us out some, we rented a bicycle built for two and rode up and down the boardwalk, the warm air on our faces. We ate chili dogs and ice cream under the fishing pier, and his eyes rested on me when he said, "I've never known a better day, Joanna."

My heart pounded in my ears.

That evening and the next, we met at sunset, laughing together and talking about whatever popped into our heads until, wonder of wonders, Eben reached for my hand! My heart beat so wildly, I wondered if he sensed it. All I could think of was our interlaced fingers.

But all too soon, we had to part ways, our private time together at an end. He asked for my address, and I happily gave it. In such a short time, we'd become so dear to each other. I tried not to cry.

Our meeting on the beach—as romantic and special as it was—birthed a renewed hope in me. After all, it was nearly a blight on any Amish girl to still be single at my age. *Ach*, but Eben Troyer had surely changed all of that. Surely he had. . . .

Then and there, I decided it was safe to go out on a limb. I agreed to be Cousin Malinda's bridesmaid, hoping with all of my heart to prove wrong my sister's pointed warning.

1

IF Joanna hadn't witnessed it, she wouldn't have believed Cousin Malinda would break down and cry on the morning of her wedding. Certainly all the preparations were stressful, and November's weather was also quite unpredictable—today was undeniably disappointing, with rain making down in sheets. *But is that reason to shed tears on your wedding day?* Joanna wondered.

Neither of the other two brides Joanna had stood up with had wept before going downstairs to make their marriage vows. But then, neither of those weddings had taken place on days with a cloudburst and deafening thunder.

Standing before the bishop with Malinda and her tall, brown-eyed Andrew, Joanna hoped her cousin wasn't moving ahead with something she might later regret. Once the sacred promises were made, there was no looking back. Marriage was to be honored for life.

Surely Cousin Malinda's tears were related instead to something other than second thoughts or cold feet. Oh, Joanna hoped so. Something to do with a blend of many emotions, maybe?

Through the windows, she saw the last vestiges of leaves falling in the downpour, the sky a slate gray. It nearly looked like nightfall, even though it was closer to noon.

Returning her attention to the bride and groom, Joanna was relieved to see Malinda look up adoringly at Andrew just as Bishop Beiler pronounced them husband and wife. "In the name of the Father, the Son, and the Holy Ghost."

After the tears, only love remains, Joanna thought, aware of the reverent spirit in the temporary house of worship. So many church members were present today, as well as extended family from other districts and even Englischer friends.

O Lord, bless Cousin Malinda and her husband, Andrew, with your loving care, Joanna prayed silently.

All during the wedding feast and the fellowshipping that afternoon, the rain continued, pouring over the eaves and streaming down the windowpanes. Then, lo and behold, it turned to sleet . . . and later to snow, with thick flakes filling the sky.

"Such a lot of weather for a single day," Joanna overheard Malinda's mother saying to Andrew's, a heavyset woman in her late fifties.

"Makes things interesting, jah?" Andrew's mother replied, making note of the edible wedding novelties for the bride and groom at the *Eck*, the special corner of the wedding table. Besides sticks of chewing gum and wrapped candies, there were little animals made from Rice Krispies and candy. And miniature buggies made from marshmallows, hitched with toothpicks to animal cracker horses.

Joanna nodded absentmindedly from the corner where she and several other single girls, including her golden-haired cousins, Ruthann and Lena, stood talking and nibbling on sweets.

Cora Jane was there, too, looking exceptionally pretty in her bright green dress and white apron. "To be honest, weather ain't the only thing amiss today," she said, looking askance at Joanna.

For goodness' sake, thought Joanna, letting the remark slide over her, even though it felt like an ocean wave threatening to topple her. True, this *was* the third time she'd served as a bridesmaid, but now that Eben Troyer was in her life, she wanted to set foolish superstition aside and just enjoy the day.

Joanna thought back to the beautiful beach where she'd met handsome Eben. How she yearned to hear his voice, the way he'd said her name as they walked together. It was easy to fall into that daydream;

she missed him terribly. She would not soon forget the delightful day at the mailbox last summer when she'd laid eyes on Eben's first letter, her name and address written in his strong hand. It was the beginning of their long-distance friendship, now blossoming into something so much more. She secretly treasured that special letter, having read and reread it before tucking it safely away in a wooden letter box in her hope chest. It was there that Joanna kept her most treasured possessions, including her writing notebooks.

Around midafternoon, copies of the German hymnal, the *Ausbund*, were passed around, and a special wedding Singing began for the newly-weds' enjoyment, with the courting-age youth sitting in pairs at the feast table. *Such a happy time*, Joanna encouraged herself, out of place though she felt at such gatherings anymore.

She put on a smile when she spied good-looking Jake Lantz, also known as Freckles Jake, sitting across the front room. The nickname arose from the freckles dotting his nose and cheekbones. His tall, robust frame proved he was hardworking, the kind of young man any Amish girl would welcome as a beau. His sandy hair and hazel eyes were identical to those of his younger brother, Jesse, who sat nearby, singing with other fellows in their late teens. Though Jake was twenty-three, both brothers were still quite single—according to the rumors, Jake had scared off a couple of girls on the first date, wanting to hold hands too soon.

Remembering that Eben had taken her hand in his the last evening they'd been together, Joanna couldn't help but smile as she sang with the others. Eben's gesture had been so natural, an outgrowth of their shared affection.

Between songs, Joanna chuckled over the candies made to look like little airplanes that decorated the table in front of her. *When did make-believe planes become the norm at Amish weddings?*

Suddenly, she was again aware of Jake's gaze and felt a wave of pity for him, feeling as sorry for him as she had for herself last year around this time, at her first wedding as a bridesmaid. No doubt Jake just wanted to marry and get on with life. *Maybe if he'd had a sister, he'd know better how to treat a girl. . . .*

Later, Joanna poured her heart into the gospel song "I Love to Tell the Story," one of her favorites. But she wasn't able to put Jake out of her mind for long. Several times over the course of the afternoon he caught her eye, and as Joanna learned later, he even went so far as to ask Malinda to pair him up with Joanna for the evening barn Singing.

"He's awful sweet on ya, cousin," Malinda herself revealed to Joanna in whispered tones prior to the evening meal.

But Joanna gave no indication she'd heard . . . nor did she say she was no longer available. Best to hold to tradition and keep Eben a secret—at least till the proper time.

After the wedding supper, Joanna and the other courting-age young folk headed to the barn for the regular Singing. The evening was still, without a hint of a breeze. If it were summer, she might be sitting out by the pond beyond their barn, bare feet in the water . . . her writing notebook on her lap. Out there, with the occasional breeze, she could keep her stories from prying eyes, especially Cora Jane's. It was one thing for Joanna to keep a daily journal, but quite another to write made-up stories, since fiction was frowned upon by the ministerial brethren.

All of that aside, Joanna had for some years delighted in spinning her imaginary yarns. There were just so many interesting ideas flitting through her head!

She glanced at her younger sister, who stood in her usual cluster of friends and cousins. Here lately, Joanna had suspected Cora Jane was getting close to a marriage proposal. Truth was, with her golden hair and big blue eyes, Cora Jane knew how to get a young man's attention, something she'd even shared back when they were confidantes. Since Joanna had met Eben, however, their sisterly chats had become a thing of the past. And maybe it was for the best, with such a secret to keep.

Joanna remembered clearly what her sister had whispered during one nighttime conversation: that it was important to let a fellow know you were interested, holding his gaze and hanging on to his every word, interjecting a comment here and there while letting him do most of the talking, especially on the first date. And all of that had come so naturally to Joanna with Eben . . . something that had never happened before.

The minute the songs were finished, Jake looked Joanna's way again, and so as not to encourage him a speck, she visited with Cousin Malinda's younger sisters. She wanted nothing more than to slip out of the barn for home, unseen. Feeling a little guilty about her deliberate aloofness, she returned his smile when she again found him looking her way. Her toes curled in her shoes.

Will he take it wrong?

Then, as if by some miracle, Cora Jane, and Malinda's younger sister, Mary Rose, walked over to the other side of the barn to talk with Jake. Feeling much relieved, Joanna wondered if Cora Jane had, perhaps, observed the silent exchange of smiles and sensed Joanna's uneasiness. Had her sister stepped in on purpose?

Looking about her, Joanna saw that she could at last exit discreetly. So she pushed open the barn door and left to walk home through the chilly night. She didn't mind the snowflakes that sprinkled her nose and lips; Joanna simply pulled her coat tighter around her, glad for her scarf and gloves.

In that moment, she had an unexpected thought, one that warmed her heart. What if she and Eben were to marry next wedding season? Which two girls would *she* choose for her bridesmaids? Joanna laughed to herself—she was putting the carriage before the horse again. She was known to have a vivid imagination, something even *Mamma* had pointed out since Joanna was but a little girl. So now Joanna questioned herself: Was it merely wishful thinking to hope her beau might propose, perhaps even via letter? Or was this just the stuff of the romantic fiction she dearly loved to read . . . and write?

Wonderful as it was to anticipate and receive Eben's letters, they were a frequent reminder that her beau lived way out in Shipshewana, where he and his extended family had farmed for generations. She was curious about his parents and siblings—his entire family, really—but hadn't had the gumption to ask, not wanting to appear forward. She sometimes feared she might mess up and write something awkward, spoiling things between them. So she was careful to see that her own letters dealt mostly with daily life and happenings in Hickory Hollow.

Joanna had taken care to capture every detail of her own beloved little hollow there in Lancaster County. She'd also written Eben about the dear folk, like Samuel and Rebecca Lapp, and Paul and Lillianne Hostetler . . . and Ella Mae Zook, the old Wise Woman so many in the area turned to with their problems. Joanna hoped she hadn't gone overboard with her portrayals or the descriptions of the landscape. It was just that she loved everything about Hickory Hollow and was holding her breath that Eben might come *there* to court her, to settle and eventually marry. So far, though, he hadn't said anything of the kind.

Picking up her pace now, she thought of Cora Jane and her steady beau, Gideon Zook. She'd seen him drop her off late at night after a long buggy ride. The memory of Cora Jane's mirth rang out in Joanna's mind—that appealing, melodious laughter.

"Do I laugh enough?" Joanna whispered into the darkness, unsure how to share her lighthearted side in letters to Eben. But there had never been a need to work to impress him. Why, joy of joys, recently Eben had started signing off, *with love.*

A mighty gut sign!

And tomorrow evening at seven o'clock, Eben had said he'd call her, having asked for the phone number of the community phone shanty situated in one of *Dat*'s fields.

So much for Cora Jane's admonition, Joanna thought with a smile.

Then a sudden concern presented itself, and she couldn't help wondering what Eben wanted to discuss by phone. *And why now?*

2

JOANNA slipped into bed well after ten o'clock that night, but she awakened before dawn with such curiosity and expectation for the day that she got right up and lit the lantern. She hurried across the room, her bare feet chilled by the draft creeping through the floorboards. Then, taking her notebook from the three-ring binder stored in her hope chest, she curled back up in bed and wrote for a good hour, till it was time to shower.

Her thoughts today were on one thing: the phone call from Eben tonight. Oh, to hear his voice again!

After dressing, she brushed her hair more than a hundred times, caught up in the notion that she wanted to look her very best, even though Eben couldn't possibly see her. Joanna was to use the outdoor phone meant primarily for emergencies and calling for a driver—necessary things that didn't include talking to a beau. Yet lots of folk did small things behind the bishop's back, saying by their actions, *What the strict bishop doesn't know won't matter.*

Even so, what *would* happen if Joanna were ever caught using the phone for personal use? Was it truly a transgression?

Parting her hair down the middle, she tightly twisted the sides before pulling her blond hair into a thick bun. Then she placed her white Kapp on her head and hurried back upstairs to make her bed and put away her writing notebook. She'd taken an unnecessary risk, leaving it out in plain sight on the bed, of all things. For sure and for certain, the phone call tonight had her all but *ferhoodled.*

19

She still had no idea why Eben wanted to call. Was it just because he missed her? His letters certainly indicated his lasting affection. She hoped hers sent the same loving message back to him.

After breakfast, she put a roast in the oven, then set about sweeping Mamma's big kitchen floor with the stiff-bristled broom. She got in the corners real good, as Mamma had taught her back when she was a little girl, scarcely as tall as the broom itself, finishing out in the catch-all utility room, which was as cluttered as she'd ever seen it. *How does such a mess happen in a single day?*

Once the floors were spotless, Cora Jane brought in a pile of mending and sat down at the kitchen table without uttering a word to Joanna or to their pleasingly plump mother. Right away, she set to work patching, not giving anyone so much as a glance. Joanna figured it was best to keep out of her sister's way, especially considering how Cora Jane had acted at Cousin Malinda's wedding.

Around ten-thirty, Joanna wiped her brow and went to wash up before peeling potatoes for a generous pot of beef stew. Taking into account Cora Jane's attitude, she'd rather cook on her own. Mamma had undoubtedly noticed the tension between them, but Joanna hoped things might calm down somewhat, now that Malinda and Andy's wedding was past. *Now that I've served as a bridesmaid yet again.*

Joanna began cutting up the potatoes, musing. If she could do anything in the kitchen, she'd choose something other than cleaning. Cooking was altogether different, because she didn't equate making meals or baking bread with housework. To her thinking, one was humdrum and uncreative, the other enjoyable. She smiled, thinking how she'd feel cooking for Eben each day.

Just at that moment, Cora Jane looked over at her. "You happy 'bout something, sister?"

Mamma turned to look, as well, blue eyes shining. "Are ya makin' enough stew so we'll have leftovers tomorrow?"

"Oh, there'll be a-plenty," replied Joanna, thankful for Mamma's intervention. "This is a double batch."

"*Gut*, 'cause I really *hate* peelin' potatoes—it's the worst thing ever," Cora Jane complained.

"Now, dear," Mamma said sweetly. "No need to say 'hate.'"

Cora Jane clammed up, eyes blinking fast. At her age, she knew better than to say things to set Mamma off, yet sometimes Cora Jane just seemed bent on being disagreeable.

But Joanna knew it would do no good to fret over her sister. She returned her attention to cutting up the roast beef, then browned the cubes in butter. When that was done, she added two large onions, canned carrots from last year's family garden, and the seasonings. She'd made the meal so many times, there was no need for a recipe. All the while, she wondered what Eben's favorite meals were. Joanna could scarcely wait to learn all there was to know about him!

Her father's intense gray eyes were fixed on the steaming bowl of stew Joanna set before him, though he characteristically said nary a word. He leaned his tall frame against the chair at the head of the table, and the four of them offered the silent table blessing. They enjoyed the hearty meal, complete with cottage cheese, fresh-baked bread, and Mamma's wonderful apple butter. For dessert, Joanna served the rest of a pumpkin pie Mamma had baked yesterday afternoon following the wedding.

Cora Jane ate without making a peep. Dat didn't say much, either—generally he said little unless he had good reason. Mamma, for her part, tried to make small talk, mostly about the cold weather and the coming snow. Joanna cherished her own private thoughts as she spooned up the delicious stew, relieved in a way that Cora Jane wasn't as talkative as usual.

Looking around the largely empty table, Joanna tried to picture Eben sitting there. Could *he* manage to get Dat talking during dinner? Very few folk could. Not even Michael Hostetler down Hickory Lane, their neighbors' genial son, who until recently had worked part-time for Dat.

"We have a few more weddings comin' up in the next two weeks," Mamma said.

Joanna nodded. "Have ya decided which cousin's wedding to attend next Thursday?"

"Ach, two weddings in the family on the selfsame day," Mamma said, shaking her head. "Happens too often, jah? Lena and Ruthann—such a hard choice to make."

Cora Jane didn't bother to look up, and Dat would leave the decision to Mamma. *Poor Mamma*, thought Joanna.

"Which wedding will Salina go to?" Joanna asked. Salina was the only married daughter in the family and already a mother to three young children. The rest of Joanna and Cora Jane's siblings were boys, all married with youngsters of their own.

Mamma's face lit up. "Now, why didn't *I* think of that? I'll ask her this afternoon."

Joanna wasn't surprised. After all, Salina stopped in quite often. So then it was settled: They would go to whichever wedding Salina chose.

Weddings abound, thought Joanna, taking another bite of pie while avoiding Cora Jane's impudent stare.

When the clouds lowered during supper that evening and a tremendous wind came up, gusting snow, Joanna knew she was in for a challenge getting out to the phone shanty several acres away. The white-out conditions were hazardous—some farmers were known to tie a rope to the house and their own hand just to go out to the barn and back in such conditions.

She hoped the snowstorm was short-lived and done by the time she needed to get to the phone. How she yearned for the lovely months of summer, when their closest neighbors could easily wander over for some watermelon or homemade ice cream and a back porch visit, or the other way around. Mamma, for instance, hadn't been over to see Ella Mae Zook or even Rachel Stoltzfus, the bishop's mother-in-law, in weeks. Joanna missed all the impromptu conversation at the end of the long day, as well as the sight of green leaves and blossoming flowers.

Joanna had never quite forgotten the impression she'd had of Ella Mae when Mamma had taken her along for tea with the Wise Woman. It was years before Ella Mae's husband passed away, when Joanna was but four and Ella Mae was still living in the farmhouse a mile or so away. Joanna couldn't help but feel comfortable in the sun-drenched kitchen so similar to Mamma's own. She'd sat across from Mamma on a wooden chair with a mound of pillows tucked beneath her, a little yellow daisy teacup and saucer set before her filled with peppermint tea.

Mamma and Ella Mae sat sipping and chatting on the other side of the table while Joanna picked up her spoon and began to stir, looking at the murky hot water.

"Here, dearie," Ella Mae said, rising just then and going to her old icebox to get a jar of real whipped cream. "This'll make your first cup of tea extra yummy." With a twinkle in her eye, Ella Mae put a dollop of the sweet white cream atop Joanna's tea. Mamma's eyes widened when Ella Mae encouraged Joanna to stick her little pointer finger in the whipped cream and lick it off.

Even then, Joanna had wondered how a woman that old could have possibly known what a child was thinking. Then and there, she sensed something special about this lady the People called wise, whose sincere and welcoming manner—and specially brewed tea—drew people like bees to roses. Particularly women who needed a caring friend and a listening ear.

Joanna smiled with the dear memory as she drew hot water after supper dishes were cleared from the table. She squirted an ample amount of dish soap into the water and swished it around. Cora Jane came over, jerked the tea towel off the rack, and stood stiff and uncommunicative, waiting to dry the dishes. Joanna sighed inwardly and listened to see if the wind outdoors might be dying down some. Less than an hour and a half left before she needed to make her trek out to the phone shack for the seven o'clock call.

When the kitchen was all redd up, Mamma suggested the three of them make chocolate chip cookies for the upcoming weekend. Cora Jane brightened immediately, voting to make snickerdoodles, her very favorite. Joanna agreed to help, knowing she'd have to watch the clock, as well as find a way to leave gracefully without raising eyebrows.

Going over to preheat the gas oven, Joanna noticed Dat get up from his chair near the heat stove and wander out to the utility room. Mamma followed, asking where he was going in such weather.

"Want to check on the livestock . . . see how the newest calves are doin'."

Her father opened the back door, and Joanna could see that the wind was not as fierce as before. And when it was time to place the cookie sheets into the oven, Mamma slipped away to the sitting room and Cora Jane went upstairs. Joanna breathed a sigh of relief.

It's now or never! She made haste to don her warmest coat, boots, woolen scarf, and gloves. Then, lickety-split, she put on her black candlesnuffer-style outer bonnet and left the house.

3

EBEN Troyer headed through the cold toward Peaceful Acres Lane wearing his old work boots and black felt hat, as well as his father's dark blue muffler. The frosty air stung his cheeks and nose, and he could smell the smoke from the new woodstove he and *Daed* had installed in the barn just a few days ago. *In time for the turn in weather.* He'd spent a good part of the day stacking hay in the loft and, later, hooking up the horse's water tank to the generator to keep it from freezing.

The rickety phone hut was a half mile from his father's farmhouse, not far enough away to warrant hitching up the horse and carriage. He had been counting the days till he talked to Joanna, and judging from the way she'd responded in her letter about their conversation tonight, he presumed she was equally excited. *A phone date, of all things!*

As he approached the shanty, he noticed his father's older brother, Solomon, standing inside and talking by lantern light. Sol's hands were moving to beat the band, which was the way he always talked.

Didn't expect this, Eben thought, searching for his pocket watch. Unable to see it, he pulled out his flashlight but then thought better of turning it on. He certainly didn't want to call attention to himself, not with talkative Uncle Solomon nearby.

So Eben hung back in the trees, waiting his turn and hearing the *clip-clop*ping of horses' hooves in the distance. Who would've guessed the weather would sour like this on the very night he'd chosen to phone Joanna. He could only imagine what it was like in Hickory Hollow.

Growing colder by the minute, he wondered how much longer his uncle would be and wished he'd worn heavier gloves. Even so, he'd wait all night if it meant hearing Joanna's sweet voice again.

He removed her letter, folded with the phone number face up. It was to some extent amusing that of all the girls he might have fallen for, Joanna Kurtz happened to live in another state. But there was no doubt in his mind she was worth any amount of distance. And as pretty and thoughtful as she was, it had initially puzzled him as to why Joanna was still single.

Has God kept her just for me? The thought was encouraging as Eben waited for Uncle Sol to complete his call, which it appeared he was doing just now. Sol hung up the receiver and opened the wooden door, then closed it right quick. But he'd forgotten his lantern and had to step back inside to retrieve it before leaving again.

I'll wait just a bit. Eben watched his uncle amble across the field toward his farmhouse. Then, lest someone else wander along to use the phone, Eben flicked on his flashlight and made his way into the shanty, his pulse quickening. After exchanging letters as their only means of communication since this past summer, he was certain this wintry night was about to warm up in a very big way.

Joanna shivered as she stood inside the narrow shed, holding her breath for the phone to ring. The light from her small flashlight began to dim, and she wished she'd put in new batteries before leaving the house.

Despite the weather, she'd arrived a few minutes before the designated time. After all, it would be a shame to have missed Eben's call. But now that she was here and the hour had passed, she wondered if something had come up on his end, maybe, to keep him from getting to the phone.

It was snowing harder, and the wind blew through the openings around the door. All the little cracks in the shanty that helped keep the place cool on the hottest days of summer made it downright frigid now.

Just when she was beginning to think he might not call after all, the phone rang. Joanna let it ring twice, so as not to appear too eager. "Hullo?" she answered, feeling terribly shy.

"Joanna?"

"Jah. Is this Eben?"

"It's so *gut* to hear your voice."

25

"Yours too."

"I'm sorry it's a little later than I'd planned, but it couldn't be helped." He explained that the phone had been tied up. "You just never know with these community telephones."

"That's all right." It was such fun hearing him, and he sounded so happy to talk to her. She wanted to flutter around; it was all she could do to stand still.

"Our neighbors to the north have a phone installed in their barn, but so far my father will have nothing to do with that."

She mentioned that some of the youth there in Hickory Hollow had cell phones. "And so do a few folk who work away from the farm."

"What do you think of that?" he asked.

"Ain't for me: I'm baptized."

He agreed, sounding somewhat relieved. "My bishop only permits them for business use," he said. "But how's it possible to enforce?"

She nodded, then laughed because he couldn't see her.

"Ach, you laugh just the way I remember," Eben said. "How've ya been, Joanna?"

"Real *gut*, and you?"

"Oh, just fine. Keepin' mighty busy here."

She loved listening to his voice, but was still curious as to why he'd wanted to call.

One thing led to another, and soon they fell easily into talking about their weeks. Then he surprised her by asking, "Would it suit for me to come visit, say, next week sometime?"

Joanna was elated. "Why, sure . . . what day are ya thinkin'?"

"Thursday or Friday, either one."

"Well, we have a wedding on Thursday, so Friday would be better."

"All right, then. I'll ride out with a Mennonite van driver who makes regular trips between here and Lancaster. I'll grab a cab from there. It'll be about ten hours to get to your place."

"Such a distance! How long can ya stay?" she asked, her heart thumping hard.

"Just overnight. Then I'll have to head back the next afternoon." He mentioned needing to get someone to cover his farm work.

"So do your parents know, then . . . 'bout us?"

"I plan to tell them in due time."

She smiled. "I haven't told anyone here, either. We still keep a bit quiet 'bout such things."

"We don't as much anymore here, but I wanted to wait to say anything till a few more things are worked out."

She wondered what things he meant. "You'll need a place to stay."

"If that's all right. Whatever's best for you and your family, Joanna."

Oh, she loved it when he said her name! "I'll see if you can stay with our neighbors, the Stoltzfuses. That is, if you're comfortable having the bishop's in-laws suspect you're here to see me."

He chuckled. "Sounds wonderful-*gut.*" Pausing, he continued, "I'd like to meet your parents, too."

Her heart leaped at the thought. *Oh, praise be!* This was getting serious! "All right."

A gust of wind suddenly pounded against the door.

"Sounds like a windstorm there," Eben said.

"Practically a blizzard."

"Will you be all right getting back to the house?" There was concern in his voice.

"I haven't far to go and I'm all bundled up, so no worries."

"Well, don't get chilled."

"I'll be quite fine, Eben," she said, not wanting to hang up just yet.

"Can't have my girl catching her death of cold," he added softly.

My girl . . .

Oh, Eben, she thought, shivering now with something more pleasant than cold.

"Say, I have an idea. What if we talked by phone like this every so often? We could set a regular time. Would ya like that?"

Would she? "Sounds ever so nice," she said, hoping her voice sounded calmer than she felt. It was happening at last . . . and just as she'd hoped. Surely he was planning to court her in earnest!

Then they were discussing several things they might do together during his short visit, and Joanna said she hoped things might warm up. "But ya never know this time of year."

"True, but no matter what, we'll get better acquainted, which is why I'm comin'. That and to meet your family."

She smiled into the phone. "I look forward to it."

"Jah . . ."

She could tell Eben was every bit as reluctant to hang up as she was. Eventually, though, she had to tell him she was afraid her flashlight was going to conk out.

"All right, then, I'll let you go." He said he'd write to let her know what time to expect him on Friday. "I hope to get an early enough start so I can arrive sometime in the afternoon."

"I'll see ya soon," she said.

"Until then," he said. "Good-bye, Joanna."

"Good-bye." Slowly she placed the receiver back in its cradle.

The flashlight dimmed, and she picked it up. She opened the shanty door and ran through the snow, hoping to get home before the light sputtered out completely. Still enraptured by the *wunnerbaar-gut* phone visit, Joanna scarcely minded the wind and cold.

Eben's coming to see me!

4

THE familiar smell of freshly baked cookies greeted Joanna when she returned to the house from the phone shanty.

"Where've *you* been?" Cora Jane asked, eyeing her sharply.

Joanna wasn't ready to reveal her news yet, not without Mamma around. "Oh, just outside."

"Well, that's obvious." Cora Jane reached for two cookies and sampled both kinds as she continued to watch her. "Well, aren't you the secret keeper!"

Joanna ignored that and took her time removing her boots and outerwear. She wanted to savor every moment of her phone chat. Nearly too good to be true!

The back door opened just then, and there was Dat, his boots tracking in snow. He wiped his feet on the rag rug near the door as usual, just as she had, and looked at her curiously as she hung up her coat and scarf. But he said nothing.

All during family worship, Cora Jane stared at Joanna, taking away some of her joy. The minute the silent prayers were finished, Joanna slipped upstairs to write in her diary, which she kept hidden between the mattress and the bedsprings.

"He's comin' to visit at long last!" Joanna whispered as she dressed for bed.

But it was hard to fall asleep, if not impossible, with Eben's voice still in her head. She cherished everything he'd said and was nearly as excited as the first time they met. Oh, she could scarcely wait to show him around Hickory Hollow!

The bitter cold and steady winds made delicate designs on the window-panes the next morning. Joanna was captivated by the frosty patterns when she awakened just as the sun rose, spraying light on them. She'd overslept, and no wonder, having replayed Eben's phone call happily in her mind throughout the night.

When should I break the news about him—and his visit—to Dat and Mamma? She pondered this while getting ready for another day of chores prior to the Lord's Day tomorrow. She took extra care to inspect her best blue church dresses on wooden wall pegs over near the dresser, thinking she'd wear one of them next Friday when Eben arrived. She wanted to look her very *bescht* since he hadn't laid eyes on her all this time.

Breakfast was applesauce, bacon, and steel-cut oatmeal, which Mamma always said had a way of sticking to your gizzard. Cousin Lena Witmer stopped by right afterward. She didn't bother knocking, just rushed in, tossing off her boots at the back door. She made her entrance into the kitchen still wearing her outer clothes, her blue eyes aflutter.

Lena grabbed Joanna's hand and hurried her upstairs to her room, where she closed the door and fell into Joanna's arms, coat, mittens, and all. "Oh, cousin, I don't know what to do!" Lena cried. "I hope you can help me."

"What's happened?" Joanna tried to comfort her, suggesting Lena sit on the bed.

Lena carried on a bit longer, then managed to wipe her tears away, though she looked terribly forlorn as she sat down. "My sister Verna was going to be my first bridesmaid, but she's been called away to Wisconsin to help with our father's ailing sister." She sighed and seemed to gather herself. "With the wedding next Thursday, I'm out in the cold."

Joanna sat beside her. "Have ya thought of askin' one of your younger sisters?"

Cousin Lena removed her black outer bonnet and fiddled with the strings. "That's just the problem: They're both lined up to be bridesmaids on that day—for Ruthann's wedding, and our neighbor, Kate Elizabeth's."

Joanna hardly knew what to say. Or think.

Again, Lena sighed, her eyes tearing up once more. She searched Joanna's face, then looked away. "I know it's awful late, but I was wondering if, well, maybe you'd consider standing up with me. Along with my cousin Mary Ruth."

Joanna wondered if her surprise registered on her face.

"I really don't want to ask anyone but you, Joanna."

So she has no other options. . . .

It may have sounded presumptuous, coming from any other cousin, but Joanna could see poor Lena's dilemma.

"Well, it's nice of you to consider me, but have ya thought of Cora Jane? She's closer in age," Joanna suggested.

Lena wrinkled her nose, then shook her head. "Ach, not sayin' anything against your sister. It's just that, well, I much prefer you, Joanna."

Joanna wondered whether she'd even have time to sew a bridesmaid dress if she consented. "What color are ya planning?" As was the custom, the two female wedding attendants would dress to match the bride.

"Plum's what I chose for under my white cape apron, since nearly all the brides wear blue anymore."

"Well, I don't have a dress that color, but—"

"Oh, I'll give you money for the fabric and thread. I'd be ever so glad to."

"It's just that, well . . . I'd need time to sew it." With Eben's visit coming up, too, Joanna would be scrambling.

"I can hem or do whatever ya need." Cousin Lena smiled. "*Denki* ever so much, Joanna! You have no idea how grateful I am."

Based on Lena's jubilant reaction, Joanna certainly did understand. And just that quickly she was committed, without even really agreeing. She must try to dismiss the notion that this was to be her fourth time as a bridesmaid, of all things. Once Cora Jane heard this, she'd say Joanna was pushing it for sure. But Joanna felt more confident than ever now, because Eben Troyer was arriving the very day after Cousin Lena's wedding. To think he was traveling nearly half a day just to see her!

What's it matter how many times I'm a bridesmaid? Joanna thought as she hugged Lena good-bye. "I'll get started with the dress first thing Monday, after the washing's hung on the line."

"Ach, I feel so much better." Lena kissed her cheek. "Denki, dearest cousin."

Joanna walked her downstairs and waited while she donned her black bonnet. Cousin Lena reached to give her another hug. "This means so much to me."

"Glad to help," Joanna said, aware that Cora Jane and Mamma were within earshot now. "I'll go and get the material and thread this afternoon yet."

Waving, Cousin Lena made her way over the snowy walkway to the waiting horse and buggy.

Just as Joanna thought she might, Cora Jane crept up behind her. "What on earth was that about?"

Joanna briefly described the pickle Cousin Lena was in.

Mamma kept silent, but Cora Jane pressed for more. "So she wants *you*, then?"

"Guess I know which wedding I'll be attending." Quickly changing the subject, Joanna asked to borrow the driving horse. But Mamma said to ask Dat, just in case he needed the mare for a trip of his own.

With Cora Jane's eyes boring into her, Joanna slipped on her winter things and headed out to the barn to talk to her father. Truth be known, she was relieved to exit the house. Glad, too, that she just might have an opportunity to talk privately with Dat about Eben's upcoming visit. Such a father-daughter chat she'd never undertaken before.

The field mules were dismantling several hay bales in the barnyard as Joanna made her way to the stable. Sliding open the door, she was greeted by the damp, earthy smell of animals and bedding straw.

She found her father freshening the foals' area. She stood back before making herself known, waiting for courage. Knowing how reserved her father was, Joanna felt tense about breaking this news.

She drew a breath, then stepped forward as Dat acknowledged her. "Can I have Krissy for an hour or so? I need to run an errand right quick."

Dat nodded his consent.

Then, while he was still forking straw from the bale, she ventured ahead and brought up Eben. "We met while at Great-Uncle Amos's funeral back last summer and have been writing since. He's from Indiana, Dat." She paused, aware that her hands were clammy inside her gloves. "And . . . somethin' else. Eben's comin' to visit next Friday."

When her father said nothing—didn't even make eye contact—Joanna tried not to make too much of it. After all, this was Dat's customary response to most things. "He wants to meet you and Mamma, if that's all right."

Her father stopped what he was doing and leaned on the pitchfork. "This is what you want, daughter?"

"I'm in agreement, jah."

Dat frowned. "Is he willing to move here and join our church?"

"I 'spect so."

Dat reached for the pitchfork and resumed his work. At last he said, "Then, jah, we'll meet him."

Joanna had to make herself be still, although she'd much rather have squealed her delight. For Dat's sake, she remained sedate and calm, at least on the outside. "Denki ever so much!"

The slightest hint of a smile crossed his face, warming her clear through. Then she turned toward the stall to get the driving horse. *A pleasant look is a good start,* she told herself.

So all was well.

Doubtless Dat would pass the word to Mamma later in the privacy of their room, so Joanna wouldn't have to go through this again with her. But as for Cora Jane . . . it would be best to tell her directly. "I'll wait till she's in a *gut* mood," Joanna murmured as she led her favorite mare out of the barn to hitch up. "Whenever that might be."

5

IN the middle of the night, Joanna dreamed she was running through a cornfield, chasing after Cora Jane, trying to catch her to tell about Eben. But in the dream, each time Joanna drew near enough, her sister darted ahead . . . relentlessly out of reach.

Joanna's heart pounded in her sleep. Oh, how she wanted to talk to Cora Jane once again, like sisters should, to say she'd never felt this way about a fellow. She tossed and turned, pulling the sheet like a rope.

Awaking with a start, Joanna was grateful to realize even in her clouded state that what she'd just experienced was not real. *Surely my sister will want to hear my news*, she thought, rising to greet the dawn.

It was the Lord's Day, and a Preaching Sunday at that. The sun's rays were just beginning to extend over the horizon, and Joanna went to raise the dark green shade at first one tall window, then the other. Instead of digging into her hope chest for her writing notebook as she liked to do, she instead felt compelled to read several psalms to start the day. Working on her story somehow didn't seem wise this morning.

Glancing across the hall at Cora Jane's partially closed bedroom door, Joanna contemplated what she ought to do. Surely by now Mamma knew about Eben's plan to visit. Dat would've told her without delay.

Joanna sighed and stared at the lineup of postcards on her dresser which she'd received from her Englischer friend, Amelia, presently in Europe. Such interesting sights and descriptions of London, Amsterdam, and Berlin—places Joanna would never see.

She reached for her Bible and read two psalms, then considered going over to awaken Cora Jane—tell her right away about Eben and be done with it. Yet with her sister so quick to find fault, news of an out-of-state beau had the potential to spoil the reverence of the day, and Joanna decided against it. *At least, not before church.*

Joanna ended up postponing her talk with Cora Jane even longer, as her sister seemed in no disposition for it. *Perhaps after the common meal?* she mused while waiting in the cold to go into church at Cousin Malinda's. Shivering, she stood with Mamma and Cora Jane and her maternal grandmother, *Mammi* Sadie, along with Salina and several of their sisters-in-law, all of them in line with the other womenfolk. Everyone was bundled up, most of them waiting with their arms wrapped around themselves for warmth.

Up ahead, Joanna spotted Cousin Lena with her own mother and two younger sisters. Despite the frosty air, Lena was smiling.

Such a happy bride to be!

Later, after the Preaching service, Joanna sought Lena out, greeting her warmly. Lena clasped Joanna's gloved hands and insisted they walk around the barn until it was time for the second seating to be served.

In the chilly air, they strolled along together. What a difference a day had made for Lena. "You're simply beaming," Joanna remarked, her breath floating before her. "You actually seem relaxed."

"I surely am." Lena flashed a big smile. "Because of you."

"Ach, don't know 'bout that."

"Well, I do!" Cousin Lena squelched a giggle, then dug into her purse and handed some bills to Joanna. "Here's *Geld* for your dress fabric, before I forget."

Joanna thanked her as she accepted the money. Lena began to describe all of the extra-special treats her mother and many aunts had planned for the wedding feast at Lena's parents' home. Joanna wished she and Cora Jane could talk so easily like this again. What had happened to make Cora Jane so tetchy? Was it truly just about Joanna's being a bridesmaid?

When they rounded the barn for the second time, Joanna noticed Cora Jane walking with Cousin Ruthann, who was also scheduled to

35

wed this week. It was clear the pair were having a confidential chat, so Joanna and Lena hurried back to the house, both of them offering to help Cousin Malinda even though neither had been assigned to kitchen duty.

"Next time," Malinda said, thanking them. "Now go *waerme*—warm up." She pointed to the heater stove, and Joanna willingly obliged.

Eventually, Lena wandered away to talk with her grandmother, who was enjoying the light meal, and Joanna headed to the glassed-in porch to visit with some younger cousins. She imagined how each girl she talked to might take the news of her Indiana beau. What might she say? But, of course, Joanna's parents were wiser than to tell it around, undoubtedly wanting to see how things went with the actual visit.

Will they like Eben?

She observed Cora Jane across the yard, still talking with Cousin Ruthann. Sighing, Joanna wondered whether her sister would mind her manners when Eben arrived. Or would Cora Jane just be Cora Jane and spoil things but *gut?*

··· ➤ ⤙ ···

Monday morning washday—*Weschdaag*—Joanna, Mamma, and Cora Jane worked together with Mammi Sadie in the cold yet sunny air to hang out all of the wet clothes by seven-thirty.

Once the chore was accomplished, Joanna hurried indoors to check on her bread dough. She planned to bake enough to share with her grandparents and Cousin Malinda, too. She ran tepid water over her nearly frostbitten hands to restore the feeling. The wet clothes would surely dry stiff as boards on such a day.

Once the bread was in the oven, Joanna began to pin her dress pattern to the plum-colored fabric on the kitchen table. She couldn't remember when she'd owned such a lovely dress. Despite the last-minute invitation, being one of Lena's bridesmaids was going to be right nice.

At that moment, Cora Jane wandered down the steps and offered to help cut out the pattern, surprising her. "I know you're in a hurry, jah?" she said.

Pleased as pie, Joanna smiled. "So nice of you. Denki." She glanced up at her sister. *Is now a good time to talk?*

"An unusual color for the bride and the attendants, ain't?" Cora Jane said, running her hand over the fabric.

"Cousin Lena wanted something different than most brides round here."

"I see that."

"She'll be a perty bride, I say."

"A nice color for you, too," Cora Jane replied. "With your blond hair and all."

Glad to work alongside her sister once again, Joanna pinned the seams, eager to sew them up on the treadle sewing machine. The neck facing wouldn't take long, nor would the hem. Lena had offered to help her mark the latter sometime this evening.

Cora Jane began pinning the tucks into the sleeves by hand, humming a hymn as she worked. Her sister's apparent cheerfulness gave Joanna the courage she required.

"I've been wanting to tell ya something," she began.

Cora Jane's head bobbed up. "Oh?"

"I've met someone."

"You've seemed awful preoccupied, so I wondered."

"He's not from round here, though."

Cora Jane frowned. "Isn't that risky?"

"Not really."

"Okay, then . . . tell me more."

Joanna smiled. "Well, he's from Indiana."

"Ach, so far away!"

"And he's comin' to visit this Friday."

"Honestly, now!"

"His name is Eben Troyer . . . and he wants to meet Dat and Mamma."

"And what about the rest of the family?" Cora Jane asked.

"No doubt he'll be happy to meet whoever is around that day."

Cora Jane fell silent. "You aren't thinkin' of going out there to live, are ya . . . if you marry?"

"I daresay he'll come here to court me, when the time comes."

"Well, I should hope so," Cora Jane said emphatically. Her forehead pinched up.

"Please, ya mustn't worry 'bout my promise to the Hickory Hollow church, if that's what you're thinkin'."

"Still, what if he wants you to go there, like some fellas in other districts? What then?" There was an edge of panic to her voice.

Joanna didn't want to get into this. Not when she and Eben hadn't really discussed it. "I'll take things as they come." She sighed. "I just wanted you to know before he arrives." She didn't dare say, "*So you'll behave yourself.*"

Cora Jane moved slowly to the windows and looked out. "Where'd ya meet this fella?"

"At the funeral last summer."

"Way back at Virginia Beach?"

"Jah."

Cora Jane turned to face her. "Where we'd planned to spend lots of time together."

"Please, Cora Jane . . ."

"I'd looked forward to it, ya know . . . but you kept disappearing." Cora Jane's expression turned accusing, her lips curved down. For the longest time, Cora Jane just stared at her. She looked almost stricken. Then her eyes became moist, which surprised Joanna no end. "Well, I'm not goin' to stick around and watch this fella steal you away."

Joanna was flabbergasted. "I never meant to upset you."

Cora Jane reached for the needle, thread, and sleeve once again. "I hope you know what you're doin' is all. I've seen the postcards from your fancy friend, traveling through Europe."

"Amelia has nothin' to do with my long-distance beau," Joanna assured her.

"It just wonders me if you're itchin' to move away from here. Maybe she's given ya a taste for the world."

Joanna didn't offer more to ease her sister's concerns—surely Cora Jane knew her better than that! Nor did she wish, worried and forlorn as Cora Jane looked, to say how wonderful it had been to receive Eben's letters for nearly five months now.

An uncomfortable silence fell between them. "So what's this fella look like?" Cora Jane finally prodded.

Eben was precious to Joanna. She couldn't bear to have her sister criticize anything about him. "I'm really not up to sharing much right now, if ya don't mind. If you stick around, you'll see him for yourself."

"Is he writing to you?"

Joanna said he was.

"But ya never breathed a word of it to me." Cora Jane grimaced. "This is nothin' like the way things used to be. I really don't know what to say."

"Why not just say you're happy for me?" Joanna's stomach was tied up in knots. "Weren't you afraid I'd never be more than a bridesmaid?"

"I *am* happy. How's that?"

Could've fooled me! Joanna looked at her. "What's happened to us, sister?" Her lower lip trembled.

"You tell me!" Cora Jane tossed the sleeve with the needle and thread stuck in it across the table, then abruptly exited the room.

Joanna could hardly believe her eyes. *Will my own sister interfere with my chance for love and marriage?*

6

ODAY'S the day, thought Eben, planning to talk with his parents during the noon meal. *Surely they suspect something's up . . . all the letters back and forth.*

He strode across the snowy yard toward the side door that led into the kitchen. Undoubtedly his father would enter the house by way of the utility room door, first stopping to take off his work boots so as not to dirty *Mamm's* spotless kitchen. Eben was careful to scrutinize his boots, as well, before heading indoors, though today he did not dally long, eager for some black *Kaffi.* Eben removed his work gloves and pulled off his boots on the back porch, leaving them near the door. The appealing aroma of washday stew hit him and, stocking footed, he made a beeline into the warm and inviting kitchen.

The kettle was shrilling as he washed his hands and dried them on the old towel Mamm left out for him and Daed to use. He caught her smiling softly, as if she suspected his reason for taking the shortcut into the kitchen. Mamm nodded and poured boiling water into a coffee cup, then carried it to the table. Eben had never made a fuss over brewed coffee or instant—it made no difference to him. He was just glad for the hot pick-me-up on such a cold morning.

Once Daed appeared, Eben found his tongue. It was long past time to forge ahead and tell them about his sweetheart residing in Lancaster County. Pretty Joanna Kurtz was the dearest girl he'd ever known.

Daed eyed his chair at the head of the table and ambled over to

40

sit down. Eben could hear his father's stomach growling even as they waited for dinner to be served. His mouth watered at the thought of the thick morsels of beef blended with potatoes, corn, and beans. Still, he sat with his hands folded under the table there in his younger brother's spot just to the left of their father. The wooden bench next to him had been scooted beneath the table, dutifully waiting for a larger family gathering. It had been Mamm's idea to offer Eben the solid chair, similar to Daed's own.

After Leroy left for the world.

Eben still recalled the emotional devastation his brother's rebellion had inflicted upon the entire family. And because Leroy's decision to leave remained mighty painful, Eben had waited this long to communicate his interest in Joanna of Hickory Hollow to his parents. Of course, it wouldn't be anywhere close to the same sort of leaving as Leroy had done. Despite that, Daed and Mamm would be greatly affected by Eben's announcement today.

"A girl in Pennsylvania, ya say?" his father replied, nearly sputtering as he set down his spoon.

Eben explained where and how they'd met. "Seemed providential."

Daed's brown eyes were suddenly serious. "I expect you'll want to bring her here to live, after you wed." He paused. "*If* ya do."

"Not sure how Joanna would feel about that." Eben had never brought up the idea to her, knowing how hard it had been on one of his girl cousins to move clear to Wisconsin a few years back. And it was plain from her letters, as well, that Joanna was quite attached to Hickory Hollow.

"We look forward to meeting her," Mamm said, and Daed agreed with a jerky bob of the head.

"You'll meet Joanna before we marry," he assured them, realizing his father's grave look of concern had everything to do with Eben's being his temporary partner in running the farm. "Of course, I'm prayin' Leroy will come back first."

"Jah, we're all still holding out hope for that," Daed said.

Daed gave Mamm a hard frown, then turned back to Eben. "I'm sure ya know, you and your bride will have to live here if Leroy doesn't return home. Your Mamm and I are dependin' on ya, son."

The very thing that kept Eben up at night returned to plague him anew, and he said no more as he pondered his father's declaration.

··· ⊱ ⊰ ···

Joanna worked alongside Mammi Sadie to get the wash indoors and folded that afternoon. She also managed to finish the plum-colored dress, all but the hemming. Because of the latter, she wasn't available to help Mamma get an early start on supper like she usually did. Tonight's meal was an oven casserole of turkey, buttery egg noodles, and mushroom soup—one of her father and Cora Jane's favorites.

Grateful to have a short break in her routine, Joanna thought of running over to Rachel Stoltzfus's before returning to set the table for Mamma.

"Looks like Cora Jane's flown the coop," Mamma remarked with a peculiar look at Joanna when she came down to the kitchen after putting away the dress.

"Most likely upset with me."

"What now?"

"I told her 'bout Eben's visit."

Joanna knew by the glint of recognition on Mamma's face that Dat had filled her in.

"Well, I should think she'd be downright pleased for ya."

Joanna nodded. "If ya don't mind, I'm going to check with Rachel about Eben staying with them for one night. All right?"

"*Gut* a place as any, I 'spect."

"I'll be right back," Joanna said, going to put on her boots and coat for the trek across the snow-covered field.

"If ya see Cora Jane anywhere, tell her to come on home," Mamma said as she followed Joanna into the utility room. "She knows better than to throw a fit like this."

Mamma's fed up, too! Joanna thought as she picked her way over the windblown snow. She wrapped her scarf more tightly to protect her face from the fierce cold. "How long before word gets out about Eben and me?" she whispered. Her precious secret had been safe for this long. She shuddered at the thought of most all the People knowing her business; the cocoon their love had grown in was dear to her. Yet that was the price of moving forward with a real-life romance. Nothing story-like about it! Of course, hard as it was to surrender their relationship to others' scrutiny, Joanna was thankful Eben was apparently ready to start seriously courting. *Just as I am . . .*

Blue patches of sky appeared through the high clouds, and she wished Eben were coming to see her when it was warmer. Certainly, there were still interesting things to do in November. Why, with all the cold they'd been having, they might even be able to go ice-skating on Samuel Lapp's pond.

She spotted the Stoltzfus farmhouse and hurried toward the driveway. Then, thinking it might be best if she didn't appear too eager when she greeted Rachel, Joanna quickly flattened her smile. No sense in Rachel's guessing right away who Eben was to her. She made her way around to the side door, turning her head away from the wind, and knocked.

"Well, goodness me! Hullo there," Rachel greeted her. "Won't ya come in?"

"Hullo, Rachel." Joanna followed her into the balmy kitchen, replete with a delicious aroma.

"What brings you out in this weather?" Rachel's face was cherry red from cooking over her woodstove. She was one of only a handful of women in the area who still cooked the old way.

"Sorry to barge in so close to supper," Joanna said. "Just wanted to ask a favor."

"Why, sure . . . anything a'tall."

"We're havin' out-of-town company this Friday . . . and, well, I wondered if you'd mind keepin' him overnight."

Rachel fixed her gaze on Joanna, a hint of a smile in the corners of her mouth. "Why sure, we'll put your guest up for ya, Joanna."

"Denki ever so much."

Rachel's curiosity was evident in the arch of her eyebrows. "Is this anyone we know?"

Joanna guessed she wouldn't be getting out of this without filling in a few details. So she did her best to satisfy Rachel and yet not come right out and say that Eben Troyer was her beau.

"Rest assured, we'll treat Eben real *gut*," Rachel said with a nod of her head.

"He'll take his meals with us, of course. You won't have to bother with that."

"Oh, 'tis no trouble—but as you wish." A smile spread across Rachel's face. "We'll look forward to meetin' your friend, for sure."

She saw right through it! Joanna thought as she turned to leave. *Just as everyone else will.* Even so, it was her job to trust that all would go well.

Still feeling hesitant, Joanna tightly pulled her old wool jacket around her and hurried back to her father's house.

7

AFTER supper, Cousin Lena arrived to mark the hem of the bridesmaid dress as she'd promised. Joanna stood like a statuette on a stool in the middle of the kitchen as Mamma observed merrily from the head of the table, where she rarely sat.

Meanwhile, Lena chattered nonstop about the many relatives coming to town for the wedding—some from the Somerset area, and others from upstate New York, near the Finger Lakes. All were first or second cousins of either Lena's mother or father and had received written invitations.

"It'll be nice to see some of my own second cousins, then, too," Mamma mentioned, putting the family tree in better perspective for Joanna.

"Which makes them Lena's second cousins once removed?"

Mamma agreed. "And yours, too."

Once the hem was precisely marked by many pins, Lena insisted on sewing it up at home for Joanna, asking to take the dress with her. "I'll press it up real nice for ya, too." Her eyes twinkled gaily.

Joanna thought Lena might be overdoing it. "It's your wedding, for goodness' sake!"

Yet after a few more exchanges, Joanna realized she wasn't going to get Lena to change her mind; there was nothing to do but let her have her way. Joanna went into the bathroom to step carefully out of her new dress, then folded it neatly. She put on her work dress again and took the lovely plum one out to the kitchen, where she watched Lena tuck it into her wicker basket. "I'll come and pick it up Wednesday afternoon, then. All right with you?"

"Sure," Lena said before marching to the wooden pegs in the utility room, where she'd hung her coat and scarf. Then, just that quickly, she was ready to go. "Denki ever so much, Joanna!" And she was out the back door to the waiting horse and carriage.

"Well, I did my best to persuade her to let me finish the hem," Joanna said, joining Mamma at the table.

"That's one strong-willed bride, I'll say." Mamma laughed softly and glanced at Cora Jane, whose back was to theirs now, where she stood near the counter. "Such traits tend to run in the family."

Joanna caught her meaning and rolled her eyes.

"How'd it go over at Abe and Rachel's?" Mamma changed the subject.

"Everything's all set."

"Sure's nice of Rachel," Mamma said rather cryptically.

Smiling briefly, Joanna agreed. "She's doin' it for you, Mamma, ya know. For her *gut* friend."

Mamma said she supposed that could be. "But even so, Rachel must be awful happy for you . . . just as I am." Mamma eyed Cora Jane again, as if she almost expected her youngest to speak up now and say something kind.

"Well, I can't wait for you to meet him," replied Joanna.

At that, Cora Jane slipped out of the room.

Mamma waited till Cora Jane was gone a few moments before saying, "Someone's definitely sufferin'. Not sure just why."

"Maybe I shouldn't have waited so long to tell her about Eben."

Mamma shrugged. "I wouldn't blame yourself. Some folk are just afflicted with a grouchy disposition."

"Comes and goes like the wind, jah?"

Mamma sighed into her hands. "It might be best if your sister's gone on Friday, like she's threatened to be."

"She said that, too?"

Mamma nodded her head. "It'd be such a shame if her attitude spoiled things for ya."

"Well, Eben comes from a long line of siblings, so surely he's encountered a *schniekich*—persnickety—sister at some time or other."

"Just hope she grows out of whatever ails her," Mamma added.

Or just plain grows up, thought Joanna.

··· ➤ ◄ ···

All day Wednesday, Joanna, her mother, and Cora Jane scoured the interior of the house as thoroughly as if they were planning to host Preaching service. They'd washed all the throw rugs the day before, having done up the rest of the laundry on washday.

Cora Jane's apparent disdain for the effort to make things spotless annoyed Joanna. She worked slowly and grudgingly; Mamma actually had her go back and redust or remop certain rooms. Although firm, Mamma was altogether patient, like a mother might be with a youngster. Joanna was grateful for her mother's example and resolved not to let her sister's sour attitude get the best of her, not with so much happiness just around the corner.

··· ➤ ◄ ···

Joanna rose early the next day to arrive at Lena's in plenty of time to offer support to the bride. Joanna offered to brush Lena's long blond hair while the other attendant, Mary Ruth Beiler, pressed Lena's white organdy cape apron one last time.

Joanna recalled Cousin Malinda's emotional pre–wedding service breakdown and smiled to herself. There was no evidence of tears for *this* bride. No, Lena seemed impatient to get on with the wedding.

Out the window, Joanna spotted Salina arriving with her husband, Noah. She wondered if Salina would have chosen to come to Lena's wedding had Joanna not been one of the wedding attendants. Nevertheless, it was good to see her and Noah looking so nicely dressed for the occasion. She loved the way they still glanced so fondly at each other.

Hours later, once the wedding feast was under way, Joanna noted which courting couples were in attendance. As beautiful as the wedding table was, she could hardly wait to get home, thinking of Eben's arrival tomorrow.

She was glad that Dat and Mamma had come, which meant Cora Jane was somewhere around the house. But because Gideon Zook evidently hadn't been invited, her sister must have had to resort to spending time upstairs talking with other girl cousins. Joanna hated to admit it, but she felt more comfortable with her sister in another room just now.

It wasn't till much later, after the evening Singing, that Joanna and Cora Jane walked home together. This was the first they'd been alone since Joanna had told her about Eben's visit, and Joanna was content to walk in silence for quite a ways.

Then, out of the blue, Cora Jane muttered something about Joanna's defying the odds. "You're pressin' your luck, sister."

"I don't see it that way."

"Well, how *do* you see it?"

Breathing deeply, Joanna felt the icy air cut into her lungs. "It's about believing, really."

"That someone's going to marry you?"

"Not just someone." She sighed. *Should I say it?*

"So your beau's comin' to propose marriage, is that what ya think?"

"That's what fellas usually do after writing to a girl so long." She'd divulged nothing more than the truth.

"Okay, so maybe he *is* going to . . . but don't forget he could take you away from Hickory Hollow forever!" Cora Jane sounded hurt. Really hurt. And Joanna didn't know what to say.

"After all, he's already taken you from me before: You never once explained your absence while we were in Virginia Beach, ya know." Her sister paused.

Joanna shook her head. "I didn't realize you were counting on me, Cora Jane—you seemed to be having plenty of fun with our cousins. Honestly, I didn't think I'd be missed."

"Well, now ya know."

Cora Jane's tone was bitter, and Joanna couldn't bring herself to apologize. Lots of older sisters kept romantic things to themselves until closer to an actual engagement. Just because Cora Jane herself had always been so open about fellows didn't mean Joanna was bound to be, as well . . . especially when she'd had so few fellows take an interest in her over the years. *And, too, I didn't want Cora Jane to ruin anything with Eben*

48

when we'd only just met, she thought. Considering her sister's present concern about his being from Indiana, Joanna didn't think she'd been wrong in that.

Cora Jane sped up the pace a bit, not saying more. And Joanna fell in step with her once again.

8

JOANNA stirred until late that night, unable to sleep. She was excited about tomorrow, yet apprehensive, too. She offered a silent prayer to God, who alone saw her troubled heart. If only Cora Jane hadn't refused to understand the need to keep Eben's affection a secret. After all, this was Joanna's first and only love. *Why can't Cora Jane understand?*

The moonlight crept under the dark shades, playing across the wide plank floor. Was Cora Jane restless tonight, as well? Joanna was too drained to go across the hall to see.

Eventually, Joanna fell asleep, although her rest was fitful.

Hours later, when it was finally time to get up, she tiptoed to Cora Jane's room, expecting her to just be waking. But the bed was neatly made, with no sign of her. *What's this?* Joanna clenched her hands. Where had her sister disappeared to at this early hour? Had she already made good on her threat to leave?

Nor was Cora Jane present at the breakfast table. And when Joanna asked Mamma where she might've gone, her mother shook her head in dismay. Dat raised his eyes fleetingly to meet Mamma's, then resumed eating his eggs and bacon.

She'll return once Eben goes home, Joanna felt sure.

After dishes were done up and put away, Joanna dressed warmly and hurried outdoors to brush and curry both the driving horses, not knowing which one she and Eben might use later. She was anxious to show him around Hickory Hollow, hoping he, too, might fall for its winsome charms. She combed the horses' thick dark manes and tails till they were beautifully smooth.

When she was satisfied they looked exceptionally well groomed, she and her father oiled the harness, working together. While Dat remained mum on the subject of Eben's visit, she did catch him looking her way several times, wearing a thoughtful expression. He'd also taken time to clean up his work boots and was wearing one of his better black felt hats instead of the old gray knit one he usually wore around the farm this time of year.

Even though there was no way Eben would arrive before four o'clock, Joanna found herself keeping an eye out for him from midmorning on. She wanted to be completely prepared in every way. Once she was satisfied all was caught up, she went to bathe and dress in her best blue dress and matching cape apron. She dabbed some light perfume behind each ear and on each wrist. Then she went through the house, scrutinizing the downstairs rooms, trying to see them through Eben's eyes as best she could.

Mammi Sadie dropped in a few minutes later, mouth pursed. "It seems that Cora Jane's run away from home," she muttered.

"I know," Joanna said, offering her grandmother a chair near the heater stove. "She's peeved."

"Joanna's beau's comin' from Indiana," explained Mamma.

Mammi Sadie's eyes lit up. She looked quizzically at Joanna. "So then it's true, what Cora Jane said."

"Cora Jane told?"

"Oh . . . lots of sisters slip up and spill the beans, 'specially about such exciting news, honey-girl."

Joanna didn't know what to think.

Soon, Mammi Sadie had her talking again, and Joanna quickly filled her in about last summer at the beach.

"Well, praise be!" Mammi made over her like a mother cat tending to her kitten. "Today? Your beau's honestly comin' today?"

Joanna said he was, but she wanted to know more about Cora Jane. "Do you know where my sister's gone?"

"Why, sure I do. She's sittin' over in my kitchen eating me out of house and home."

"Ach, now." Mamma's shoulders visibly relaxed. "*Gut.*"

"Is she comin' back anytime soon?" Joanna asked.

"She's in a foul mood. So I didn't dare ask," said Mammi Sadie.

"Well, better keep her over there, then." Mamma gave Joanna a knowing look. "We sure don't want any fussing today."

Mamma doesn't want to run Eben off is what! Joanna had to smile at how much his visit seemed to mean to her mother and grandmother.

"Tell Cora Jane she's welcome to have supper with us, if she'd like," Joanna offered.

Mamma shook her head. "Do ya really think that's a schmaert idea?"

Joanna wondered. "Well, I dislike excluding her."

"Looks to me like she's doin' that herself, ain't so?" Mammi Sadie said, accepting the hot coffee Mamma offered.

"Jah, 'tis best to leave her be," Mamma said firmly.

"All right, then." Joanna looked out the window from sheer habit. "Keep Cora Jane occupied."

"Oh, will I ever," Mammi Sadie agreed. "There's plenty of patching and whatnot that needs done."

Won't she just love that? Joanna grimaced for her sister, then poured herself some hot water for tea and wandered into the front room, letting Mammi and Mamma talk alone for now. She stood at the window facing the road and peered out. Heavy gray clouds had moved in, and delicate flakes drifted in the air like bits of onion skin. She hoped the snow slowed by the time Eben arrived so they could have a ride around Hickory Hollow, but she didn't want to dictate their activities. Whatever they did was up to him, even though he was their guest.

Now, if only Cora Jane would behave herself and quit causing a silent rumpus!

By five o'clock, Joanna had almost given up on Eben's arrival in time for her delicious meal. She was warming the potato rolls she and Mamma had taken great care to make when she heard her mother let out a little gasp.

Turning, Joanna saw a bright yellow cab pull up to the end of the lane. "Ach, he's here . . . Eben's here!"

Mamma rose and went to the window, smoothing her apron. "He certainly is."

"Are ya nervous, too, Mamma?"

They laughed, acknowledging their shared anxiety, and Joanna's eyes locked with hers.

"Oh, Mamma, pray nothin' goes awry." Joanna fussed with her hair, smoothing the middle part.

"*Puh*, what could go wrong?"

Joanna dared not ponder that. Instead, she asked, "Do I look presentable?"

"You're fine, dear. You look just fine." Her mother smiled and waved her toward the door. "Go on now. Meet your beau."

Reminding herself to breathe, Joanna went to the door, her heart beating double-time. Only in the pages of her stories had she ever experienced a moment like this before. Mere romantic imaginings . . .

Joanna spotted Eben strolling up the lane, carrying a dark duffel bag. He wore a black frock coat and black felt hat, as though for Sunday go-to-meeting. By all indications, he was coming around the back of the house, the way everyone else did in Hickory Hollow. And oh, did he ever look handsome!

Joanna made herself move slowly to greet him, glad to see the lineup of coats and boots was still tidy from her morning redding up. A *marvel!* Now, standing a few feet from the closed door, she stared at it, nearly boring a hole with her anticipation as she waited for the knock to come.

A thickening band of clouds had blown in with the afternoon, depriving the area of color. The change in weather had occurred just since Eben had arrived in Lancaster city. Joanna's Hickory Hollow looked pale gray beneath the gloomy sky as he paid the cabbie, then walked toward the Kurtz home. He'd checked the address twice for good measure. At long last, the day he'd waited for had come.

Eben took note of the well-kept older farmhouse, similar to his own father's abode. The horse fences had been newly whitewashed, and someone had just recently swept off the long walkway around to the back door, where he assumed he ought to go and knock. Would Joanna herself open the door? If so, how would she greet him?

Relax, Eben told himself. *This is the girl who writes you every single week.*

The reminder was encouraging. And now the moment had come. He stood tall, pushed his feet together, and took a deep breath. *O Lord, bless this time with my sweetheart-girl*, he prayed.

He raised his hand and knocked on the back door with what sounded like confidence, even to him.

9

JOANNA opened the back door, and there stood her beau, a broad smile on his face.

"*Willkumm*, Eben." She'd never meant anything more.

"Hullo, Joanna . . . it's wonderful to see you again."

"You too." Her cheeks warmed at his words. "Come inside." She opened the door wider.

"Mighty cold here, ain't?" he commented as he removed his boots.

"Jah, 'tis," she said. "Was it this wintry in Shipshewana this morning?"

"Not nearly, and it was mighty early when I left." He shook his head, still smiling. "Driver said you might be getting a big snowstorm here."

Joanna led him through the outer room to the kitchen. Just seeing him again, sensing the lovely feeling of attachment between them, she wished he might get snowed in here for days on end.

Then, remembering her mother was sitting nearby, Joanna introduced her. "Eben, this is my mother, Rhoda Kurtz."

Eben set down his duffel bag and shook her hand. "Denki for allowing me to visit your daughter."

Mamma's eyes glinted her approval. "I daresay you've had yourself a long day." She rose and went to the stove. "Would ya like something hot to drink? Coffee, tea . . . some cocoa?"

Eben kindly accepted some coffee, and Joanna offered to take his coat and hat, which he gave her. She turned toward the utility room but thought better of it. Eben's outer clothes ought to be hung elsewhere. They looked so nice . . . and new. Surely he hadn't put himself out just for her!

Joanna slipped into the sitting room and hung Eben's coat in there, then, returning, she found Eben and Mamma talking quite freely, and she felt momentarily sad that Cora Jane wasn't around to meet him, too.

"My husband's still in the barn, but he'll be along soon," Mamma was saying.

Joanna eventually showed Eben into the sitting room, knowing Mamma wouldn't mind setting the table and putting supper on for the four of them. Joanna had so enjoyed preparing the special meal, delicious recipes in the family for generations: dinner in a dish and Hickory Hollow salad. Dessert was lemon sponge pie, which she dearly loved to make and eat.

"I'm eager for you to meet my father," Joanna said as they sat down. "Just a little warning, though—he's quiet. Rarely says much."

"Ah, I have uncles like that." He laughed a little. "You kinda get to know what they're thinkin' after a while."

"That's exactly right."

Eben smiled at her and leaned forward slightly. "You're even prettier than when I first met ya, Joanna."

She lowered her head. "Ach, Eben . . ."

"You truly are," he said, reaching for her hand. "After supper, I say we go riding . . . just the two of us."

She agreed, unable to pull her eyes away from his.

"We'll have us a nice time," he said.

She knew they would. Goodness, she knew it as well as her own name! Then, hearing Mamma in the kitchen, she let go of his hand and settled back in the chair.

Eben winked at her before looking around, resting his hands on the upholstered arms of the chair—Mamma's favorite. "A pleasant spot, jah?" He glanced toward the corner windows.

"Mamma likes to read her devotional books and the Bible here where the light streams in."

He picked up a magazine with the title *Ladies Journal: Inspiration and Encouragement by Women of Faith.* He thumbed through and stopped at a particular page. "Well, look at this—an article on natural homesteading."

Joanna leaned over to see.

"It mentions the bugs folks need in a healthy garden. How 'bout that?"

This brought a fond chuckle; then he began to read from the article. "Listen to this: 'Hoverflies and chalcids will consume aphids, white flies, and stinkbugs' . . . oh, and even grasshoppers in alyssum." He looked at her. "Do you plant alyssum?"

"In the late spring, jah." She found it interesting how casual and familiar they were together. "May I see that article?"

He handed her the magazine, holding it open. "Looks like men might even enjoy some of these columns. My father would, I think," he added. "He's not much for reading, though. Mostly the Bible."

"Same with mine. But he does faithfully read *The Budget* and the *Farmers' Almanac*—just not in that order."

In a few minutes, Mamma softly called them for supper, though without coming into the room, honoring their privacy. They rose and walked into the kitchen just as Joanna's father was entering the back door.

May this supper go well, prayed Joanna.

She could hardly wait to share her meal with Eben. But then the back door opened once again, and Cora Jane stepped inside, as if she'd never gone anywhere at all.

Suddenly realizing that Mamma had set the table with only four plates, Joanna scrambled quickly to the cupboard and pulled out another for Cora Jane. It would never do for her sister to think she wasn't wanted, not after spending all day with Mammi Sadie next door, undoubtedly stewing.

But Cora Jane caught her eye just then and saw what Joanna was doing. She raised an eyebrow as Joanna placed the plate and an extra set of utensils on the table. *This is sure to set her off again!*

By the time Dat came into the kitchen after washing up, Joanna didn't know whom to introduce to Eben first. But it was her sister who looked the most interested, standing in the middle of the room and trying not to be conspicuous in her scrutiny of Joanna's beau.

"Cora Jane, I'd like you to meet Eben Troyer from Shipshewana," Joanna said, finding her voice. "Eben, this is my sister Cora Jane."

"Hullo." Eben offered to shake her hand, which she did with a pleasant enough smile. "It's nice to finally meet you and your family . . . put faces to names, ya know."

"Willkumm to Hickory Hollow," Cora Jane said, eyeing the table again.

She went to her regular spot to the left of Dat, who'd dried his hands and was moseying around Eben's duffel bag to the head of the table now without stopping to speak.

"Dat, this is my friend . . . Eben Troyer," Joanna said, holding her breath for what he might say.

Her father said hullo agreeably, then stuck out his hand to shake Eben's. "Gut to meet ya."

"Please call me Nate," Dat said as he took his seat. "That'll be just fine."

Cora Jane attempted to squelch the smirk that appeared at this but failed. Joanna was on pins and needles as she went around the table to the right of Mamma, where she sat with Eben on her opposite side.

So the suppertime setting was lopsided, instead of the way Joanna had envisioned things earlier, without her sister present. At least Cora Jane had shown some respect and come home to meet Eben. Yet Joanna still wasn't convinced that was such a good thing.

Eben found the unspoken interplay between Joanna and her younger sister curious. There was certainly an undercurrent of tension between them, yet Joanna hadn't referred much in her letters to Cora Jane or to her older, married siblings, all of whom had two or more children of their own. She had written mostly about the sister named Salina and her *three S's*, as Joanna liked to call her young nephew and two nieces. And Joanna had also told of an English friend named Amelia, who played the fiddle, as well as an elderly woman nicknamed the Wise Woman and other folk who lived there in the hollow.

Eben listened as Rhoda Kurtz praised Joanna's cooking skills, finding it somewhat humorous. After all, his taste buds were definitely in the know, and right this very minute, too.

"Joanna cooks and bakes near everything from scratch," Rhoda added.

"'Cept for her pizzas," Cora Jane said, leaping into the conversation, her eyes sparkling mischief.

Eben felt Joanna stiffen on the wooden bench next to him.

"Oh jah, the store-bought tomato sauce," Rhoda defended Joanna. "Well, all the womenfolk use it."

Eben glanced at Nate Kurtz, a seeming caricature with a healthy appetite. His graying beard had somehow managed to grow in the shape of a V, something Eben hadn't seen before. It almost looked as though someone had taken a scissors and trimmed it, and in a droll way, it complemented the man's reserved demeanor.

"Is this your first visit to Lancaster County?" asked Joanna's mother, obviously changing the subject, and abruptly at that.

"Sure is," Eben said as he turned to smile at Joanna.

"Had ya thought of comin' sooner . . . to meet us, I mean?" Cora Jane said, her eyes fixed on her sister.

Eben had to laugh. "Oh, many times."

Dear Joanna fidgeted next to him.

"Couldn't get away before now," he explained. "Bein' my father's right hand, so to speak." He thought now was as good a time as any to let Joanna and her family know about his dilemma. "You see, my younger brother's away from the fold . . . left us two years ago. My father had him pegged to be his partner in running the farm, which hasn't happened. Not just yet."

Cora Jane's eyes widened, as did Nate's. Eben didn't look at Joanna or her mother just now.

"Is that why you didn't come to court my sister right away?" Cora Jane asked.

Her father looked at her, face vexed. "Daughter . . ." he said softly, though the warning in his tone was clear enough. Then, turning toward Eben, he said, "You do plan to move here in time, ain't?"

Eben nodded. "That's my intention." He drew a long breath. "Once my brother returns home."

Cora Jane was looking at Joanna now, no doubt sending messages with her big eyes. It reminded Eben of Leroy, who'd always sat across from him at the table, pulling faces.

"Well, you must know by now that Joanna's already made her baptismal vow to God and the church here," Rhoda remarked. "In accordance with *our* bishop."

"So how's this ever goin' to work, then?" Cora Jane blurted.

"Sister, please!" Joanna said, nearly coming up off the bench.

Cora Jane's head went down and Nate's shot up. Rhoda quickly rose and hurried to the stove, where she reached for the coffeepot. She returned to the table and began to pour it rather shakily into everyone's cups, whether they'd asked for more or not.

Eben felt it was on him to say something to calm things down. "All of my family, and many others in our community, are prayin' for my brother Leroy to return to his senses, to join church."

"The Lord God is sovereign," Rhoda said firmly, turning to carry the coffeepot back to the stove.

"He certainly is," agreed Eben.

"In all His ways," Nate Kurtz added.

Eben made a mental note to privately ask Joanna's father his permission to court her on Hickory Hollow soil. Given the concerned reaction at the table just now, that seemed like the wisest approach. *Best to stick with my original plan.*

10

JOANNA was surprised when Mamma let Cora Jane know that she alone was to be responsible for clearing the table and redding up the supper dishes.

Meanwhile, Joanna managed to keep her composure until Dat took Eben outside to the barn. "You had no right to speak up like that, Cora Jane! What were ya thinkin', for pity's sake?"

Cora Jane still sat at the table, leaning her head into her hands.

"Now, girls," Mamma said, getting up to look outside. "This'll never do. Let's make this a pleasant time."

"Well, Eben's trouble." Cora Jane rose from her seat. "He is . . . you'll see."

"Listen here, I'd never think of talkin' up to your beau like that."

"Well, don't ya think it's a *gut* thing I did?"

Joanna left the kitchen to go and sit where she and Eben had enjoyed a quiet and relaxed moment, prior to supper. *Before Cora Jane came home!* She sat there, not knowing what to do. Would Eben take the next van out of here tonight yet? She wouldn't blame him if he called for a driver immediately. What sort of hornet's nest had he walked into? *Ach, I hope he isn't thinking the selfsame thing!*

She folded her hands, trying to soothe herself by taking deep breaths. Sometimes it was a good idea to just breathe, especially when feeling fit to be tied. Joanna looked out the window at the rising moon. *Eben never told me about Leroy's role in all of this*, she thought, feeling sad.

Even so, Eben was here now, and she believed he'd meant business about courting her. He had also been honest enough to share his quandary. So shouldn't she simply make the best of their time together? Surely things would work out eventually.

Sighing, Joanna wished Cora Jane had just stayed put next door with *Dawdi* and Mammi for the day.

··· ➤ ➤ ···

Eben came inside to warm his hands by the heater stove and urged Joanna to dress "extra warm tonight." Joanna layered up quickly, happy at the thought of going out. And then, with a word of good-bye to Mamma and Cora Jane, Eben picked up his duffel bag and they headed out together. Joanna was surprised to see the sleigh waiting and ready. Evidently, Dat and Eben had hitched Krissy up to the one-horse open sleigh as a treat.

"Thought it'd be fun to see the area while it's snowing," Eben said, guiding her by the elbow as they made their way over the slippery sidewalk and across the driveway.

Even though she was fully capable of getting into the sleigh on her own, Joanna accepted his help, a feeling of relief settling on her. *At least he's not ready to rush right home,* she thought.

Nightfall was approaching as they set out for the evening, turning west on Hickory Lane. Snow was falling more gently now.

She smiled at Eben and was surprised to see he was looking at her, his soft brown eyes seeking her out. "I want to apologize for my sister's impertinence at supper," she said, then paused. "I'm awful sorry."

"I didn't mind, really," he said kindly. "Maybe it's all for the best . . . getting things out in the open right away, ya know?"

"Well, I'm sure her outspokenness bothered my parents. And me."

Eben reached for her hand. He held it close against his chest. "I don't mind a plainspoken woman at all, 'specially when she's speakin' what she believes in."

Joanna couldn't imagine her father saying something like that. Most men she knew felt just the opposite—they wanted their women to be passive and obedient. And even though her own father was a man of little speech, he was most definitely the family patriarch. He made all of the big decisions. Mamma was fairly placid when it came to Dat.

They were coming up now on Samuel and Rebecca Lapp's sandstone house. Seeing the downstairs windows glowing with old-fashioned amber light made her think of the Lapps' adopted daughter, Katie, who lived in the English world, not far from Hickory Hollow. Since she was shunned, Katie was still very much out of arm's reach of the People.

"There's a nice big pond out behind the Lapps' barn," she told Eben. "I've skated on it many times."

"Maybe we could go before my ride leaves tomorrow afternoon. Would ya like that?"

She smiled, delighted he was so accommodating. "That'd be wonderful—*gut*."

Riding a little ways beyond Samuel and Rebecca's home, Joanna pointed out their bishop's farmhouse. "John Beiler was a young widower, but eventually he remarried a much younger woman," Joanna mentioned. "You'll be stayin' at his wife's parents' house tonight—Abe and Rachel Stoltzfus are just across the field from us."

"Then I guess it might not be a *gut* idea to be out all hours, jah?" He winked and playfully pulled her closer.

"I didn't mean that," she chuckled, explaining that Rachel had said the back door would be unlocked. "You can sleep in the downstairs guest bedroom, just to the right of the kitchen. She'll keep a lantern lit for ya."

"So we *do* have all night, then." Eben kissed her gloved hand.

"If we don't mind getting frostbit."

His laughter filled the sky. "I won't let you get too cold, believe me," he said, pointing to the woolen lap blankets. "Your father saw to it that I was well supplied."

Which means Dat approves of Eben. "The two of you conspired, then?"

"In so many words."

Joanna caught his meaning and had to smile. He must not mind Dat's reticence, she decided.

"He wasn't reluctant to give his blessing when I asked," Eben surprised her by saying. "But I made it clear where the courting will take place. And now we must pray fervently for Leroy's return."

She wished things didn't depend upon his brother's actions. But she was hesitant to say so.

"Where to now?" he asked when they came to a crossroads.

"I know! The one-room schoolhouse is comin' up soon," she said, pointing with her free hand. "You'll see it in the moonlight."

"Did you ever teach school after eighth-grade graduation?" he said.

"I was never asked, but my sister Salina did for three years before she was engaged."

"What about Cora Jane?" he asked. "Did she?"

"There was some talk of it, but she was passed over for one of our cousins."

"And why was that?"

Joanna didn't want to shed more negative light on her sister. "Cora Jane just wasn't ready."

"Too blunt . . . is that it?"

"Maybe so."

Eben slowed the horse a bit. "If your school board's anything like ours, I understand. They tend to have rather inflexible expectations."

She agreed as they pulled into the school yard. Eben helped Joanna down from the sleigh, keeping her hand in his even after she was safely down.

Eben slipped his arm around Joanna while they peered into the windows of the little schoolhouse. She pointed to the large plaque on the wall, just over the chalkboard: *Trust in the Lord.*

"It's been there for as long as I can remember," she said. Joanna was talkative, even expressive, and he liked the way she strung her phrases together—made him think she was well read, although she never mentioned books. Certainly her letters were exceptional. She wrote in a manner he'd never encountered before, as if she were sharing her very heart on the page.

"Come, Eben, I want to show you where I used to sit and eat my snack during afternoon recess." She tugged on his hand, and he loved that she seemed so comfortable with him.

He followed her around to the front of the school, near the steps. "Were you a shy girl?"

"Well, I still am . . . sometimes." She smiled up at him, blinking her eyes.

"*Most* of the time, right?"

"S'pose so." She led him to the swing on the far left. "Right here. This was always my spot," she told him. "I liked to swing as hard as I could, sometimes leaning back and lookin' down at the ground almost upside down, just a-yearnin' for that giddy feeling in my stomach. Know what I mean?"

Did he ever! "I did that hundreds of times." He paused. "So you took your snacks to the swing?"

"I put my lunchbox on the ground until I got tired of swinging fast; then I dillydallied and ate my snacks later, dragging my feet in the dirt."

"Ah, but only after you tired yourself out."

"My classmates didn't call me *schpassich* for nothin'." Her laugh was delicate in the cold air.

"I don't find you peculiar at all, Joanna."

"Well, you're still getting to know me, jah?"

Eben stepped near, reaching for her again and catching the scent of her perfume. "I can't wait till we have more time for that. And . . . I'm thinkin' our courtship shouldn't last too long." Looking into Joanna's eyes, he was incredibly drawn to her. He wanted to take her in his arms right then and there. He had to purposely force away the thought of kissing her parted lips.

"We best be goin'," she said, apparently sensing what he was feeling. "There's so much more to see."

Sighing inwardly, he agreed. There was plenty of time to demonstrate his affection for her—a whole lifetime ahead. *Lord willing.*

Snow was falling harder now, and it made him remember the woolen blankets, which he unfolded and placed over her once Joanna was settled back in the sleigh. "Let me know if you're still chilly. All right?" he said, loving the sweet, reserved way she had about her.

Joanna nodded without speaking, and he wondered if she, too, had yearned for him to hold her close back at the schoolhouse.

They made a complete circle of Hickory Hollow, and Joanna pointed out one fond landmark after another. She told interesting stories, too, about her many kinfolk, her interactions with Englischers at market . . . and a beautifully secluded spot called Weaver's Creek, set back from the road. She said she hoped they'd have time to at least drive by there before he left tomorrow. The way she talked, there was no doubt in his mind she was extremely attached to this small speck on the map. No, a girl like Joanna wouldn't think of leaving her home. She shouldn't have to.

Our very future lies in my brother's hands. . . .

11

A LONG about eleven o'clock that night, Joanna realized she had very little sensation in her fingers and toes. She and Eben had gotten caught up in conversation about his hope to move to Hickory Hollow to live and work. He had a real interest in becoming an apprentice for a smithy, and he wanted to meet the local blacksmith tomorrow. Of course, farming was definitely in Eben's blood, so that was also an option, if they could just find a parcel of land. But considering the lack of available farmland, it was unlikely.

Just then he leaned his face against hers. "Time to get you home," he said. "I'll unhitch while you get warmed up."

"Don't ya want to go directly to Abe Stoltzfus's place? It's on the way back to Dat's." She was thinking of him.

"But then you'll be stuck unhitching by yourself," he said, clearly unhappy about that.

"Won't take much, really. Maybe I'll get Cora Jane to help me."

He chuckled. "You wouldn't."

"No," she said, smiling. "I'm not that brave."

"I really hate to leave ya with that chore on such a cold night." He paused. "Why don't we just head back to your house?" he suggested. "And I'll unhitch while you warm up indoors. Then, once the horse is stabled, I'll come inside for a while."

She touched his arm. "And I'll make ya some hot cocoa."

"We'll sit in your mother's kitchen and talk a bit longer, jah?"

Joanna could tell he liked this idea. "*Gut,* then."

··· ➤ ≺ ···

Eben unhitched the mare faster than Joanna expected—surely his fingers were as stiff and numb as her own, and gloves made it even harder to maneuver. Yet presently she could see him leading Krissy back to the barn.

She paced in front of the heater stove, remembering what Eben had said about appreciating a frank woman. His response still surprised her. Evidently Joanna had worried about Cora Jane's candor for nothing.

Looking across the field, she wondered if Rachel Stoltzfus had remembered to light the lantern in the kitchen. She strained to see, and sure enough, it looked like she had. Joanna could just make out the kitchen windows from where she stood. She might simply point Eben in the right direction and let him walk over there on his own, once he'd had a good chance to thaw out. It wouldn't do for them to say their farewell for the night outside Abe's farmhouse anyway, for goodness' sake. Nor would it do for them to get too cozy here in Mamma's kitchen. The way Eben was talking, he might be stuck in Shipshewana working with his father for who knew how much longer yet.

So I mustn't let him kiss me. Joanna didn't want to be sorry later, if for some reason Leroy Troyer didn't return home to partner with his father. *In case Eben can't leave there. . . .*

No, she didn't want to risk giving away her first kiss.

There had been many moments in Eben's life when his head had ruled his emotions, but tonight hadn't been one of them. Eager to get back to Joanna, he pushed hard against the barn door, closing it soundly. He was grateful for the time he'd spent earlier with Nate Kurtz. *My future father-in-law, if all goes well.*

Glancing toward the house, he could see movement through the back door window—was Joanna standing there, waiting? Poor thing, if she was even half as frozen as he was. He tramped through the fresh snow as he made his way back to the house, ready for the hot chocolate. And a few more precious moments with Joanna, as well. He needed to slow down, he thought, lest they spend all their time cuddling. Much as he longed to hold her close, they had so little time together; he wanted to learn as much about her as possible—keep her talking. And, if he wasn't

67

mistaken, there seemed to be something she was holding back from him, something she was hiding, though he couldn't put his finger on it.

Eben thanked Joanna for the large mug of cocoa and plate of cookies. She'd lit the gas lamp over the table so that the light spread across the room and poured into part of the small sitting area where they'd first sat when he arrived. Seeing her again now, in this place, he marveled at how dear she'd become to him since that first evening by the ocean. He realized anew how fortunate he was that she was still single, not snatched up and married years ago.

Joanna came over to the table and sat next to him on the bench. She smiled without speaking as she began to sip her own cocoa, but her eyes danced in the warmth of the kitchen.

"I enjoyed seein' Hickory Hollow," he said.

"Would be nice if you could see it in the daytime, too."

He agreed. Then he thought to ask the name of their blacksmith. "I'd like to talk to him right quick tomorrow, if you don't mind."

"I'm sure Smithy Riehl would be happy to meet you and talk shop."

"Of course I'd like to work in some fun for us, too," he went on. "I've been wondering . . . do you have an extra pair of skates big enough for my feet?" he asked, wishing he didn't have to leave so soon.

"I'm sure we do somewhere."

He nodded. "How well do you skate?"

She ducked her head, shy again. "Salina says I'm perty *gut*."

"I'll bet you are." Eben reached for a chocolate chip cookie. "So we'll go skating bright and early tomorrow."

"After a nice hot breakfast, jah?"

"If you're cooking, it'll be delicious."

She blushed and nodded. "What's your mother usually make for breakfast?" she asked.

He realized just then that, other than Leroy, he hadn't talked much about his own family. "Anything from oatmeal to chicken and waffles and gravy. Sometimes scrambled eggs with ham."

"Sounds filling."

"I'd like you to meet Mamm sometime . . . and Daed, too."

"That'd be real nice."

"I hope it can be soon." He sensed her sudden hesitance. Who could blame her, after what he'd revealed at supper? "Don't worry. Something will work out, Joanna." He reached for her hand. "I believe God has a plan for our lives . . . yours and mine—together."

Slowly, she smiled. "I've felt that way, too."

"So we'll just trust in that, jah?" He leaned near. "All right?"

After a time she asked if he'd like more cocoa, but because it was growing late and he was mindful of the Stoltzfuses' kindly gesture for the night, he said he should head over there.

Quickly, Joanna offered him a flashlight from the lowest cupboard. "This'll help ya see your way."

They walked hand in hand out to the utility room, where he turned and thanked her again for the delicious drink and the evening. "I'll see ya tomorrow." He paused. "My sweetheart," he added in a whisper, reaching for her.

"*Gut Nacht*, Eben." She stepped back ever so slightly, and he knew right then that he didn't dare stay any longer. He picked up his duffel bag.

"*Da Herr sei mit du*—God be with you, Joanna." With that, he reached for his black felt hat from the nearest wooden peg, then pushed open the back door and stepped out into the frosty night.

12

THE moment Eben left, Joanna went upstairs to find Cora Jane near the doorway to her bedroom. "You're wasting your time with Eben," she declared.

Joanna walked past her sister, letting it go—she wasn't about to allow anyone to spoil her lovely evening.

"I'm serious. How can ya go out ridin' when he basically told you he's uncertain he can ever move here?"

Hearing her own fears verbalized, Joanna shuddered.

"*How*, Joanna?"

Turning slowly, she measured what she ought to say. "Why are you makin' this your business, sister?"

"I hate to see you get hurt . . . and you will."

"You seem so sure," Joanna said.

"I'm just good at tellin' the truth."

Suddenly exhausted, Joanna motioned toward her room. "Good night, Cora Jane. *Ich geh noch em Bett*—I'm goin' to bed."

Her sister was big-eyed but mum as Joanna closed her door and leaned hard against it in the darkness.

"*I hate to see you get hurt*," Cora Jane had said.

Oh, what Joanna wouldn't give to erase those words.

But how, when her sister's fears were her very own?

--- ➤ ➣ ---

Eben made his way over the snow-covered ground to the Stoltzfus house, glad for the flashlight. He flicked it off and moved quietly into the dimly lit kitchen, still carrying his duffel bag. There, he found a lantern and a welcoming note, which reminded him of his own mother's hospitality.

Recalling where Joanna had said he was to sleep, Eben carried the lantern through the kitchen and toward the front room, into the guest bedroom on the right. Then, raising the wick a bit, he sat on the bed and opened his Bible to Matthew's gospel and began to read as he did each night.

After several chapters, his eyes felt scratchy, and he closed them. He recalled a long-ago afternoon. He and young Leroy had been in charge of bringing home the herd for milking. Leroy had carried a long stick, shaking it back and forth over the emerald-green pastureland as they headed toward Daed's big bank barn.

Eben had seen it first: a single-engine plane buzzing overhead. But it was Leroy whose wide eyes were filled with craving as he stopped suddenly to raise his stick and trace the plane's path across the sky, like an artist's brush on a vast blue canvas. Then and there, he stated, "Mark my words, Eben. One day I'm goin' to fly like a bird."

At the time, Eben had thought his brother meant he wanted to be a passenger on a flight someday. But no, even then Leroy's heart must have been set on being a pilot.

Years later, in the wee hours one night, the distinct sound of Leroy's tennis shoes squeaking in the upstairs hallway would record itself in Eben's brain. Stiffening under the covers, Eben had heard Leroy descend the stairs and knew better than to rush after him or attempt to call out to stop him. Eben hadn't even considered alerting their parents. No, when morning came, they all knew Leroy was gone.

Shaking off the miserable recollection, Eben began to pray the prayer he'd offered up ever since Leroy jumped the fence. But this night, he did so more earnestly than ever before: O Lord, hear my prayer for my brother. Lead him back to us in your will and time, for your sake.

Eben paused, thinking how to phrase what he wanted to add.

And for Leroy's sake, too . . . as well as Joanna's and mine. Amen.

Joanna awakened full of anticipation the next morning. She slipped on her white cotton bathrobe, then raised the shade to peer out, welcoming the rosy daybreak. Another inch of snow had fallen in the night, making a soft covering over yesterday's accumulation. The beauty made her think of Eben, just a field away. Was he also up early, contemplating their day together?

Looking down, Joanna saw where a small fox, or perhaps a young deer, had cut across the newly fallen snow toward the pastureland, its tracks meandering around a walnut tree in the side yard. This time of year had always been bittersweet for her—the year had matured to its eleventh month, and wedding season was in full swing. The season brought joy to most families, but melancholy to the women who'd been passed over . . . another reminder of romantic rejection.

She moved from the window and returned to the small table next to her unmade bed. *Have I grown this year in the fear and admonition of the Lord?* She prayed so, and sat next to the window to read a single psalm before asking for a blessing on the day.

··· ➤ ◄ ···

Joanna began to make a nice hot breakfast to start things off, even though Cora Jane's eyes were sending a silent message that Joanna was merely endeavoring to impress Eben.

Then, of all things, Cora Jane hurried off to cook breakfast next door, first making a mumbled effort to say where she'd be before leaving by way of the back door.

"You know your little sister," Mamma said, excusing her to Joanna.

Joanna tried not to pay attention to the slight, keeping her focus on Eben's imminent arrival. With a fork, she lifted a slice of bacon in the pan to make sure it was perfectly crisp.

When Eben arrived and the food was ready, she and Mamma worked quickly to get everything on the table nice and hot. Then, eager to dig in, Dat led the silent prayer before the four of them enjoyed the tasty spread.

Surprisingly, Eben and Dat had plenty to say to each other during the breakfast of fruit, sticky buns, fried eggs, bacon, and blueberry pancakes. They discussed not just the weather, but the upcoming farm auctions, which made Joanna smile.

Dat likes him!

Mamma was also relaxed compared to last evening and seemed to know without being told that Joanna and Eben had plans for the remainder of his visit. In fact, Mamma practically shooed them out the door, saying she'd do the dishes alone. "Have yourselves a real nice time."

"Denki. We will, Mamma," Joanna said before settling into the sleigh amidst many warm lap robes, thanks once again to Dat. She was thrilled to be alone again with Eben—she'd never felt so comfortable with anyone.

Not far up the road, Joanna finally decided to reveal her love for writing. She'd wanted to wait for the ideal time.

"Stories? Really?" He was all smiles.

"And some poetry, too."

"Well, I'm not surprised, given your letters—they're always so interesting. I really look forward to them."

She didn't mention that other people—especially her circle letter pen pals—had told her they also enjoyed her descriptive letters. "But my stories are just for fun, kinda like your picture taking. I don't share them with anyone."

"So . . . a secret writer." He appeared to mull that over, then asked, "Do you ever write anyone you know into your stories? Me, for instance?"

She flirted back. "As a matter of fact . . ."

"Well, now I'm going to have to read them for certain."

"Oh, you think so?" She laughed, but truly she was delighted.

"What's to hide?"

"No secrets," Joanna said, more thankful than ever for her wonderful beau, someone with whom she could share all of her heart.

Their first stop was Smithy Riehl's blacksmith shop. Joanna was happy to see the stocky middle-aged man grip Eben's hand in a friendly handshake as he offered to show him around. Not wanting to listen in, she walked to the house and visited the smithy's wife, Leah, who was busy mending a pair of her husband's pants. Joanna sat and kept her company, all the while hoping Eben's visit here might bring a promise of work from the highly respected blacksmith.

"That's a fine young man you've got there," Leah said, eyes smiling. "From round here?"

"Indiana," Joanna was quick to say.

"Oh, is that right?"

She nodded, knowing the grapevine would be swinging soon. "I can help ya mend while I wait."

Leah gave her some socks to darn, and the two women sat silently working, although Joanna couldn't help noticing Leah's frequent glances at her.

Later, when Joanna and Eben were on their way to the pond behind Samuel Lapp's barn, Eben volunteered some of what he and the smithy had discussed, including the fact that Eben was encouraged to do some apprentice work with the blacksmith back home.

"Have you been interested in blacksmithing for long?" Joanna asked.

"Well, I learned a few things from our smithy back home one summer, during my teens." Eben explained that his father had urged him and his brothers to learn a trade, along with farming. "Daed always said, 'Ya just never know when it might come in handy.'"

Joanna felt reassured by the fact that her beau was planning ahead for their future as a married couple. As they rode along the familiar back roads, she realized just how wonderful life in Hickory Hollow would be with Eben by her side.

When they came upon Weaver's Creek, Joanna pointed out the lovely spot, so pretty with the dusting of snow on the boulder in the middle of the creek. "Once you're settled here, I'll show you round the whole area," she said. "It's a little too cold today."

"I'll get myself back here the minute I can," Eben promised, reaching for her gloved hand. "Do you trust me, Joanna?" His eyes searched hers.

She nodded her head, relishing his nearness, already dreading his departure. *How I'll miss him!*

Eben was relieved to busy himself with parking the horse and sleigh while Joanna dashed to the Lapps' big house to ask permission to skate out back. He wasn't so keen on riding around in an open sleigh, letting the People here see Joanna with a virtual stranger. The last thing Eben wanted was to have folk murmuring about Joanna's romance with an out-of-state boy. *Hopefully I won't be one for long,* he told himself.

Waiting near the horse, he eyed the two-story bank barn over yonder. The more time he spent with Joanna, the more he knew they were meant to be together. Surely the wedge that was keeping them apart for now would vanish in good time, leaving Eben free to depart Shipshewana.

The Lapps' pond belonged entirely to Joanna and Eben, a novelty for Joanna, who had never skated there without at least a dozen or more other youth sharing the patch of ice. The sun rose higher in the sky, and she enjoyed the warmth on her back as she and Eben couple-skated, flying over the frozen surface together. But what she liked most was his strong arm around her waist, guiding her, supporting her as they went . . . connecting them as a unit. It was as if he had always been there for her.

What'll I do when he leaves?

She made herself reject the miserable thought, wishing the sun might slow its steady climb.

⋯ ➤ ⬱ ⋯

After the noon meal of hearty chicken corn soup, Eben suggested they go walking around her father's property. He said it with a wink that told Joanna there was more on his mind than merely seeing Dat's farmland.

She liked his more casual appearance today, his combed hair free of its more formal black felt hat, and a warm jacket instead of the dressier frock coat he'd arrived in yesterday. Oh, to think of all they had seen and done in the space of not even twenty-four hours! She doubted she'd sleep tonight with thoughts of Eben rushing over her. How could she turn off such strong feelings, just because he was gone from sight? He'd managed to impress himself upon her heart, and there wasn't anything she could do about it.

They walked leisurely, dawdling as they picked their way over the field lane that ran along the perimeter of Dat's vast acreage. Eben held her hand like he might never let it go, and more times than she could count, their arms touched, sending shivers down her spine.

"There's where I got your phone call." She pointed to the old shanty to the left, clear out in the silver field.

He smiled down at her, reminding her that he would always call her every other Friday at seven o'clock.

"Guess I'd better make sure my flashlight has plenty of fresh batteries," she said.

He laughed lightly, and when they looked at each other, neither seemed to want to turn away.

"Will ya wait for me, Joanna?" he asked, serious but hopeful.

"Jah," she said softly, knowing his words were more of a promise than a question.

"For certain?"

She assured him with her smile.

And when it came time to part, Eben took her tenderly into his arms. For the sweetest moment ever, she felt the beating of his heart.

"I'll write to you, my darling," he whispered.

Much as she loved writing, she dreaded the thought of returning to that way of communicating when his nearness was just so lovely, the very answer to her heart's cry. And when he said her name, she raised her face to his, still wrapped in his strong arms.

"Oh, Joanna, I'll miss ya so."

Tears sprang to her eyes as he searched her face, lingering over her brow, her eyes . . . and then her lips. She couldn't help it; her resolve flew far away, and she longed for his kiss.

A crow cawed loudly over their heads, and just that quick, Joanna shifted slightly, offering her cheek instead of what he'd surely prefer. And what she, too, so yearned for. Oh, to know the feel of his lips on her own! *When Eben's my husband, I'll know,* she reminded herself. *We must wait. . . .*

She slipped gently out of his arms, smiling to comfort him. And he followed her, reaching again for her hand as they walked more quickly now to the phone shack, where Eben made his call for the cab. Too soon he'd be taken away from her, all the way to Indiana.

13

THAT night, Joanna put pen to paper, writing the story of her heart. She included every emotion she'd felt during Eben's wonderful visit, and after she outened the lamp, she could scarcely sleep, reliving again and again how he'd held her . . . and the sweet desire she saw so vividly in his eyes.

As days passed, she attended still more weddings, assisting in the kitchen at several, and looked forward to the weekly quilting circle at Mary Beiler's. Joanna's older brothers and Dat worked to shred cornstalks for bedding and attended packed-out farm sales as far away as the eastern county line and into Honey Brook. Other older Amish farmers, weary of the cold, headed south to places like Pinecraft, Florida, and other sunny climes, once wedding season was past.

Joanna and Cora Jane said precious little to each other all the while. Joanna had learned soon enough that things went more smoothly that way. She enjoyed going next door to sit with Dawdi Joseph twice a week, giving Mammi Sadie time to run errands or just to have a slice of pie and a quiet afternoon with her older sisters or Mamma. Joanna cherished the time with her Dawdi, though his memory seemed to be weakening. His recollection of Bible verses was perfect, but he was often hard-pressed to remember where Mammi had gone off to, or what they'd been up to just a day before. *How long before he won't recognize me anymore?* she sometimes wondered.

Besides time with her *Grosseldre*, Joanna also anticipated her occasional visits to see Cousin Malinda. And every other Friday evening a few minutes before seven o'clock, she dashed off to the phone shack to receive Eben's calls, ignoring the looks Cora Jane sent her way.

Yet as wonderful as the phone calls were, Joanna pined for Eben. Joanna recalled his suggestion that they trust God for their future. So much hinged on a day too far ahead . . . at least for her liking. How she longed to hear the three words he hadn't said. Was he waiting for just the right moment to say "I love you"?

Upon his return from visiting Joanna, Eben had been pleasantly surprised when his father agreed to let him take a day off from farm duties each week to work as an apprentice with the local smithy.

The area blacksmith shop where Amish farmers came to have their horses newly shod was set back a ways from the main farmhouse, with its own lane. In just a short time, Eben had discovered how much he liked the work—everything about it from trimming and filing horses' hooves with clippers and rasp, to measuring the new shoe against the hoof, and then heating it on the blazing anvil. Eben worked mighty hard, too—an experienced smithy could shoe a horse in less than an hour, shoeing anywhere between six and eight horses during the space of a typical day. Eben was determined to learn the particular skills involved, anxious to move forward with the hope of working alongside the Hickory Hollow smithy one day.

Yet as Eben joked with customers and busily went about his duties, he couldn't quash the concern that ever hovered in the back of his mind: His splendid plans for the future were for naught if Leroy did not return.

Joanna fretted as the months dragged on without another visit from Eben. Winter melted into spring, and still he stayed away. Was he stepping back? To his credit, he continued to call her, and his letters arrived with the same frequency. He wrote of working with his father to run their big dairy operation, and also told about his apprenticeship with the smithy. Promising as that was, nothing further was said about Leroy or any type of backup plan if his brother didn't come home.

Joanna assumed that with so much responsibility resting on his shoulders, Eben was sacrificing any free time to write to her, and she was grateful. She did wonder if her worries were the fault of her active imagination. Or was she actually reading between the lines? Surely his thinking hadn't changed. Surely the hope of leaving Shipshewana still remained strong.

Trying not to lose heart, she occupied her time by making quilted potholders and embroidered pillowcases for market, as well as helping around the house and next door, too, at the *Dawdi Haus*. She was thankful for the opportunity to earn extra money at the Bird-in-Hand Farmers Market.

As for her sister, when Cora Jane wasn't sewing market goods with Joanna, she was still accepting buggy rides from the same fellow—Gideon Zook. Joanna envied the frequency of their outings under the stars, remembering that one sweet November evening in the sleigh with Eben Troyer. Oh, she hoped Eben still felt the same way about her! With all of her heart, she did.

One March day, Joanna was delighted to receive a letter from her English friend, Amelia Devries. Not wanting to alert—or alarm—Cora Jane, she took the letter to her bedroom and closed the door, settling onto the chair next to the window. Feeling secure there, she began to read.

> *Dear Joanna,*
>
> *Thanks so much for your recent correspondence!*
>
> *I hope you're doing well . . . and still writing your wonderful stories. You might be surprised, but I often think about the one you shared with me when I was there visiting last summer. It was quite compelling—your characters seemed so very real!*
>
> *Have you ever thought of getting your stories published? If so, I would be the first to encourage you to do whatever it takes.*
>
> *Just recently, my own mother received a book-publishing contract. Mom jokingly says that if she can do it, anyone can. Of course—like you—she has been writing secretly for quite some time. So this is by no means a sudden success. . . .*

Joanna smiled at Amelia's enthusiasm but was also cautious not to let the remarks go to her head. And she wasn't about to get herself an agent or move heaven and earth to get published, not when seeking publication was frowned on by many Plain communities. It was the farthest thing from Joanna's mind.

Yet there were times when she privately considered what it might be like for other people to read her work . . . but precisely what form that might take, she really had no idea.

It was April now—ten months since Joanna had first met her beau—and the flowering shrubs were starting to burst forth alongside Hickory Lane. A horse's neigh caught Joanna's attention where she sat at Mamma's table beneath the gaslight, writing yet another letter to Eben. She was glad to have the house to herself this evening. Thankful, too, that Cora Jane had followed Mamma out the back door after supper dishes were put away, to hurry over the dirt field road to visit Mattie Beiler, longtime Amish midwife.

Joanna smiled as she signed off: *Yours always, Joanna.* It was a good thing her nosy sister couldn't be here to peer over her shoulder! Cora Jane had made it clear over the past months that she still frowned on Joanna's Indiana beau. It didn't help Eben's case when he was still stuck in Shipshewana.

Barefoot, Joanna rose and made her way to the rear screen door, where she looked out at the hazy sky, the humidity obscuring the sunset. Over in the pasture, eight mules meandered toward the barn—dark, lumbering figures against the coming twilight.

She stared at them, sighing. It was such a long time since she'd delighted in snuggling with Eben, his smile ever so dear in her memory. More and more like just a pleasant dream. Her heart had never ached for someone like this. They were supposedly a couple. Yet at such lonely times, Joanna feared that nothing more might come of their long-distance courtship. After all, Eben had made only that one visit.

If we could just have more time together!

Their days at the beach and last November's visit and their phone calls were hardly enough to sustain a near engagement. Their relationship needed a shot in the arm—they needed to see each other again, face-to-face. And more frequently, too.

Surely Eben also feels this way.

Joanna noticed a golden barn cat squeezing beneath the newly painted white porch banister. All the while her father and his two older brothers discussed feed prices in their lineup of hickory rocking chairs. They also speculated who might get the most cuttings of alfalfa come summer.

Leaning her head against the doorjamb, she enjoyed the sweet fragrance of Uncle Ervin's pipe tobacco, though neither her father nor Uncle Gideon had ever taken up the habit. *Bishop John disapproves.*

Joanna sometimes wondered about Eben's bishop. Her beau rarely mentioned these kinds of things in his letters. Was their man of God patient and measured . . . kind? Or unyielding and stern, as she knew some to be—like their own bishop, John Beiler? Would it be difficult for Eben to transfer his church membership here, to relocate to Hickory Hollow at the appropriate time?

Joanna didn't see Mamma and Cora Jane anywhere just yet. Mattie's husband had recently remodeled the kitchens in both the main house and the Dawdi Haus, and Mattie wanted to show them to Mamma. Nearly all the Amishwomen nearby had beautiful kitchens resembling most any modern one—except, of course, the stove and refrigerator ran on propane gas. Mattie had gone on about the "perty oak woodwork" this morning while having coffee here, and that had apparently sent Joanna's mother running over there. The two friends were known to work well together, putting up jellies or jams in the space of a few hours, even after the day's chores were done. And oh, the stories that flew from their lips . . . especially from Mattie's, telling all about the many babies she'd caught through the years.

Heading back indoors, Joanna gathered up her letter to Eben and went to her room, placing it in the middle dresser drawer for now. Her heart beat faster at the thought of his reading it in just a few days.

Smoothing her hair bun, Joanna headed back downstairs and exited by way of the front door so as not to interrupt her father and uncles. She skirted the main house to visit her grandparents in the adjoining Dawdi Haus. Mammi Sadie often baked sweet cherry desserts—a favorite fruit of Joanna's—and thinking of warm cherry cobbler with a dollop of vanilla ice cream on top made her quicken her steps.

There was no need to knock on the back door—she'd been told for years by Mammi to "chust come in," which she did, pushing on the screen door and stepping inside.

Sure enough, Dawdi and Mammi were seated at their kitchen table having dessert—still like best friends after all these years. "Hullo," Joanna said softly. "Thought I'd drop by . . . see how you're doin'."

"Oh, fine . . . fine," Dawdi said, a bit droopy eyed as he forked up another bite. "Pull up a chair, won't ya?"

"Denki." She did just that as her grandmother dished up an ample portion of cherry cobbler and placed it on one of several dessert plates nearby on the table, just waiting for company. *The best baker round Hickory Hollow, hands down.*

Mammi Sadie looked flushed and reached into her dress sleeve to produce a white hankie, fanning herself with it. "A *gut* strong breeze would help to blow this humidity out of here, jah?"

Joanna agreed as she took another forkful of the dessert, glad she'd come over. "Have yous had evening prayer and Bible reading yet?" she asked.

Dawdi Joseph smacked his lips. "*Gut* thinkin'. Sadie, where's the old *Biewel?*" He winked at Joanna. "Might as well let our young whipper-snapper here do the readin'."

"Well, my German's not so *gut*," Joanna warned.

"Mine ain't much to boast about, neither." Dawdi motioned toward the bookcase. "Look for the bookmark," he added.

Joanna rose and went to the shelf where the Bible for daily use was stored, as well as the old family Biewel with tattered edges. She lightly touched the latter, recalling that it had possibly come over in 1737 from Switzerland with some of their ancestors on the *Charming Nancy*. The Lancaster Mennonite Historical Society would love to have it for their secured archives, if they knew.

Picking up the newer Bible, she found the spot in Psalms and returned to the table. She wished her grandparents used the English Bible so they could more easily understand the verses, like Eben said he did. Some of the young people around here did the same.

"'O Lord God of my salvation, I have cried day and night before thee: Let my prayer come before thee: incline thine ear unto my cry. . . . '"

When she'd finished, she closed the Bible reverently, finding it curious that the reading was so fitting for her tonight. How good of the Lord God to be mindful of her sadness. Silently, Joanna breathed a thankful prayer.

"Nice of ya to read for us," Mammi Sadie said, scooping more ice cream and plopping another spoonful on Joanna's plate without asking.

She knows I crave homemade ice cream!

Dawdi Joseph peered over his glasses. "Better save some for Reuben, or he'll be disappointed when he gets here."

Mammi's mouth dropped open. "Joseph, dear, your brother passed away nearly two years ago."

"What're ya talking 'bout, Sadie Mae?"

Mammi gave Joanna a quick frown, her cloudy blue eyes dim with concern.

"I just talked to Reuben—yesterday, in fact. Why, sure I did." Dawdi shook his head repeatedly, his face perspiring. "You keep gettin' things mixed up." He continued mumbling. "You were off somewheres baking pies and whatnot."

Wisely, Mammi Sadie said no more, her lips tightly pressed. Joanna had seen her handle worse things before, sometimes talking gently to Dawdi when he was disturbed or confused due to memory issues. Things like *"I know it's hard, Joseph,"* or *"I'll stay right here till you feel better."*

Mammi Sadie was as kind as Ella Mae Zook, and Joanna was glad she and Dawdi lived so close in their final years.

Later on, after Dawdi Joseph wandered into the sitting room and Joanna was alone with Mammi, she asked about Dawdi's fixation on the past. "His memory is so sharp 'bout the olden days, ain't?"

"Seems to be the way of aging," Mammi replied. "For some of us, at least."

Joanna felt sorry for her grandfather but knew he was in the best of care with Mammi Sadie, whose mind was as clear as a bell. "You let me know when you'd like some time off, jah?" Joanna offered. "I'm happy to sit with him more than a couple times a week."

"I'm all right, really."

"Well, ya need to get out, too, don't forget."

Mammi reached across the table and touched her hand. "I daresay it's you, Joanna, who needs to get out more often, dear."

She nodded, guessing her grandmother had heard it from Mamma. "S'posin' you're right."

"Which reminds me, your cousin Malinda asked 'bout you the other day."

"Oh?" Joanna perked up. "Is she all right?"

"I think so, but she misses her family at times, like some young brides do."

"I should go see her more often." Joanna finished up her dessert.

"Jah, I think she'd like that."

Joanna pushed her chair back and thanked her grandmother for the tasty dessert. Then, making her way toward the back door, she called "Gut Nacht" to Dawdi and decided to go see Cousin Malinda tomorrow. Malinda's parents and younger siblings lived clear over on the other side of the hollow, so no wonder she sometimes seemed lonely.

Might cheer us both up.

14

W ELL, lookee here!" Malinda said, smiling after supper the next evening as she opened the back door and met Joanna on the porch. Her blond hair was parted perfectly in the middle and neatly pinned into a thick bun at the base of her slender neck. Beads of perspiration glistened on her temples.

"I've been missin' ya." Joanna kissed her cousin's moist cheek.

"Everything all right?"

"Oh jah . . . just keepin' busy with planting the family vegetable garden and whatnot." Joanna followed Malinda around to the potting shed in the side yard. *"The heart of my garden,"* Malinda liked to say. In the summer, it was a cool spot to relax or pray amidst stacked pots, drawers filled with seed packets, and book-sized shelves ideal for storing gardening magazines and guides. There were snips, pruners, and trowels in an old clay pot. Birdseed, sprayers, several spare buckets, hoes, rakes, and shovels, as well as kneeling pads, were well organized in many nooks and crannies. And along one windowless wall, Malinda had a pegboard where she stored garden shears, scissors, and a hammer for small repairs. She even had a comfortable old rocker in the corner.

Joanna's cousin lit a small lantern and pulled out two wooden stools, and they settled in for a heart-to-heart talk beside the wheelbarrows and a push mower.

"Are ya goin' to the quilting bee tomorrow?" Joanna asked, noticing the way fair Malinda beamed in the lantern's light.

"Maybe next time. I'm helpin' my neighbor with spring house cleaning."

"We're hopin' to finish up one real perty friendship quilt," Joanna added. Malinda continued to smile.

Looking at her, Joanna sensed she had something on her mind. "You want to tell me something?"

Malinda glanced over her shoulder, toward the barn. "Honestly, you might not be surprised at all." She paused a second, her eyes twinkling. "So far I've only told Andy."

Joanna's heart leaped up. "Oh, I think I can guess."

"Can ya, now?"

Nodding, Joanna said, "Are you expecting a baby?"

Malinda clapped her hands and laughed softly. "Well, aren't you the schmaert one."

"Oh, such wonderful-*gut* news!" Joanna nearly toppled the stool in her hurry to embrace her cousin. "I'm so happy for ya."

Malinda's face radiated joy. "Just think . . . our first little one, comin' in early November."

Tears sprang to Joanna's eyes. Oh, to be married like Malinda and starting a family! She could just picture herself confiding the same sort of lovely news to her cousin, once she was wed to Eben.

Returning to her stool, Joanna ventured a quick look at Malinda's middle, which as of yet showed no signs of the wondrous news. She imagined how it might feel to have her own tiny babe growing so close to her heart.

Malinda continued talking. "I suppose it's much too early to be makin' cradle afghans and other baby things. Even so, I've already started jotting down names."

"I'd be doin' the same thing if I was in your shoes." Just that quick, Joanna noticed they were both barefoot, and they laughed heartily.

"Dare I ask how things are progressing with your beau?" Malinda's expression turned quite sober.

The question was certainly warranted, but Joanna was caught off guard. She shrugged, feeling the need to keep mum.

"Ah, now, there must be *something*." Malinda leaned forward, clearly wanting to coax it out of her. Joanna recognized that look as one she'd seen on Mamma's face, as well. "I'll keep quiet, promise," Malinda assured her.

"There's nothin' much to tell."

Malinda frowned, her gaze more scrutinizing. "Aw, cousin."

"No, really."

Malinda relented. "All right, then. But I'll keep you in my prayers."

Joanna forced a smile. She disliked pushing her cousin away, but what could she say?

Darkness began to settle in. "No one knows I'm gone from the house," she said. "Might I borrow a flashlight to head back?"

"Of course." Malinda rose and motioned for Joanna to follow her. "But before ya go, I want to show you something I found in the attic during my recent airing of some stored items. This find was quite unexpected, I'll say."

"What is it?"

"Ach, you'll see." Malinda's smile was mysterious. "I'm just sure you'll be delighted . . . 'specially once you're engaged to your young man."

"Ya mean, it's for me?"

"Oh, Mammi Kurtz insists."

"You've talked to our grandmother 'bout this?"

Malinda nodded as they walked through the yard. "It'll make you ever so happy, believe me."

Joanna followed behind her cousin, thinking she should ask the question she'd already posed to several family members in a sort of poll. She wanted to include some of the responses in the story she was writing, the longest one to date. She enjoyed observing people—*real* people—storing away the images in her mind. This had been a hobby since childhood, when she watched others wherever she went, be it the one-room Amish schoolhouse, Sunday Preaching, or at the roadside vegetable stand where Englischers stopped by. Only later had Joanna started recasting these remembrances into fiction on the pages of her notebook.

Joanna and Malinda strolled back to the house, and Joanna was aware of the stars appearing one by one. Insects fluttered against the screen door, hungry for the light. She recalled the small bees she'd seen curled up, asleep, the other day inside the creamy-yellow rose petals along the side of the house. *The wonders of spring . . .*

Joanna paused on the back porch, leaning on the railing. "Have ya ever considered what's been the happiest time of your life, so far?"

Malinda wrapped her arm around a porch post and closed her eyes for a moment. Then, laughing softly, she opened them. "Frankly, I don't have to think hard 'bout that. It's the day I married Andy."

Joanna was mighty happy to hear it, particularly considering how very emotional Malinda had been. Goodness, to think she'd misread her cousin so completely! "Several of the womenfolk have said their happiest moment was becoming a mother for the first time," Joanna told her.

"I guess I'll know that soon enough."

Joanna hugged her. "It does me *gut* seein' ya so contented."

Malinda studied her for a moment. "Why did ya ask, Joanna?"

"Oh, just something I'm curious about." She pressed forward. "I like to know what others think . . . maybe because I like to write stories."

"Stories?"

"Jah . . . it's a secret I've kept from nearly everyone. Well, 'cept Eben and my friend Amelia." Pausing now, Joanna hoped she wasn't making a mistake by revealing this to her cousin. Yet Malinda had always been one to keep a confidence.

"I daresay you've been a curious sort since you were born."

"Guess you're right. But now I'm starting to wonder if I should've kept it to myself and not told Eben at all."

Malinda bit her lip thoughtfully. "Well, I've never heard of a fiction writer amongst the People."

"Me neither. Well, least not in Lancaster County so much."

"Bishop John doesn't want us to think too highly of ourselves, ya know—Scripture has a lot to say on that."

"Jah, 'tis best to stay humble."

"S'pose if you wrote stories to help others . . ."

"That's an idea," Joanna agreed. "But so far they're really only for me." She was quite relieved Malinda didn't seem to think any less of her for her confession. "Truth be told, I'm concerned my beau might be backin' away from me a bit."

"Whatever do ya mean?"

Joanna didn't know if she should say more.

"If anything, at least from what I've heard, the Indiana Amish are less strict in some ways than we are." Malinda smiled endearingly. "Are ya sure he's become aloof?"

Joanna shook her head. "Just a feeling."

"Maybe you're worrying too much."

Her cousin had a point. "Maybe so."

Together, they made their way indoors, through the kitchen, then upstairs to one of the guest bedrooms. Malinda moved to a lovely oak blanket chest just beyond the footboard of a double bed. Carefully, she lifted several blankets and other linens off the top and placed them on a nearby chair. Then, smiling, she raised up the prettiest double wedding ring quilt Joanna had ever seen, all done in reds, purples, and blues. "Just look at this."

"For goodness' sake!" Joanna peered at the exquisite work of art. "It's breathtaking." She reached to hold one end, and Malinda held the other as she inched back to exhibit the entire length of the beautiful quilt.

"Mammi Kurtz says it's a family heirloom."

"And in perfect condition—must not have been used as a covering at night."

"That's exactly what I thought," Malinda said. "But it was somehow misplaced for forty years."

Joanna stared appreciatively at the large interlocking circles. "Such a wonderful-*gut* discovery you've made."

"Well, I don't plan to keep it," Malinda said.

"Oh, but you must!"

"Remember what I told ya?" Malinda's eyes were soft. "Mammi insists that it goes to you."

"*You're* the newlywed in the family," Joanna protested.

"That's kind of you, but I already have plenty of quilts."

Joanna studied her cousin. "Are ya sure?"

"There's no arguing with our grandmother."

"Or you either, ain't so?" Joanna was delighted.

"Besides, there's an interesting story behind this quilt."

"They say every quilt has one."

Malinda nodded her head slowly, eyes twinkling. "It's not just any story, mind you."

Joanna was all ears. "Well, no wonder. Just look at it."

"I don't mean the colors or the stitchin'."

"Oh?"

"Mammi Kurtz says it has a spiritual legacy. And," she said more softly, "there's something of a mystery about it."

"Did Mammi tell you?"

"She said it was a known secret many years ago, but it was forgotten when the quilt disappeared."

"Now you've got me wondering." She searched the quilt for any initials. "Mammi must know who made it, jah?"

"She says it was made in the late 1920s by one of our great-great-aunts."

"That long ago?"

Malinda laid it out on the bed, and Joanna knelt to trace her finger over the familiar pattern, marveling at the choice of such a bold combination of colors. "It's really not much different from our present-day double wedding ring pattern, jah?"

Malinda agreed and knelt on the other side of the bed. "And just look how straight the stitches are. I'm told it was done by only one quilter, if you can imagine that."

"What an enormous undertaking," whispered Joanna.

They fell silent for a time, admiring the family treasure. Joanna let herself imagine the woman, their talented ancestor, who'd lovingly taken the time to make this quilt. To think Malinda had rescued this heirloom from the attic. And, even better yet, Mammi Kurtz wanted Joanna to have it!

Her cousin's and grandmother's sentiments touched Joanna deeply. "Denki," she managed to say. "Thank you ever so much." Did this mean they no longer believed she was destined to be a Maidel?

Her cousin offered to keep the quilt until Joanna could retrieve it in the buggy another day, and Joanna thanked her as they walked downstairs and then out to the porch. A loud chorus of crickets and the scent of honeysuckle filled the air. They spotted Andy coming out of the stable.

Malinda gave her a sweet hug and a flashlight. "Don't wait so long to visit again, all right?"

Joanna said she'd stop by tomorrow, after the quilting bee. She waved, then made her way down the porch steps. She felt nearly giddy, not only about Malinda's pregnancy, but the special quilt. Such a wonderful gift! Indeed, the idea of placing it in her very own hope chest did much to renew Joanna's hope.

She looked forward to hearing what Mammi Kurtz knew about the tale behind such a quilt. *Soon, very soon.*

15

DRIVING horses trotted up and down Peaceful Acres Lane, the thuds of their hooves accentuated by the evening's quiet. Eben wiped his forehead on the back of his shirt sleeve before he opened the mailbox on the front porch of his father's white clapboard farmhouse. Hoping for a letter from Joanna, he was surprised to find a mighty big stack and wondered why Mamm hadn't come out to check for mail before supper.

A single letter caught his glance as he thumbed through the ads and bills. Looking closer, Eben could hardly believe his eyes. *Leroy's hand-writing—and a letter addressed to me?*

Quickly, he opened it, holding his breath. How long had it been since he'd heard from Leroy? As best as he could recall, it had been a good six months since his twenty-four-year-old brother had written.

Not wasting a second, Eben walked around the side of the house, peering closer in the dim light of dusk to read the short letter. He felt a surge of excitement at the final lines. *I'll be home a day or so after you get this, and not anytime too soon. I'll look forward to seeing you and Mamm and Daed, too. We'll have a fine reunion. Best regards, your little brother, Leroy.*

Eben refolded the letter and squinted toward the barn and the out-buildings, including the woodshed, where he and his brother-in-law had spent several hours chopping wood this morning. "Glory be! A reunion, then?" Eben muttered aloud, making his way around the side of the house, toward the door. "What's on his mind?"

Set back on the narrow country lane and surrounded by two hundred acres of farm and grazing land, the Troyer house was grand and welcoming. His parents and two generations of paternal grandparents before them had built the place up from scratch, tilling and cultivating the soil, raising pigs and chickens, and milking a small herd of cows to provide for the family and to make a living. The house itself was over a hundred years old, and Eben knew first-hand what that meant, having helped with the constant repairs through the years.

He reached for the door leading to the combination screened-in porch and catch-all utility room. The mud room, Mamm called it.

"Is Leroy comin' to claim his rightful place?" Eben wondered aloud as he stepped inside. If so, what an answer to his prayers of the two and a half years since Leroy forsook his upbringing, yearning for higher education. The bishop had preached about advanced learning in a sermon not long afterward, urging young people to avoid it like the plague. *"There's a reason why college is called 'higher education,'"* the minister had declared. To him the word *higher* indicated a desire for self-advancement and disobedience to God. As if high school and college weren't enough, Leroy had even learned to fly a plane, far and free.

Free . . .

Leroy was apparently that—liberated and modern—to the detriment of his own family and close friends. And to Leroy himself. Initial word had spread right quick through their community: Will Troyer's youngest boy had finally gone fancy.

Still gripping the letter, Eben considered the wisdom of revealing this news to his parents. Twice now Leroy had mentioned returning for a visit, but something had come up each time to postpone it. Eben certainly didn't relish putting his mother through the heartache again, not the way she'd gone around nearly holding her breath, for pity's sake. And it had been just as tough for Daed, poor man. No, it was best to simply wait and see what happened. See if fancy-pants Leroy followed through this time.

Eben pushed the letter into his pocket and tore the envelope in half, placing it in the trash receptacle under the kitchen sink. His dear mother sat in the small room adjacent to the kitchen, her nose in a book—an Amish love story, it looked to be. She said nary a word over there in the corner, all snug in her overstuffed chair, surrounded by devotional magazines and the weekly newspaper, *Die Botschaft*.

Eben headed to his bedroom upstairs at the end of the long hall. It was still early enough this evening to write to Joanna. What he wouldn't give to tell her this news—was the dreadful holdup on their formal courtship finally at an end?

Goodness, if any girl deserved a proper one, it was Joanna, sweet as a honeycomb. And with each month that drifted by and with every letter he wrote, Eben felt downright aggravated at not being able to give his girl so much as an update. There simply had been no word from Leroy . . . till now.

When Joanna arrived home from Cousin Malinda's, she rushed upstairs and noticed Cora Jane lingering near her doorway, looking rather sheepish. "What're ya doin'," she asked, her suspicions rising.

"Just thinkin' is all."

Joanna excused herself and slipped past her sister. Closing her door, she immediately went to her hope chest to see if her binder of story notebooks was still safely concealed.

Satisfied nothing was amiss, she shook off the prickles of concern and headed downstairs in time for family worship.

Cora Jane had already gathered with their parents in the front room as Joanna came in and sat in her usual chair near the windows. Cora Jane was scrunched up nearly in a ball over in the far chair, her head turned toward the window. Was she thinking about her beau, just maybe?

Settling in across from Mamma, Joanna envisioned each spot where their older siblings had always sat around the front room for morning and evening family worship. Having five older brothers and two sisters, Joanna knew plenty about siblings and their personality clashes, but she also knew that no two siblings were ever alike. Again, she glanced at Cora Jane, wondering how *she* might react to hearing about the heirloom quilt.

Joanna tried to picture Eben and his family beginning their evening prayers, too. And his siblings—six in all, he'd told her—a mixture of sisters and brothers. Did they read and pray every morning and evening as her family did? Except for Eben, all but his younger brother were married. And also like Joanna, he was the next to youngest. *Another common bond between us.*

As for herself, for now, Joanna was quite content to be one of the last two children living at home. She had it worked so she was the sole person getting the mail every afternoon, for one thing. Surprisingly, that had helped to keep questions about Eben's plight to a minimum. *Thus far, anyway . . .*

Presently, Daed began to read the old Biewel in the firm voice he always used for reading God's Word. He placed his callused hands just so on the thin pages. Mamma sat humbly with her pink hands folded in her lap as Joanna listened, watching her sister fidget.

The Good Book had always held an important place in her parents' hearts, and in Joanna's, too. Dat had shared the Scriptures in this manner with the family from their earliest childhood on, starting and ending each day with prayer and Bible reading.

Someday Eben will want to share the Word of God with our children. In her mind's eye, Joanna saw herself sitting next to Eben as he read to the family—how many children? Oh, she longed to move ahead, to be done with her single and sometimes lonely life. She longed to be loved.

Later, when it was time to kneel for prayer, Joanna offered silent thanks for Cousin Malinda's fun discovery of the quilt, and she also prayed for Eben's wayward brother, Leroy.

After Dat said amen, Mamma headed to the kitchen, and Dat shuffled out to the barn one last time.

Joanna said good-night to Cora Jane and hurried upstairs to her own bedroom. *If only tomorrow had wings,* she thought, eager to get her hands on the stunning wedding quilt.

Carefully, she lit the gas lamp in her room and went to the window that faced west, toward Indiana. *I miss you, Eben. . . .* For the longest time, she stood there, looking out.

Then, perceiving someone else in the room, she turned to see Cora Jane in the doorway, her golden hair cascading over both shoulders, a brush in her hand. "May I come in?"

"Sure," Joanna replied. "Want me to brush your hair?"

"Would ya?" Cora Jane's face lit up momentarily.

Joanna motioned for her to sit on the sturdy cane chair near the window. "It's been a long time," she said quietly. *Too long . . .*

Cora Jane sat nice and still, saying no more. Looking at her sister just then, Joanna felt cheerless to think the two of them had been at something of a standstill since Joanna met Eben in Virginia. She tried to make small talk as she brushed Cora Jane's beautiful hair, mentioning things like the next trip to the bakery and wanting to go and see Mammi Kurtz sometime soon. Things that didn't hold a candle to what they'd shared before, sometimes late into the night, lying on each other's beds.

But Cora Jane didn't speak at all.

Joanna shaped the words in her mind: *I'm sorry we're at odds*, she thought sadly. But tonight Joanna believed she could not bridge the gap if she'd wanted to. Cora Jane knew how she felt. Her sister was immovable in her thinking that Eben would never come here to live . . . that he was being less than forthright with Joanna.

Holding Cora Jane's heavy hair in her left hand, Joanna brushed with long, sweeping strokes, again and again. *We've fallen apart*, she mused, hoping this gesture might somehow demonstrate her care for Cora Jane.

And because her sister remained silent, Joanna let her mind wander back to Eben as she continued to brush. Long as it had been since she'd seen him, she wished she had just one picture of Eben. But in keeping with their strict *Ordnung*—the church ordinance—she had none.

I scarcely remember what you look like, my love. . . .

16

AFTER Cora Jane left the room, Joanna raised the lid on her hope chest—there was scarcely enough room inside for the heirloom quilt. "I'll make a place somewhere," she whispered, eager to have the wonderful handiwork in her possession.

Then, digging deeper, she carefully removed a wooden letter box, a gift on her twenty-first birthday from Salina. Every letter Eben had ever sent was safely concealed inside.

She found her favorite—one he'd written in early winter—intending to read it for the hundredth time. She'd marked it with a pink heart on the envelope, so when she missed him the most she could always find it amongst his many letters.

Dearest Joanna,

How are you?

You might laugh at this, but I can hardly wait to see if there's a letter from you every other day or so. Denki for writing as often as you do . . . it's always wonderful-good to hear from you!

Here lately I've been getting up earlier than usual, going with my father to nearby farm sales. But even though I'm fairly busy this winter, I'm never too busy to write to you at night, my sweetheart.

I love being with you! And I wish I could see you again . . . soon.

She stopped reading and held the letter close, pondering his final words. "That's the closest he's ever come to sayin' 'I love you,'" she said softly, wishing with all of her heart he'd tell her so in person. *Oh, to have that as a memory!*

She slipped the stationery back into the envelope and found its spot again, then closed the pretty letter box, slipping it under two knotted comforters and other linens. Joanna then took out the large three-ring binder where she kept her many writings and removed her blue notebook. She carried it to her bed, eager to reread the scenes she'd written yesterday. It hadn't taken long to learn that what seemed good on a particular day often read much differently the next. So she spent time reworking her sentences and paragraphs many times over—*a rewriter,* she liked to call herself.

Joanna tucked her feet beneath the long dress and apron, wishing her church district wasn't so strict. However much some might frown on her spending hours each week bent over her notebook, she loved to express herself that way and couldn't see anything wrong with it. What was she to do? She knew of only one Amish church district, one not far from Harrisburg, whose bishop had given a baptized Amishwoman permission to publish her novels, but they were based on the Plain life, so Joanna guessed that made them all right.

Writing had always been something she did just for herself, but since Amelia's suggestion, the desire to be published sometimes tugged at Joanna during the day when she helped Mamma bake bread or sew. And at night, too, when it poked at her . . . in her dreams. Truth be known, if she could have anything at all, she longed to see something meaningful come from her writing. That, and to marry Eben Troyer.

When she wasn't writing an actual story, she loved jotting down character traits and descriptions of people. Also ideas, things that popped into her head, including questions to explore, like the one she'd asked Cousin Malinda earlier today.

Just yesterday she'd asked Mamma's opinion about the happiest time of *her* life, too, but the question was met with raised eyebrows, as if her mother were saying, *"Think about something useful, child."*

Joanna's oldest brother, Hank, married for some time, had given her a ragged frown when she'd asked him the same thing. He'd spouted his response all too quickly. *"That's easy enough! Courting age,"* he'd said, perhaps implying that marrieds were strapped with responsibilities.

97

But it was the Wise Woman, Ella Mae Zook, who gave the most profound answer of all. *"For me, right now—this moment—is the very best time."* She'd spoken with a faltering smile. *"At my advanced age, I've already learned the hardest lessons, or should have, anyway. Everything we learn when we're young is useful for the years ahead. Unfortunately, sometimes we never really learn the life lessons we're supposed to. Sad but all too true, don't you agree?"*

Frail Ella Mae hadn't spelled out what those lessons were, but Joanna understood her well enough to know she meant the gifts of the Spirit found in Scripture: love, joy, peace, longsuffering, gentleness, goodness, and faith. Some folk called them the simple gifts.

Joanna whispered to herself, "Cherish each and every moment. That's what Ella Mae meant."

She took up her pen, continuing to work on her longest story to date, about an Amish couple deeply in love and separated by several states: *At their first reunion, they talked long into the night, sharing their truest hearts.*

Hearing a sudden creak behind her, she turned and saw Cora Jane standing on this side of the doorway, inching away.

Quickly, Joanna closed her notebook. "How long have you been there?" she asked, her voice quivering.

"Sounds like ya have a guilty conscience." Cora Jane was staring at the notebook.

"Oh, sister . . ."

Cora Jane folded her arms. "Just take what I'm about to say as a warning."

Joanna shifted forward on the bed. "You really can't go through life bossing and judging everyone in sight. It's not your place."

"I've seen you filling pages and pages, sister. Sure doesn't look like a letter to me . . . nor a diary. Who exactly are these people—and places—you're writing about? Did ya make them up?"

Joanna blushed; she'd been caught. "So you're sneaking round, snooping over my shoulder?"

"Then it *is* a story, jah?"

"Writing stories doesn't hurt anyone!" Joanna justified her secret passion to Cora Jane, just as she'd always done to herself. Beyond flustered, she locked eyes with her sister. "I must answer to the Lord God and no one else for what I do. And I don't believe writing the stories in my heart and mind is wrong, not really."

"Have it your way," Cora Jane said. "It sure seems you're bent on that. But what I don't understand is why you've kept this secret from me all this time. You shut me out of your life even before Eben came along, ain't?"

Joanna groaned but said nothing more.

"Why, Joanna? 'Specially if there's nothin' wrong with it, as you say?" Cora Jane demanded. "First your worldly friend, Amelia, then a faraway beau, and now this fiction writing! Next thing, you'll be slippin' away from the People and running off to the fancy English world. It's like I scarcely know you anymore." With that, she turned and fled the room.

Joanna moved to the door and closed it soundly. Her sister was absolutely wrong to lump Amelia and Eben together with her love for writing. *Oh, if only I'd been more careful!*

A torrent of emotions plagued Joanna as she returned to her cozy nest on the bed. She found her place and tried to begin again. But her sister's critical words echoed in her mind, clamoring for consideration until Joanna put her pen down and leaned back on the pillow, tears spilling down her cheeks.

17

JOANNA was startled awake the next morning at her mother's call up the stairs. "*Kumme* now, Joanna, and help make breakfast!"

"All right, Mamma." Joanna stretched, yawned, and got out of bed, still feeling groggy. She stepped across the hall to peek in at her sister, who was still in bed. "Cora Jane, time to wake up. Mamma needs us."

"I heard her," Cora Jane said sleepily, rolling over, her golden hair sprawled out all over the pillow. "She called for *you!*"

With a sigh, Joanna hurried to wash up. She recognized that Cora Jane was still rather young and in the process of maturing. But sometimes her prickly edges were hard to overlook, especially when she confronted others as she had Joanna last night.

Choosing to wear her gray choring dress, Joanna then quickly brushed her long hair and wove it into a tight bun, pinning it securely. No sense risking getting hair in the scrambled eggs!

Peering into her dresser mirror, she noticed how bright her eyes looked after a night's sweet dreams of Eben. *Closer in my dreams than in reality.*

Suddenly it occurred to her that Ella Mae Zook might be someone she ought to consider talking to about her beau. After all, the Wise Woman lived just over the cornfield, so it was easy to visit without having to bother hitching up the horse and buggy.

Even though Ella Mae was one of her mother's dearest friends, Joanna believed the older woman kept all shared confidences—she was a trustworthy soul. And ever so forthright, too, freely speaking her mind . . . even to the point of being downright *batzich*—spunky. So interesting, because the woman was nothing like Joanna's own mother, nor any of the other respected womenfolk in Hickory Hollow. Joanna privately wondered if the Wise Woman managed to get by with her plucky nature because she was much too old to be put off church.

"'Tis a *gut* thing," Joanna whispered as she set the white organdy Kapp on her head.

Dare I tell her about Eben's predicament?

Perhaps Ella Mae might have some advice to give about their long-distance romance. Might it help to simply voice her sheer frustration?

Joanna decided to test the waters later this week and see what wisdom Ella Mae might offer her . . . over peppermint tea. At this point, any counsel would be welcome!

Cora Jane conspicuously picked at her bacon and eggs at the breakfast table, apparently also lacking any appetite for Mamma's homemade sticky buns. Joanna wondered what ailed her. Was she still upset over last night, or was she dreading the quilting bee today over at Mary Beiler's? Last Thursday one of Mary's Ohio cousins, Linda Jean, had showed up wearing a bright pink dress, unlike any color ever seen round Lancaster County. Cora Jane brought attention to it in a most critical way, causing a stir at the quilting frame.

Chagrined, Joanna had felt for her sister and wished Cora Jane might show more kindness. *"What if we simply made it our heart's work to pray more and judge less?"* Ella Mae had once said, years ago. And Joanna had never forgotten.

"I think I'll stay home today," Cora Jane announced across the table from Joanna. "Dat could use some help outside, ain't?" She looked at their father, who wiped his mouth with the back of his sleeve.

"Well, now," Dat said, "I thought you were headin' to the bishop's for the quilting bee." He glanced first at Mamma, then back at Cora Jane. "All of yous."

"That's right, Cora Jane. We're going to help finish the friendship quilt we started last week. And we need you." Mamma meant business. But so did Cora Jane, her eyes widening even as she sat there.

"But I ain't feelin' so *gut*," Cora Jane replied, sighing dramatically and placing both hands on her cheeks.

"Just that quick, you're sick?" Mamma shook her head; she knew Cora Jane all too well. "If you're under the weather, I know just the thing to get ya feelin' up to snuff. A big tablespoon of cod liver oil should cure that in short order."

Cora Jane pulled a hard frown. The matter was quite settled.

"The boys and I will finish planting Elam Lapp's potato field by supper-time," Dat said casually, obviously attempting to squash any more tetchiness from Cora Jane.

"Next comes the cultivating," Mamma added, eyes still fixed on Cora Jane, who had managed to sit up tall and straight, the mere threat of fish oil lingering in the air. "You'll be mighty busy, too, with spreading manure on the vegetable gardens," she said to Dat, the ordeal of breakfast clearly behind them.

Joanna smiled as she listened to her parents' everyday small talk. A kindly person was a content one. Sooner or later, Cora Jane would understand that, too.

Eben sat down to breakfast, waiting for Mamm to take her seat near Daed. There was much on his mind, not the least of which was Leroy's letter. Keeping the news to himself was exhausting. It was as if the secret were weighing him down . . . refusing to be disregarded.

Glancing up, he saw his mother shaking her head. Then, slowly, she waved two pieces of paper, one in each hand. "What's this here, Eben?" she asked, frowning as she came to the table. "Did Leroy write to you?"

Eben recognized the envelope he'd ripped in half last night. He had no choice but to fess up. "Ach, Mamm, I didn't want to get your hopes up." He glanced at his father, sitting squarely at the head of the table.

"Oh?" Daed said, his brow creasing into a hard line. "What're ya talking 'bout?"

"Leroy says he's comin' home . . . maybe as soon as today."

Mamm's face broke into a smile. "Well, praise be!"

"I don't know much else. He really didn't say a lot."

"'Tis best not to jump to conclusions, Mamma," his father urged.

"It's been a long time comin'," Eben added. "Not to mention all the prayin'."

"That's the truth." Daed motioned for Mamm to take her place so he could offer the silent prayer.

She quickly slipped onto the bench, and Daed folded his hands and bowed his head low. Eben did the same, heart beating fast. He'd hurt his mother, and just when he'd tried to spare her further pain. During the silent table blessing, he prayed that Leroy's visit would be providential.

After the amen, Eben reached for the nearest platter and offered it to his father, then helped himself. He was grateful for the exceptionally hearty breakfast of cornmeal mush and sausage Mamm had taken the time to make.

He wondered how long it had been since Leroy had enjoyed such a breakfast but didn't feel sorry for him. After all, Leroy had pushed the boundaries even as a youngster; it was his own unwise decision to leave the People.

Even so, Eben hoped his brother had reconsidered all the time he'd spent rubbing shoulders with the world. Might he be ready to settle down at last and assume his expected place on the farm?

What I wouldn't give for that! Eben thought, assuming such a thing was highly unlikely. No, something else had to be up with Leroy. Why *was* he coming?

18

JOANNA'S mother breezed through the back door and began gathering up her basket of quilting supplies. "'Bout ready?"

"Perty soon, jah." Joanna wiped off the counter and turned to the table, where she had her own quilting needles and thimble in a little box, ready to tuck into her sewing bag.

"Don't want to be late," Mamma replied.

Cora Jane was the one dawdling, still in her room. "I'll see what's keepin' my sister." Joanna hurried to the bottom of the stairs. "We're hitched and ready to go," she called up.

Joanna waited a moment, giving Cora Jane time to respond. She heard only the creak of footsteps, but they weren't moving toward the stairs, so she called again, "Are ya comin', sister?"

A long silence.

At last, her sister replied, "I'll be right down."

"We'll be waiting." Turning, Joanna headed back through the kitchen, her navy blue canvas sewing bag slung over her shoulder and her writing notebook tucked safely inside. The notebook was her "insurance," in case of a lull in activity. That way, Joanna could go somewhere alone and write if she wanted to, and no one would be the wiser.

Hurrying out the back door, Joanna could hardly wait to get to Beilers'. Bishop John and Mary seemed to go out of their way to make the quilters feel welcome every week. And Joanna loved seeing their darling children, especially making over the younger ones.

The day was already quite warm as Joanna walked across the yard, taking in the sweep of land in all directions. Spring had its own unique smell, a freshness and earthiness found in no other season.

Joanna stepped into the carriage and sat beside Mamma. "Cora Jane says she's comin'."

"She'd better make it snappy. We're running behind." Mamma smoothed her cape apron over her long dress. "You're lookin' perky, Joanna."

For many reasons, she certainly felt good. "I'm eager to see how the friendship quilt turned out—all pieced together." Joanna thought, too, of Mary's ailing grandfather. "And it'll be *gut* to hear how Abram Stoltzfus is doin' this week."

"Sadly, word has it he's declining quickly . . . awful confused these days." Mamma glanced at the house, a glint of frustration in her eyes. No question Cora Jane was a slowpoke today. "Mary says her Dawdi clearly remembers what he did years ago as a youngster, but he can't recall his own grandchildren's names." She sighed loudly. "'Tis the saddest thing."

"Jah." Joanna thought of her own Dawdi Joseph. "Old folk tend to live in the past, ain't so?"

Her mother gave a sudden frown, leaning around Joanna to stare at the house again. "For pity's sake, where's Cora Jane? Slow as molasses in January!"

"She might be feelin' embarrassed 'bout last week."

"Well, we're not leaving here without her," Mamma declared.

Joanna resumed talking about Mamma's ailing father, saying he seemed to need more rest than ever before. "Mammi says he takes two or more naps a day."

"And the older he gets, the more he'll want to doze," Mamma agreed. "Seems elderly folk and wee tykes require more sleep than the rest of us."

Just then, Mamma brightened as Cora Jane burst out the back door and sped across the yard, her skirt tail flying.

"Ach, I'm ready!" Cora Jane called, nearly leaping into the carriage. She sat down with a thump, taking more than her share of space. Then she leaned back dramatically. "I shouldn't have rushed so!"

Joanna sputtered at that. Did she really have to make a spectacle of herself?

"Cora Jane, we've been sitting out here waitin' for ya," Mamma rebuked. "You best be more considerate in the future, hear?"

Cora Jane nodded slowly.

"I mean it," Mamma added, the reins taut in her hands.

Cora Jane gave Joanna a quick look.

Joanna hoped things would go well *this* quilting frolic. Far as she could tell, Cora Jane had gone from being rather lethargic at the breakfast table to just a mite too spunky now.

Hickory Lane was busier than usual with horses and carriages. Amish neighbors waved as they passed, and here and there small children ran barefoot after the carriage. Others skipped rope beneath shade trees or played jacks on the front porch, where it was still cool. And all the while, Joanna felt she was holding her breath, wondering how Cora Jane might behave today.

Yet neither her mother nor her sister made a peep, and the sound of the horse's *clip-clop*ping helped relax Joanna somewhat. She particularly enjoyed the sight of little red squirrels climbing trees along the roadside. Cows roamed the grazing land, and mule teams worked the soil, plowing and chasing sunshine.

The day was going to be unusually warm. Joanna was glad she'd thought to bring along her bandana for the ride home later this afternoon. She might even loosen her hair bun, although she'd never think of undoing it entirely in public. Looking at the sky, she hoped for the possibility of a rain shower. *Just maybe,* she thought, feeling terribly cramped with three in the seat.

Then, quite unexpectedly, Cora Jane folded her hands and looked at their mother. "Ach, Mamma . . . I'm real sorry for makin' a scene last week over Linda Jean," she said humbly. "Honestly."

A sweet smile spread across Mamma's face. "Well, dear, maybe ya didn't realize that pink is an approved color for Amish dresses in some areas of Ohio."

Cora Jane hung her head. "It just looked so awful worldly," she replied, staring at her lap, her tone softer now. "Such a loud color."

Joanna wasn't sure she ought to put her nose into the conversation. She waited for a moment, then quietly suggested that there were many different church ordinances, even within a five-mile radius in Lancaster

County. Maybe Cora Jane wasn't too aware of this, not being baptized yet.

"Just none that permits pink for courting-age girls, jah?" replied Cora Jane, raising her eyes.

"That's absolutely right," Mamma said.

The discussion triggered a curiosity in Joanna. What color dresses did Eben's mother and sisters wear in Shipshewana? Oh, she'd love to know more about his family and their church ordinances, too. Then she scolded herself, knowing she had no need to consider any of that, at least not for herself.

Yet, what if Eben *did* ask her to come to live in Shipshewana after all? What would she say to that?

19

JOANNA was pleasantly surprised by Cora Jane's change in attitude as she worked cheerfully with the other women amidst the chatter, using her tiny quilting needle at the frame. Cora Jane also went out of her way to show extra patience when Mary Beiler's youngest children were a bit rambunctious under the table during the noon meal. She got down on the floor, where she reached around the little girl and whispered something. Whatever Cora Jane said made the child's face light up like a lantern, and the child settled right down and played with her rag dolls more calmly from then on.

When no one was paying much attention, Joanna slipped outside with her sewing bag to the family carriage to write a few things in her notebook. She could get inspiration at the oddest times and was ever so glad she'd thought to bring the notebook and a pen along today.

Stepping into the buggy, she sat and opened her canvas sewing bag— but the notebook was gone. "*Wu is es?*—Where is it?" she whispered, looking behind the seat. Had it somehow fallen out of the bag? She peered into the rear section of the carriage.

Joanna's heart flickered. Her writing notebook was nowhere to be seen! Wracking her brain, she wondered if she'd dropped it back home, perhaps when getting into the buggy. Could that be? But no, she'd had it with her when they arrived here and when she helped Mamma carry her quilting basket into the bishop's house. She was fairly certain of that.

Her mind in a whirl, Joanna searched every inch of the carriage, then got out and hurried down the driveway leading to Hickory Lane. And as she went, she lamented ever bringing the notebook at all, especially when it contained a love story. Besides that, it was unwise to have brought it to the bishop's own house, of all places! *Why didn't I think of that?*

She fumed at herself and fretted, her head hurting as she stood at the edge of the road. And a dreadful thought came to her: Maybe she hadn't lost it after all.

"Did someone purposely take my notebook?" Joanna whispered, remembering Cora Jane's warning last night.

··· ➤ ≺ ···

It was difficult to concentrate the rest of the afternoon. Joanna dropped stitches and was so distracted at one point, she even pricked her finger, causing a drop of blood to fall onto the quilt. Mary Beiler hopped out of her chair like she'd been stung by a wasp, her prayer cap strings flying, and went to get a cold washrag to dab at the spot.

"I'm awful sorry," Joanna apologized. "I truly am."

"Don't worry," Mary assured her as she worked feverishly on the stain, though eventually she gave up on getting it out completely. "This could happen to anyone."

Joanna groaned. "I've ruined the quilt," she said, worrying a thread loose.

"No, no. Ain't the worst thing, really," Mary insisted as she leaned down to nearly touch her forehead to Joanna's.

Mamma spoke up from farther down the frame. "The spot will come out, dear," and several heads popped up, nodding. "You'll see," Mamma added, her brow wrinkling with empathy.

Cora Jane averted her gaze and pressed her lips together in a flat line, appearing as concerned as Joanna felt.

Joanna looked once more to her mother for support, glad for Mamm's merciful expression, although still painfully aware of the all-too-noticeable blemish on the quilt. Right in front of Joanna's nose, too!

Alas, she had no one to blame but herself. She'd been a *Dummkopp* to bring her story notebook along. Yet never before had anything disappeared from her bag, for pity's sake!

Pondering the whole situation again, Joanna felt even more mortified. *Ach, I should've known better!*

The ride home seemed considerably longer than usual as Joanna squinted into the late-afternoon sun. She could hardly wait to get home to see if she'd dropped her notebook in the yard or left it on the kitchen table. But although she didn't dare ask to look inside Cora Jane's own sewing bag, she was certain it looked more rigid than when her sister had climbed into the carriage that morning. In fact, Joanna was sure she could see the outline of her notebook tucked inside.

She chided herself—Joanna had never been one to falsely accuse someone. Yet who else was nosy enough to take it?

Thank goodness there was not a speck of conversation in the carriage as they rode. Joanna was so worked up, she was intentionally drawing slow, deep breaths, lest she spout off. She glanced again at Cora Jane, who looked at her quizzically but still said nothing.

Finally, when they pulled into the lane leading to the house, Joanna remembered the quilt waiting for her at Cousin Malinda's. "Mamma, would ya mind leaving the horse and carriage hitched up?" she asked. At this, both Cora Jane and Mamma looked surprised. "I need to go to Malinda's right quick," Joanna explained, not wanting to say why.

"But *I* need to go somewhere, too," Cora Jane piped up. "Why can't ya just walk over to Malinda's?"

"Well, I have to bring something back with me," Joanna said. "Something too heavy to carry."

"All right, then," Mamma said, appearing weary from the long day. "Make it quick so Cora Jane can get her errand run, too."

"Where are you headed?" Joanna asked her sister, wondering if perhaps she'd simply asked for the carriage to be difficult.

"Oh, you'll see," Cora Jane said mysteriously. "In due time."

Not interested in playing along, Joanna shook her head. "I shouldn't be long" was all she said.

Mamma, who'd surely detected the tension between them, asked Cora Jane, "Did ya enjoy yourself more so today, dear?"

"It was nice seein' everyone again," Cora Jane replied. "And we finished up the friendship quilt, 'cept for the hem, ain't so?"

"That we did," said Mamma, letting go of the reins as she eyed Cora Jane. "I'm sure you'll want to host some quilting frolics of your own one day."

"When I'm married?" Cora Jane said, a smile playing on her lips.

"From what I've heard, a wedding might not be too far off," Mamma replied with a sly look.

"Now, Mamma!" Cora Jane laughed, which solidified what Joanna— and obviously their mother, too—had strongly suspected: Cora Jane was planning to be a bride, maybe as soon as this fall.

Before me, Joanna thought with a sinking feeling.

While Cora Jane tied the horse to the hitching post, Joanna retraced her steps into the house, trying not to be conspicuous. The notebook was not on the back walkway or on the lawn, so she made her way inside and looked all over the kitchen, the table and counters, and even under the wooden benches, trembling now. *All the hours of writing, for naught!* She peeked out the window and saw Cora Jane standing near the horse, her own sewing bag over her shoulder.

Crestfallen, Joanna snatched up the flashlight she'd borrowed from Cousin Malinda last evening and headed back outside. She saw Cora Jane running to catch up with Mamma, who was walking to the stable, most likely to let Dat know they were back. Since Joanna had already asked Mamma for the buggy, she went out and untied the horse, then got back inside the carriage, sitting on the far right side this time as she picked up the reins. Her emotions were all jumbled up between the regretful loss of her notebook and the anticipation of bringing the wedding quilt home. *I shouldn't accept it*, she thought as she drove to Malinda's, *not if Cora Jane's getting married this fall*.

Even if Eben were to move to Hickory Hollow tomorrow, Joanna wondered if he could get established in a job quickly enough for them to wed come November.

Thinking then of her plan to seek some perspective from Ella Mae, Joanna continued on to her cousin's house. Soon, the lovely heirloom quilt would be in her possession.

My beautiful wedding quilt . . .

20

EBEN and his father were shoveling out the dung in the stable when a white Mustang convertible with black stripes along the side whooshed into the lane. Taken off guard, Eben realized Leroy had just arrived.

"Well, what do ya know?" Daed said, going to stand in the doorway of the barn.

"Looks like he's got himself a girlfriend," Eben muttered next to Daed. "Guess we should go and wash up, jah?"

"For certain!" His father fell into step right behind him, pulling his gloves off and tossing them on the lawn near the well pump.

Eben waved at Leroy. "Willkumm home, *Bruder!*" he called, motioning for Leroy and the pretty redhead to go inside. Eben waited his turn as Daed lathered his hands at the pump. "Been muckin' out the barn, so need to wash up *gut* before we shake hands."

Leroy's face broke into a frown, and he exchanged glances with the petite young woman. Eben took his turn with a bar of soap at the well pump before hurrying indoors to alert his mother to their company. "Leroy's back—has a lady friend along."

"Leroy's *here?*" Mamm's eyes grew big as she ran her hands over her Kapp and bodice.

"Comin' up the porch steps."

"Hullo, son. Good to have ya home," Daed said as he pushed his big hand into Leroy's.

Eben didn't want to gawk, but his brother looked taller than he remembered, broader shoulders, too. Was it the petite young woman at his side? He went over to shake Leroy's hand while Mamm hovered near, smiling like she didn't know what else to do or say . . . tears springing to her eyes.

"Daed . . . Mamm, I want you to meet Debbie," said Leroy, slipping his arm around her. "Mrs. Debbie Troyer."

Mrs. Troyer? Eben's heart sank at Leroy's news.

"You're married?" Mamm blurted.

"Two weeks tomorrow." Leroy grinned down at his bride, who had the thickest, darkest eyelashes Eben had ever seen.

"This is . . . well, a surprise," Daed said, managing a smile and shaking Debbie's hand.

Polite though his father was, Eben could tell he was masking his disappointment.

Debbie offered a warm smile of her own. "I'm real pleased to meet you, sir. I wanted to before the wedding, but it was so difficult for Leroy to get away."

Mamm intervened somewhat by directing them into the kitchen, waving Leroy toward the bench. Then, her face mighty pink, she offered a seat to Debbie, as well, and something to eat. "We can't have our new daughter-in-law goin' hungry, now, can we?" Like Daed, she was clearly flustered.

They sat around the table, except for Mamm, who made her way to the gas-powered refrigerator to pull out a pitcher of lemonade and some apples to slice. Freshly baked bread, butter, and several choices of jams were next, Eben guessed. And a pie, too, soon enough.

In the meantime, Leroy was talking a mile a minute, now that the ice was broken. But when Eben looked at Leroy and his bride and how very happy they seemed together, it made him think of Joanna's dress brushing against him as they strolled along the beach, hand in hand . . . and of reaching to hold her tenderly on her father's field road.

Any hope he'd had for marrying her in Pennsylvania and living there was gone. His father needed him here, working the farm. There was no one else to rely upon. And as much as Joanna loved Hickory Hollow, he couldn't think of asking her to leave to settle down and marry out here. Could he?

I'm locked in!

Discouraged, Eben looked down the table at Leroy, clean-shaven and wearing pressed navy slacks and a pale yellow shirt. Daed needed *someone*, and it sure wasn't going to be Leroy.

Never was, thought Eben miserably.

··· ➤ ◄ ···

When Joanna arrived at Malinda's, she found her pressing two Kapps in the kitchen, humming a song from the old Ausbund.

"Knock, knock," Joanna called to her.

Malinda looked up and quickly put the iron back on the stove. "Was wondering if you were goin' to make it yet today."

"Wouldn't've missed coming."

"I wrapped your quilt in brown paper," Malinda told her, going to the sitting room around the corner to retrieve it. "You can store it as is, if you want."

"Denki."

Malinda leaned down to set the wrapped quilt on the kitchen table. "Would ya like some meadow tea or lemonade?"

"I really can't stay long. Cora Jane's waiting for me to return with the horse and buggy."

"How's she doin' these days?"

Joanna considered what to say. "Well enough, I daresay . . . though the reason for that ain't common knowledge, so keep it under your bonnet for now."

"A wedding, maybe?"

Sighing, Joanna forced a smile, then looked away. "You didn't hear it from me."

Malinda tilted her head, eyeing her. "You look sad 'bout it, Joanna. Are ya?"

"Oh, not so much sad as concerned." She bit her lip.

"Do ya know Cora Jane's fella?"

"I do, but honestly her beau ain't the worry." She paused and looked down at the quilt. "That's all I best be sayin'."

"I won't press, but I'm here if you need to talk more."

Joanna was grateful but didn't know where she'd even begin. "I appreci-

114

ate that . . . really, I do." All of a sudden, she could no longer restrain her emotions. Sobbing like her heart might break, she flew into her cousin's open arms.

··· ➤ ➤ ···

A young elk grazed just beyond the woodshed, out near a stand of trees as Eben dutifully followed along with Leroy and his fancy wife on a tour of the farm. It was surprising how Daed was going overboard in his hospitality. He'd insisted on showing his new daughter-in-law around, leaving Eben in the dust and practically doting on Leroy and his bride. In fact, Eben felt more like the visitor than his father's dependable right-hand man.

He had long guessed that Daed preferred Leroy, not only as a son but as a potential business partner. Yet Eben had diligently worked to do Daed's bidding while ticking off the days, weeks, and months until he could see Joanna again. Their inferior approach to courtship had become wearisome, although he had attempted to hold his own with letter writing, eager to keep Joanna happy. She'd never complained, and he knew she was patiently waiting for him. He looked forward to their phone chats every other week.

Sadly, in the space of a few short minutes, the miles between them had grown to an impossible distance with the knowledge that Leroy wasn't coming home to stay.

The foursome headed into the birthing area to see the new calves, but Eben's attention wandered as he thought of the difficult letter he must write to his sweetheart-girl. However would he break the terrible news? He could visualize starting one letter after another, only to crumple them up. Was there any way to let Joanna down gently, so as not to break her heart?

She doesn't deserve this, he told himself while Daed showed Leroy and his wife the birthing stall. Daed thought of their dairy cattle as his pets; the whole family did—except Leroy. No, it was apparent that farming had never clicked with his brother.

Eben shook with anger that had simmered for months now. He'd marked time, waited for Leroy to decide to be Amish or not—working himself to the bone. And for what? Only to learn he was going nowhere, and least of all to Hickory Hollow.

Eben forced air through his lips. Let his father finish up the ridiculous tour. Let his brother show his bride the very farm he'd rejected!

A letter won't do—I have to explain things to Joanna in person! The realization burst into his head as he made a detour out of the barn to head to the house, swatting away mosquitoes as he went. Joanna would have to leave the community she so dearly loved to come here and marry him . . . *if* she was even willing to do so.

Inside the house, Eben dashed through the kitchen to his room. How fast could he get to Hickory Hollow and back? He wished he hadn't wasted any time trailing behind his father, brother, and new wife out there. Then he chuckled bitterly. Why, Leroy could fly him to Lancaster County in nothing flat!

What *would* it be like to arrive at Joanna's side in such a short amount of time? But air travel was forbidden by the bishop—Eben would travel as other Plain people did over long distances, by taxi-van or bus. First, though, he would have to line up someone to cover his farm work.

Letting his imagination run away, he envisioned showing up at the Kurtz farm once again and taking Joanna into his arms, holding her ever so close. And this time, he'd never let her go.

Knowing how impatient Cora Jane could be, Joanna quickly dried her eyes and thanked Malinda for a shoulder to cry on. She bade farewell to her cousin, whose eyes shone with concern as Joanna stepped out the door with the large quilt in her arms. With the greatest care, Joanna placed it in the back of the buggy. *The prettiest quilt I've ever seen,* she thought, glancing back toward the house with a wave at Cousin Malinda. She went around the buggy to untie the horse.

"Come again soon!" Malinda called, her hand held high.

"I surely will," Joanna said as she climbed into the enclosed carriage. She reached for the reins and clicked her tongue to get the horse moving. Oh, if only she'd held back her tears for dear Malinda's sake! The poor thing didn't need any stress now. Joanna promised herself to keep in touch with Malinda through the next months of waiting for the baby's arrival. And with the thought of a sweet infant, Joanna imagined a narrative that featured a brand-new baby. Ah, she'd love to write such a story . . . but her notebook had vanished. Such a dreadful loss!

When she arrived home, Cora Jane was standing in the lane, wearing a displeased expression, her large tan sewing bag draped over her shoulder. Joanna got out without offering a civility, and her sister got in without saying a word.

Upset, Joanna hurried to the house and went inside to start supper. And just that minute, it dawned on her: *Ach, no! I left the heirloom quilt in the back of the buggy!*

Without a second thought, she dashed outside, running down the long lane to the road, calling for Cora Jane to stop. "Come back, sister!" But the horse was nearly galloping as the carriage sped away.

21

JOANNA returned to the house, crestfallen and out of sorts. So ferhoodled she was today! She joined her mother at the kitchen table to peel a pile of potatoes.

"Where's Cora Jane headed?" she asked Mamma.

Mamma looked up, her eyes questioning. "Why do you ask?"

"She was in such a big hurry."

"As *you* were earlier."

Mamma's reply caught her off guard. "I just went to Cousin Malinda's is all," Joanna said. "I said I'd be by today after the quilting."

"Well, I have no idea what Cora Jane has in mind."

Joanna told about the old family quilt Cousin Malinda had discovered. "I went there to pick it up." She paused. "Evidently Mammi Kurtz wants me to have it."

A quick smile spread across Mamma's face. "That's awful nice." Mamma peered around the kitchen, as if expecting to see the quilt nearby. "Where're ya keepin' it?"

"I accidentally left it in the back of the buggy."

Mamma's expression was inquisitive. "Have ya told Cora Jane yet?"

Shaking her head, Joanna continued to scrape out the eyes of the potatoes. Did Mamma think her sister should have the quilt instead?

Mamma placed her freshly peeled potatoes in her apron to carry them to the sink to rinse. "I'm sure curious 'bout that quilt."

Joanna repeated what Malinda had said regarding how old it might be, though she didn't say a word about how special it was, nor that Malinda had suggested it had something of a story.

Mamma inquired about the pattern and the color scheme, and Joanna was happy to share all of that.

"Where do ya plan to put it?" Mamma asked.

"Oh, prob'ly in my hope chest."

"Well, why not use it?" Mamma looked surprisingly serious.

"I don't . . . I mean, I'm thinkin' I'll just wait awhile." Something seemed off beam about having a wedding ring quilt spread across her bed, especially when things with Eben seemed at a standstill.

"Till you're wed, ya mean?"

Joanna didn't look up, for fear she might see reservation, even doubt, in Mamma's eyes. "It's been a while, for sure, but I can still hope things work out, ain't?"

"One can always hope." The halting way her mother said it left Joanna believing her mother had lost faith in her beau. Had Cora Jane swayed Mamma to her thinking? Certainly now at twenty-five, most young Amishwomen would have accepted their singleness.

But Eben loves me, Joanna reminded herself.

⋯ ➤ ⬿ ⋯

The late-afternoon sun was still bright when Cora Jane returned home. Joanna spotted her from the kitchen window, where she was still working with Mamma. "I'll help her unhitch the horse," she told Mamma right quick. "And I'll bring in that quilt, too." She wanted to talk to her sister without Mamma or anyone else overhearing.

Cora Jane looked surprised as Joanna approached.

"Where'd ya go in such a hurry?" asked Joanna, wasting no time.

Cora Jane kept mum as she unhooked the back hold strap on her side of the horse.

Joanna unfastened the tugs, her jaw clenched. "I asked you a question."

Cora Jane shrugged, shifting her feet. "Guess you'll know soon enough."

"For pity's sake, Cora Jane, what's gotten into you?"

"I'd say pity's a *gut* way to put it."

"Why on earth can't ya say where you've been?" Joanna demanded, her stomach in nervous knots.

There was a long pause in which Cora Jane's face turned pale. "To see the deacon," she finally admitted.

"Whatever for?" asked Joanna.

"With proof. I think you know what I mean."

Joanna could scarcely speak for lack of air. She struggled with what to say—how to say it. "You didn't!"

Cora Jane nodded slowly. "You're a baptized church member, expected to follow the rules. Ain't so?"

"You honestly didn't take my notebook over there, did ya?"

Together, they held the shafts, and Cora Jane led the horse out, away from the carriage.

How could she? Joanna stared at her sister.

Soon misery began to overtake Cora Jane's countenance. Still standing next to the horse, she said, "I had no choice." Her voice was a near whisper. "Under the Lord God, ya know."

You little snitch!

"Is it really your job to judge—to help the Lord out?" Joanna thought of poor Mary's Ohio cousin and her pink dress. Where would Cora Jane's self-righteousness end?

"It's just one more sign, sister."

"A sign . . . of what?"

"I fear you're walkin' the fence." Cora Jane frowned sadly.

Breathing a prayer for patience, Joanna shook her head. "No, Cora Jane. There's no need to worry 'bout any of that," she said, tears welling up. "You betrayed me, and you know it!"

Cora Jane dodged Joanna's glare and looked toward the house with a sigh. "Preacher Yoder will drop by sometime this week to speak with you on behalf of the ailing deacon."

"You have no idea what you've done. How could a sister do this to a sister?" Joanna fought back tears. *"How?"*

"What about the ministerial brethren?" Cora Jane said quietly. "How could you transgress against *them*?" With that, she led the horse up toward the stable.

Joanna's chest felt tight as she walked back to the buggy, to the front seat, where she snatched up Cora Jane's entire sewing bag, the story notebook tucked inside. Then, with a huff, she moved outside to the very back of the buggy and retrieved the old quilt. She made the effort to carry both the large quilt and Cora Jane's bag across the yard.

Inside, Joanna couldn't bring herself to make eye contact with Mamma when she hurried through the kitchen. The pain in her heart knew no bounds as she made her way upstairs, to the privacy of her room.

The bedroom was strewn with sunlight, a contrast to Joanna's despondent mood. Tenderly, she unwrapped the quilt and placed it on her bed. Then she promptly emptied the contents of Cora Jane's sewing bag beside it. Sure enough: There lay her treasured notebook. She opened it and was stunned to see the first pages gone.

The start of my best and longest story!

She wanted to weep and wail. But she was not a child; she shouldn't let her emotions get the best of her. The truth was, she'd gotten caught at last, and at the hands of her own sister, which hurt worst of all.

"Everything all right in here?" Mamma asked, standing primly in the doorway. She frowned into the room.

Joanna sighed. Dare she spill out her woes to Mamma? She simply wasn't one to share much with her mother, maybe because of her own need for privacy . . . particularly when it came to her writing. "Just upset, I guess."

Mamma stepped into the bedroom and wiped her hands on her long black apron. "Your face is nearly purple." Mamma looked curiously at the sewing notions strewn on the bed, and at Cora Jane's bag lying there, too.

"I'll be fine, honest."

"Jah?"

Although devastated at the thought of anyone unsympathetic reading her stories, Joanna was also relieved Mamma wouldn't press for answers. She motioned to her bed. "Here's the wedding quilt I was tellin' about."

Her mother moved closer and sat on the bed to inspect not only its pattern, but the stitching on both sides. Eyes wide, she searched the top and bottom bordered hems for any indication of its maker, much as Joanna first had at Cousin Malinda's. "It's special, all right," Mamma said at last, eyes glistening. "An enduring connection to our relatives of yore."

"I felt that way, too, when Malinda first showed it to me."

They nodded in unison. And, in that strangely sweet moment, Joanna almost had the courage to open her heart to let the anguish of Cora Jane's disloyalty overflow.

Then, thinking better of it, she said only, "I'd rather Cora Jane not see this just yet. Not today, anyway."

Mamma grimaced but didn't ask why. Silently, she rose. "I'm happy for you . . . being able to call this quilt your own."

Joanna gave a tentative smile, thankful Cora Jane had kept herself outside—away from the house for this long. It was the very least she could do.

22

THE next morning was cooler, with wispy clouds hugging the sky. "A *fine fishing day*," Joanna's Dat might say, if he wasn't all tied up this Friday with field work, as all the local farmers were.

Joanna was also occupied, rolling out pie dough with Mamma at the kitchen table while Cora Jane organized the sewing room upstairs.

From where she sat, Joanna could see clear out to the road and beyond, past the neighbor to the south, who was repairing the roof of their springhouse. She gazed over at the expanse of acreage to the edge of her newlywed cousin's freshly plowed cornfield. Maybe she'd go over there and help once the baby arrived. Such a special time that would be this fall, caring for a brand-new infant. Of course, Malinda would have plenty of help from the rest of her family, too.

Joanna let herself imagine other people's lives, as she often did when doing menial tasks. Why did Malinda seem so lonely when she'd married her best friend and sweetheart? That was one thing Joanna didn't quite understand.

Raising her eyes again to the window, she was jolted back to reality. Her breath caught in her throat. *No!* Preacher Yoder had just turned into the lane.

"Well, what's this?" Mamma sputtered, getting up to go to the back door.

Joanna's heart beat ever so hard as she remembered Cora Jane's declaration. *Preacher didn't waste any time!*

Soon their tall minister was standing on the back stoop, his bearded face looking mighty grim as he asked to speak to Joanna.

Mamma's cheerful expression changed quickly to shock; nevertheless, she motioned calmly to her.

Never had a minister come to call on account of Joanna. Anxious, she stood and walked to the screen door, wishing she could hide in the cold cellar below the house.

"*Guder Mariye*," Preacher Yoder said. Then, just as quickly, he asked her to walk to the well pump with him, in plain view, as was customary.

She nodded respectfully, her hands clammy. Mindful to walk slightly behind him, she willed herself to breathe.

"It's come to my attention that you're writing make-believe stories." The minister got right to the point. "And thanks to your notebook, I've seen it with my own eyes."

"'Tis true." She nodded.

"And . . . seems to me you're putting yourself into one of them, jah?" He didn't let her answer but continued on. "That Troyer boy from Indiana is in there, too. Not hard to see that, even when the names are different."

She didn't know how to respond, or if she should.

"I wouldn't get any ideas, now, about asking permission to transfer your church membership out there, not with this secret ambition you're hiding." Preacher Yoder's eyes penetrated hers.

She lowered her eyes; he certainly wasn't finished.

"Do you understand why I've come here, Joanna?"

She raised her head and saw how solemn his expression was. With his black coat and trousers, he looked ready to conduct a funeral.

"Nee, not entirely," she said softly. Since her baptism, Joanna had been careful to follow the Old Ways in everything but this. Even so, writing her stories was one thing; sharing them in print was quite another. Yet hadn't she been tempted to do that very thing?

Preacher paused, then after a great, deep breath, he went on. "Writing such stories is a waste of time, but it also appears that you're a-hankerin' to get them published."

Joanna trembled under his stern gaze. "So far, I've written them only for myself."

"Well, that may be, but there is more than one note about possible publishers written in the margins of your notebook." He paused. "Is your fancy English friend, Amelia, encouraging you to seek publication?"

"She has." Joanna's heart wavered. "But I've yet to look into it."

"Far better for you to keep in mind your vow to God and the Hickory Hollow church. No need letting an outsider influence you toward the world. And no need getting puffed up about your writing, neither."

"Is it considered a sin to put stories down on paper, then?" She looked over her shoulder, back toward the house. "I know such creativity is frowned upon . . . but not forbidden, jah?"

Preacher Yoder's responding frown was so harsh it enveloped his whole face. "Your attitude concerns me. I see rebellion in you, Joanna—the worst sin of all. The origin of all wickedness."

She was stunned. Did an innocent question make her rebellious? "I didn't mean to come across as—"

"You're a baptized child of God, are you not?"

"Jah." She bowed her head. "Forgive me for speaking out of turn, Preacher."

"It's been some time since I've encountered an attempt at compliance and stubborn insistence in the selfsame breath. Joanna, you must never talk back to a man of God," he stated firmly. "Doing so could eventually get ya shunned."

Despite her shock at this, another question sprang to mind: Was there a difference between telling a story out loud and putting it down on paper? How many storytellers did she know in the hollow? Yet they had not been silenced for sharing interesting tales at quilting bees and work frolics and such. Nor had they been threatened with excommunication.

Joanna pondered whether or not to voice her question. Certainly she did not want to push things, like Rebecca Lapp's adopted daughter, Katie, had some years ago. Katie was still under the *Bann*.

"Is tellin' stories out loud also considered a sin, then?" she asked in what she hoped was a meek tone, looking at him again.

He pursed his lips, deep furrows still evident in his brow. The preacher seemed more frustrated than indignant now that she had the gall to continue to speak up. But he did not pacify her by saying her writings were either forbidden or a sin. "If this type of questioning continues, you will be called upon to repent before the church membership."

Do I sound defiant? Joanna honestly wondered—she'd been too perplexed to remain silent.

Preacher Yoder gave a swift jerk of his head, signaling the end of the conversation. Then, without another word, he marched to his waiting horse and carriage, a profile in black except for his straw hat.

In a daze, Joanna tried to sort out what he'd actually said. She was fairly sure she was expected to stop writing her stories, yet he hadn't specifically said it was against the church ordinance. Nor had he declared it a sin. But getting published: The preacher had been mighty clear on *that* point.

Ach, I've never been so embarrassed in my life!

Trying to calm down from the upsetting visit, she looked up and noticed Cora Jane standing at an open upstairs window. Joanna was shocked to think she might have listened in on the private conversation. Reddening, Cora Jane inched back, away from sight.

What's come over her?

With a moan, Joanna turned away from the house. She stared at the clouds toward the northeast. Never before had she felt so alone.

So it's come to this. Joanna reached for the hem of her apron to dry her tears. The emptiness in her heart needed to be filled, and she yearned for Eben's loving arms, imagining what it would be like to have him with her now, walking together once again.

She poured out her heart in prayer. *O Lord, how can I give up what brings me such enjoyment?*

23

STILL shaky from her meeting with Preacher Yoder, Joanna darted into the small bathroom off the kitchen, where she washed her face. She stood at the sink and stared into the modest cabinet mirror, letting water drip off her chin. Her distress threatened even more tears, but she set her jaw and splashed cold water on her eyes and forehead.

She was thankful for indoor plumbing on such a day. Four decades ago, her family was using the wooden outhouse, which still stood a ways from the barn. Ah, the wonderful-good conveniences the ministerial brethren had permitted back then. Considering that, she wondered when individual creativity might be allowed. Would story writing—and music, like Katie's guitar playing—always be frowned upon? Now, sadly, her story would languish, forever unfinished. *Ironic.* She hoped that wouldn't be the case with her real-life love story.

She hadn't received a letter from Eben in the past couple days, and the knowledge compounded her misery.

After drying her face, Joanna turned to the window and moved the plain white curtains aside to look at the lush green lawn, carefully tended each week by her and Cora Jane. They'd also planted the brightly colored petunias along the walkway and around the well pump on the eastern edge. Alas, the old pump would always be a reminder now of Preacher Yoder's stern admonition.

Evidently, she was considered a transgressor in his eyes. Yet Joanna wasn't herself convinced. And she wished with all her heart that the minister would've answered her questions—now she was so confused. Did he think Joanna was merely a *ferhoodled* female? She'd sometimes overheard other men in authority talk so about their womenfolk, which had privately triggered her resentment, though she hadn't "given place to the devil" and acted on it. Still, she couldn't imagine Eben referring to her that way . . . nor her own father.

Joanna rushed through her indoor chores, avoiding Mamma as best she could. She simply could not reveal what had happened today, not the way she felt. But she needed comfort terribly, and thankfully she knew where to seek it. As miserable as Joanna felt, she could hardly wait to leave the house, to escape both her mother's questioning eyes and her sister's pained expression. She detested what Cora Jane had done. Yet she also knew that pursuing revenge was not the way of forgiveness.

Joanna headed on foot around the barn after the noon meal and cut through the field lane that bordered her father's cornfield. She relived Preacher Yoder's awful visit as she trudged over the lengthy pasture to the other side of their property.

How could she ever forgive Cora Jane? Yet she must.

Birds gathered in masses in the trees, calling back and forth, then flew together in a great gray cloud against the sky. They seemed to mock her.

When Joanna finally arrived at Ella Mae Zook's little house, she spotted the white-haired woman on the back porch, watering her potted red geraniums with a galvanized watering can. Several years had come and gone since many pretty annuals blossomed in the beds along the walkway and porch. But Ella Mae's knee joints could no longer tolerate bending to weed a garden.

Ella Mae looked up and gave a smile as Joanna made her way across the backyard. "Well, now, I *thought* that was you." She looked neat and proper in her green dress and black apron, graying hair in a low bun and her crisp white organdy Kapp over the widening middle part. "Nice to see ya, dearie. Come sit with me on the porch."

"Hullo, Ella Mae," Joanna said as she approached the elderly woman. "I've been wantin' to visit you."

"Glad ya dropped by, then." Ella Mae led the way up the steps, going to her own rocking chair near the far end of the white banister. "You're lookin' a bit *schlimm*, dear girl." Gingerly, she eased herself into the rocker.

"Do I?"

"Serious as ever I've seen ya."

Joanna took her seat on the only other rocker. Leaning back, she sighed, glad for the quiet and the peaceful landscape beyond the barn. "Honestly, I scarcely know where to start."

"Well, the beginning's always a *gut* place, ain't?"

Joanna crossed her legs and glanced at her dusty bare feet. She felt so comfortable with Ella Mae, who was certainly the best listener Joanna had ever known. "All right," she said, glad they were alone. "When you were a girl, did ya ever love someone who lived outside the community?"

"I never cared two cents for any Englischer boys, if that's what ya mean."

Joanna waved her hand. "No, no . . . I didn't mean to imply that." She scooted forward a bit. "What I meant was, did ya ever care for an *Amish* fella who lived in a different church district . . . maybe even in another state?"

"Can't say that I did." Ella Mae shook her head. "Never met any young fellas outside this community back in my own courting days."

Forging ahead, Joanna confided about Eben Troyer and all of the important details surrounding their long-distance courtship since their meeting on the beach and his visit last November. "Even though he wants to move here, things just aren't movin' forward like I thought . . . actually, they don't seem to be moving at all."

"Ain't surprising, really," Ella Mae said softly, blue eyes peering over her glasses.

Disheartened, Joanna hoped she might explain.

"Problems can arise in a long-distance courtship," Ella Mae said, no longer rocking. "Misunderstandings, for one thing. And sometimes a couple doesn't always mesh because of the different church ordinances, for another. What one bishop allows, the other doesn't—so there's some fittin' in that must happen over time."

Joanna wondered if Eben's bishop considered writing fiction a problem, but she quickly dismissed that.

"And there can be certain challenges to face by havin' to move far away from family and friends, too."

Joanna knew this—why, even Cousin Malinda seemed lonesome at times.

"What *I'm* wonderin' is, aren't there any nice fellas in Hickory Hollow?" Ella Mae asked, chuckling a little, her dimples showing.

"That's a *gut* question."

"Well, then?"

Joanna considered that. "But what if you've already fallen in love with someone else?" There. She'd said it.

"Guess it's just as easy to fall for a young man right here at home as anywhere, jah?"

Joanna felt discouraged. Ella Mae didn't seem to understand—the young men around here had had their chance, but none of them had shown much interest. No one had, in fact, till Eben. Yet the Wise Woman's questions lodged in Joanna's mind. Truth was, there would be no such difficulties for her and Eben . . . at least not once he finally arrived to court her. He'd never hinted at any worries about what the move would mean for him, or any concerns related to the Ordnung there in the hollow. On the other hand, he had never really written about anything controversial. Maybe he simply took things as they came.

"Problems can arise in a long-distance courtship. . . ."

Ella Mae's words continued to resonate in Joanna's mind later, as she walked back through the cornfield toward home, feeling worse for the visit. She glanced over at the top of the phone shack where she and Eben secretly talked.

Will he call again tonight?

··· ➤ ➤ ···

"Oh, *gut*, you're home," Mamma said the minute Joanna walked in the back door. "I need ya to take a casserole and some fresh bread over to Mammi Kurtz right quick. Your father's already hitched up the team."

"I'll be glad to," Joanna replied, noting that Cora Jane was down on all fours, washing the kitchen floor. *Truly glad . . .*

"I would go, but Rachel Stoltzfus is comin' over any minute now, bringing ideas for the school's benefit auction next month." Mamma bustled around, gathering up the long loaf of bread, some strawberry jam, and the hot dish, putting everything in a large basket. "Hope it's not too heavy." She handed it to Joanna.

"No . . . I can manage."

"Just so ya know, your Mammi Kurtz ain't feelin' well," Mamma added. "Might not be a *gut* idea to stay long, ya hear?"

Joanna nodded, promising not to tire Mammi out. She did wish she could ask about the story behind the double wedding ring quilt, but it sounded like that would have to wait.

She glanced at her sister before leaving the kitchen with the food basket. Cora Jane kept scrubbing all the while, never once looking up, like she was taking out some frustration on the wood floor.

Joanna's Mammi Kurtz was the topping on any cake. She wasn't just dear, she was considerate, too. And beautiful for her age. Her skin was fair and unflawed, except for the wrinkles, and she wore her prayer cap pushed toward the back of her graying head.

"Well, aren't you nice, Joanna." Her grandmother got up from her comfortable chair in the tidy corner of the small kitchen, setting *The Budget* aside.

"No need to cook tonight," Joanna said.

Mammi shuffled over and touched her arm. "How'd your Mamma know I was under the weather?"

"Let's see." Joanna glanced at the ceiling. "From that trusty ol' grapevine, perhaps?"

Her grandmother gave a little laugh, then teetered a bit. Right quick, Joanna helped her back to her chair. "Maybe I should stay awhile and help ya serve supper," Joanna offered. "If ya would like."

"Ain't necessary, really. Fannie will be checkin' up, like always." Her daughter-in-law Fannie lived in the main farmhouse with her husband and children.

"If you're sure, then."

"Oh jah . . . ever so sure." Mammi nodded, though she looked pale.

"But before ya leave, I wondered what ya thought of the wedding quilt Malinda found."

"It's astonishingly perty. I love havin' it, Mammi."

"Didja know your name's the same as the great-great-aunt who made it?"

"Really?"

"'Tis true . . . and Joanna wasn't a typical Amish name in those days." Mammi crossed her hands over her bosom. "That's why I thought you should have the quilt."

Not because she thought I'd be marrying anytime soon. . . .

"It's beautifully made," Joanna said.

"Oh, it's just the most wonderful quilt . . . for more than one important reason."

"Sometime, I'd like to hear more 'bout it," she ventured, heeding Mamma's wishes about staying too long.

"We'll need some time alone for that," Mammi said, her eyes flashing a secret. "Just the two of us."

"I'll look forward to it." Joanna set the hot dish on the back burner for warming later. "You sure it's all right for me to leave?"

"Abseelutt." Despite her ashen face, Mammi was emphatic. "Come by anytime, dear."

Joanna went to give her a kiss on the cheek. "Be sure to tell Dawdi or Fannie to bring ya over to see Mammi Sadie sometime, all right?"

"That I will." Mammi's smile was precious. "And you tell your Mamma that Dawdi and I are grateful for the delicious supper. Smells awful *gut*."

"I will." With that, Joanna headed for the back door. Knowing her name was the same as the quilt maker's tickled her no end. Moreover, considering the preacher's visit—and Ella Mae's depressing remarks about long-distance romances—it was the nicest thing Joanna had heard all day.

Now, what else did Mammi know about that extra-special quilt?

24

ONE after another, cars with impatient drivers rushed past the horse and carriage as Joanna reined the mare closer to the safety of the shoulder. Yet she didn't hurry the horse whatsoever. She needed this time to contemplate all the many events of this Friday.

Ella Mae's words continued to turn in Joanna's head, begging for attention, even though Joanna wished to push them aside. She turned her thoughts back to the quilt. It was odd, but she wondered if the wedding quilt was somehow destined to have been passed along through the family to her . . . if for no other reason than to offset her doubts. She honestly didn't know what to think about the young man who loved her but who seemingly had no plan of action that would permit them to marry anytime soon. Even so, the quilt from the past encouraged her.

She tried to picture her great-great-aunt—surely as resourceful and diligent as Joanna's own mother and grandmothers—sewing and humming as she worked . . . perhaps praying? Oh, she felt so reassured by the thought. It was almost as if the Lord was whispering in her ear, *All is well, my child.*

Her soul had to be silenced so Joanna could hear the still, small voice of God. Only then could she relinquish the reins of her life to her heavenly Father . . . and breathe a grateful prayer.

Joanna had just rounded the bend leading toward the fork in the road—the left side headed to Hickory Lane—when she noticed a young man walking on the other side, going in the same direction she was. He turned slightly, and she realized it was Freckles Jake.

Well, of all things!

He smiled and waved, and without a smidgen of hesitation, he called to her, "Joanna! Would ya mind giving me a lift?"

"Any other time, but I need to get home quickly."

His face fell. "All right, then."

Immediately, she felt guilty. Would it really be so bad to take him home or wherever he was headed? She thought better of it. "Well, if you're not goin' too far out of my way," she said, slowing the horse.

"Mighty kind of you," he said and thanked her.

She veered the horse off the road and stopped so Jake could hop in on the left. She hoped he'd stay put over there and not slide toward her for any funny business. Though for all the rumors, she'd never encountered anything out of the ordinary with him.

"Where're ya goin'?" she asked, suddenly feeling shy with him sharing the seat.

"Over yonder, past your father's farm—to Ella Mae's."

She was shocked, because she didn't know a young man would admit to going to see the Wise Woman. "Interesting," she replied, unable to keep her smile in check.

"Why's that?" The late-afternoon sun poured in on him, making his hair look redder than usual.

"Ach, I don't know," she said, embarrassed.

"Well, I think you do." He was grinning.

"Ella Mae's one terrific listener, for sure." *We all need to talk to someone,* she thought.

He shrugged.

"I can take you there, if you'd like."

"No, that's all right. I'll just get out at your place and go through the cornfield, if ya don't mind." He removed his straw hat, running his hand across the top of it. Then, glancing at her, he said, "I appreciate the ride."

"Don't mind at all."

He started to say something, then stopped and donned his hat. She was relieved. What if he asked if she was going to the next Singing? She didn't want to hurt him.

134

Besides, I belong to someone else, she thought. *Don't I?*

Her visit to Ella Mae's had certainly stirred up some issues. That and meeting with Jake on the road today—it was almost as if he'd turned up to reinforce the Wise Woman's remarks about local boys.

A few minutes later, they turned into her father's lane. "Here we are," she said, amazed how quickly Jake bounded out of the buggy, like he wanted to impress her. Then, before saying another word, he tied up the horse.

She turned to thank Jake for this small and unexpected favor and found him right behind her. His hazel eyes sparkled as he grinned at her. "Pleased to help . . . anytime, really." Then, crossing the barnyard, he turned to wave—twice.

Laughing a little at Jake's eagerness, Joanna headed around the side of the house and was completely astonished to see someone sitting on the back porch steps. There, looking altogether handsome, was none other than Eben Troyer!

25

"HULLO, Joanna." Eben remained seated for a moment, reconsidering his visit in the awkwardness of the moment. Had he done the right thing showing up unannounced?

But Joanna's contagious smile lifted the roof right off his heart, and he rose to meet her. "Ach, Eben . . . I . . . when did ya get here?" she stuttered, searching his face.

"A few minutes ago."

She was staring with disbelief, and if he wasn't mistaken, there were silent tears in her pretty eyes. "Ach, it's so *gut* to see you again! Does anyone know you're here?" She looked about her.

"I knocked, but no one came to the door. So I sat myself down to wait, and now you're here." He wanted to pull her into his arms and kiss her right there in broad daylight, but that wasn't called for. For one thing, he'd come bearing bad news. And for another, he couldn't easily dismiss the jovial fellow who had been riding with Joanna. Eben had never seen someone so smitten. He wondered why she hadn't introduced him before he ran off.

"Care to go walkin'?" he said.

"Or we could take the carriage." Joanna's eyes sparkled, and he saw again how exceptionally pretty she was. "We could walk along Weaver's Creek, if you'd like."

He didn't have the heart to tell her there was no time for riding like last time. Besides, lingering at the creek would simply prolong things. "I really can't stay," he said, pushing the words out.

Her face turned pale. "Why not?"

"I have a round-trip bus ticket. Gotta leave today." He couldn't bear her disappointed expression.

"I don't understand."

"We need to talk over some important things." He motioned toward the field lane on this side of the cornfield, where they'd walked in the cold and snow last November. Now that he was here, seeing her . . . he wanted to reach for her hand and feel it nestled in his, the way they'd walked before. Eben found it hard to voice what he'd come to say. Not hard, no—nearly impossible.

Joanna looked up at him as they headed across the driveway, a frown piercing her lovely face. And it was then he realized he was walking much too fast. He must slow down, slow everything down and take his time—*their time*—so he wouldn't regret it later. He had to first muster the courage to tell her how disappointed he was, soothe her with his own sadness, somehow.

He forged ahead. "My plans have suddenly changed, Joanna. Things are out of my control." He felt her stiffen as they walked beside each other, the electricity still evident between them.

"What do you mean?"

"You know I'd hoped to court you here." Eben drew a breath. Could he get the words out without making a fool of himself? "But circumstances have gotten in the way." His voice sounded foreign even to him. "It's become impossible for me to move to Hickory Hollow, after all."

Her eyes widened. "What's happened?"

He had to make her understand, so he tried again. "Leroy has thrown a wrench into everything. He got himself married to an outsider—brought her home to meet the family just yesterday."

"So . . . he's not comin' back, then?"

He shook his head. "I prayed he would get fed up with English life and come home to work with our father—and take my place."

She nodded her head slowly. "And there's no other choice but for you to stay put there?"

"My father can't manage on his own."

137

She fell silent as they walked farther away from the house.

After a time, he felt compelled to answer the unspoken question hanging between them. "I just had to come see ya, Joanna. I couldn't put this to you in a letter." If only she hadn't written so often about her great fondness for Hickory Hollow, this whole thing would've been much easier! "You deserved better, so I wanted to come here, to tell you in person."

"I don't know what to say." She stared at the ground for the longest time.

"What if you could move to Shipshewana?"

She immediately looked horrified, as if it was unthinkable. "I've never really considered it, Eben." She sighed audibly. "Thought you wanted to—"

"I know it's a lot to ask."

She shook her head, eyes glistening.

"You all right?" he asked, touching her elbow.

She flinched slightly. Then, raising her head to the sky, she pursed her lips and glanced toward a farm in the near distance . . . then smiled faintly.

What was this expression? Was she actually relieved they were parting ways?

He waited for her to say more, but when she continued in her silence, he remembered the auburn-haired young man who'd enthusiastically waved good-bye to her. No question, that fellow was sweet on Joanna.

Understandably so . . .

Somehow he found the courage to ask, "What is your bishop's stance on transferring church membership?" He hadn't wanted to broach this topic, didn't want to put her on the spot. He did recall her mother's pointed response to this during the last visit, but he needed to hear directly from Joanna.

"Bishop John's mighty strict," she stated, then paused like she was struggling terribly. "No, I doubt I'd be permitted to leave . . . now."

Eben wished he hadn't asked.

Joanna was so stunned she could scarcely speak. *He came all this way just to say good-bye?* She could not grasp this terrible turn of events. Truth was, Eben seemed at a loss to say more about his dilemma, simply blaming his brother Leroy for this mess. And the fact that Eben had asked, nearly out of the blue, if she'd move to Shipshewana . . . *What timing!* She was too embarrassed to tell him about the preacher's warning, especially now, when Eben seemed to be breaking up with her. Oh, how she loved him! How could she let him just give up on their relationship—everything they'd meant to each other?

Even so, she'd made a vow to God and to *this* church district, so there was no considering a move away to Indiana. Certainly not when Preacher Yoder's counsel burned in her ears.

Considering everything, it didn't make a whit of sense to keep walking like this, dragging out the inevitable. Her heart was being torn further with every step.

"I'm truly sorry it's come to this, Joanna," Eben said quietly. "I just see no way out . . . not anymore."

Because I'm not able to move to Indiana, she thought, knowing she'd pushed herself into a corner because of her love for writing. No, Leroy wasn't the only one who'd created this problem.

Joanna couldn't look at Eben for fear he might see her dismay.

They walked another few minutes without talking. She felt like Mamma's pressure cooker as the chasm between them grew by the second.

"I kept hopin' to see us together somehow," he said glumly. "I can't say enough how sorry I am."

"I'm sorry, too," she said, hoping he'd understand how much she cared for him. But she didn't dare ask anything more . . . she felt she was being as pushy as Jake was said to be. If only she could erase all the months of their separation and turn the clock back to the evening they'd first met in Virginia. When the world seemed to tilt as the sun fell into the ocean. When he'd whispered into her hair . . .

They were approaching the far perimeter of her father's field, where the grazing land bordered Ella Mae's son-in-law's property. Feeling forlorn and terribly helpless, Joanna looked toward the Wise Woman's Dawdi Haus again and remembered her pointed caution. True to form, she had not minced words. *"Complications,"* Ella Mae had said about long-distance relationships.

Joanna wanted to turn around and hurry back to the house, put this painful visit behind her. But in that moment, she spotted Jake Lantz sitting with Ella Mae under a shade tree on a double glider. *Can he see us out here?* she wondered, hoping not. As it was, Eben might very well be peeved at her being with Jake earlier. She almost wondered if she ought to say something, clarify that Jake had asked *her* for a ride—that he was nothing but a casual friend, if that. But might that only draw attention to Jake? Oh, she didn't know what to do!

"We should prob'ly head back," Eben said. "I need to call for a cab soon."

Her heart sank as she pointed to the telephone shanty in the next field over. The very spot where she'd looked forward to going to hear his voice. She sighed, choking back tears.

Eben offered a nod, then headed off in that direction.

Observing him walk, his posture so straight, his black suspenders perfectly crisscrossed against his white short-sleeved shirt—*he wore his for*-gut *clothes again*—Joanna refused to cry. *"Either a fella wants ya or he doesn't,"* she'd heard Ella Mae say some years ago. *"No sense in pleading for what's goin' to fizzle anyways."*

No, Joanna wouldn't fight for what could not be, and she wouldn't fret over him, not in his presence, anyhow.

She would sorely miss his calls and the many letters postmarked from Shipshewana. They had become such an important part of her weeks . . . her life.

In the depths of her heart, Joanna knew this parting meant much more than losing a beau. Joanna felt her last chance to marry for love slipping away.

Brokenhearted, she watched Eben open the wooden door to the shanty and reach for the telephone.

26

E BEN'S hand shook as he pulled the number for the cab company out of his pocket and attempted to dial the phone. *Worst day of my life.*

He stopped and hung up, still gripping the receiver as he stared out the lone window. If he did succeed in acquiring transportation back to the bus depot, he would sit there for a couple of hours until time to board for the overnight return trip—squander his precious time with Joanna. Yet there was nothing more to say; she seemed upset by his presence . . . even put out with him. It had been so long since he'd seen her, he wasn't sure he was reading her correctly. Was she sad he was calling off their plans? Angry?

We're almost like strangers.

He prayed for wisdom. Life had come crashing down indeed. And here he was, muddling through when he ought to be moving heaven and earth to win Joanna's heart and make her his bride.

Lifting the receiver again, he managed to dial this time. He went through the motions of speaking to someone at the dispatch office, asking for a ride within the hour, hoping that might give him a bit more time here—to make sure Joanna was all right. Although at the rate he was going, he wasn't certain she wanted him around at all. And who could blame her? He'd written her love letters, promising things based on mere hope . . . things he now knew he couldn't fulfill. *"Ich hab en Hutsch draus gemacht*," he whispered, glancing at his watch. There was no doubt in Eben's mind: He *had* made a mess of it.

Joanna was in such a bad way, she couldn't bring herself to stand there and wait for Eben to finish up his call. To preserve her sense of propriety, she walked back to the house and began to unhitch the horse, wondering where her parents and Cora Jane were keeping themselves.

She forced her thoughts away from the ragged ache that hadn't let up since she realized Eben was returning to Indiana, taking back his promise of love and a future together. Why hadn't she told on herself about the visit from Preacher Yoder . . . the complication *she'd* caused by not explaining herself? Why not, when their courtship was already coming to a painful end?

In a few minutes, Jake appeared again on this side of the barnyard, having returned through Dat's field. As before, his face glowed at seeing her. "Say, let me help ya, Joanna." And before she could politely refuse, he began to assist with the heavy harness. She hoped Eben wouldn't get the wrong idea, if he were to spot them working together. But then, realizing that was a ridiculous worry now, she dismissed it. After all, Eben had just let her go, so why should she fret? It might even be providential for Eben to see her with Jake.

Just that quickly, Joanna felt chagrined. No way did she wish jealousy on Eben. But she did wish she could erase his words and return to the days of their romance, however stalled. At least then the sting in her heart would not be so sharp.

In that moment, Cousin Malinda's husband, Andy, came rumbling down the road in his hay wagon. He slowed at the end of the lane, then called to her. "Joanna, come *schnell*! Hop aboard!" Something was obviously wrong. And without hesitation, she dashed to the road, leaving Jake behind.

Andy was hatless, his blond hair sticking out every which way like he'd run his hands through it.

"*Was fehlt?*" she asked.

"Mammi Kurtz collapsed in the kitchen . . . seriously injured her hip," Andy explained.

"Ach, no!" Joanna had seen how unsteady her grandmother had been earlier. *I should've stayed with her!* "Are my parents and Cora Jane over there already?"

"Jah, and your mother needs help with Dawdi, 'specially once the ambulance arrives."

Joanna felt terrible for not making sure her grandmother was all right. For more reasons than one, she should not have come home.

However anxious she was to be with her family, she also didn't want to leave just yet . . . not without saying good-bye to Eben.

Looking back, she saw him heading toward the house, within a few yards of Jake and the horse and carriage. She groaned inwardly, knowing Jake was a talkative sort. It was anyone's guess what he'd chew the fat about . . . and what Eben might say to him.

She asked Andy to wait a minute, then hurried to Eben. "My grandmother's fallen—might have a broken bone," she said. "I'm needed over there."

Disappointment seemed to cloud his countenance as she offered a quick farewell.

Unexpectedly, he reached for her hand and gave it a quick squeeze. "*Gott* be with you, Joanna," he said simply.

She tried to give him a smile in return, then, knowing it was best not to linger, headed back to Andy, who hoisted her up and into the wagon.

The horse moved forward, and Joanna looked back to Eben . . . just in time to see him shake Jake's hand. The two of them turned and were standing shoulder to shoulder, looking altogether befuddled as she rode away. If Joanna hadn't felt so miserable right then, seeing Jake and Eben together like that might've struck her as almost comical.

"Looks like it's just us," Jake said after introducing himself, helping Eben lead the horse to the stable. "Most folk call me Freckles Jake . . . guess you can, too."

Eben, still reeling with emotion, felt momentarily thankful Jake was being so down-home and relaxed. *Like Leroy always was* . . .

"*Gut* to meet ya, Freckles Jake. I'm Eben Troyer."

Jake removed his straw hat and scratched his head. "That's a family name we don't hear much round here."

Eben nodded. "I'm from Indiana . . . Shipshewana, to be exact."

"Ah, so you're the fella who visited last year." Jake grinned now, planting his hat back on. "Nice to put a name to a face."

"Have you lived here your whole life?" Eben asked.

"Born and bred." Jake straightened and pushed out his chest. "We here in Hickory Hollow are mighty proud—well, in a *gut* sort of way—of our secluded little spot, hidden away from the English world. 'Tis hard to find, if you don't know where you're goin'."

Eben could vouch for that. The cab driver today had never even heard of Hickory Lane and didn't know it was east of Intercourse Village—*a strange name for a town,* Eben thought. *Thank goodness for the cabbie's GPS.*

"Well, what do ya think of our hollow?" Jake asked, looking him over but good as they walked out of the stable.

"I see why folk like it." *Joanna especially.*

"Looks like you've got some time on your hands, what with Joanna carted off and all."

If Eben had been in a better mood, he would have chuckled. "Not much time, actually."

"All right, then. You gonna spend it standing lookin' like you're lost?"

Something about this young man demanded his attention. "I like you, Jake. I truly do." He clapped his hand on Jake's shoulder, feeling the muscles there. No question this was a hardworking, responsible fellow. "What can ya tell me about your Ordnung here? How strict is your bishop, for starters?"

A frown appeared on Jake's face. "Oh, now, you don't want to fool with the likes of Bishop John Beiler."

"So . . . mighty strict, then?"

Jake bobbed his head. "Imposed the harshest shunning anywhere some years ago. A young girl wouldn't submit to the church over her music."

Eben's ears perked up. "Really, now?"

"She ended up leavin'—took her guitar with her."

Eben didn't need to hear how harsh they'd treated her, but he did wonder about the types of vows required at church baptism. "Some churches want their members to stay put in the same district their whole life."

"Jah, that's pretty much what we've got right here."

Eben considered that, his mind going a hundred miles an hour. "Ever know anyone who managed to get permission to move to another Amish church?" No doubt the reason for his questions was apparent to Jake, but Eben couldn't help asking.

"Well, a few . . . sure. But they were members in good standing." Jake studied him hard. "Why do ya ask?"

"Curious is all." Eben couldn't help but wonder why Joanna had said so emphatically otherwise. Had she purposely misrepresented the bishop? Surely not. And he couldn't imagine a girl like Joanna not being highly regarded in the church.

No, Eben knew the real truth. She simply was not interested in leaving her beloved home . . . not even to marry him.

27

As she rode to her grandparents' house, Joanna could still picture Eben with Jake, standing at the end of the lane. She squelched the urge to cry, knowing she must be strong for her mother . . . and for poor Dawdi, who would surely want to go along in the ambulance with Mammi. That's just how he was these days—hardly let her out of his sight.

I'll be the one to stay home with him.

Tears sprang to her eyes as she considered both the unforeseen breakup with Eben and now Mammi's terrible fall. Truly, Joanna could hardly hold herself together.

Eben spotted the yellow cab coming this way and immediately regretted having to leave. If only he could have come here under much different circumstances. Like his visit last wedding season. Yet, knowing what he did now, he could see she was not willing to commit, not when it meant a move. Otherwise, why would she not say there were exceptions to membership transfers? She'd lost interest in him . . . perhaps in part because of the friendly fellow beside him.

"Mighty nice talkin' with ya," Jake said, moseying onto the road with a wave as he headed toward home.

"You too." The encounter with Jake had seemed meant to be.

Eben opened the back door of the cab and got in, watching Joanna's house fade from sight as they sped away. He took in the springtime views, especially noticing the well-tended lawns and surrounding flower gardens—every farmhouse here was pristine and tidy, too. Not that his community back home wasn't as well cared for, of course . . . it just struck him that each and every property here was remarkably maintained.

No wonder Joanna adores the area.

With a glance into the rearview mirror, the cabbie asked if he had kinfolk here.

"No."

"Ah . . . a girlfriend, maybe?"

"Not anymore." Eben shrugged. "It didn't work out."

"Sorry, man."

No more than I am, Eben thought. *My whole future was bound up in Joanna Kurtz.*

"Remember, there are lots of other good fish in the sea," the driver said with another glance over his shoulder and a sympathetic smile.

Eben considered that. Meeting Joanna had seemed providential—so much that he had trusted in it completely.

As they drove a bit farther, he noticed a large farmhouse where an ambulance was parked in the lane, as well as several gray buggies, a van, and the same hay wagon that had come for Joanna.

He caught sight of Joanna herself standing on the front porch, opening her arms to an older man. Was it her Dawdi? Watching her comfort him, Eben swallowed the lump in his throat, touched by her compassion.

Oh, dear Joanna, he thought sadly. *What have I done, letting you go?*

Just as Joanna had guessed, she was left in charge of her grandfather as a vanload of various relatives, including her parents and Cora Jane, followed the ambulance with Mammi inside to the hospital. She helped get Dawdi settled in a rocker on the front porch, where he'd insisted on being positioned facing west, in the direction the ambulance had gone.

"Would ya like something cold to drink?" She concentrated on doting on her grandfather, glad to have something to occupy her mind.

Dawdi smiled a little, his blue-gray eyes still moist from weeping. She supposed, as tenderhearted as he was, he might sit out here and cry some more. "There's a pitcher of lemonade in there," he said.

"I'll get some for ya."

"You're as thoughtful as your Mammi, ya know?" he surprised her by saying.

"That's awful nice." Joanna remembered again Eben's disheartening visit. Lots of girls would've questioned him even further—talked up to him, perhaps. Cora Jane would have!

While Dawdi drank his lemonade and kept cool outdoors, Joanna put the casserole she'd delivered earlier into the oven to reheat. Once she'd set the table for two and checked on Dawdi again, she wandered to the sitting area in the kitchen alcove and noticed her Mammi's devotional book open and lying upside down. Looking at it, Joanna began to read the selection for the day from Psalm 29:11, surprised by its pertinence. *"The Lord will give strength unto his people; the Lord will bless his people with peace."*

Still holding the book, she sat down in Mammi's chair. "I long for your peace, O Lord . . . I truly do." She stifled her urge to cry as she looked with fondness around this little corner where Mammi loved to sit and read. "With God's help, I'll get through this unbearable time," she whispered, wishing Eben Troyer safe travels home. She did not harbor any bitterness toward him, not one speck: Eben was a good man, she knew. But she was hurt terribly and longed to receive the peace spoken of in the psalm. She leaned her head back, hoping her grandmother would be all right. *Let her know you're with her, O Lord.*

After a time, Joanna went to stir the casserole, making sure it was hot enough to serve. And she burst into tears, realizing she would never cook such a supper for Eben.

The man in front of Eben on the bus smelled of cigarettes. Now that he thought of it, Eben realized that Leroy had smelled a bit like smoke, too. Surely his brother hadn't gravitated toward that kind of habit. But then, Leroy had dabbled in plenty of things since he'd attended high school and college.

Eben looked out the window, the sky already dimming as the sun dropped low, flicking light between thousands of tree trunks as they headed west.

Back to where I came from . . .

He'd learned more about the Hickory Hollow church district in a few short moments with Jake than he had in all the months of courting Joanna by letter. But then, Eben hadn't probed about her community, so it wasn't fair to measure in that way. Joanna was a responder—she had never been pushy or forward like some girls. No, Joanna was kind and patient, and she certainly hadn't deserved being put through the wringer today. What a rotten outcome for someone so wonderful.

Squinting into the fading sunlight, Eben thought it served him right if Jake Lantz *was* interested in Joanna. Considering how forthright and congenial the young man was, Eben almost hoped he'd pursue her. At least then he'd know Joanna would have a fine husband.

He closed his eyes, again seeing Joanna's sweet face when first she'd seen him sitting there on the back porch. Repeatedly, he made himself remember only her demure and cheerful expression . . . the way she looked before he'd opened his mouth and ruined everything. He resented the pain in his heart, for it was his own doing.

Rest eluded him. Eben opened his eyes and stared out the window at the landscape along the highway, a greenish-brown blur as the bus sped along faster and faster toward home. *Away from my dearest love,* he thought as the wind rushed past the windows.

After supper, Joanna sat in her grandmother's chair and listened as Dawdi Kurtz read the old German Bible. She wondered when someone might return to give some word of Mammi.

Not surprisingly, Dawdi eventually called it an early night and headed off to bed in the downstairs sleeping room. Her grandfather was a quiet man who lived his life inside his head and disliked engaging in much conversation—like Joanna's own father. Sleep was Dawdi's way of coping with his great concern for Mammi, now far away in the hospital. *Amongst Englischers . . .*

Feeling restless, Joanna wandered upstairs to look at the rooms that had been set up by Fannie and her husband to look nearly identical to those in the main farmhouse, where decades before, Joanna's grandparents had nurtured and raised their children. The more spacious bedroom was presently arranged as a comfortable guest room, and the smallest was a sewing room. Just as in the bigger house next door, the larger bedroom was situated directly over the kitchen for the best warmth during the cold months. The room still looked the same as when Mammi and Dawdi had moved here to the slightly smaller Dawdi Haus, right after Cora Jane was born. Joanna's mother had needed some extra care from her own mother, so Joanna was brought here at the age of seven to spend a week. At that time, Mammi Kurtz had shown her a secret opening in the wall, a concealed bookshelf where she'd kept her diaries and a New Testament in English. There was also a file of old letters—"relics," Mammi had called them—and an assortment of books, including one titled *Voice of the Heart*, by John Newton.

Knowing Mammi wouldn't mind if she poked around a bit, Joanna made her way to the crevice in the wall. There, just as she remembered, was the small hideaway, now filled with still more books. Joanna looked more closely and noticed that some were novels—"*made-up stories*," as Preacher Yoder had described them. Then, opening one of the devotional books, Joanna saw two letters tucked inside, both on parchment. The words *Aunt Joanna* were beautifully written on the strip of paper wrapped around them.

"Is this my namesake?" Joanna whispered, noting the June 1932 date on the letter. Surely this confirmed it was written by the aunt who'd made the double wedding ring quilt. Joanna sighed. *I'll ask Mammi if I can read these sometime.*

She slipped the letters back into the book and closed the small door. The discovery of letters from the other Joanna was so interesting, especially right on the heels of having received the quilt. Why *had* Mamma chosen to name her after this woman whose letters were so special that Mammi Kurtz had saved them all these years?

Sitting on her grandparents' old bed, Joanna contemplated her heritage—so many devout folk, like her two sets of grandparents. Wise folk . . . like Ella Mae Zook.

She leaned back on the bed and looked up at the ceiling. She thought again of the Wise Woman's surprising advice. "She was right," Joanna whispered, letting her tears flow freely now that she was alone.

28

IN many ways, Joanna was thankful she hadn't told Cora Jane or Mamma about Eben Troyer's recent visit. She was an emotional mess, and while she did her best to conceal her heartache, she was also aware of her parents' concern. So she tried to hide how she felt during the day, grateful for the time she had to herself while Mamma went to the hospital to visit Mammi Kurtz, who had indeed shattered her hip and was facing a lengthy recovery.

Adding to Joanna's pain was the rift between her and her sister. Never before had Joanna known such discord in their home. She and Cora Jane actively avoided each other. Mamm had stepped in to keep the flame from blazing out of control, ordering housework so that the two sisters were never thrown together—at least, not alone. The girls' work outdoors was even more conducive to the standoff, as they rarely crossed paths. If one was weeding and hoeing the vegetable garden, the other carried feed or water to the barn animals. Joanna wondered if things could ever be made right between them.

After two solid months of melancholy, Joanna was exhausted from crying each night, weary of her grief. She decided to make the effort to go on a van trip with other youth in the church district in mid-June—a tour of the Ephrata Cloister National Historic Landmark. The tour would help her get her mind off herself. Besides, it was time to dismiss Eben Troyer and get on with living.

On the way back from Ephrata, Freckles Jake asked to sit beside her,

151

and amidst inquisitive looks from the other girls, Joanna agreed. *They think he's trouble.* But Joanna wasn't the sort of young woman who would put up with anything inappropriate from a fellow, so she ignored the initial stares. As for her opinion, thus far the only real drawback was his age. Jake was turning twenty-four in the fall, a full year younger than Joanna.

Pretty soon, Jake was telling her one story after another, weaving together people and places until everything else around them seemed to fade. She was thoroughly entertained and amused, though she hadn't the least idea if the stories were true or not. Really, it didn't matter—she'd so desperately needed to laugh again!

Jake appeared delighted by her response and asked if she'd go riding with him. Joanna agreed but didn't commit to when that might be—still, she found herself actually looking forward to some more time with this fellow storyteller.

As for her own stories, Joanna had managed by sheer willpower to refrain from writing since Preacher Yoder's visit, but her resolve was waning—she was that eager to express herself once more. And late that night, after returning from the trip to Ephrata, she could hold off no longer. Jake's remarkable tales had stirred up her creativity all over again.

She pressed a doorstop beneath her closed door and pulled out the writing notebook from the binder in the hope chest. What if she could replace the first pages of her most recent story by rewriting the opening? And as she recast it, she realized her turns of phrase were actually better than those in the former attempt. *How strange is that?* Joanna mused, happily writing for more than an hour, the words pouring onto the page. As before, she was transported to another place, losing all sense of time . . . and loving every minute.

Never once did she consider the need to be repentant for this breach, nor did she feel guilty. If she could just finish this one last love story, she would cease her writing for good.

The very next night, and the next, Joanna engaged in the same activity, writing frantically in the secret haven of her room until she was helplessly drawn back into her old pattern of daily creating a make-believe world on paper. But she'd wised up considerably, vigilant now to hide her notebook, not wanting anyone to read the sad pages of her fictitious love story and guess that her own romance had also come to a painful end.

··· ❧ ❧ ···

On a sultry Saturday near the close of June, Joanna longed for a breeze as she dressed for her first real date with Jake. Oh, to have a nice big overhead fan, like the one Ephraim Yoder had recently installed at the General Store! Not electric, of course, but run by an air compressor.

She eyed two recent notes on her dresser, both from Jake. He'd sent them in the last week, mostly humorous anecdotes intended, she was sure, to make her smile. She guessed he'd picked up on her appreciation for his "tellin's"—the snippets of stories he so obviously delighted in sharing.

Before checking her hair one last time, she lightly dabbed a rose scent behind each ear, then walked primly downstairs. Cora Jane had already left to meet her beau, or so Joanna assumed, and Mamma sat on the back porch with Dat, both eating tapioca pudding as Joanna made her way outside. She waved shyly as she left, catching Mamma's eye. "I won't be late," she said softly, and Dat nodded, fidgeting.

They must suspect I'm going out with a new fellow, she thought. *If so, they must be relieved.* She'd moped around the house long enough. *That's all behind me now.* She wished she hadn't put all her eggs in one basket with Eben. But there had never been anyone else for her . . . till now.

Presently, she walked barefoot down the lane, the evening still warm enough that no wrap was needed for later. An owl hooted somewhere high in the dusky cottonwood, and Joanna felt his keen gaze on her.

Will Jake entertain me with his stories again? she wondered as flecks of the past crossed her mind. *Will he help me forget Eben?*

··· ❧ ❧ ···

Eben felt like he was swimming underwater as he trotted his driving horse on the way to pick up Ada Kemp. It was his first social outing since he'd returned from Lancaster County. At the thought, he heaved a sigh. "Wonder what Joanna's doing tonight," he said aloud, realizing he'd have to quit thinking about his former sweetheart. Wouldn't be fair to any other girl he started seeing.

The evening sky was a hazy blue, and the sound of crickets already filled the air. He forced himself to think about nineteen-year-old Ada Kemp, his date tonight. *Ain't the smartest thing I've ever done,* he decided, knowing the pickle he'd gotten himself in by smiling at Ada last week at Sunday Singing. Ada's older brother had taken notice and twisted Eben's arm into asking her out. *Well, not actually twisted,* Eben thought.

He urged the horse onward as he grew closer to Ada's green-shuttered farmhouse. If she even remembered to show up at the preappointed spot, he hardly knew what to say to her.

Maybe she'll forget. . . .

He was out of practice; it had been some time since he'd gone through the motions of a typical courtship. Eben frowned, still disgusted with himself for unintentionally leading Joanna on for so long. For that he was the most sorry of all.

"If I could just go back and do everything differently," he muttered, yet he realized the end result would be the same. The exact same wretched outcome. He shook his head at the depressing thought, and just then spotted Ada walking this way, wearing a bright lavender dress—a salve for sore eyes. She smiled demurely but didn't wave . . . and he couldn't help himself: He missed Joanna all the more.

Joanna hadn't realized how strong Jake Lantz was until he offered his hand to help her into his open buggy. She felt featherlight as he pulled her up, and she was soon at ease as he remarked on the especially warm temperatures and the fact that there were no storms brewing tonight in any direction. "It'll make for a nice buggy ride." The way he said it, so casual like, made her feel even more relaxed.

She was equally surprised to see the black leather bucket seats and plush carpet he'd installed. Trying not to smile too broadly, she thought, *You just never know what a day will bring!*

"Did ya have a nice big supper?" Jake asked, looking mighty fit in his black broadfall trousers, white shirt, and black vest. He hadn't worn his straw hat this time, his clean hair blowing gently in the slight breeze.

Was he asking if she wanted a snack? Joanna wanted to be polite, not sound like a pig. "I had plenty to eat, jah."

"That so?" He gave her a mischievous grin. "I've noticed you always make room for ice cream."

"Really, now?"

"Well, you've eaten your fair share at the youth gatherings."

She chuckled but felt a little embarrassed, realizing he had been watching her for quite some time.

They talked about other things. Then Jake brought up her grandmother's fall and the day he'd met Eben. "Do you mind if I ask if you're still in touch with him?"

He certainly had every right to know if she was free to date. And for some reason she felt comfortable enough to say that Eben was gone from her life. "We wrote back and forth for a long time, though," Joanna added.

Jake looked at her again, concern in his eyes. "You sound upset."

"I sure am!"

He smiled quickly. "That's all right—I don't mind bein' your punching bag . . . if that's what ya need."

She shook her head, looking away. "Sorry. It ain't like that. Shouldn't've said anything."

"'Tis all right. You're feelin' better already, jah?"

Goodness, he'd seen right through her. "Guess I do."

The horse pulled them faster, nearly at a gallop, and Joanna glimpsed flashes of black soil between the rows of soybeans on either side of the road. No question, Jake was showing off. And just how had he known she loved a good joyride? *What else does he know about me, for pity's sake?*

29

JOANNA thoroughly enjoyed a double-scoop peach ice cream cone at Lapp Valley Farm, where she and Jake used the convenient drive-through. Jake was determined to treat her, which was quite nice, even though she suspected he was hungry for some dessert himself.

Over the course of the next few hours, they managed to talk about everything from English tourists they'd met to what it would be like to live in a house with air-conditioning on such a humid night. She was especially relieved that Jake hadn't spoiled things by reaching for her hand or slipping his arm around her. Had the Wise Woman counseled him on the proper way to date, just maybe?

And Jake did not bring up Eben again during the zippy ride past Amish farmland. For that, Joanna was grateful. She was even more surprised later, when Jake pulled over on the side of the road, near Weaver's Creek—the very spot she'd wanted to bring her former beau.

"What're we doin' here?" she asked.

"You'll see." He offered to help her down. "Follow me."

They walked single file through the high grass, toward the wide, wooded creek bed. He scrambled to the top of the largest boulder and sat there like a tall bird. He smiled, watching her from his perch. "Oh, here, do ya need some help?"

"I'm fine," she said, laughing. And she was. She could easily climb up there to join him.

When she'd sat down in the small spot left for her, she soon saw why he'd brought her here.

"Shh, just watch," he whispered.

As the light dimmed, the sun melted the sky into pinks and gold, the rosy hue filling the shadows and the stream itself. Colors she'd never seen before were reflected in the water. Adding to that near-magical glow were the sparkles of hundreds of lightning bugs. *Fireflies*, Eben had called them in a letter. But Joanna had never seen them like this with Eben. No, her evening with Jake was far different than a date with a letter . . . or a phone booth! And Joanna rather liked it.

··· ➤ ◄ ···

Eben initially thought Ada might be rather shy, but as the evening progressed, he discovered he'd been quite wrong. She seemed to feel the need to fill even the smallest gaps of silence. She also had a strange habit of wringing her hands, just like his tetchy *Grossmammi* on his mother's side. Both habits made him wish he'd stayed home.

Ada was saying something now about her best friend planting an extra big crop of celery seedlings, starting tomorrow. "Ya know what that means, ain't?" Her voice rose to a crescendo.

He knew, all right.

She jabbered on about this unnamed friend of hers, even though Eben knew perfectly well it was Dottie Miller, having seen Ada come into Singings and other get-togethers with her sisters and this good friend. *So Dottie's getting hitched,* he thought, guessing one young woman after another would marry during this November. And if Eben didn't get on the stick and get serious about finding a bride, he'd end up having to look at the new crop of sixteen-year-olds next thing.

He must've chuckled at the thought, because Ada looked over at him. Then, oh, the laugh she gave! It was the most harsh-sounding, peculiar laugh he'd ever heard before, sharp as shattered glass. Why hadn't he noticed this prior to asking her out? Eben held tightly to the reins and reminded himself that he'd been the one who'd asked her to go riding tonight.

By the time they arrived at his brother-in-law's place to meet another couple for a tournament of Ping-Pong, Eben was annoyed, though he knew he must be a gentleman and make the evening pleasant for her. He was not one to throw in the towel quickly.

So they played doubles in the cool basement—girls against the guys, and later couples against each other. The beautiful girl opposite Ada reminded him of Joanna in looks and demeanor, and he had to be careful not to stare, lest her boyfriend think he was coveting.

As the Ping-Pong wound down, Eben's sister-in-law made popcorn and surprised them with some homemade strawberry ice cream for the occasion. The time of refreshment and visiting was dominated by Ada, yet in spite of the chatty girl by his side, Eben felt downright lonely. Was this how he'd always feel without Joanna in his life?

There was talk of another tournament—some other evening—and Ada leaped up a little in what Eben assumed was excitement at the idea. The other couple readily agreed, but Eben was reluctant. He saw the disappointment in Ada's dark brown eyes but had to be true to himself. He was not going anywhere again with Ada Kemp. It was wrong to let her think he was interested in anything more than friendship.

Minutes after Eben had seen her home, he removed his black vest and rolled up his white shirt sleeves, nearly as tired as if he'd filled silo all day. The leisurely ride home was just what he needed . . . and the blessed silence. "What a mistake," he whispered, vowing not to get himself into such a pickle again.

--- ➤ ◄ ---

Cora Jane surprised Joanna by waiting up for her that night, perched on the edge of Joanna's own bed. "Heard you might've gone out with Freckles Jake," Cora Jane said, eyes wide. "Did ya?"

"I'm awful tired, if ya don't mind."

"You sure don't look it."

Joanna went to the window, her back to her sister. "Well, I *am*." Did her sister suddenly think that all was well between them because Eben was no longer a part of Joanna's life?

"Did he kiss ya?"

Joanna whirled around. "You know better than that!" She caught her breath. "Takes two for that."

Cora Jane began to laugh, then clapped her hand over her mouth, stifling her own giggles. "You should see your face, sister. I mean, honestly!"

"This isn't funny."

"Ach, your face is."

"I'd like to get ready for bed now, Cora Jane." Joanna didn't even think to ask if she'd had a good time with Gid. It was the last thing on her mind with her sister acting so foolish.

But Cora Jane continued to sit there, calming down some and looking more serious.

Joanna pointed toward the door. "I mean it," she said. "I'd like some privacy."

"What . . . so you can dream 'bout Jake Lantz?"

Joanna shook her head in disgust. "When will you ever grow up?"

"Are you just too *old* to have fun . . . is that it?" Cora Jane rose and stood at the door, leaning her head against the doorjamb. "How could you possibly go out with the likes of that boy?"

"He's a gentleman, that's how."

"Well, ain't what our cousins are sayin'. . . . Goodness, all the girls are avoiding him."

"People can change."

"But not Jake," said Cora Jane.

"How would you know?"

"I'm smart enough to listen to *gut* advice," Cora Jane shot back.

Joanna stood her ground. "I'm tellin' you he's nothin' at all like the rumors."

The two of them glared at each other, but the resentment Joanna felt wasn't because of Jake. "I think you owe me an apology, sister." She'd endured Cora Jane's silence and near gloomy outlook for far too long . . . holding in her hurt the best she could. "You know precisely what I'm talking about."

"Why, because I called the preacher's attention to your disobedience?"

"Wasn't necessary and you know it."

"No?" Cora Jane shrugged. "Since when are you the rule maker?"

It was all Joanna could do not to retaliate and say, *Since when are you?* But she bit her lip and kept silent. She turned away. The encounter with Cora Jane was beginning to cloud her special time away. Not wanting to ask her sister to leave the room again, Joanna went to sit in the chair near the window, and when she turned around, wondering how she was going to keep her peace, Cora Jane was gone.

··· ➤ ◄ ···

Joanna wished for a lock on her door as she wrote long into the night, remembering the beauty surrounding her at Weaver's Creek. Yet the evening's charms mingled with sadness at her loss of Eben, and she wrote with all the more fervor—only *this* story must have a happy ending.

She felt carried away to her lovely fictional world, like a character snatched away from another completely different place, where things of the heart were shared and treasured for always. Where there was no speck of pain or sadness over lost love. Just as always before, Joanna reveled in her precious creation.

Sometime later, after she'd put away her notebook, she dressed for bed, slipping into the lightweight blue gown she'd sewn a few weeks ago. Then she pulled out a box of greeting cards and found one to send to Mammi Kurtz, who was still in a rehab hospital in Lancaster. Each week, Joanna enjoyed sending a card with her own special made-up poem, hoping it might bring her grandmother some cheer. Joanna's mother had commented on the cards, which she'd seen when she'd gone to visit, saying how pleased Mammi was to receive them.

While writing this poem, Joanna wondered if anyone else amongst the People might see her poetry. If so, would they report her to the ministerial brethren the way Cora Jane had? She hoped it wasn't against the church ordinance to write little rhyming encouragements, too!

When she was finished, she pulled out the wooden letter box in the hope chest and contemplated what to do with Eben's many letters and cards. But the more she considered it, the more she knew she couldn't part with any of it just yet. Maybe someday.

Something else weighed on her. Pleasant as he was, she didn't know if she ought to go out with Jake again, except that all the other fellows who were unspoken for were even younger than he was. She'd so wanted to be married this wedding season. *But not to just anyone . . .*

Joanna turned out the gas lantern and slipped into bed, sighing. As her eyes slowly grew accustomed to the dark, it struck her that she might simply enjoy occasional dates with Jake Lantz, if he was willing. What could it hurt? But she should let him know next time they saw each other that she was only interested in a casual friendship until she was completely over Eben Troyer.

How will Jake feel about that? she wondered. *Is that fair to him?*

30

THE following Wednesday morning, Joanna worked with Cora Jane and Mamma—and Ella Mae's daughter-in-law, Mattie Beiler—to transplant celery seedlings from the nearby Amish greenhouse. Afterward, Joanna stopped at the end of the lane to mail a get-well card to Mammi Kurtz. Then, setting off on foot so she wouldn't tie up the family carriage, she went to visit Cousin Malinda.

A quarter mile along, here came Jake Lantz in his pony cart, waving to beat the band. He slowed and stopped in the middle of the road. "Hullo," she said. It was clear by his smile he was happy to see her.

"We meet again," he said.

Recalling what she'd wanted to tell him, she suddenly felt bashful. "Nice day, jah?"

"Ideal for helping the deacon. He's still under the weather, ya know."

She knew all too well. He'd been ill since April.

"Thought I'd take up some of the slack over there with barn chores and whatnot."

Nodding, she smiled. "*Gut* of you."

He glanced up the road like he had something on his mind. "I sure had a great time last Saturday. I'd like to take you out again, if that's all right."

Here was her moment to speak up, but by the happiness in his eyes, he surely wouldn't want to hear anything but a positive response. "When were ya thinkin'?" She amazed herself.

"How 'bout we go riding after the Singing this coming Sunday night?"

161

She'd guessed that's what he might suggest. "Preaching's at Andy and Malinda's, ya know."

"Jah, heard Andy's sweepin' out the upper level of his barn come Saturday, so I'll go over there and lend a hand."

"I was just headin' there now . . . to help Malinda wash down the walls and whatnot," she added.

"Nearly forgot you're kin to them," Jake said as he reined in the anxious pony. "So will ya go with me, then . . . Sunday night?"

Another carriage was coming this way, so she had to make up her mind. Joanna smiled right quick. "Jah, I'll go."

His face burst into a grin and off he went. And, if Joanna wasn't mistaken, she heard him say, "Glory be."

"What *am* I doin'?" she whispered, moving back to the side of the road to let the coming horse and carriage pass.

———

Joanna enjoyed the walk to Cousin Malinda's less for having bumped into Jake, and she stewed now about not having the courage to say what she should. *This Sunday I will, for certain*, she promised herself as she took in the stands of hardwood trees near the white horse fences of Andy King's land and the open pasture beyond. Indeed, it was a splendid day.

Malinda was outside weeding her marigolds and asters, a patch of yellows and purples, when Joanna came up the driveway. "I've come to give you a hand," Joanna called.

Malinda was red cheeked in the blazing sun. She wiped her damp brow with the back of her palm, her plain blue scarf having slipped back. "Ach, so *gut* to see ya. Sure, you can help."

They worked together to finish up the bed so that it was free of even a single weed for the coming Lord's Day. Of course, knowing Malinda, by Saturday she would go back and do the same thing where needed.

Once inside, they cleaned the house from the top of each room down, dusting, sweeping, washing, and making everything tidy and spotless. Joanna felt a hushed reverence about their work, knowing that this farmhouse would become a temporary place of worship this Sunday.

After the noon meal, Malinda's twin sisters, Anna and Becky, joined them in beating rugs and sweeping every inch of the front and back porches before hosing them down. They finished off by cleaning the windows and screens, as well.

Later, once Joanna and Malinda were alone again, they enjoyed a tall glass of meadow tea, which hit the spot, as Mamma liked to say. Malinda dropped into the rocking chair on the shady back porch with a sigh. "Thanks to you and my sisters, I'm a little ahead of things," she said, fanning herself.

"Glad we could pitch in."

Malinda asked about her family and Cora Jane, and Joanna told her about planting the celery.

"Oh, Joanna . . . I hope Cora Jane's getting married this fall isn't hard on you," said Malinda.

"Bein' she's younger than me by a mile?"

There was a sweetness in Malinda's concerned expression. "Maybe I shouldn't have said anything."

"No . . . no, that's all right." *We're more than cousins . . . we're friends.*

They sipped their iced tea, watching the breeze move through the tops of trees and the birds flitting about.

Then Malinda said softly, "I'm afraid I've got a rather prickly topic to bring up. I heard something the other week that's hard to believe."

Joanna froze and stared at her glass, wondering what on earth.

"Did Preacher Yoder come and talk to you?"

"Jah, he dropped by a couple months ago . . . about my stories."

Malinda studied her. "Is everything all right?"

"For now, jah."

"I've been concerned awhile but wasn't sure if it was true."

"Oh, true enough." Joanna told on herself. Somehow it was different talking about difficult things with Malinda. *A far cry from talking to Cora Jane.*

"You must have a real gift for writing."

Stunned, she looked at Malinda. "What?"

"Evidently the deacon's wife read part of your story and was quite taken by your talent."

"She did—she *is?*"

Malinda nodded and took a sip from her glass.

"How'd ya hear this?"

"My mother mentioned it last weekend, when she was over to help me put up beans."

"Good grief, I wonder who else knows?" Joanna felt it strange to hear someone talk about her private writing like this.

"Word spreads, ya know?" Malinda encouraged her.

Jah, ain't that the truth.

Joanna watched Malinda closely, wishing she hadn't said anything just now. So, was everyone talking about this? Had it gotten to the grapevine? She cringed at the thought.

Malinda continued along the same lines. "Seems kind of peculiar that on one hand, the preacher wants you to put a stop to your creativity, and on the other, the deacon's wife is praising your work."

"Odd, indeed." And that, Joanna thought, was all she ought to say.

31

JOANNA could hardly wait to see her grandmother that Friday when she learned Mammi Kurtz had at last been released from rehab. Fannie and the rest of the family had requested permission for the rehabilitation hospital to dismiss her to their aid. With the help of a home care nurse several times a week, they planned to look after Mammi together.

Hurrying through her morning chores, Joanna got a ride to Mammi Kurtz's with her father, who was on his way to see the smithy. "Mammi must be delighted to be back home again," she said, making small talk.

He nodded so slightly she almost missed it.

"Do ya happen to know anything 'bout my namesake?" she asked, wondering if she might be able to get him talking. "The aunt I was named after?"

"You might ask your grandmother Kurtz. She'd know best. I don't remember her so well."

"I hope to but don't want to tire Mammi out, ya know."

He neither nodded nor commented.

After that, she remained quiet till they pulled over onto the side of the road, at the turnoff to the driveway. "Denki, Dat . . . I'll walk home later."

His eyes registered her words, and he gave another nod. "See ya then."

From the street, the white clapboard house looked tall and narrow. Large oak trees flanked the east side of the lawn. A small shed and big barn out back, as well as the curing house over near a grove of trees, rounded out the property. The lawn had been recently cut; whoever had used the push mower last needed to sharpen the blade before the next mowing.

Three small children came running out the front door to meet Joanna—her married sister Salina's three—Stephen, Sylvia, and Susan— all adorable towheads. "*Aendi* Joanna!" they called, flinging their arms around her long skirt.

"Come see the sweets Mamma made. Hurry!" said almost six-year-old Stephen in *Deitsch*.

"Could it be sugar cookies, maybe?" Joanna played along.

"Nee . . . come see," said Sylvia, her eyes dancing.

"What can it be?" Joanna scampered after them, hurrying around the side of the house to go in the back way. "Sticky buns, maybe?"

"Whoopie pies—chocolate ones!" tiny Susan exclaimed as all of them burst into the kitchen.

Salina gently shushed them as they entered, then greeted Joanna.

"Hullo, sister," Joanna said, the little girls still hanging on her.

"A warm welcome, jah?" Salina fanned herself with a white hankie.

"How's Mammi Kurtz?" Joanna asked once the children were settled at the table, swinging their bare legs beneath the blue-and-white-checkered oilcloth.

Salina set a large whoopie pie on a napkin in front of each of them. Then she motioned for Joanna to follow her to the bedroom just around the corner. There sat her grandmother in a straight-backed cane chair, head bowed and sound asleep. "She's all tuckered out, which is understandable," whispered Salina, leaning near.

"Can she walk without help?"

"She uses a walker okay, but she shouldn't be alone . . . that's why I'm here today." Salina smiled and touched Joanna's arm. "Would ya mind checkin' on Dawdi for me?"

"Front room?"

"Jah, there by the screen door, to get the best breeze. He's not too keen on sittin' on the back porch when the children are here."

"No doubt the commotion wears on him." Joanna could understand that—Salina's busy three were definitely a handful. She went to the largest room and found her grandfather sitting there, wide-awake. "You all right, Dawdi?" she asked, going over to him.

He said nothing but blinked his eyes at her, and a small smile inched past his lips.

"Okay, then."

Going back to the bedroom, she stood in the doorway. "Dawdi looks to be just fine."

"*Gut*," Salina replied. "Never hurts to check, ya know . . . at their age." She looked lovingly down at Mammi. "Pains me to see them suffer like this." She sighed.

Joanna agreed. "So the family's takin' turns with Mammi?"

Salina nodded and moved toward the door to join Joanna. "We have it all arranged. I'll show you the chart."

Joanna hoped she might be called upon to help, too.

"Here 'tis." Salina found the paper on the kitchen counter, next to the whoopie pies. "Help yourself," she said as Joanna eyed the goodies.

"Denki, think I will." Joanna took a bite and, oh, it was heavenly . . . melted in her mouth.

"Before I forget, Mammi mentioned how much your cards—especially your poems—meant to her in the hospital. In case she forgets to tell ya, I thought you should know."

"That's why I wrote them," Joanna replied. "To bring some cheer."

"Well, they surely did that," Salina said. "She even read two of them to me. Saved each and every one."

Joanna was pleased but didn't want to let on. All this talk about her writing here lately had her unnerved.

The children were giggling and becoming rambunctious now.

"Too much sugar," Salina was quick to say.

As much as their silliness seemed to annoy Salina, it had the opposite effect on Joanna. Watching them act up, poking one another and bursting into laughter, made her yearn even more for children of her own one day. "How 'bout I get them washed up and take them out to see the new calves? Leave ya be with Mammi for a while?"

Salina looked relieved. "You're a lifesaver, Joanna."

"Not to worry." She set to work wiping off each little set of hands before permitting them to leave the table.

Salina picked up a basket of mending, then headed back to Mammi Kurtz.

They had been observing the new calves for a good twenty minutes or so when Stephen said, "I'm awful hungry, Aendi Joanna."

"Didn't ya just have a snack?" She smiled down at him, ruffling his flaxen hair.

"Can't remember," he said, straight-faced.

"He's *always* hungry," Sylvia piped up from where she was crouched near the smallest calf.

Spoken like a little sister! Joanna got a kick out of the interaction between those two. "Is he, now?" she asked.

"Oh, jah." Sylvia dramatically nodded her head up and down.

"I'm hungry, too," little Susan said, blinking her blue eyes at Joanna.

"I know!" Stephen announced. "Let's get some milk from the cooler."

Joanna agreed, thinking that would stall the children from returning to the house just yet. Salina had looked tired, like she might enjoy a bit more time alone with their grandparents. Joanna, too, was eager for a visit with her grandmother, but that could wait if necessary.

While they were in the milk house, Stephen gulped down a full glass of the fresh raw milk. Then, looking at her with a white moustache, he asked, "Will you tell us a story, Aendi?"

She began to protest. "I'm not a storyteller like Rebecca Lapp or . . ." She stopped before saying Jake Lantz's name.

"*I* heard ya were." Stephen was frowning.

"Well, now, who's sayin' that?"

"The deacon's wife," Stephen said, standing on tiptoes now as he held his empty glass up for more milk. "Heard her tell Grandmammi Mast so."

Joanna found this ever so curious. *So much for that!*

"So will ya tell us a story?" he pleaded.

She guessed it would be all right, especially if she told a Bible story. What could that hurt?

Eben had already spent too much time at the harness shop, overhearing his neighbor Micah Hershberger talk enthusiastically about a group of older folk from their community who were thinking of buying up a row of condos in Virginia Beach.

Where I met Joanna, thought Eben.

"When's this?" he asked, though he needed to get back to the farm. Still, Eben was mighty curious.

"Oh, in the next month or so," Levi, the harness shopkeeper, replied.

"'Least before wedding season, anyways," another neighbor, Elias Schrock, remarked.

At this, Micah shook his head. "Seems there must be quite a few condos available right now . . . same thing's goin' on in Florida."

"The housing market's in a heap of hurt," Eben offered.

"Might be the ideal time to snatch up some property, then," Micah said with a tug on his peppery beard.

Levi nodded. "Wouldn't wait too long to seal the deal, either. Not if you're serious."

"Well, these folks certainly are," Micah said.

Eben wondered just who he was talking about. He hadn't heard anyone mention this. "Well, my Daed's goin' to think I'm playin' hooky," he said, then moseyed toward the door.

"Say, I heard Leroy got married," said Levi, following him.

"That he did."

"So the world got him, then?"

Eben nodded. "Sorry to say."

"Well, now, I'll bet you are." Levi gave him a sympathetic smile. "Word has it you had someone mighty special over in Lancaster County."

Eben wouldn't deny it.

"So is she comin' out here sooner or later . . . or is that all over now?" Levi was known to pry, and he was doing a mighty fine job of it.

It wouldn't do any good to explain the problem. Besides, it wasn't Levi's place to ask. Eben shrugged off the question. "Best be headin' on home."

"Tell your Daed hullo for me, ya hear?" Levi called, turning to greet the man who'd just entered the shop.

"I'll do that." Eben closed the door behind him and made his way to the horse and carriage parked behind the shop. He looked to the east, wondering what Joanna was up to this hot summer day. Were they having a Preaching Sunday this weekend? Was she going to Singings yet again?

Eben untied his horse, then hopped into the enclosed black buggy and backed out of the spot. All the way home, he smelled the fragrance of honeysuckle and wondered if he'd been right about Jake Lantz's seeming admiration for Joanna. And if so, had Jake made a move to court her? The questions in his head continued until he saw Ada Kemp and her mother in another buggy, coming this way. Ada leaned forward suddenly when she caught his eye, smiling and waving at him. He was polite and gave a slow wave of his own. After their first and only date, he'd taken two other girls out, and knowing how fast the grapevine was, Ada most likely had heard about it.

Eben wasn't interested in leaving a long line of spurned women. But the truth was, none of them compared with Joanna . . . not a one. Maybe he just needed to continue his search. For sure and for certain, he needed someone to fill up Joanna's place in his heart.

I have no other choice.

32

JOANNA was very sure Salina's threesome had grown taller just in the space of two days. Mamma often said children grew faster in the summer months—*"like weeds"*—and looking at her nieces and nephew, Joanna couldn't help but agree.

Strolling about the backyard between the time Preaching service ended and the shared meal began, Joanna enjoyed the shade from several tall trees. She spied Salina and a couple other young mothers with their youngsters and went over to talk to them. Joanna's nephew Stephen was on the verge of being grouped with other boys his age—first graders come this fall. For now, though, he still played with his little sisters and young cousins, chasing them around the tree trunks and teasing the girls, some of whom were playing with their little white handkerchief dollies.

Joanna noticed Cora Jane on the other side of the yard with a few teenage girls, including Mattie Beiler's granddaughters Martha, Julia, and Susie. Martha and Julia looked at Jake Lantz and his younger brother, Jesse, with disdain when the guys walked by with a handful of other courting-age young men. Joanna wondered if Susie and Julia had perhaps been two of the girls who'd complained about Jake's forwardness. Would he behave differently now, were he to go riding with either of them?

Over on the long back porch, Mary Beiler crept alongside her elderly grandfather Abram Stoltzfus, searching for a chair for him. *Bless their hearts.* Joanna watched them tenderly, missing her own grandparents today. Dawdi Joseph hadn't felt well enough to attend, so Mammi Sadie had stayed home with him. And of course her Kurtz grandparents hadn't come, either, and probably wouldn't until Mammi was more sure of herself with her walker. Dawdi Kurtz refused to leave her, even though someone was there caring for her—he'd missed her terribly while she was in the hospital. Joanna wondered what Bishop John thought of that. Did he ever send the preachers out to talk to elderly and infirm members about missing church?

"You're deep in thought, ain't?" Salina leaned to whisper to Joanna.

"Guess I am . . . sorry."

"Couldn't help but notice you and Cora Jane sitting far apart during church today," Salina said, moving closer to Joanna beneath the shade tree to talk more privately. "You girls still at odds?"

"It'll pass."

"Well, I should hope so, after all this time . . . ain't the best example for the other young folk, ya know."

"No, s'pose not."

Salina frowned and made eye contact. "There *is* something bothering you, Joanna. I hear it in your voice."

She didn't want to criticize her younger sister on the Lord's Day, especially. "Best just pray 'bout it, jah?"

"Watch and pray, Scripture says." Salina was smiling too broadly.

"Ach, don't be so *labbich*, sister."

"Ya think I'm silly, do ya?" Salina said, rolling her eyes. "Hard not to see what's goin' on round us, jah?"

Joanna had never thought of her older sister as a *Schnuffelbox*—busybody—but today she certainly did seem to know what was going on with nearly everyone.

The two of them laughed softly, and then Salina really cut loose, which made Joanna laugh even harder. Laughter felt good; she couldn't deny it. And she knew it was wrong to harbor bitterness toward Cora Jane . . . or anyone.

Eben willingly helped his older brothers construct the temporary tables for the common Sunday meal at their father's house, using three wooden church benches for each table. First, they placed the benches side by side, then raised them using a hidden trestle. The very moment each table was put together, the womenfolk began setting down plates and drinking glasses.

When the tables were in place, Eben spotted Daed come inside and remove his straw hat out of reverence. His eyebrows rose when he caught Eben's eye. He came right over and patted him on the back, saying nary a word. It was Daed's way of expressing gratitude. And it was still interesting to Eben that nearly the minute Leroy and his wife left for their own home, Daed's demeanor had returned to normal. Although it *was* clear his parents were pained through to the heart over Leroy's decision to leave the Amish life for good. Daed wore the regret on his face every waking hour.

To think Leroy's offspring will never experience the Plain life . . . never be taught the Old Ways. Eben couldn't begin to imagine that.

"Have ya heard 'bout the birthday doin's for the bishop's wife next month?" Salina asked Joanna.

"Didn't know. Does Mamma?"

"I think so. Everyone's talking 'bout it."

Everyone? Once again, Salina was in the know. "Where and when will it be held?"

"At Bishop John's—on August eighteenth. A Saturday."

"Must not be a surprise party, then."

"Oh, believe me, it was supposed to be." Salina smiled. "But the cat managed to get out of the bag."

Joanna understood. "Must be a special birthday, ain't?" She'd lost track, since birthdays weren't celebrated all too often, particularly not too fancy-like.

"Mary's turnin' twenty-five."

My age, thought Joanna with a shock, watching young Stephen pull on Sylvia's apron strings. How could she have forgotten?

A light breeze swept over the lawn, rustling leaves above her head, letting dappled light through. A squirrel scampered to the highest branch and daringly pattered out to nearly the end of the limb. Joanna enjoyed watching the little animals and thought suddenly of Eben, who'd once written about caring for a wounded squirrel when he was a boy.

Oh, Eben . . .

Would he forever be just on the edge of her thoughts? He had been such a huge part of her life for too long to expect that she was over him. No, she couldn't fool herself into thinking she was fine, because she was far from it.

"Before I forget, can ya help Mammi Kurtz this Tuesday for a few hours—get the noon meal started and whatnot?" asked Salina, bringing Joanna out of her reverie. "She's already doin' so much better since returning home."

"Sure . . . I'd like that."

"All right, then, I'll let Fannie know. She has to run an errand for the deacon's wife."

Joanna perked up her ears. Fannie Kurtz rarely interacted with Sallie, the deacon's shy wife. "What's Dawdi doin' to keep himself busy?"

"Hovering, mostly, like a worried old hen."

"Aw, so sweet, jah?"

Salina nodded. "Still lovebirds after all these years."

Lovebirds . . . The word whirled in her head. *Will I ever know that kind of love?*

The noontime siren sounded in the distance, reminding Eben that along with the sun's progress across the sky each day—and the occasional pocket watch—there was more than one way to tell the time on Peaceful Acres Lane this Lord's Day. He'd heard, though, that the siren wasn't always prompt—sometimes it was early, depending on the fellow who was in charge of pulling the lanyard. Eben grinned at the very notion as he stood over near the woodshed with other young men his age, waiting till the first seating of ministerial brethren and older couples had an opportunity to eat the light meal inside.

It was such a beastly hot day, Eben wondered why they hadn't set up the tables on the lawn, like two weeks ago when church was held at his uncle Isaac's place, just a mile up the road.

Eben stood with hands clasped behind him, like several of the more pious young men did, determined not to let hunger pangs get the best of them on the Lord's Day. He listened as Cousin Chester talked about having just landed a job on the west side of Elkhart, doing some welding work. But it wasn't hard to notice the faltering way Chester was describing this sudden change of work. It was almost like he was leaving the area.

Then Eben began to piece things together. Anyone would have to be blind not to have seen Emma Miller's swollen eyes earlier as she waited in line for the service with her mother and younger sisters. Had Chester broken up with his longtime girlfriend? Eben observed his cousin gesturing with his big hands, apparently overcompensating as he told about the "wunnerbaar-*gut* job" he'd landed.

Eben felt downright sorry for him, and for poor Emma, too, knowing something of what they were going through. *If* he was correct about their circumstances.

Emma Miller was an attractive girl and awfully nice, but Chester had gotten to her first, years ago, preventing Eben from pursuing her himself. But now . . .

His head was spinning with what to do. How long should he wait for Emma to get over Chester? Eben had his own reasons for not rushing into something serious. It hadn't been long since he'd hoped to make Joanna his bride.

Even so, he hoped Emma might be at the Singing tonight, although he seriously doubted it. *Girls tend to wait awhile,* he thought and wondered how long before Emma might go out again . . . or was she so upset with Chester that it didn't matter?

33

AFTER the Singing in Andy King's big barn, Joanna discreetly slipped out with Jake to his courting carriage. He set her at ease at once by sharing a funny anecdote about what a sound sleeper his brother Jesse was, even during an afternoon nap. He insisted that Jesse could sleep through thunder and lightning, and even a tornado. Jake described the scene, just today, prior to coming to Singing—how he'd shaken Jesse and hollered at him, finally resorting to pulling him across the floor by one leg. At last, Jesse woke up. "What're ya doin' to me, Bruder?" he'd yelled. "Couldn't ya see I was sleepin'?"

Laughing as she pictured the scene, Joanna momentarily forgot her plan to come clean about wanting no more than a friendship with Jake.

They talked in a relaxed manner as they rode behind several other carriages, the sounds of chatter and laughter filling up the night. He asked her what sorts of things she liked to read, and whether she liked to cook or bake better. So many questions . . . he sure seemed eager to get to know her.

But Jake wasn't Eben, and Joanna knew it wasn't right to keep accepting dates with him. So, breathing a silent prayer for wisdom, she pressed forward. "I've enjoyed spendin' time with you, Jake," she said so softly she scarcely heard herself.

He looked at her with a smile. "Same here."

"And I like you—"

"I like you, too, Joanna," he broke in.

She felt so bad for him . . . hated saying what must be said. "But I'd prefer to just be friends, if ya don't mind."

"Well, we're already that, jah?"

She nodded. "But how would ya feel if we were to stay only friends for a while? Till I have enough time to—"

"To forget about Eben?" He turned away and looked at the road now; the horse's head bobbed up and down.

"I'm sorry, Jake . . . I really am."

"No need," he said, sounding more upbeat. "Why don't we see where this leads?"

She pondered that. "Maybe in time, jah. I don't want to be thinking 'bout him when I'm with you."

"Well, then?" He chuckled, breaking the tension.

She paused. "I hope you understand, Jake."

"I certainly do," he replied. "But I'd like to keep seein' you, Joanna . . . as a friend, of course." He smiled over at her. "All right?"

As long as he understands, what can it hurt?

Much later, when they were heading back toward Hickory Lane, Jake mentioned how much he appreciated her honesty. "I truly do," he said.

Then, turning into her lane, Jake said, "I can see why Eben was so taken with you, Joanna."

She blushed and was glad he couldn't really see her face in the darkness.

He leaped out of the carriage and raced around to help her down on the left side. "Sweet dreams," he said as he walked her around toward the back door. Then, turning, he told her good-night and made his way back to the waiting horse and open buggy.

Joanna realized she felt relieved to have a good friend in Jake, and that he understood. *I did the right thing by telling him.* She went to sit on one of the rockers on the back porch and watched ten thousand stars light up the summer sky. It made her think again of Eben and wonder if he, too, was stargazing this warm, muggy night.

··· ❧ ❦ ···

Mammi Kurtz's face shone with joy as Joanna walked into the kitchen the following Tuesday morning. "I'm Fannie's substitute today," Joanna said, going over to greet her grandmother with a smile. "Did Salina tell ya?"

"No, but Fannie did, before she left." Mammi sat in a comfortable chair near the wide-open window, drinking root beer. She held up her glass. "Would ya care for some?"

Joanna thanked her and went to get a glass from the cupboard. She reached for the pitcher from the counter and poured a half glass, then returned to pull out Dawdi's chair from the table and turned it to face Mammi. "How're ya feelin' today?"

"So much better. Fannie insists I walk back and forth the whole length of the driveway now." Mammi told of the home-care nurse's visits, as well. "I do believe I'm getting back to normal. Slow but sure."

"And Dawdi—how is he?"

A beautiful smile appeared. "Since I've been home, he's doin' all right." Mammi mentioned he was in their room resting, having his morning nap. "A bit clingy, though, I have to say."

Joanna was pleased they were alone—the perfect chance to mention the quilt from Cousin Malinda. And after they'd talked about Mammi's hospital experience and all the kindly Englischers she'd met there, Joanna asked about the tale behind the quilt made by her great-great-aunt. "I'm really curious, Mammi. Why'd you want *me* to have it?"

Mammi nodded and looked more serious now. "Well, because your namesake—I'll call her Aunt Joanna to make things simpler—made that double wedding ring quilt in the midst of great disappointment . . . out of sheer faith."

"What do ya mean?" Joanna was determined to persuade Mammi to at last tell her everything she knew.

"She was nearing her fortieth birthday and had never married," Mammi explained. "And although it was her heart's desire, your aunt had been labeled a Maidel by then."

Joanna listened intently, her heart breaking for a relative she'd never known.

"Aunt Joanna wrote all about 'the ache' in her heart, as she described her disillusionment at being passed over during her courting-age years."

Joanna was intrigued—it sounded like the seeds for a good story. "Where'd she write this?"

"In two letters to her younger sister."

"Did she also keep a diary?"

"Oh, I'm sure. Most folk did in that day."

Joanna admitted that she'd looked in the special cubby in the wall upstairs, in their former bedroom. "I saw a devotional book with two letters in it. Were they hers?"

"Snoopin', were ya?" Mammi teased.

"Well, I didn't read them."

"That's all right. I've nothin' to hide, dear girl. Least of all from you." Mammi readjusted herself in her chair. "I'm surprised I never thought to have ya read them."

"Oh, could I?"

"Sure, go on up and get them. But before ya do, I'd like you to know why you were named after this particular relative."

Ever so delighted, Joanna said, "I understand the name Joanna was rather unusual in her time. Cousin Malinda said as much."

"Oh my, was it ever. But it certainly fit her—she was a pretty unique soul," Mammi said. "And such faith was involved in makin' a wedding quilt for herself. Unheard of in those days."

"Because everyone had given up on her marrying?"

Mammi's eyes glistened. "That's right."

Joanna felt even more drawn to this woman who'd left such a precious spiritual inheritance. *For me.* "So it must've been hearing about Aunt Joanna's courage that caught Mamma's attention, and the reason she decided to name me after her."

"Jah—ain't it the dearest thing?"

"And kind of peculiar, too, if ya think 'bout it," Joanna said softly.

"Why's that, honey-girl?"

Joanna took a deep breath. "Well, because my own beau and I parted ways."

"Ach, I'm so sorry. Shouldn't have said anything."

"No, no, it's all right. Hadn't you heard this, Mammi?"

"Jah, I believe I did." Mammi sighed. "But it was some time ago now."

"Well, to be honest, it seems like just yesterday to me. I'm still strug-gling with it."

Mammi frowned amiably. "This young man . . . you must've loved him very much."

Joanna nodded thoughtfully as she remembered all the letters, the good times she and Eben had spent together, however short. "I know he loved me, too." Joanna opened up even more and explained that Eben had been hoping to come here to live and work, to become established in the community while courting her. "But all of that fell through when his youngest brother married an Englischer and refused the partnership with his father."

"No wonder you're sad. Sounds to me like the two of you had your future all planned out."

"We did." Joanna was relieved to share with her grandmother, who seemed to understand. *At last someone cares.* Mammi Kurtz was quite sympathetic about Eben, unlike Ella Mae Zook had been.

"Have you ever considered goin' out there to be with *him?*" Mammi asked, surprising her.

"I really don't see how." *Not with Preacher Yoder's warning to me.*

"If he still loves you, I mean," Mammi added.

"He tried to ask if I would, but at the time, well . . ." Joanna's voice trailed off as she remembered again the dreadful moment. Eben *had* asked her about moving, hadn't he? Yet he'd seemed so hesitant, almost apologetic. And she . . . she knew it would never be allowed, though she hadn't explained why. "We haven't even written each other since April," she murmured. "I'd thought of it—but I don't want to be forward."

Mammi shrugged. "Well, you should read the letters your namesake wrote to her sister if you think that."

Hearing this, Joanna got up from her chair that quick. "I'll be right back!" She hurried upstairs, opened the hidden spot in the wall, and found the letters. Then, returning to the kitchen, she placed them in front of her on the table, suddenly feeling nervous.

"Go on, it's all right," Mammi coaxed. "Read them in the right order."

Joanna looked at the dates in each postmark and opened the earliest one. She began to read with great interest this account from the past, from one sister's heart to another.

My dear sister Miriam,

Since our visit, I've been a-pondering many things. For one, I realize it is important for each of us to become humble, like a little child, so much so that we cry out to our Father in heaven, looking to Him for guidance first and foremost. We must reach for His hand each and every day. Just as you said, it's the only way to live a happy life in the midst of disappointment. And I say, it's the only way to live life, period.

Joanna finished the letter, which continued in a similar vein. But apart from what Mammi Kurtz had just told her about this woman of great faith, Joanna didn't know why her great-great-aunt had written in such devout terms. Had her sister counseled her about being single?

"Are ya ready for the next one?" Mammi asked, her voice gentle.

Joanna removed the letter from its envelope and unfolded it, suddenly trembling as she began to read.

Dearest Miriam,

Since your last letter, I've taken your advice and decided to put out a fleece of sorts, like Gideon of old. I realize some folk will think I'm all but ferhoodled. But to demonstrate my belief that God will hear and answer my heart's cry, even now as I've just marked forty years of life, I've started to piece together a double wedding ring quilt. Some might poke fun behind my back, but that's all right. And I'm not superstitious enough to think that once it's finished, I shouldn't spread it on my own bed, even though at my age I have no prospects for a beau. Fact is, I'm going to do just that!

So, coupled with my earnest prayers, I'm putting my confidence to work, so to speak. "Faith with feet," I read somewhere. True, this is not the typical Amish way. Even so, I believe that when the Lord God puts a desire in a person's heart—remember Psalm 37:4?—it's there for a reason and ought to be acted upon.

I'll keep you informed as time goes along. And I'm telling you right now, I won't be shy when the Good Lord brings a beau to my door!

I wait and pray with expectancy for the husband He has chosen for me.

> *With love,*
> *Your sister, Joanna*

Blinking back tears, Joanna looked over at her grandmother. "What an amazing woman, jah?"

Mammi nodded her head, face solemn. "She certainly was . . . and God not only heard her heart's prayer, but gave her two children—twins, a boy and a girl—a double blessing, to be sure."

Joanna couldn't help asking—she had to know. "How long after the quilt was completed did she wed?"

"One year," Mammi said. "She married a lovely man, a widower who was only three years older . . . and a respected preacher, as well."

"With that kind of faith, she must've been a wonderful-*gut* preacher's wife."

Now Mammi was brushing away tears. "We have an inspiring heritage, ain't so?"

The Good Lord had known, all the way back to the day her great-great-aunt Joanna was threading her little quilting needle, that on this day, these many years later, another much younger Joanna would be deeply touched by the unseen yet very real bond between them.

Joanna remembered the line toward the end of the last letter. *I won't be shy. . . .* "With as much pluck as she seemed to have . . . did Aunt Joanna pop the question to the widowed preacher, just maybe?"

"As the story goes," Mammi said, the most encouraging smile on her pink face.

"Denki for sharing this with me."

"Happy to, dear girl."

"Aunt Joanna's quilt is a mighty special one, I'll say."

"Special indeed," said Mammi, a twinkle in her eye.

34

EBEN had lined up two dates with two different girls for the next couple of weekends, well into the middle of July. Maybe filling up his free time might help him recover more quickly from his loss of Joanna, though so far that plan hadn't been working. And since Emma Miller, Cousin Chester's former fiancée, was by no means interested in mingling with any new fellows, Eben was stuck with asking out much younger, and rather immature, girls.

Each Friday since returning home, he'd thought of Joanna when the usual time rolled around to call her. By now, though, he had lost track of which Friday it was, and for that he was sorry. He'd thought he would always remember the every-other-week pattern.

Life had plodded along for him. He scarcely had any leisure, what with threshing in full swing and his father depending more and more on Eben's decision making.

Since Leroy's visit, his letters had become increasingly frequent, which Eben found curious. Now that Leroy was married and had completely severed himself from Amish life, did he miss it?

But it was a mistake to entertain such thoughts. Besides, Eben had gotten a good look at Leroy's Mustang convertible and his English wife. Mrs. Debbie Troyer was by no means inclined to think of becoming Plain, even if her husband might begin to regret his decision in years to come. No, it was hard to comprehend why Leroy now wrote to Eben each week. Was he merely making up for lost time?

··· ❯ ❮ ···

One night in mid-July, a couple weeks after Joanna's enlightening visit with Mammi Kurtz, she gently removed the large double wedding ring quilt from her hope chest and placed it on her bed. Of course, with the summer heat almost unbearable upstairs, there was no way she'd use it to cover herself, but placing it there felt like a celebratory act.

When she'd taken care to lay it out just so, she knelt beside her bed and prayed as earnestly as Great-Great-Aunt Joanna had prayed so many years ago. Silently, she poured out her heart to God, sorry for not having prayed for His will in her life before now, especially in regard to a husband. She asked for a broken and contrite spirit, acknowledging her part in the wall that had come between her and her sister. *Please, Lord, forgive me for my own unkind attitude. . . .*

In the quiet, Joanna also confessed her repeated defiance toward the ministerial brethren when it came to her writing—whatever she might think of it. *Lead me in every aspect of my life . . . just as you led my namesake.*

After a while, Joanna rose and sat on the only chair in the room. Her heart felt lighter somehow as she began to knit soft white baby booties for Cousin Malinda's coming child. She had also been crocheting a pale-yellow-and-mint-green cradle afghan, which she picked up now and then, taking her time and praying all the while for this new little one.

The minutes passed, and she glanced up to see Cora Jane lingering in the hallway, her long hair down and clad in her lightweight house robe. Her sister looked like she wanted to come in. "It's all right," Joanna said, motioning to her.

Cora Jane blinked her eyes as she gawked at the quilt. "I must've missed something," she said, face puzzled. "Did ya secretly get married?"

Joanna laughed softly. "No."

"Well, what's this doin' here?"

"I've decided, why not just enjoy it while I wait?"

Cora Jane's eyes fluttered. "Wait for what?"

"Well, for a husband."

"And you think this quilt will make that happen?"

"Nee—not at all." She smiled at her sister. "But it will happen in God's time." Quickly, she shared the story behind the old quilt, glad for the opportunity to finally tell her.

Nodding slowly, Cora Jane gathered up her hair and pushed it over one shoulder. "You wonder me, sister."

I understand that feeling. But Joanna kept the thought to herself.

In the following days, Joanna wished there was a way to broach the topic of her namesake with Mamma. On one of the last Tuesdays in July, she helped finish up the ironing while baking several loaves of bread. Her mother put up a batch of green beans with Cora Jane and talked about the peaches and plums that were coming on soon. Mamma hoped they'd make lots of extra jam, along with canning the fruit.

The heat was so sweltering, Joanna suggested they take their noon meal under the shade tree in the backyard. "How about a nice picnic instead of a hot meal today?"

Cora Jane nixed the idea, arguing that Dat and their older brothers helping cultivate the cornfield needed a big, tasty meal to keep up their strength. "A sandwich just isn't enough."

Mamma gave Joanna an agreeable look. "What a nice idea, though," she said while Cora Jane glowered. "Another day, maybe?"

"Well, Dat's not goin' to want to sit on a blanket on the ground anytime soon, is he?" Cora Jane piped up again. "His back's out of whack again, what with all the field work."

"That's true," Mamma said. "But still, it was a lovely thought your sister had. And your father and I can always sit on lawn chairs out there, ya know." She wasn't going to let Cora Jane have the final say on this—that was clear.

Joanna braced for another spirited remark from her sister, but when none came, she offered her best smile to Cora Jane, who held her gaze, then suddenly looked sad.

"So what should we make for dinner, then?" asked Mamma.

Joanna observed her sister more closely. Something wasn't right. Cora Jane's lower lip quivered as she moved to the window and stood there looking out, her shoulders heaving.

Then, of all things, she left the kitchen and went running across the side lawn to the celery patch.

"What on earth?" Mamma said.

"I'll see to her," Joanna said, leaving the ironing board set up. She rushed out the back door.

It was so stifling out there under the noontime sun, Joanna hardly wanted to move, let alone run after her surly sister. But run she did, determined to talk to Cora Jane . . . and find out why she'd gone to stand in the middle of the celery patch, holding herself around the middle and weeping like she'd lost her best friend.

"Cora Jane . . . honey, what's a-matter?" Joanna said softly, standing back a ways.

"Leave me be!"

"I just want to help."

"Ain't nothin' you or anyone can do," Cora Jane sobbed.

Joanna saw Mamma step out on the back porch down yonder. "You're terribly upset," Joanna said more softly. "I know you are."

Cora Jane leaned over, still holding her stomach like she might be sick. Then she did a strange thing. She fell to her knees and began to yank up young celery stalks, as many as she could grab with both hands, weeping. "I never should've planted these! Never!"

"Aw, sister . . ." Joanna felt like crying now, too. "I'm ever so sorry."

Cora Jane turned to look at her, letting the plants fall on the rich, dark soil. "I was a fool." She wiped her tear-streaked face with her grimy hands. "That's all I am. A fool, I tell ya."

"Come with me." Joanna held out her arms, moving closer. "Won't ya, please?"

Her poor sister sat back on her heels in the dirt, surrounded by uprooted plants. "We'll never need this much celery come fall."

"Maybe things'll turn around."

"That's impossible." Cora Jane pulled her tan-colored bandana off and sat there with her soiled hands on her head. "Just leave me be."

"You're in no shape to sit out here. Besides, you'll get cooked by the sun," Joanna persisted, stepping near. "I want you to come inside with me. How about I draw you a nice cool bath?"

"I don't deserve that. I'm *gut* for nothin'!"

"That's not true," Joanna said gently. "You heard me, Cora Jane. Get up and come inside."

"I'm done for, that's what."

Joanna reached down and assisted her sister into a standing position. "Your heart's all broken apart, but you won't let whatever's happened get the best of ya. I know you, sister."

Cora Jane turned, her lower lip trembling, and looked at Joanna. Then she flung her arms around her, just as Joanna had done with Cousin Malinda, crying like she might never stop. Joanna held on to her as she sobbed, her whole body quaking with every gasp. The day had come crashing down around them.

"Go ahead and cry," Joanna managed to say. "That's all right. . . ."

Once she could gently pry Cora Jane loose enough to walk her back toward the house, Joanna knew it was a good thing the noon meal wouldn't be outside with their father and brothers relaxing on the back lawn in the shade of ancient trees. No, a picnic was not a good idea on this wretched day.

35

CORA Jane went to lie down in her room that afternoon, needing some time alone. Joanna truly hoped she'd find a way to rest.

Returning to her own room, Joanna looked up at the creak of floorboards and saw Mamma standing in the doorway, a frown on her face as she stared down at the bed.

"I've noticed you put the quilt on your bed," Mamma observed. "Can't help but wonder if that has something to do with Cora Jane's tears today."

"I decided to bring out the quilt from my hope chest is all," Joanna explained, standing at the foot of her bed. "A while after Mammi Kurtz told me the story behind it." She tried to keep her voice calm, her sister's cries still in her ears. "And I hope you understand, Mamma, my quilt isn't what set Cora Jane off." She looked toward the ceiling and heaved a sigh. "I feel sure this was coming on for a while now."

"What was?" Mamma's eyes narrowed as she stood near the dresser, her arms folded.

Joanna sighed, feeling a bit hesitant. "Apparently my sister's without a beau."

Mamma's jaw dropped. She glanced toward the hallway, to Cora Jane's bedroom. "So there'll be no wedding?"

"Jah . . . she didn't tell me a lot, but she made that much clear."

Mamma looked fatigued, dark circles beneath her eyes. "I didn't mean to make it sound like I was accusing you, dear." Her mother lowered herself onto the bed and sat there gingerly, as if she didn't want to mash the heirloom quilt. "Since we're alone, I'd like to talk to you 'bout something else altogether."

Joanna went around the bed and sat on the other side, wondering.

"I want to tell you a little something about your namesake, Great-Aunt Joanna Kurtz."

"I'd like that." Joanna didn't need to say that Mammi Kurtz had already told her a few things when she'd shared about the quilt itself.

For a moment, Mamma was very still, looking out the window, then back at the quilt, smoothing it gently with her right hand. "Your father mentioned you'd brought it up to him once."

Joanna remembered. "Jah, I've been curious for a long time."

"From what I knew of your father's great-aunt, well, I'd have to say I was impressed. She was a unique woman, and in some ways, a woman who put me to shame . . . her unusually strong faith and all." Mamma sighed. "She knew what she wanted and clung to prayer."

"You've given me a special gift, Mamma . . . with my name." Joanna felt the lump in her throat.

"The name suits ya," Mamma said, looking at her from across the bed. "As does this quilt."

Joanna ran her fingers over one of the double wedding ring patterns. Then, pausing, she covered Mamma's hand with her own. "This time together, talkin' like this, I mean . . . it's just awful nice. Denki."

Mamma rose and came around the bed, placing both hands lightly on Joanna's shoulders. "I see your faith at work in displaying this quilt, even without a serious beau," she said quietly. "You surely do resemble your namesake, Joanna. I'm ever so thankful for that."

Joanna raised her eyes to Mamma's and held her gaze. "I believe the Lord God has a plan for me," she whispered. "Just as He did for my namesake."

Mamma nodded sweetly. "I believe that, too, Joanna, dear."

Truly, she had never felt so close to her mother.

··· ➤ ≼ ···

Cora Jane stayed home from all youth-related activities for the next few weekends, as did Joanna. Not knowing how to draw her sister out, Joanna wrote short poems of encouragement and slipped them under her bedroom door at night. Rhyming poems with such titles as "My Sister, My Friend," and "From My Heart to Yours."

Cora Jane actually brought up the "nice poetry" one night in mid-August after their parents had gone to bed. Joanna had drifted over to her room, hoping to strike up a conversation, and with a small smile, Cora Jane had invited her in. Ever so slowly, Cora Jane began to open up, sharing what she believed had gone wrong between her and Gideon. "But I can't blame my beau for everything. It takes two to make things work well," Cora Jane said, grimacing.

"Now that I'm this far away from our breakup, I can see better that we weren't right together." Cora Jane tilted her head and looked hard at Joanna. She opened her mouth, then shook her head.

"What is it, sister?"

Cora Jane pursed her lips for a moment. "Well, since we're talking so openly . . . but I really hesitate to bring this up."

"Say what's on your mind."

"Just wondered if ya think Eben was well suited to you."

Joanna pressed her fingers to her temples, then ran her hands through her long hair. "I know we'd be engaged by now, or possibly even married . . . if it weren't for his father's need for a farming partner."

Cora Jane nodded sympathetically. "Seems like something should've worked out for you two." She sighed. *"Something."*

Joanna couldn't let herself think that way. "The past is behind us."

"Did he ever ask you to move there, even though it would take some doin'?"

"He mentioned it, but I knew it was out of the question." She stopped for a moment, realizing that what she was about to say surely implicated Cora Jane. "After Preacher Yoder talked so straight to me, I knew I couldn't leave Hickory Hollow."

"The preacher said you couldn't?" Cora Jane's eyes grew wide as quarters.

"He suggested it, jah. Said I shouldn't get any ideas to transfer my membership out to Indiana . . . not with my story writing."

Her sister's gaze dropped, her face losing its color. "And to think I caused much of that."

"Not entirely. I should've taken heed, thought twice about it, for sure. It's not easy, believe me, turning my back on something I've enjoyed so much. The writer's muse is a powerful thing. But I have stopped writing stories—I don't want to continue doing something others dear to me consider wrong. Lately I've been writing poetry instead, hoping maybe I can honor the Lord in that."

Cora Jane turned and held out her hand. "Do you still resent me for tellin' on you?"

Joanna's breath caught in her throat. She reached for her sister's hand and pressed it gently, letting the gesture speak the loving truth. "I forgave ya some weeks ago. And . . . are you still angry with me for pushing you away after Eben came along?"

Cora Jane shook her head slowly. "Who could ever stay angry at a sister like you?"

"I should've told ya from the first, but my relationship with Eben seemed so fragile and new. 'Specially with the distance between us, I was afraid things wouldn't work out if we were watched too closely."

"Truth be known, I was jealous of you for bein' so self-assured, as if you thought you could just keep accepting invitations from brides like that, always bein' a bridesmaid . . . and not heeding tradition."

It felt good to set things right. Cora Jane had made it clear she was sorry, and in time, the sting from her sister's betrayal would surely lessen.

But it was Cora Jane's remark that something should've worked out with Eben that gave Joanna a fleeting feeling of warmth. At the same time, it was also a miserable reminder of what had been lost. Even if she had a glint of hope, she could see no way to fan it into flame.

36

AUGUST peaches were coming on almost faster than Mamma could keep up. For that reason, neighbors Mattie, Ella Mae, and Rachel came over for a canning bee right after breakfast Tuesday. Mamma, Joanna, and Cora Jane helped set up an assembly line for peeling and pitting. They gave Ella Mae the most comfortable chair in the house, situating her away from the sunny windows.

They jabbered in Pennsylvania Dutch, midwife Mattie telling stories about the babies she'd delivered—and three she'd nearly lost—over the many years. Rachel and Mamma listened but blushed and rolled their eyes at times, no doubt because Joanna and Cora Jane were present.

Once Rachel could get a word in, she shared the plans for her daughter Mary's upcoming birthday. "The children are all makin' little cards to hang up on a string, over the kitchen doorway . . . like at Christmastime."

"Aw, that's nice," Mamma said, placing the sliced peaches in slightly salty water to preserve their natural color.

"The bishop's son Levi is quite the artist," Rachel added. "Hard to know how that'll turn out, with his father overseein' things."

"Just maybe he'll see the benefit of this wondrous gift from the Good Lord," Ella Mae said. "That's what."

The room went silent, and Rachel and Mamma exchanged concerned glances. But Joanna knew, as did all the others, that the Wise Woman exercised no restraint in speaking her mind.

Eventually, the talk turned to putting up pears and plums in the coming days and weeks, and making jam, too. Mattie complained a little about needing to patch her husband's work pants by hand. "An unpleasant task, ya know," she said, sighing.

"Ach, just be thankful your husband still lives," widow Ella Mae muttered to her daughter, though they'd all heard.

Later, Rachel mentioned *der Debbich*—the bedspread—she was looking forward to making come fall. "I'm doing it in blues and yellows, with a perty black border that'll make the colors stand right out."

Ella Mae said she'd laid eyes on a hand-woven coverlet made from wool at an antique shop in Bird-in-Hand recently. "Carded and spun by hand, too," she said, dimples showing.

"That'd be a real chore, spinning," Cora Jane said pleasantly. Though still somewhat downcast at times, her overall mood seemed much better since her heart-to-heart with Joanna a couple nights ago.

When it came time to stop and make the noon meal, Mamma took charge of the kitchen, requesting some help from Cora Jane, Rachel, and Mattie. She'd asked Joanna in advance to keep Ella Mae company, so Joanna led the older woman into the small sitting area around the corner from the kitchen.

"How you doin', dearie?" Ella Mae asked once she was settled in Mamma's chair.

"All right some days . . . others, not so *gut*. It's the way of life, I'm learning."

"Heard your young man came twice to see ya, ain't?"

Jake must've told her. . . .

"Well, once to visit and once to part ways."

"That so?" Ella Mae scratched her head. "Now, wait a minute . . . didn't I hear that, too?"

Everyone's heard by now, thought Joanna.

"Thing is, I can't seem to forget him, even though I've tried." She shared that she'd gone out with a fellow from around here. "Someone lots of fun, and a really convincing storyteller, too." She wondered if Ella Mae might guess whom she meant, although that wasn't why she'd mentioned Jake in so many words.

"Ah, I daresay I know just who you're talking 'bout. A right nice boy, he is."

Joanna wouldn't say Jake's name, thinking it could tempt Ella Mae to divulge a confidence. But she gave a little nod. "Honestly, though, it'll be mighty hard to forget Eben Troyer."

By the look in Ella Mae's eyes, the wheels inside her head were turning. "Are ya wantin' to know what I'll say to that?"

Joanna was taken off guard. "I didn't bring it up for counsel, no."

"Why don't you tell me more 'bout this young man who's captured your heart."

This time Joanna did not hesitate from beginning to end, every last detail she felt comfortable sharing. "But now I don't know how to be round anyone but him."

Ella Mae observed her intently, then asked if she'd ever thought of going out to Indiana. "To meet his family, I mean. Surprise him like he did you, maybe?"

"I'm stuck here, I'm afraid."

"Well, that just ain't true, dear girl. No one's stuck anywhere unless they choose to be. The Lord God guides those who are moving forward." Such startling words . . . words that resonated in the depths of Joanna's heart.

In that moment, she remembered how impressed Eben had been with Cora Jane's frankness—he'd even indicated that he liked a woman with gumption.

"Ever ponder Ruth's pledge to her mother-in-law, Naomi, in the book of Ruth?" Ella Mae asked, seemingly out of the blue.

"Not really, why?"

"Well, just listen to this." Ella Mae wore a smile on her wrinkled face. "'For whither thou goest, I will go; and where thou lodgest, I will lodge: thy people shall be my people, and thy God my God,'" Ella Mae recited.

Joanna recalled hearing that plenty of times in Preacher Yoder's wedding sermons.

"So now, if it was *gut* enough for a young widow to declare to her mother-in-law, why not a girl to the man she loves?" Ella Mae locked eyes with hers. "Chust think 'bout it, Joanna. That, and pray 'bout it, too."

··· ➤ ➤ ···

All the rest of the day, and throughout that week, Joanna thought and prayed and thought some more, until that Friday evening. She'd purposely gone walking on the field lanes where she and Eben had strolled together, hand in hand. Again, Ella Mae's words came back to her, like an echo. Then suddenly, they stopped.

The phone was ringing in the little shanty in Dat's field.

Joanna froze right there. *Is Eben calling? Can it be?*

Heart hammering, she ran through the cornfield, rushing past the countless rows, thrusting the stalks away from her face as she ran faster and faster.

The phone continued its ringing, like a clanging cowbell in the distance, as she groped her way toward its beautiful sound.

Think, think, Joanna! Which Friday is it? Which?

Then, stopping for a second, she knew. "Oh, Eben . . .!"

The ringing continued as she peered on tiptoe over the tops of the tasseled corn, the tall telephone shack before her like a lighthouse in a vast green sea.

She moved forward, dashing to the shack. There, she pushed open the wooden door as the phone continued to ring. Reaching for it, she felt faint at the prospect of Eben's voice on the line. But wasn't he long gone from her?

Still, she had to know. Lifting the receiver off its cradle, she managed a hello.

Just then, like a feather flying away in the breeze, Joanna heard the line click as the phone went dead. And her heart sank.

Was it you, Eben?

She couldn't help wondering how long the phone had been ringing, perhaps even before she'd come within earshot. Feeling weak, Joanna leaned against the familiar wall, staring straight out the only window at the sky with its billowing clouds. And she cried, unashamed.

"O dear Lord in heaven," she wept. "I don't know what to do . . . or where to turn. Eben's in my constant thoughts. Please remove my love for him, if it's your will." She reached to touch the black receiver, recalling Eben's voice in her ear, oh, so many times. "If you have a different plan, will you make that path clear and ever so straight . . . and lead me back to Eben? Amen."

When she'd managed to dry her eyes and gather her wits, Joanna headed through the maze of cornstalks, over the field lanes, and past the corncrib toward home.

37

THE afternoon birthday celebration for the bishop's wife the next day turned out to be a hen's party with a mystery meal, complete with cryptic descriptions of the menu items and various group games, including Dutch Blitz for all twenty or so women present. The atmosphere was as festive as any Joanna had ever been a part of, and jovial, too. For a while she actually forgot herself and entered into the gaiety, relishing the fun.

Dear Mary, wearing her best royal blue dress and matching cape apron, looked a bit sheepish about receiving so many pretty cards, as well as a few handmade gifts from close relatives and friends. As gracious as Joanna had always known her to be, Mary dutifully thanked each of them before the party disbanded.

On the way out the back door, Joanna was surprised when Preacher Yoder's round-faced wife, Lovina, stopped her and quietly said her husband wanted to meet with her again. "But he's goin' on a trip, so it won't be for a week or so."

Why's she telling me this now—so I can worry myself sick?

"He wants you to know he'll contact your father when the time is right," the older woman added, a serious look on her face.

Joanna felt self-conscious about being singled out like this, especially at such a happy gathering. "Is this concerning—"

"He'll speak directly to *you*," Lovina Yoder said, touching her arm. "All in *gut* time."

Nodding, Joanna said she'd wait to hear further from her father about

196

this. But now her stomach was churning. How long would she have to wait for the next scolding? At least she could honestly tell the preacher about her prayer of contrition . . . and about having turned her back on writing make-believe stories, hard as it was. Something she'd decided to do to demonstrate her willing heart before God, and her love for the People.

"Denki," Joanna said softly, though really there was nothing to thank her for.

"Have a nice day," the preacher's wife said, smiling now.

Nice day? How on earth?

Joanna was relieved Cora Jane hadn't attended this get-together. Cora Jane was feeling crushed enough for having started all this by going to the deacon in the first place. But Salina was there, although she hadn't observed Joanna's encounter with Lovina. Here she came just now, out the back door, having stayed inside a bit longer to visit with the birthday girl.

"Can I get a ride home?" Salina asked Joanna, hurrying her pace. "I should prob'ly walk, but I need to start supper soon."

"Sure."

On the ride there, Joanna relived the unpleasant encounter with Lovina Yoder, whom she rarely spoke to, considering the woman's age and stature in the community.

"You're awful quiet," Salina said. "Hope ya don't mind goin' out of your way."

"Not at all."

Up ahead, Joanna noticed Jake and his brother Jesse driving their market wagon home. Jake spotted her and waved.

She watched as Jake headed down the way, toward the Lantz home. *Are we merely friends?* she mused, wondering if this was a swift answer to yesterday's prayer in the phone shack. *Should I let him court me after all?*

Salina sighed and it brought Joanna's attention back inside the buggy. "I'm feelin' tired today."

"The heat's getting to all of us, jah?"

Salina agreed. "Ain't that the truth, though we can't complain compared to the high temperatures they've been having in Ohio and Indiana this week."

Indiana . . . Had Salina mentioned that state for any particular reason? But her sister went on to talk about a number of circle letters she was writing to distant cousins out there in the Midwest. "Didja know we have a third cousin named Maria Riegsecker who lives in Shipshewana?"

Joanna sucked in a breath at the mention of Eben's hometown. "Never heard of her," she managed to say.

"Jah, she was a Witmer like Mamma but married into an Indiana family. She's been askin' for Noah and me to come visit and bring the children, too. She runs a candle store and wants me to come and pick out whatever I'd like."

"How nice," Joanna replied absently. *Maria?* Had Eben ever mentioned her before? She didn't recall. "How long have you been writing circle letters with her?"

"Four years now. Maria's awful nice—kindhearted and generous. Says she has lots of empty bedrooms just waiting to be filled up when we visit."

"Sounds like you'd have a *gut* time."

"I think so, too, but getting Noah to take off during the summer is out of the question."

"How old a woman is Maria?"

"Mamma's age, I'd guess, although I really don't know."

"She makes candles, ya say?"

"All kinds of colors and scents. Hundreds of 'em, and they sell right off the shelves in her little shop above their stable."

"Sounds pretty," Joanna said. "I hope you can go sometime, Salina."

"Maria lives right off the main street, she says, within walking distance of the Blue Gate Bakery, where she likes to go to purchase apple dumplings and pecan rolls."

"Now you're makin' my mouth water!" Joanna smiled. "If you go, I'll send along some money for you to pick out a candle or two for me, all right?"

"Well, by the sound of it, Maria would be happy to treat anyone in the family," Salina said. "You could come, too . . . help look after the children, maybe?"

Just thinking of being anywhere in the vicinity of Eben's neighborhood and not seeing him tore at Joanna's heart. "I don't know how I could get away, even in the fall," she said.

They were coming up on Salina's house—Joanna could see the front yard jutting into view, just around the next bend. All this talk of

Shipshewana was making her head spin. It was a good thing she was close to dropping Salina off.

"Nice to see you havin' a *gut* time today at Mary's."

Joanna nodded. "I did." *Except for the preacher's wife.*

"Say, if you'd ever like to join in on Maria's circle letter, just let me know." Salina paused, then opened her pocketbook and fished for a notepad and pen. "Here, I'll jot down her address for ya, if you'd like."

It was funny seeing Salina so insistent, but Joanna did like the idea of writing to someone who was creative with something other than flowers or quilts. "Sure, I'll be glad to write her," she said, not sure when she'd have time.

"Denki for the ride, sister!" With that, Salina got out of the carriage and walked toward the house, waving without turning around.

Looking at the slip of paper in her hand, Joanna saw that the street name was Peaceful Acres Lane. *Same as Eben's address!*

"First the phone rings nearly off the hook . . . then I spot Jake. And now this," she said to herself as she hurried the horse toward home. She thought of the beautiful quilt and smiled as she recalled her prayer last night, asking God to make the path clear. Goodness, but the path, if it could be called that, was all *ranklich*—tangled up!

38

THE following Saturday, Joanna went riding again with Jake. When she asked, he confessed that the tales he told were true ones, some of which he'd heard from his grandfather. "He liked to embellish nearly everything," Jake told her.

"So they're family stories, then?"

"Oh jah, who'd ever think of makin' such things up? Real life is much stranger than fiction, ain't?"

Fiction. There it was again.

"Have you ever read a made-up book?" she asked.

"Oh, maybe a handful of mystery novels." He glanced at her, looking mighty dapper in his white dress shirt and black vest. "Have you?"

"Well, since we're becoming such *gut* friends, I'll tell ya a little secret." He leaned his head over. "I'm all ears."

"I've read quite a few novels, actually."

"Love stories, maybe?" He chuckled. "Make-believe—all lies, ya know."

"But a reflection of our relationship with the great Lover of our souls, I like to think," she stated.

He looked surprised, then nodded, evidently in agreement.

They were getting along so well, Joanna was thankful she'd agreed to continue seeing him. Maybe Jake *was* the answer to her prayer. Maybe in time he could help her forget Eben, once and for all.

That night, she and Cora Jane whispered and giggled, and Joanna told her all about Jake's convincing tellings. But she kept back their discussion about fiction, still sensitive about her former story writing. Would she be up to facing Preacher Yoder when he returned? Joanna couldn't help but worry about what he had up his sleeve.

After the ironing was done on Tuesday, Joanna and Cora Jane went over to Mammi Sadie's and helped her put up sweet corn all afternoon. It was the hottest day in August thus far, but none of them complained, not with the thought of delicious canned corn to enjoy come autumn and winter.

While the corn was simmering, Joanna slipped her grandmother a little poem of encouragement she'd written earlier that morning upon arising, knowing how stressful Dawdi's situation was for dear Mammi. His mind was slipping more often these days.

"Well, aren't *you* nice!" Mammi Sadie said, opening the poem. She read it silently, tears springing to her eyes, then opened her ample arms to Joanna, who couldn't help feeling ever so joyful at this heartfelt response.

"Heard you've written a lot of these poems for various folks," she said.

Joanna was reticent to own up. "Oh, it's just something I do to spread cheer." *And keeps me honest before the Lord God, too,* she thought, wishing her passion for story writing would fade for good.

Dawdi Joseph began to babble about his brothers and other relatives who'd passed away. But when he talked of his school days, his eyes sparkled, especially as he recalled the happy memory of helping raise cocker spaniel puppies to sell.

"Did ya ever get attached to any of the pups?" Cora Jane asked, drawing him out as he sat near the back door, just rocking.

"Oh jah . . . there was one black one with the saddest eyes you ever did see, and the way he'd just sit and look at ya, cock his little head, and nearly talk to ya . . . well, it warms my heart." Dawdi's shoulders rose and fell as he took a deep breath, revisiting the past. "In the end, that one went to our neighbors down the way. Mighty nice, too."

"You must've visited him sometimes, then, jah?" Joanna asked, hoping to keep their grandfather with them in the present a while longer.

"Why, sure I did."

"What did you name him—or did you?" Cora Jane asked, smiling at Joanna and giving her a knowing glance.

Dawdi nodded. "Called him Jigger. My, my, what an active pup he was. It seemed right."

"'Cause he nearly danced a jig when you saw him?" asked Joanna. She enjoyed seeing Dawdi so caught up in the recollection.

"Oh, goodness, did he ever." Dawdi went quiet and stopped rocking. Then, stretching his arms, he yawned and started murmuring, like he was talking to himself again—the way he often did these days.

"When was the last time you saw Jigger, Dawdi?" asked Cora Jane.

"Well, now, I 'spect he's round here somewhere." He scooted back his chair, straining his head to look. "Here, Jigger, ol' boy . . . c'mon to your friend Joseph. Here, Jigger . . . Jigger."

Heart breaking, Joanna had to turn away. She wondered if Mary Beiler's own Dawdi Abram ever lost track like this. As she recalled, Mary hadn't mentioned him at her birthday party. Perhaps because it was meant to be a very happy day.

Only eight women showed up at Mary's for the weekly quilting frolic. Joanna and Cora Jane helped stretch out the quilt, and then all of them worked to put it into the big frame. Because Mary was left-handed, she sat at one of the corners of her choosing and the rest of them filled in, finding their spots across from or near sisters or cousins. Cora Jane whispered that she wanted to sit right next to Joanna, which pleased Joanna no end. In time it would be like they'd never had a falling out at all.

Neither Ella Mae nor Mattie was in attendance. When Joanna asked about both women, Mary said Ella Mae was suffering with a miserable summer cold, and Mattie had stayed home to look after her. "A woman that age has to be careful, ya know?" Mary said as she picked up her thimble and needle.

Joanna agreed and smiled over at her. *Dear Mary, always thinking of others.*

And then, as though Mary had been privy to Joanna and Ella Mae's talk the day they'd put up peaches with Mamma, she said she'd been reading in the Old Testament. "The book of Ruth, actually . . . and it just struck me again how much love Ruth had for Naomi."

"For whither thou goest, I will go. . . ." Joanna hadn't forgotten that verse, either. It felt to her like yet another nudge back to Eben, and she

wondered if she ought to make a list of everything pointing in his direction. *Then maybe I should make another list for Jake.*

"What're you thinking 'bout?" Cora Jane leaned over to ask.

"Why, was I smiling at nothin' again?"

Cora Jane giggled a little. "It's like I can read your expressions anymore."

"Well, that's what sisters do, jah?"

Cora Jane nodded and glanced at her again, all smiles.

That night after family worship, Joanna read the entire book of Ruth, lingering on the verse Ella Mae had quoted.

"*Is* this a sign from God?" she whispered, staring at the tall gas lamp with its shiny glass chimney from her spot on the bed.

Then, admiring the old wedding quilt again, she thanked the Lord God for this legacy of faith passed down to her. And for divine guidance in her life.

She rose and placed her Bible back on the dresser, and as she turned, her eyes fell on the hope chest. *I ought to put my writing notebooks somewhere else,* she thought. They were such a temptation. So many feelings raced through her, she scarcely knew what to think.

She started when a knock came at the door. "Come in, Cora Jane," she said.

"Well, it's Mamma."

Stepping to the door, Joanna opened it. "Jah?"

"Your father's receiving a visit from Preacher Yoder on behalf of our elderly deacon." Mamma's face looked pale in the lamp's amber light. "Preacher wants you there, too."

Lovina Yoder's words flew back to her, and Joanna dreaded what was to come. "When's he comin' by?"

"One of these mornings, your father says."

"I'll be ready."

Mamma frowned hard, her lower lip trembling. "Sorry to be the one to tell ya. Your father, well . . ."

"I know—he's a busy man," Joanna said, excusing his wariness.

Nodding, Mamma patted Joanna's arm. "I'm here, if ya want to talk 'bout it."

These were the gentle words she needed to hear. "I'm not afraid, Mamma. All right? Please don't worry."

"I'll pray." Mamma turned to leave.

"Denki," Joanna said, wishing her story writing hadn't caused such a stir and put an ache in her mother's heart. *And poor Dat's, as well.*

39

T HE light coming from within the barn Thursday evening was a stark contrast to that of the gas lamp in the kitchen. Eben's father had summoned him to the makeshift office in one corner of the old barn for an unexpected *"meeting, of sorts"*—or so Daed had called it. The lantern light glowed eerily on such a dark night, and the animals were restless. Eben could sense something amiss, and not only in the atmosphere. His father's face was unusually grim.

For the past few weeks, Eben had noticed something quite different about his father and even considered perhaps Daed might be ill. Yet it was the oddest thing—some days he seemed entirely optimistic, then the next day downright dreary. Eben had never known Daed to be unsettled like this, and he wondered what might be on his mind. Maybe he was going to bring up some newfangled gadget that would make work easier for them both. If so, was it something the bishop approved?

Daed awaited him, sitting slumped at his beat-up wooden desk. He looked tired . . . defeated.

What's troubling him?

Immediately, Eben thought of Leroy. Had his father received news from him? But then again, what could be worse than Leroy's leaving the People, his heart no longer kneeling in contrition before almighty God?

So why'd Mamm urge me here on his behalf? Eben wondered as he entered the murky glow of light. "You wanted to see me, Daed?"

"Pull up a chair, son." His father sat straighter, filling his lungs slowly. "Need to bend your ear awhile."

Eben took a seat, ready to listen.

"I've come to a hard decision. One I've been mulling over for long enough now."

Eben's shoulders tensed into knots as he braced for the news that, nearly overnight, had the power to grow gray hair in his father's beard, and plant more crinkles around Daed's eyes and mouth. The weight of it had seemingly cloaked him with a gray pallor.

"Some days ya get the bear, other days the bear gets you," Daed began.

Never before had Eben heard this saying from Daed's lips—so uncharacteristic of him. What could it possibly mean?

Even though Joanna had pleaded with her mother not to worry, she had tossed about for half the night, doing plenty of that herself. And upon rising the next morning, her legs felt as wobbly as newborn calves. She made her way downstairs to shower and dress, then helped Mamma make breakfast. All the while, she kept her eye out for an early arrival by Preacher Yoder, in case he chose to appear today. It was well-known in the hollow that Preacher Yoder liked to arrive early, often surprising folk as he checked up a bit.

But Preacher didn't come that day or the next, and Joanna couldn't have been more apprehensive if she were expecting the bishop himself.

After the Sunday Singing, the first one in September, Joanna noticed Cora Jane talking with Mary Rose Witmer and two other cousins across the barn. Joanna managed to catch her sister's eye and motioned to her. "Come join us," she mouthed, thinking it might be fun to include Cora Jane in small talk with her and Jake.

Once Cora Jane came over and made a little circle of three, Jake told a story about a bunch of fellows who'd gotten their feet tied up while they were sleeping at a campout one night. They'd ended up tripping all over themselves when they got up in the morning—falling flat on their faces.

"Why on earth?" Cora Jane asked, inching in closer.

Jake grinned. "Well, it's like this: They were all getting hitched that comin' week. The single fellas tend to pick on the ones who are published to be married, ya know."

206

"There are so many pranks for the groom, ain't so?" Cora Jane said. "Oh, tell us another prank you've heard."

With that, Jake was off, this time with a tale about another cousin. Cora Jane's eyes were big as he wrapped up, and then one topic of conversation shifted effortlessly into another, until they were talking easily about shared interests. Cora Jane seemed to be genuinely enjoying herself, and Joanna could see how exceptionally taken Jake was with Cora Jane's spunk.

Joanna felt amused at being left far behind in this exchange. And later, when Jake asked if Joanna minded if they gave Cora Jane a ride home, too, Cora Jane protested demurely. But it was quite obvious there was a real spark between her and Jake, and Joanna realized she didn't mind in the least.

Jake seemed to enjoy the attention of both girls as they rode along in his handsome open carriage. Joanna couldn't keep from smiling as she looked back and forth between Jake and Cora Jane, like a witness to a Ping-Pong match. She was smashed like cheese in a sandwich between the two of them, and as they talked animatedly, she noticed that this was the third time they'd passed the house and not stopped to let Cora Jane out.

Eventually, as the hour grew late, Cora Jane graciously suggested she should be getting home. Joanna didn't object because she wanted to talk with Jake for a bit once her sister left for the house. She would be ever so cautious, though, in how she phrased things.

When asked, Jake didn't deny the attraction. Joanna gave him the green light to pursue courting Cora Jane. "If you'd like to."

"Are you sure 'bout this?" he asked, leaning closer. "I'd never want to hurt you, Joanna."

"We have a deal, remember? Just friends."

He nodded much too emphatically, and she couldn't help but laugh. "I'm perfectly fine if you want to take my sister out."

Jake studied her. "Only if you're absolutely certain."

"I am. And just think, if you two end up together, we'll be brother and sister, which is even better than friends, jah?"

He chuckled. "Not always. Sometimes siblings can be a pain in the neck, if you know what I mean."

While that was certainly true enough, Joanna didn't admit to it—not now, given the way Cora Jane and she were getting along so well.

A crescent moon appeared over the cornfield to the east, and Jake kindly mentioned that it was probably time to call it a night. He came around the open carriage, helped Joanna down, and walked her partway up the lane, just as he had always done before. But tonight, Joanna guessed, was to be the very last time.

··· ➤ ◂ ···

Cora Jane's lantern was still lit and burning when Joanna slipped over to her room. Her sister's hair was a sheet of flowing flaxen over one side of her pale pink nightgown. She sat in bed and smiled immediately. "Did Jake tell more stories after I left? I must've missed some *gut* ones, jah?"

"Are you honestly sayin' that's what you want to know?"

Cora Jane's eyes glimmered. "What else is there to ask?"

"Oh, well . . . I wouldn't want to spoil the fun."

"For me or for you?" Laughing softly, Cora Jane reached for her hand. "You do know something, don't you?"

"Maybe."

"Goodness' sake!" Cora Jane blushed.

They were both laughing now, and it felt like old times. Cora Jane patted her side of the bed, inviting Joanna to stay awhile longer.

"Jake is *gut* for you, ain't so?" Cora Jane said as she turned on her side to look Joanna square in the face.

"I never thought I could be friends with a fella, ya know? It's kind of peculiar."

Cora Jane was suddenly quiet.

"He's learned some important courting lessons," Joanna said. "Knows how to behave on a date, for sure."

"I wondered 'bout that. But it's pretty obvious he got some *gut* advice from somewhere."

Joanna didn't mention Ella Mae Zook or that she knew Jake had gone to talk to her last April.

"He's grown up a lot—maybe because of bein' friends with you, Joanna."

She shrugged. "Who's to say?"

"And the two of you have something big in common, jah?" said Cora Jane. "A real love of stories."

"That we do." Sliding her hand beneath the pillow, Joanna began to relax. "He tells them so freely."

"Do you miss your story writing terribly?" Cora Jane's voice was soft, even regretful.

"Not as much as at first. If I didn't have my poetry to fall back on, I'd miss it even more. The Lord's given me another way to express my creativity, I guess."

"Well, no matter what you write, it's a gift."

This surprised Joanna. "What a nice thing to say."

"Nice . . . and mighty confusing, too, ain't?" Cora Jane glanced at the small clock on her bed shelf.

Nodding, Joanna refused to think about the confusing part, feeling quite sure she knew what was coming with Preacher Yoder's impending visit.

"You'd better head for bed," Cora Jane said, "or you'll end up falling asleep in your clothes right here."

Joanna opened her sleepy eyes and looked over at her sister. "I'm glad we can talk like this again."

"Me too."

With that, Joanna got up, said good-night, and walked to her own room. Once there, although feeling tired, she lit her lantern and settled into bed to read from the book of Proverbs. After a time, she bowed her head and folded her hands in a prayer of thanksgiving for God's goodness and grace in all of their lives. Then she outened the gas lamp.

But sleep did not come quickly. For one thing, she had a hard time dismissing the conversation with Ella Mae the day they'd canned peaches. For another, she couldn't forget the letters her namesake had written to her own sister Miriam.

Lying there in the darkened room, Joanna stared at the open window, welcoming the cool night air. She had carefully folded back the heirloom quilt, along with the sheet, and relished the slight breeze on her cotton gown.

And then, as if a nudge had come from heaven, an unexpected idea dropped into her heart. *Oh jah.* Joanna knew exactly what she wanted to tell Preacher Yoder, Lord willing, once he revealed what was on his mind. It was ever so plain to her just now.

But dare she speak up yet again?

40

ASINGLE blunt knock came at the back door the next day, just as Joanna and her mother were sitting down to catch a breath after having hung out an extra large washing. They'd also baked two more loaves of bread than usual, and on such a warm day, too.

Mamma looked sideways at Joanna and got up to move toward the screen door, where Preacher Yoder stood in his usual black attire, his straw hat in hand, jaw set.

I must surely be in trouble again. Joanna slunk down in her chair at the table, where she'd fluted the edges of two pie shells she planned to fill with early apples. When she glanced up, she could see the old well pump behind the preacher, in the backyard. She cringed, remembering the minister's last visit.

Meanwhile, Mamma was telling him Dat had gone. "Went over to Noah's place not fifteen minutes ago."

Joanna held her breath and hoped Preacher Yoder might simply offer to return at a more suitable time.

"Joanna, dear," Mamma called, turning to reveal a flushed face.

She left the piecrusts there on the table. *I'll hear what he has to say and be done with it,* Joanna told herself.

But before she could get out to the utility room door, Preacher Yoder strode into the kitchen with Mamma following behind like a chubby little bird.

"Joanna," he said, not cracking a smile. "I have something to tell you."

She refused the urge to flinch and instead met him at the table when Mamma gave a slight shift of her hand, indicating they should sit. Joanna sat where Cora Jane usually did, on the long bench facing the windows, and Mamma sat across from her in her own chair, with Preacher Yoder presumptuously at the head of the table, in Dat's place.

Preacher folded his callused hands on the table and stared at them for a moment. "You are quite fond of writing, as I understand it."

Joanna slowly raised her eyes to his. This was ground they'd already covered.

"And you continue to write even now, according to the deacon's wife, Sallie, and others."

"Only poetry." She took the risk and defended herself in what she dearly hoped was a respectful tone. "Little poems to cheer folk up."

He nodded, his expression less severe than at the last visit. "So I hear."

"I've given up my story writing—gave it up before the Lord God and heavenly Father." She longed to jump ahead and tell him what had helped to prompt her decision, but she refrained, thinking it unwise. She curled her toes under the table.

"Sallie is so impressed by those little poems, she's suggested I encourage you to submit some of them to the *Ladies Journal*." He pulled out a piece of paper and handed it to her. It gave an editor's name and the address for submissions.

Joanna could hardly speak. "My writings . . . published?"

"Your *poetry*."

She was stunned at this turn of events. Mamma beamed at her across the table, and her short, quick nod of the head meant that Joanna should say something. But news of this sort had been the farthest thing from her mind on such a day. "Are *you* . . . is she ever so sure?"

"Sallie?" Preacher grinned. "I'm told several women were in agreement with her."

Joanna thought then of the way Fannie's visit to the deacon's wife had been somewhat downplayed by Mammi Kurtz. Now that Joanna thought of it, she wondered if Cora Jane might also have been involved.

Beyond pleased, Joanna shook her head as she tried to absorb all of this. And, lo and behold, the very question she'd so wanted to ask just flew from her mind. Gone in the wake of this wonderful-*gut* surprise.

"I'll leave it up to you to pursue this, if you wish," Preacher added. "With my blessing . . . and Bishop John's, too."

The bishop's?

She nodded, still overwhelmed at this turn of events. It wasn't difficult to think of which poem to present to the magazine editors. A pleasant tremor went through her. What if it ended up in print for the whole world to see? *Her* world . . . the Plain community at large.

Then, before Joanna could say more, Mamma offered to bring each of them a slice of warm bread with strawberry jam, and soon Joanna and the preacher found themselves sitting alone at the table, just looking at each other.

Something about the way he ran his fingers up and down his suspenders made her think of Eben. And in that moment, Joanna knew she could indeed confide in Preacher Yoder.

Eben enjoyed nibbling the fresh cinnamon sticky bun his mother had made earlier that morning, though he allowed himself only one. He hadn't second-guessed the things Daed had put to him the other night in the barn. None of his older brothers had blinked an eye at Daed's decision, which still surprised Eben. Yet he reeled with the news and felt it was only right to contact Leroy about it, as well.

"You and your father have to fill silo yet," his mother said, offering more to eat.

"That and the vet's comin' to check the cows' blood for TB and brucel-losis in a couple of days," Eben mentioned. Knowing how sluggish eating between meals made him, he politely refused any more mouthwatering treats and hurried back out to help his father.

Eyeing the phone shack, a brown dot in the distance, he determined it was time to give Leroy a call.

Later tonight.

The time had come for Joanna to share with Preacher Yoder what she'd felt led to do. "No matter how things turn out, I want to do this for the Lord God . . . and out of respect for the brethren," she began.

A confused frown crossed the minister's brow. "Speak plainly," he urged.

She glanced at Mamma, now over at the sink, then back at the minister. "After prayer, I am willing to sacrifice my story writing for the rest of my life, for a transfer of membership to another state," she said with all the courage she could gather.

"To which church?"

She told him quietly.

"Well, I can't promise, but I'll bring it up with Bishop John." His composed countenance spoke volumes, and she felt heartened.

Mamma returned to the table carrying a plate with two thick slices of bread and set it down, along with a jar of jam.

Joanna continued, being more direct than she'd ever been with anyone in spiritual authority. In turn, the preacher made it equally clear that she was permitted to continue writing her poetry as long as it was done to offer encouragement.

"Daughter?" Mamma said after a time, looking baffled as she sat there. "Why a request to transfer to another church?"

Holding off on revealing her entire plan, Joanna explained that she didn't know yet if transferring would even be necessary. "But I'll know soon enough."

It was only then that Joanna saw the bewilderment lift, and tenderness and understanding shone in Mamma's dear eyes.

41

JOANNA hadn't really foreseen how anxious she would be to locate the Troyer farm in thriving, green Shipshewana. By the time she arrived Friday—in a van full of other Amish heading for various towns in Indiana—and had acquired a taxicab, she was beginning to feel the effects of the exceedingly long day, tired yet buoyed by the excitement of her surprise visit. The worry came from not knowing what her former beau might do or say when she arrived without warning.

What if he has a steady girlfriend by now? Joanna asked herself, then attempted to squash the dreadful notion. Oh, surely not! Yet the voice of reason crept back in, and she realized that Eben could very well have moved on with a new sweetheart. What would keep him from doing so?

Either way, she had to know for certain. And if not, was he still thinking of her, missing her . . . wishing there was a miraculous way for them to be together? Well, here she was, and all of their distance keeping was behind them. Although Joanna no longer wrote down her romantic imaginings about happily-ever-afters, she still liked to contemplate different scenarios. No one could keep her from writing stories in her head, so to speak. And she did just that as she enjoyed the ride along the rural roads, all of which were numbered county roads rather than streets with names, like those in Hickory Hollow.

Weary as she was, she longed to lean her head back in the cab, but she would not have time to undo her hair bun and tidy it up before seeing Eben and meeting his family. *If that even happens.* The thought of being introduced to his parents hadn't been something she'd mentally prepared herself for at all. And thinking just now how awkward that might turn out to be for all of them, Joanna wondered why she hadn't considered it before now. *Was I in too much of a hurry?* she wondered, thinking back to last Monday and the preacher's visit.

Mamma had quizzed her at length after their minister left with strawberry jam on his shirt. She'd been unable to suppress her smile or her animation. In fact, Joanna had never imagined her mother so aflutter about Joanna's hope of reuniting with Eben. Mamma, of course, had mixed feelings of both joy and sadness—and, oh, how she fretted about the risk Joanna was taking!

"I *have* to do this," Joanna had explained, citing her namesake as the inspiration for her daring plan to go to Indiana. "Did ya know my ancestor proposed marriage to the man she eventually married?"

Mamma grimaced and said she wasn't certain that information was factual, but Joanna insisted Mammi Kurtz knew all about it.

Once Joanna had finished sharing her intention, she asked Mamma not to tell Dat. "Only you and Cora Jane will know," Joanna said. "Promise?"

Mamma looked askance, as if to say, *"You're asking this?"*

"I'll tell Cora Jane myself," she assured Mamma.

"Well, and that's far better, I daresay. Sister to sister." Mamma fell silent for a time. "Your father would never agree to let you go, if he knew."

"Another reason why it's probably best for him not to. After all, aren't I old enough to decide?"

"He'd say it isn't becoming of you to chase after a beau."

Doubtless Mamma was right. Except that Eben Troyer hadn't been just any beau. Joanna wholly trusted that God had planted this desire in her heart . . . and now she must fulfill it.

The cabbie pulled into a long, tree-lined lane. "Here we are, miss."

She paid the bill and double-checked the address she'd come to know so well. "Denki," she said and got out.

The cab pulled away quickly, and she was left appraising the grand lawns and the Troyer house itself. There was a strange hush surrounding the place as Joanna walked timidly up the lane, carrying her small overnight case. Was it just her imagination, or was her heartbeat audible?

Flecks of sunlight dappled the flower gardens beneath enormous, leafy oak trees along the left side of the house and the wraparound porch. And, now that she was nearer, Joanna noticed several Amishmen strolling along the opposite side yard, talking in Deitsch. If she wasn't mistaken, one of them mentioned something about a "big doin's" coming up soon on these premises. What could that mean? Perhaps a landmark birthday for either of Eben's parents, like the celebration thrown for Mary Beiler? Or someone's wedding anniversary?

She focused again on the three-story house, noting the arch of a tree limb reaching like a protective wing over a white gazebo with gingerbread latticework along the bottom. The air was fragrant with climbing pink roses on two white arbors, and there were several martin birdhouses positioned on the lawn. She searched for any sign of Eben, hoping she might spot him near the barn set off to the west.

There was a white sports car parked in the very back, and surprised, she wondered whose it was. A black-and-white tabby meowed loudly at her, then ran and hid under the back porch, as if daring her to play hide-and-seek.

With a knock on the screen door, Joanna peered into the wide summer porch and beyond, into the long kitchen. She saw no one. Then, just as she was wondering if anyone was at home, she heard someone calling and turned to see a red-haired English woman wearing white walking shorts and a bright red sleeveless blouse. A cross pendant hung around her slender neck.

"May I help you?" the young woman asked, pushing her lovely hair behind one ear.

Joanna noticed the sparkling diamond ring on her left hand and wondered if this might be Leroy's bride. "I'm a friend of Eben's," she said. "Thought I'd surprise him with a visit."

The petite woman glanced curiously at Joanna's overnight bag and shook her head. "I'm sorry, but Eben's out of town for a few days. Left this morning."

"Oh," Joanna said, heart sinking. "I've missed him, I guess."

Looking her over, the younger woman frowned for a moment, her eyes searching Joanna's face. Then she turned as if she was going to call to someone, but just as suddenly turning back. She touched Joanna's hand. "Excuse me, but you wouldn't be . . ." She paused. "Are you Joanna?"

"Jah." She shook her head enthusiastically, pleased the woman knew her name. *A gut sign, for sure!* "And might you be Eben's new sister-in-law?"

"I am." The pretty woman nodded, smiling now. "Debbie's my name." She shook Joanna's hand. "I'm just along for the ride, I guess you could say . . . here to help my husband and his family organize and sort through a lifetime of accumulation."

Sort through?

"What do you mean?" Joanna asked, astonished.

"Leroy's parents are auctioning off the farm this coming week—moving to Virginia Beach. So we're dividing up the items they don't want to sell. Sentimental things, you know . . . things that should remain in the family."

Joanna wondered when this had come about, and how it would impact Eben. Her head was whirling. She wanted to ask if Debbie truly knew what she was talking about, because it sounded unbelievable. Such strange things she was telling her . . . so very hard to comprehend. Eben's father was selling his farm?

Just then a young man in blue jeans and a gray T-shirt appeared from the barn, heading this way. He looked enough like Eben to be his brother, and his gait reminded Joanna of the first time she'd seen Eben walking along the beach, snapping pictures. In that surreal moment, she wondered what had ever become of those pictures. Had Eben saved them? She so yearned to see them . . . to see him.

Debbie introduced Leroy to her, and he was quick to offer a hand-shake in greeting. Then he slapped his forehead, laughing hard. When he'd managed to stop long enough to speak, he said, "You'll never guess where Eben is right now." He paused a moment. "He hopped on an early-morning van to Lancaster."

Joanna thought her heart might stop right then and there.

Leroy was still chuckling, and Debbie looked as shocked as Joanna felt, obviously just hearing about this amazing coincidence for the first time. "Well, like we say here, don't this beat all?" Leroy said amidst more laughter.

"What's he plannin' to do there?" Joanna's voice sounded far away to her.

Leroy ran his hands through his hair and looked at the sky, then back at her, a glint in his eye.

Suddenly, she knew. Debbie had mentioned an auction here. So Eben had gone looking for her—to tell her the news that he was unshackled at last!

But Joanna didn't wish to hear any more of the details from either Leroy or his wife. No, she wanted to wait to hear all of this from Eben himself. *Dear, dear Eben!*

She noticed the cell phone clipped to Leroy's pocket. "Might I use your phone right quick?" she asked, wanting to contact Cousin Maria before it got dark.

Leroy gladly handed it to her and showed her how to use it. She made the call to see if she could spend the night with the candlemaker before catching an early van home tomorrow, explaining that she was Salina's sister, which opened the door to Maria's heart extra wide. Or so it seemed by the sound of delight in her voice.

Still flabbergasted by the day's unfolding events, Joanna thanked Leroy for the use of his phone. When he offered to drive her to Maria's, with Debbie accompanying them, she wasn't sure what to say. This was the man whose foolishness, his discarding of his Amish heritage, had kept her and Eben apart. But forgiveness was a way of life, the very core of their beliefs. She had to overlook what he'd done, knowing people made their own choices, whether for God or the world. "All right," she said, agreeing. "I appreciate it."

"Won't Eben be surprised when he finds out you're *here?*" Debbie said over her shoulder as they climbed into the sporty car.

The realization shook Joanna anew.

42

EBEN quickened his pace up the driveway, anticipating seeing Joanna after all their months apart. He dismissed any notions of her being engaged to Jake Lantz or any other young man, for that matter, although if he were honest with himself, he knew he should be worried. Right now his entire focus was on winning back her heart, if that's what it took, now that he was finally able to relocate here to Joanna's splendid little corner of the world.

A low stone wall along one side of the lane leading to the house was coated with thick moss, and behind it a long double row of marigolds flourished. The windmill beyond the barnyard creaked in a cadence that reminded him of Daed's own, and Eben breathed in the familiar aroma of soil mixed with the fertilizer of more than two hundred years as the sun leaned toward the horizon.

Rhoda Kurtz was sitting out on the back porch when he arrived at the door. She let out a gasp when she spotted him, getting up from her chair right quick to come over and babble something about Joanna's not being home. "She's out of town," Rhoda said, seemingly too shy to meet his eyes.

"I should've written to say I was comin'. . . ." Eben felt his shoulders slump as the breath left him for a moment. "When will she return?"

Again, Rhoda acted altogether bashful. Was she the type of woman who needed the cushion of others? Eben knew plenty of womenfolk like that, but this apparent change in Rhoda took him aback.

"Not exactly sure when she'll be home," Rhoda said hesitantly.

"Well, I'll be glad to wait and see her, if you don't think she'd mind."

She nodded, again behaving in a completely different manner than the first time he'd visited here.

Eben asked if she knew where he might spend the night. Immediately, Rhoda mentioned Rachel Stoltzfus, saying she'd be more than happy to go over there with him. "They'll be pleased to put you up again," she insisted.

"Don't want to put anyone out."

"Oh, no worries 'bout that," she was quick to say. "Let me get you something cold to drink—you look all in."

He lowered his duffel bag onto the porch and turned to gaze out toward the barn, perspiring as he stood in the dying sunlight. It had been equally as hot back home. He wondered how Leroy and Debbie and all the other family members were getting along while dividing up the spoils. He was actually relieved not to be present for all of that, although he wouldn't have minded having some of the garden tools—shovels, trowels, and such. Things his father's hands had touched all the many years. As for personal effects and furnishings, he desired nothing like that from Daed, who'd given him steady employment since his late teens while asking very little by way of room and board, allowing Eben to stash away much of his earnings.

Eben sighed and realized how tired he was. He watched Nate Kurtz bringing in the field mules, a dark profile against the meadow, where lightning bugs twinkled as far as the eye could see. Eben guessed he'd gone back out to labor after supper, just as Eben's own father often did. *No more,* he thought, wondering how long it would take for his parents to adjust to retirement once the farm sold next week at auction to another Plain family. Daed had been winding down awhile, he'd told Eben that night in the glow of the barn's lantern. And he'd waited for several years, just to be sure this was what he and Mamm wanted. And now, he said, it was.

Eben knew all too well the daily strain, year after year, required in farming the old way—using mule or horsepower to plow, cultivate, and harvest, instead of tractors like the English. Lots of Amish farmers lasted only twenty or twenty-five years anymore before selling their land to their youngest son, or other kin, to keep the fertile soil in the family.

"Here's something to wet your whistle," Rhoda said as she handed him a tall glass of ice-cold root beer. "Made it just last week."

"Denki." He felt terribly nervous around Joanna's mother, just as she seemed to be around him. Joanna was the important ingredient in the social equation, and she was absent. But gone where?

Rhoda asked if he'd like to sit a spell till Nate came in and washed up. "He'll be surprised to see ya, too."

Eben didn't have to guess what that meant. And he hardly knew where to look, because when Rhoda spoke, she avoided his eyes, which signaled something. *What?*

Then a terrible fear gripped him. Was Joanna spoken for? Could that be the reason for her mother's peculiar manner?

Rhoda seemed restless as she got up yet again. "Would ya like some pie, maybe?"

"Oh, that's not necessary," Eben said, trying to be polite, although he was hungry, having devoured his sandwich, apple, and nearly a whole stalk of celery in the van hours ago.

But Rhoda didn't seem to pay any mind and headed back inside again, fanning herself now with her black apron.

Cora Jane was wandering through the meadow when he looked that way, barefoot and swinging her arms. Strands of her blond hair hung out from beneath her royal blue bandana. She had been picking golden daisies and was waving them in the breeze as she came closer. Then, just that quick, she caught sight of him and began to run toward the house.

"What on earth are ya doin' here?" Her expression was one of total disbelief.

He laughed. "That's an interesting way to say hullo." This was the plucky sister, he recalled.

"No, I'm *serious* . . . why are ya here, Eben Troyer?"

"Came to see Joanna."

"I see that." She blinked her eyes and frowned toward the back door. Then, coming closer, she whispered behind her free hand, "I was told not to tell a soul this . . . but I think you should know that my sister has gone lookin' for *you.*"

"She what?"

"She's out in your neck of the woods." Cora Jane nodded her head. "She made us all promise not to say anything. Not even Dat knows where she went."

221

Eben couldn't believe it. "I'm here and she's there?"

"Jah, but remember, you never heard it from me."

"Glad for the tip."

She stood there looking at him, a smile on her face now. "Something else," she whispered again, then paused, weighing her words, he thought. "Joanna's in love with you, Eben—she never stopped."

With that, she hurried to open the screen door and headed inside.

He couldn't have imagined this in his best dreams. Yet what had precipitated this sudden move by Joanna toward him? And what on earth had possessed her to go to Shipshewana without letting him know first?

Rhoda reappeared with a tray of goodies—pie and cookies. Must Eben now pretend he didn't know Joanna's whereabouts while he made small talk? He accepted a generous slice of peach pie and thanked her, picking up a fork from the tray, as well.

No wonder Joanna's mother acted so strange!

He could hardly sit there and eat his pie, even though it tasted truly terrific. Rhoda said hardly a word, and he wondered how much longer before Nate came and joined them, as Rhoda had suggested he might.

Out of habit, Eben pulled out his pocket watch, the light in the sky diminishing with every tick of a second. It was just a few minutes till seven o'clock—he'd been traveling nearly all day.

Has Joanna really gone to Indiana . . . could it be?

"Such a quiet evening, ain't?" Rhoda said for lack of anything else much to say. "Ever so peaceful here."

"Fridays are like this back home, too," he said, thinking of his family. Would they come here to meet Joanna and her kin someday?

Friday!

The awareness was an alarm bell in his memory. Eben nearly leaped out of his chair, spilling a bit of his pie, which he leaned down to pick up before returning his dessert plate to the tray on a small table nearby. Then, despite the fact that most likely he'd raise Rhoda's eyebrows by his impulsive actions, Eben hastily excused himself, not looking back to see the startled expression that surely played across her face.

He took off running across the yard, toward the dusty field road. Though the little phone shanty was now nearly hidden by cornstalks taller than his head, he knew the way.

43

JOANNA sighed, shaking away the doubts. No, she was not as out-spoken as Cora Jane . . . nor was she as self-assured as her forebear Aunt Joanna. Still, she couldn't reject the curious pull she felt toward the phone booth down Peaceful Acres Lane from Maria Riegsecker's house. Joanna had to see where Eben went to call her, thinking it might make her feel a little closer to him tonight.

"You might have to wait to use it, though," Maria had said with a smile. "Sometimes that happens, 'specially on a Friday evening." She meant the more traditional young men used it as a matter of course to connect with their girls. Others less adhering to the church ordinance used cell phones.

Joanna had not commented on that one iota. Now that she was here in Eben's neighborhood—now that she knew Eben was free to court her and move to Hickory Hollow if he chose to—she felt compelled to see the shanty where he had always phoned her on Fridays at seven o'clock.

It was close to that time even now.

As she walked along the roadside, she saw that the door to the small lean-to was standing open. Once inside, she pushed the door shut. Then, without thinking or second-guessing herself, she raised her hand to the black receiver. Slowly, she lifted it out of its cradle and dialed the opera-tor, ready to use the code Maria had given her for the eventual billing.

There was little hope that anyone would be in the area of the cornstalk-concealed phone shed to even hear the phone ring, let alone answer and go to track Eben down at her parents' house. But Joanna wasn't thinking like herself just now; she was doing what Cora Jane might do. "Or my namesake," she said aloud.

Eben literally jumped when he heard the phone jangle the first time. He shoved the wooden door open at the second ring and picked the receiver right up. "Hullo?"

Silence.

"Anybody there?" he asked.

Then softly, he heard her voice. "Is that you, Eben?"

"Jah . . . Joanna?"

She said it was. "I came to see you in Shipshewana."

"And I'm here in Hickory Hollow, as you now know."

They laughed at the wonderful unlikeliness of it all.

She told him of having met Leroy and Debbie and sounded like she was starting to cry, and trying not to. "I'm standing in your phone booth, not far from your father's house."

"Ach, Joanna . . . this is *erschtaunlich*—astonishing!"

"I came to Indiana to let you know I might be able to transfer my membership to your church." Her voice cracked.

He contemplated what all this meant and wished he were next to her now, able to show her how pleased he was. "Well, whoever thought we'd go to see each other . . . and on the same day?" he managed to say, wanting to sound strong so that she could be.

"Stranger than what ya might read in a storybook, ain't?"

"I want you in my life, Joanna. I'd rather talk to you this way or write to you by letter than be with any other girl. But all that's goin' to change, if you'll have me."

"Have you? Oh, Eben, don't ya know . . . I love you?" she said, warming his heart.

"I wanted to wait to say those words to you in person." He wished she were here in his arms this minute.

"Well, I want to hear them *now*," she declared.

Cora Jane's spirit had rubbed off on her. "All right," he said, grinning into the phone. "I love you, Joanna Kurtz, with all of my heart. And I want to make you my bride."

There was a sudden, poignant silence. He held his breath.

224

"Will ya ask me again when I see you tomorrow?" she said, surprising him once more.

"I certainly will," he said. "And you know what I think? We need to preserve these phone shacks somehow. Maybe I could take a few pictures."

Her laughter was so sweet. "For posterity, jah."

They laughed together, blending their mirth as the Friday evening sun set. And it was all Eben could do to say good-bye when the time came.

Joanna spied Eben sitting on the front porch waiting for her as she arrived home the next day. She made herself walk, not run, across the front lawn, and when he saw her, he fairly flew off the porch swing and hurried down the steps to meet her.

"Willkumm home," he said, looking well rested and as handsome as she'd remembered.

"You too." She smiled as she moved into his open arms, letting him hold her. "I thought I'd never get here."

"I know *that* feeling." He chuckled. "My sweet Joanna."

She loved being so close to him, after having been apart all this time. But this was not the place to be so intimate.

Soon they were walking back to the porch, where he told her all that he'd been doing today. "I've lined up a place to start workin'—for Smithy Riehl. I'll start next week, just as soon as I get my things moved here."

She was thrilled, hanging on to his every word. "Will you stay with him and his wife, maybe?"

"That's part of the deal, too." Eben seemed mighty pleased.

She kept waiting to hear the longed-for words but was happy to take in the exciting plans he'd set in place in such a short time.

Eben also talked further about his father's decision to sell the farm. "It's such backbreaking work for my poor Daed," he concluded.

She fully understood yet was stunned at how this had all come together . . . and for their benefit, of all things!

"And, just so ya know, he did offer me the farm to purchase. But I turned it down, hoping you were still single."

"You gave it up for me?"

This took her breath away. And now her heart yearned to tell what she'd sacrificed for God—and for him, as well—but Joanna thought better of it. *Maybe I'll wait till my poems are published in the magazine . . . Lord willing!*

"You and I—this whole thing—is an answer to prayer," he told her.

She nodded in agreement, wanting to pinch herself.

He reached for her hand. "So now that we're together here . . . will you marry me, Joanna?"

The words startled her briefly. But then she smiled into his dear face. "What took ya so long?" she replied.

He winked at her, clearly enjoying her spunk. He leaned over and kissed her lightly, and then again. "Is the coming wedding season too soon?" His eyes still lingered on hers. "All right with you?"

"Can we possibly be ready by then?" There were so many plans to be made—where they would live, most important. Suddenly, Joanna remembered the ample celery patch and wondered if Cora Jane would mind if she used it.

"I'll work to make that happen, my love." He slipped his arm around her and pulled her ever so near, kissing her again for even longer, not seeming to care what the neighbors thought.

And snuggling next to him . . . neither did she.

Epilogue

WITHIN weeks of Eben's move to Hickory Hollow, my younger sister confided that Jake Lantz was quickly becoming a serious beau. Cora Jane also said it was more than all right to use her celery crop for the traditional creamed-celery casserole at my wedding feast. I couldn't help myself—I slipped in my all-important question then and there. "Will ya consider bein' my bridesmaid, sister? It would mean ever so much."

A mischievous smile appeared on her pretty face. "Why, sure, I'd love to." She reached to hug me, and we laughed till tears clouded our eyes.

Both Eben and Jake have had numerous opportunities to get acquainted at church and at youth gatherings. We've even talked of going on double dates here before too long. Such *gut* times we'll have together!

Meanwhile, Mammi Kurtz has shown a great deal of interest in Eben, asking me about his attendance at Preaching services and the like. She, too, suspects we'll be published after church one of these November weeks. And I know Mamma and Dat do, too.

As for the double wedding ring quilt that has graced my bed, I've decided to wash it up real nice and set it aside for Eben's and my wedding night. I'll tell my darling the story of the determined woman in my family tree who wholeheartedly believed that we're all here by design . . . that none of us is an accident in God's eyes. Our heavenly Father's hand is at work in all of our comings and goings—and in the choice of a life mate.

Prior to their move to Virginia, I went with Eben to Shipshewana to meet his congenial parents. They were so encouraging about our eventual

227

union, they even invited us to come visit them once they're settled there. That way, we'll come full circle and go walking along the beach where we met. Eben says we might want to go for our first wedding anniversary, as well.

Thinking of anniversaries, Cousin Malinda had her first baby, a boy, the week before her anniversary. Andy said it was right fine with him whenever the Good Lord wanted to bless them with such a healthy baby. And Malinda says Baby Aaron's day of birth definitely ties for first place in happiness with the day she and Andy married.

As for me, I've continued to attend the weekly quilting frolics, where Mamma says a wedding quilt is in the making. I haven't had the heart to tell them I already have one that I cherish, instead letting Mamma guide the decision as to the pattern and color scheme. It's something I will look forward to as a thoughtful gesture, to be sure. Besides, a bride can always use more than one quilt in the house!

Once Eben and I are wed, we will stay with my parents till springtime, as is our custom. Eben has been hard at work with Smitty Riehl, so he's already making money here, adding to his savings, along with some funds his kindly parents gave us from the sale of their farm. Even though there is no land available to purchase in the hollow, we've got our eye on a smaller house not far from the bishop's.

Yesterday, the deacon's wife, Sallie, and Fannie surprised me when they showed up at the house, bringing several copies of the *Ladies Journal*. They could hardly quit chattering and quickly turned to the page featuring two of my poems.

Zwee—two! Who would ever have thought this possible?

When I showed Eben later, he asked me to sit near him and read them aloud, which I happily did, although toward the last stanza I could scarcely see the words through my joyful tears. It was a good thing I'd memorized the rest. He kissed my cheek and I cried all the harder, such happy tears.

Then he showed me the numerous digital pictures on his camera, including the ones he took that first night on the beach—a striking series of the ocean, sky, and the dark ship on the horizon. And one more: a distant shot of a forlorn-looking Amish girl sitting with her feet pushed deep into the sand.

"So you *did* take my picture," I teased.

"But I never got it printed—in keeping with the Ordnung, ya know." He smiled as he showed me the zoom button on his fancy camera. "I couldn't say how many times I looked at this picture of you up close. First thing every morning and the last thing at night," he admitted.

His picture taking reminded me of my story writing, a lovely yet swiftly fading memory. After all, I was too busy living my happy ending to have any regrets.

Now, if I *were* still writing fiction, I'd start by penning something like this for the opening lines to my own personal love story: *"Three times a bridesmaid, never a bride." That's just what my younger sister said about me—in front of our engaged cousins, no less. . . .*

Author's Note

SINCE my early teens, I've heard the saying "Always a bridesmaid, never a bride," but I didn't know all those years ago how that well-known saying might entice me as a novelist to discover Joanna's unique story path. I delighted in developing the characters of Joanna Kurtz (oh, the writing side of her!) and her feisty younger sister, Cora Jane. Not to mention their devoted mother, Rhoda . . . and the *wunnerbaar* Eben Troyer. I also especially enjoyed revisiting the character of Ella Mae Zook, Hickory Hollow's Wise Woman.

I offer enduring gratitude to my dear husband, Dave, my brainstorming partner and first editor, who in every way helps make my deadlines achievable.

My sincerest appreciation also extends to the stellar staff at Bethany House Publishers, whose collective expertise guides and encourages me, and who ultimately share the pleasure of publishing stories for legions of devoted reader-friends. Thanks primarily to Jim and Ann Parrish, David Horton, Steve Oates, Rochelle Glöege, Debra Larsen, and Helen Motter—you are all truly gifted!

Many thanks to Mary Jane Hoober, gracious innkeeper of the Peaceful Acres Bed-and-Breakfast in Shipshewana, Indiana, who offered invaluable insights into the Indiana Amish for this particular book. During an autumn respite, my family and I thoroughly enjoyed staying at this lovely inn, the source of Eben Troyer's fictitious street address: Peaceful Acres Lane.

The brief reference to John Newton's book *Voice of the Heart* was inspired by the cherished copy given to me by Aunt Ada Reba Bachman before her Homegoing nearly three years ago.

Special thanks to my cousin Dave Buchwalter for the gift of an heirloom friendship quilt made in 1927 for my maternal grandparents . . . the seed that planted the family quilt subplot in this story. I am so grateful!

Denki to my faithful assistants and consultants—Amish and Mennonite alike. I am forever thankful for your prayers and encouragement, as well as to Barbara Birch for meticulous proofreading, and to Dale Birch and Dave and Janet Buchwalter for research help and faithful prayers.

To our magnificent and all-wise heavenly Father be all blessing and honor . . . *Soli deo Gloria.*

The
Secret Keeper

For
Jackie Green,
with love.

And . . .
for all of my devoted reader-friends
whose heart's cry is to live more simply—
if not Amish,
then a more peaceable life.

Prologue

TODAY'S the day I'll tell them.

I parked my car beneath the brilliantly red sugar maple tree at the impressive Connecticut estate—my childhood home. It was a yearly custom for my parents to throw a dinner party to celebrate my October birthday.

Twenty-five and still trying to fit in . . . somewhere.

I glanced at the console and spotted a pile of mail tucked away there, including a card from Marnie Lapp in Lancaster County. *May this be the best birthday ever, dear Jenny!* she'd written beneath her name.

A chance meeting several years ago while on vacation, and curiously enough, Marnie and I had become friends. Despite being Amish, she was one of my closest confidantes.

Getting out of the car, I drew a deep breath and strolled toward the formal entrance. At the grand double doors, I paused to muster up the required poise, straightened my breezy floral skirt, and pushed back my shoulder-length auburn hair. Ready or not, I reached for the gleaming handle and stepped inside the two-story foyer.

My older sister, Kiersten, greeted me, her brown-eyed gaze lingering with unconcealed disapproval on my high-necked blouse and open-toed sandals. "Happy birthday, sister," she said, waving me into the intimate gathering room near the dining room. "Mom's knocked herself out, as usual." Then, pausing as we passed through the doorway, she added,

"Oh, and I should warn you. Robb brought along a colleague from work. His name is Frank." Her eyes communicated the message *Not my fault!*

So my brother-in-law, Dr. Robb Newburg, was obviously as concerned as Mom about my single state.

I cringed. Now what? How could I possibly reveal my plans?

Attempting to conjure up some enthusiasm, I smiled as Robb rose from his comfortable perch and rushed over to extend his hand. He turned to introduce a good-looking, very tall blond man.

Frank gave me an engaging smile. "It's great to meet you," he said, all charm.

"Thanks for joining us," I replied politely even as my heart sank. I didn't like the idea of postponing my inevitable news. This was supposed to be the night I actually dared to be honest with everyone.

"My sister's something straight out of the nineteenth century," Kiersten declared. "In case you wondered, Frank." She punctuated her remark with foolish laughter.

Ah . . . Kiersten. True to form, interlacing her banter with shards of truth. She glanced coyly at Robb, who smiled back at me, apologizing with his blue-gray eyes.

"Um, what's so special about *this* century?" I asked, glancing over at my brother, Cameron, and his girlfriend, Tracie Wells. "High-tech gadgets aren't everything."

Kiersten simpered as she fingered her diamond earring.

"Does this mean you *still* don't have a cell phone?" asked Cameron, feigning pain when Tracie poked him.

"Life is far less complicated without one," I replied.

My own family. After all these years, they still didn't know what made me tick.

In the corner of the room, our father was hunched over one of his many research books, oblivious to the undercurrents. *All the better. Wouldn't want to spoil things for Mom.* Such parties translated to fun and socializing for her—the more, the better. Dad, however, preferred to immerse himself in his work as a research scientist for a pharmaceutical company, more at home with books than with people.

I went over to say hi. "What're you studying, Dad?"

He glanced up as if just realizing I was there. He blinked at me, a vague look on his face, apparently still deep in thought about his book. So typical of my cerebral father. "Hi, Jenny."

Not "Happy birthday, honey."

Then Mom appeared in the dining room archway, impeccably coifed, pretty eyes smiling. She was ready to serve dinner and motioned gracefully without a word, contentedly leading the way.

The chandeliered space was adorned with silver streamers, and matching candles flickered across the gleaming table. We'd celebrated numerous birthdays here in Mom's favorite room, yet I'd never stopped feeling out of place.

Once we were all seated, I tried to make conversation with my mother, but she was eager to talk about an upcoming gala instead.

The prime rib was wonderful. But with Frank seated next to me at the table, it wasn't easy negotiating our forced meeting. Really, Mom? The uncomfortable pauses between Frank's upbeat comments—and his attempt to ask me out—were the last things I needed at my final dinner party in the modern world.

And sitting there with my family gathered near, I wondered, If I were to disappear, would they even notice?

After dinner, my mother produced a spectacular chocolate layer cake and lit the birthday candles. Kiersten studied me like a lab tech with a specimen while Mom coaxed me to blow out my candles, as if I were still six. "The evening's not perfect without a birthday wish. Make it a good one, Jenny."

Making wishes was the easy part. It was the end result that was iffy. Despite that, I closed my eyes to appease her, knowing all too well my mother's dearest wish—that I'd settle down and marry. The sooner, the better.

I puffed out the candles, but my wish had nothing to do with a man— not that I was opposed to marriage and a family of my own. More times than I could count, I'd imagined what it would be like to live in a simpler era, when people actually listened to one another.

The ideal world . . .

But there would be no announcement tonight. Hours after the superb meal, we parted ways and I drove to my modest condo on the outskirts of Essex. Inside, I hurried to my bedroom and sat on a chair to reread

Marnie's card. Remembering the serene Pennsylvania setting that was her home, I savored the thoughtful birthday greeting, then scanned the sparsely furnished room where I'd hatched my secret plan.

Not even my closest friends had seen my room. Not that they were missing much by their standards. My cherished decorating style was essentially Early Attic.

I breathed out the number of my years, "Twenty-five," and rose to reach for my scuffed antique silver brush on the simple dresser. I pulled it vigorously through my hair, eager to lose myself in something other than my parents' decked-out home or frivolous table chatter. I stared into the antique oval dresser mirror, recalling how Kiersten *always* introduced me: *"My sister's an old soul. . . ."*

Absolutely, I agreed. *I was born too late.*

Turning from the mirror, I strolled to the cozy window seat and opened its top. Inside were scores of clippings from my subscription to a Lancaster newspaper, arranged by categories I'd labeled more than a decade ago. I recalled the first time I'd heard of the Amish. I was only eleven when I was transfixed by a TV documentary.

People actually live and dress that way?

Mom hadn't known how to react back then; my fascination with the simple life perplexed her. *"What can they be thinking—no cars, no electricity, and even some outhouses?"* she'd mused aloud.

Regardless, by the time I was fourteen, I'd devoured everything written about the People, including novels with Amish settings. I yearned to know why the Plain folk continued to live as though they were locked in time. Several years later, my first road trip had led me to Lancaster County, where I had returned each summer thereafter, walking barefoot along the dusty byways and stopping at roadside vegetable and fruit stands, relishing the way the sweet, juicy peaches split right open. What fun it was to make small talk with the more outgoing Amish girls. I met Marnie Lapp at one such stand, and she agreed to exchange letters with me, apparently curious about why an Englisher girl was so taken with all things Plain.

Oh, hers was such a gloriously peaceful world, one firmly grounded in the past. I sincerely desired the stability of Amish tradition and hoped my own personal issues might simply disappear in such an established, dependable community. I'd held that hope within me for years now—I'd even committed it to prayer. *After all, God gives His children the desires of their hearts.*

If only my earthly family—my parents, especially—had taken the time to really try to understand me.

"Bloom where you're planted," Mom had often insisted while I was growing up, but what if you were planted in the wrong soil? What then?

I was very sure I knew the answer. And I was willing to give up everything to follow my dream. Never had I felt so free.

1

REBECCA Lapp felt so numb and stiff she could scarcely move. It was past three o'clock in the morning according to the wind-up clock on the small table near the headboard. Breathless from the harrowing dream, she worried, *Is it a warning?*

Slowly, lest she awaken Samuel, she inched her way up to a sitting position, her eyes wide against the darkened room. But her heart was a lump of lead. She pondered her dream in a stupor, wishing she could release the misery.

Minutes ticked by, and at last she inched out of bed, creeping to the dresser a few feet away. She probed the area with her fingers in search of the box of matches. Clumsily, she managed to light the small kerosene lantern. The wing of flame faltered, then blazed brightly.

Just a silly dream, she assured herself. *Everything's fine—I haven't been found out.* Besides, most dreams had no particular meaning; she knew that.

Samuel's snoring was familiar and steady, even comforting, as Rebecca reached for her warm bathrobe on the wooden wall peg and wandered down the hall to Katie's former bedroom. She stepped inside and perused the vacant room by lantern light. Breathing deeply, she felt sure there was still a hint of Katie's lilac-scented potpourri. Mrs. Daniel Fisher had been blissfully married now for six years and kept busy with four-year-old Samuel Dan, known mostly as Sammy, and his baby sister, Kate Marie, eighteen months old next week. Other than her blond hair—so like her *Dat*'s—little Kate was the spitting image of her pretty *Mamma,* though

Kate Marie wasn't the most Amish-sounding name Katie might have chosen.

Close enough, Rebecca mused.

She still could not shake the notion that the dream might be prophetic. Samuel and their sons—Elam, Eli, and Benjamin—would surely think so. After all, she *was* pushing the boundaries of the *Bann*, going over to see shunned Katie and the children now and then these past few months. *If I'm caught, I'll be accused of hindering the effect of* die Meinding, Rebecca thought. She didn't want to stand in the way of God's work in her wayward daughter's life, yet Katie's was the harshest shunning in all of Lancaster County. Rebecca was terribly conflicted—wanting to obey the church ordinance while also heeding her heart's cry to see Katie and the grandbabies.

She set the lantern on the end table and tiptoed to the neatly made bed and knelt there. Goodness' sake, there was plenty to pray about, considering that her niece, twenty-one-year-old Marnie Lapp, had dropped by unexpectedly last week, all rosy cheeked and talking up a storm, *babblich* as ever. It seemed she had befriended an out-of-state *Englischer*—a young woman named Jenny Burns—and written her letters for several years. Oddly, the outsider had sold off near everything she owned somewhere in Connecticut—even her car. To top things off, she was coming to live in Lancaster County as an Amish seeker and needed a place to stay for a while, till the bishop acknowledged her as a convert. *"I was wondering if she might rent one of your empty bedrooms,"* Marnie had suggested, her blue eyes ever so hopeful.

Another one of Marnie's rather ferhoodled *ideas . . .*

Marnie had clasped her hands as she stood fidgeting in the utility room just beyond the kitchen, a fallen gold leaf stuck to her black woolen shawl like a curious posy. From the look on her niece's face, there was not a doubt in Rebecca's mind that Marnie was thrilled about the prospect, outsider though Jenny Burns was.

Rebecca had never known any of the People to open their homes for the purpose of giving a stranger time to learn the Old Ways and *Deitsch*, too—certainly not with the hope of joining church. When she'd mentioned the idea to her husband after Marnie left, Samuel was not keen on the idea, though in the end he'd taken up the matter with Bishop John Beiler.

Presently, she bowed her head and pressed her hands together. Rebecca hardly knew what to pray. "Almighty God, grant divine guidance and grace in this peculiar matter," she whispered. "And help us know how to proceed. We want to do the right and wise thing, to glorify thy name."

⸱⸱⸱ ➤ ➤ ⸱⸱⸱

The day following her birthday, Jenny had given her two weeks' notice at Always Antiques, where she'd worked as an appraiser since college graduation. While neither her job nor her home state of Connecticut had any real hold on her, she would miss her friends, especially Pamela and Dorie Kennedy, two sisters she'd known since childhood. It was a significant blessing that her condo lease was finally up. She would also miss Woodbury—the antiques capital of Connecticut, about forty minutes away—and beautiful Essex. Her parents' estate was located a mere block from the Connecticut River. *Rushing . . . like time's own swift current*, she thought while making a list of things to pack.

Her soul was starving for a sensible, more solicitous life. Since her first visit to Lancaster County years ago, Jenny had decided to make it her home, but she hadn't seen her way clear until now. Thanks to Marnie's working behind the scenes, finding her a place to live, she was finally able to move ahead. The Amish life offered what Jenny longed for: more time to savor each moment, slow the torrent of time, and grow as a child of God. She was ready to embrace a unique people, one set apart.

Perhaps one day her own family would come to accept this near-constant yearning in her bones. Up until now, they'd barely endured her obsession with the past, frowning at her frustration with ever-changing modern society.

But now Jenny was sure she had the ultimate answer. "Hickory Hollow," she breathed.

In the diffused autumn light, she caught herself staring at the old pine desk in the corner of her bedroom, where she'd stored a beloved album from the past. The memory of creating it tugged at her, as did the thought of leaving it behind. But her heartache of that time had since mended—the split had come more than two years ago. She had moved forward, glad to have more than survived the demise of her first love.

I'd do everything differently, given the chance, she vowed.

She went to the desk and removed the cherished scrapbook. Taking her time, she memorized each page of the romance represented there. Every picture, every memento—the movie stubs, photos of flea market events, and visits to the Mystic Aquarium . . . the bits and pieces of two remarkable years.

She headed to the living room and built a blistering fire in the quaint fireplace. Without another thought, she tossed the album into the flames. "Good-bye, Kyle Jackson," she whispered. "Good-bye forever."

Jenny could hear the beating of her own heart. That small, fragile sound made her wish for peaceful Lancaster County more than ever. *Heaven on earth*, she thought, counting the days until she could finally move.

She watched the moon rise and settle into the trees beyond her living room window while the familiar question persisted: *Can I really do this?*

Suddenly, Jenny remembered what Marnie Lapp had penned in a recent letter: *My dear friend, there's only one way to find out!*

2

THAT'S right, Hickory Hollow," Jenny Burns repeated for the cab driver outside the Lancaster train station. The short, balding cabbie looked completely baffled, so she opened her purse and located the house address on Hickory Lane.

Tired from the long trip, Jenny recalled the cell phone joke her brother had made two weeks ago at her birthday party. Surely the cab driver had a smartphone, or at the very least, a GPS. He shuffled to the trunk of the cab and opened it, then *thwomp*ed her large suitcase inside. He glanced at her as if to say, *"Whatcha got in there, Missy? An elephant?"* Then he closed the trunk and waved her toward the backseat. "I'm sure if it's in the area, we'll find it."

Carrying her purse and smaller bag, Jenny slipped inside the cab. She could have happily described the golden vale of a place—the fertile, sheltered hollow bounded on the north by the Old Philadelphia Pike and on the south by the Lincoln Highway.

Jenny buckled up and realized she'd only visited here in summertime. Presently, the air was swollen with the scent of sun-drenched autumn and, unmistakably, manure. "It must be harvesttime," she murmured.

"Excuse me?" the cabbie said.

"Uh, nothing."

"Ah, here we are." The cabbie pointed to the small screen on his dash. "You were right. That's Hickory Lane, over there to the east."

Soon they were off, heading toward Bird-in-Hand. Along the way, they encountered a number of gray horse-drawn, boxlike buggies, with two carrying young children who peered out the back. One young girl squinted at them, her eyes smiling when the cab passed the carriage on the left. The little girl's white cap was tilted askew on her head.

"Welcome to Amishland," the cabbie grumbled. He shook his head with something close to disgust. "I don't get it, and I never will."

"I think theirs is a noble way of life," Jenny said, surprised by his attitude and feeling defensive.

"Are you kidding? Can you imagine living Amish? I mean, seriously."

"It works for them," she replied. "Has for more than three hundred years."

He muttered something. Then he said more audibly, "I know an Amish fellow who got fed up with the church and left." He looked at her in the rearview mirror. "Know why?"

Miffed, she merely shook her head.

Mr. Cabbie tapped his forehead. "Told me he wasn't permitted to think for himself."

Some fit in and some don't, she thought.

"He wanted a high school education—a no-no for Amish. When he left, he got his GED and went on to college. Wanted to be a lawyer, I guess. An odd career for an Amishman."

"Well, this country could use some *honest* attorneys." She smiled at herself.

"Last I heard, he had a nice big house over near Eden—opposite direction from where we're headed." The cabbie nodded his head. "This fellow just wasn't cut out to be Plain." He glanced at her in the rearview mirror. "Know much about the Amish?" he asked.

"I've met a few Plain women . . . bought tomatoes and cukes at their roadside stands."

The highway narrowed as they headed through Smoketown, then entered Bird-in-Hand proper, past the Old Village Store on the left and the farmers market on the right.

"All I know is that they make my job harder, clogging up the roads," he said. "Why they don't just get cars, I'll never understand."

"How much farther?" Jenny was ready to end the stream of criticism.

"Not too far. By the looks of it, Hickory Hollow's east of Intercourse Village."

She made herself relax. Thankfully, the cabbie was less keen on chattering now. Jenny enjoyed the sun's warmth as she watched the landscape whiz past, thinking ahead to riding in a horse-drawn carriage with Marnie. She was captivated by the eight-mule teams and the Amishmen working the fields, sporting straw hats, their suspenders crisscrossed against dark blue, green, or gray shirts.

Like in the books I've read . . .

From what Marnie Lapp had said, her aunt Rebecca was the ideal person to mentor Jenny, at least until she found her own place. *"You'll like her,"* Marnie had predicted in the last letter. *"For sure and for certain."*

Jenny's own resolve still surprised her, particularly the sale of her car a few days ago, after having already sold most of her household possessions and dispensable personal effects at area consignment stores following her birthday. She only regretted not being more specific with her parents, especially her mother, although as it turned out, her mother seemed as distracted as her father, most likely finalizing her latest gala. Mom had looked up from her list, her mind seemingly miles away. *"Where are you going again?"*

Jenny had hesitated. *"I'll get in touch once I'm there."*

Mom's frown was inscribed on Jenny's memory; she could see the confused expression even now. *"Well . . . whatever you think is best, dear."* She paused, fixing Jenny with a look of concern. *"Is everything okay?"*

Jenny opened her mouth, wondering if she shouldn't just come clean, but before she could answer, her mother suddenly remembered something and reached for her cell phone, raising her finger. *"Hold that thought."*

It occurred to her not for the first time that it might be weeks before her mother even realized she was gone.

Kiersten had been indifferent, more concerned with Jenny's supposed snub of Frank, her husband's *"really wonderful associate"*—she'd seemed more anxious than usual to get off the phone. And Cameron had just assumed Jenny was taking an extended vacation. *"Must be nice . . ."*

And while she'd tried to tell him it wasn't that at all, Jenny believed in her heart that saying anything more would be a mistake. They would just try to talk her out of moving to Amish farmland, abandoning the materialistic English world. *Their beautiful world.*

When the cab made the right turn onto Cattail Road, Jenny's skin prickled, and she wondered how close the Lapp farmhouse might be. She saw what looked like a waterwheel near a creek. For an instant, she wished for her camera, but she'd sold that, too.

Leaning back again, she remembered working on a little lap quilt as a young teen while her sister played video games with their brother and neighborhood friends. *I was passionate about simple things while everyone else was into high tech.*

She thought of various fancy things she could have brought along—makeup, for one. And toiletries. But those weren't for a dedicated Amishwoman, as she intended to be. She'd walked out on her lipstick, her jewelry, most of her clothes, even her books.

It's time to live. Forget the stuff.

Just that quick, it occurred to her that Marnie might have forgotten to set things in place. Her emotions imploded. Surely not! Arranging things with the Lapps was vital—there was no backup plan. Oh, why was she thinking this way? If she couldn't trust Marnie to follow through, whom could she trust? *And given Marnie's excitement . . .*

Despite that, corresponding by letter about the arrangement now seemed terribly risky. Why hadn't Jenny gotten confirmation before she jumped?

Her heart pounded as she considered again the major changes ahead—changes that she was willing to make. *For the rest of my life . . . if the People will have me.*

She forced her gaze toward the heavens. *Lord, if you've put this desire in my heart, then here I am.*

Besides Jenny's strong feeling about all this, Marnie had nearly promised that her aunt Rebecca was the key to Jenny's pursuit. The Amish life lived under the watchful care of Samuel and Rebecca Lapp would lead Jenny aright, solve her lifelong desire. In every way, she was coming home.

3

REBECCA Lapp lingered in Ella Mae Zook's snug kitchen longer than usual early that afternoon. During the past few days, she'd observed a perceptible change in her elderly friend, and Rebecca hadn't been the only one to notice. Indeed, Ella Mae still held her slight shoulders straight and smiled most readily, so there wasn't anything physical that Rebecca could credit this feeling to. But there *was* something.

Standing near the back door, Rebecca knew she should head across the field in case her niece's English friend arrived early. "I'd be happy to bring supper over later," Rebecca offered, resting both hands on the back of the wooden kitchen chair. "You just say the word."

Ella Mae smiled. Her middle part appeared wider and her hair whiter in the streaming light from the window. "*Ach*, ya musn't baby me, hear? Ain't nothin' wrong that some hot peppermint tea can't cure."

"You sure, now?"

"Go on, Rebecca dear. Time to greet the young seeker-woman. She'll need all the encouragement you can give her." Ella Mae pressed her crinkled hand to her high forehead. "What's her name again?"

"Jennifer Burns, but I'm told she goes by Jenny."

"A nice enough name." Ella Mae looked out the window, her cane hooked on her scrawny arm.

"Well, the name's not the point," Rebecca added good-naturedly. "What matters is what she's made of."

"Mm-hmm," Ella Mae agreed. "Ain't many fancy folk who fit in with us, ya know."

Ella Mae had always been one to cling to her own strong opinions, even when most folk would have stood down—Samuel had once said as much years ago, when Ella Mae was causing a stink with the deacon at the time. But Ella Mae had never suppressed her view on things when it came to speaking up for what was right. At least what was right and good in *her* eyes, which meant she didn't always line up with the *Ordnung* or the bishop, either. Yet the usually stern Bishop Beiler let her be—she was too old to be put off church.

Rebecca looked away and spotted a drawing of a carved pumpkin on the refrigerator, doubtless the work of one of Ella Mae's many great-great-grandchildren. The pumpkin's smile had one tooth showing on top and two on the bottom, all staggered perfectly. She was a bit surprised Ella Mae kept it up, knowing how the older woman felt about anything to do with Halloween.

"It's not what ya think," Ella Mae said, breaking the quiet.

Rebecca blinked. "The jack-o'-lantern?" She returned her gaze to the fragile woman sitting at the table.

"Ach, no, for pity's sake."

"What, then?"

"The reason I'm so tetchy." Ella Mae pointed to the chair across from her, and Rebecca pulled it out and sat down. "I hate to say anything, but when I heard what Marnie was up to, getting you and Samuel involved, well . . ."

"Marnie talked to you?"

"Twice already."

"Ah . . . you must be worried 'bout us opening our home to a stranger."

Ella Mae fixed her eyes on Rebecca. "That ain't the half of it."

Things always went more smoothly when Ella Mae's side of the conversation was permitted to trickle out without interruption. So Rebecca waited, quite aware of her friend's crumpled brow. Deep concern was embedded there.

"Think of it, Rebecca. The woman's a worldly outsider. Have ya thought of getting some instruction on this from the ministers? A seeker sure ain't something we hear of every day."

"Samuel and Bishop John put their heads together a couple days ago, so that's taken care of, I daresay."

Ella Mae stared at her fingers. "I'm surprised that Samuel agreed."

Rebecca cleared her throat.

"*Did* he, Rebecca?"

"Not at first, *nee*."

"And now?"

"He's warming up to it; that's all I best say."

"Well, then, 'tis better . . . I s'pose."

"We'll just have to rest in that."

Ella Mae nodded slowly, her frown still evident. "I think ya could be askin' for trouble."

"Are you wondering 'bout her Proving? All the time it might take?"

"For certain." Ella Mae paused, shifting her weight in the chair. "And she's unmarried, ain't?"

"Far as I know." Rebecca looked right at her. "So then, you must think she's comin' here out of curiosity."

"Maybe. Or could be she wants to find herself a Plain husband."

Rebecca sighed. "Well, yes, I'd assume so if she wants to be Amish herself. But I really don't think marriage is her first priority."

"Well, aren't most seekers *married* couples with young children searching for a different lifestyle, lookin' to be set apart from the modern world?" Ella Mae leaned hard on the table, her face suddenly all washed out.

Rebecca nodded, mindful of her friend's serious expression. "*Jah.* Sometimes they're a-hankerin' for a church that meets their standards. Or they want their children to experience working the soil, raising their own crops—like the Englischer pioneers did, ya know." Rebecca smoothed out the placemat. "And some single men come seeking, too . . . wantin' wives to cook and keep house. Something, I guess, that's not very common anymore in the English world."

"But a single woman arranging to come here on her own? It's mighty suspect, I'll say," Ella Mae said. "I wonder what her family thinks of it."

"Well, just maybe her motives are untainted. After all, Marnie would surely know, since they've been exchanging letters for a number of years."

Ella Mae gave an odd little half smile and shook her head. "You'll be the first to know where her heart is, Rebecca. Just think on that."

Rebecca felt the weight of it. "You want me to watch for certain signs, is that it?"

"All I'm sayin' is keep your eyes and ears open." Ella Mae reached across to tap Rebecca's hand with her own. "The Good Lord may indeed have entrusted this seeker to you and Samuel. That's where it all starts—in the soul of a person."

"I can only guide her as far as she is teachable . . . or pliable."

"And I can tell ya one thing: She won't be as tenderhearted toward the church as our own young ones, growin' up in the ways of the Lord God." Ella Mae paused, her small blue eyes seeking out Rebecca's. "Any idea 'bout this Jenny's upbringing?"

"Only what Marnie says. Evidently she was taken to church as a child by her aunt and uncle for a few years, but her parents stepped in and decided she'd had enough religion."

"Might be, then, that she'll have a lot of catchin' up to do."

"I'd guess she will, although Marnie indicated she'd found a small church she enjoyed attending on her own after leavin' home."

"Regardless of how it turns out, you've got your work cut out for ya, Rebecca. I wouldn't want to be in your shoes. I 'spect she'll last a month, maybe two."

The Wise Woman was probably right. It wouldn't do to get too fond of the young woman, the way Marnie had.

Ella Mae insisted on serving more peppermint tea with raw honey before Rebecca was free to go. And all the while, Rebecca mulled the Old Wise Woman's words. Had God truly handpicked her and Samuel to look after young Jenny Burns's heart?

Rebecca inhaled and raised her shoulders, not sure she was up to such a task. That was a parent's calling, as she knew quite well. And she'd failed dreadfully with Katie, her only daughter.

Why'd the Good Lord choose me?

"Looks like it's one of the next big farmhouses on this side of the road," the cabbie announced, looking over his shoulder at Jenny. "Wait a minute. You're not coming here to *stay* with the Amish, are you?"

"As a matter of fact, I am."

He scratched the side of his head. "Well, I'll be!"

She inhaled slowly. "I plan to join the church if they'll have me."

He spun around to crane his neck at her. "You *cannot* be serious."

"Actually, I am."

He looked back to the road and reached up to rub the round circle of pink flesh on top of his head. "But why?"

She felt no obligation to share her reasons. "I just am."

"Well, you're in for some mighty hard labor. From sunup to sundown is what I heard."

She looked out the window. *I'm not afraid of hard work.*

Just then, they turned into Samuel Lapp's lane. She spotted the name on the large mailbox out front.

"Welcome to your new life."

"Thanks," she said, opening her purse to pay him.

He took the money and counted it carefully. "I wish you the best— you're going to need it."

She disregarded his comment and gave him a smile. "Have a pleasant afternoon."

He nodded quickly and got out to open the trunk and set the oversized suitcase on the ground. He pulled out a card from his trousers and pointed to the phone number. "In case things don't work out, here's your ticket out of Plainville . . . back to the real world. Of course, there aren't any phones, so you'll have to find a neighbor to—"

"Thanks again," Jenny interrupted, relieved to have arrived at the Lapps'. She waved away his business card. *Why would I possibly need it?*

4

REBECCA observed the Englischer's hefty suitcase as the slender young woman pulled it behind her, coming up the lane toward the house. She looked like she was planning to stay a good long time, just as Marnie had said. The seeker's abundantly thick hair was a lovely auburn hue, similar to Katie's—radiant as the sun's golden beams caught it.

Dear Gott *in heaven* . . . It took her breath away.

Rebecca remembered walking up this long driveway to the house as a young bride. Now it was as if a part of her were walking it again. *Ever so starry-eyed . . . like this dear girl*, she thought.

Rebecca hurried around the side of the house toward the attractive young woman even as Ella Mae's earlier call for prudence crossed her mind.

"*Willkumm*," Rebecca called, finding her voice. "You must be Jenny Burns."

"Yes, and you're Rebecca Lapp, aren't you?" The girl's sweet face lit up, and she let go of the suitcase and stuck out her hand to shake Rebecca's.

"I surely am," Rebecca said, then looked up the road. "I 'spect Marnie will stop by any minute."

"Oh, I hope so." Jenny's light brown eyes shone as she took in the adjacent countryside. With a great sigh, she said, "It's perfectly gorgeous here, Rebecca."

"Samuel and I think so. The Lord's beauty everywhere ya look, ain't?"

Jenny nodded enthusiastically.

Rebecca asked, "Can I help you with one of your bags?"

"Thanks, but I packed as light as possible, knowing I'll be sewing some Amish clothes." The girl frowned at her own large suitcase. "It really doesn't look like it, though."

Smiling, Rebecca said, "That's quite all right. You'll have plenty of room upstairs for all your things."

"I can't express my gratitude to you enough, Rebecca—and to your husband. I am truly thankful."

Jenny Burns looked as modest, even as Plain, as many of the Mennonite ladies Rebecca encountered at the Bird-in-Hand Farmers Market. She didn't ask but assumed Jenny meant she wanted to start dressing Amish right away. "Well, *kumme mit*, and I'll show you where you're goin' to stay."

Jenny beamed as she said, "You'll have to overlook my enthusiasm. I've been living for this day for a long time."

Never before had Rebecca encountered anyone so thoroughly taken with the notion of Amish life. Already she liked Jenny very much. She just hoped the young woman wouldn't be disappointed. Had she set the People up on a pedestal, like so many Englischers did? And, as pretty as Jenny was, why on earth wasn't she already hitched up? Guessing such information might be forthcoming, she led Jenny into their hundred-and-fifty-year-old farmhouse, built by Samuel's forebear Joseph Lapp and his stonemason friend.

It'd be right nice, Rebecca decided, if she had a manual to follow. She wondered, for instance, how long she was expected to converse in English with Jenny. And was it her place to start teaching Deitsch? After all, if Jenny was serious about becoming a convert, she'd have to learn the language.

For now, though, Rebecca simply led the way upstairs to the room Katie had occupied for twenty years, prior to leaving Hickory Hollow. Her heart sank to her toes as she remembered those happy, happy days, raising her darling girl there on the farm.

Ach, she thought. Why hadn't she considered this situation more carefully, consenting to having a stranger stay in this very special room? All of a sudden, she felt downright disloyal to her adopted daughter.

What have I done?

Jenny tiptoed as if walking on holy ground. How could she not stare as she passed through the surprisingly modern-looking kitchen, into the large sitting room, toward the steep stairway? She assumed the appliances were gas powered, yet they looked like something one might buy at a regular kitchen store. *Interesting!*

The hallway walls were the delicate gray color she'd expected—not drab at all in person—and the wide-plank floorboards had a quaint hammered look, possibly original to the old farmhouse. Jenny shivered with pleasure. She was here, settling into an Old Order Amish house and making it her home for the foreseeable future.

Inside the airy bedroom, she admired the rich wood molding on the doorjamb and took note of the dark green shades neatly rolled up on both windows. The hand-stitched navy, green, maroon, and yellow bed quilt was definitely the Double Nine Patch pattern—she recognized it thanks to a similar quilt that once hung in the antique shop back in Essex, where she'd lovingly eyed it for weeks until it was sold.

There was something tangibly beautiful in the atmosphere. Was it just her? Or was there truly something special about finally being here? She could not keep from smiling.

Jenny could hardly wait to join the ranks of Amishwomen. She envisioned the many canning bees and quilting frolics. The cordial gossip and close friendships to come. She felt her burdens lifting and sighed gratefully.

All is well, at last!

⋯ ➤ ⬿ ⋯

Marnie Lapp assumed it was best in every respect to give Jenny time to settle in with Aunt Rebecca. But it was all she could manage, making herself stay put at home with *Mamm* with her friend so near.

"I do hope someone's alerted Bishop John 'bout all this," Marnie's mother said while they crimped peanut butter cookies with forks. Mamm's tone suggested she was skeptical. "Don't ya think it's unusual, really? I mean, just think of it."

Marnie repeated what Aunt Rebecca had said about Bishop John and Uncle Samuel talking things over recently. "Why not trust the Lord God and the ministerial brethren, too?"

"So then, Bishop John's all right with this?"

"From what I've heard. He says it's up to Jenny Burns to live Amish and learn our ways for the time being. When she finishes her Proving time, we'll know better where things stand."

"Well, someone's got a lot to teach her—how to dress, how to speak our language, and the rules of the Ordnung. Why, she probably doesn't even know how to hitch a horse to a carriage!" Mamm's blue eyes widened. "Has anyone even considered that?"

Marnie nodded.

"So are you thinkin' of teaching her, then, Marnie?"

"Me?" She laughed, knowing full well she was not the best choice, at least for the hitching up. Not with her own clumsiness when it came to horses, buggies, and other moving things. "Maybe Uncle Samuel can help out—with the hitchin', anyways."

"Well, I'd be careful 'bout assuming that." Her mother looked too pink in the face. "Your uncle is awful busy running his big dairy farm."

"Maybe Cousin Andrew's a better choice, then."

"Oh, ya want *Andrew* to show her, do ya?" Mamm's eyes narrowed to slits. "*Puh*, he's got enough to worry 'bout, much less a wannabe convert—a single one at that! An Englischer's the *last* thing he needs."

"I'm not sayin' anything 'bout courtin', Mamm."

Marnie sighed. She certainly couldn't argue the point. And she *had* been straight with Jenny that finding a husband, if she was so inclined, would be very difficult considering just about everything. After all, most young Amishwomen were married in their early twenties, if not earlier. Jenny was already past the normal marrying age, and it would be some time before she could be baptized. Marnie wondered how Jenny Burns would be accepted by any of the older single fellows, as well as by Marnie's own family. *Especially Dat.*

Marnie's father was particularly apprehensive where the English were concerned. He disliked having much to do with them, even though more and more Amish were interacting with the world nowadays, working alongside them out of necessity, due to dwindling farmland.

"Have you told Dat 'bout Jenny's comin'?" Marnie ventured.

"Just yesterday," Mamm said, wiping her hands on her work apron. "Waited till the last minute, I guess."

Marnie understood. "Maybe Jenny will change Dat's mind about fancy folk."

Mamm waved her hand. "Not likely."

"You don't know her like I do. She's serious 'bout all this," Marnie said. "Jenny even discussed with me how she oughta dress today, when she first arrived."

"Did she, now?"

"She wanted to start off on the right foot. She even sold her car."

Her mother's head turned quickly. "Well, it sounds like she's mighty sure of herself."

"Oh, she is, believe me. This is everything she wants."

Mamm went to the oven, opened it, and removed a pumpkin pie.

"Smells awful *gut*."

"You always say that, Marnie." Mamm smiled. "Never fails."

"What could be better than pumpkin goodies in autumn?" Marnie loved October more than all the other eleven months wrapped up together. She'd felt that way since she was a wee girl, watching the trees, anxious to see the green turn to red, orange, and gold. So she marked this wonderful-good fall day and excused herself to head down Hickory Lane. "I'm itchin' to see my English-turned-Amish friend."

"I assumed so," Mamm replied, a glint of curiosity in her eyes. "But you'll return to help with supper, ain't?"

Marnie promised to.

"And just in case you get any ideas 'bout bringing her back here today, I think Rebecca's the best one to help Jenny get situated. All right?"

"I want to check on her, is all."

"Like I said, Rebecca can acclimate her just fine."

Goodness, but her mother sounded adamant. Marnie almost wished she'd told her mother more about the letters she and Jenny had written over the years. But, no, it was all right to have a few secrets.

"I won't be gone long," she told Mamm and went out the back door.

Jenny must be having the time of her life, thought Marnie, wondering if it was smart to pave the way too smoothly for a seeker. Any seeker, really. Jenny's struggle to adjust to the Plain life and insight would ultimately make her *niedrich*—humble—and stronger spiritually. *She'll have to look to God each and every day*, Marnie mused, hastening her step. *Just as we all do.*

5

WHILE unpacking, Jenny added several more things to her mental checklist. High on the list was asking Rebecca about the requirements for the Proving. That, and what things would be asked of Jenny at her baptism, some time from now. The day could not come soon enough.

Jenny went to the oak dresser and slid open a drawer. There was plenty of space for her undergarments there, as well as room beneath the wooden wall pegs for her plain black shoes. And her sneakers, which were appropriate for daily wear, since she knew that Marnie wore them, too. While Jenny hadn't brought along any makeup, she couldn't resist packing some light perfume, which she presently placed on a small tray on the dresser.

Enjoying this time to herself after the hectic day of travel, she opened her daily journal and turned to a fresh new page.

From this day forward, I, Jennifer Burns, will faithfully attempt to mimic Rebecca Lapp and the other Amishwomen here in Hickory Hollow for my Proving. My clothes, hair, and manner must reflect Gelassenheit—a compliant and submissive spirit. In short, I will give up my own wants and desires and yield to the ways of the People. And to God.

I promise to abandon the English world and its modern conveniences, including driving a car, using electricity, and anything related to the

World Wide Web, among other things. All in favor of the Anabaptist life and the Old Ways.

With the help of my heavenly Father, I write this with a reverent heart.

—*Jennifer Burns*

Jenny reviewed the entry. It was rather formal, much like her own mother. Even the navy blue journal, hardback and with thick, high-quality pages, seemed to lend an air of sophistication not in keeping with simplicity.

She sighed, realizing the challenges that lay ahead, especially when it came to romance and the prospect of marriage. Marnie had made it clear that finding an Amish husband would prove difficult, if not impossible. Unless Jenny was willing to marry one of the widowers with children, most eligible men were already taken.

To think I'm nearly an old maid!

But Jenny could readily admit, if only to herself, that she hoped to be the exception to the rule. If not, and she was to live a Plain and single life till the end of her days, then so be it. Becoming an Amish convert had never been about finding a husband, but she certainly *desired* to share her life with someone. And she sincerely believed that with God, all things were possible.

Jenny admired matronly Rebecca in her blue dress and full black cape apron as they sat happily in the adorable little sewing room on the upper floor. The afternoon light sifted in through the west-facing windows, making the room even more pleasant. Their conversation about homemade dress patterns might have been anything but fascinating to someone outside Hickory Hollow, but for Jenny, this was what she'd dreamed of doing here—and so much more.

Creating her own pattern was something she hadn't really considered, although she fully intended to make her own clothes. She'd taken quite a few sewing classes and believed she was up to the task. *Using a treadle sewing machine will be interesting!*

Rebecca raised her own well-worn pattern for Jenny to inspect. It was obviously much too large for Jenny's slender figure. *The only thing missing in this sweet, homey moment is a cup of espresso,* Jenny thought as the afternoon slump began to set in. Her day, after all, had started very early when she'd caught a cab to Old Saybrook, where she had boarded the train at a little past eight o'clock. Then, close to noon, she'd transferred to the Philadelphia train and traveled on to Lancaster, arriving in just five hours total. Without a car, it was the most direct route.

After they'd discussed dress patterns and appropriate colors, Jenny asked, "What requirements must I meet to be baptized, after the Proving time?"

"Well, Samuel met with our bishop 'bout this. He says there are a number of expectations—and spiritual qualities—to fulfill."

Jenny was anxious to know.

"The church ordinance, what we call our Ordnung, must be followed at all times," explained Rebecca. "These are the unwritten rules determined by the membership and the bishop himself. That includes everything from how we dress and work to the order of the Preachin' service every other Sunday."

Jenny was familiar with this from her previous study. "What else?"

"You must learn to speak Deitsch, our German dialect; hitch up a driving horse to a carriage and be able to handle the horse well on the road; and attend work frolics and canning bees—in other words, fit in with our womenfolk. And like all of us, you must live in a way that exemplifies the teachings of our Lord Jesus Christ in the Sermon on the Mount."

Jenny listened carefully.

"You prob'ly know there's no jewelry, including rings and fancy wrist-watches, although some wear plainer-looking watches."

The list was growing as Rebecca continued. Flying in planes was prohibited, as was joining secular organizations, filing a lawsuit, riding in a car on Sunday, and worldly pleasures such as TV, radios, and going to movies. Yet none of this was a surprise to Jenny.

"In all you do, keep yourself separated from the world and adhere to the collective wisdom of the People . . . and the Lord God," Rebecca said. "We teach our little ones to bend their will—give it up in complete submission."

Gelassenheit, Jenny thought, remembering what she'd written in her journal soon after arriving. She'd read about this, but hearing it directly from one who lived by that principle brought it home loud and clear.

Can I lay down all of my own wants and wishes for the sake of the People? she wondered.

"You'll be under the covering of Samuel and me," Rebecca added. "At least for the time of your Proving."

"Like a daughter?"

Rebecca's face flushed. "Well, not exactly, but looked after, for sure. Bishop John believes his wife, Mary, will be a *gut* mentor for you, as well." Rebecca paused. "She's in need of a mother's helper every so often, so as I understand it, you'll be over there occasionally. Marnie said you're trustworthy, so that's why you got the job."

"I'll do whatever the bishop thinks is best." Jenny recalled what Marnie had shared by letter about the Hickory Hollow bishop. The man was younger than most bishops, but John Beiler was apparently as strict as any bishop in the region. *If you look guilty, you are guilty*, Marnie had written. Jenny thought it was a strange stance on things, and sincerely hoped she would meet with his approval.

"Your Proving can be as short as six months and as long as two years. It'll depend on how quickly you consistently demonstrate the attitudes and skills I mentioned," Rebecca said.

Then, as if a light had gone off in her brain, Rebecca leaped from her chair. "Ach, how could I have forgotten? Our Katie's dresses and aprons might just fit ya, Jenny. *Kumme mit!*" She waved her into the hallway and toward the master bedroom.

Following closely, Jenny was perplexed. Why would Rebecca offer her daughter's clothes? Had Katie outgrown them? But Jenny was sure Marnie hadn't mentioned any children still living at home.

Not wanting to be meddlesome, Jenny was quiet as she waited in Rebecca's spacious room, where the older woman leaned down to open the large cedar chest at the foot of the bed.

"Ah, just lookee here." Rebecca pulled out a royal blue dress, holding it up momentarily before setting it aside almost reverently, draping it over the polished footboard. Then another long dress appeared, this one a deep green, and soon another—a fairly dull gray, and finally, a plum-colored dress. Had this Katie passed away, by chance? Why else were the dresses tucked away so lovingly in the beautiful chest?

"Why don't ya try these on?" Rebecca said. "It'll save ya from sewin' up some right quick."

"Are you sure?" Jenny was stunned yet pleased. Then again, she wasn't all that certain, second-guessing how she should react. Could she actually bring herself to wear a deceased woman's clothing? A strange lump nearly choked her as she struggled with the thought.

Rebecca handed her the dresses. "They'll need pressing, of course. You won't want to be seen in them publicly till ya do."

"Thank you, Rebecca." She looked at the dresses, limp on her arm. *I guess . . .*

"They're yours to wear, if they fit."

After trying on the blue dress, she returned to Rebecca's bedroom, still feeling a little queasy. She was very anxious to know about the former owner of these dresses but didn't want to offend her helpful hostess. Rebecca began to show her how to position and pin twenty-seven straight pins—no more, no less—to attach the top half of the apron to the waistline of the bottom half.

"Have you ever stuck yourself?" she asked, unable to erase the thought of Rebecca's daughter.

"Oh, rarely." Rebecca smiled. "And once you pin on your apron dozens of times, you prob'ly won't, either."

When they finished, Rebecca removed all the pins and had Jenny try to replicate what she'd done, handing her the pins in a plastic box. But it wasn't as easy as it looked.

Rebecca grinned when Jenny asked if there was a tall mirror around. "Just some hand mirrors," she told her with a tilt of her head, hazel eyes sparkling with mischief. "But if ya must see yourself fully, you could go out to the springhouse pond and see what ya look like Amish."

Jenny blushed and hoped she didn't sound vain. "Oh, that's all right."

"Next, would it be too pushy to talk about your bangs?" Rebecca asked kindly.

Jenny blew her bangs off her forehead. "You've probably never had such a dilemma, right?" There were no bangs on Amishwomen in the pictures or movies she'd seen, nor on the cable channel reality shows.

"Jah, that's so," Rebecca answered. "We train our wee girls' hair to part from early on—without bangs, of course. Then as it grows, it's twisted off to the side and into the hair bun." She went on to explain that the more conservative Amishwomen wore their hair bun low on their neck. "And the more progressive put them up a bit higher." Here, Rebecca's eyes twinkled a smile. "We don't have much to do with them, though."

Jenny knew from Marnie that the Hickory Hollow Amish were stricter than some conservative groups—it was interesting to realize how that affected even the smallest things. Yet she was eager to do up her own hair like Rebecca's. She doubted this aspect of her venture into Plain life would be difficult or even sacrificial, since she'd always loved wearing long homemade skirts and modest blouses. But her wispy bangs were definitely a problem.

"I s'pose we can wet them down till they grow out," Rebecca suggested, dimples in her plump cheeks.

"Or plaster them with hairspray." Jenny laughed.

At the mention of hairspray, Rebecca let out a chortle. "I really doubt there's any round here."

"Oh, sorry. Of course not." She felt silly. "Guess I forgot myself for a moment."

"You could try pinning them down, I s'pose."

"Are you permitted to wear bobby pins?"

"For our hair, sure. But we use straight pins to secure our *Kapps*."

"The prayer bonnets?"

"We don't call them that," Rebecca said gently. "They're actually prayer veilings, but we just refer to them as a cap." She paused. "Once you're baptized, you'll begin wearing yours."

Jenny nodded, glad she knew a few things.

"Would ya like to have a tour of the farm, then?" asked Rebecca.

"I'd love to! It's my first time visiting an Amish farm." Jenny wanted to go exploring immediately, eager to take it all in—the hen house, the large two-story barn, and the most appealing stone springhouse, not far from the Lapps' big house.

Yet where was Marnie—wasn't she coming?

I'll ask her about the clothes I'm wearing. She'll know about Katie.

Jenny wanted to do everything at once—take the farm tour with

Rebecca, talk with Marnie, and go and sit on the quiet front porch to soak in what she'd already heard and encountered. Though the surroundings were peaceful, she suddenly felt as if she were on sensory overload and needed time to process.

What a completely different world!

Glancing toward the barn, she realized she hadn't met Rebecca's husband yet. *Samuel Lapp—an ideal name for a strong, loving Amish father.* Yet she knew so little about him. When she inquired, Rebecca nodded cheerfully. "Oh, you'll meet him soon enough—and our eldest son, Elam, along with several of our young nephews, too. Our younger sons, Eli and Benjamin, drop by with their families often, sometimes to pitch in and help." She waved her hand. "It takes a *gut* many to fulfill the many requirements of running a dairy farm."

"I've read some articles about it."

"Sounds like you've done your homework." Rebecca's round face spread wide with her smile. "If not before, you'll see Samuel when it's time for supper, after milkin'," she said. "We have an assigned spot for each meal. You'll sit on the opposite side of me, right where our Katie always used to sit."

Jenny glanced at the sawbuck table. "Katie? Your . . . daughter, you mean?"

Rebecca bowed her head. "Sorry, guess ya don't know 'bout her."

Know what?

Just that quickly, Rebecca raised her chin. "Come. I'll show you the rest of the house."

And with that, Jenny decided she had better start walking on eggshells where Rebecca's daughter was concerned. Despite the books she'd read, she was evidently still ignorant of some Old Order social dynamics, though she was ready to learn.

I've staked my whole life on it!

6

MARNIE Lapp held her breath and managed to avert a sneeze as she walked along the road to Uncle Samuel Lapp's place. She wondered how Jenny was managing so far. She liked the idea of having another friend around who was still single. Talking in person with Jenny Burns during a few days each of the past summers had been a treat after trading letters. Even so, Jenny hadn't shared much at all about her love life, or lack of it, and Marnie had kept quiet that she was nearly engaged to a handsome Amish beau—Roy Flaud—who lived and worked over in Bird-in-Hand. Even so, the two girls had clicked from Jenny's first stroll past Marnie's roadside vegetable stand.

The young Englischer was downright interesting, but despite her fondness for simple things, she wasn't much different from other English folk Marnie had met. She had a streak of pride, which must eventually be suppressed. Just like Marnie's own sneeze.

Most Englischers didn't realize that being Amish wasn't just about dressing Plain, riding in carriages, and living simply. No indeed. The Amish way primarily involved obedience to the community and to God. If Jenny wanted to join church, she would soon have to learn to deal with her strong will and submit to the rules of the Ordnung and the bishop.

Marnie let herself enjoy the fall breeze and clear skies. The start of Amish wedding season was just days away, and she already knew of several weddings she wanted to attend—all for first cousins. As for herself, she didn't dare think too far ahead, considering her own beau had indicated they'd most likely wait till next year to marry.

Returning her thoughts to Jenny, she whispered, "If I weren't Amish by birth, would *I* want to join from the outside?"

It was hard to imagine Jenny's gumption in quitting her job to come here. And Marnie wasn't sure how she'd chosen to tell her family. Jenny had been mum on all that, and Marnie figured it wasn't her place to probe, anyway.

With the exception of Jenny, there was only one other person Marnie had known to leave home and family. And in that moment, it dawned on her how odd it was that Katie Lapp and Jenny Burns had seemingly exchanged places, unbeknownst to each other. Jenny was, no doubt, staying in Katie's former room . . . left empty when Katie, excommunicated and shunned by the People, had turned to the Mennonite church.

One out; one in.

"Who would've thought?" Marnie said aloud. It wasn't that she'd consciously planned any of this, picking the Lapps' place for Jenny's temporary residence. It was her mother who'd insisted that Rebecca was the best choice for Jenny's mentor. And the bishop had agreed.

Marnie froze suddenly at a horrid thought. What if Jenny didn't make it through the Proving? She certainly hadn't given it much consideration till this moment. But no! She must dismiss the very possibility, because there should never be another time of deep sorrow for poor Rebecca, not after losing Katie. Still, the painful thought persisted, and Marnie had to shoo it away like a wasp.

Surely that won't happen. Surely not.

Marnie took hope in the fact that Jenny was utterly determined to succeed as a seeker. After all, she hadn't moved here on impulse. No, she'd formulated the move for some time, saving money and planning the smallest details, looking to the heavenly Father for guidance. So surely there was no worry that Jenny might fail to become one with the People.

None at all.

Marnie waved and hurried her step when she saw Jenny running down Lapps' long lane toward the road, in full Amish attire, minus the Kapp.

"Well, look at that," she whispered. Marnie waved again and felt her heart soar. Where on earth had Jenny gotten a dress and apron so quickly?

"Hi, Marnie!" Jenny called to her, a big smile on her face.

"Hullo! Looks like ya made it."

"Still can't believe I'm actually here. Better pinch me fast!"

Marnie opened her arms and hugged her friend. "I'm ever so glad." She looked her over but good. "Ach, we're nearly twins, 'cept for your bangs."

"I've been letting them grow, but obviously they aren't there yet." Jenny laughed. "Rebecca helped me pin them down, as you can see."

"Did ya really need thirty bobby pins?"

Their laughter blended like apple cider and ginger ale as they headed back toward the house.

"Are you already unpacked?" Marnie asked.

"Almost."

Asking what things she'd brought, Marnie was still amazed that courageous Jenny had actually made the move. To think she'd willingly abandoned electricity and her car!

Jenny recited the various items she couldn't part with: two poetry books, her Bible and a devotional book, and a thick white bathrobe with matching slippers. "That's why I brought a large suitcase." She lowered her voice. "I think Rebecca was startled at its size."

"Did you bring any pictures of your family?"

"A few, yes."

Marnie smiled and suggested they sit on the front porch chairs Rebecca still had out, despite the chillier days. "I'm very curious to see."

"Well, I'm equally curious, Marnie. Is it okay for you to look at pictures of my family when you can't have any of yours?"

"I can understand why you might think that," Marnie said as two bobby pins slid from Jenny's bangs.

"Oh dear." Jenny picked them up and tried to put them back again. "I can hardly wait until my hair looks like yours."

"I can tell ya one thing for certain: Patience will become your closest friend during the Proving."

Jenny laughed. "Oh, I'm sure of that."

"So how are ya getting along with Aunt Rebecca?"

"She's very thoughtful." Jenny paused and cast her gaze toward the sky. "I do think she wonders what I'm doing here, however."

"Well, I can't imagine switchin' places with ya."

Jenny's smile spread across her pretty face. "Here I am! But I can't help wondering . . . do I really look Amish?"

Marnie laughed. "You look as Plain as I do. And you're goin' to fit in just fine here."

"I appreciate the vote of confidence."

Marnie frowned. "Did you ever doubt it?"

Jenny shook her head.

"Honestly, not many seekers stick around, from what I've heard—at least in other areas where this sort of thing is more common."

"I'll take it a day at a time."

"*Gut* idea."

"Jah, really *gut*."

Marnie laughed out loud. "Ach, you've picked up some Deitsch, then."

"I recognize a few of the simpler words and phrases already, thanks to two years of high school German."

"Remember, understanding and speaking are different things." Marnie reached to give her a hug. "You'll catch on eventually."

"I certainly hope so."

"Oh, you will." Marnie tried not to smile too big. "But first . . . I know exactly the place to take ya for a peek at yourself."

Jenny brightened. "Really?"

"Just you follow me."

7

AN autumn breeze trembled the treetops, creating a leafy shower below as Jenny followed tall, lean Marnie around the Lapps' old sandstone house. "I'd really like to see the springhouse up close," she said, intrigued by her earlier glimpse of it. "Rebecca says it's the closest thing to a full-length mirror."

"The springhouse pond?" Marnie turned and gave her a surprised look. "Why, that's precisely where we're headed."

"Perfect, then," Jenny replied happily.

Marnie stopped walking abruptly as they made their way down the lane. Grinning, she said, "Lookee there." She pointed in the direction of the large double-decker barn. A striking young Amishman with blond hair and wearing a straw hat was walking toward the main door. "My cousin Andrew Lapp is here, helping with milking this afternoon. He does occasionally, when he's caught up on his own work." She shielded her eyes from the sun. "You'll like Andrew . . . everyone does."

"If he's your cousin, he must be nice."

"Oh, believe me, Andrew left *nice* in the dust."

"He lives here in Hickory Hollow?"

"Rents a room from his parents." Marnie nodded. "Andrew says he baches it."

Jenny shook her head. "What's that mean?"

"Well, just that he's still a bachelor at twenty-nine. Guess he never found the right girl, but he keeps real busy with his welding business and helping Uncle Samuel, too."

"I thought Amish were *expected* to marry young."

Marnie laughed. "Jah, but every now and then a persnickety one comes along. Like Cousin Andrew."

Jenny watched him for a moment and then noticed Marnie looking at *her*. Marnie's eyes sparkled knowingly. "He's a real catch, but a lot of girls have tried to get his attention, believe me. Even so, he claims to be holdin' out for the right one. We tell him he's gonna hold out till his dyin' breath!"

As they continued down the hill, Jenny observed Marnie—her gentle mannerisms, her soft way of speaking—glad to be getting to know her even better, here on her own turf.

"Be careful on these steps," Marnie said, motioning toward the steep stone walkway leading down to the pond. "They're often slick."

Jenny loved how the site was set apart from the rest of the farm in a haven of sorts. The treed area provided exactly the right amount of shade, and the rock-walled springhouse and small spring-fed pond looked like the ideal place to relax or even pray.

"There." Marnie waved a hand gracefully toward the clear, placid water. "See for yourself what ya look like . . . in nature's mirror."

Jenny peered down at herself, feeling a little shy. *Amazing!* she thought. *I could actually pass myself off as Amish.*

"Well, what do ya think?" Marnie had moved closer.

"Like the saying goes—the clothes make the man. Well, the woman."

"'Tis the truth!"

They had a laugh, although it was Jenny who laughed longer. "I almost forgot the old me."

"You'll have plenty of time for that, Jenny."

Jenny stared into the pond, suddenly thinking that Pamela and Dorie would never believe what she was up to, despite knowing how keen she was on old-fashioned things. A lump sprang into her throat, surprising her. *I'll miss them.*

Ultimately, her friends would find other friends and fill the gap. And perhaps they'd understand something of her passion once she wrote and explained herself. *Maybe . . .*

Jenny stepped back from her reflection in the pond. "I'm curious to know about Katie, the Lapps' daughter. What happened to her?"

"Ach, she was shunned—and a mighty harsh shunning it was, too. All this happened almost seven years ago now, when Katie refused to destroy her guitar . . . and her music. She was even so brazen as to stand up our bishop, John Beiler, on their wedding day. Many think it enraged him when she jilted him, literally running away." Tears sprang to Marnie's eyes. "It was a very sad time for everyone."

"So she lives elsewhere?"

"Just on the edge of Hickory Hollow, with her husband, Daniel Fisher, who's also under the *Bann*. We're not s'posed to visit them in their home, exchange money, or take anything from their hand to ours."

"Wow—that's serious." Jenny looked down at her dress. "Does it matter, then, that I'm wearing Katie's former clothes?"

Marnie stared. "They're Katie's?"

Nodding, Jenny admitted they were.

"No, that won't hurt a thing," Marnie assured her. "Ain't like Katie's rebellion can affect you."

Jenny wondered how strict the same bishop would be with her. And knowing all this put her on edge. Would there be much grace for even the most innocent of mistakes? She sighed. "Is shunning very common?"

"It depends on the severity of the transgression. Of course, if you don't get baptized, you can't be shunned." Marnie leaned closer and whispered, "Katie Lapp was considered practically dead to the People for nearly a year during her initial shunning."

Jenny shivered at the thought. "That's horrible."

"Things loosened up slightly after that, but we never see her around here."

"So what happens if I fail my Proving?" Jenny had to know. "Could I be kicked out . . . like Katie?"

"Fail?" Marnie frowned, then grinned quickly. "Don't ya worry . . . there's no way that'll happen!" Marnie waved her toward the little rock building beside the pond. "Have ya ever seen the inside of a springhouse?"

"No."

"Come, then, I'll show ya."

They went to the small door and Marnie opened it. Stooping, they entered the damp room. Off to the right side, there was a long rectangular section on the ground, where spring water was rimmed by a cement ledge.

"Aunt Rebecca sometimes refrigerates milk cans and crocks of food in the cold water there," Marnie said, showing her the areas of deep and shallow water.

"It's charming." Jenny loved the quiet, private little space. She touched her face to make sure she wasn't dreaming.

Marnie folded her arms, all smiles. "I thought you might like to see it. My mother wishes we had one on our property. Anyone who has a spring has a blessed thing, she says."

"Must be wonderful for keeping things nice and cold."

"Jah, that's just what we used them for," Marnie agreed. "'Course now we have other ways of doing that," she explained. "We rent space in our English neighbors' big freezer just west of here."

"Really? It's not an inconvenience?"

Marnie shrugged. "Oh, we're used to taking food elsewhere. It's not so bad, really."

"Do you also use the phone at your English neighbors' sometimes?"

"Not as often as you might think." Marnie explained there was a phone shanty positioned in a field, camouflaged by trees and tall bushes. "Our bishop doesn't like to flaunt it, he says." She opened the door to exit the springhouse. "You'll meet him on Sunday, at Preachin' service."

"I'll look forward to that."

"Oh, wait—on second thought, you might not meet him then, after all. He's visiting another church district this weekend."

Jenny fell into step with her Amish friend. "I love everything about Hickory Hollow. There's no crazy rushing here, like in the English world."

"Oh, trust me, you should see some of us early on market days, or hurryin' off to church . . . 'specially those with big families, who have to hitch up two horses to two carriages and pile all the little ones inside, if they don't take an open spring wagon." Marnie chuckled.

Jenny wondered if she would be expected to talk the way Marnie did when she spoke English, with 'tis and lest and such. "I expect I've got a lot to learn. Speaking of which, are you up for teaching me to speak Pennsylvania Dutch?"

"Oh, I doubt you'll need to be taught it formally. You'll just pick it up over time."

Jenny wasn't so sure. "Well, about that. Is there a bookstore where I can purchase a Pennsylvania German dictionary?"

"Gordonville Book Store, not far from here. We'll go over there sometime soon if ya want."

"Great, thanks."

"*Denki,*" Marnie said with a smile. "Say *Denki.*"

"Jah, sorry," Jenny said, which made them both smile.

8

AFTER coming up the springhouse steps, Jenny followed Marnie back to the house, where Rebecca was waiting for them, sitting barefoot on the back step.

"Would ya like to meet my husband, Samuel?" Rebecca asked, observing both girls.

"Sure she would," Marnie replied. "And don't forget to introduce her to the others working in the barn—including my boy cousins."

Jenny noticed the furtive looks exchanged between Marnie and Rebecca. "If it's no trouble," she hastened to add.

"If the herd's calm, maybe you could start helpin' with the four o'clock milking," Marnie suggested.

"Now, dear," Rebecca said, hazel eyes widening, "no need to scare Jenny off her first day here, is there?"

Marnie shrugged, mischief on her face.

What's to be afraid of? Jenny wondered.

"Marnie." Rebecca shook her head. "Jenny won't need to help with milkin'. She'll work with me in the house—where we womenfolk belong." She gave Jenny a reassuring smile, yet Jenny felt somewhat disappointed.

"I'll fit in wherever you need me," Jenny remarked with a glance at Marnie. "So put me to work wherever you wish."

Rebecca nodded. "Even so, the men do most of the milkin'."

"Ah, you've been spared." Marnie laughed as she motioned for Rebecca and Jenny to follow her to the barn.

Rebecca nodded sweetly. "Has anyone thought to let the bishop and his wife know Jenny's arrived?" She asked this in a way that made Jenny think the good woman wanted Marnie to hurry off to the bishop's at that very moment.

"Well, *I* haven't," Marnie said. "And I doubt Mamm has yet, either."

Rebecca brushed her hands against her long black apron. "Might be nice if Jenny got acquainted with them real soon."

Marnie agreed and reached for the barn door, then heaved it open. She looked back at Jenny. "If he doesn't drop by in the next few days, it's not because he doesn't want to welcome you. Just remember that."

"Sure, there's plenty of time," Jenny replied.

With that, they stepped into the muggy barn, and Jenny got her first strong whiff of the smells of livestock, hay, and manure. And at that moment, she was quite glad Rebecca had spared her, as Marnie had so aptly put it.

Marnie found Uncle Samuel with his bushy brown beard pitching hay over in the stable, along with clean-shaven Cousin Andrew. Both men were wearing their oldest, rattiest straw work hats, though in a few weeks they would don their black felt hats for winter. Secretly, she preferred the looks of those over the straw hats.

Aunt Rebecca stepped forward and introduced Jenny to Uncle Samuel, who'd propped up his pitchfork against the wall, wiped his hand on his black work trousers, and offered it to the seeker. He smiled only briefly before his lips returned to a flat, hard line.

Jenny was the first to speak. "I'm pleased to meet you."

"Same to you."

Marnie was satisfied by her uncle's initial reception, though she wasn't sure how her cousin would handle things. Jenny was awfully pretty, but Andrew had been around lots of attractive Amishwomen. Of course, no Amishman in his right mind had any business taking a shine to Jenny unless she was entirely committed to joining church.

"Cousin Andrew," said Marnie gently, "this is my English friend, Jenny Burns."

His blue-eyed gaze honed in on her auburn bangs. "Fancy, then, ya say?"

"Well, she'd rather *not* be," Marnie said. "'Least not anymore."

"Is that right?" Andrew's face was sober. "Are ya here to join us as a people separated from the world, then?"

Jenny nodded enthusiastically. "I certainly am."

"Well, let me be the first to congratulate you." Andrew stuck out his hand, and Jenny shook it. "I'm sure my uncle and aunt will see to it that you get along well here as ya learn the ways of the Lord God . . . and the church."

Marnie felt much lighter, relieved that her friend was being received so hospitably. She gave her cousin an approving nod. "Let's show you round the stable," she said to Jenny. "You'll want to meet the driving horses—learn their names and let them get used to ya."

"It's nice to meet you both," Jenny said to the men, and Marnie noted that Aunt Rebecca was struggling not to smile too broadly as she fell in step with the seeker.

Jenny drank in each new vista—the old corncrib, the woodshed, and the glassy pond behind the two-story barn. The first hours here had flown like mere moments.

She followed Rebecca's example, washing her hands thoroughly at the well pump before going into the kitchen and scrubbing her hands there, as well. The whole chicken the women had prepared earlier was roasting, filling the kitchen with a delicious aroma as they set to work on the remaining supper items. Rebecca also recited a recipe for homemade lemonade so Jenny could write it down.

"Tomorrow I'll show you how to make bread," Rebecca told her. "We'll make egg noodles from scratch, too, here before long."

"This is so wonderful. Denki."

"*Wunnerbaar,*" Rebecca said with a small smile.

Jenny dipped her head with gratitude. "My mom didn't want me underfoot in her kitchen, so I never learned to bake at all. She loves to cook, but she's more focused on gourmet dinners than typical home cooking."

"I daresay you might not have been so willing to cook and bake with me had you come a few years sooner," Rebecca tittered, explaining how, at that time, Samuel had removed the old woodstove and remodeled the entire kitchen. "It was the talk of the hollow for a while. 'Specially when we put in a full bathroom off the back of the house."

"Marnie mentioned that in one of her letters. It wasn't long before others jumped on the idea, too, right?"

"Marnie told ya?"

"I doubt I'd be here if it weren't for your niece. She really helped make it possible." Jenny paused. "I'm sure she never shared anything you'd be uncomfortable with . . . or that wasn't common knowledge."

"Well, I should hope not." A shadow flitted across Rebecca's face.

"You can rest assured of that." Jenny gave her a smile.

"There's plenty of tittle-tattle round here, I'm afraid. Be forewarned."

It was human nature to want to share gossip, especially at social gatherings, Jenny thought. But to hear Rebecca admit this so freely made her a little sad.

"You look surprised," Rebecca said as she tossed a dish towel over her ample shoulder. "Remember, we certainly ain't perfect."

Jenny caught her breath.

"Did ya think otherwise?"

The People were God-fearing—Jenny believed that with all of her heart, no matter what Rebecca might say. For now, though, Jenny would leave things be.

"Hope you're not lookin' for the ideal church, Jenny. Please say you ain't."

Jenny considered that. "Well, the Amish church has to be better than some I've visited."

Rebecca looked away, then back at Jenny. "Keep in mind, once a person steps into a church fellowship, ach, it's no longer perfect. None of us is without fault, ya know. There was only one who was sinless—God's Son, the Lord Jesus Christ."

Jenny knew this. Still, didn't she have every right to believe in the worth of the Amish church? What was so wrong with that?

9

JENNY had expected paper plates and plastic spoons and forks. Instead, she and Rebecca laid the table with a green-and-white-checkered oilcloth and pretty flatware, along with simple yet lovely white dishes. There were white paper napkins beneath each gleaming fork, and glass tumblers filled with the delicious lemonade, made by Jenny herself.

Samuel came inside for supper with a quick smile for Rebecca, then removed his straw hat, placing it on the peg inside the door before heading directly to the washbasin. Soon, he took his place at the head of the table and waited silently for Rebecca and Jenny to bring over the chicken and potatoes.

Before he bowed his head and folded his hands, he said, "Let's give thanks," which they all did. Jenny held back tears during the long silent prayer, grateful to just be sitting here tonight.

When the prayer was over, Samuel gave a little cough and then reached for the large serving fork to choose his piece of chicken. Rebecca asked Jenny to pass the large oval dishes of potatoes and buttered peas once she'd served herself.

Jenny was surprised at how few words were spoken during the meal; she wondered if Samuel might ask about her family, or something about her English life. But no such questions came, and she slowly began to relax and enjoy the meal. The truth of the matter was that Samuel was a busy man—he did mention to Rebecca that he and a few others would be cleaning the milking equipment right after supper. "Andrew's comin' back to help me scrub out the bulk tank tonight, too."

"Is the vet still due tomorrow?" Rebecca asked quietly.

"Well, it's scheduled, so he'd better. I don't have time to fool around waitin' for him this time." Samuel reached for his lemonade and took a long drink. When he was done, he wiped his mouth on his sleeve.

"We have a guest, dear," Rebecca said, reaching for his napkin and fluttering it at him.

Then, and only then, did Samuel cast a look Jenny's way. She didn't know if she ought to smile or not, given the man's disposition.

"It's been quite a day," Rebecca said.

"Lots to do yet tonight, so I'll be goin' back out to the barn, soon as dessert's served."

Will he compliment Rebecca—or me—on the meal? Jenny wondered.

Then, as if Rebecca had thought the same thing, she told her husband that both she and Jenny had prepared the food. "Jenny's a right *gut* help, she is."

Samuel kept chewing, his eyes cast down. He muttered something in Deitsch.

Rebecca looked at Jenny and shrugged. "Soon enough you'll pick up what's bein' said."

"What's that?" Samuel raised his head suddenly.

Jenny considered his response as Rebecca spoke to him in Deitsch. It would be very interesting to understand some of the asides the Lapps shared. In fact, she was sure that's what Rebecca meant.

"What 'bout church?" Samuel asked.

"Well, she'll come along with us, ain't so?" Rebecca offered a warm smile to Jenny.

Samuel smacked his lips and leaned back in his chair. "I didn't mean that. Shouldn't ya tell her what to expect?"

"Well, why not explain things now?"

"You go right ahead, Rebecca."

Jenny heard her sigh. "There must be a lot on your mind, Samuel."

He didn't say there was or there wasn't. But the awkwardness continued even after he asked for another serving of chicken.

Jenny was beginning to think Samuel viewed her as an intruder. Or was it just his way? *I don't have to be liked immediately,* she decided, glad for women like Rebecca and Marnie.

"We have leftover bread pudding, dear." Rebecca broke the stillness. "Would ya care for some, Samuel?"

He gave a bob of his head, and Rebecca rose quickly to get it from the stove, where she'd had it reheating.

Jenny's first meal with Marnie's relatives certainly had been eye-opening, but she was not faint of heart. She was here for the long haul—and nothing whatsoever was going to change her mind!

Rebecca gritted her teeth and served Samuel his black coffee. She offered some to Jenny, who politely refused. It kept her awake if she drank coffee too late in the day, Jenny said.

Smiling sympathetically, Rebecca hoped the seeker wouldn't be put off by Samuel's unfriendly manner. Heaven knew his temper could rise, and she found herself thinking again of Katie and the precious grandchildren she'd managed to see a handful of times in the past months. Samuel would pitch a fit, for sure, if he got word of it. *I best be more careful.*

"I'm goin' to show Jenny how to hitch up the driving horse to the family carriage after supper, if ya don't mind," said Rebecca.

Samuel shook his head. "Just remember you'll have to unhitch, too." He finished his bread pudding, then downed the rest of his coffee. "Why not wait till daylight, Rebecca?"

She had her reasons.

Samuel didn't press further, and he leaned forward for the second silent prayer. As he again bowed his head, Rebecca and Jenny did the same.

10

JENNY felt as tight as a fiddle string and wasn't ready yet to fall asleep. The palpable strain at the supper table between Samuel and Rebecca still troubled her. Besides that, Rebecca had become flustered while teaching the names of the various parts of the equipment for hitching up—the harness, bridle, back hold straps, shafts, and the like. In the end, Jenny had merely watched and tried to comprehend. Last she'd looked, the horse and carriage were still parked in the driveway.

Presently, she sat in bed, writing in her journal, three full pages. When she was finished, she shuffled out of bed to the hallway. *What if I went out and sat on the front porch? Would it bother the Lapps?*

The present tranquility was the kind she'd longed for back home. That, and nearly everything else Hickory Hollow had to offer. Turning again to her room, she realized she could see herself in one of the bedroom windows; the gas lamp glowed on the table beside her. She stared at the silky canary yellow nightgown in the reflection and sighed. "I don't look like I belong here," she whispered. Sooner or later, she'd have to sew a long cotton nightgown to sleep in.

What does Marnie wear to bed?

She admired herself again. It was the only pretty nightie she'd brought along. *Just for tonight—I'll wear it one last time.* The truth was Jenny adored beautiful sleepwear and wondered who would ever know.

But she also wanted to be wholly Plain, from the inside out—from her inner heart and ideals to her external attire.

"I'll discard this little number tomorrow," she promised herself.

She thought then of her mother, who would be aghast if she knew Jenny was living here at all. As would Kiersten, whose opinion as the older sister always prevailed. What she said was to be respected . . . never questioned. *She'll be wondering a great deal now,* Jenny thought, a little sad. *Since I'm missing . . .*

As for Cameron, his response would be the worst. *"Out-and-out ridicule,"* as Rebecca Lapp or Marnie might say. Jenny groaned. If the Lapps knew the behind-the-curtains Burns family dynamics—well, lucky for them they didn't.

Jenny's father was the only one who might not mind her running off to the Amish. But how would anyone ever know for sure? When it came to anything other than his work, he had little time to spare. He took not noticing to new levels.

But she didn't need to imagine what her friends might think. Dorie, especially, would think she'd flipped out. *"You're crazy, Jen,"* she would laughingly say, but she'd mean it if she knew.

So it's best I kept it to myself.

She did plan to write letters to them eventually—they deserved as much. Cameron was the only one Jenny wasn't sure about contacting. After all, her mother would inform the rest of the family without delay.

Jenny regretted the way she'd left things with them unfinished, but there was no room for second-guessing. She thought of all the resourceful gleanings she'd received from Rebecca in her shining kitchen. She'd even learned how to trim a kerosene lantern wick, light it, and put it out. To top things off, there was even more in store after Samuel's evening Bible reading. Rebecca had Jenny sit next to her at the table and taught her some basic needlepoint, something she'd seen her aunt do years before. Jenny had taken to it tonight like a child to her first taste of chocolate.

I've missed so much by being born English.

Tomorrow was Halloween, but Amish people wouldn't think of celebrating the day. Regardless, Rebecca said they had pumpkins to deliver for pies and invited Jenny to help distribute them in the neighborhood.

Fondly, she looked around the room. So this was not a *deceased* daughter's former bedroom, although Marnie had whispered before she left that

Katie had been considered practically dead to the People. The idea of such a severe shunning made Jenny clench her teeth. Poor Katie!

She extinguished the lantern and moved back to the window, inching closer to see the moon-drenched grazing land and the pasture beyond. It was hard to stop thinking about Samuel and Rebecca's daughter.

Suddenly, Jenny spotted someone dash outside and get into the waiting carriage. She peered closer and saw that it was Rebecca.

Lowering herself, Jenny crouched and watched, wondering where the woman of the house was hurrying off to at this late hour. It struck Jenny as not only strange but rather eerie.

Incredibly curious, Jenny considered waiting up until Rebecca returned. But she felt so exhausted, it was difficult not to return to bed and stretch out beneath the sheet and quilt. She gently traced the quilt's pattern and its stitching, not forgetting to thank God for this remarkable dream come true.

Then, with a deliberate sigh, Jenny relaxed and gave in to blessed sleep against the embroidered pillowcase.

··· ➤ ◄ ···

The matching white ceramic lamps on either side of the burgundy-and-white-checked sofa cast such brightness upon the front room, Rebecca had to squint as she sat there with darling brown-eyed Katie. The light gleamed in the otherwise darkened house until, ever so slowly, her eyes became accustomed to it.

Electric, Rebecca thought with regret, although she must not let her concern overtake her. She was altogether pleased her daughter had stayed up to see her, as they'd planned two weeks ago.

"You look tired, Mamma." Katie was curled at one end of the sofa in her soft blue bathrobe, holding tiny, sleeping Kate Marie. The toddler's blond hair fell in lovely ringlets.

"Never too tired to see you." Unable to resist, she scooted over and touched her granddaughter's smooth cheek with her finger. "Just look at the little sweetie—she's growin' so fast, jah?"

"You must see the changes more than we do." Katie stroked her little one's locks.

"Well, no doubt." *Ain't like I wouldn't visit every day if I could*, Rebecca thought.

"Does Dat know you've started coming to see us?" asked Katie.

"I've managed to keep it from him."

"What will happen if . . . "

Rebecca's dream came to mind. "That's why my visits must be after dark."

"Oh, Mamma. This sneaking around seems so unnecessary."

"Well, the Bann's to be upheld." Rebecca felt suddenly guilty again. "By most of us, that is."

Katie shook her head and pushed her hands through her own auburn hair. "It's just been—"

"Too long since you saw your father . . . your brothers?" Rebecca asked. "That could all change, if only—"

"Mamma, *please*. We're happy in our new church. We're doing God's bidding. We believe that." Katie placed her sleeping daughter onto the sofa and leaned back. "And we've started a Bible study."

"Ach, really?"

"Daniel felt the Lord nudging him to invite anyone seeking to delve into Christ's teachings."

"Is that so?"

"You're welcome to come, too, Mamma. We'd love to have you."

"Well, I . . ."

"Just think about it, all right?"

Rebecca thought two seconds and knew there was no way she'd be permitted to attend, even if she wanted to. Yet she was torn.

They sat there quietly, Rebecca's thoughts churning. Thoughts she could not voice.

"When's Benjamin planning to take over the farm for Dat?" asked Katie out of the blue. "I thought he was nearly ready to do that several years ago."

Rebecca explained that Katie's youngest brother helped Samuel daily to run the dairy farm, along with a few of his cousins. "Keep in mind that when Benjamin married, his father-in-law helped them buy their own place."

"So you and Dat will continue to live where you are, then?"

"For the time bein', jah." Rebecca wondered when Katie had last seen her three brothers, especially Benjamin, whom she was always closest to. "Do the boys keep in touch with you at all?" she asked.

"Just Eli—mostly a note now and then from his wife." Katie looked away, biting her lips and squinting her eyes. "Elam's written me off. . . ." she whispered.

All the People did, Rebecca thought miserably, thankful for the bishop's lifting the Bann slightly so they could correspond by mail, though only a few did so.

Then, looking down at tiny Kate Marie, Katie smiled. "I think she's starting to resemble Daniel a little, don't you, Mamma?"

She finds her joy wherever she can. . . .

Rebecca agreed and leaned forward a bit. "Her looks are changing, that's for sure."

"Here lately, people have been saying so, though I've thought it, too."

"Sammy's always looked more like you, with his auburn hair," Rebecca said, a lump still in her throat. "To think he's never met his *Dawdi* Samuel."

"No, sad but true."

They pushed past their grief over the Bann and talked about the children, mostly everyday things—how little Kate was beginning to put more and more sentences together. Rebecca didn't say it but wondered if any of those were Deitsch.

Katie's face beamed suddenly and she lowered her voice. "Mamma, I'm expecting a baby again. We found out just this week."

"Such happy news. Any chance of twins?"

Laughing softly, Katie said, "You must really want doubles, Mamma."

"Why do ya say that?"

"Well, this isn't the first time you've mentioned it."

Rebecca had to chortle. "Is that right?" She knew it was true.

Katie nodded and looked again at her precious girl, whose pudgy arm twitched as she rolled to face the sofa. "Whatever the Lord sees fit to give us, Daniel and I'll be ever so happy."

"You look real *gut,* dear one. Healthy as always."

"The doctor says so," replied Katie, going on to say the baby was due the first week in May. Katie smiled. "Little Kate will likely still be in diapers."

"And you'll have your hands full for sure."

"I don't mind one bit. I love being a wife and mother," Katie said, yawning.

Just not an Amish one, thought Rebecca.

"Oh, and not to change the subject, but I heard you and Dat were keeping an Englischer over at the house."

"That's right. She arrived just today."

"Someone from the outside who wants to join the Amish church?"

Rebecca said it was so. "How'd ya hear?"

"Daniel's sister Annie."

Elam's wife. Nodding, Rebecca replied, "Jenny Burns is awful nice, I'll say that. And she seems sincere, too."

Katie was still.

"This is so rare, ya know, we hardly know how to go 'bout it," Rebecca volunteered.

"Surely Bishop John has a plan, jah?"

Rebecca loved it when Katie slipped back into her old ways of expression. "That he does. John Beiler's told your father it's a matter of letting Jenny learn our ways at her own pace."

"So Dat's all right with it?"

"Well, he's cautious."

"No wonder."

"Can't be too careful," Rebecca said. "But I don't mean there's anything to worry 'bout. Just that Jenny must fit in with the membership before she'll be given the chance to become one of us."

"Does she speak any Deitsch?"

"Only a word or two. But from what I can tell, she's determined to do what's necessary."

"Where'd you put her—which room?"

Rebecca paused. "Does it matter to ya, daughter?"

"Not really."

"Well, since your old room's the largest besides ours, I offered her that." A shadow crossed Katie's face, and for that instant, Rebecca worried she'd made a blunder in doing so. "Is that all right, dear?"

"Of course. Why would I mind?"

Rebecca was mighty sure she did. "It's too late to change things," she said, wishing she'd brought it up with Katie before now. "She's nicely settled."

"Really, Mamma, it's all right." Katie drew a long breath. "I just hope she finds whatever she's looking for."

"Jah, and who's to know what that might be."

"It's hard to think of an Englischer wanting to be Amish," Katie said in a near whisper.

Hard indeed, Rebecca thought sadly.

11

JENNY dreamed she was scrambling eggs and frying German sausage, and she awakened to the same delectable aromas. She guessed Rebecca Lapp was up already and making breakfast for Samuel.

And I'm still in bed!

She peered at her watch on the bedside table. *Six o'clock!*

There had been no discussion about what her morning chores were to be, or how early she should rise. She was told yesterday that Samuel would have a bite before going out for the early morning milking at four o'clock, which meant this must be a more substantial breakfast that Rebecca was preparing.

"Remember, we're not here by accident," Rebecca had said yesterday while they worked together in the sewing room. *"Just like these dress patterns have a purpose, so do we. . . ."*

Jenny pushed back the bed quilt and rose to go to the window. Lifting the green shade, she stared out at the beauty dawning before her eyes.

"I'm here for a purpose," she said softly.

Today she wanted to help Rebecca in any way she could. Her first priority was here at home, learning the ways of an Amishwoman. Speaking and comprehending their language was an essential part of that. *If I can just get my hands on a Pennsylvania German dictionary.*

She went to the dresser to get her brush and tried to remember how to put her hair back the way Rebecca had done it up yesterday. But she kept failing, and her bangs were a nuisance. *I need a larger mirror!*

291

She decided to try again to pull her bangs back to accommodate a full middle part, perhaps downstairs in the bathroom. Except that the cabinet mirror there might not be much help, either, considering it was rather small. Despite that, it was better than nothing, so she would just slip down there in her modest bathrobe, hopefully unnoticed, and shower or wash up before dressing. Swiftly, she gathered her things.

Rebecca greeted her as she hurried through the kitchen to the bathroom, and Jenny noticed the dark circles under her eyes. "No need to rush, Jenny. The men will be outdoors for a while yet." She explained that she sometimes liked to offer a nice hot breakfast to Elam and her nephews. "It's not always the same young men each day, since most of them have other part-time jobs."

Jenny couldn't help wondering how late Rebecca had stayed out last night . . . and where she'd gone at that hour. But it wasn't her place to inquire, and she made her way into the bathroom for her shower and hung her silky nightgown over her bathrobe on the door hook.

When she'd finished, she wrapped her hair in a towel and dried off, then stepped into one of Katie's discarded dresses, recalling the small spring-fed pond by the springhouse. She couldn't run off to look at herself in its reflection each morning. She'd have to trust Marnie's assessment that doing her hair the Amish way would become second nature in time.

Marnie could hardly wait to finish cooking breakfast in her sick mother's stead. Mamm was resting this morning, nursing a bad headache. Marnie assumed it was another migraine, so it was also up to her to get the lunches packed for her three school-age siblings, and in a big hurry, too.

Once the kitchen was redded up and her younger siblings were out the door, she washed the floors by hand in the utility room, kitchen, and the small sitting room near the front room. Then, while they were drying, she went upstairs and sat down to write a letter to her beau, Roy Flaud, who had invited her to attend an area Bible study next Tuesday evening. He'd written that he would pick her up, if she wanted to go.

Not wanting to turn him down, she'd thought about it overnight, unable to sleep. It was odd, really, because naught but a week or so ago she had heard Cousin Emmalyn—Andrew's nineteen-year-old sister—talking about a couple holding such meetings, somewhere on the outskirts of Hickory Hollow. The concern was that some of the unbaptized Amish young folk might head over there out of curiosity. *And eventually wander out of the Amish church.*

"If Emmalyn got wind that I attended that meeting, I'd be all but cooked," she whispered. "And that would be the end of Roy and me." The thought of anything tearing them apart made her head hurt. *Like poor Mamm's!*

Quickly, Marnie took a pen from her desk drawer and began to write to her darling.

> *Dear Roy,*
>
> *I was glad to receive your letter yesterday afternoon. Right away, I wanted to write you back to thank you for the invitation. But honestly, it's not a good idea for me to go to the Bible study. I don't want to have trouble brewing with my parents. Or worse, with the ministers here. I hope you understand.*
>
> *As you know, my father is not progressive in any manner, shape, or form—we've discussed this, you and I. Besides, if word got out to Bishop John, well, I'd have some fast explaining to do, even though I'm in my Rumschpringe like you.*
>
> *It would break my heart for anything to divide us, Roy. I look forward to seeing you again. I'll wait to hear from you to find out when that might be.*
>
> *I'm really sorry about not joining you.*
>
> > *Yours always,*
> > *Marnie Lapp*

She folded the letter and slipped it into an envelope, glad she'd kept her romance secret for all this time. Oh, goodness, she hoped this problematic invitation wasn't just the tip of the haystack!

--- ✺ ✺ ---

Jenny offered to wash the big black griddle for Rebecca as the smell of baking bread permeated the kitchen. The breakfast they'd served to

Samuel, Elam, and three of the Lapps' teenage nephews was heartier than any Jenny had eaten in recent memory. Along with fried potatoes, scrambled eggs, and sausage, there was also orange juice, black coffee, and a snitz pie Rebecca had made yesterday.

The young men hardly made eye contact as they dug into their food. And just as he had last night, Samuel still seemed tentative about talking to Jenny, which didn't surprise her. *I'm still a stranger.*

She was finishing up the dishes while Rebecca dried when suddenly a frustrated stream of Deitsch came pouring from within the bathroom.

"Ach no!" Rebecca said, turning crimson and darting toward the bathroom door.

What's happening? Jenny wondered.

Rebecca talked through the door in their language. *Another private conversation,* Jenny mused.

At last the door opened narrowly, and Rebecca squeezed inside, disappearing behind it. More muffled talking ensued. Jenny hoped Samuel hadn't become ill.

Then Samuel emerged from the room, his head bowed as he scurried away like a terrified mouse toward the utility room and out the back door.

What's going on? Jenny thought as she returned to scouring the sink.

After a few moments, Rebecca called to her. "Will you come in here, please, Jenny?"

"Coming." She stepped into the bathroom. There, she found Rebecca gingerly holding up the silky yellow nightie by the straps. "Is this . . . uh, little item yours, dear?"

Jenny gasped and felt her face flush. "Oh, I forgot to—"

Rebecca's eyes were beyond serious. "We have but one bathroom in this house, as ya know." The woman looked absolutely appalled. "That's all I'll be sayin' about this."

"Really, I'm so terribly sorry. It won't happen again," Jenny assured Rebecca—and herself.

··· ➤ ➤ ···

During the bumpy ride in the spring wagon to haul the plump and beautiful pumpkins, Jenny's embarrassment followed her like a stalking dog. But just as Rebecca had stated, she did not mention the incident further.

"What does your family think of your decision to come here?" asked Rebecca after a while. "They must be shocked." Her hands were tight on the reins.

Jenny drew a long breath and slowly let it out. "Actually, they don't know."

Rebecca turned toward her, frowning. "Whatever do ya mean? You didn't tell them?"

She shook her head. "I knew they'd try to talk me out of coming."

Rebecca sighed loudly. "So they *could've*?"

"I worried they'd pressure me to change my mind, yes."

The older woman raised her eyebrows. "And why's that?"

"It's not that I'm easily talked out of something, if that's what you think." Even to Jenny's ears, the words sounded defensive.

"Nee?" Rebecca gave her a doubtful look. "Are ya sure?"

Jenny nodded. "This kind of life is all I've wanted since I was a girl."

"But you can't just disappear from your family and not tell them what's in your heart."

"You don't know my family, Rebecca."

"True. But even so."

The conversation made Jenny feel even worse than she'd felt earlier, when Samuel had found her nightgown.

"I did tell my mother I was leaving town for a while."

Rebecca's pretty eyes became even more sober. "So you really don't know if you're goin' to stay put, then."

"I *do* know."

"I'm confused, dear. And I wonder if you're not equally so."

Jenny's frustration was mounting. "I told my mother I'd contact her in a few weeks."

"Yet you didn't tell her where you are or what you're doing." Rebecca's face drooped as though with sadness. "This is so peculiar to me."

Jenny sat up taller in the wagon. "You don't understand."

"You're certainly right."

A lengthy and embarrassing pause followed. Then quietly, slowly, Jenny tried to explain. "My family is nothing like yours, Rebecca. I've never felt like I fit in with my parents or sister and brother."

"Never felt like it, or just never did?"

"Both, I guess."

Rebecca reached over and patted her knee like Jenny was a child. "I don't mean to question. I just wonder if your Mamm wouldn't rather know where you are."

Jenny stared at the road, seeing the grooves on the other side, where carriage wheels had worn down the pavement. Rebecca had no idea how aloof her family was. She sighed. "Do you think I can make it through the Proving?"

"Considering what you've told me, I'd be hesitant to say."

"You mean because I haven't been forthcoming with my family?"

Rebecca smiled faintly. "The truth is always best, no matter what a stir it might cause."

"I believe that, too. I even meant to tell them, but . . ." Jenny mentally kicked herself. She'd known all along what she should have done.

I just didn't do it.

12

REBECCA and Jenny stopped first at the home of Preacher Ephraim Yoder and his wife, Lovina, where Rebecca introduced Jenny to the reserved older couple before dropping off two pumpkins. Jenny was astonished at the length of the minister's tapered brown beard, speckled with gray. But despite his bristly brows, his deep-set eyes smiled a convincing welcome, and she believed he was a kind and gentle man. Lovina only eyed her at first, warming up more slowly before eventually offering chocolate chip cookies and hot coffee. Jenny was happy to sit at their table and nibble on the snack and sip the black coffee. But she wondered if they viewed her as a distraction since they were required to speak English in her presence. *I won't take it personally,* she thought as she noticed the Scripture wall calendar nearby. *They'll grow to trust me . . . to know me.*

The Lapps' driving horse, a black mare named Star, reared her beautiful head as they got back into the wagon. And when Rebecca reached for the reins and the horse began to move forward, Jenny noticed how very taut the reins were.

This horse is raring to go! Would she ever be able to control such a spirited animal?

Soon, they were coming up on Nate and Rhoda Kurtz's farmhouse, the Lapps' neighbors to the south of their cornfield. Rhoda Kurtz was nearly as welcoming as Lovina had been, but still somewhat guarded, with only an occasional forced smile. Nate Kurtz, on the other hand, scarcely acknowledged Jenny, saying nothing at all.

When they returned to the wagon, Rebecca explained that was Nate's reticent way. "Don't feel bad. Some folk are nearly tongue-tied around Englischers, 'specially here in our little neck of the woods."

"Who can blame them?"

"And there are a number of farmers who basically speak with their eyes and hands. Guess they don't feel it necessary to talk much."

"My father's a little like that," Jenny said. "When he does speak, it's mostly about things no one else really comprehends or cares to discuss."

"Well, I feel for ya, then." Rebecca went on to say her husband was nothing like that—"quite the opposite. But there's no guessin' where Samuel stands on any issue."

"He was real quiet at supper yesterday."

"Oh, you just wait till he gets to know ya. He'll nearly talk your ear off."

Jenny wondered how long it would be before that might happen. Samuel Lapp wasn't just cautious; he was opposed to her being there. Of that, Jenny was almost certain.

In a few minutes, they made another delivery, this time to Samuel's brother's farmhouse, where they were met at the door by a young blond woman. "We've got more pumpkins than we know what to do with," the girl said as she stood in the doorway, obviously blocking their entry. "Dat suggested we just put them on the English neighbors' front porches." She frowned at Jenny, and Rebecca intervened.

"Jenny, this is my niece Emmalyn Lapp, Andrew's younger sister—you met Andrew at our place yesterday."

Jenny nodded and smiled. "Another of Marnie's many cousins."

Emmalyn stared back. "You must be the fancy friend."

"Well, I *was* fancy. And I am Marnie's friend, jah."

Emmalyn shrugged. "Dressin' the part doesn't make it so."

Jenny wholeheartedly agreed. "I would love to have been born Amish, like you." She'd put it right out there, wondering how Andrew's sassy sister might respond.

But Emmalyn merely folded her arms and turned to her aunt Rebecca. "I'll let Mamm know you dropped by."

"Are ya sure your mother doesn't want this pumpkin?" Rebecca was still holding it. "'Cause she ordered it from me."

Emmalyn shook her head. "Why not give it to her yourself, then? See if she takes it."

"Just tell your mother I was here." Rebecca put the pumpkin down, and that was that.

Her jaw set, Rebecca made no excuses for Emmalyn, like she had for Nate Kurtz. She simply got into the wagon, picked up the reins, and clicked her cheek.

Jenny felt chagrined at Emmalyn's rudeness and barbed remarks. *Some people are just a nuisance!*

She wondered if Rebecca was all right but didn't know her well enough to ask. So she looked the other way, watching the world of Hickory Hollow pass at a snail's pace.

The final stop was Bishop John Beiler's spacious farmhouse. His young wife, a rather plump but pretty woman named Mary, was giving her three youngest children a morning snack of juice and crackers when they arrived. Rebecca had mentioned the girls on the way into the house: chubby Mary Mae, just turned five—Mary's first child with the formerly widowed bishop; petite Emily, who was three; and little Anna, eighteen months. There were five other children with the bishop's first wife, Rebecca had said, most of them school age now. However, Hickory John and Nancy, the two oldest, both worked for other Amish families—Nancy in Sugarcreek, Ohio, where she assisted the bishop's elderly aunt.

It was quite an effort for Rebecca to talk over little Anna's cries. Nevertheless, she did her best, stating that Jenny was the seeker her niece Marnie had helped bring to Hickory Hollow. "I wanted you to meet her."

"Ach, you'll have to excuse my little one today," Mary said, her blond hair falling out of the bun in several places. "She had a fitful night and is a little out of sorts today."

"I well remember such times with my own youngsters, so don't fret," Rebecca said, leaning over to stroke the older girl's fair hair.

Jenny smiled at tiny Anna, whose golden hair was pulled back into braids fastened into a thin knot on the back of her head. Jenny pulled a silly face, which made the tot cease her crying at once.

"Well, that's much better," Mary said, kissing her daughter's wet cheeks.

The women talked further, and later Rebecca offered to carry in the pumpkin. "Is the back porch all right?"

Mary agreed as she switched Anna to her other hip. "It's awful nice of you to drop by, Rebecca."

"You'll be able to make several big pies, ain't?" Rebecca said before heading out to the spring wagon for the pumpkin, leaving Jenny alone with Mary and the children.

"We've all been so curious 'bout you, Jenny Burns. I hope you're finding a *gut* willkumm here," Mary said, her angelic smile filling her round face. "Are ya?"

The pleasant woman's comments made Jenny feel warm all over. "Thanks, er . . . Denki. So far I've only met a few neighbors, but Rebecca's been just wonderful."

"There's no one quite as kind—or long-suffering—as Rebecca Lapp, I agree." Mary set Anna down on the floor to play with Emily. "We've got quite a few folk asking 'bout you," she mentioned. "Everyone's very interested. In a *gut* way, of course."

Jenny knew what she meant. And when she saw Rebecca coming up the back steps with the large pumpkin, she scurried to the door. "Here, let me help," she said, thankful to have this distraction.

"I've got it," Rebecca said, gently placing the pumpkin on the floor. "There ya be, Mary."

"I'll get some money right quick," Mary said as she searched her dress pockets.

"Ach, there's no charge for the bishop's family." Rebecca wiped her hands on her black apron. "'Tis an offering of thanksgiving."

"Well, aren't you nice!" Mary lightly touched Rebecca's arm. "Denki to you and to Samuel, too." Mary's girls were quiet now as they stared up at Jenny with three sets of blue eyes.

"Your girls are precious," Jenny said, wishing they might stay longer.

"I think they must like you." Mary punctuated her words with a nod and a smile.

"Maybe they've never seen such unruly bangs." Jenny reached up and felt for the bobby pins.

Mary shook her head. "Oh, I didn't mean that. . . ."

"The bangs *are* a problem. But it's just a matter of time." Jenny smiled at Rebecca.

"Time is the key to many things, don't forget," Mary said with the sweetest smile.

"I'm real happy to meet you, Mary." Jenny offered to shake her hand.

"We'll get better acquainted soon," Mary replied, receiving the hand-shake. "Has Rebecca talked with you 'bout coming to help me now and then with the little girls?"

"She has, and I'd love to." Jenny smiled and waved.

After she and Rebecca had made the loop at the top of the driveway and headed back out to the road, Rebecca remarked, "I've never heard young Anna carry on like that before, just so ya know."

"Oh, that didn't bother me."

"Workin' as a mother's helper might be a *gut* way to learn Deitsch quicker," added Rebecca. "Since the children are learning to speak it, too."

"It's going to take some time, like Mary said. Jah?" Jenny enjoyed using the word.

"I daresay you're right."

Hesitantly, Jenny forged ahead. "What about your husband—is he really okay with me staying at the house?"

Rebecca paused for a moment. "Oh, never ya mind Samuel. He'll come around . . . in time."

So I was right. Her being here *had* created conflict between them. *Heaven knows there's enough of that.*

Then, recalling the earlier incident at the Lapps', she cringed again at the blunder with the yellow nightie. Here it was her first full day in Amish country, and she'd already made a fool of herself. And to think it was her reluctant host who'd discovered the gaffe!

13

JENNY sighed and stretched and dragged out of bed when the alarm sounded at five o'clock Friday morning. Her third full day here, and already she felt fatigued from the dawn-to-dusk routine of cooking from scratch—three big meals a day. In her entire life she'd never minced so many onions. Nor had she boiled and then chopped so many eggs. There were numerous recipes to master, all of which Rebecca had stored in her head. Not a single recipe written down! The woman was a living, walking miracle, the way she managed all that was expected of her.

And there's no chance, even at my young age, I can even dream of keeping up with her!

Rebecca had taught Jenny how to beat rugs, iron with a gas iron, gather eggs, and scrub wood floors on all fours. And, oh, the mountain of mending! She'd also shown Jenny how to make bread, but thus far Jenny's bread looked nothing like Rebecca's: plumped up on top, done to perfection.

Jenny sat up in bed with a start. Just yesterday, she'd darned one of Samuel's socks completely shut. Rebecca hadn't seemed to mind and had a good laugh over it. She'd simply handed Jenny a seam ripper and, with a smile, requested she reopen the closure. And Jenny had started all over again.

Along with indoor chores, Jenny had also assisted Rebecca with the daily customers who knocked on the back door, coming to purchase a variety of jams and jellies. She quickly learned that Rebecca Lapp's preserves were known all over Lancaster County.

But the temptation to beat herself up with her own yardstick of perfection persisted. *I'm not a wimp . . . I'll get used to all of this. I have to!*

Eventually, she pulled herself out of bed and dressed, glad to have showered the night before. When her hair was brushed and swept back into a thick bun, she hurried downstairs to help Rebecca make the hot breakfast for Samuel and whoever happened to stay around. They never knew how many of the Lapps' nephews would appear for any given meal, but Rebecca had warned that this was the norm. Anyone was welcome, and Samuel was grateful for the help.

Plenty of room at the table, too, Jenny thought.

After the breakfast dishes were washed and dried and placed back in the cupboard, Jenny was pleased to see a blue van pull into the driveway. Marnie jumped out, wearing a big smile, and came around to the back door.

"Are we going to the bookstore?" Jenny asked when she met her there.

"Jah, but I can't be gone for long. Need to get back to help Mamm cook for the weekend," Marnie told her.

"Same here." Still, Jenny jumped at the chance to go. She found Rebecca in the sewing room upstairs, cutting out fabric for Samuel's new work pants. "Do ya mind if I go with Marnie to Gordonville to the bookstore?"

"Just right quick, jah? We have lots of pies to bake this afternoon." Then Rebecca waved her off.

"Denki," Jenny said and hurried to her room to grab her purse. She dashed back downstairs, where she followed Marnie outdoors and into the nearly empty van. It was hard to imagine how Rebecca had juggled all the indoor duties prior to Jenny's coming. The thought of it boggled her mind.

Too bad Katie isn't allowed to drop by and help, she thought, still puzzled by the day-to-day consequences of the shunning.

··· ➤ ◄ ···

At the bookstore, Jenny found a veritable storehouse of reading material—everything from Amish school curriculum to realistic fiction for children, such as *The Pineapple Quilt* and *The Only Sister.*

Marnie tugged at her arm playfully, reminding her of the urgency to return home, and led her to the stack of paperback dictionaries. With a grin of assurance, she placed one firmly in Jenny's hands. "Here 'tis. Your road map to speaking fluent Deitsch. This will help ya make more sense of what you're already soaking up."

Pleased, Jenny could hardly wait to look up various words she'd heard repeatedly since her arrival, words like *ferhoodled* and *Nachtmohl*.

The chatter in the van en route to Hickory Hollow increased greatly when two Amishwomen climbed aboard after waving down the driver outside the nearby Amish shoe store. Despite her fatigue and their talking, Jenny would not be deterred from her hunt through the dictionary. She quickly learned that *Nachtmohl* was Holy Communion, which she hoped, even prayed, to be eligible for as a bona fide church member.

Will I endure the Proving? she wondered, the test stretching out before her like a grueling path. And to think she'd only lived Amish for a few days!

Marnie could see how captivated Jenny was by the dictionary, so she let her browse through it while she talked with the womenfolk in the van. "Jah, she's here to stay," Marnie told them in Deitsch when they inquired. "There's no question in my mind."

"Honestly, it's hard to think of goin' from the fancy English world to ours," Ella Mae Zook's married granddaughter Rachel Glick said, casting furtive looks Jenny's way.

"Oh, I agree," Marnie replied. "Just think of all you'd have to give up: cars, phones, television . . . pretty clothes."

"Honestly, what would make someone from the outside want to join our church?" Rachel's aunt asked.

Marnie wasn't free to divulge Jenny's confidences. That was for her friend to share later, once she had steady footing amongst the People. "Maybe someday she'll tell you."

This caused Rachel to roll her eyes, then shake her head. "Makes not a whit of sense, if ya ask me."

"She's not askin' you." Marnie smiled.

"Well, aren't you something?" Rachel teased.

"Sorry," Marnie offered. "Hope I didn't sound mouthy."

The other women exchanged glances.

304

"She's learnin' our language, so very soon we'll be including Jenny in all our conversations," Marnie added hastily, not wanting to exclude a friend.

Rachel was quick to nod her head.

"What lengths would you go . . . to make a dream come true?" Marnie asked in an attempt to change the tone of the conversation.

"Not sure." Rachel frowned. "Why?"

Marnie went on to say she thought Jenny Burns had done nearly the impossible, moving heaven and earth to get here. "It's remarkable, really."

The women nodded, now staring at the back of Jenny's head as she read her dictionary.

Jenny chose that moment to enter their chatter. "Why's the spelling for *ferhoodled* different?" she asked, turning to face Marnie. "I was paging through and stumbled upon a spelling I've never seen before in books."

"Show me." Marnie leaned over to look at the book.

"It's spelled *v–e–r–h–u–d–d–e–l–t*," Jenny said, showing her the word and the meaning—confused, entangled, mixed-up.

"Oh, that's not surprising, really."

Jenny looked at her, puzzled.

"Some of my circle letter friends in Ohio, for instance, spell our words completely different," Marnie explained. "It's not like German, where there's a set standard for spelling."

Jenny grimaced. "Uniformity would be helpful."

Marnie could see that she was struggling—and not just with words in a dictionary. No, Jenny looked sleep deprived.

"You all right?" Marnie whispered.

"Sure, why?"

"Just checkin'."

A few minutes later, the driver took an unexpected turn, and they headed down the road where her shunned cousin, Katie, and her husband, Dan, had now lived for more than five years. "Look over there," Marnie said softly, pointing. "That's Katie's house."

Jenny turned quickly to look.

There was the familiar meadow, with the creek running through it in the background. Although she'd never darkened the door of the place, Marnie found the clapboard house rather appealing. "Perty, ain't?"

Jenny nodded, still staring as they passed. "And no one's allowed to visit her?"

She shook her head. "It's all part of the Bann." Marnie felt sad just saying it.

"Can't anything be done to alter it?" asked Jenny. She certainly was one to nose out the facts.

"Aside from Katie offering a kneeling confession in front of the membership, what's done is done." Marnie wished she hadn't brought it up. She'd been little more than a schoolgirl when Katie left, yet the pain of separation still tore at her own heart.

14

THE driver dropped Marnie and Jenny off at Uncle Samuel's, and they strolled up the lane toward the house. "Let me know if there's anything you need, all right?" Marnie said.

Jenny tapped the dictionary. "I think this is going to help."

"Remember, you'll pick up our language faster by listening and attempting to speak it."

Jenny nodded, but her face looked downcast.

"What is it?"

"This has nothing to do with speaking Deitsch." Jenny seemed hesitant.

"Go on."

"I'm wondering. How do you think Rebecca's daughter would feel about my wearing her Amish clothes?"

"Goodness, I doubt she'd care."

"You're sure?"

Marnie nodded. "Katie's moved on. I guarantee it. Maybe you'll run into her at market or somewhere. She's a spunky sort."

"Does she stay in touch with any of her family?"

Marnie paused. "Bishop John allows written correspondence, as I understand it."

"The Bann seems cruel."

"I'm sure ya think so. But the shunning's for the purpose of bringing a wayward church member back into the fold. And it works, at least for some folk." She could see that Jenny was unconvinced. "Of course, Katie ran off for different reasons than most—wanted to search for her birth mother, of all things."

"She wasn't born Amish?" Jenny's face was suddenly ashen.

"No."

"This must be so hard for everyone who loved her."

"*Loves*," Marnie insisted. "Ach, my heart breaks for Aunt Rebecca, the Mamma who raised her. I can't abide the thought of losing a grown daughter to the world."

Jenny glanced away, and if Marnie wasn't mistaken, there was a tear in her eye. In this awkward moment, was Jenny thinking of her own family back in Connecticut? Here she'd left everything behind for the Amish life, and Katie had done just the opposite.

A heavy sorrow settled in the pit of Marnie's stomach. Was this another common strand attaching Jenny to Katie, like stitches in a quilt?

··· ⊱ ⊰ ···

Dancing splotches of light scattered over the road as Samuel Lapp drove the enclosed family carriage to the Preaching service on Sunday morning. The smell of tilled black earth and a predawn rain fused in the atmosphere as Jenny sat on the back bench of the buggy, peering out at the road behind them. She felt like a modern-day pilgrim watching at least a half dozen other such carriages form a gray caravan. Along the way, she noticed signs posted near mailboxes or at the end of lanes: *Bunnies for Sale, Rubber Stamp Supplies,* and *Firewood for Sale—No Sunday Sales!*

Jenny spotted a young Amish boy on in-line skates who held on to a long rope, attached to the back of one buggy. He couldn't have been more than eight years old as he skated his way to church. She was tempted to ask Rebecca, sitting up front to the left of her husband, if this was even safe. It certainly looked like fun, and the boy held on tightly as he swung way out and around when the horse and carriage made the turn left.

"Oh, stink!" Jenny heard Rebecca say.

"What is it?" Samuel replied.

"I left my best hankie at home."

"Well, is that any reason to be upset?"

Rebecca went silent.

"You want me to turn the horse round and go back, is that it?" Samuel said in the irritated tone Jenny had heard before.

"Nee, go on," Rebecca replied. "It's my fault for rushin' around so."

"You're sure, now?"

"We'll be late for church otherwise." Rebecca sighed. "No, I'll make do."

Samuel was quiet for a few moments; then Jenny heard his breathy "Haw," as he directed the horse to turn left into the deacon's lane.

This close now, she realized that the carriage pulling the skater was crowded in the back with young children. *One way to accommodate an extra passenger!* she thought, grinning.

The sun shone through the oak trees along one side of the deacon's driveway. Jenny squinted at the sky and felt hesitant yet joyful at the thought of attending her first-ever Amish church service. She'd gone to bed *"with the chickens"* last night, as Rebecca had strongly urged. Jenny had been staying up much too late, unable to rise and shine by five o'clock each morning. *"There are no shortcuts to becoming Amish,"* Rebecca had gently pointed out to her. Consequently, there had been no late-night session with her journal yesterday, either.

Still, anything worth doing is worth doing right, Jenny decided, embracing Rebecca's philosophy as she fell in step with her mentor. Jenny felt a little unsettled knowing the blue dress and white cape apron she wore today was the one Katie had worn for her botched wedding to Bishop John Beiler. Jenny wished Rebecca hadn't spilled the beans earlier, while they cooked breakfast together. *Why tell me?* Jenny wondered and decided she would sew her own Sunday clothes as soon as possible.

She followed Rebecca to the line of women and children, which included a number of small boys. Jenny enjoyed the cool air and the overall feeling of anticipation. She expected the church meeting to be a reverent one. Since much of the service would be in German, Rebecca had informed her of the order and explained what would transpire. Even though Jenny was dressed like the rest of the women, she was still con-sidered a visitor. An English one, at that. She would be thought of this way until she was a full-fledged member of the Hickory Hollow Amish church. *After my Proving,* she thought, standing with Rebecca until the long line began to shift toward the back door of the farmhouse. Rebecca whispered that it was time for her to take her place with the unbaptized teenaged girls, at the back of the line.

On her way there, Jenny couldn't help noticing Andrew Lapp in the procession of men. Besides Samuel and several of Samuel's nephews, Andrew was one of the few men she recognized. *Besides Preacher Yoder.* That man had offered a kind smile and a dip of his head earlier when he had arrived with Lovina.

Near the tail end of the line, a young woman motioned for her to step ahead of her, making Jenny the fifth from the last. "Denki," she whispered, and the girl nodded but did not smile.

Marnie held her breath as she observed Jenny Burns. Goodness, she'd failed to tell Jenny not to look over at the menfolk. You just didn't do that on Sunday mornings, when everyone's mind—and heart—was supposed to be fixed on worship. She didn't think Jenny was actually eyeing the young men, of course. There was so much the seeker would have to learn in order to be thought of as humble and submissive! Glancing over at the men lined up for church wasn't going to make the best first impression.

Ach, but Jenny has a good heart. All the letters Marnie had saved surely pointed to that. Marnie glimpsed her again and noted that Jenny looked better rested than on Friday, which was wonderful-*gut*. There was not much worse than being dog tired on a Preaching Sunday!

Prior to leaving to stand with the unbaptized girls, she said softly to her mother, "Mamm. I want you to meet my friend Jenny today."

"Ach, must I?"

"She's my *friend*, Mamm."

Her mother was quiet for a moment, then looked away.

"Isn't it about time?" Marnie whispered. "She's been here five days already."

"Well, might make better sense to see if she stays around."

It bothered her that Mamm wasn't interested in welcoming Jenny with open arms. *She just doesn't want to meet her,* Marnie thought glumly, glancing back at her English friend again.

I must talk to Jenny before the common meal, Marnie decided, lest the seeker make a serious misstep.

··· ❧ ❧ ···

Jenny quickly decided, once the hymns were finished, that the back of the large front room of the deacon's house was a perfect spot for a newcomer to fight sleep. Which Jenny certainly did, though less because she was tired and more because she was discouraged. Thanks to Mr. Zimmerman's high school German class, she had an idea what the first and the second sermons were about, but her head was hurting with the effort required to comprehend even that. And she didn't think she could sit for another minute, let alone the next full hour. Her seat was numb and her back ached from the hard wooden bench. If it wasn't so difficult, it would have been comical, especially since she'd read this very thing about Englishers who'd visited Amish church meetings.

She noticed Rebecca and her married sisters, as well as Marnie and her mother and younger siblings, all sitting straight as pins. She hoped to meet Marnie's family today, as well as a myriad of others. Yet she knew she would need to wait for them to make the first move—pushing into this cloistered community was not the best way to be accepted.

When eventually everyone turned to kneel at their bench, she did the same thing, surprised her legs actually worked, as anesthetized as they'd become. She thought of all the times she and Kyle Jackson had gone to college football games, taking along flat bleacher pillows to sit on. She liked the idea of having one for the Preaching service in two weeks.

Will I even last that long, Lord? she mused, aware of her stomach's rumbling while everyone else prayed silently. *Will I manage to abandon my selfish upbringing and cushy modern lifestyle to bow my knee in contrition and meekness as a baptized Amishwoman?*

15

AFTER the service, Jenny was told there was to be a meeting for only church members. Those who were not baptized headed to the screened-in back porch behind the kitchen. A few teen girls in identical blue dresses to Jenny's looked shyly at her in passing before wandering down the steps and over to the barn in a cluster. The boys, matching in black trousers and coats with white shirts buttoned to the neck, sauntered in the opposite direction, toward the woodshed.

Jenny pulled on the black shawl Rebecca had loaned her for the day and waited on the porch with a handful of small children who sat along the wall on a padded bench. Several eyed her while talking softly among themselves in Deitsch. In time, two of the older little girls popped up and began a quiet clapping game, spinning around in between claps, their organdy aprons fluttering about. Jenny wished she could speak their language—she longed to interact, feeling again like the outsider she was. But she continued to watch the well-behaved, even demure youngsters from her corner.

Sighing, Jenny wished again that she'd grown up here. She wouldn't have so much catching up to do. *And I'd be able to handle the long Preaching service, too!* Her previously easy life had spoiled her, making this entry into the Amish world more challenging than she'd ever imagined.

She looked off toward the distant hills, the landscape shining with the freshness of the day. Birds tweeted and horses neighed in the stable, the sounds of nature blending with the intermittent laughter coming from the nearby woodshed. In the background was the steady drone of the preacher's voice as he spoke to those still in the house.

It was some time later, when the private meeting adjourned, that Jenny was greeted by Emmalyn Lapp, who wore a maroon-colored dress with her white apron and Kapp. Her golden blond hair was perfectly parted in the middle and neatly slicked back on either side.

"Hi, Emmalyn," said Jenny, hoping she might be more pleasant this encounter.

"Wie geht's?" Emmalyn asked, her pale blue eyes wide.

"I'm fine—how are you?"

"Ah, so you *do* know." The teenager smirked. "Wunnerbaar-*gut.*"

"I'm slow but sure."

"But are you as hungry as I am?" Emmalyn moved her head gracefully in the direction of the kitchen.

"I'm starving. How do you say that in Deitsch?" Jenny laughed softly.

"Did ya understand anything the preachers said?" Emmalyn asked, seemingly ignoring Jenny's question.

"Not much."

Emmalyn pulled her shawl closer, a slow smile on her face. "If you want to ward off your hunger, just go in and help yourself to some slices of lunchmeat or cheese and whatnot."

"Really?"

"Just to hold you over, ya know."

Jenny didn't have to be told twice. She moved past Emmalyn and went inside, caving in to her hunger pangs. She reached for two slices of bologna and one of Swiss cheese, rolled them up, and took a bite. Then, seeing a pile of bread, she took a slice of that, as well.

On the way back to the porch, she noticed the bishop's wife staring at her. Not only Mary Beiler, but also Andrew was looking her way—and grimacing.

She kept going, her head down a little, and made her way back outside, taking another bite of her delicious snack as she went.

Emmalyn was no longer in sight when Jenny returned to the porch, so she stood over in the corner, pushing the meat and cheese into the bread and folding it over to make a half sandwich. She was thankful for Emmalyn's suggestion as she nibbled away but could hardly remember a worse Sunday worship experience. Was she just impatient . . . in need of humility? *I want to be one of them*, she thought. *If I have the fortitude.*

She thought again of the backbreaking service.

"Uh, Jenny Burns, isn't it?"

She whirled around as Andrew Lapp stepped onto the porch.

She wiped her mouth on the back of her hand and refrained from eating the last delectable bite.

He moved toward her, eyes narrowing. "You're partaking of food before the brethren?"

She nodded, not sure she ought to say it was Emmalyn who'd given her the go-ahead. "Is it all right? I mean—"

"Well, now, the first seating for the shared meal is always for the ministers and folk up in years," he informed her.

"But I thought it was all right to . . ." But, no, she wasn't going to throw his sister under the bus, even though it seemed evident Emmalyn had deliberately misled her.

"The second seating is for younger marrieds and single young people. You'll likely sit with my aunt Rebecca and her sisters." His direct words did not match his mannerly tone. He had a thoughtful way about him, Jenny noticed, and it comforted her, especially now.

"Denki, Andrew. I really appreciate knowing."

At that moment, Lovina Yoder appeared in the doorway, blinking and twisting the front of her apron into a knot. "Ach, I . . ." the preacher's wife murmured, then hurried back inside.

Jenny had no clue what was wrong. "I'm terribly confused." She looked up at Andrew, who still offered his calming presence.

His blue eyes held her gaze. "Ask me anything at all."

"I've obviously made a mistake by preempting the meal with a snack."

His eyes twinkled suddenly. "And did ya pray a blessing over this nibble?"

"Actually, I did not." She paused and noticed a couple of young women looking out the window. One of them was the bishop's wife. She cringed. "Are we not supposed to be . . . talking?"

Andrew drew in a long breath and folded his arms. "The age-old rule is that women are to congregate with like women on Preachin' Sundays— married women together, and single women with others who are single."

"So the men and women mustn't mingle on Sunday?"

He was nodding slowly, still gazing intently at her. "Not before or after the Preachin' service, nee."

"Gotcha," she said, forgetting momentarily that she was supposed to be a quaint, soft-spoken Amishwoman.

He smiled, his lips parting. "You'll catch on soon enough, Jenny."

"That's encouraging, thanks."

"Do ya mean Denki?"

"Jah, and that, too."

"*Da Herr sei mit du.*" Andrew turned to head down the back steps, toward the woodshed.

I'll have to look that up, Jenny told herself. Did he mean *God be with you,* perhaps? She ate the last of the unsanctified snack and watched Andrew go, hoping he would keep walking and not look back and see her still staring.

16

JENNY hoped neither Andrew Lapp nor anyone else was observing her later that afternoon as she watched Marnie's father, Chester Lapp, hitch up the driving horse and carriage. Chester eyed her warily while he and Marnie slowly backed the driving horse between the shafts as, all the while, Marnie described the process in English. Jenny tried hard to remember the various steps, aware of the hollow feeling in the pit of her stomach. How many times would she have to be shown this before she could do it herself?

Once the horse and carriage were successfully hitched, Chester Lapp called for his family to get settled inside for the ride home. Marnie quickly introduced Jenny to her mother, Peggy, who seemed reluctant to shake her hand and greet her. Then, that quickly, Marnie was waving as she climbed into the back with her younger siblings. "I'll see ya sometime this week, all right?" Marnie said.

Jenny nodded. "It was nice to meet your parents today."

Marnie smiled apologetically. "Keep your chin up, Jenny!"

"Denki," Jenny replied and trudged over to the deacon's house, where Rebecca stood waiting patiently, a compassionate smile on her face. "Would it be possible to write down the steps for hitching up?" Jenny asked her. "Might be a good idea."

"Of course, but I think you'll learn better just by doin'," Rebecca said.

Sure doesn't seem that way.

"I daresay you're fretting yourself, ain't so?"

316

Jenny couldn't verbalize the truth—that she was afraid she'd never get it right.

"You have plenty of time, remember?" Rebecca motioned her inside. "Come now, I'd like you to meet some of my friends before they leave for home."

Not in the best frame of mind to socialize, she followed Rebecca into the house, where an elderly woman sat in an oak pressed-back chair near the window, holding her cane just so. Her small blue eyes shone as Jenny approached her.

Rebecca leaned down near the older woman. "Ella Mae, this is our seeker, Jenny Burns," she said. Then, turning to Jenny, she said, "And, Jenny, I'd like you to meet my lifelong friend, Ella Mae Zook."

The white-haired woman stretched out her gnarled hand. "Hullo, Jenny Burns. It's *gut* to meet ya."

"Jenny's from Connecticut," Rebecca added, straightening to her full height.

"Well, dearie, you're a long ways from home," Ella Mae said. "Ain't so?"

Jenny hadn't thought of it quite like that. "It would take a very long time by horse and buggy, absolutely." She smiled down at the petite woman.

"Did ya have a nice trip here?" asked Ella Mae.

Jenny told how excited she'd been last Tuesday. "That day is a complete blur to me."

Ella Mae cocked her head. "You have a little accent, don't you?"

"No one's ever mentioned it." Jenny was actually charmed by the diminutive lady, who had a smile that was a fascinating blend of reassurance and mischief. *"She's never met a seeker,"* Jenny recalled Marnie telling her. *Not in her lifetime. I'm a rarity.*

"You'll have to drop by and have a cup of my peppermint tea sometime," Ella Mae said in her delicate voice. "I'd like to hear your story."

Jenny was taken aback, but seeing her lovely smile reappear, she assumed the woman was only being friendly.

"I'm quite serious," Ella Mae added. "Do come visit me anytime."

"Thanks, um . . . Denki. How nice of you!"

"It's time we got acquainted."

Jenny nodded, feeling better suddenly, though she didn't know exactly why. Ella Mae's demeanor was as much of an encouragement to her as Andrew's had been earlier.

"Why not go 'n' see her on Tuesday, after Monday washday?" Rebecca suggested.

"Tuesday it shall be," Ella Mae piped up even before Jenny could agree.

And Jenny did so with a cautious smile. *Is this Rebecca's idea?* she wondered.

During the ride to the Lapp farm, Jenny again sat in the back of the buggy. It wasn't long before she noticed the same carriage with the boy skater attached by rope, coming fast upon them, about to pass them on the narrow stretch of road. The driver was a middle-aged man with a bushy dark brown beard that protruded out over his chest. And if she wasn't mistaken, he was looking over at her, grinning. Instantly uncomfortable, she looked away. *Who is that?*

When they pulled into the Lapps' lane, Jenny offered to help unhitch the horse, but Rebecca intervened and suggested Jenny'd had enough for one day. She urged her to spend some quiet time alone in her room, which Jenny welcomed. She had been so busy the past two days, she'd failed to write in her journal, so she sat on the bed and began to jot down her thoughts.

> *It's amazing what a person can absorb in a few days' time. I never gave butchering chickens much thought, but now I can pluck feathers and prepare the bird for cooking. Rebecca knows how to break a chicken's neck humanely, with the least amount of pain for the bird. She is a stronger woman than she appears and can do this chore without help . . . whereas I could hardly watch the first time. I tried to think of having nothing to eat but that poor full-grown chicken. Guess I'll need to think like a homesteader if I want to fit in here.*
>
> *Rebecca told me that sometimes the weakest chicken will get pecked to death by the others, and I've wondered if I'll end up like that, too. I don't mean that anyone's really picking on me . . . well, except Emmalyn Lapp, who obviously set me up today before the common meal. Thankfully, her brother Andrew didn't think poorly of me for eating ahead of time.*

Or then again, he may have concealed what he truly thinks. Who knows what any of them are whispering about now.

At times like this, I can't help thinking about my former home. I'm even starting to miss my family—I wish I hadn't kept them in the dark about coming here.

There are moments I don't even know what I think anymore, other than the fact that Andrew Lapp has to be the best-looking Amish—or English—guy anywhere!

··· ➤ ◄ ···

"Our young seeker is discouraged," Rebecca told Samuel as they rested in their room that afternoon. "I can see it on her face."

Samuel was still for a while, his eyes closed. Then he drew a slow breath. "Jenny Burns is not solely your responsibility, Rebecca."

She knew as much and was glad Jenny would ultimately be overseen by the bishop. Even so, she wanted to see the young woman succeed more than anything. Well, almost. Her thoughts flew to Katie, as they often did on the Lord's Day. Pity's sake, they'd lost one girl from the Amish church. Oh, she hoped she could manage to keep concealing the visits. It was imperative, though she never thought of going to see dearest Katie as actually sinning. *But the ministerial brethren would certainly think so. As would Samuel . . .*

"Have ya thought of lettin' things run their course?" Samuel said drowsily. "Have ya?"

She looked at him in surprise, her mind still on Katie. "What?" Her throat was terribly dry.

"Jenny must find her own way," he said.

Goodness, she was relieved. Although she hadn't thought that way at all since the young woman had walked through the back door and into her life. *Their lives.*

"Are ya napping now, Rebecca?" her husband asked, rolling over to peep at her before he shut his eyes again.

"Not just yet."

"Well, what do you think 'bout what I said? Are ya deaf, or just playin' like it?"

"I don't know what to say."

He smiled, his eyes still closed. "I think ya do." Sighing, he adjusted the pillow. "You're getting too attached to her, I daresay."

Rebecca shrugged. He was probably right.

"If she fails, you'll be terribly troubled, jah?"

"Well, she won't."

"You don't know that for sure." His eyes flicked open. "Mark my words, Rebecca. You'll get your heart all bound up in Jenny . . . won't be *gut* for ya. You hear?"

She'd heard but she also had high hopes. "The girl needs help if she's goin' to get through to her baptism."

"That's what I'm talking 'bout."

Rebecca turned and stared at the dresser and the gas lantern. Then and there, she remembered her dream from a couple of weeks ago and trembled. She was thankful when Samuel slipped his burly arm around her and held her that way till she fell fast asleep at last.

···➤ ≺···

Marnie left the house soon after they arrived home, as she often did on a Sunday afternoon. Even on a fairly chilly afternoon such as this, she liked to get out and walk. It was easiest to sort through her thoughts when she was alone beneath the sky and sun. Sometimes, too, Roy came by in his open buggy, soaring down Hickory Lane. *Just maybe.*

She hoped with all of her heart he'd understood what she'd written in her letter, which he would have received by now. There was enough time for him to have replied, as well, but she knew he was busy helping his father these days, baling corn fodder for stable bedding.

Still, it nagged at her that he and his family seemed to be moving in the opposite direction of the Old Order. She couldn't help but wonder if Roy's parents were as interested in the Bible studies as Roy was.

She couldn't fret her afternoon away, but she hoped to know the answers, and surely she would, soon enough. "If Roy drops by," she whispered, nearly holding her breath every time a courting buggy made the bend in the road and headed this way. Oh, what she'd give to feel her hand in his on this beautiful November Lord's Day!

17

THE following Tuesday morning, Jenny was reminded of her visit with Ella Mae Zook. Rebecca brought it up right after she said *Guder Mariye* when Jenny appeared in the kitchen to help with cooking.

Jenny repeated the words, which meant good morning. She smiled as she recalled how Rebecca had been spending more time teaching her Deitsch since just Sunday evening, when they'd sat down together following supper. Jenny had noticed an almost maternal change in Rebecca's demeanor and was delighted for the extra help. Samuel, on the other hand, seemed quieter than ever, but Jenny assumed the reverence of the Lord's Day had something to do with it. *Except his reticence has continued into the week*, she thought.

"There's a bit of ironing and mending to do after breakfast," Rebecca said. "Then we'll clean the main level of the house before making the noon meal. And, while we work, why don't we practice speaking Deitsch?"

Jenny was heartened. "I'd like that. Denki."

"We'll start with a review of the more common expressions, then go over some household words."

It was great how Rebecca was jumping on board with Jenny's goal. She hurried to get the flour out of the pantry, and on the way noticed Andrew Lapp through the window, walking across the yard toward the barn. He was waving his straw hat at something, and she caught herself smiling. For the life of her, she couldn't understand why such a handsome guy was still single, especially in Amish country. She remembered what Marnie had said—something about a number of young women trying to catch his eye but failing. Andrew's being unattached was a mystery, indeed.

When Samuel and two of his nephews came in for breakfast, Jenny wondered if Andrew might also join them. But when she glanced out the window again, she saw his spring wagon heading up the road. Not once had he shared a meal there since her arrival. But then again, he came to help sporadically; undoubtedly he had to return to his own work.

Besides, it was silly to set her eyes on a man, no matter how appealing he seemed to be. *I don't need any distractions!*

"Eli needs my help repairing his horse fence this afternoon," Samuel stated to Rebecca during breakfast. "I'd like ya to groom Ol' Molasses for me." She nodded quickly, then glanced at Jenny. "We did have plans already to go 'n' see Ella Mae."

"You'll just have to postpone" came Samuel's swift reply. "You can't be takin' the oldest horse out on the road anyways. He will have his fill of miles by then."

Rebecca was torn between wanting to say something privately to Samuel and demonstrating her willingness to submit in all matters. *Especially now,* with Jenny observing. How else was the young woman going to learn to be a good wife someday?

"Maybe I'll send Jenny over there on foot by herself," she replied mildly. She didn't want to spoil Jenny's plans, and Ella Mae would be expecting her, even looking forward to the visit.

"Maybe she could stay home and work on hitchin' up instead," Samuel shot back. "Or spend time helping you with groomin'. 'Tis the best way to bond with a horse, ya know."

Rebecca stiffened, resenting his tone but refusing to let it get the best of her. *Why is he so blunt?*

She simply nodded again and cut into the sausage and scrambled eggs on her plate. Oh, she hoped Jenny understood that Samuel was a kind man and good husband, not as demanding as he seemed here lately. Sadly, his benevolent side had all but disappeared.

⋯ ➤ ⬅ ⋯

Jenny realized Rebecca was doing her husband's bidding and sacrificing the time for her own chores by grooming the aging horse. She accompanied Rebecca out to the stable, offering to help. Thus far, Jenny had seen no sign of any delayed resistance to Samuel's earlier demands, which surprised her. Hearing Samuel bark his orders at the table had given her a headache. In fact, she wanted to mention something to Rebecca but knew she'd better not. Observing the woman's meek behavior with her husband reinforced what Marnie had written in her letters about the importance of submission in marriage and in the community. *Surrendering her will,* thought Jenny. *Resigning selfish wishes and desires in the silence of the soul.*

After Rebecca shooed her back to the house to clean up the kitchen, Jenny wished she could hurry down to the little springhouse to collect her thoughts . . . and pray for humility. *And to reside quietly in Christ.* Because if a future husband ever spoke that way to her, she *knew* she would stand up to him. The core of her heart was anything but obedient. *Far from it.*

"Mom talks right over Dad," she whispered. *Yet she's devoted to him.* But everyone interrupted and talked over everyone. She considered the twenty-four-hour news shows on TV and talk radio . . . even conversations with co-workers or friends.

At that moment, Jenny could see a marked difference between her father and Samuel Lapp. One was well satisfied to let a woman have her say, and the other had to have the upper hand.

She recalled Samuel's remark that she ought to stay home to practice hitching up. Actually, it was the last thing Jenny wanted to do this afternoon. Would discounting his wishes be stubborn and haughty?

I'll ask Ella Mae about submission, Jenny decided, wishing she had the right to wander at will today. A brisk walk might help her get past the frustration over Samuel's insistence. But could she find her way around Hickory Hollow without Rebecca's help?

The air was chilly and a light wind had come up as Jenny set out to follow Rebecca's directions down Hickory Lane and beyond. Rebecca had said Ella Mae was known for her specially brewed peppermint tea, which would be waiting for Jenny upon her arrival, *"to warm you up."*

The way Rebecca had rebounded from the earlier conversation with

Samuel still surprised Jenny, even though nothing more had been said at the noon meal. She was beginning to think her own skin must be too thin. As good-natured and compliant as Rebecca was, she must have already forgotten or even overlooked Samuel's words.

Jenny planned to note in her journal the times when Rebecca acquiesced to Samuel. She'd never known such a humble spirit. It just wasn't human nature to be that way.

She heard a horse *clip-clop*ping behind her but didn't want to glance over her shoulder, in case it was a man driving this way. She was still finding her way through the labyrinth of social expectations. *I don't want to make another misstep!*

Next thing she knew, the horse was slowing to keep pace with her as she walked quickly along the roadside. Uncomfortable as it was, she did not dare turn to look.

"Hullo there." The voice was surprisingly familiar.

She spied Andrew Lapp there, riding in his spring wagon. He held the reins taut, his muscular arms parallel to his knees.

"*Wie bischt?*"

"*Yuscht* fine, and you?" she replied, wondering why she felt so light-hearted around a man she hardly knew.

"Say, I believe you're comin' along with your Amish."

"Denki, but it's pretty jumbled."

"We all begin somewhere, ain't?"

She wondered if he was going to offer her a ride and almost hoped so. Was it written on her face?

"Are ya headin' anywhere in particular?" he asked, and there was that twinkle again. Was he really just a flirt?

"Out for a long walk."

"But not aimlessly walkin', jah?" He chuckled. "You remind me of someone." He slowed the horse even more. "Spunky . . . and with the same color of hair."

"Anyone I might know?"

"Well, now, I'm tryin' to think who 'tis."

She laughed softly. Was he fishing to see what she knew about Katie Lapp Fisher? Marnie had said on Sunday that Jenny could be mistaken for Katie's sister.

She kept walking, picking up her speed a little now and wondering if he'd make his horse follow suit.

"How're things goin' so far?"

"Wunnerbaar-*gut*," she replied.

"Glad to hear it."

"By the way, I'm headed to Ella Mae Zook's—am I going the right way?"

"You certainly are. Not much farther now before you turn to the north." Andrew grinned and cued his horse to trot, giving her a big wave before he moved along. "*Hatyee*—so long, Jenny!"

She fought a smile of her own, unable to get a read on his peculiar actions. What made this man tick?

18

JENNY passed by Marnie's house on the way to Ella Mae's but didn't see her friend anywhere outdoors. *Probably busy helping her mother prepare food for one of the first of many Thursday weddings,* she thought, remembering what Marnie had said last time.

A row of potted orange mums on the front porch steps caught her eye with its colorful display. Marnie had written more than a month ago about going to a nearby greenhouse to purchase autumn plants from their Amish neighbor, Maryanna, whose young children helped her prepare orders for customers.

The wind rose even more by the time Jenny made the right-hand turn at the far end of Nate Kurtz's massive cornfield, where she could finally see the farmhouse Rebecca had so perfectly described.

Ella Mae Zook, minus her cane, greeted Jenny on the small white porch off her side of the complex of houses attached to the main one. She ushered Jenny inside out of the cold, into a pleasantly snug kitchen that smelled appealingly of peppermint. A yellow ceramic teapot adorned with a yellow-and-green tea cozy awaited on the counter.

Jenny took off her black shawl and outer bonnet, both of which belonged to Rebecca. "Where would you like me to hang them?" she asked politely.

"There's an empty hook over yonder." Ella Mae pointed toward the back door, her expression serious.

Is she scrutinizing me, too? The older woman seemed guarded, similar to almost everyone else Jenny had encountered in the past week.

"How was the walk over?" asked Ella Mae, going to the counter and opening a cupboard above her white head. She reached for two teacups and set them on the counter.

Jenny said she'd enjoyed it very much, then quickly explained that Rebecca Lapp had stayed home to help her husband groom a horse.

"That's all right. Rebecca comes here quite often." She pulled out the chair and seated Jenny as if she were an honored guest. The gesture was sweet and reminded Jenny of something her mother might do. "Would ya care for some homemade pastries with your tea, Jenny?"

"I'd love some. Denki."

Ella Mae's eyes brightened. "Well, you sound nearly Amish."

"I have a feeling I'll speak Deitsch long before I'm able to embody the spirit of submission. Like Rebecca . . . and the other women in the community."

Ella Mae nodded. "That quality comes more easily for some, I'll admit." She carried the teacups to the small table, each one perched on its matching saucer, and set one in front of Jenny on a place mat embroidered with yellow roses. Her wrinkled hand trembled, which caused the other cup and saucer to jingle as she situated it on her own place mat directly across from Jenny. "Our mothers here begin training their wee tots in obedience from the time a child is two. You won't see many *rutschich* little ones at the table, for example. They're taught to sit still and be patient."

"Do you mean submission can be taught?"

Ella Mae smiled. "To a clean slate—a young child—jah. Although some youngsters have stronger wills than others, of course. They're taught to recite this old school verse and take it to heart: 'I must be a Christian child, gentle, patient, meek and mild; must be honest, simple, true, in my words and actions, too. I must cheerfully obey, giving up my will and way. . . . Must remember God can view all I think and all I do.'"

Jenny considered Ella Mae's remarks and the traditional poem.

"Are ya havin' some trouble with this?" Ella Mae gently asked.

"It's just that I know myself too well." Jenny was reluctant to say more.

"Chust remember the Lord God knows your heart better than you know it yourself."

It was hard not to like this woman. "And He still loves us, in spite of ourselves," Jenny added.

"*Jah*, despite our shortcomings."

They sipped their tea; several cups' worth, it was so tasty. A large plate of treats graced the middle of the table, including two Jenny didn't recognize. Her generous hostess seemed happy to name them off: pineapple cookies and walnut drops. There were sand tarts, as well.

"You're spoiling me," Jenny said.

"Well, now, you've been through a rough week, I s'pose. So why not sit back and enjoy?"

Jenny agreed. "You're very kind, thank you."

Ella Mae dipped her head and demurely peeked up at her. "I'm awful glad you came, or I would've been takin' tea alone this afternoon."

"Do you have tea at different times of day like the Brits do?"

"I honestly don't know what they do over there, dearie. I've been known to drink tea three times in a day, sometimes with my noon meal, which is considered dinnertime amongst the Amish."

Jenny smiled. "Marnie filled me in on that and many other things before I made the decision to come here."

"Marnie's a *gut* and faithful friend."

"*Jah*, and it's almost as if we've grown up together."

"Did you see each other a few times before you started writing letters?"

"Actually, it was after we first met that we began exchanging letters. Each summer after that, we've visited at the Bird-in-Hand Farmers Market, taking several walks together."

"But you never stayed in an Amish home till now?"

"No." She didn't say that Marnie's mother had been nervous about her daughter being friends with an Englisher.

"It must be quite the experience, livin' in an Amish house."

"It's different than I thought."

"In what ways?"

Jenny mentioned the nearly nonstop work, as well as the specific duties required of women versus men. "There's so much cooking. No matter how much food Rebecca and I prepare, there are rarely leftovers."

Ella Mae tittered. "There aren't many shy folk at the table round here. Second and third helpings are mighty common."

They talked about the current wedding season, and Ella Mae mentioned she had three great-granddaughters getting married between this Thursday and the middle of December. "Thankfully, they all didn't choose the same day!"

"Could you possibly attend more than one wedding in a day?" Jenny asked.

"Well, that's just the thing . . . ya can, but not the whole day, ya know." Ella Mae reached for another sand tart she'd been eyeing. "It's all right to eat a few of these, ya know. They're ever so thin."

Jenny smiled. "I noticed that, too. Trust me, these cookies are an art form. You should see mine—well, maybe not. They're at least five times thicker."

Ella Mae gave a wave of her hand. "Ach, I have little else to do nowadays. My eyes are wearin' out, so I don't do tatting or embroidery anymore." She looked about the kitchen and the small sitting room adjoining. "I much prefer to bake, and the more I do, the thinner my sand tarts get, I daresay."

Jenny wondered if, at times, even baking posed a challenge for the frail-looking woman.

"Growing old has its moments." Ella Mae's voice grew weary. "Times of reckoning, for sure and for certain."

"Do you have any regrets?" Jenny asked, hoping she wasn't being too prying.

"Honestly, if I think on it, I'm embarrassed by some of my youthful decisions." Ella Mae paused to touch one of the strings of her Kapp. "And, if I may be so bold to say, some of the church's, too."

Jenny was so surprised, she didn't know what to make of this.

"Ach, but you're startin' out . . . chust comin' into the Old Ways." Ella Mae turned her face to the window. "I'd never want to discourage you on your journey. Never."

"Rebecca tells me the People aren't perfect—no church is," Jenny said.

"And she's right." Ella Mae reached over and took hold of her hand. Her eyes welled up as she searched Jenny's face and gently squeezed her fingers. "Never forget that, dearie. Keep your eyes fixed on the Lord Jesus, and you'll never be disappointed."

The words of the Wise Woman, as Rebecca said she was called, settled in as Jenny thanked Ella Mae for inviting her to the lovely tea, then reached for the shawl and bonnet before heading out the door into the cold air. Even colder now that the sun was concealed by a long, flimsy cloud, like a windblown bridal veil.

She's embarrassed by some of the church's decisions. Jenny stood silently on the porch, letting Ella Mae's poignant words linger. At the very least, she hoped she might return for another visit. Perhaps she might become a helpful friend to the elderly woman who had affected her so deeply, moving her in ways Jenny did not fully comprehend.

Was she giving me a warning? Jenny wondered as she walked down the narrow sidewalk. Then again, Ella Mae had stated that she didn't want to discourage Jenny.

She turned to look back at the little dwelling built onto the larger house, which belonged to Ella Mae's daughter Mattie Beiler. And as she did, she noticed a man with a very bushy brown beard walking out of the main farmhouse across the small yard. When he spotted her there, his ruddy face broke into a broad smile.

"Aren't you Jenny Burns, the seeker from Connecticut?" he asked, coming her way.

"Yes, uh . . . jah." She'd seen him before—the middle-aged man in the buggy that had passed them on Sunday after church. This was the father of the boy who had skated to and from Preaching.

"Well, I'm mighty pleased to meet ya." He stuck out his big callused hand. "Hezekiah Stoltzfus is my name. Just call me Hezzy, if you don't mind."

"Denki." She quickly let go of his hand.

"I'm Mary Beiler's uncle, just over pickin' up some mending." He nodded in what Jenny assumed was the direction of the bishop's place. "I go over there to help the minister out some with the livestock and whatnot all." He glanced back toward Mattie Beiler's house. "Ya might not know the bishop and Ella Mae's son-in-law, David, are brothers." He laughed heartily. "Goodness knows, nearly all of us are related here in the hollow."

She gave him what she hoped was a polite smile, noticing how dark his beard was compared to his peppered, graying hair. It crossed her mind that he might be using hair dye on his beard, assuming an Amishman would do such a thing. "Well, I'd better get going."

"I'm headin' out, too . . . why don't I give you a lift, Jenny?"

Yikes, she thought, wondering how to get out of this gracefully. No way was she getting into his carriage. Next thing, all of Hickory Hollow would have her linked to this older man!

She was thinking of what to say so as not to offend him when she heard the squeak of Ella Mae's screen door, followed by her thin voice. "Jenny, dear?"

"Excuse me, please," she said, grateful for this unexpected yet convenient distraction. She ran back to Ella Mae's house. "What is it?" Jenny asked.

"Won't ya come inside for a moment?" Ella Mae pushed the door open wider and eyed Hezekiah, who appeared to be waiting for Jenny's answer.

"Thank you," Jenny whispered, trying to keep a straight face, even though Ella Mae did not. She remembered her manners and turned to offer a polite wave to the man, who nodded, seemingly disappointed, but there was a hopeful glint in his eyes.

"*Gut* to meet ya. Maybe another time?"

"Have a nice day!" Jenny practically blurted. And then, when the door was closed, Jenny breathed a sigh of relief. "You saved me!"

Ella Mae's grin was mischievous. "You stay right here till he's *gut* and gone, if ya'd like."

"Believe me, you don't have to ask twice." And Jenny thanked the Wise Woman once again.

19

J ENNY followed Ella Mae through the connecting door to her married daughter's farmhouse. There, she was introduced to Mattie Beiler, who'd only just returned from visiting a sick relative. The woman looked as though she was in her sixties—evidently her husband, David, was the bishop's much older brother.

"Mattie's helped deliver many a baby here locally," the Wise Woman said.

"Your mother certainly is a lovely person," Jenny said as she shook Mattie's hand and smiled back at Ella Mae.

"I agree," replied Mattie. "And her peppermint tea's not bad, either."

They laughed, exchanging glances.

Like every other Amishwoman Jenny had visited, Mattie offered a treat, along with something to drink. Almost without waiting for their response, Mattie began to pour some hot coffee. "I heard from my sister-in-law Mary—the bishop's wife—that she'd like you to stay with her three youngest children tomorrow morning, Jenny. She needs to run some errands for a couple of hours."

Jenny asked what time she should be over there.

"Right after breakfast is fine. The bishop's place is real close to Samuel and Rebecca's—right across the field, in fact," Mattie said.

"Yes, I've been there." Jenny glanced at Ella Mae. "And anyway, I managed to find *this* house, didn't I?"

That brought a chuckle from both women, and the three of them sat down and sipped black coffee and had some fresh-baked oatmeal-and-raisin cookies. A few minutes later, Mattie brought out little cakes topped with coconut, and some tempting butterscotch cookies, too. Jenny was starting to think the women who lived in this house were always either baking or eating!

"I noticed Hezzy out there talkin' to ya," Mattie said, looking right at Jenny. "He's Mary's widowed uncle—has a whole passel of children. But he's just friendly."

"He means well," Ella Mae added, looking tired.

Jenny wondered if she might have overstayed her welcome. "I should get back to help Rebecca," she said, smiling her thanks again to Ella Mae. "The goodies were delicious," she told Mattie. "I'm going to get fat if I keep snacking like this."

"Well, have yourself a nice walk back," Mattie said. "And if Hezzy swings round to catch ya on the road, don't be timid 'bout talkin' to him."

"Oh, for pity's sake, Mattie," said Ella Mae. "Leave the girl be! She's just begun her Proving, remember?"

Mattie was grinning. "Puh! I have my opinion and you have yours, ain't?"

"Isn't that the truth?" replied Ella Mae.

Jenny laughed, but she wasn't keen on the idea of going back to the Lapps' without the covering of a carriage—a place to hide from Hezzy's very wide grin. If only she'd hurry and learn how to hitch up a horse!

All the way up Hickory Lane, she was vividly aware of the many carriages and wagons coming and going. She even held her breath as they passed—and was quite relieved when they did.

Marnie was more than pleased when a letter arrived in the afternoon mail from Roy Flaud. Her heart fluttered to beat the band. *Glory be!* He'd kindly offered to meet her at her cousin's wedding on Thursday morning. Marnie could hardly wait to see him again, she missed him so.

I'd like to talk to you further about the house meeting I mentioned in my earlier note, he'd written toward the middle of the page. Roy went on about how it was something he'd contemplated a lot. *I feel we ought to go as an engaged couple . . . making our own choices.*

She read further, realizing that it was just as clear from the rest of the letter that Roy wanted her to reconsider her stance. *Maybe he'd best talk to Dat about this,* she thought. *Dare I even suggest that?*

Roy was so very important to her; she knew without a doubt he loved her. But it was peculiar that he was pushing her this way. She'd pondered more than a few times that he hadn't been baptized into his Bird-in-Hand church district yet. But then, neither had she joined church in Hickory Hollow, waiting to follow her beau's lead. Still, being solidly Amish was as serious a matter for Marnie as it was to her parents.

A shiver ran down her back at the thought of upsetting her father over such a thing. *Never!* she promised herself, recalling his rage over her older brother's brief flirtation with the fancy world.

Rebecca had long since finished grooming Ol' Molasses. Presently, she made preparations for supper without Jenny's help, wondering what was keeping her. She continued chopping the onions, celery, and carrots for her thick stew, aware of the vacant spot at the counter where Jenny usually worked. Rebecca pursed her lips to keep them from quivering. What was wrong with her, checking the wall clock every five minutes? Was she already that wrapped up in the seeker?

She brushed such thoughts aside and tried to focus more on understanding why Jenny had kept her family in the dark about coming here. *Was it really because they hold enough sway over her to change her mind? Or is there something else, something she hasn't yet revealed?*

Rebecca stopped her work to wipe her forehead with a hankie. Goodness, maybe she ought to take to heart Ella Mae's initial concerns about Jenny's motives—whatever they might be. Even so, if the young woman was staying in Hickory Hollow only to search for an Amish husband, her demeanor and attitude did not lend itself to those leanings.

Truth be told, Jenny's auburn hair and personality were a constant reminder of Katie, who had also left her family to follow her heart. Rebecca's breath caught in her throat.

Dearest Katie, living out her days as a Mennonite. Sighing deeply, Rebecca couldn't help but wonder if her adopted daughter ever missed her former Amish life, the heritage of her childhood. *The life Samuel and I gave her.*

Rebecca gathered up the chopped vegetables from the wooden cutting board and placed them in a large bowl, then added some cubed beef for the stew. Silently, she offered up a plea for Dan and Katie's return to the church of their families.

How much longer, O Lord?

··· ➤ ➤ ···

I managed to catch up with my chores as soon as I arrived back from the interesting visit with Ella Mae Zook—and her daughter Mattie Beiler. Dived right into baking some pumpkin walnut bread and twelve dozen chocolate macaroons, which Rebecca plans to take to market tomorrow while I help the bishop's wife with her youngest children.

Also, after supper, I helped mend Samuel's shirts with Rebecca, who didn't talk as much as she usually does while we worked. I caught her looking at me rather suspiciously once or twice. Is something bothering her?

And, because I really want my own clothing, instead of wearing Katie's old dresses, I cut out two—one blue, one green. It was strange, having the house so quiet while I worked in Rebecca's small sewing room down the hall, but both Samuel and Rebecca seemed extra tired today. Maybe grooming the horse wore Rebecca out, and now, in retrospect, I wish I would have stayed to help her. Such a hardworking woman! Yet I so enjoyed spending time with Ella Mae. I can see why everyone refers to her as the Old Wise Woman.

As for tomorrow, I'm nervous about taking care of the bishop's kids, wanting to do everything exactly as Mary wishes. I've never cared for the children of someone "anointed by God," as I've heard the People describe the bishop.

To think I've yet to even meet this revered man!

As often as she committed tomorrow to the Lord, Jenny had difficulty shaking off her apprehension of the man who'd put Katie and her husband under the dreaded veil of the shunning.

20

REBECCA hardly made eye contact with Jenny during breakfast preparations the next morning, though she was cordial enough. Perhaps she was only tired—Rebecca looked worn out, despite the fact she was typically a whirlwind of energy. Considering this, Jenny felt reluctant to leave the house to help Mary Beiler today, even though Mattie Beiler had said Jenny was expected over at the bishop's. It seemed strange that Jenny hadn't heard directly from Mary about this. Was it the Amish way for one person to tell another until the information found its way to the correct set of ears?

No need for cell phones here!

Rebecca quietly handed Jenny a platter of pancakes to carry to the table. Her hostess's rather sudden detachment weighed on Jenny. What had changed between them?

When Jenny arrived at the Beilers' farmhouse, the back door was standing open, but the storm door was closed. So she knocked softly, her pulse fluttering like a hummingbird in her throat.

I'll be working for the man who holds my very future in his hands!

No one came, and she knocked harder, hoping Mattie hadn't gotten her wires crossed about Jenny's being needed this morning.

Should she keep knocking?

Unsure of herself, Jenny raised her hand again, and at that second Mary appeared, coming this way through the utility room. She beamed when she spotted Jenny and appeared dressed for errands in a pretty maroon dress and matching apron. Her black outer bonnet was already perched on her blond head, its black strings hanging down the front.

"Oh, *gut*, you did get the message from my sister-in-law. Mattie said you'd be visiting Ella Mae yesterday." Mary smiled. "The girls are lookin' forward to seeing you again. Emily and Anna are playing with their dollies in the playpen." She continued, saying Jenny didn't have to entertain them. "Just be close by if they need anything." Mary waved at Mary Mae, who sat at the table coloring.

Jenny wondered why the two younger girls were confined so, but she didn't ask.

"You'll find fresh-baked cookies in the cookie jar," Mary said, pointing to the counter on the left side of the sink. "John's out in the barn, feeding the livestock. He won't be inside till I return to cook the noon meal. But if ya need anything, just holler."

Jenny nodded, careful to pay close attention.

"If you wouldn't mind peeling those potatoes for me, that'd be a mighty big help." She indicated the mound on the counter in a large plastic mixing bowl. "Mary Mae likes to scrub 'em, so she'll be a *gut* little helper."

"Sure, that's fine," Jenny replied, glancing at the three darling girls sitting so quietly.

Mary reached down and touched the baby's head. "You children behave yourselves for Jenny, won't ya now?" The girls looked up at her solemnly as Mary repeated her instructions for them in Deitsch.

"I love their names," Jenny said.

Mary smiled and blushed a bit as she reached for her black woolen shawl and tied her black bonnet under her round chin. She picked up a wicker basket with a blue-and-white-checked cloth covering over it. "Like I said, I'll be back shortly. Denki ever so much, Jenny."

"Take your time." Jenny followed her to the back door, wondering if she should secure it behind her. Not knowing for sure, she locked it anyway.

Mary dashed out to the waiting horse and family carriage, her heavy wrap swooshing against her calves.

Just knowing she would likely not encounter the bishop today put

Jenny more at ease. Turning back to the two younger girls, she sat on the wood bench on one side of the long table and smiled down into the playpen at them.

"*Wu is Dat?*" three-year-old Emily asked, grinning at her coyly, then standing and leaning her little head against the playpen railing.

"Your daddy's outside," Jenny said in English. She hadn't brought along the Deitsch dictionary and couldn't piece together anything the child could understand.

"Dawdi?" the little girl said.

"Nee, not Dawdi . . . Dat."

Oh, was this ever frustrating! Mary Mae looked at her curiously, then said something softly to Emily, which seemed to satisfy the younger girl. *Maybe this will work out after all,* Jenny thought.

A half hour later, someone startled her with a knock at the back door. Jenny looked up in the midst of playing dolls with the girls. There stood Hezekiah Stoltzfus, peering in against the pane of glass, jiggling the door handle.

"Oh boy," she whispered, glancing back at the girls as she made her way through the kitchen.

"Yes, what is it?" she asked through the door, keeping it closed—she wanted to be known as a principled young woman in this place of conservative expectations.

"Is Bishop John around anywhere?" he asked, surprise evident on his face, as well.

"Mary said he's in the barn."

Hezekiah smiled and straightened up. "Well, all right, then." With that, he turned and hurried across the lawn.

She closed the inside door, which made the utility room less bright, but she felt better about it.

Remembering the potatoes, Jenny began to wash and set about peeling them, amazed at the happy sound of the unintelligible murmurings between the adorable little girls in the corner.

In a few minutes, Mary Mae slid off the bench, scooted a chair over to the sink, and crawled up on it to stand next to Jenny. Very soon the two of them had a system going as the heap of potatoes on the counter began to diminish in size. Mary Mae washed them and passed them on to the opposite sink for peeling by Jenny. The long strips piled up quickly in the second sink.

While she worked, Mary Mae chattered to Jenny in Deitsch, as though Jenny understood. It was so endearing. She loved having this opportunity to work alongside such a small Amish girl.

If my sister saw this, she'd be shocked speechless!

When Jenny finished peeling the potatoes, she washed her hands, dried them, and checked on little Anna, who'd fallen asleep on one of the cloth dolls in a corner of the playpen.

Meanwhile, Emily continued playing in the opposite corner, talking quietly to her doll. Mary Mae went to a hutchlike buffet on the other side of the kitchen, opened the second drawer, and pulled out some construction paper and a blunt pair of scissors. Then, without being told, she slid onto the wood bench and sat at the table.

This job is a piece of cake. As Jenny wandered into what Rebecca called the front room, she wished Mary had assigned her more housework. A large German family Bible lay on top of a beautiful wooden writing desk, but she didn't touch it, only admired it.

In the near corner stood a tall oak cupboard, obviously custom made and quite old, though not an antique. She was especially drawn to the tea sets and decorative plates inside, all lined up in a colorful fashion in their respective grooves.

Seeing these items reminded her of the shop in Essex, where she'd enjoyed the parade of furnishings and trinkets from long ago. It had been fun to assist the customers who had come to purchase antiques. *Cherishing the past.*

Jenny wandered back toward the kitchen, through the small room just beyond the front room, and smiled to see a rocker made of beautiful bleached willow branches. It crossed her mind to sit in it to see how comfortable it was, but Mary hadn't actually said to make herself at home. Not like most of the women she'd baby-sat for as a teenager, who had shown her the soda in the fridge and offered stacks of movies to peruse.

Just then she noticed Hezekiah Stoltzfus walking outdoors with another man, presumably the bishop, who looked younger than she'd envisioned. Better looking, too—tall, blond, with the predictable full beard of a married Amishman.

The two men stood and talked for a short time before getting into Hezekiah's carriage and riding off.

"The bishop must trust me a lot," Jenny whispered.

Had Rebecca put a good word in for her? Why else would Bishop Beiler be comfortable with a near stranger in charge of his youngest children?

Mary Mae's head leaned close to her paper and scissors as she worked to cut out various shapes. Jenny strolled about the kitchen, intrigued by the unusual wall clock with fanciful black trim and the large pastoral calendar hanging on the back of the cellar door. If their cold cellar was anything like Rebecca Lapp's, there were rows and rows of canning jars lining the shelves down there. *"As many as eight hundred,"* Rebecca had said.

Jenny noticed a slip of paper in the center of the gas-powered fridge and tried to read the Deitsch: *Dan un Katie Fisher hawwe Gemee an die Haus.* The names startled her—it was something about Rebecca's son-in-law and daughter. And as Jenny read the Deitsch, she realized she understood it—even *Gemee*, which she'd heard Marnie say. The words were similar to their German counterparts. Evidently Dan and Katie Fisher were having meetings of some kind in their house. *Bible studies, perhaps?* Jenny wondered. She knew this wouldn't be acceptable in Hickory Hollow, but Dan and Katie were shunned.

What's the purpose of this note?

Jenny was so curious, she determined to find a way to ask Rebecca about it. *As if she'd know . . .* Then Jenny realized that was silly. Neither Samuel nor Rebecca would likely be aware of this.

Would Marnie know?

"*Gucke, Maidel.*" Mary Mae's voice broke into her thoughts. The little girl smiled and pointed to her cutout design.

"Oh, it's very pretty," Jenny said. Then, trying to communicate better, she went over and lightly touched the art before pointing to her own smile. She so wanted to talk to Mary Mae, but the language barrier was just that—an obstruction between herself and the sweet girl.

Jenny sat on the bench next to her and picked up a green crayon, drawing a smiley face in the upper right-hand corner of one of the sheets of paper. "Jah?"

Mary Mae's eyes sparkled. "Jah," she replied, bobbing her head up and down. She reached for the coloring book and pointed to the right side, babbling nonstop in Deitsch as she poked the page closest to Jenny.

"You want me to color with you," Jenny said, happy to indulge.

Some time later, Emily began to squirm and stood up waiting quietly for Jenny to give the nod that she could get out of the playpen. When Jenny got up to get her, Emily had already leaned over the railing and climbed out.

Unable to resist, Jenny offered her a hand and brought her over to look at Mary Mae's artwork. She sat down with Emily next to her, and was surprised when Mary Mae put a blue crayon in Emily's hand and turned the page, talking to her in Deitsch. "It's always nice to share with your sister," Jenny said, smiling again at the five-year-old, delighted at this gesture. The youngster obviously exemplified the training of her Amish mother. Sharing was precious, but it had to be taught.

Jenny heard a commotion outside and turned toward the kitchen window. Unbelievably, a cow ambled past, heading down the driveway. "Oh no!"

Another cow came along, right behind. Glancing at Anna, still asleep in the playpen, and the two older girls sitting at the table, Jenny hurried to the utility room to look out the windows there. A third Holstein bellowed after the first two. She unlocked the back door and stared out. It certainly appeared the barnyard fence was broken or someone had accidently left a gate open. What else could have happened?

Jenny's first inclination was to rush and secure the barnyard fence, but then she looked toward the road and saw the trio of cows lumbering down that way.

Oh, what should I do? She wrung her apron hem, distraught. *Dare I leave the girls alone and attempt to bring back the cows?*

21

REBECCA Lapp gasped. She could see three black-and-white heifers rambling down the middle of Hickory Lane. "Samuel, *kumme schnell!*" she called out the back door, then reached for an old jacket and hurried for the steps.

In no time, Samuel flew out the barn door and came running across the yard, this way.

"Someone's cows got out," she hollered, not waiting for Samuel to catch up. But he quickly outran her, headed straight for the road. "Pity's sake, whose are they?"

Samuel kept going, taking off his straw hat and calling, "Coboss! Shoo . . . get on home now." He blocked their way, waving at the lead cow. "Coboss!"

"Oh, goodness. Ain't the bishop's, are they?"

Samuel nodded. "Certainly are."

Rebecca's heart sank. Surely this had nothing to do with Jenny Burns. *Ach, mercy no . . . surely not!*

··· ➤ ➤ ···

Jenny felt nervous about leaving the children unattended and went back to the kitchen to check on Anna, who remained sound asleep, her little head cushioned by a light blanket.

Smiling, Jenny reached for Emily and motioned for Mary Mae to come along with her, as well. She led them to the utility room, where she swiftly helped Emily put on her coat and a small black winter bonnet while Mary

Mae dressed herself. Jenny then slipped on Rebecca's shawl and woolen scarf before hurrying outside with both girls.

"See there?" Jenny pointed to the barnyard and tried to explain what she assumed had happened. And she soon verified what she'd suspected— the barn gate was open just enough for the cows to wander out. Had more escaped than she'd seen?

Reaching up, she secured the gate and heard voices in the field behind her. She and the girls turned to see Samuel Lapp herding three cows across the harvested cornfield, Rebecca coming close behind, her cheeks bright pink from the cold.

"Oh, good, the cows are back," Jenny said, relieved. *I think we'd better open the gate again,* she thought as Mary Mae and Emily clapped their hands, all smiles.

Once the cows were safely corralled, Jenny invited Samuel and Rebecca indoors to warm up. She offered them the hot coffee already on the stove, and Rebecca suggested they ought to wait around for Bishop John and Mary to return. Jenny wasn't sure why they felt the need but was glad to see Rebecca acting more like her old self.

Samuel played with Emily, bouncing her on his knee till she could hardly stop giggling. Mary Mae showed off her coloring pictures and cutout designs first to Rebecca, then to Samuel before placing them on the refrigerator with magnets of pigs and cows.

Jenny was tempted to show Rebecca the refrigerator note about Dan and Katie's house meetings but decided against it, not knowing how Samuel might react to that sort of news. *I can only imagine. . . .*

Later, when Mary returned, Rebecca was quick to tell her what good care Jenny had given the girls. "She even managed to keep an eye on the cows—got the gate closed before more scurried off."

Mary nodded and looked pleased as she took it all in. But before long, Jenny noticed Mary glance at the fridge, frown, and rise promptly to remove the note. Without saying a word, Mary opened the cupboard and slipped the note inside.

So she didn't *want me to see it . . . let alone Samuel and Rebecca!*

--- ➤ ◄ ---

343

The feast began shortly after Marnie's cousin Linda Ebersol's three-hour wedding service the next day. Marnie blushed when she caught Roy gazing fondly at her from across the room. Her heart did a little flutter, and she thought ahead to that evening's barn Singing for the courting-age youth. *Many of them are couples like Roy and me.*

But she didn't have to endure the long afternoon hours waiting for that particular gathering to bring them face-to-face, or for the feel of her small hand in his. After the delicious meal and a brief time of hymn singing, Roy gave her a sign with his brown eyes and a meaningful dip of his head. He slipped out the back door, intending for her to follow, which she did, after donning her warmest woolen coat and black outer bonnet and gloves.

"Oh, Marnie. I could hardly wait to be alone like this," Roy said as he led her around behind the big barn, where the sun shone against the white wood slats and made it more tolerable to be out in the cold.

She smiled, longing to say the same thing back but letting him do the talking instead. And just that quick, he was leaning closer, smiling down at her, blocking the sun from her eyes. She looked up at him, taking in the arch of his brow, the intensity of his gaze . . . and all the while her heart pounded nearly out of her ears.

"The Lord Gott is ever near, Marnie," Roy whispered. "As close to you—and to me—as we are now. Closer, really." He paused a second. "And I believe He wants us to understand how much He cares for us through the experiences we're havin'."

"What experiences?" She could hardly speak.

"The one I'm askin' you to share with me." He leaned ever near, his breath on her face. "Marnie, I want you to go with me to the house meeting I wrote you about. More than anything."

"But—"

Roy tilted his head and sweetly kissed her cheek. Then, moving slightly back, he looked deep into her eyes. "Will ya do this . . . for me? Just this once?"

"I'd do anything for ya, Roy . . . you know that."

"Then you'll go?"

Those pleading eyes of his . . . how he adored her. She simply could not refuse her darling beau. "Jah, I'll go along. But only once."

His face beamed as he leaned down to kiss her other cheek. "You've made me a very happy man today, my sweetheart-girl."

Oh, she wanted to wrap her arms around his neck and never let go. "When's the meeting?" she asked, folding her hands against her wrap.

"I'll pick you up next Tuesday evening, round six-thirty." He reached for her right hand and began removing her glove.

"What're ya doin', Roy?"

"You'll see." He raised her smooth, bare hand to his lips and kissed the back of it so tenderly she thought she might cry.

"I love you so," Roy said, pressing her hand to his chest. "You know that, don't ya?"

Marnie smiled and nodded her head, locking eyes with her future husband. "You sure know how to change my mind, ain't so?"

And concerns of her father's displeasure flew fast away.

22

THE following Monday, Jenny helped Rebecca run the dirty laundry through the wringer washer. It was so tedious and time-consuming, she actually missed using an automatic washer and dryer. As the two women worked side by side, they talked about the remainder of the wedding season, as well as other upcoming church-related activities.

Finally, after considering it to death, Jenny got up the nerve to tell Rebecca about the strange note she'd seen on Mary Beiler's refrigerator. "I wondered if I should say anything," Jenny said quietly. "I don't want to be inappropriate."

"Well, I'm glad ya spoke up." Rebecca's naturally rosy cheeks drained of color.

"What do you think it means—or isn't it important now that they're . . . um, outside Amish jurisdiction?"

Rebecca nodded slowly. "S'posin' if I'd seen it, maybe I'd know who wrote it. That'd be a clue."

"I guess there's a lot I don't understand about being Amish."

"Never mind that, Jenny. Either the bishop was informing Mary, or vice versa, is my guess."

"A warning?" asked Jenny.

"Katie and her husband are adults," Rebecca said, frowning. "What they do is their business."

Jenny wasn't surprised at her response. On one hand, Rebecca had every right to be defensive. Yet on the other, shouldn't she reflect the mindset behind the shunning and in line with the church ordinance? *And the bishop.*

"Maybe I shouldn't have brought it up," Jenny said.

"Nee, I'm glad ya did." Rebecca took out another of Samuel's shirts before she said more. "It's just that I sometimes feel awful sorry for Katie. Same for Daniel."

Jenny heard the pain in her voice. "I'm sure you miss them terribly."

Rebecca pressed her lips together and said nothing for a moment. "More than I could ever say."

"I shouldn't ask this, but do you exchange letters sometimes?"

"Now and then," she replied, adding quickly, "'cause writing letters is allowed."

Jenny noticed an odd blink of Rebecca's eyes and a twitch of her head. Was the probing question out of order?

"Talking about this makes you sad, I can see that." Jenny sighed. "I'm sorry for that."

Rebecca remained silent. And Jenny decided to say no more regarding the agonizing topic.

··· ➤ ➤ ···

The afternoon was perfect for drying clothes on the line, thanks to a brilliant sun and a steady breeze. Jenny finished sewing the last of her new dresses while Rebecca worked on the final three pink roses on a pillowcase to be sold at market.

Rebecca set down her work at the kitchen table and mentioned that the bishop had dropped by that morning to speak to Samuel. "He was mighty impressed with your '*gut* judgment' last week when his cows got out."

"I'm sure he was equally grateful for your help, and Samuel's, in bringing them back."

"Jah, that, too . . . but he's been tellin' everyone what you did, Jenny." Rebecca's eyes were serious. "You did well. Wasn't like it was a planned test."

But a test, all the same.

They worked silently for a time, and Jenny let Rebecca's words sink in. To think this had come from a man she still had not had the occasion to meet.

Seemingly out of the blue, Rebecca said, "We must always work to improve ourselves, ya know. It's one of the best goals."

"Where does grace come into play?"

"Ah, the age-old question of God's grace versus our obedience to His commandments. Many mistake obedience for tryin' to work one's way into the kingdom," Rebecca said solemnly.

Jenny wished she weren't so hung up on whether she was doing the right thing. "Do you think the Lord sometimes wants us to move out of our comfort zone?"

"Depends on what ya mean."

"I've been thinking," Jenny said hesitantly. "What would you say if I invited my parents to visit me here?"

Rebecca's needle stopped in midair, and she looked toward the window. Was it just Jenny's imagination, or was Rebecca trying to gather her wits? "Perfectly fine with me." Rebecca put down her sewing and looked right at her.

"I've been considering it for a while."

"Well, I'd say that's a wonderful-*gut* idea, Jenny. It may be time your family knows your plans, ain't?"

"I've gone back and forth—even had a dream about it. It feels right to me now. And I'm more confident about talking to them."

"'Tis *gut*." Rebecca fixed her eyes on her.

Just then Jenny saw Marnie coming down the road. She excused herself and dashed out to grab the shawl off the wooden peg.

Marnie saw her waving and headed into the lane. "Hullo, Jenny. Wie geht's?"

"*Recht gut.*"

Marnie smiled at Jenny's reply, and they chattered happily, though mostly in English. Marnie noted how well Jenny was picking up common phrases in Deitsch.

"How was your cousin's wedding?" asked Jenny.

Marnie filled her in on the special day, her eyes alight when she revealed that her boyfriend from Bird-in-Hand had spent the whole day with her. "And . . . we've got some interesting plans. But that's all I best be sayin'."

"A boyfriend, you say?" Jenny smiled. "Sounds to me as though you have more than one secret!"

"Most definitely . . . and I hope I don't catch it later."

"You aren't going to run off and get married, are you?"

"Goodness, I wouldn't miss out on havin' a regular wedding. Not for anything." Marnie grinned.

"Great, since I'd like to attend."

Marnie asked if she had the pictures of her family. "Not to pester, but I'd like to see 'em."

"Oh, I'm happy to show you." Jenny invited her into the house, stopping for Marnie to greet Rebecca, who was still sewing at the table.

When they were upstairs, Jenny latched the bedroom door and went to the dresser to retrieve a small book of photos. "It's the only album I brought," she said, going to sit with Marnie on the edge of the bed. "Funny, but I haven't looked at it even once since I arrived."

"Really?" Marnie cocked her head. "Do ya think it will make ya miss your family more?"

Jenny hadn't thought of that. "I guess we'll find out, jah?"

Marnie placed her hand on top of the album. "Seriously, I don't have to see it today."

"Don't be silly; I want you to." Jenny opened the book and displayed more than a dozen pictures of her parents, Kiersten and Robb, and Cameron. Slowly, she flipped through the snapshots, answering Marnie's questions about who was who and the events surrounding each photo. It was nice to see Marnie so interested.

Then, turning to the last page, Jenny was shocked to see a shot of Kyle Jackson and herself smiling, cheek to cheek. "What's this doing here?" she muttered. *I thought I destroyed all the pictures!*

"Who's *that?*" Marnie peered closer, her Kapp strings falling forward. "Just a guy."

"Well, it looks like you're in love with him."

Jenny recalled the special evening and all the joy surrounding that day of her college graduation. Kyle had surprised her, flying in with her parents and brother. Jenny remembered the way he'd leaned close to her right as the picture was taken, how he had smelled of spicy cologne.

She felt overwhelmed at the clarity of the memory and the many emotions the picture evoked.

"Jenny . . . are you all right?"

"I *did* love him, Marnie," she whispered, tears welling up. "I loved him very much."

"And by the looks of you, maybe ya still do?" Marnie touched her arm.

"Actually, I don't know why I said that. It's ridiculous." She explained that the relationship had ended sadly—he couldn't understand her passion for the Plain life, the one thing she longed for. "But that was two years ago," she added. "He's apologized since for not handling our breakup with more tact. He's not a bad guy . . . just not the one."

"Your first love, then?"

Jenny nodded.

"Roy's mine." Marnie shook her head and looked at the ceiling. "Honestly, I don't know how I'd manage without him. Ach, I shouldn't have said that. Don't mean to make things hard—"

"Don't worry," Jenny assured her. "I'm happy for you."

Marnie opened her mouth to say something but stopped and shook her head.

"What is it?" asked Jenny.

"Just thinking, is all."

Jenny wondered how long Marnie had been dating Roy but didn't ask, thinking perhaps she and Marnie had shared enough for one visit. "Would you care for a snack?"

"Sure, I'm always ready for sweets."

Jenny put away the album, still shocked the photo of her and Kyle had managed to follow her here. *Our best picture together, too.*

Leading Marnie downstairs, Jenny felt embarrassed that she'd mentioned Kyle Jackson. Considering the reason for their breakup, he was the last person she ever wanted to talk about in the midst of her adjustment to Amish life.

23

As was her custom following Bible reading and silent prayers, Jenny usually spent the rest of the evening prior to bedtime in her room reading her devotional book or writing in her journal.

Tonight, however, she decided to go ahead with the letter she had been formulating in her mind for days. *Time to tell all.*

Dear Mom and Dad,

Thanks for your patience. You're probably wondering what I've been up to. I hope you will try to understand what I've been doing for the past nearly two weeks. And where I'm living.

Do you remember when I pleaded for an Amish bonnet for my twelfth birthday, Mom? You somehow managed to purchase a handmade one, and I proudly displayed it on my dresser mirror.

Well, my goal is to own—and wear—a real head covering someday: the Old Order Amish kind. So I'm renting a room from Samuel and Rebecca Lapp, who live in a small area of Lancaster County called Hickory Hollow, just east of Bird-in-Hand, Pennsylvania. I'm surrounded by farmland, and I love it. My hope is to live, dress, and work here as a baptized Amishwoman for the rest of my life.

This isn't an easy path, but it's my heart's desire . . . and perhaps you're not too surprised. Haven't I always loved the countryside and doing things the old-fashioned way?

I'd really love for you to visit me here and to meet the Lapps and the other wonderful people I've come to know. Samuel and Rebecca have encouraged me to invite you, so you'll be very welcome.

Please reply to me at the return address on the envelope.

With love from your daughter,
Jenny

She held her breath thinking how her mother, especially, might receive the news. Rereading her letter, Jenny felt it was a bit stiff, even unemotional. But not knowing any other way to relate to her parents, she folded it and placed it in the bedside table drawer.

What if Mom and Dad show up and want to take me home? she thought unexpectedly. She could almost hear her father expressing his concern about certain cults or brainwashing.

Will they try to interfere?

Jenny felt restless. Once or twice before, she'd contemplated going down to the springhouse to pray, and tonight she needed the fresh, cold air. So, taking her flashlight downstairs, she slipped on her warm outer bonnet and Rebecca's shawl. She opened the back door, thankful it didn't squeak, and made her way over the walkway and toward the peaceful haven. How she looked forward to talking with God! She yearned for more humility and for divine help in caring less about how she appeared to others. *It's prideful to worry so,* she thought, still hung up on the possibility of future faux pas . . . even her hair, though she was slowly getting used to not peering into a mirror each morning. She seemed to be in a tug-of-war with submission. Could she ever be as meek and obedient as Rebecca?

Turning off her flashlight, she knelt near the pond adjacent to the entrance of the little springhouse. Jenny folded her hands and bowed her head. "Dear Lord," she began to pray quietly, "my heart is bursting with thanksgiving tonight. I'm so grateful for your constant help . . . your continual presence."

She raised her eyes to the dark sky and watched the stars appear, one by one. "Please soften my parents to my plans," she whispered. "Prepare them for my letter. I know it will be strange, but if it is your will, please help them understand my heart for the very first time. . . ."

She paused. Just then across the pond, she saw a flicker of white. Was someone there?

Peering into the murky darkness, she saw what looked like the figure of a man perched on the stone wall near the water. Concerned, she stood quickly and hurried toward the steps away from the springhouse.

"Jenny . . . is that you?"

The voice was deep and familiar.

She turned. "Andrew Lapp?" Her reply echoed against the pond's surface.

"I didn't mean to frighten you," he said, coming her way, his flashlight guiding his steps.

"What are you doing here?" she asked, rattled at the knowledge she hadn't been alone.

"I come here to pray, too. Have for years."

She nodded dumbly, still trying to get over her surprise at being discovered here . . . and by him.

His chuckle lifted into the night. "Did I disturb you?"

She opened her mouth to answer but smiled instead.

"No better place to be alone with the Lord God, in my opinion," he said. He stood there looking at her, and she remembered bumping into him on the porch at Preaching service that first Sunday. "It's a wonderful-*gut* spot."

"Jah," she said softly.

"When it's bitter cold, I sometimes sneak inside the springhouse to finish my prayin'."

A twig cracked loudly in the near distance, and Andrew turned to look.

Jenny thought she saw movement in the trees along Hickory Lane. "Is someone watching us?" she whispered, unnerved.

"Prob'ly just a small critter." He smiled down at her. "I hope you're not nervous."

She was surprised he'd noticed. "I guess I am," she replied. "I wrote to my parents tonight, and I'm a little worried what they'll do when they read the letter."

"Just a *little* worried?"

She laughed timidly. "Okay, a lot."

"And why's that?"

"I doubt they'll understand." *They never have. . . .*

He was still for a moment. "But Gott does, don't forget."

"Denki for the reminder."

He inhaled audibly. "And, Jenny . . . something else."

"Jah?"

"I'm prayin' for you, too."

She blushed and wondered whether he could tell in the glow of the flashlight. "That's so kind of you."

"Honestly, I doubt I could do what you're settin' out to do. I mean, if the tables were turned and I was tryin' to find my way in the English world . . ."

"Thank goodness you aren't," she blurted before thinking. "I mean—"

"Don't fret; I think I know what you meant."

"Denki."

"You're one very thankful woman, I daresay." Andrew stepped back slightly. "Well, I'd best be on my way now. *Gut Nacht*, Jenny."

She almost hated to see him go. Waiting for a moment, she knelt again on the cold cement. But try as she might, she could not recover her prayerful attitude, not when she could hear Andrew's footsteps heading up the rocky wall toward the plowed cornfield.

So the private little area was not exclusively hers. A *shared altar of sorts*, she thought, feeling not at all disappointed by the discovery, but surprisingly warm inside. Warm . . . yet tentative.

Jenny rose, turned on her flashlight, and made her way back to the farmhouse.

⋯ ⋟ ⋞ ⋯

Before going to bed, Jenny composed a letter to her friends Pamela and Dorie—the two sisters were roommates. While she wrote, she prayed their reactions, especially Dorie's, wouldn't be as negative as she feared. *Though justly deserved.*

Jenny considered inviting them to Hickory Hollow, too. But she decided against it before sealing the envelope and placing it in the drawer with the letter to her parents.

Later, as she nestled beneath the bed quilts, it was neither her parents nor Pamela and Dorie who occupied her thoughts. Rather, the memory of Andrew Lapp's emergence from the darkness at the springhouse looped round and round in Jenny's head.

24

THE Bird-in-Hand Farmers Market parking lot was crammed with cars, SUVs, and minivans Wednesday morning. Jenny presumed the milder weather had coaxed people out of their homes this mid-November day. After the cold snap of the past two days, the sun felt wonderfully warm, and there was not a cloud in the alluring blue sky.

Jenny and Rebecca carried in the carefully ironed embroidered pillowcases and hand-quilted potholders and matching place mats from the carriage, hoping to sell them within the first few hours. Two teen girls, obviously tourists, looked Jenny over, staring at her Amish garb. It wasn't the first time—there had been glares and pointing, even smothered laughter. All the same, Jenny felt embarrassed for the many Englishers who'd ever made fun of anyone unlike themselves.

Rebecca stopped to introduce Jenny to a number of vendor friends, including Elizabeth Miller and her pretty strawberry-blond daughter Tessie at Country Crafters. She also stopped at Groff's Candies and Aunt Ruthie's Specialties. But it was Emmalyn Lapp who caught Jenny's notice as Jenny took care to place the handmade items in the correct piles on the display table. Jenny was pleased as she stepped back to take a better look, glad she'd come to help Rebecca today.

Jenny kept tabs on Emmalyn out of the corner of her eye as the young woman inched closer. So as not to postpone the inevitable meeting, Jenny told Rebecca she would be right back and wandered over to the booth where Emmalyn was selling wooden horses and other handmade toys. "How are you, Emmalyn? I thought I'd come say hi."

"I saw *you* the other night," Emmalyn said, not bothering with a greeting.

"When?"

"Just think about it. . . ." Emmalyn's voice held a strange tone.

"What are you talking about?"

"You've honestly forgotten?" Emmalyn glowered. "You were with Andrew at the springhouse pond."

So she was there, too, snooping around!

Jenny refused to honor her accusing tone with a response. She glanced back at Rebecca, whose hands were moving rapidly as she talked in Deitsch.

"Don't get too close to my brother" came the angry words.

Jenny shivered. What was wrong with this girl?

A young Amish mother with identical twin boys tucked into a double stroller rushed past them, apologizing as she went.

"Listen, Emmalyn, I don't understand what you want from me."

"I want nothin', and the same goes for my brother. You're not one of us, Jenny Burns. Just keep that in mind." And Emmalyn turned away.

Jenny took that as her cue to return to Rebecca, quite aware of her pounding heart.

Despite the long day at market, Rebecca was determined that evening to make good on her latest note to Katie. She waited till Samuel was asleep to get out of bed and take her clothes downstairs. In the kitchen, she turned on the smallest gas lamp and tiptoed to the bathroom to change out of her nightgown.

She went to the utility room and reached for her warmest black coat and gray scarf, along with her waterproof mittens, which kept her hands cozier than the ones she'd knitted last winter.

Then, moving quietly out the back door, she was conscious of the shuffle of her shoes against the pavement. The air was brisk and a slight gust of wind made her shudder as she hurried down the lane, deciding to go on foot.

Oh, she ached for Katie and the little ones again. Her heart throbbed every single day, missing them. Allowing one or two weeks to pass between visits was becoming an unbearable situation, because each visit made her yearn for more, like someone with a sweet tooth needing more and more sugar.

She didn't dare talk about this terrible loneliness with Samuel. But without saying their names, she alluded to them now and then. She suspected that making reference to their daughter and her family by name would hurt Samuel, and she refused to let him know just how much their shunned daughter occupied her thoughts. Rebecca's elderly mother had once told her without blinking an eye that most folk will do what they believe is best for themselves, no matter what's expected. *"They just do what they think is right, when all's said and done."*

In the shadows, Rebecca looked about her, hoping she could manage yet another furtive visit up the road. She dared not pray to that end, though, not when she was being disobedient. Oh, such a tear down the middle of her soul!

She sometimes wondered what her own sisters or mother would do in a similar place. Die Meinding had broken her heart, for certain. But the dreadful experience had also served to remind her how much she loved Katie.

Rebecca would do whatever it took to stay in touch with her daughter. If only the bishop could understand the very heart of her and kindly look the other way!

Jenny quickly realized it was cooler again tonight as she made her way to pray near the springhouse once more. As before, she walked the path that snaked away from the house, down an incline toward the wide stone steps. She crept toward the spot and then knelt and prayed silently, in case Andrew was concealed from view, bringing his own petitions before God. *Praying for others . . . and for me.*

Tonight Jenny was pleading for wisdom in dealing with Andrew's own sister in addition to her usual plea for a humble heart. Despite Jenny's attempt to focus on God, Emmalyn's sharp words continued to resound in her mind. Nevertheless, Jenny asked the Lord to *"tender her heart,"* as Rebecca Lapp had once said.

The night was hushed and still, except for the sound of two hoot owls calling from the branches of distant trees, and the occasional tinkle of tack and traces as unseen courting buggies passed by. The sky was filled with sharp white stars. Embracing the tranquility, Jenny wished everyone might have the opportunity to know and absorb such peace, at least for a moment.

She eventually rose and headed toward the stone steps, noticing an amber light in the kitchen window as she stepped onto the driveway. Had someone gotten up and discovered she was missing from her room? She couldn't imagine it, since she kept her bedroom door closed even when she was gone.

Jenny heard quick footsteps on the driveway and turned to look. Was Emmalyn spying again?

Something rose up in her in spite of her prayers for a peaceful, gentle spirit. Irritated, Jenny followed the footsteps of the figure, a woman hurrying along the roadside without even a flashlight. When Jenny was within perhaps a quarter block of her, she realized the silhouette was too matronly to be Emmalyn.

This must be Rebecca, decided Jenny, although she couldn't know for sure. But why on earth would Rebecca Lapp get up after going to bed and rush off to parts unknown?

Jenny followed the mystery woman until she came to the crossroad that curved south, toward the house where Katie and her husband lived. She remembered Marnie's pointing it out the day they'd gone to the Gordonville Book Store.

The woman picked up her pace as she approached the familiar house. Hanging back, Jenny watched as the woman gently patted the mailbox. *What was that?* From this distance, Jenny couldn't be sure what she was seeing.

Then, suddenly, she felt a sneeze coming on and pinched her nose tightly shut. But try as she might, a wheeze slipped out, and the sound was magnified in the vacuum of night.

The woman stopped and turned in Jenny's direction. "Who's there?" she called.

Rebecca's voice.

Jenny stepped gingerly behind a tree trunk, trying to avoid uneven roots protruding from the ground.

"Hullo?" Rebecca said, moving away from the walkway, the welcoming porch light behind her. "Is someone there?" She was not giving up.

Heart thrumming, Jenny struggled, unsure what to do. Rebecca's gait was decisive as she approached the tree, not ten yards away. Rebecca would keep coming until she discovered Jenny's hiding place.

At last, stepping out of the shadows into the soft, pale light of the moon, Jenny said softly, "Rebecca, it's me—Jenny."

The older woman inhaled sharply and seemed to grow a few inches. "Why are you followin' me?"

"I wasn't—I mean . . ." Jenny was surprised at her sharp tone.

"Go back now, and erase this from your mind."

Shaken, Jenny turned and began to walk toward Hickory Lane, confused by what she had just witnessed.

25

JENNY had never felt so perplexed as she showered and washed her hair before bed. When she'd dried off, she slipped on one of three cotton nightgowns she had sewn with Rebecca's help since the incident with her fancy one. Instead of discarding the problem nightie, however, she'd placed it in a zipped pocket of her suitcase, which lay beneath the bed.

She replayed the uncomfortable encounter with Rebecca in front of Katie's house. Annoying thoughts kept her from sleeping, so she turned the gas lamp back on and sat up in bed with her devotional book.

What was Rebecca doing?

Jenny reviewed all that Rebecca had taught her regarding obedience and submission—the highest calling. Wasn't Katie under the Bann, shunned for life? If so, wasn't it disobedient for Rebecca to visit her daughter's home?

Much later, as Jenny was dozing off, the lamp still on, she heard someone knock at her bedroom door. "Are you awake, Jenny?"

Quickly, she opened the door to Rebecca, who hurried inside and closed it behind her. "I'm glad you're still up." She sat on the edge of Jenny's bed, cheeks cherry red from the cold. "As you know, it took great trust when Samuel and I opened our home to you." Rebecca's hazel eyes looked dark in the dim light. She bit her lip and continued, "Ach, if anyone happened to get wind of this, I'd be persecuted right along with Katie. The bishop would put his foot down, and I would no longer be able to correspond with my daughter and family, let alone risk seeing them face-to-face."

She sighed heavily. "Staying away from them is something I can't adhere to—not any longer. Of course, my family would never forgive me if I ended up shunned like Katie and Dan."

Jenny's heart broke for her. Yet Rebecca knew the rules. How could Jenny offer comfort?

"Other bishops might be more lenient to a parent in my position, but it's hard to be sure," Rebecca said. "Bishop John is mighty strict, so you must keep my secret. Will you, Jenny? Will you keep this to yourself?"

Jenny drew back, shocked. "What if the People were to find out, though, and discovered that I knew all along but didn't say anything? What then?" she managed to say. "I don't want you to be shunned, Rebecca. How could I live with myself, knowing I was party to that? But I—"

"You're wonderin' if *you're* at risk, being a seeker 'n' all."

Jenny nodded, disheartened at the thought. And this after her few strides forward these past weeks. "The bishop wouldn't give me much, or any, leeway."

"Nee—none at all." Rebecca lowered her head. "I won't lie to ya. Keepin' my secret and being found out will *verfalle*—put you to ruin."

The two women stared sadly at each other. Rebecca looked away first. "But I *have* been careful. Ain't been caught yet."

I caught you, Jenny thought. "Not by the ministers, no."

Rebecca nodded circumspectly. "I can't keep my distance from my Katie-girl." She went on to add in a whisper how she loved her grand-children, Sammy and Kate Marie. "You just don't know." Her lower lip quivered as a single tear spilled down her cheek. "Please forget what you saw tonight. Promise me."

Jenny trembled. "You're asking me to defy the Ordnung."

"Still, you're not baptized yet, don't ya see? You're not under the ruling of the church."

"But I'm striving to be. It's everything I hope for."

Rebecca rose, her shoulders stooped as she trudged to the door. Silently, she turned to look down at Jenny. Her face was solemn. "I beg you not to say a word." Then she opened the door and left the room.

Jenny blew out the gas lamp and curled up in the warm bed. She made an effort to understand how a devout believer like Rebecca could justify violating the Bann. As honorable as the woman had appeared to be—and considering the attributes she'd repeatedly urged Jenny to follow as an Amish seeker—the thought was nearly profane.

Exhausted, Jenny prayed yet could find no peace. Everything she'd believed about Rebecca Lapp had come crashing to the ground.

The next morning, Rebecca awoke to the sound of Samuel whispering his prayers in Deitsch. When she opened her eyes, she saw him sitting next to her in bed, two pillows propped behind him. She listened, not letting on she was awake, and was shocked to hear that he knew of Dan and Katie's home Bible studies. *Of all things!*

Samuel sounded distraught as his voice cracked when speaking to the Almighty about his excommunicated daughter and her husband. Rebecca couldn't help wondering how on earth he'd heard about this.

She waited for his amen, then moved a bit, stretching. "You're awake early, dear," she said quietly.

He leaned down with a sigh and kissed her, then sat back up. "Lots to be in prayer 'bout this mornin'."

"Oh?"

"Bishop John stopped over yesterday and shared some mighty surprising news. Seems lately our son-in-law has been the instigator of a house gathering."

Now was not the time to share that she'd been invited to one of them by Katie herself.

"Bishop wants to find out if some of our young folk are goin' over there . . . hearin' Mennonite doctrine."

"What's that mean?"

"Declaring one's salvation, which is only the Lord God's to declare."

"Jah . . . on the Judgment Day," she agreed with him.

"We have the hope of salvation, sure, but it's wrong to go round sayin' you're saved like Daniel Fisher's teachin'."

Rebecca had heard all this before, back when Katie up and left the Amish church. Even six years later, she and Dan were quite outspoken about their beliefs. "What's the bishop plannin' to do?" she asked.

"Well, for one, Preacher Yoder's goin' over there next time they meet, to spy things out."

She bristled. "Makin' a list of our folk?"

"Sure sounds like it."

"Bishop must be desperate, then." *Not surprising,* she thought.

"Now, Rebecca, watch what ya say," Samuel reprimanded. "John Beiler's the anointed minister of God."

"Jah, Samuel. Ever so sorry." She felt like a hypocrite down to her very bones—knew it as sure as she ought to be getting up right now and dressing for the day.

Yet this coming on the heels of the events of last evening nearly paralyzed her—how could she not have known this might happen? She realized she ought to be very thankful it wasn't one of the People but rather Jenny Burns who had found her out. Rebecca yearned to cover up with the many quilts, burrowing down where she'd be safe from prying eyes.

Will Jenny keep mum? she wondered as Samuel rose and went to put on his old work trousers.

Rebecca hoped so, but she did not pray it. She knew better.

She also knew that if she was *schmaert,* she'd write her daughter a letter saying she must be more careful about her visits . . . or not go anymore at all.

The sun was concealed by a gray blanket of clouds as bleak as her spirit that morning. Jenny knelt on the cold wide-plank floor and poured out her heart. Even though the ministerial brethren were unaware, hadn't she already broken the rules of the Proving? Yet coming clean to alleviate the guilt of her knowledge would cause even more pain. Not just for herself, but for Rebecca and her family, who'd already been through the wringer.

Jenny remained in a contrite position, asking for forgiveness, knowing she must trust in divine wisdom and not *"unto her own understanding."*

Rebecca's pleas for confidentiality plagued her, and Jenny prayed all the harder, filled with despair. What if she'd never heard any footsteps last evening . . . never followed them up Hickory Lane?

I must put it out of my mind like Rebecca urged. But can I live with myself?

Over the ensuing days, Jenny's relationship with Rebecca continued to decline. Although they worked side by side in the kitchen when Jenny wasn't helping the bishop's wife, the once warm and inviting camaraderie had all but disappeared. Meanwhile, Rebecca seemed more weary than ever. Was it the love burden or the deceit she carried?

However unwilling, Jenny felt like an accomplice, a seeker with merely a righteous face. Yet when she pictured herself revealing Rebecca's transgression to even Samuel, her knees locked and her back straightened. *I am not humble, nor am I obedient.*

Still, her silence was only part of the sin, and Jenny was stuck between an impenetrable wall and a boulder, with no breathing room.

Rebecca welcomed Jenny's help washday morning, but she was relieved when Jenny left early to go baby-sit the bishop's little girls. She needed a reprieve from the disappointed looks poor Jenny could no longer disguise. She felt just wretched, praying for forgiveness even as she willfully refused to comply with the Bann. She knew herself too well to change that, barring locking herself in the attic and crawling into the old wooden trunk. *Where Katie's pink satin baby gown was first discovered . . .*

Rebecca leaned over the big basin in the cellar and let the tears fall. There was simply no place to turn.

Jenny was almost positive Rebecca was sobbing her eyes out somewhere in the house. She'd seemed despondent since their talk in Jenny's bedroom. *Katie's room,* thought Jenny, never quite able to forget.

When Jenny arrived at her neighbors', Mary Beiler greeted her at the back door, saying she wanted to introduce Jenny to the bishop. The timing was unnerving. And when the tall, rather attractive bishop appeared out of the kitchen, holding little Anna, Jenny felt out of sorts and didn't know how to address the man she'd wanted to meet all this time.

"Our little ones enjoy having you baby-sit," the man of God said as he extended his right hand. His eyes were discerning yet kind, and his voice did not thunder down the fiery brimstone she knew she deserved. "Denki, Jenny."

She tried to work her facial muscles into what she hoped was a convincing smile. "I love taking care of your little girls." She didn't have to say it, but the words flowed freely. It was the only aspect of this delayed meeting that felt natural.

"I commend you for wanting to be one of the People," the bishop surprised her by saying. "Not many succeed, you must know."

This wasn't exactly what she needed to hear, but Jenny found herself nodding. "The way of Gelassenheit is not easy."

"Nee," he whispered, bowing his head. "We must die daily to our wants and desires, as the Scriptures instruct."

She was dying all right, with nearly every breath.

"Before I forget, there were two young ladies—Englischers in their twenties, I'd guess—lookin' for you earlier." The bishop shifted sweet Anna in his arms.

"This morning?"

"Jah. Said they'd gotten lost and needed the right address."

Could it be Pamela and Dorie? Jenny wondered, a surge of excitement rising after the bishop left for the barn and Mary headed for the waiting horse and buggy. Seeing her dear friends again might help Jenny get her mind off herself, if only for a while.

Rebecca told the dolled-up Englischer sisters at her front door that Jenny was indeed staying there. "But I'm sorry she's not home right now." To think they'd already been over to the bishop's place, and less than an hour ago, too. How on earth had they gotten lost in such a small area as Hickory Hollow?

"We drove to the end of West Cattail Road," the older and shorter of the two sisters explained, seemingly flustered. She wore a dizzying display of colors—a salmon-hued sweater and a lime-green scarf showed beneath her rust-colored leather jacket.

"Then we turned west onto the highway and circled all the way back to that town with the odd name." The younger woman dabbed at her very thin eyebrows.

"Ah, 'tis Intercourse Village," Rebecca prompted her. "Jenny's just over yonder, behind the plowed field, taking care of the bishop's children. You can go over there if you'd like."

"Thanks," they said in chorus, then returned to their bright red car in their pencil-thin blue jeans.

Why'd they come? As she hung up the cold, wet washing in the cellar, Rebecca couldn't help thinking the fancy girls' surprise appearance might be useful to her. Why, if Jenny Burns threw in the towel and abandoned her attempt to become Amish, it might just save Rebecca's skin.

Oh, but she felt guilty for thinking that way. Sighing, she shook her head, downright disgusted with herself.

26

JENNY squealed with joy when she answered the knock at the back door and saw Pamela and Dorie Kennedy standing there. Quickly, she pushed the door open.

Pamela's jaw dropped as Dorie bent to better inspect Jenny's long dress and apron. For a moment, the three of them simply gawked at one another.

Dorie was the first to find her voice. "Whoa, Jen. You've turned . . . *Amish*!"

Pamela reached for Jenny, who returned the hug, followed by Dorie, who nearly squeezed the life out of her before they all shared in a group hug. Standing back again, Pamela's blue eyes shone. "You really, really look the part, Jen."

"Bravo!" Dorie was clapping.

Then, remembering the bishop's children, Jenny cringed and held her pointer finger over her lips. "I forgot," she whispered, "two of the kids are sleeping." She gestured to Dorie and Pamela to follow her into the utility room, closing the door behind them. "It's so good to see you two! You must have read my letter."

"Did we ever!" Dorie teased with a roll of her pretty green eyes.

Pamela smiled sweetly, apparently unable to stop staring at Jenny's clothes. Dorie touched the fabric of her dress. "What're we going to do with you, girl?"

"Hmm . . . you're not into vintage?" Jenny joked, feeling flushed.

"Your new look, it's just so, well . . ." Dorie paused.

"Plain?" Jenny said.

"I think you look pretty," Pamela spoke up. "In an Old World sort of way."

Jenny explained that she didn't know if it was a good idea to invite them in. "I'm not sure what the bishop's wife would say."

"That's okay," Pamela said. "We don't mean to barge in."

They stood and talked there in the outer room while Jenny glanced at the children in the kitchen from time to time.

"You look like you fit right in here," Dorie said.

"Except for my dreadful bangs." Jenny patted her head. "I'm still growing them out."

"Listen, if that's your one and only flaw, you're good." Pamela fluffed her own chin-length hair.

"Oh, there's far more to being an Amish seeker than meets the eye," Jenny said as they quickly caught up on one another's lives. This included Pamela's exciting new job as a publicist for a celebrity author, and Dorie's purchase of a townhome in Hartford, near Mark Twain's former house.

"I'm going to have a new roommate."

"You're parting ways?" Jenny asked, surprised.

"It's time," Dorie said with a smile.

"Any serious guys on the horizon?" asked Jenny.

"Career first," Pamela said. "Romance can wait."

"What about *your* life here?" Dorie probed. "Aren't you tired of getting up with the chickens?"

Jenny laughed. "Who could ever adjust to that?"

"Are you saying there's hope?" Pamela asked.

Jenny's gaze swept the narrow room. "I'm living the simple life, as you can see. There's nothing quite like it."

An awkward pause settled in, and Pamela's face darkened. "Seriously, Jenny . . . when are you coming home?"

"Dorie, honey . . ." Pamela eyed her sister. "Be nice."

"Um, that *was* nice."

They were both looking at her, waiting for an answer.

"I explained everything in my letter. You read it, right?"

Dorie nodded. "Sure, but now that you're here . . . I mean, *really?*"

Jenny's heart sank but she smiled anyway. "I'm very happy."

There was another pause.

Dorie sighed, followed by a subtle shake of the head. They must believe she'd lost it. "So . . . do you have to wear that funky black apron all the time?"

"This?" Jenny smoothed her apron. "All the women wear them. White on Sundays for single women, though, for Preaching service."

"There's probably a lot we don't get, Dorie," Pamela said. "Right, Jenny?" She bobbed her head.

Dorie frowned. "Well, I'm worried about you."

Pamela touched Jenny's arm. "Your mom's worried, too."

"You've talked to her?"

Pamela nodded and exchanged glances with Dorie. "The truth?"

"Always."

"Your mom's flipped out." Pamela's eyes were serious again.

Dorie added, "She sent us on a reconnaissance mission."

"Sniffing out what I'm really up to?"

"In so many words," Dorie admitted.

"And was there a reward involved?" Jenny laughed but felt ill.

"Oh, Jen . . ." Pamela said, looking cheerless.

"She offered us cash," Dorie said, a humorous glint in her eyes. "But we refused."

"It's nice to have friends who can't be bought off." Jenny chuckled but felt she had to change the subject. "Would you like something to drink? I could bring something out here," she offered, but they shook their heads and politely declined.

"We'd better get going," said Pamela. "Any parting words?"

"In Deitsch or otherwise?" Jenny said, relieved the awkward reunion was coming to an end.

"English is good," Dorie replied.

"Just greet my parents for me." Jenny paused, thinking there was more she'd like to relay to her family.

"By the way, your brother has a new girlfriend," Pamela said. "He broke it off with Tracie."

Jenny was sorry to hear it. "Wow, I thought she was the one for Cameron."

"Oh, you know, things happen," Pamela said, looking as miserable as

Jenny felt. "Hey, maybe you could visit for Christmas and get the whole scoop."

Dorie grinned. "Yeah, and be sure to wear your cute Amish outfit, okay?"

Jenny heard little Anna stirring in the playpen. "I'd better get going—thanks for coming to visit."

Pamela said, "We're staying at the Hampton Inn over on Greenfield Road if you want to do anything this afternoon."

"Wish you'd given me a heads-up. I'm busy all day today."

"Well, if you change your mind, just text us," Pamela said. "Oh, wait, I forgot—"

"No cell phone," Jenny reminded.

Dorie grimaced. "You're really cut off, Jen."

"It's not so bad."

Dorie shook her head. "Maybe not for you."

Pamela gave her a sad little smile. "Nice seeing you, Jen. Take care."

They embraced quickly, instinctively.

Jenny sighed. It was no fun saying good-bye to her faithful friends. This was the hard part of separating oneself from the world. Samuel Lapp had read aloud from the English Bible on this very subject just last evening. *"The tearing away is never easy,"* he'd added while looking over his spectacles at her. *Tearing away from the English world . . . and from my wicked self.*

She smiled and waved as her friends looked back at her, the shock still evident on their fair faces. She watched them go for what might be the last time, a lump in her throat. But what gave her even more pause was the fact that her family hadn't had the nerve, or the interest, to come visit themselves.

27

WITH a bit of trepidation, Marnie Lapp waited for her beau beneath a cluster of willows near the road Tuesday evening. Roy Flaud brightened when he jumped out of the passenger van wearing his Sunday-go-to-meeting clothes. He helped her in with a silent grin.

They talked quietly in Deitsch as the paid driver pulled forward. Marnie felt the energy between them when Roy reached for her hand. "I didn't bring along a Bible," she told him. "S'pose that's all right?"

He removed a small Testament from his coat pocket. "We'll share."

She thought he might kiss her cheek right then, Roy seemed so pleased. Was it being with her or anticipation for the meeting he was so impatient to attend?

"I'm reading chapter eleven in Luke's Gospel, the part about lighting a candle and hiding it under a bushel basket," he said. "Have ya seen that verse?"

"Can't say I have."

He opened his New Testament to a bookmarked page. "Here, read it for yourself." He pointed to verse thirty-three.

She wondered why this was so important, but she took time to look at it all the same. Then, nodding, she handed the Testament back. "'Tis *verninfdich.*"

"Jah, I agree. It *does* make sense to display a light for all to see." Roy's eyes brightened and he slid closer to her.

"Why did ya want me to read that?" she asked.

"The Lord's shown me truths in the four Gospels that I've missed my whole life."

Marnie didn't know what to think of this. Weren't the ministerial brethren supposed to be the ones to impart the knowledge of Scripture?

Roy leaned back, still holding the thin little book. He said no more on the topic, and Marnie hoped that was the end of it.

Turning off Hickory Lane, they drove down a meandering road, past meadows where black-and-white heifers roamed. In the distance, a yard light illuminated a graceful row of poplars that served as a windbreak for a nearby redbrick farmhouse, and Marnie began to wish for the first lovely snowfall. Now that wedding season was in full swing, she could also start to dream of her own wedding day . . . next year.

"You're awful quiet, Marnie." Roy pressed his shoulder against hers.

"Just thinkin'."

"'Bout us, I hope."

She looked at him, smiling. "Always."

"*Gut*," he whispered. "Me too."

She thrilled to his words as he searched her face. Leaning in next to him, she whispered, "We'd best behave ourselves in public, ya know."

He bobbed his head right quick and let go of her hand, folding his arms over his chest. "*Gut* idea."

She suppressed a laugh and turned to gaze out the window, so happy. "Where are we goin', anyways?" She had noticed some familiar terrain along the way, but here there were no streetlights.

"Ever hear of Daniel Fisher?" Roy asked as the van turned into a driveway.

"There's a bunch of 'em." She had to smile. "But sounds Amish, ain't?" She looked outside again, then noticed the little porch light and gasped. "You've brought me to my shunned relatives' house?"

He shook his head. "Who do ya mean?"

"Dan and Katie—they're my first cousins." Oh, she could've cried, and now the driver had turned around, gawking at them but thankfully not able to understand what they were saying. Yet he could surely see her downturned face.

Marnie pressed her hand to her heart. "I can't go in there, Roy. I just can't."

"We'll talk outside." Roy reached for the door.

Marnie shook her head. "I think we best be stayin' right here."

"Sweetheart, please."

She had been taught to obey her father, older brothers . . . and her fiancé, too. So, reluctantly and with a heavy heart, Marnie followed Roy and stepped down, out of the van. Roy went around and paid the driver, instructing him to return in two hours.

He must not care how I feel, Marnie thought.

The van backed up slowly, then pulled out onto the road and sped away while she and Roy stood off to the side of the driveway by a tall tree. Marnie bit her tongue and tried her best not to argue with her beloved. As much as she knew she'd be in terrible trouble with her father, she did not want to spoil the evening, although she feared she already had.

"No one will ever know you're here," Roy coaxed. "I promise."

"My cousins will know . . . and so will God."

"But your cousins won't tell on ya, and the Lord will be mighty pleased."

"And you really think my father won't hear 'bout this?" she asked in what she hoped was a meek voice.

"Just follow me, love." He kissed her forehead. "You won't be sorry."

Marnie walked to the front porch with him, fretting the whole way. Was she doing the right thing? And what on earth was she to say to Cousin Katie?

Jenny took mental notes while Samuel balanced his old German *Biewel* on his knee, sitting there in the front room with Rebecca. It was Samuel's idea to read one verse first in German and then in English. *"Reading from the Psalms that way is something he likes to do,"* Rebecca had mentioned earlier.

Jenny's guilt tore at her heart. She could not bring herself to look at Rebecca during the reading. She had offered her silence up to God, praying to be forgiven. She wondered if Rebecca was also compelled to ask for mercy each time she hurried off to see Katie against the bishop's wishes. By the looks of her, the woman was under tremendous strain, perhaps even losing weight. Jenny felt moved to pray for her during the silent prayer time, offering her entire entreaty on behalf of poor Rebecca.

When they were finished, Samuel rose with some effort, put the Bible on a nearby table, and headed back through the kitchen to the door. In a few minutes, though, he returned to tell Jenny she ought to go out and observe Andrew unhitch one of Samuel's road horses. "Andrew's the one to watch," he said, and Rebecca, in turn, encouraged Jenny, as well.

"I'll get my scarf and gloves." Jenny felt odd about going. After all, it had been eight days since she'd encountered Andrew down at the spring-house pond, which must be frozen over by now, with the cold weather.

When she'd put on Rebecca's old work coat and boots, Jenny made her way outdoors and across the yard to the driveway. The cold pricked her face and she adjusted her scarf. She realized Samuel had returned to the barn to finish cleaning the milk house, since Andrew was working alone to unhook the straps on the back of the horse.

"Samuel suggested I come to watch," she said as she neared the horse.

Andrew chuckled. "Actually, it was *my* idea," he was quick to say. "Go round to the other side of the mare, won't ya?"

She followed his instructions, trying extra hard to do things correctly this time. Jenny concentrated on helping him unhook the traces and tuck them into the harness around the back of Star.

"Have ya been outdoors prayin'?" Andrew asked casually.

"It's been too cold." She hoped that would lessen any fears he might have about being caught with her.

"I haven't gone there to pray lately, either," he said.

Yet I've been praying more than ever, she thought, though naturally she didn't wish to reveal why.

"There were some Englischers lookin' for ya here lately."

"That Amish grapevine is astonishing, jah?"

"Well, I didn't hear this secondhand," Andrew said, still working on his side. "A red sports car stopped, and the lady driver asked me for directions."

"Must have been my friend Pamela Kennedy," she volunteered.

"She was real chatty, I'll say."

Jenny smiled. "That's Pamela, all right. Her sister's quite personable, too."

"They did seem nice. Not like some tourists who manage to find their way to Hickory Hollow." Andrew paused and looked over at her. "Did they come to take ya home?"

"I think they would have liked to, but it wasn't the main reason they came."

"Oh?"

She nodded slowly. "My parents sent them."

Andrew sucked in a breath and straightened. "Your family misses ya, then?"

She laughed. "I wouldn't say that exactly."

He didn't press further.

"The truth is, no one back home can believe I've walked away from my former life." She sighed. "I doubt it's the last trick my parents will pull."

He didn't respond. Did he think she was disrespectful?

Andrew asked her to help him hold the shafts and lead the horse out and away from them. For some reason, the maneuver was easier than her previous attempts, even though this time it was by lantern light.

Andrew pushed the carriage over a ways, and together they walked the horse to the stable. As they went, Andrew took a sugar cube from his pocket and handed it to Jenny. "Here, give her this, all right?"

"Denki."

He added, "The more you bond with the horses, the better."

It wasn't the first time she'd heard this. "I don't have a lot of free time," she told him. "Rebecca—and Mary—keep me very busy."

"Well, every chance you get, come out to the stable and help groom or feed the horses. Eventually, they'll become more accustomed to you and actually work with ya, makin' it easier to hitch up."

She thanked Andrew for the advice and stepped back, waiting for him to lead Star into her stall. Once the horse was secured, she held out the sugar cube on her flat palm.

"No need to be afraid," Andrew said, holding the lantern.

She's so much bigger than I am. . . .

"Go ahead . . . talk to her," Andrew gently urged.

Jenny felt silly, even awkward. "That's a good girl," she whispered.

"Don't be shy," Andrew said. "Go on."

"But I am shy."

He tilted his head, sizing things up. "All right, then, maybe you can practice when no one's round. Will ya?"

"Sure, I'll try it."

Andrew grinned. "There's something else you might like to help with." He explained that his uncle Chester Lapp's golden Labrador, Posey, had followed Marnie down the lane earlier and hadn't returned. "Chester's worried she might've gotten hit by a car, up near Route 340. I've already looked all along Hickory Lane searchin' for her," Andrew said, concern in his voice.

"I'd be glad to help you look."

Andrew raised the lantern a bit. "It's not too late, is it?"

"I might need something to warm me up first. How about some hot cocoa or coffee? Would you care for something?"

"I sure would."

His enthusiasm surprised her. And Jenny hoped Rebecca wouldn't be too shocked to see Andrew following her into the house, all smiles as he was right now.

28

WHY'D I let Roy talk me into this? Marnie froze in place and glanced at her beau standing next to her. What on earth would she say to Cousins Dan and Katie?

It's been so long. . . .

Her mouth was cotton, and she trembled at the thought of breaking the church ordinance. *I'm taking a big risk.*

The front door opened and Cousin Katie appeared, wearing a gracefully long print dress, her hair in a bun covered by a formal Mennonite veiling. Her pretty face broke into a smile and soft brown eyes widened when she realized it was Marnie. Without hesitation, Katie stepped down onto the porch and reached to hug her. Roy moved aside, giving them some privacy.

"Cousin Marnie . . . oh, sweetie," Katie murmured into her ear. "I've missed you just terribly."

Marnie nodded her head, scarcely able to speak. Oh, the happiness of this reunion! "I thought I'd never see you again," Marnie whispered. And she felt it might be the one and only time, so she let herself enjoy this precious moment.

They looked into each other's beaming, tear-streaked faces. *The Bann kept us apart,* thought Marnie, won over as always before by Katie's warmth and love.

"Are ya happy, cousin?" asked Marnie with a glance at the door, which had been closed.

"Oh goodness, incredibly so, and counting my blessings every day! Wait till you see our little boy, Sammy, and baby Kate."

"Well, I'm really not s'posed to be here, ya know," Marnie said, not that she had to explain.

"You've come for the Bible study, then?" Katie's eyes still glistened.

"It was my beau's idea."

"Well, it doesn't matter whose it was; I'm so glad you're here." Katie turned and welcomed her inside. "Come and take a seat next to him."

As resistant as she'd been to attending, Marnie experienced such comfort talking with her dearest cousin. It was all she could do to keep her mind on the Scripture reading, at least for the first few minutes. She also noticed two other Amish courting couples present—one of the girls was the bishop's niece Naomi Beiler, but none of them looked at all ill at ease. Marnie was curious to know what Roy thought of that.

Katie's husband, Daniel, hadn't changed much since she'd last seen him. His hair was still quite fair and, oh goodness, those blueberry eyes Katie had always referred to. Marnie couldn't help remembering what close friends Katie and Mary Stoltzfus Beiler had been in years past, since they were tiny girls. *"Friends for life,"* they'd always said of each other. Now to think Mary was the bishop's wife and mother to his children . . . and Katie was far removed from the People.

She sighed as Dan read the entire third chapter of the Gospel of John. Katie sat next to him in the circle of chairs.Marnie couldn't help also watching her auburn-haired cousin, whose proper Mennonite head covering looked so different than the Amish one Katie had once worn—a squared-off cup shape with pleats ironed in on the sides.

Does she adhere to any of her Amish upbringing? Marnie wondered, trying not to stare at the darling couple.

Just then Roy held his New Testament out before her so she could follow along. She'd better pay closer attention, but it was ever so hard, considering the years she'd lost with her cousin and friend.

"'The Father loveth the Son, and hath given all things into his hand,'" Cousin Daniel read again, his face radiant. "'He that believeth on the Son hath everlasting life. . . .'"

Marnie drank in the verse as if she were hearing it for the first time.

A sermonlike talk followed. Daniel reminded her of a preacher, without the singsong approach. It was surprising how relaxed and conversational he was as he spoke. He seemed to know just what to say about the chapter he'd read, focusing primarily on the final verses.

How can this be? Marnie wondered, nearly in awe.

"The verse means precisely what it says," Daniel emphasized, leaning forward in his chair and folding his hands between his knees. "We have eternal life through Jesus Christ alone." He continued, his eyes shining as he shared the "great joy and amazing peace" he'd found in "accepting this truth and receiving Jesus as my own Savior and Lord." He paused to look around the circle, compassion on his handsome face. Dan's deep voice grew softer then. "I have found a love I'd never known before, my good friends. And I'm thrilled to share it with all of you."

Marnie noticed one of the Amish girls struggling not to cry, her lower lip quivering as Daniel continued his testimony, sharing his personal background in the Old Order Amish community . . . and later, his excommunication. There was scarcely a dry eye in the room. Even Marnie had to hold her breath to keep from being overwhelmed. Anyone could see that Dan's and Katie's experience with God had changed their lives.

When Daniel asked them to bow their heads while he led in prayer, Marnie felt a great yearning to be alone in her room to pray privately. The incredibly tender way she felt just now, there was so much she wanted to tell the Lord God.

Afterward, Katie and Dan played their guitars, leading the group in a slow version of "Amazing Grace." Now it was Marnie who could scarcely keep her tears in check as she blended her voice in unison with the others. To think the bishop had renounced their expressive playing.

Following the final prayer, Katie invited all of them to the cheery kitchen for homemade refreshments: carrot and nut cake, vanilla ice cream, and root beer. Marnie was surprised how the folk there kept talking in hushed tones while they mingled—some of them praying for each other aloud. Clearly, they were eager to linger.

When everyone was served, Katie silently motioned for Marnie to follow her upstairs. Still profoundly touched by Daniel's words and the Scriptures he'd shared, Marnie looked fondly down at Katie's darling children, an auburn-haired boy and a girl with blond ringlets, both sleeping soundly.

"Oh, honey-girl," Katie said as she slipped her arm around Marnie's waist. "Go ahead, my sweet cousin. It's all right to cry. . . ."

Unable to speak, Marnie wept for the pain Katie and Dan had suffered for the sake of their obvious love for Jesus. And yet immense joy was written on their dear faces.

Later, when she'd composed herself, Katie opened her arms and hugged and kissed her. "I hope you'll come again, Marnie. You're always welcome here."

"Denki," she eked out.

Katie leaned down and peered into her eyes. "Are you baptized, cousin?" she asked softly.

"Not yet."

Katie seemed to sigh. "Then you can't be reprimanded for visiting us."

"Pray for me, won't ya, Katie?" Marnie told her how harsh her father had been toward Marnie's older brother. "If I'm found out, I'll be in trouble."

Katie promised to pray daily. "You can count on me." She wiped Marnie's tears with both thumbs. "All right?"

Katie had such an appealing way about her—she stirred up the atmosphere with her love of people. Only a woman like Katie could believe the cure for her own sadness due to the Bann was in making others happy. She remained the cousin Marnie had always loved, even though they were not blood kin. Truth be known, folk had been drawn to Katie since she first arrived in Hickory Hollow as a rosy infant with Uncle Samuel and Aunt Rebecca, who'd claimed her as their own nearly thirty years ago.

"Our home is open to you, if you ever just want to come and stay awhile." Katie told Marnie that one of the bishop's nieces was considering doing the same thing.

Marnie nodded gratefully, knowing in her heart that, with or without Roy's wanting to return, there was nothing anyone could do or say to keep her away from the next meeting.

29

ANDREW Lapp's flashlight paved their way with a white circle of light as Jenny kept pace with him. "How long has your uncle had Posey?"

"Not long, which might be the reason she's run off. You see, Uncle Chester's a real stickler for obedience, not excluding his pets."

"So Posey must be a pup?"

"Jah, the runt of the litter. She comes from a long line of pedigreed Labs owned by my Dat's family for several generations."

"Interesting."

Andrew nodded and looked her way. "My uncle also has two golden retrievers for hunting small game, Skip and Sparky."

Trying to be helpful, Jenny asked, "Could Posey have followed Marnie?"

"I doubt that, 'cause Uncle Chester said Marnie left in a van, headed somewhere. It's a mystery why Posey's still missin'."

Jenny purposely breathed through her nose and tried to keep from shivering as she walked. The moon was a delicate light behind a stream of clouds, but the night was very still. She listened for anything that might sound like a puppy.

Up the road, they heard the fast trot of a horse with an enclosed buggy behind it, bright lights on both sides. "Someone's late for supper," Andrew joked.

"Can you differentiate between one neighbor's buggy and another's?" she asked.

"Sometimes, jah . . . after you're around the different road horses."

Jenny wondered if she'd ever reach that point and, intrigued by this, forgot to call out for Marnie's father's dog. She liked Andrew's willingness to answer her questions and his free and easy style, much like his casual stride.

Another horse and carriage approached now and began to slow. "Can you tell whose horse it is from here?" she asked Andrew.

"If it was daylight, I could."

"Hullo there" came a low male voice.

Jenny looked closer and could see an older man waving through the windshield.

"Who's there?" Andrew called, stepping closer to the shoulder with Jenny.

"It's Preacher Yoder." The horse halted in the middle of the road. "You two headed somewhere?" The man had slid over and was looking out at them from the passenger side of the front seat.

"Just out searchin' for Uncle Chester's Labrador. Did ya happen to see a small yellow pup anywhere?" Andrew asked.

"Wasn't payin' any mind, to tell the truth."

Andrew chuckled. "Aren't you usually in bed at this hour?"

"Bishop sent me out on an assignment."

"Well, don't let us keep ya, then."

"That's all right—got what I needed." The preacher nodded his head.

"Gut Nacht," Andrew said, and Jenny repeated it.

After the horse pulled forward and headed on, Andrew said, "Wonder why he's out after dark."

Jenny wondered the same, as well as what reason the bishop might have for sending the preacher. *Bishop Beiler's nice enough*, she thought, thinking back to their brief meeting and having seen him around the farm on days she baby-sat there. It was still hard to imagine that Bishop John was as stern as Marnie and others made him out to be.

"I've been wantin' to mention something, Jenny," Andrew said after they'd walked awhile without speaking. "I daresay you're paying us Amish folk a big compliment."

"You think so?"

He paused a moment and looked at her, his flashlight still shining on the road. "I don't know any other Englischers who'd give up everything to do what you're doin', or fight so hard to be Amish."

She didn't know what to say.

"It can't be easy for ya. And I admire your courage."

"With the Lord's help, I'm doing my best." She never would have thought she'd feel comfortable talking like this with him, especially as attractive as he was. "I appreciate your prayers."

"It's the least I can do, Jenny." He laughed again. "That, and help ya learn to hitch up."

"I must be a slow learner."

He asked her to count for him in Deitsch and she smiled, happily able to get to *zwelf*—twelve.

"Lots of Amish folk mix up their numbers with English, did ya know that?"

"I'm not surprised."

"My own brother would have to think a second to say the Deitsch for, say, ninety-five."

Jenny wondered if that had come about because so many men now worked among Englishers, away from the Amish community.

Andrew asked her to run through some of the easier sociable questions, the same ones Rebecca had gone over with her, and Jenny remembered each one. It struck her funny that Andrew seemed so pleased about it, even energized by her small triumph.

"You're doin' very well, Jenny. Won't be long and you'll be talking up a storm like the rest of us."

"Deitsch is slowly starting to make sense. I just wish some of the other things would, too."

"Like what?"

She wasn't sure she should say. After all, he wasn't sharing *his* inner struggles. And, too, they hardly knew each other.

"Well, if you really want to know."

"I do," he said quietly.

"I'm not sure how well I'm emulating the seemingly ingrained attributes I've observed in the People." She thought suddenly of Rebecca's visit to her daughter, Katie. "Well, in *most* of them."

"Not sure who you're talking 'bout, but I don't know anyone born into this world with a pure heart."

His words echoed in her mind as they continued walking farther away from the Lapps' farm. *"We're not perfect,"* Rebecca had once said.

In the distance, Jenny thought she heard a shrill whining, and she stopped walking to listen more closely. "Did you hear that?"

Andrew pitched forward, cupping his ear.

Jenny held her breath for a few seconds. There it was again. "Sounds like there might be a lost pup over that way."

They turned off the road to hurry through a pasture in the direction of the crying. According to Andrew, this was Nate Kurtz's meadow. She was thankful for the large flashlight, not wanting to step in a cow pie!

Jenny glanced at Andrew as they picked over the uneven ground and nearly tripped. He put his arm out and reached for her gloved hand.

"You all right?" he asked, still holding her hand.

"Jah." She laughed. "I'm fine, thanks. Denki," she said and slid her hand gently out of his.

Self-conscious now, they walked in total stillness. And Jenny almost forgot to listen for the puppy's cries.

30

"JENNY left with Andrew Lapp after makin' hot cocoa for him," Rebecca told Samuel as they sat at the kitchen table that evening.

"'Twas the oddest thing, Andrew askin' for her like that." Samuel went on, indicating that he'd thought their nephew only wanted to help her learn the unhitching process. "Tricked me, I guess."

"Oh now." Rebecca sprinkled a few more miniature marshmallows on the hot chocolate in Samuel's big brown mug.

"You just don't know, do ya, with these young folk?"

"Jenny's not someone he should be takin' a shining to, is she?"

"May God grant him wisdom if he does." Samuel stirred in the marshmallows with his spoon. "They'd best be waitin' till she's safely baptized before any formal courting."

Safely baptized.

Rebecca tensed up and wondered what Jenny would reveal when Preacher Yoder asked her the *most* important question, after the six weeks of instruction for baptism next summer. *If she's invited to take part.* She shivered and her husband looked up, his brow furrowed.

"What is it, dear?" Samuel raised his sturdy mug to his lips.

She tried to calm herself. "What are the chances Jenny Burns will last round here?"

He drank slowly and lowered his cup. "That's one question I'll leave with the Good Lord." Samuel locked eyes with her. "He alone knows the intent and purposes of the heart."

"'Tis best, jah." She suddenly felt almost too weak to sit there as Samuel's eyes continued to probe hers. *Does he suspect?*

"I've noticed some tension between you and Jenny here lately," Samuel added. "I think it's wise you keep her at a cautious distance."

She said nothing to that.

"I approve of the way you're heedin' my advice, dear."

Lowering her gaze, Rebecca felt all the more guilty.

··· ➤ ◄ ···

"I hope ya don't think I was too forward back there," Andrew said as he and Jenny stood in Nate Kurtz's field. They'd stopped walking when Jenny heard another sound in the distance.

Jenny blushed and was thankful the flashlight wasn't shining in her direction. "Listen," she said. "I just heard it again."

Andrew turned off the flashlight. The moon skimmed out of a translucent cloud, brightening the landscape somewhat. Then the piercing cries came once more, and Jenny darted off in that direction, not waiting for Andrew.

Posey sounds hurt!

When Jenny found her, the poor thing was trapped, her collar caught on a raised tree root. "Quick, Andrew! Help me pry her loose," she called as he approached. She worked the thin root back and forth rapidly, trying her best to break the pup free. "Do you have a pocketknife?"

He did, and when Posey was free at last, she held the whimpering pup close, carrying her back across the field, toward the road. She snuggled her face into the pup's downy body.

"Posey's shivering," she told Andrew, feeling the cold seeping out of the furry pet.

"And you must be cold, too, Jenny." He took off his heavy outer coat and draped it gently over her, tucking the pup underneath. "Uncle Chester's place isn't too far from here," he assured her. "We'll get warmed up there before I take ya back to Uncle Samuel's. How's that?"

She was shocked that Andrew would shed his coat in such cold, but it had been a long time since Jenny had felt so cared for. How could she object?

··· ➤ ◄ ···

Three buggies were parked alongside Marnie's driveway when Jenny and Andrew arrived. The puppy had stopped crying as they hurried around to the backyard, toward the house. Jenny was anxious to take a closer look at Posey in the light of a gas lamp.

The house was abuzz with the sounds of Deitsch and people eating. Marnie's robust father turned and gawked at them when they entered the kitchen, which looked very much like Rebecca Lapp's with its linoleum flooring and long trestle table and wooden benches.

Spotting the pup, Marnie's father nearly leaped out of his chair at the head of the table, coming quickly to greet Andrew and Jenny. But it was the pup that Chester wanted, and he reached under Posey to lift her out of Jenny's arms.

Tall Chester Lapp smiled and shook her hand firmly. "Denki ever so much." His face beamed as he cradled Posey in his strong left arm. "She ain't hurt, is she?" He looked the pup over and stroked her head. Posey's pink tongue gave Chester's cheek a lick, and he grinned again.

"A happy outcome for one vivacious pup," Marnie's mother, Peggy, said, coming over to thank Jenny, as well. She glanced suspiciously at Andrew as he removed his coat from around Jenny's shoulders. "Denki for your help." She looked up at Chester. "I can't tell ya how happy you've made my husband—and all of us."

Jenny smiled. "I'm glad Posey didn't get stuck out in the cold all night." Based on the reception, she felt like she'd accomplished something important here.

"Won't ya join us for some warm apple betty and coffee?" Peggy asked, a bright expression on her plump face.

Andrew accepted without conferring with Jenny, which tickled her. "We've been walkin' all over creation," he told them, offering Jenny a seat at the far end of the table. "So this'll be right *gut*." He, in turn, sat across from her, on the side with his middle-aged uncles.

In a few short minutes, they learned that everyone present had been out looking for Posey. "Till the womenfolk turned into popsicles," Chester Lapp said, sitting back in his chair, still holding his pup with one hand. He forked up some dessert and smacked his lips. "I would guess Marnie'll be home here fairly quick," he said, then began introducing Jenny to his relatives.

Peggy explained that Marnie's younger siblings were already tucked into bed. "For school tomorrow. You'll just have to come another time and meet them."

Jenny said she would enjoy that. But it was the delighted expression on Andrew's face whenever he looked her way that stayed in Jenny's mind long after Andrew drove her home in a borrowed carriage.

··· ➤ ◄ ···

When Jenny slipped in the Lapps' back door, she was surprised to see Rebecca still up, lifting a pie from the oven.

Straightening, Rebecca said, "You've been gone a *gut* while."

Jenny realized the late-night baking was probably an excuse to be there when she arrived. She explained she'd gone to help Andrew look for Chester Lapp's dog, Posey.

"Ah, that silly pup—he's gone head over heels over her." Rebecca seemed to know.

"That's the one." She said they'd found Posey and taken her home.

"You must've seen Marnie, then?"

She didn't think she should reveal that Marnie had just been coming home in a van from a date. "Right as I was heading back here," she said vaguely.

"You two are getting along nicely, ain't so?"

Jenny nodded and said they were. "Say, I was wondering . . . did I happen to get any mail earlier?" It had been a while since she'd written to her parents, but Jenny wasn't certain they would actually write, especially when her mother had sent Dorie and Pamela after her. All the same, she could hope.

"No letters that I've seen." Rebecca placed the pie on a cooling rack and moved to the sink to wash her hands. "Are ya lookin' for something in particular?"

Jenny shrugged, not saying more. Her mind was overflowing with many pleasant things—she wanted to savor the evening rather than lose herself in small talk. She excused herself, eager to go upstairs and write in her journal.

Okay, this may sound earthshaking, but I think I might be falling in love again. The trick is that before I can be of real interest to anyone here in Hickory Hollow—including the very likeable Andrew Lapp—I must first be baptized into the church. At least, before I can be courted officially.

On the buggy ride back to Samuel Lapp's farm, would you believe that it began to snow softly, just like in the movies? I sat on the left side of the seat and watched Andrew handle the horse out of the corner of my eye. We had several heavy woolen lap blankets tucked around us to keep us warm. I've never experienced anything quite like it. Something more ethereal than romantic, but I'm getting way ahead of myself!

It was especially nice bumping into Marnie and her beau, whom she introduced to Andrew and me, although she was a little reticent about doing so, there at the end of her father's lane. Marnie's eyebrows soared when she saw Andrew at the reins and me sitting in the buggy with him.

All in all, it's been an incredibly interesting day. If only it didn't have to end!

Now I need to get myself settled down after that coffee—don't I know better than to have caffeine so late? Time to read my Bible and pray for God's guidance. And to sleep . . . if I can!

··· ❦ ···

Marnie felt it coming.

"You know better than to let the puppy out of the utility room," her father scolded, raising his voice even as Marnie's uncles and aunts were out on the back porch saying their good-byes to Mamm. "What were ya thinkin', daughter?"

"I'll be more careful," she replied with a slight bow of her head.

"You'd better be," her father muttered, heading toward the stairs.

"I really am sorry, *Daed.*" She followed him.

He kept going, ignoring her.

Part of her heart was broken anew each time he turned his back on her—more times than she could remember to count. *I'll be more careful with your precious pet,* she thought sadly. *But you won't keep me from Cousin Dan Fisher's meetings.*

Going to the kitchen to see cute little Posey, Marnie leaned down and lifted her into her arms, then slid onto her regular spot on the hard bench. She stared at the dark sky through the window—her relatives were still talking outside. Tears threatened to spill as she snuggled with the puppy. "Nosy Posey," she whispered. "You just had to see where I was goin' tonight and who I was with, didn't ya?"

Did Daed see Roy, too?

She worried that, because of her father's involvement in helping to start up the Bank of Bird-in-Hand, which appealed to Plain folk, he knew many Amish farmers and businessmen over where Roy and his family lived. Still, it was far better for Daed to recognize Roy as one of the prominent, progressive Flaud family than for him to hear where Roy had taken her this most inspiring night.

31

JENNY was delighted when Rebecca invited her to go along to the Bird-in-Hand Farmers Market the next morning to help tend the cash register at Groff's Candies. The vendor, a friend of Rebecca's, was sick at home with the flu. So it was decided that Jenny would do the financial transactions and Rebecca would help the customers find what they were looking for among the homemade fudges, nuts, dried fruits, and brittles. Jenny asked if Rebecca was going to sell some of her jams and jellies, as well.

Rebecca shook her head. "The vendors don't work that way," she explained. "I'll just sell them at the house, like always."

Jenny was glad for the opportunity to get out for a good part of the day, wanting to clear her head. Today had her second-guessing why her mother hadn't written back. Not even a Thanksgiving card, the perfect excuse to get in touch.

Is she just waiting for me to fail . . . and return home?

··�➤ ◄··

This being the day before Thanksgiving, the marketplace was packed with patrons—young and old, couples and singles, and a number of families. The air smelled of fudge and freshly popped popcorn and, around certain men, sweet-smelling pipe tobacco.

Jenny had been told by both Rebecca and Marnie that Amish folk did not observe Thanksgiving Day, *"not like the English."* Instead, the day was typically taken up with all-day weddings, one of which Samuel and Rebecca would be attending tomorrow, in honor of their niece Susannah Lapp.

So I'll spend the day by myself, Jenny thought, reliving the many times she and Kiersten had helped debone the turkey for their mother after dinner, always searching for the wishbone. *Will I miss being there this year?*

Jenny worked nearly nonstop ringing up dozens of purchases. She didn't bother to look for Emmalyn Lapp this time and was relieved when a few hours passed and Andrew's sister had not appeared.

She did notice, however, a tall, brown-haired young man who very easily could have passed for Kyle Jackson's brother or cousin. She felt momentary surprise, then scolded herself, quite positive Kyle was nowhere near Lancaster County. *He's long gone from my life.*

Later, Ella Mae Zook and Mattie Beiler came by to say hello, each taking a small sample of homemade fudge. They stood there oohing about it, and Ella Mae's eyes danced at the rich taste. The Wise Woman appeared to be more spunky today than the last time Jenny had seen her, and Jenny smiled as she artfully reached for another piece while Mattie was talking with Rebecca.

"Do you know how *gut* this is for the arteries?" Ella Mae said with a chuckle. "'Specially if ya eat enough of it?"

Jenny played along. "So . . . how much is enough?"

"Oh, just let your sweet tooth decide."

The woman was adorable, and Jenny wished she had the opportunity to bump into her every day. "It's fun to see you, Ella Mae. Come by anytime." Jenny smiled at herself—she was starting to sound like Rebecca.

"I think it's time *you* dropped by for some tea again, Jenny." Ella Mae turned things around as she was known to do. "Will ya?"

"When I'm able to get free, sure."

"How 'bout tomorrow? Or are you goin' with Samuel and Rebecca to the wedding?"

"I haven't been invited," she replied, glancing at Rebecca, who was still gabbing with Mattie. "Do you know if anyone serves turkey on Thanksgiving Day around here?"

"Only if it's Amish roast—ya know, cooked turkey or chicken mixed with stuffing. Same as what's served at the wedding feasts." Ella Mae blinked her small eyes. "But now, if it's turkey you want, I could make ya some."

She felt silly for saying anything. "Oh, I don't want you to go to any work! Especially not on my account."

"Well, you just make sure ya come for dinner tomorrow, hear?"

Rebecca turned away from Mattie to focus on them. "What's this?" she said. "Did I hear you two makin' plans?"

"She's comin' for the noon meal tomorrow," Ella Mae informed Mattie. "We're havin' us a Thanksgiving feast!"

Rebecca's eyelashes fluttered. "I beg your pardon?"

"We can't have the poor thing all alone on an English holiday, now, can we? She's gonna have family back home enjoying turkey and mashed potatoes and gravy and whatnot all. The least we can do is give her some turkey roast, ain't so?"

Mattie shook her head, and Jenny had the impression the midwife wasn't surprised at anything her mother proposed.

"What can I bring to help?" Jenny asked, hoping she wouldn't suggest a loaf of homemade bread, knowing her own track record.

"Just yourself." Ella Mae's white head bobbed up and down. "Leave everything to Mattie and me."

Rebecca's smile spread to her ears, and Jenny could hear her trying to squelch her snickers. "So we'll have a feast at the wedding, and so will yous."

"And why not? It's mighty close to a month since Jenny came to us. I daresay a celebration's in order."

Jenny blushed.

"Goodness' sake, Ella Mae," muttered Rebecca as she went over to help a customer. The young woman's cozy red sweat suit reminded Jenny of one she'd once had, and for that single second, she missed wearing sweats.

"There'll be pecan pie and pumpkin, too. I know what Englischers like to eat," Ella Mae said, her face beaming mischief. "Drop by round eleven-thirty—come hungry."

"Denki," said Jenny, her mouth watering.

Mattie went over to her mother, and the older woman reached for her arm and headed off. A few steps forward and she turned to wink at Jenny. *She's got something up her sleeve.* Jenny was very sure.

··· ➤ ◄ ···

After supper, Jenny slipped outside under a canopy of stars. She had missed her peaceful prayer time at the springhouse. The night was mild, and since Rebecca wasn't on the list of kitchen workers for the wedding tomorrow, both she and Samuel were relaxing in their rocking chairs by the heater stove in the kitchen. Jenny wanted to give the couple some time alone, especially because she'd heard them talking in an obvious code during the meal, Deitsch words and phrases mixed in with English. Unknown to them, she'd managed to piece together some of it. Evidently, the bishop and the deacon had pulled together a short list of young people who'd attended a Bible study last evening. Jenny recalled the note on the fridge at the bishop's house. Was this talk about Dan and Katie's meeting?

She was glad the evening was so temperate compared to last night's tromp through Hickory Hollow to look for Posey. She thought of the Wise Woman's visit at market earlier and her generous invitation. Why had Ella Mae seemed to seek her out, and in front of both Mattie and Rebecca, no less? And what was all the talk about celebrating? Jenny didn't feel she deserved it. *I haven't yet accomplished what I've set out to do.*

Jenny carried a lengthy mental list as she walked down the lane to the springhouse steps. She needed to pray for guidance. She no longer had the confidence of her first days at the Lapps', uncertain she was able to do all that was needed to make her Amish dream a reality.

32

THANKSGIVING morning, Jenny spent the first couple of hours trying to make two loaves of bread that wouldn't collapse like a sinkhole. Much earlier, even before breakfast, she'd gone out to groom Ol' Molasses and narrowly missed being kicked. The day was off to quite a start.

She had started long before Samuel and Rebecca left for the wedding to gather the ingredients, mix them, and punch down the dough. Jenny needed all the practice she could get, and while she waited for the dough to rise the second time, she sewed.

The thought occurred to her that she might write to her mother again, or to Kiersten for the first time. But she didn't want to appear desperate. The silence on their end was becoming deafening, but she couldn't blame them, could she? She was the one who'd left without saying what she was up to. *Neurotically guarded.*

With every stitch she made, her prayer was for wisdom in following her heart here. Jenny didn't want to think she was second-guessing her resolve, but she knew she was. "I'm only half Amish, if that," she whispered. "When will it register on the inside?"

When it was time, she carefully patted the dough into the loaf pans, hoping for success. When, oh when, would it happen? If she couldn't even make a decent loaf of bread, how would she ever manage a kitchen as an Amish wife and mother?

If I'm fortunate enough to ever marry.

··· ➤ ◄ ···

Marnie wished to goodness her parents had reserved their criticisms for a different day. The three of them had ridden together in one buggy to Susannah Lapp's wedding earlier that morning. Her father's sharp words on the way there had spoiled the service for her, and she'd fretted and stewed ever since. Presently, her head throbbed, and her thoughts were spinning at the revelation that someone had seen her and Roy over at Dan and Katie's.

And if that wasn't enough, her father's spy, whoever he was, recognized Roy as the son of a progressive Amish businessman. Marnie sighed, knowing she was in twice as thick a stew. *"You are a very poor example to your younger siblings. Des is arig—bad!"* her father had said, his face red with anger. *"You must not continue seein' that Flaud fella, and you will stay away from the Fishers' place, too."*

She could hardly hold her head up the rest of the morning, even when it was time to file out of the house before the wedding feast and cluster with the single girls, all of whom had serious beaus.

How quickly things had come to a halt. And worse, the precious feelings she'd had at Cousin Katie's must be left to flicker away. Marnie was a captive in her own home, cut off from her beloved and prohibited from following her newfound faith. What could she do?

Suddenly, Katie's invitation to stay with them began to look like an actual possibility . . . a place of refuge. Her mind turned around the idea again and again, but there was no easy answer.

The crisp air felt good as Marnie stood with the other young women her age under the overhang of the stable. Her cousin Mandie glanced at her, then gave her a closer look.

"Are you ill?" Mandie asked as they waited.

"Do I look it?"

Her cousin nodded her blond head. "I've been worried 'bout ya all mornin', Marnie. You all right?"

Oh, the questions! They only served to make her feel sorry for herself. "I'll be fine," she told Mandie, but she knew she wouldn't. If Marnie was to submit to her father, she would be miserable the rest of her life. And if she defied him, she might lose the love of her family.

···➤◄···

It was close to eleven o'clock when Jenny opened the oven and removed the steaming loaf. But as before, the bread had flopped in the middle. "What am I doing wrong?"

Disgusted, she refused to give up. Tomorrow she would try again, and she would leave extra money with the weekly rent payment for Rebecca to replace the wasted ingredients.

Jenny ran upstairs to change into a clean dress, having spilled milk and flour on both her apron and her dress. "I'm a sight," she said, trying to put the baking disaster out of her mind.

It was going to be the strangest Thanksgiving ever, but hadn't she counted the cost before coming here? It was her choice, after all, to separate from her world in an attempt to live a life in unity with God and the People. In so doing, Jenny had lost her family.

Just like Katie . . .

···➤◄···

"Ach, are you sure?" Rebecca asked Rachel Stoltzfus, the bishop's mother-in-law, who had ridden along with her and Samuel to the wedding. They were sitting alone at the table, having just finished their dessert of delicious white cake, and the topic of Katie and Dan's invitation had come up.

Rachel removed a lace-edged hankie from beneath her sleeve and leaned close to Rebecca, whispering. "Word has it your daughter's offered to open up her home to two of our teenage girls."

"You don't mean it!"

"Just ask Lovina Yoder."

Rebecca found it difficult to consider talking to their preacher's wife about such a matter. "Ach, this is *greislich*—dreadful."

"Jah, indeed."

"Why would Dan and Katie do such a thing?" She could not for the life of her understand what they were thinking.

"Well, when ya believe in something so strongly that you're willin' to leave family and home to pursue it, ya never know what's next." Rachel wiped her brow with her hankie. "Once this gets out, I'm afraid we could see a whole bunch of young folk movin' away."

"Why's that?"

Rachel turned to glance over her plump shoulder, then looked back at Rebecca. "Some are sayin' the bishop's gonna empty out the church. You can read between the lines, ain't?"

"Too strict?" Rebecca bent near Rachel's ear to say it.

"Seems so."

"Well, we've always known that. What's different?"

"Modern ways are creepin' in—smartphones and iPads and whatnot all. Word has it the young folk are talkin' privately amongst themselves about their questions—and the bishop. Something 'bout goin' viral."

Rebecca shuddered to think her own daughter was paving the way for an exit, if that's what was happening. Could it be true? It was ever so hard to believe that more than just a couple of girls might want to leave Hickory Hollow. "Are ya sure this isn't tittle-tattle?"

"Ain't gossip." Rachel shook her head. "Like I said, if ya don't believe me, go an' talk to Lovina."

"Oh, dear me." Reaching to cover Rachel's wrinkled hand with her own, Rebecca knew it was high time to write Katie a letter. And she would do so the very minute she returned home today.

Jenny was surprised to see Emmalyn Lapp already there at Ella Mae's when she arrived. The Amish teen was down on the floor playing with three young children, whom Ella Mae quickly introduced as Mattie's grandchildren—Ella Mae's "greats."

Did the Wise Woman know Emmalyn was coming? Jenny wondered. *Did she plan this?* Jenny offered to help set the table in the larger house, but Ella Mae insisted that Mattie had already finished doing that. "You just relax and enjoy the family atmosphere," Ella Mae said with a smile. Yet how could Jenny, with Emmalyn there?

Eventually she learned that Emmalyn had chosen not to attend the wedding today, so at Ella Mae's invitation, she'd come to help entertain the children.

Interesting, Jenny thought.

After spending time in Ella Mae's kitchen and carrying over several hot dishes to the main house, Jenny was relieved when Mattie called all of them next door to be seated. Emmalyn went to sit with the youngest children at the far end, away from Jenny.

David and Mattie Beiler and their grandchildren were there, as well as the bishop's wife, Mary, with six of the bishop's children still living at home. It surprised Jenny to see Mary Beiler without her husband, but someone said that the bishop had gone to marry Samuel and Rebecca's niece to her longtime beau, Adam Miller.

All the same, Jenny wondered why Mary and the children were there and not at the wedding. *What's going on?*

Marnie felt altogether blue by the time the wedding feast was finished. It was hard not to remember how happy she'd been at Cousin Linda Ebersol's wedding with Roy two weeks ago. How she'd loved spending the day with him!

Naomi Beiler, who had also gone to the Fishers' Bible study, smiled from across the room. Marnie rose and went to her, and Naomi suggested they go for a walk. "I can't breathe in here anymore," Naomi whispered.

Agreeing to go, Marnie hoped she wasn't in for more bad news. The day had been fraught with enough emotion. "Are you enjoyin' yourself at all?" she asked as they made their way up the road.

"Not much." Naomi sniffled.

"You too?"

Naomi nodded slowly. "I had such wunnerbaar-*gut* plans, but they're upset now 'cause I got found out. Did ya know Preacher Yoder was over there in the shadows watchin' all of us file into Dan and Katie's Tuesday night?"

"Jah, I heard someone was spyin'. Didn't know it was Preacher Yoder, though."

"What're you gonna do, Marnie?"

She shrugged. "What *can* I do? We'll just have to quit goin', is all."

"Well, you might not know it, but I've decided to take Katie up on her invitation to move in over there." Naomi was fuming.

Marnie stopped walking, shocked. "You'd do that—you'd up and leave your family?"

Naomi jerked on her Kapp strings till one of them popped right off. "Just look what I did," she said and burst into tears. "Just look. . . ."

"Maybe it's a sign." Marnie wished she could comfort her.

"I want a different life, one like Katie's and Dan's," Naomi insisted. "Don't ya see how happy they are?" She paused to brush back tears. "Just think 'bout it. Most of the men I know are sour faced, and the womenfolk, well, the happiest times are when we're all workin' at a quilting bee or whatnot." Naomi started walking again.

Marnie listened but did not agree. "Maybe you're only seekin' out the miserable ones. Could that be?"

Naomi said she didn't know. "*Gut* thing I ain't baptized. I can fly away . . . if I get the gumption to."

Marnie didn't comment. Still, she felt awful bad for Naomi. She would have the ministerial brethren breathing down her neck now for sure.

"Don't let me sway you, though, Marnie." Naomi slowed her pace in spite of the cold. "You've got your own mind to make up."

"Does the bishop know you're movin' to Fishers'?"

"How can he not know?" Naomi whimpered. "The way the grapevine goes."

"Well, this is the first *I've* heard it."

Naomi merely bobbed her head, her face wrinkling as if to cry, and Marnie reached for her hand.

33

AFTER the memorable Thanksgiving feast, Jenny helped Emmalyn dress Mattie's three small grandchildren, putting on their coats, knit hats, scarves, and mittens. They dashed out the back door, along with Emmalyn and Jenny, too, into the big yard, where mature trees rimmed the area to the north. One in particular had an inviting circular wooden seat built at its base. Though the air was brisk, the sun was strong and warm. The lone boy and two little girls ran around the tree, flapping arms held high, then would sit down for a few seconds on the wooden seat before popping back up to run again.

It looked to Jenny like they were pretending to be either birds or butterflies. Perhaps the boy was the bird and the girls were young butterflies fresh out of cocoons. She stood just a few yards back from Emmalyn, unsure if she dared subject herself to Andrew's sister again. *So far, so good,* she thought, looking at the sky and wondering what her family was doing today, besides eating themselves into oblivion.

"It was awful nice of Ella Mae and Mattie to celebrate an Englischer's holiday with you," Emmalyn finally said, her eyes meeting Jenny's.

"It certainly was."

"Never saw that happen before round here. Prob'ly never will again."

"It really wasn't necessary," Jenny said. "But I appreciate it."

"Well, you've given up a lot to come here, I 'spect."

"In some ways, yes . . . er, jah."

Emmalyn fell silent and the children's playful sounds filled the yard.

The boy had no problem fitting in with his sisters, Jenny noticed, and she remembered her own brother's futile attempts to mesh with her and Kiersten when they were kids. It had basically been Cameron against the two of them from early on. Then later, Kiersten had teamed up with Cameron against Jenny. *Someone was always on the outside looking in,* she realized, feeling sad as she watched the Amish youngsters play so delightfully together. Rebecca might say it was all in the upbringing, and Jenny had to agree.

"Have ya learned the shortcut for makin' butter?" Emmalyn asked unexpectedly.

"No," Jenny said, not sure where this was coming from.

"You just pour some fresh cream in a canning jar and make sure the lid's on real tight, then put it in the washing machine."

After the trick Emmalyn had pulled after the first shared meal, Jenny looked at her skeptically. "You're not pulling my leg, are you?"

"Just ask Ella Mae—she does it sometimes, too."

Jenny still wasn't sure if Emmalyn was actually serious, so she changed the subject to baby-sitting. "Looks like you're having fun today with the Beiler grandkids."

"Oh jah. But 'tween you and me, it all depends on *die Kinner*—the children." Emmalyn glanced back at her. "How do ya like takin' care of the bishop's youngest?"

"They're very sweet."

Emmalyn nodded. "I've kinda wondered how ya got that job, considering . . ."

Emmalyn's words always had a way of jabbing. "I really don't know," Jenny replied softly, gently, the way Rebecca had taught her. Above all she wanted *"the ornament of a meek and quiet spirit."*

Soon, the bishop's eleven-year-old son Jacob and five-year-old daughter Mary Mae came outside to play, too. They had not even the slightest hesitation to join the others, and they all swooped and darted about like barn swallows in flight.

Why can't I merge into Amish life like that? Jenny wondered, a little envious of the fluid motions of their interaction.

Emmalyn went to sit on the seat at the base of the tree, and the children clapped their hands and treated her like a princess. Sunbeams dappled the front of Emmalyn's hair, making it look like spun gold. Was there such a thing as Amish royalty? Jenny imagined that if there were dandelions to decorate Emmalyn's hair, the girls might have made a crown with them.

They adore her. . . .

Jenny turned to go inside, contemplating the odd dichotomy. Was it true that children often sensed whom they could trust and who was real or fake?

Is Emmalyn only difficult around me?

⋯ ➤ ➤ ⋯

Naomi's cheeks and nose were red with the burning cold as she and Marnie approached the bride's parents' home. "Do you think of me as a person who'd openly disobey?" Marnie probed.

"Well, if you're thinkin' thataway, then maybe so. Are you planning to?"

She couldn't tell Naomi her plans, because she wasn't sure of them herself.

"What if Roy asks you to leave the Amish with him—I mean, if *he's* leavin'?"

"He's never confided that." Shaking her head, Marnie felt sick at the thought. "I look at what's happened with the breach 'tween Cousin Katie and her parents and brothers. It's awful sad, ya know. And it's not changin' anytime soon. Dan and Katie aren't comin' back to bow their knee and repent. Prob'ly never," said Marnie.

"It's like I said: They're happy in their new church community. God is their King, not the bishop."

Marnie gasped. "You think like that?"

"Sometimes it seems like that." Naomi said it straight-faced. "I've heard a lot of the other youth are getting fed up, too."

Marnie didn't want to defame their bishop's position. "They'd better be careful what they say. Bishop John was chosen by divine lot—God ordained."

Naomi didn't bow her head in shame, but she nodded slowly. "It's all so hard to understand. But Dan Fisher's teachin' from the New Testament makes sense to me."

"I agree, but it's all woven together like a well-made basket. Don't

403

forget, you can't have one without the other—faith without family. And vice versa."

Naomi hissed, "That's silly, Marnie, and you know it. It's the Lord who's the center of our faith."

Marnie didn't say more. She felt nearly frozen from their long walk and was anxious to get warmed up.

"I'll be prayin' for ya," Naomi said as they went.

Marnie thanked her and hurried around to the back door, surprised to see most of the young couples had disappeared from the bride's house. *Must be in the barn or the stable.*

Her parents, however, were sitting in the front room speaking with Bishop John Beiler. When Marnie spotted him, the man of God looked at her with fiery eyes, and she was helpless not to meet his gaze.

He knows everything!

··· ➤ ◄ ···

Ella Mae was dropping a sugar cube into her coffee cup as Jenny returned to the Beilers' large farmhouse. Emmalyn had gone over to pick up the toys at Ella Mae's.

Mattie motioned Jenny back to the table, where the adults had settled in for coffee and another helping of pumpkin pie. Two of the bishop's children, Levi and Susie, were playing dominoes at the far end of the table.

"Is it getting colder out?" asked Mattie.

"It's pretty nice in the sun," Jenny told them.

"And the little ones are bundled up, so they should be all right," Mattie replied.

Ella Mae scooted over next to Jenny. "Mary has something she'd like to say," she said softly. The frail woman leaned forward to get Mary's attention. "Tell Jenny what ya told me earlier."

"Well, sure." Mary looked like she'd been put on the spot. "Bishop John has been askin' me to talk to you."

Jenny tensed up.

"There's something goin' on . . . well, how should I say this?" Mary paused. "The bishop's aware of one of our former church member's inter-action with—"

"Just come out and say it," Ella Mae interrupted.

Please, no, thought Jenny, clasping her hands beneath the table. Oh, she felt nauseous, recalling that fateful night, following Rebecca in the dark, up the long road. Then, discovering the secret and wishing for all the world she'd never known the forbidden pull between mother and daughter.

"Have you met Naomi Beiler yet?" asked Mary. "She's our niece . . . the bishop's blood kin."

"Jah, once." Jenny's heart pounded. Was this about Naomi or Rebecca? She held her breath.

"Would ya like to befriend her, maybe?" Mary continued, explaining that the bishop was concerned about her and thought Jenny's fervor for the Amish life might benefit his "rather wayward" niece. "We're concerned she's planning to leave the hollow."

Jenny was startled by the request, just as she'd been surprised at being entrusted with the bishop and Mary's little girls so early in her Proving time. "What would you suggest?"

Mary went on, saying she'd thought about perhaps having Naomi over to show Jenny how to do piecework for quilting on one of the days when Jenny was caring for the girls. "How's that?"

"That'd be great—I've always wanted to learn to piece a quilt."

"*Gut* then, I'll let John know. I'm so glad I got the chance to talk with you today. Denki, Jenny. This will mean so much to him—to us both."

"If Jenny can work a miracle, that is," Ella Mae piped up, a half smile on her face.

Jenny offered a smile of her own to Mary, her heartbeat slowing again in relief that Rebecca Lapp wasn't going to be the topic of conversation. But she was very curious about what the bishop thought she as a seeker might do for his niece.

Naomi has grown up Amish, so how can I possibly be of help?

34

JENNY relished her time with Ella Mae's charming family, as well as everyone else present. She learned from Mary that she and the children hadn't been invited to the wedding where the bishop presided. "I imagine there were enough folk there without our brood," Mary chuckled.

All of them divided up in groups and played Dutch Blitz for an hour or more, and she quickly understood why David Beiler called the game habit-forming. Jenny would have stayed longer, but an idea had come to mind that she was eager to pursue. Somewhere in a nearby field, there was a phone shanty, she'd been told—one concealed by a clump of tall bushes. Assuming Jenny could locate it, she would try to get in touch with her family. *If I can keep up my courage.*

She wanted to share a little with them about her exceptional Thanksgiving Day. *Remarkable in every way,* Jenny thought as she again thanked Ella Mae, and David and Mattie, too. She felt like she was actually part of the Amish community here at last.

The lengthy walk back across the field toward the Lapps' was a haze of delight. These people really cared about her. And that dear, sweet Ella Mae—the special meal really had been her doing.

Today would have been perfect, if it weren't for my jumpy conscience. Jenny relived her initial fearful reaction to Mary Beiler's comments. "What will I say if I'm ever confronted about Rebecca?" she whispered into the cold air, breath spiraling up. Her stomach turned, but at least for now, she would continue to honor Rebecca's plea for silence.

Jenny had been home for only a few minutes when she heard a knock at the back door. Looking out, she saw Andrew Lapp with a wrapped package in hand. She opened the door. "Hello, Andrew," she said, hoping she didn't seem overeager to see him.

"I have something for ya," he said, inching the present toward her. He was dressed as if he were going to church.

"Is it my birthday?" She laughed a little, feeling awkward but pleased.

"Just got to thinkin' you might be a little homesick, ya know . . . today." He looked quite serious. "I hoped I'd catch ya before Samuel and Rebecca returned home, maybe." His smile was as addictive—if not more so—as the fast-moving game at the Beilers' earlier.

"I don't know what to say," she replied.

"You don't have to say anything—just accept it." He grinned.

"Denki, Andrew." *How sweet is this?*

"I'd invite you in, but . . ."

He agreed and nodded. "I understand, and I'll be on my way."

"Oh, before you go," she said, "do you happen to know where the nearest phone shanty is located?"

He removed his black felt hat, then glanced back at her, eyes twinkling. "You know what? What if I just took ya over there?"

"Oh, would you mind?"

"*Gaar net*—not at all!"

"Okay, I'll just grab my coat." She set the gift on a small table near the door.

"All right, then." He held her gaze for a second longer than necessary, then stepped back and headed for the waiting horse and buggy.

Closing the door, Jenny donned Rebecca's old coat and outer black bonnet. She tied it quickly beneath her chin and looked curiously at the gift with the card attached. *I'll wait to open it,* she decided before hurrying outside.

Jenny felt each movement of Andrew's trotting mare. *Or is it a gallop?* Certainly the horse was going faster than any she'd encountered before.

Maybe it was just Andrew's way of showing how adept he was at handling his beautiful ebony horse.

"I should've opened your present back there," she blurted out. "I'm really sorry."

Andrew shook his head and smiled at her. *Always smiling.* "No hurry. It'll still be there when you return."

She thought of his sister's strange butter-making shortcut and almost asked Andrew if he'd ever heard of such a thing, then thought better of it.

He turned off Hickory Lane and headed north a little ways before pulling over onto the shoulder. The horse came to a halt close to a thick cluster of bushes that nearly obscured the phone booth. "Here 'tis. And if you plan to make a call out of state, you'll need my code." He explained that he would receive the bill later, and she could pay him back at some point. "Least if it's a long chat." He winked at her.

He suspects what I'm up to!

"Oh, I'll reimburse you, no matter what." Thanks to his flirting, she felt like a schoolgirl.

As she made her way around the bushes, Jenny suddenly wondered if making the call was a good idea after all. Besides, why would she risk spoiling such a wonderful day?

In spite of that, she felt compelled to place the call. She opened the wooden door and slipped into the narrow space, where she picked up the receiver and gave the code, then dialed.

Her heart in her throat, she nearly hung up at the sound of the first ring. One . . . two . . . and three.

Where was everyone? Hadn't they had their usual celebration?

Then, just as she was feeling dejected to be missing out on whatever it was her family was doing, Kiersten answered. "Burns residence."

"Hey, sis . . . it's Jenny."

"Jenny who?" Kiersten laughed.

"Happy Thanksgiving to you, too," she said. "Just wanted to greet you and everyone."

"Cool . . . thanks." Kiersten paused. "The same to you, Jen."

"Did the family get together?"

"Yep, and Cameron's here with his new girl and her baby."

"A child?"

Kiersten sighed. "It's a long story."

"Well, I hope he's happy."

"Yes, and happiness always counts, doesn't it?"

"I mean it," Jenny said.

Kiersten seemed to whisper to someone else. "It's Jen, calling from Amishville."

Feeling strange at this, Jenny said, "Kiersten, is Mom there?"

"She's in the kitchen, but I'll get her. And don't break her heart again, okay?"

"What's that supposed to mean?"

"You should know—you wrote the letter, right?"

"Kiersten . . ."

"Well, I hope you're calling to say you're done with your super-crazy stunt."

Jenny couldn't speak. Was it always going to be like this? It was all she could do to remain meek and mild with her sister. *Like boot camp for the emotions,* she thought.

"You *are* coming home, aren't you?" Kiersten added.

Maybe for a visit someday . . . if I survive this call.

"Jenny? Are you there?"

"Jah . . . er, yes."

"Oh, that's just great—now you're talking Amish, too?"

"Kiersten, just please get Mom, okay?" Talking to her sister was as exhausting as she remembered.

There was a silence broken by muffled talking here and there, and what seemed like an endless wait for her mother. Was Kiersten filling Mom in on everything she'd just said?

At last, Jenny heard her mom's voice. "Hi, sweetheart. Are you all right?"

"Hi, Mom. Yes, I'm fine. It's wonderful to hear you. And happy Thanksgiving!"

"The same to you. How nice of you to call."

"I've been wanting to talk to you. Kiersten said you received my letter."

A long pause. Then, "It was a complete shock. No matter how you look at it, Jenny, I never saw it coming."

You should have . . . all my life. "I didn't mean to hurt you." She thought

409

she might choke up. "I wanted you to know where I am . . . that I'm safe and very happy."

"Just not here, honey." Her mother sighed into the phone. "Pamela and Dorie seemed to think you were . . . well, doing okay."

"I wish you hadn't sent them, but it was good to visit." She forced a laugh. "I think they were sorry they came, though."

"Oh no . . . no. They never said that."

They reported back?!

"Jenny, darling, when are you coming home?"

"I don't plan to, Mom." Hadn't she made this clear in the letter? "Not if I'm accepted as an Amish convert."

"What are you thinking, dear?" Her mother sighed. "You're not Amish."

"Not yet, no." Jenny's patience was being put to the test. "I'm sorry this is upsetting to you, Mom."

"More than you know, honey."

"Is Dad upset, too?" She had to ask.

"Oh, you know your father. It takes a lot to trouble him."

"Well, tell him I called, okay?"

"Sure, dear. And please keep in touch."

Jenny nodded, tears threatening as she squeaked her response.

"Call anytime," her mother said. Then, before Jenny could fully find her voice, "Good-bye."

What a disaster. Gently she put the receiver back, buried her head in her hands, and sobbed, glad for the privacy of the closed door. For all the years Jenny had tried so hard to be known and accepted, she wept.

35

JENNY wished she'd had the sense to carry a hankie under her sleeve, like Rebecca. She had no other option but to lift her apron hem and wipe her eyes and face on the back, then dab at her nose. "I'm a mess," she muttered. She'd indulged her pity party for too long.

Once she felt more composed, she pushed the phone shanty door open and was startled but pleased to see Andrew a few yards away, looking concerned. "Guess my call took longer than planned," she said with a weak smile.

"Jenny?" He tilted his head, eyes searching hers. "Are you all right?"

She couldn't tell him without more tears, so she shook her head and moved out of the phone booth. She fell in step with him out to the road, where he accompanied her to the opposite side of the buggy and helped her up, holding her hand. "Denki," she said when she was in and straightening her black apron.

Andrew hurried around the front to hop in on the driver's side. "How 'bout a short ride—see the area?" He seemed to read her and know that she needed some tender care.

"Sure, but I don't want to take up your time."

"No problem. I took off work for Adam and Susannah's wedding—same one Samuel and Rebecca attended." He looked at her then, a concerned expression on his face. "I'd really like to make ya smile today, Jenny . . . somehow or other."

She felt her cheeks redden. "That's very nice of you."

411

"I'm not just sayin' that," he added.

Jenny felt the familiar thrill of being pursued—and wasn't Andrew doing just that? She was comforted by their small talk as they toured Hickory Hollow. Oddly, all of this seemed more real to her than the frustrating phone call home. And far more pleasant.

"Adam Miller, the groom, is a cousin to Tessie, a relative of mine. Tessie was also at the wedding with her four older sisters and all their husbands, and she was askin' about you, Jenny. Awful curious, I daresay." He shrugged sheepishly before adding, "Anyhow, Tessie's wonderin' if there's anything she can do to help you get better adjusted here. She'd really like to."

"That's so thoughtful—please tell her I appreciate it."

"Why don't *you* tell her? She'll be at the quiltin' bee over at Mary Beiler's next week."

"Perfect, then, I will." Jenny was dying to ask why his own sister wasn't as considerate. "I had dinner today with the bishop's wife and children at David and Mattie Beiler's house. Ella Mae was there . . . Emmalyn, too."

He nodded as if he'd known.

"It was Ella Mae's idea to cook a Thanksgiving Day feast for me," she explained.

"Not surprising."

Jenny agreed and folded her hands. "Everyone likes the Wise Woman."

"Well, and you can see why."

She really wanted to talk further about Emmalyn, but since he didn't go there, she dropped the idea.

They rode all the way up past the Hickory Hollow schoolhouse on the right side of the road before getting to Route 340. "I want to show you the school where I attended as a boy," Andrew said, slowing the horse to a stop. "Several of my girl cousins were in the grades below me, but they were more like sisters. And growin' up around so many girls and other young women in the church district, I had plenty of opportunity to get to know them. But none of the suitable girls appealed to me . . . for a bride." He was quiet for a moment, his head forward, eyes on the road. "I've been accused more than once of bein' too picky."

She wondered where he was going with this, and there was a long moment as he seemed to measure her, as though judging whether he should continue in a similar vein. "Do you mind if I'm frank with you, Jenny? I mean, I don't want to offend you . . . or give you the wrong idea."

"Honesty's good," she managed to say, suddenly feeling a bit tense.

Andrew coughed nervously. "I respect your courage . . . actually everything about you." He turned to face her. "I admire how you stick to your chores and practices that have to be foreign to you, doin' so with kindness—and even *gut* humor. But most of all, with a gracious spirit. Truth be told, you're the kind of girl I've been lookin' for." He stopped for a moment, frowning a bit. "But you prob'ly won't be here a year from now, will ya?"

She was completely taken aback and had to scramble to gather her wits. "Only if I don't learn to bake a better loaf of bread." She tried to laugh but it came out as a sigh. How had they arrived at such a serious discussion? "You know, all the other girls around here can cook and can and bake and think like an Amishwoman. They have me beat hands down."

"But they don't have your sweet personality, or your determination— least not the girls I know." His expression was solemn. "So many of our young folk are mighty curious about the modern world, tryin' to get out of the church. And here you are, trying to get in."

"Maybe they've taken their Plain heritage for granted." She looked at the barns and the dairy cattle, envying anyone who'd grown up here. "I have so much catching up to do, beginning with the language."

"But that's comin' along much better."

"Well, slowly."

"And you're learnin' to hitch up, ain't so?" he said kindly. "For that matter, I've been thinkin' we could have ya try hitching up a pony to a pony cart, to make things easier. What do ya say?"

We . . .

"Whatever works best for someone who's all thumbs with a harness," she replied, pondering this. "Any ideas on bread making, as well?"

He chuckled. "Whoever said a girl has to be an expert in the kitchen?"

"*Amish* girls, of course!" Now she was laughing with him.

Andrew looked down at her folded hands and then back at the road. "None of the things you mentioned are as important as a person's heart," he said, pausing. "I'd like to get to know ya better, Jenny . . . if that's all right."

The day of her baptism had never seemed so distant. *"You're not one of us,"* Emmalyn had pointed out that day at market. "As a friend?" she asked softly.

"Of course."

"Will it be a problem for you, spending time with a seeker like me?"

"If young couples see each other secretly, why can't we?" He smiled at her, so striking in his black felt hat and black coat. "We could meet at the springhouse once a week . . . to pray, then to talk or walk, depending on the weather."

She thought again of Emmalyn. "I probably shouldn't say this. . . ." Her voice trailed off.

"Say whatever you like, Jenny."

Her heart warmed to this thoughtful man. "Your younger sister seems leery of me."

He nodded, his expression reflective. "S'pose she is, jah."

Jenny held her breath. Had she spoken out of turn?

"I take it Emmalyn hasn't told ya why."

Jenny shook her head. "We *did* chat this afternoon while watching Ella Mae's great-grandchildren playing outside." *And she was nicer today. . . .*

"I may tell you 'bout all that someday," Andrew said quietly. "When you and I know each other better."

Jenny acquiesced but remained very curious.

When Jenny saw that Samuel and Rebecca were already home, she suggested Andrew let her out on the road. She thanked him for the ride and for the gift, promising to go in and open it right away.

"Will ya meet me next Thursday evening at the springhouse pond, then?"

She smiled. "I'll look forward to it."

"Till then," he said, getting out of the carriage to help her down. His smile touched her heart, and he released her quickly before she hurried through the front yard and around to the back of the house.

Her heart fell when she stepped inside and noticed the present was missing. Had Rebecca found it? Oh, Jenny wished she'd taken it directly to her room. What was she thinking, leaving it out?

Going into the utility room, she removed her outer clothes and hung them on the specified wooden pegs. Then she looked to see if Rebecca was anywhere in the kitchen, which thankfully remained empty. Tiptoeing in, she spotted Andrew's gift on the kitchen table, the card still tucked under the ribbon, with only her name printed on the front. *Whew,* she thought, taking it upstairs to her room and closing the door.

What will I tell Rebecca if she asks?

An impious thought crossed her mind. After all, she was keeping Rebecca's secret, so wasn't it fair to expect her to do the same?

Jenny unwrapped Andrew's gift and was tickled to see a hardcover devotional book, *Streams in the Desert.* She opened to the front page. Andrew had written an inscription: *To Jenny Burns. May God grant you the peace your heart craves here in Hickory Hollow—for always. Sincerely, Andrew Lapp.*

"For always," she whispered, realizing it was his way of saying that he hoped she would still be here in a year, if not forever.

"How considerate," she murmured as she paged through the devotional book. It surprised her that he seemed so in tune with her spiritual yearnings. He, too, enjoyed communing in prayer with God.

Andrew's card was next, and she purposely hesitated to open it. Didn't she already care too much for him?

She held the envelope and stared at her name in his strong, flowing handwriting. What could he possibly have written inside?

36

"YOU simply cannot do it!" Marnie's friend Tessie Miller said, shaking her head as they walked home late that night from the barn Singing after Susannah's wedding. "You'll be sorry—I just know it."

Marnie refused to cry, afraid her tears would freeze on her cold cheeks. "But I love him. I'd follow Roy anywhere."

"To Bird-in-Hand, then? To his progressive church?" Tessie bit her lip. "You'll be the next Katie Lapp."

"Naomi Beiler and I might share a room over at Fishers', till we're able to get out on our own."

Tessie wrinkled her pretty little nose. "You mean till you're married. But why not just stay home till then? It'd spare your family the heartache."

"Oh, Tessie . . . I'm in a fog. No matter what, I'm cooked." Marnie wrapped her scarf closer to her mouth and tried not to breathe in the frigid air. A half moon glistened in the heavens. "Since the preacher knows—and the bishop, too—soon everyone will. I don't think I could bear bein' looked down on."

"Just be thankful you can't be shunned." Tessie shivered noticeably.

"Small comfort."

Tessie went on, urging Marnie not to move in with Katie and Dan, insisting it would be a blight on her. "It'll look like you're in favor of their leavin' the People."

"Maybe so."

"Just bide your time. Please don't go an' live at Fishers'."

Marnie hugged herself, glad for a warm coat and scarf. She looked at the clear sky. "Isn't it peculiar, really, how someone like Jenny Burns can come in and be so devoted after only a month's time?"

"Does it make ya feel guilty?"

"Something awful." Marnie pondered that. Oh, the irony of it all, when she'd played such a big part in Jenny's life-altering choice. "Makes me wonder what's wrong with me."

"Well, it's not like you're going fancy. You'll still be Amish."

"Daed won't think much of the difference. He'll say I'm scarcely Amish, wanting to attend Bible studies with my beau and all."

Tessie nodded. "And I still say you'll be honoring the Old Ways, no matter."

"If only my father could look at it the way you do." *The way I do . . .*

"Besides, wouldn't he want you to marry for love?" Tessie asked.

"I'd hope so." Marnie wished the night weren't so cold and the walk home so far. And she wished, too, that she might see her sweet beau again. But how?

Maybe Ella Mae will have some ideas, she thought, determined to visit the Old Wise Woman, and soon.

··· ⋟ ⋞ ···

It was late when Jenny reread the card wishing her A *happy English Thanksgiving.* Andrew had also printed the reference to a Scripture verse at the bottom, below his name. She didn't even have to look it up, because it was one she had memorized a few years ago.

"Psalm 84:11," she murmured. "'The Lord will give grace and glory: no good thing will he withhold from them that walk uprightly.'"

She bowed her head and thanked God for bringing so many new and wonderful Plain friends into her life. *Especially Marnie and Andrew,* she added with a smile.

Then she sat down on her bed and wrote a short note of thanks to Andrew, determined to mail it in the morning.

··· ⋟ ⋞ ···

The atmosphere in the house was so tense by Saturday that Marnie hurried through her chores, not saying much to Mamm. As soon as she

417

was finished dusting and dry mopping, she went to her room and locked the door, longing for solitude . . . and to be held in Roy's arms.

She pulled out a page of stationery and began to share her thoughts with him.

Dear Roy,

I hope you are doing well. How I miss you!

You must know that I love you dearly, and nothing has changed, except our present circumstances. I've been found out—Preacher Yoder saw me at last week's Bible study. Honestly, though, I can scarcely handle the pressure here at home—the disapproving glances, the harsh words from Daed. Mamm struggles not to say much, yet I see the pain in her eyes. My parents are sorely disappointed, and that's the hardest of all.

The Fishers' meetings are off-limits for the time being, so I cannot go with you, at least not as long as I'm living here.

Ironically, Katie has invited me, along with another girl, to stay with her family until you and I wed next year. Can you believe this? It would be against my parents' wishes, and I don't know what to do. My heart belongs to God, and soon to you, my dear Roy. What do you suggest?

When you write back, please send your letter to Ella Mae Zook, who will get it to me. She'll soon know about this plan . . . and I appreciate your understanding and prayers.

> *With all my love,*
> *your girl, Marnie Lapp*

⸱⸱ ➤ ⬅ ⸱⸱

The Wednesday after Thanksgiving was blustery with snow and arctic wind. Jenny headed across the field to baby-sit for the bishop's youngest girls. She'd taken Rebecca's advice and worn an extra layer of long underwear beneath her dress. *"Lots of the womenfolk do, at least this time of year,"* Rebecca had said, indicating that some of the younger women even wore leggings under their skirts if they worked out in the barn.

She leaned into the bone-chilling wind, fondly recalling Andrew's gift, which she'd been reading daily. She found it most interesting that Rebecca had not mentioned the gift or card, though she assumed both

Rebecca and her husband must have surmised who had dropped by in their absence. *Who else?*

When Jenny arrived at the bishop's, she removed her boots and coat and put them neatly away in the utility room. The farmhouse was becoming familiar to her, and she cherished her time there with the girls.

Emily raised her arms to be picked up, saying, "*Aendi*," and patting Jenny's cold cheek as Mary came smiling into the kitchen.

Jenny twirled Emily around and set her down to play on the floor with some blocks. At the playpen, Jenny leaned down to tousle Anna's silky hair, cooing at her in Deitsch, "*Mei lieblich Boppli*—my adorable baby."

"You're getting more confident with our language, I see," Mary said.

"It's about time, jah?" Jenny laughed softly, and Emily looked up at her, chattering in Deitsch, asking what their snack would be.

"Chocolate *Millich*," Jenny replied.

Emily grinned back at her.

"You're makin' *gut* strides forward, Jenny. Wunnerbaar!" Mary reached for her purse. "By the way, Mary Mae is over at my sister's house playin' with her preschool cousins this morning."

"Okay, be sure to tell her I missed her."

Mary nodded. "I surely will. And I won't be gone more than a few hours—Naomi should be here very soon." She kissed each child, then smiled at Jenny. "I hope you'll get along nicely with Naomi."

"I'm looking forward to it," Jenny said, wondering just how far on the fringe the bishop's niece really was.

After a few minutes, Naomi Beiler arrived at the back door, carrying a big quilted bag. Jenny went out to greet her, playing hostess as Mary and Rebecca always did. "Did you walk over, too?" she asked.

"Jah, but not very far . . . just from up the way." Naomi pointed east. "Feels like a snowstorm comin'."

"I noticed that fresh, crisp smell hanging in the air."

"Jah, we'll get it when it comes," Naomi said, grinning. "Mamma always says that. My father likes to walk through the field in the springtime and pray, 'Lord, give us all the rain we need, and not one more drop.'"

Jenny liked hearing that, another example of the People's profound trust.

When Naomi had hung up her coat and scarf, she came into the kitchen and sat on the opposite side of the table, her back to the window. She talked in Deitsch to Emily, who smiled brightly and jabbered about her block tower.

With the children happily settled, Jenny poured some hot coffee for Naomi and herself. And Naomi shared some pumpkin cookies she'd made before coming, offering them to Emily, too.

"Aunt Mary Beiler urged me to get acquainted with ya," Naomi said with a glance at Emily, who wasn't paying attention and couldn't understand English, anyway. "She hopes you and I might become friends in due time."

Jenny nodded, smiling. "She told me that, too."

"How long have you wanted to be Amish, if ya don't mind me askin'?" Naomi leaned her elbows on the table, her fists under her chin.

"Since I was fairly young."

Naomi wanted to know what triggered it, and Jenny said she thought that at first it had come from an appreciation for the culture and a craving for a simpler life. "Things changed, though, as I grew older. I became disillusioned with modern society . . . felt I belonged in a different era." She studied Naomi, who began removing colorful squares of fabric from her bag, placing them on the table. "Can you understand that?" Jenny really wanted to know.

"Makes me all ferhoodled, really." Naomi stared at the ceiling and shook her head. "Honestly, I must be just the opposite of you."

Jenny glanced over at baby Anna, who was babbling softly and playing with her toys. "We're all different," she told Naomi. "I know that much."

"Ain't that the truth?" Naomi slowly began to open up. "I really just hope to learn how to make it out in the fancy world . . . someday. With a little help, though."

"So you're leaving Hickory Hollow?"

"When it's time."

Jenny watched Naomi move the cloth squares around to her liking. "What would make you change your mind? Anything?"

Naomi looked up suddenly, her pale blue eyes meeting Jenny's. "I can't imagine what."

"Well, until you do go, I like the idea of being friends."

Naomi reached for two squares, trading them with two others. "Ain't that I'm ungrateful . . . I hope ya understand." She again raised her eyes to Jenny. "My beau wants to leave, too." She said it softly, almost reverently, like it was a well-guarded secret. "And here you are, Jenny . . . from the outside and wanting to be . . . well, like us."

"Remember, it's human nature to want something other than what we already have, right?"

"I guess that's true. Rarely are we content with what we're given." Naomi smiled. "For example, I'd like to wear pretty necklaces and learn to drive a car." She fixed her gaze on Jenny. "I think everyone's curious to know how you gave up your wheels."

"Oh, it wasn't easy," Jenny admitted. "I sometimes wonder if one reason I have such trouble hitching up is that I subconsciously miss my car. Actually, I've never voiced that to a soul."

"Not to worry. I won't make a peep."

Jenny helped Naomi rearrange the squares an assortment of ways. "It's always seemed to me that Amish folk are the salt of the earth, you know."

"Well, sometimes we're more earth than salt," Naomi replied, laughing. "As you're finding out."

Naomi's remarks echoed in Jenny's mind until well after Mary Beiler returned from her errands.

37

REBECCA got up much earlier than usual the next morning, not knowing where to keep the letter Katie had sent. Well, now there were *two*—both private responses to Rebecca's earlier one saying she'd heard from Rachel Stoltzfus that Dan and Katie were causing a stir with their Bible studies. Katie, bless her heart, had jumped to the conclusion that the bishop must be "under conviction from God," putting such clamps on the youth who were in Rumschpringe and entitled to decide spiritual things for themselves. Katie had even gone so far as to encourage Rebecca *and* Samuel to come to their Tuesday night Bible studies, which were growing so rapidly Daniel had to borrow more folding chairs from their church. *Forget the bishop's demands, Mamma . . . please! Trust the Lord instead,* Katie had written.

Thus things had begun to change between Rebecca and her daughter—she'd felt it clearly the last time she'd gone over there, during the dark phase of the moon. Rebecca had felt so guilty during her walk there, fearful of being caught by someone other than Jenny, she'd nearly returned home, shaken. All Katie had talked about during the visit was the spiritual renewal they, and those who were attending their Bible study, were experiencing.

Presently, Rebecca sat in the front room near the heater stove to reread Katie's most recent letters while the house was ever so still. She'd considered destroying them, but wouldn't she be wiping out the last remnants of their relationship in doing so? *What's it matter whether we're seeing eye to eye?*

It was truly peculiar to think that Katie and Dan were praying just as hard for her and Samuel to "see the light of God's truth" as Rebecca was for them to return to their Amish heritage, "to stay in Jesus."

In the end, she went and hid the letters upstairs in the sewing room, in a drawer where she kept extra pillowcases. Knowing him, Samuel would never look there.

Jenny awakened with the pleasant thought of seeing Andrew Lapp later that evening. How quickly the week had passed, yet she still struggled with concerns about not measuring up to the People's standards, domestic and otherwise. She was beginning to wonder if her own yardstick was perhaps too high, considering she compared her cooking ability to Rebecca Lapp's. She felt it was a good idea for her to meet with her new prayer partner to continue to ask for divine help and patience in her struggle.

As for the secret she carried, Jenny had convinced herself that it was best to turn a blind eye to Rebecca's nighttime comings and goings. In fact, Jenny now closed her shades at dusk to keep from spotting her. She did, however, want to know more about Rebecca's daughter. Shockingly, the shunned young woman had somehow managed to convince Marnie Lapp to move in over there sometime after the New Year. Marnie had told her yesterday afternoon, only hours after Jenny had returned from talking with Naomi about *her* wishes.

Jenny and Marnie had walked down near the springhouse, as Marnie had been anxious not to be overheard. She was experiencing mixed emotions, she'd said, loving her family—and not wanting to hurt or disappoint them—and wanting to do what she believed was God's will. The whole thing put Jenny on edge, and she'd told Marnie so. She didn't want to lose her closest friend. Jenny wondered if Marnie had been influenced to make this decision by Katie and her husband. But Marnie was her own person—Jenny knew that to be true. So, hard as it was to grasp, it must be that Marnie actually *wanted* to live with the shunned couple until she married Roy Flaud.

"I won't be able to visit you there," she'd told Marnie, who promised to

visit Jenny at Samuel and Rebecca's. Yet Jenny wasn't convinced things would ever be the same.

Getting out of bed, she put on her slippers and strolled to the windows to pull up the dark green shades. She looked out, glimpsing the first rays of dawn on the far horizon, and suddenly realized if she positioned herself in the window just so, she could see all the way down to the springhouse. There was a dusting of snow on the pond, and her heart warmed once more at Andrew's surprise invitation. *He's willing to take a chance on me.* She wondered if meeting him had been providential, as Ella Mae liked to say.

Jenny went to the dresser for her brush. When she pulled back her hair, she noticed her bangs had grown enough to pin back more easily. She reached for one of her newly sewn dresses, glad for Rebecca's treadle sewing machine. Funny, but working the ancient contraption was already old hat to her. *Who knew?*

At least she was making some progress, because Jenny's talks with Andrew made her all the more determined to pass her Proving with flying colors.

… ➤ ◄ …

As Andrew had indicated, Jenny was glad to meet several of his female relatives at the quilting circle that morning at Mary Beiler's, including his own mother, Maggie Lapp. Andrew's tall, slender cousin Tessie Miller was present, too, her pretty reddish-blond hair parted down the middle and pulled back on both sides like Jenny's. Tessie smiled gaily when she spotted Jenny and hurried over to talk with her.

Jenny was quick to say how grateful she was for Tessie's offer to help her get her bearings in the community.

"Cousin Andrew must've told ya, then?" Tessie asked, her delicate blue-green eyes questioning.

Jenny wondered if it was okay to confide that Andrew had spoken with her. Glancing about, she nodded and noticed the other women still appeared very curious.

Tessie stepped near. "I think he's got his eye on ya, Jenny. I guessed as much your very first Sunday." Her eyes sparkled with fun. "I saw you two talkin' out on the porch—remember?"

Jenny certainly did but wasn't about to say so.

When it was time to sit at the quilting frame, Tessie and Marnie decided to "share Jenny," as they said, with one sitting on either side of her. They guided her patiently as they demonstrated how to use the small needle.

As they worked, Jenny still sensed the gaze of the other women, especially Rebecca and her quilting partner, Maggie Lapp, Andrew's attractive mother, who kept one eye on the quilt—and the other on the seeker in their midst.

··· ➤ ➤ ···

The evening air was icy, but without snow, and Jenny easily made her way down the lane to the springhouse steps. It crossed her mind that Andrew might not remember their prayer appointment. Even if he didn't show up, she would pray alone. Whether she bowed her head and heart in the privacy of her room or outdoors, this quiet time was the highlight of her day.

Christmas was coming soon, and she wanted God's direction on how to connect with her family back home. This had been on her mind for days now because, for the most part, gifts weren't typically exchanged among Amish adults, and she wanted to respect that. On the other hand, she doubted her family would understand not receiving gifts from her, just as they didn't comprehend any other aspect of her choice to be Plain. She wanted to honor them in some special way, as well as demonstrate her love. But how?

"Hullo, Jenny," Andrew called quietly to her from the murkiness.

She followed the steps to the entrance of the springhouse, where he stood with his flashlight shining on the ground. "You're early," Jenny remarked.

He nodded and motioned her inside. "I've just been here a few minutes."

She hesitated about going into the small space with him; it seemed nearly too intimate. "We could pray outside, too."

"Jah, but you'll be warmer in there."

Not wanting to dispute him, Jenny stepped inside, where he offered her the only wooden ledge, with just enough room for one. He insisted she sit and be comfortable while he stooped across from her, near the waters of the spring.

"Is this a good idea?" she said, thinking suddenly of Emmalyn. With the flashlight lighting up the space, could their shadows be seen from outside?

425

"All's well." He hunkered down as he folded his hands.

They began to pray, silently at first and then aloud, with Andrew leading in prayer "for wisdom on the part of the restless youth in the church." He prayed a while about that as Jenny offered her silent agreement.

Later, Jenny gave praise for God's many blessings, large and small, and then asked for help in knowing how to respectfully approach her family over the Christmas holidays.

Their prayer time was short and to the point, and even though she'd felt a bit uncomfortable about letting Andrew hear her prayers, Jenny soon realized she no longer clenched her folded hands. Praying with Andrew was quite exciting, and very sweet, too, although she did still feel somewhat anxious about being alone with him, not wanting anyone to mistake their intentions.

"I received your thank-you note," Andrew said as he reached for the flashlight and rose to open the door. "You didn't have to do that, ya know."

"And neither did you," she said, referring to his gift. "I've been reading the devotional book morning and night and really enjoying it."

He smiled, looking even more handsome tonight. "It's a timeless classic. My older brothers and their wives use the same one each morning."

"I can see why." She loved talking with him but thought they should be going.

"I'll see you here next week, if you'd like," he said.

"If it's milder weather, we should pray outdoors, jah?" She knew he'd understand.

He agreed, smiling. "Do ya mind if I write to you between our prayer visits?"

Just the way he said it made her heart smile. "Okay."

"I won't put my name or return address on the envelope . . . for obvious reasons."

"*Gut* idea," she said. "And before I forget, how much was the long-distance phone call?"

"I haven't gotten the bill yet, but let's just forget about it."

"Um . . . we had a deal." She didn't want to renege.

"I'll let you know when it comes."

"Denki, Andrew. Gut Nacht." She headed out the door as he held it open. Without looking back, she hurried toward the stairs as she heard him go in the opposite direction.

As she walked toward the house, she decided that their prayer rendezvous would probably seem peculiar to anyone but the two of them. And she wouldn't enter Rebecca's kitchen before removing the pleased smile from her face. From her current vantage point, she could see Samuel and Rebecca presently having their own devotional time.

Jenny slipped into the stable to see the driving horses again, as she had been doing at Andrew's suggestion. She realized once more how fond Andrew was of her, even though the pretext for their relationship was friendship. *That, and prayer partners.*

38

MARNIE knew just the person to confide in on Friday afternoon. It was either that or burst. Besides, she was dying to know if Roy had sent a reply, and today was the first chance she'd had to ask.

"I can't think of not bein' with my beau," she told the Wise Woman, trying to contain her emotions at the pretty tea table with yellow rose paper napkins and matching placemats.

"'Course ya can't, Marnie. Your heart's all bound up in him, ain't so?"

Marnie wiped a tear from her cheek. "Did ya feel that way, too, when you first met your husband?"

"Oh jah . . . ages ago." Ella Mae leaned nearer. "And ya want to know a little secret?"

Marnie quickly nodded her head.

"Every single one of us feels that way in the blush of first love. I did, so did your Mamma and Dat—same with your grandparents, too. It's the way the Good Lord made us."

Marnie thought on that. "So what happens when we're told we can't be with the young man we love . . . what then?"

"Are ya grown-up enough to make your own decision about love? Are ya trustin' God for that important choice?" Ella Mae stirred the peppermint tea in her delicate cup. "Are ya, dearie?"

"I have no doubt Roy's the one for me," Marnie said, meaning it.

Ella Mae shrugged her slight shoulders. "That's your answer, then. Ya know what you must do."

She bowed her head. "Why's it such a struggle?"

"Believe in God's Word and live your life accordingly . . . however the Lord leads."

"Even if that means disregarding my father's wishes?"

"Well, it ain't like your father was the most obedient young man there ever was."

"What are ya sayin'?"

"Your father went up against his own Dat—your Dawdi Lapp—back when he was a young fella."

Marnie had never heard this.

"I'll just say there was quite the *Uffruhr*—uproar—in the woodshed, and for days at a time, too." Ella Mae blinked her eyes and squinted into the window's light, a mask of memories on her wrinkled face.

"Now ya've got me wonderin'."

"Had plenty to do with your father courtin' a girl he loved."

"My Mamm?"

Ella Mae nodded. "Your Dat won out, too . . . which was a mighty *gut* thing, jah?"

Marnie sniffed and agreed.

"I daresay you've got some of his fine stubbornness in ya, dearie."

For some reason, hearing this made Marnie feel better. "Denki, Ella Mae. I think I needed to come see ya today."

"Believe ya did, too, Marnie."

Ella Mae rose and brought the teapot over. "I've been wondering 'bout your friend Jenny Burns. How's she doin'?"

Marnie tittered. "Honestly? I think better than most of us."

"Why's that?"

"She just seems so settled, despite what she calls 'some botched attempts' to do what comes naturally to the womenfolk."

"And learnin' to speak our language?"

"Inches forward at a time, she likes to say."

"How's her sock darning comin' along?"

"Well, she hasn't sewn any shut this week, she said. I'm only tellin' ya because you asked . . . not to make fun." Marnie explained that she felt sure Jenny would keep trying. "She wants to meet Aunt Rebecca's standards for everything."

"Well, that'd be hard for any of us, jah?" Ella Mae was grinning.

"Ach, for sure. But I've never heard her say anything 'bout giving up or turnin' tail and running home."

"If ya don't give up, you haven't lost. Tell her that, won't ya?"

Marnie smiled. "I've always liked that proverb." She sipped some more tea.

"I'd hate to see her get discouraged," Ella Mae added.

Marnie nodded, feeling exactly the same.

"Someone whispered she's got herself a fella already," Ella Mae said, surprising her.

"Ach, I really doubt it—she's not a church member."

Ella Mae smiled thinly. "Best not be sayin' more, then."

"But you must!" Marnie said, knowing she could trust Ella Mae. "What do you know . . . and who told ya?"

"My lips are sealed. See?" Ella Mae pressed her lips tightly together and blinked her little eyes.

Marnie groaned.

"Jenny'll tell ya when she's ready, jah?"

Marnie knew better than to ask again. But then, thinking back to seeing Jenny with Cousin Andrew the night Posey had gone missing, she had a glimmer of an idea. Could it be Cousin Andrew might open his heart, even a crack, to let in someone like Jenny?

Later, when they'd had some delicious finger cakes, Ella Mae gave her Roy's letter, addressed as Marnie had suggested. "I wouldn't tell just anyone this, but by the looks of his handwriting, this is one determined young man." Ella Mae chuckled. "I believe your little ones will be mighty strong willed, too . . . a *gut* thing, mind you, when they're molded and shaped for the Lord."

"Do ya think it's a problem he's not as conservative as we are?"

"Pity's sake, Marnie, there're many kinds of Amish." Ella Mae waved a wrinkled hand in the air. "Those of us who love Jehovah God worship Him alone, ain't so?"

Marnie pondered that as she walked toward home, realizing what the Wise Woman meant. And, unable to wait a minute longer, she tore Roy's letter open and savored each word, tears threatening as she learned that he was in favor of her moving in with Dan and Katie Fisher. And not once did he refer to the Fishers' Bann.

430

··· ➤ ◄ ···

That afternoon Jenny did her best to darn another sock, practicing her very lacking skill. She sat with Rebecca in the cheery sewing room, soaking in the warmth from the windows like a cat in a sunbeam.

But the more she tried, the worse things got, and her pinpricked fingers hurt. *I'm fooling myself if I think I'm leaving this sock in better shape than I found it!* Still, she was determined. "Do you know of an Amishwoman who can't darn socks?" she asked Rebecca with a deliberate shake of her head.

"Well, to be honest, no."

Rebecca reached across the table. "Here, let me have a look-see." She examined the sock this way and that, even lowering her reading glasses to better scrutinize.

The elongated inspection frustrated Jenny further, and she got up and stood near the window. "This is ridiculous," she muttered. "How long have I been here, and I still can't do this chore?"

"Well, you do very nicely with other sewing, and your embroidery's coming along, too." Rebecca put her glasses back on. "Mustn't forget that."

"But I can't embroider my way through life here."

"Well, you must keep at it." Rebecca slid the sock and needle across the table. "Mustn't be too hard on yourself, Jenny. Remember, you haven't been doin' this for very long yet."

"Some days it seems like it's been forever."

Rebecca's head bobbed up. "Ach, Jenny . . . you're discouraged. That's all."

The last thing she wanted to do was return to her chair and keep darning.

"Try 'n' relax, all right?"

Reluctantly, Jenny returned to the table and sat down, leaving the sock where it was. She leaned back and sighed.

"Just give yourself more time, won't ya?" Rebecca removed her glasses and wiped her eyes. "I daresay you're doin' your best—trust the Lord God." She stopped for a moment, turning to look out the window. "Don't forget the Old Ways are worth learnin', Jenny. I can't impress that on you enough." She nodded her head. "Worth their weight in gold."

Somewhat encouraged, Jenny reached for the sock and picked up her needle, wanting to keep trying . . . and at more than just this task. And as she began again, she asked Rebecca what she might do to support herself.

"Ya mean, if you stay single?"

Jenny nodded.

"Well, you could embroider some." Rebecca smiled, glancing over at her. "And ya haven't cracked any eggs yet, now, have ya?"

"Maybe I could raise chickens."

"Or get some tips from one neighbor up the road—she made out perty well runnin' a greenhouse. Of course, she rented out her land to an Amish farmer, too."

I have no land, Jenny thought, glad she had saved more than a year's worth of income. She hadn't known, however, that she'd be so reliant on it. She'd definitely need to make a living of some kind here in Hickory Hollow.

Rebecca had gone over to see Ella Mae late in the afternoon, leaving Jenny to make supper. But Jenny became distracted with mashing potatoes, forgetting to keep an eye on the creamed chipped beef. By the time she smelled the burning, it was too late. Stopping what she was doing, she turned off the gas and removed the ruined main dish. She carried the smoldering mess to the trash, hoping to get the burn out of the pan before Rebecca returned. If only the scorched smell in the house would dissipate before Samuel came in for the meal.

I'm losing ground, she thought, aggravated with herself. *I'm getting worse instead of better!*

That evening, after a supper of mashed potatoes and reheated stew, Jenny allowed her mind to wander during Bible reading and silent prayers. She needed to write in her journal—she might feel better if she dumped her annoying thoughts . . . got the negativity off her chest.

> *Hard as I try, I'm still a failure compared to the other women here. Even the bishop's school-age daughters can cook better than I can!*
>
> *Marnie came by this afternoon, and when I told her about my woes with bread baking, she was very kind, as always, and suggested that I might be trying too hard. But how is that possible?*

Marnie was happier than last time I saw her. I think she has a new lease on life, because her fiancé has given his blessing on her move to Katie and Dan Fisher's, whenever she's ready. I can't wrap my brain around this. Roy must be drifting away from the Amish himself, to encourage this. It's inconceivable to think my first Amish friend might soon be fancy!

The Amish teens who do seem more settled closely follow in their parents' footsteps. Marnie and Naomi seem more interested in exerting their own wills, though. Most adults disapprove, including Rebecca . . . and the bishop and Mary. If Samuel Lapp opened up and spoke his mind, I'm sure he'd be opposed, too. It's odd how he reminds me of my own father in that way.

I sometimes wonder if this business with Marnie, especially, has affected me on some level.

There is much for me to contemplate while Rebecca keeps me busy. To top things off, we're hosting the Preaching service here on December 16, and there is a long list of chores to accomplish. All the walls must be washed down, the windows cleaned, and Rebecca said at supper tonight that some of the upstairs rooms will need a fresh coat of paint, as well. She announced this while the residual odor of my burned chipped beef was still strong in our noses. My mother and sister would think this is an omen, and maybe it is—at the very least it's a sign that I need to work harder at reaching my goal.

Sigh . . . why is it so hard to be Amish?

39

JENNY didn't know why she was startled when she got the Saturday mail, especially when Andrew Lapp had said he would write. It was a remarkable experience to read Andrew's journal-like letter, a chronicling of his daily welding work and his various English and Amish customers. And she anticipated her next visit to the springhouse with her unexpected prayer partner even while she spent time with Naomi at her parents' house, once Jenny's chores were finished.

She considered Andrew's letter, newsy and interesting. Only slightly romantic. *As it should be*, she told herself as she leaned over the sink to dig out black spots in a large potato. A committed church member like Andrew would follow the ordinance to a tee.

She found herself feeling very happy he'd written, choosing to take time for her. And couldn't help being a little hopeful that courtship might follow someday.

··· ➤ ◄ ···

Jenny experienced a week of fewer bread-baking fiascos, thankful Rebecca was encouraging and even seemed to be warming to her again. Had Rebecca stopped visiting Katie, perhaps?

This early December morning was exceptionally sunny and not as chilly as previous days. The sun played across the snowy fields, casting regular shadows along the horse fence and nearby trees.

Jenny was struck with an idea as she stood on the back steps and waved to Rebecca, who left in the family carriage to visit her daughter-in-law Annie, Daniel Fisher's sister. Samuel, for his part, was hitching up the spring wagon to go help his youngest son, Benjamin, haul a large quantity of feed bags from the nearby mill.

As Jenny observed the experienced Amishman, she wondered if she dared attempt what she was thinking. Nevertheless, why *not* practice what she'd repeatedly been taught?

She waited until Samuel pulled out of the driveway to dress warmly, yanking on boots and a heavy coat and scarf. Then she hurried to the stable and chose her favorite black pony, Josie, and curried her, just as Samuel always did before taking a horse or pony out on the road. She led the pretty young mare down the driveway and tied her to the hitching post before heading back for the cart stored in the upper level of the double-decker barn.

When she was ready, Jenny followed the same instructions she'd been given for hitching a road horse to the family carriage, thinking this should be a good test of her ability. And without anyone prompting her, either!

The process took longer than she'd hoped, but Jenny refused to give up as she hooked up the pony to the cart. *I can do this,* she told herself, giving Josie a sugar cube for being so patient.

At long last, when Jenny was ready to take a spin, she double-checked every aspect of the process one more time. Then, smiling at her accomplishment, she untied Josie and brought the driving lines back, climbed into the pony cart—and off she went.

Annie was busy in her sun-drenched kitchen making egg noodles when Rebecca arrived through the creaky back door. Her dark chestnut brown hair peeked out from beneath her Kapp. "Hullo, Annie dear!"

"Come on in," Annie called, her cheeks white with soft dustings of flour. "Well, and it looks like you already are." She gave a mellow laugh and opened her slender arms to Rebecca, offering a hug. "You're just in time to help me, if you'd like."

"Sure, anytime," said Rebecca, removing her winter layers. "That's why I'm here . . . and for the company, too."

Cheerful and lovely as always, Annie nodded demurely as she waved Rebecca inside. "Awful nice seein' ya, Mamm."

"You too."

They exchanged comments about the bright, sunny day, and how young Daniel was off to school, enjoying first grade. Rebecca wondered but would never inquire why he was still their only child. *Thus far.*

She and Annie worked to roll out the stiff, smooth dough onto an old tablecloth. As each layer of rolled dough was complete, they let the noodles continue to dry, turning them over and later cutting them with a sharp butcher knife to make fine strips. Afterward, Rebecca shook the noodles apart so they did not stick together.

Rebecca had always liked Annie—like a daughter in many ways, and ever so pleasant. *No wonder my son was head over heels for her when they started courting,* she remembered, smiling even now. Annie was the kind of girl who was just plain good-natured.

"Mamma's aunt Miriam isn't too well these days," Annie confided. "Mamma says she came to visit her the other day, and Miriam couldn't remember if she was comin' to see her or leavin', the poor thing."

"Ach, that is sad. Painful to see, ain't?"

Annie nodded. "Hard to understand why some elderly folk are clear-minded right up to the end, and others, well . . ." Her voice trailed away. "But the dear Lord knows."

Rebecca agreed, struck again by how tenderhearted Annie was and always had been.

They talked of the quilting bee at Mary Beiler's house for a while. Then, during a lull in the conversation, Rebecca asked, "Have ya heard 'bout your brother's Bible study groups?"

Annie said she had. "Elam thinks it's mighty bold of Daniel to invite anyone who wants to come, knowin' plenty of our young folk might wander over there."

"Well, if they ain't baptized yet, what's the worry?" Instantly Rebecca froze. *Did I really just let that fly out of my mouth?*

Annie gave her a startled look but didn't say more on the subject. "Heard Katie's expecting a baby again. Wish we could see her and the children . . . and Dan." She said the latter in a whisper, with a little catch in her voice.

The dear girl.

"We've been prayin' the bishop might ease the Bann on Katie and Dan—even lift it entirely." Annie bowed her head. "Would be such a help to the family, ya know."

Rebecca sighed, not daring to discuss it. She did wonder, however, exactly who'd shared the news of Katie's coming babe with Annie. Could it be Annie's mother knew? Surely that was so. It was hard to imagine the elder Fishers not knowing something so important. Like Annie, surely they, too, were missing the chance to know Dan and Katie's little ones.

Before leaving, Rebecca handed Annie a basketful of peach and pear jams. "Come see us anytime," she said, giving her a quick hug.

"Oh, we will. Denki for stoppin' in, Mamm."

"Why don't yous come for Christmas dinner?" Rebecca said quickly.

"Well, we would, but Mamma's been askin' us to go *there* this year." Annie's eyes were sad. "Ach, sorry. We'd really love to . . . but maybe for Second Christmas instead?"

Rebecca agreed, glad their church district observed the visiting holiday right away after Christmas, on December twenty-sixth. All the Amish shops in Hickory Hollow and surrounding areas would be closed for the occasion. "Jah, it'll be nice to look forward to that." *Ever so nice.*

"I can't promise till I talk to Elam, of course, but I'll let you know. If not Second Christmas, then for sure New Year's."

Rebecca assumed the latter was the soonest they'd make it over, which was fine. Between Annie's parents and grandparents, and all of Elam's and her siblings, she and Elam would have many invitations. Rebecca couldn't help wondering if Dan and Katie had ever invited them over there.

She waved and made her way out the door to the waiting horse and carriage.

Jenny was excited to be riding down Hickory Lane in the pony cart. She did feel a bit strange, though, a grown woman sitting cross-legged like this, the black strings from her outer bonnet fluttering over her shoulder.

Jenny admired the sky, delighting in the day. Across the way, horses silently milled about the pasture, two of them trotting now, long tails flying.

Suddenly—*crack, snap*—and a lurch!

Josie galloped off free, away from the pony cart!

"Oh no," Jenny muttered, disgusted. "How'd that happen?"

There Jenny sat, stranded in the middle of the road and feeling embarrassed and upset. Scrambling out of the cart, she called to the spirited pony only to watch her trot through a hole in the neighbors' horse fence.

And if that wasn't bad enough, she could see Andrew Lapp and his sister Emmalyn coming this way in Andrew's open buggy. He was waving as he slowed the horse, apparently ready to jump down from the carriage and onto the road.

"For pity's sake, Jenny . . . what happened to ya?"

She explained quietly, painfully aware of Emmalyn, who was still perched there in her brother's buggy. *More fuel for ridicule,* Jenny thought miserably.

"Here, let's get the cart off the road some," said Andrew, pulling it over to the shoulder.

Then, before either of them could say more, Emmalyn got down and offered to bring the pony back. "Is that Josie over there?" She pointed beyond the fence.

"Jah." Jenny wondered how she knew. As Emmalyn hurried off to catch the pony, Jenny turned back to Andrew, relieved there wasn't a hint of mockery on his face. "I did everything I've been taught about hitching up," she declared.

"Never mind all that," Andrew said, brushing it away. "I'm just glad we came along when we did."

Jenny mustered a smile. "I am, too."

"And not just to help you, neither." A slow grin crept across his face. "I'm very happy to see you in the daylight again." He chuckled. "I mean that."

She blushed a little as she realized their secret meetings would always be under the covering of night. "It *is* kind of nice, I admit," she said as she shaded her eyes and glanced at the sky.

"You mustn't get down on yourself over this, okay?" He assured her that it could happen to anyone who was still getting used to hitching up, though Jenny knew he was being kind. "With enough practice, you'll be an expert soon enough."

"That's what you think!"

They both had a good laugh, and when he reached for her hand, standing in front of her as if to block his sister's view, Jenny was the one trying not to smile too much.

"I look forward to our prayer time this evening," he said, releasing her hand as he stepped back.

Jenny agreed, watching Emmalyn bound across the snowy meadow with the pony, coming this way. She led Josie around to the break in the fence, then out to the road. With both Andrew and Emmalyn to talk Jenny through it, the three of them had Josie hitched up solidly in no time.

When it was time to part, Jenny and Andrew simultaneously said good-bye in Deitsch, and they laughed again, more softly this time. And as he returned to his horse and buggy, Jenny noticed a hint of a smile on Emmalyn's face. It seemed Andrew's youngest sister was no longer an adversary.

40

REBECCA slipped out to the back porch after evening Bible. She wondered where Jenny had gone. Here lately on Thursday evenings, she'd noticed her missing from the house. Not that she cared one way or the other—she guessed the poor thing needed to get outdoors alone, perhaps to sort out her thoughts. The seeker was spinning her wheels some, and it was clear that she might be questioning her resolve. Was the Amish life really what Jenny wanted? Of course, it didn't help that she'd become disheartened due to Marnie's and Naomi's sudden interest in moving away. *And my own shortcomings, as well, no doubt,* Rebecca thought sadly.

One thing was sure, the half moon was a glimmering splendor tonight, and Rebecca drank in the sight as she admired the stars, taking a deep breath of frosty air out on the back porch.

Later, when she heard Jenny's soft steps coming up from the spring-house, Rebecca slipped back inside.

··· ❥ ❦ ···

For each and every day that week, Rebecca felt like she was doing the same things over and over again. Did Jenny feel it, too? That is, until Katie's letter arrived with an idea she wanted to explore. Her little boy's one and only Christmas wish was to meet his Dawdi Samuel, and Katie wanted Rebecca to think about that.

Talk it over with Dat. After all, he is Sammy's namesake. Please pray about it, too.

We'd like to come for Christmas dinner at your house. I would prepare a meal for you and Dat here, but Dan and I have already gone over that and realize it's out of the question, given the rules of the shunning. Don't ask Dat—just tell him. Okay, I'm smiling at that last line, but please do think about it.

> *With our love,*
> *Katie*

Rebecca shuddered at the very notion of telling Samuel, who didn't even know she'd been corresponding with their daughter, let alone met and held their darling Fisher grandchildren. Knowing her husband was a stickler for the Ordnung, Rebecca couldn't see how he would bend even this far. And if by some marvel he did so, what would the ministerial brethren think of it?

Of course, if she and Samuel could meet all the requirements for having Dan and Katie there for a meal—eat at separate tables and not pass the food directly from their own hands to Katie's and Dan's—perhaps Samuel might just agree. Oh, she hoped so. With all of her heart, she did.

Still, Rebecca was certain that, just because it was permitted in the letter of the law, such a visit—even at Christmas—would not be looked upon favorably by their stern bishop.

··· ➤ ➤ ···

Jenny wasn't sure how it came up at the springhouse pond Thursday evening, but she and Andrew had been talking about the Amish way to celebrate Christmas, and she found herself confiding in him. They sat on the stone wall, watching the moon's likeness glitter on the pond's partially frozen surface. "I've been freaking out lately, Andrew," she told him. "Do you know what that means?"

He chuckled a little. "Only that you need more encouragement, ain't?"

"I feel like I'm on the edge, unable to cut it here." She paused and sighed. "It's everything I want, but—"

"Jenny, listen. Samuel wants to shepherd you a bit—show you how to hitch one of the ponies up to the pony cart. It's like you've passed some sort of test with him, I'm thinkin'."

"Samuel? Are you sure?"

"He wants to help you, Jenny. Hitching up is just the first step in his, well, fatherly role with you."

She'd never had a word alone with the man . . . wasn't sure he could actually conduct a conversation with her. "I'm astonished but really glad to hear it."

"Samuel Lapp's a mighty fine mentor. Do you trust me when I say this?" He reached for her mittened hand. "I know you will be a *gut* Amishwoman someday. And now, clearly Samuel believes it, too."

"Denki," she managed, thrilling at her hand in his.

"And, since you shared with me, I'd like to tell you why Emmalyn is so protective."

He hadn't let go of her hand, and she was intrigued by the urgency in his voice. They certainly were not doing much praying tonight!

Andrew began by saying he'd once fallen in love with a sweet Amish girl, whom he'd courted for some time. She was devout and they'd planned to marry. "In fact, it was just three weeks from our wedding— three weeks to the day—when she told me she'd set her eyes on the world and wanted to leave the hollow." He paused briefly. "And of course, me."

"I'm so sorry." She shook her head. What else could she say?

"That was several years ago."

"So thus your sister's concern over an outsider—*me*—spending time with you."

He nodded, cupping her hand in both of his. Finally he released it, saying it was time they started to pray, but he began by reciting the Lord's Prayer, first in English, followed by his first language.

Andrew lingered much longer than ever before, and after they said good-night, Jenny considered why he was still single: Marnie and Naomi weren't the first young people to grumble over joining church. And knowing how pressed to the wall she'd been recently, unsettled and on the periphery and not fully Amish herself, Jenny was scared. She did not want to break Andrew's heart . . . again.

··· ➤ ◄ ···

During a breakfast of Rebecca's tasty mush made from cornmeal and sausage the next morning, Samuel asked Jenny to go out with him to hitch up the pony cart. *Just as Andrew said*, she thought. *Should've waited to do this with Samuel!*

Jenny was surprised at how patient, even nurturing, Samuel was with both the frisky pony and with Jenny herself.

"You've had quite a time of it here, ain't?" he said, petting Josie's mane. "Farm life is a big adjustment for a city girl." She smiled, pleased he was actually talking with her.

"Well, and not only that." He held the short shafts and backed the pony into them.

Of course, Samuel didn't need to point out her English upbringing, but she knew he meant as much. "I'm looking forward to your hosting church here this Sunday," she said, making small talk.

"'Tis a big responsibility, and one not to be taken lightly. We believe this old farmhouse will become the house of worship for the day. An honor and a blessing, to be sure."

"I understand Rebecca's sisters are coming Saturday to help prepare the food to be served at the meals."

"Including the pies." Samuel grinned and then his face turned solemn. "It is our desire to be at peace with Gott and the church."

Jenny understood by now that the unity of the congregation was highly desired—even necessary—before each Preaching service. "I pray it will be so," she said.

The sky was speckled with cotton-ball clouds, and the wind began to pick up as, with Samuel's assistance, she helped where she could. The weather had turned colder overnight, marching toward deep winter, and it reminded her of the passage of time.

Jenny felt the familiar pang of disappointment as she watched Samuel's hands move expertly through the process. It was as if the Amish world was a complicated tango, moving here and there in perfect rhythm, and she still didn't know the steps.

When they were finished, Samuel suggested she hop in and go up the road a piece. "Chust *fer Schpass*—for fun."

She got in and picked up the lines. "Like this?" she asked, recalling her own short-lived jaunt up the road, thankful the grapevine hadn't spread word of the mishap to the Lapps' ears.

"You'll do fine if ya stay on the *rechts* side of the road."

"I can remember that. Denki," she said and was off.

Although the ride was satisfying and fun, Jenny had a hard time thinking of anything but Andrew's rescuing her the last time she'd done this. To think last night he had shared so personally with her about his heartache. *Especially the reason behind it.*

He'd asked if she trusted him, but she wasn't sure she trusted her own heart anymore.

···➤ ◄···

Marnie strolled to the barn, carrying a weight of worry. She'd spent all morning cleaning house with her mother and mentally rehearsing what she wanted to say to Daed. And she questioned why God had planted this powerful longing to know Him better if it was so frowned upon.

"I wish I had no heart, it aches so." The words from *Little Women*, which she'd just recently reread, resonated in her mind.

She pushed open the barn door and crept inside, but when she asked her older brother where Daed was, Jacob pointed to the milk house. Nodding, she headed across the way and approached the doorway. She could hear her father muttering as he scrubbed down the bulk milk tank.

"Daed?" she said. "Can I talk to ya?"

He raised his head. "What's on your mind?"

She froze.

"Marnie?" He looked at her with searing gray eyes. "Speak up if you're gonna talk."

She'd dreaded this and now she wished she hadn't thought she was so brave. "Maybe you've heard from the grapevine."

"For pity's sake, you're gonna have to talk louder, Marnie!"

She wished he wouldn't talk so, at least to her. "I want to move out," she declared in her strongest voice. "After Christmas, I'll go an' stay with Dan and Katie Fisher . . . just till Roy Flaud and I wed."

"Well, if you're that determined, why wait?"

She gasped, but he couldn't have heard, not with his head halfway into the tank. *So that's his first response?*

"Thought it'd be nice to stay round for Christmas, is all." She felt all in and close to tears. "I don't want to disobey you, but I love Roy. I truly do."

Daed kept on cleaning, not looking up.

"I thought it'd bring less shame on you and Mamm this way."

"Shame on *us*? But not on yourself, Marnie?" Daed rose and straightened to his full height. "Daughter, you are not behavin' at all the way your mother and I raised ya to be." He shook his head and stared her down.

She saw the crow's feet near his eyes, the wrinkle lines around his chapped lips. She remembered Ella Mae's comments about her youthful father, so long ago. Still, it made her sad that she was the reason for Daed's somber face just now.

"You're such *gut* friends with that seeker-girl. Why can't ya be more like Jenny Burns?" he bellowed, his face brighter than a red beet. "That's all I have to say!"

Marnie turned and left the milk house, running as hard as she could through the meadow, aware of the snow-laden earth beneath her feet. She ran till she had no breath left in her before stopping to rest, panting and leaning against the coarse tree bark on Samuel Lapp's property. *I came all that way,* she realized, turning to look back but refusing to think poorly of her father. No, she put herself right into his old work boots and knew, without a doubt, that she would feel the selfsame way if her daughter stood up to her like this.

Poor man, as staunch as he is, he does deserve a daughter like Jenny!

41

AFTER the Preaching service and the shared meal, Jenny and Marnie worked up a sweat with Rebecca and her sisters in the assembly line in the steamy kitchen. Jenny's mind was still reeling, attempting to understand both German sermons that morning, although she'd caught a few more words and phrases than two weeks ago. She was most impressed by the fervency of the People's singing from the *Ausbund* hymnal—it would take some time for her to learn the Gregorian-like chanting of the melancholy songs of the Anabaptist martyrs.

"You're lost in thought," Jenny whispered to her friend.

"I am?"

Jenny smiled. "I think we need to talk . . . alone."

Marnie agreed. "You don't know the half."

Cringing, Jenny passed the newly dried dishes to Rebecca's younger sister, who carefully stacked them in a large box with padding for each plate. Rebecca had explained that this same enormous set of dishes was transported from house to house for weddings, funerals, and the shared meal following church.

Once they were finished cleaning up and the place looked as spotless as it had last night, Jenny invited Marnie upstairs to her room until Chester and Peggy were ready to leave for home. "You look like you might burst," Jenny said when they'd closed the bedroom door. "Are you all right, Marnie?"

Staring down at her folded hands there where she sat on the bed,

Marnie shook her head. "My father chewed me out the other day in the milk house." She quickly told everything to Jenny, who felt sadder with each word. "I should've known better than to spill the beans on myself," Marnie said as she raised shimmering eyes.

Jenny didn't know how to console her but moved to sit next to her, head bowed. "You wanted to tell him where your heart is, jah? Wanted him to understand."

"Right. I wasn't there to ask his blessing. I knew he'd never give that."

"I'm so sorry," Jenny said as Marnie sniffled. "Maybe in time, things will change between you and your father."

"I'm not holdin' my breath."

They talked quietly a while longer. Then Marnie asked, "It's prob'ly none of my business, but do you have a special fella?"

Jenny frowned. "Why do you ask?"

"Well, not sure I should say."

"Why not?" Jenny was astonished.

"It's just that Ella Mae said something 'bout it."

"The Wise Woman?"

Marnie glanced at her, smiling. "There is someone, ain't so?"

Jenny knew she couldn't let things go any further now with Andrew. Not with her situation still so up in the air. If Marnie and Naomi—even Katie—weren't cut out to be Amish, how could she as an Englisher ever hope to belong? She sighed.

Thankfully, at that moment, Jenny heard Rebecca calling through the door. "Marnie's family is ready to leave."

Marnie reached for Jenny's hand. "I'd better get goin'."

"Keep in touch, okay?"

Nodding, Marnie wiped her eyes, promising to do just that. "Christmas is comin' fast now, and I wanted my last days at home to be happy ones." She sighed as she stood and straightened her pretty white apron. "I really did."

"Let's not give up hope for that." Jenny rose and joined her, heading down the stairs and out the back door with her dear friend, a lump in her own throat. She closed her eyes for a second in the glare of the sun.

Marnie gave her a quick hug, whispering in her ear, "I'll see you again soon."

447

"*Zimmlich glei*—very soon." She watched Marnie hurry to the waiting carriage.

The low buzz of a plane made her glance up, and Jenny remembered the fit she'd thrown as a young girl, about to take her first flight. It struck her, even then, as so very wrong to defy nature—hurtling through space in a canister with wings.

Sighing now for Marnie, she turned to go back to the house and spotted Emmalyn on the porch in her black woolen shawl, her head cocked just so. When Jenny approached her, she actually smiled.

"Thanks for bringing Josie back," Jenny said.

Emmalyn shrugged. "'Twas nothin'."

"And for keeping it to yourself, too," Jenny added, smiling back at her.

··· ➤ ◄ ···

After the long day, extended by all the visiting that followed that afternoon, Rebecca was glad to get off her feet and sit by the heater stove with Samuel. They'd had their evening Bible reading and prayer, and Jenny had gone upstairs for the night. It was just the two of them, rocking away their cares and keeping toasty warm.

"'Twas a *gut* Lord's Day." Rebecca looked over at her husband's relaxed profile, the peppery gray flecks evident in his beard.

He nodded in rhythm with his hickory rocking chair. "'Twas inspiring to hear the bishop preach on the young folk heedin' the call of Christ, jah?"

"Seemed like he was pickin' on them from where I sat."

"Aw, now."

"No, seriously, Bishop John's got it in for the youth."

"Well, and for *gut* reason, ya know."

Oh, she knew. "Hate to see Chester Lapp's family go through what we did with Katie."

Samuel shook his head right quick. "But it won't be anywhere near the same, Rebecca, with Marnie yet to be baptized."

She quit talking about it, thinking now might be the time to tell him about Katie's latest letter.

"What if we did something different this year for Christmas?" she heard herself say.

"You mean the boys and their families ain't comin' for dinner?"

"Elam and Annie are goin' to *her* folks'." She paused. "All our sons and their families are welcome, sure . . . but what about our grandson Sammy . . . and his baby sister, Kate?"

Samuel grimaced. "What do ya mean?"

"Dan and Katie's little boy wants nothin' more than to meet you for Christmas this year. He told his mother so."

Samuel pondered that, rubbing his chin and threading his fingers through his beard. "How old would this youngster be now?"

"Four—and with a hankerin' to see his Dawdi for the first time." She held her breath. *What will Samuel say?*

"You said that already." He was either miffed or glib.

"Ain't like we're shunning *him*," she added, then waited. He'd have to say something, one way or the other.

"How do ya know this, Rebecca?" His voice was stern, yet there was also a note of something else. Was it curiosity?

She told him about Katie's letter.

Samuel rocked all the harder and she braced for the whole thing to fall back into her lap. *Katie should've known better than to get her hopes up. Or poor little Sammy's, either.*

Rebecca forced her mind away from what she dearly hoped for, trying her best to set her thoughts on today's main sermon again and how heated Bishop John had been. Not a single head was nodding to sleep during *that* two-hour sermon, for sure, though the small children had gotten fidgety. Rebecca had passed a dish of crackers to all the families with little ones before going later to fetch a tall glass of cold water for the same children. Then she'd carried up a fresh glass of water for Bishop John Beiler, too, who rarely preached except at weddings and funerals. Today, however, he'd had plenty to say.

Samuel coughed a little. "Tell Katie that's all right with me," he said at last. "And not a word 'bout this to anyone, ya hear?"

Rebecca tried not to act surprised. "All right," she replied, her heart hammering happily. "I'll write her back first thing tomorrow."

Or better yet, I'll tell her in person!

42

JENNY stood in the utility room at the bishop's house the following Tuesday morning, hanging up her long coat and scarf. She was uncertain if she ought to enter the kitchen, because Bishop John and Mary were arguing, obviously unaware Jenny was within earshot. She'd come to baby-sit as planned but was mortified to be stuck there eavesdropping.

"How many young people are we goin' to push away, John?" Mary asked, her voice pinched.

"There's a standard to be upheld under God. You know it as well as I do, dear. The tradition of our forefathers is part of our very foundation" was the unyielding reply.

"But think 'bout it this way—these are God-fearing youth. Marnie and Naomi have been raised in the faith, just as you said. All they want is to seek God and to read the Scriptures in order to understand for themselves. Times are a-changin', John. You and I both know it."

"Righteousness must be utmost, Mary. Are ya listenin' to yourself?"

"You surely realize there are more of our young people who are spiritually hungry."

"Jah, I reckoned as much from the preacher's list."

"Well, and there're even more folk interested in studyin' the Bible." Mary no longer sounded desperate but sad. "I can't even see Katie, and she was my very best friend. It's been too many years, John. *Years!*"

"We're not talking 'bout the Bann now."

"Maybe not, but isn't it all wrapped up together?" Mary said, a catch in her voice. "I daresay it is."

There was a long pause; then Mary said more quietly, "If I may be so bold, John, I wonder sometimes if you put the severe shun on Katie Lapp because she stood you up on your wedding day. Ach, but is that possible, love?"

The bishop sighed audibly. "Mary . . . I . . ."

Another pause ensued.

"Have you held a grudge against Katie—and Dan, too—all these years?"

There was no response from the bishop.

"This is all I'll say about this, John. But honestly, it might be time to let go of past hurts, ain't so?" The words were brave, but Mary sounded so meek in the way she spoke to her husband.

The sound of chair legs screeching against the floor made Jenny jump. Apparently the discussion was over. She wondered when she could make her entrance without giving away that she'd overheard them. Or should she simply leave and come back later?

Too late—she heard footsteps coming and realized the bishop was heading for the utility room. *Oh no!* Her moment of escape had passed. Her teeth were clenched, heart pounding . . . and just that quick, she was standing face-to-face with the man of God.

"Well, I forgot you were comin' today," John Beiler said, leaning over to grab his brown work coat. He stood up, a quick smile on his face. "And I'm mighty glad ya did, Jenny."

She stood there awkwardly, waiting for him to continue, wearing what must have looked like a ridiculous kind of smile.

He gave her the most scrutinizing stare as he leisurely buttoned his coat. Then he said something about a "peculiar sighting" last Sunday evening. "I won't say who saw her, but it seems Rebecca was headed somewhere in the direction of Dan and Katie Fisher's place, and in an awful big hurry."

She took a small breath and slowly let it out. *So Rebecca has visited Katie again. . . .*

Jenny remembered following Rebecca through the shadows toward the very doorstep of her shunned daughter's home . . . and Rebecca's heartbreaking plea for silence later that same night. *She's a loving mother . . . how can she be expected to stay away from her only daughter?*

Jenny nearly gasped with the weight of her knowledge. Was this the moment of truth?

John Beiler took a step closer, his words falling with slow deliberation. "If you know something 'bout Rebecca, I'd expect you to tell me." His eyes were so piercing, she stepped back slightly.

Does he know? Jenny swallowed hard, wishing she might keep her secret, to defend poor Rebecca. Yet how could she do so and fulfill the conditions of her Proving?

Lord, please help me. . . .

Unexpectedly, she heard a giggle and Emily appeared in the doorway, her blond hair braided all around her petite head. "Aendi Jenny," she said, lifting her arms up.

Jenny leaned down to pick her up and squeezed her tight. Had Mary sent her? Emily wrapped her arms around Jenny's neck and hugged her back, jabbering in Deitsch.

The bishop locked eyes with Jenny for a second, then headed out the back door toward the barn. *He's testing me.* Jenny was certain.

In order to succeed in her Proving, Jenny must confess what she knew— which would betray her hostess's secret and trust. What a horrid quandary!

She carried Emily into the warm kitchen. Mary's face was crimson as she placed more Cheerios on Anna's high chair tray, but she didn't look at Jenny. "Looks like you're right on time, Jenny." Mary came to give Emily a kiss in Jenny's arms. "This one's been anxiously waitin' for ya."

"We'll have fun together," Jenny said, feeling jittery. She set Emily down at the table near Mary Mae, who was doing a maze from a book of activities.

Mary gathered up her purse and a carryall, still not making eye contact. "'Jenny, Jenny,' is nearly all Emily talks 'bout these days."

Forcing another smile for sweet Emily's sake, Jenny slipped her arm around the little girl, angry at the bishop for putting her on the spot, and upset at Rebecca for asking her to promise.

She worried for her own and dear Rebecca's future. *What will happen to her?*

··· ➤ ➤ ···

"Is something wrong, Rebecca?" her husband asked later that week while they dressed for bed.

"Well, I wonder if I shouldn't have told Eli and Benjamin that Dan and Katie are comin' for Christmas dinner."

"Why's that?" Samuel pulled on his blue corduroy bathrobe, his face anxious. Surely he suspected something.

"They're concerned 'bout it."

"What the bishop'll say if he gets wind, ya mean?"

She nodded and sat on the side of the bed. "Oh, Samuel, this is one sorry situation."

"I'm beginning to think the same thing. I mean, if a man can't grant his own grandson's Christmas wish, what sort of Dawdi is he?"

Rebecca was relieved to hear it.

"Er dutt mir leed!" Samuel said, referring to the bishop.

"I'm sorry for him, too . . . in a peculiar sort of way."

Samuel got into bed and propped himself up with a pillow before leaning his head back. "Kumme, Rebecca, let's have a word of prayer 'bout this. Look to Gott to work things out."

"I don't think it'd be the worst thing that ever happened if Dan and Katie and their babes are the only ones at our table Christmas Day."

"And Jenny, too, don't forget."

"Jah, and Jenny," she said, smiling at Samuel.

"She's almost like family, ya know."

Rebecca couldn't help but agree. "It'd be so nice for her to meet our long-lost girl, ain't?"

Samuel coaxed her next to him, patting the side of the bed. "I was just now thinkin' the same thing." Once she was situated there, rutching around to get her pillows plumped just so, he reached for her hand.

Thank the dear Lord in heaven. Rebecca sighed as her husband began to pray.

43

JENNY slogged through the next few days before Christmas. She had never attended more fun-loving "frolics and doin's" in her life—cookie exchanges and pie-baking bees galore, as well as helping the bishop's youngest children make colorful paper chains to decorate the windows and string across the doorjambs. She lost herself for a full week in a party atmosphere that seemed only more wonderful because it lacked the razzle-dazzle of the modern world. And each night, she wrote about the day's quaint and meaningful activities in her journal.

She also wrote about the bishop's stern remark—and how it was eating her alive.

In lieu of gifts, she sent pretty cards to her family, with long handwritten letters. And two days before Christmas, she received a store-bought card in the mail from Andrew. He'd written at the bottom about a special gift planned for her, wanting to know the best day and time to give it. *Sometime alone with you, Jenny, just the two of us. Maybe we could meet at the springhouse on Second Christmas, instead of waiting till Thursday?*

She hadn't given her answer yet—she felt nervous about it, although she cherished every spare minute he offered, and his letters, too, which came more frequently. *And now this exquisite card. I don't deserve this . . . now especially.*

On the afternoon of Christmas Eve, she helped Rebecca kill the fatted goose. Together they worked to pluck the feathers and clean it "right *gut*," as Rebecca liked to say. When the bird was ready for stuffing and baking, they carried it down to the springhouse in a sealed container and set it in the ice-cold water inside. Early tomorrow, they'd make Rebecca's tasty dressing and get it all set for baking.

There was plenty of opportunity for dessert making, and Jenny assisted Rebecca with tapioca pudding, bread-crumb pudding, and two kinds of pies—pecan and Dutch apple—careful to measure the ingredients, hoping not to spoil a single part of tomorrow's feast. She had much to make up for.

The intent look on Rebecca's face made Jenny realize again how very important this meal and the reunion were to her. Samuel, too, had talked of removing the hard wooden benches and bringing over some more comfortable chairs from the empty Dawdi Haus. Of course, a separate table would be necessary for their shunned family members, in keeping with the Ordnung.

Will the bishop find out—and then what?

Jenny was experiencing some unanticipated emotions, as well—stressed on the one hand, yet also wanting everything to be perfectly polished and prepared for Katie, whose room she had inhabited all these weeks now.

As soon as the breakfast dishes were cleared off and washed and dried Christmas morning, Jenny laid out a green table cloth for the meal. The day thus far had been a far cry from the holiday of her upbringing, but she had not missed the mountain of gifts beneath a shining artificial tree, or the mess of wrapping paper and ribbons piled high in the corner.

Instead, Samuel had talked of the Christ child, the dear Lord Jesus, and had taken time to read the Gospel of Luke's account of Jesus' birth. "'And so it was, that, while they were there, the days were accomplished that she should be delivered. And she brought forth her firstborn son, and wrapped him in swaddling clothes, and laid him in a manger; because there was no room for them in the inn,'" Samuel read, his voice gentling on the last line.

Jenny tried not to tear up as she considered the Savior who'd come to offer redemption. She listened along with the Lapps' eldest son, Elam, and the cousins who had come as usual to help Samuel with the morning milking. The fact that they had stayed this long was a treat for Samuel and Rebecca, who knew the men's families were waiting for them back home.

Jenny hoped with all of her heart that it was the start of an extra-special day for them. And she prayed the same, trusting that Bishop John wouldn't see the car parked in the driveway, or hear eventual rumors and spoil things.

Families are precious. . . .

··· ➢ ➤ ···

Everything was ready for Daniel and Katie's arrival with the children, including a small wrapped gift on Sammy's and Kate Marie's dinner plates. Rebecca felt her cheeks flush, yet refused to be on pins and needles over this longed-for reunion.

Jenny, meanwhile, was still cutting pickles at the kitchen counter and placing them prettily on a red-hued Carnival glass relish plate. Rebecca went over and slipped her arm through Jenny's and whispered, "I think this might be a day to remember." Tears filled her eyes, and she smiled through the veil. "I'm so glad you can meet my Katie-girl."

Jenny nodded, and then they heard the car turn into the driveway.

"They must be here," Rebecca said, moving forward to the window, eager to get a glimpse.

Just then Samuel came downstairs, all spiffy like it was a church day, and he and Rebecca moved swiftly to the utility room, where they stood like excited children. *Our hearts on our sleeves . . .*

Jenny hung back in the kitchen to observe, undoubtedly not wanting to interfere, and Rebecca hoped she didn't feel strange about being present.

Rebecca noticed Samuel's chin quiver as he opened the door without waiting for the knock. And, oh, such happiness on little Sammy's face as his tall, handsome Dat carried him inside and presented him to Samuel, who reached out his big callused hand. "Hullo, Sammy," she heard Samuel say. "*En hallicher Grischtdaag!*"

Merry Christmas, thought Rebecca. *Ach, so very true!*

Tiny Kate Marie, in her mother's arms, reached toward both Samuel and Rebecca, stretching her chubby hands to Samuel's big beard. Samuel's hearty laughter made Rebecca blink back tears as she took her grand-daughter from Katie and motioned all of them into the kitchen. Ah, the feel of this darling child in her arms!

Katie removed the children's coats, hats, and scarves as all the while

Samuel and little Sammy held hands. The blond boy stared up silently in awe at the grandpa he'd never met.

Jenny couldn't pull her gaze from the tender scene, riveted by it. What she was witnessing was a family's heart mending before her eyes. She wanted to rejoice in this major step forward, and she prayed that the man of God might pay attention to his wife's encouraging, even convicting words, especially at Christmastime. Was it possible that a family man like John Beiler might soften his heart at this time of year?

And then she recalled his pointed words to her and trembled.

"I've heard so much about you, Jenny," Katie said when Rebecca introduced her, and Jenny had stepped out of the shadows. "Such nice things, too," she added, the brightest smile on her lovely face.

"Merry Christmas to you and your family," Jenny said as she shook Katie's slender hand. "It's wonderful you're here."

Rebecca stood nearby, nodding and smiling.

It must seem like forever, Jenny thought.

Katie was looking all around the kitchen, observing what Jenny assumed she hadn't seen since the advent of her shunning. "It's so good to be home again, Mamma. It truly is." Her voice broke and she turned to reach for Rebecca, embracing her mother as her shoulders heaved with silent sobs.

Daniel, meanwhile, was holding baby Kate Marie over near the doorway to the kitchen, with little Sammy near, his mouth puckered and his big blue eyes regarding everyone.

Soon they were seated at their separate tables, although no one would have known, considering the tablecloth stretched all the way down and over the larger one. Tiny Kate was propped up safely in a booster chair Rebecca kept in the pantry for her other young grandchildren, playing with the bouncy red ribbon on her present.

Jenny and Rebecca brought over the large serving plate with the goose, browned perfectly, and all the steaming hot side dishes. There was dried corn casserole, green beans with ham bits and diced onions, mashed potatoes and rich gravy, chowchow, the relish dish with two kinds of homemade pickles—sweet and dill—and rolls still warm from the oven.

The silent prayer was longer than usual, and Jenny supposed it had much to do with the celebratory spirit of the day . . . and the homecoming of this cherished family.

At the end of the prayer, little Sammy got down from his chair and went to sit on his Dawdi Samuel's knee, sitting there for the longest time while Samuel beamed. It looked like the youngster had his heart set on remaining there for the entire meal, until Dan intervened when the chowchow was being passed around, coaxing Sammy back to his plate with the small wrapped present, which Jenny knew was a set of washable markers.

The table conversation was scarce at first as everyone enjoyed the spectacular meal. But later, when appetites were satisfied, the talk turned almost urgent, as if the principal players were all too aware of the space of time between now and their last visit here. Dan and Samuel, especially, filled in any existing lulls, as if determined no moments be wasted.

After the dessert dishes were cleared away and the children's faces and hands were wiped clean, Katie spoke quietly to Jenny over near the sink, where she and Katie were washing and drying. Katie had urged Rebecca to go into the front room with Samuel and Dan and the children, insisting on helping clean up.

With hands deep in the sudsy water, Katie asked Jenny what had made her interested in living in the Amish community. "Did you have some experience with the People prior to coming?"

"Some." She nodded. "I've been studying the Plain people since I was a girl. And I met Marnie, your cousin, at a roadside stand a few years ago, as well—my first personal link. I guess you could say I've always had a big hole in my heart . . . growing up English."

Katie's eyebrows rose. "How interesting." She brought up the fact that while she herself had loved her Amish childhood, she had never felt a deep connection to the Old Ways. "But I guess you know by now I was adopted." She laughed softly. "If you think about it, I was born fancy."

Jenny said she understood.

"I just hope you're not trying to find the ideal setup, you know." Katie frowned as she handed Jenny the next washed plate. "I mean, in the church and the community here."

"Your mother warned me the same way."

Katie dried her hands. She touched her white cupped prayer cap and smiled. "A person can live for the Lord Jesus anywhere, really. The Amish don't have a corner on piety, as I'm sure you know."

Jenny listened—Katie was certainly outspoken.

Later, when they'd finished, they wandered over to the window and stood there looking out. "People can embrace the simple lifestyle just about anywhere." Katie went on to say she and Dan had encountered searching souls from many walks of life. "Folk reexamining their entire approach to life . . . everything from wanting to downsize to rejecting materialism, or less modest ways of dress."

Jenny agreed but wondered why Katie was making such a point of this. For Jenny, the attraction to Plain living had to do with all those things, but especially faith. *There's no place else I'd rather be.* . . . Which made the thought of what was to come all the harder.

44

THE morning after Christmas, Andrew came to breakfast for the first time, along with Samuel's other nephews. Jenny took pause at the irony of it all. She had not slept much the night before, knowing what she must do . . . today.

After breakfast, Andrew asked if she could walk out to his buggy. "I'd like to give you something. I didn't want to wait till tonight."

Another gift, she thought, feeling unworthy and guessing this must be the Christmas present he'd mentioned recently.

Today he demonstrated no hesitation about being seen alone with her, although they went to the side of his enclosed carriage opposite the house, where he offered the gift more privately. She thought of apologizing for not having a gift for him, but then, she hadn't given anything but cards to anyone this year, her family included.

"This is something I wanted myself for a long time," he said as she removed the festive bow and gift wrap to find a Deitsch version of the Bible. "I have one just like it."

She was stunned. "Andrew, this is priceless!" She opened it reverently to see her name printed there and the date.

"It's been more than twenty years in the makin', I'm told. Wycliffe Bible Translators have been working on this important project in Sugarcreek, Ohio—first came the New Testament, and now the rest of the Bible. They got the help of Pennsylvania Dutch linguists to double-check every word, every sentence."

Jenny pressed the Bible to her heart and held it there. "This is the best present ever, Andrew. Denki so much."

He smiled and shook his head. "A blessed Christmas to ya, one day late." Andrew walked around the buggy with her, then got in and waved. "I'll see ya tonight for our prayer time."

She nearly choked, realizing she might not be there. Still, it was impossible to tell him here and now, to reveal that she had decided that she was leaving as soon as she could get a bus ticket home. "Oh, before I forget, I want to pay you for the phone call."

He shook his head and insisted she not worry about it.

"I really want to," she argued.

But he refused, smiling infectiously in the way she had come to know so well.

"Denki again, and have a good day, Andrew." She turned to head for the house, her spirit dismayed. *Thanks for everything.*

"Till then," she heard him call softly.

Jenny's heart ached as she shuffled back inside. She sat with Rebecca at the kitchen table, painfully aware she was letting everyone down—especially herself. And Rebecca had no idea, which was best for now, since she was still caught up in reliving yesterday's reunion, her face shining with the lingering joy of it.

Struggling with her emotions, Jenny had to look away. She could not bear this.

Rebecca wiped tears from her plump pink cheeks. "Ain't many Christmases I'll keep close in my heart like that one," she said. "For always."

Jenny wanted so badly to say how happy she was for her, but a dark, nearly suffocating curtain of anxiety hung around her. "I need to make a phone call," she said at last. She would miss the bright and sunny kitchen, and Rebecca, too. But she would not miss her failures here.

"Must you right now?" Rebecca's expression revealed more than curiosity.

"I'll be back to help you prepare the noon meal." *Then I'll start packing.*

"Ach, take your time, dear. Looks like a perty day, in spite of the cold," remarked Rebecca. "A nice mornin' for a long walk."

Jenny glanced at the sky, where snow clouds hovered on the northwest horizon. "We might be in for a storm," she said, stating it the way Marnie liked to. *Oh, Marnie,* she thought. *We're leaving the very same week.* . . .

When she'd finished her coffee, Jenny hurried up to her room to get her purse. Back downstairs, she took time to layer up for the trek to the phone shanty, aware of Rebecca's inquisitive looks, though they were indisputably more about Jenny's earlier visit with Andrew than anything else. She walked to the back door with one look back at Rebecca, who sat staring absently at her second cup of coffee, plump hands curved around it.

It's wrong of me to keep enjoying her good graces! Jenny convinced herself once more of that as she walked down the drive, past the heavenly little springhouse and pond, then turned onto Hickory Lane. And suddenly, she remembered the cabbie's words as he dropped her off at that very spot. *"In case things don't work out, here's your ticket out of Plainville . . . back to the real world."* She hadn't taken his business card at the time, thinking she'd never need it.

No matter how much she wished and prayed, the Lord wasn't coming down to help her make a decent loaf of bread or successfully hitch up a driving horse. Nor would He stop Marnie and Naomi from leaving, or protect Jenny from having to be honest with the bishop. *God's not lifting the Bann from Dan and Katie, either—nor will He keep it from Rebecca.*

She attempted to keep her emotions in check. Hadn't she become more adept at that, wanting to emulate the other women here—their generally stoic approach?

Only a few more hours remained . . . then she could release her sorrow.

Jenny took her time heading for the phone shanty, remembering all too happily walking that way with Andrew to search for Chester Lapp's beloved pup. Today was definitely colder, and dense gray clouds were rolling in quickly. If she was to get out of here before the storm hit, she needed to keep moving.

She loved Hickory Hollow, here for only two months, yet it felt like nearly a lifetime. *The life I always dreamed of* . . . She had met the most wonderful people—Rebecca, Ella Mae, Marnie, and Andrew—and learned things she never would have learned elsewhere. She had planned to stay forever but hadn't even made it to the new year.

At that moment, she noticed a car coming this way, a tan Ford.

Stepping off onto the right shoulder, she lowered her head as she'd seen Amishwomen do when a vehicle approached.

The car slowed and then stopped. "Excuse me, miss," a male driver said, the window down. "I wonder if you might help me locate the Lapp residence."

The voice sounded surprisingly familiar, and Jenny glanced up to see a dark-haired man, his face shielded partly by the visor. Her heart pumped hard.

Can it be?

"Which Lapps are you looking for?" she asked, her voice shaky. "There are quite a few around here."

The man held up an envelope. "Samuel and Rebecca Lapp," he replied, smiling.

Her breath caught in her throat as she recognized this very handsome young man.

Marnie had a serious case of cabin fever. She'd stayed home yesterday cooking and serving Christmas dinner, then helped her mother get caught up on some much-needed sewing for Daed, once the kinfolk cleared out and left for home. Now she was in the process of making a list of things she wanted to take over to Fishers' in a few days. She also wanted to see Jenny, feeling bad about how she had complicated her seeker-friend's life. *I should be more supportive.* She also had a wall hanging she'd made and planned to give as a belated gift.

Marnie got her warmest coat and scarf and headed down Hickory Lane to visit Jenny for a while that Wednesday afternoon, assuming that if her friend was busy redding up after the Christmas festivities, she might just stay and help.

But almost as soon as she left the front yard and was making her way onto the road, Marnie spotted a tan vehicle stopped in the middle. The dark-haired driver was leaning out the window, talking to Jenny!

What the world?

Marnie hurried her pace, but when Jenny walked over to the car, Marnie hung back a bit, not sure what she was seeing.

Thinking better of it, she turned and went to look in the mailbox and discovered a letter from Roy. *How bold of him—he's honestly dared to send one directly here?* Her heart fluttered with happiness, and glancing down the road again, she decided to go back to the stable and warm up a bit while reading the letter. Oh, was she ever glad she'd found this before Mamm came to check the mail, although Marnie was sure her mother would never keep one of Roy's letters from her, disappointed in Marnie though she was.

She perched herself on an old bench near chestnut-colored Willis, her favorite driving horse, and read the letter. Roy wanted Marnie to think about meeting him at his church in Bird-in-Hand, once she'd settled in at Fishers'. *I'm trying to decide on the right one for us to join. As you know, I want God's will in all of this,* he'd written.

His church? Marnie put her head down on her knees and gritted her teeth. Like Roy, she yearned to seek the Lord more fully, but this would only compound problems. After her father's reaction in the milk house, she knew that for certain.

Something had to give, but what? And on this day after Christmas, with Jenny down the road talking to an Englischer, Marnie had an ominous feeling some very big changes were coming. And fast.

45

K YLE?" Jenny was shocked at the sight of her former fiancé.
Kyle Jackson's brown eyes searched hers; then he studied her
Amish dress and apron. "Looks like you did it," he said quietly. "You
pulled it off, Jenny."

She approached his car. He looked the same, although his brown hair
was longer than she remembered. Suddenly feeling ill at ease, she slipped
a hand into her coat pocket. "What are you doing here, Kyle?"

"I just happened to be in the area. . . ." He grinned at his own joke,
the same old bravado, only now it felt out of place.

"I'm serious. How did you find—" She stopped. "Wait. Did my mom
give you the address? Or was it Pamela or Dorie?" She was upset. "Oh,
maybe it was Kiersten."

"Jenny." He hesitated a second, glancing toward the road, then back
at her. "They're all concerned, of course. But that's not why I'm here."

She let that sink in. "So . . . my *mom* sent you?"

"No, Jen. It's not like that."

He explained that he'd contacted her mom a few weeks ago and was
told Jenny had "made the leap to the Amish," as he put it. "Then, when
I said I wanted to visit you, she was excited and gave me the envelope
you sent her, with the return address for the Lapps."

Taking a step back, Jenny took a deep breath—*why today?*—and slowly
let it out.

Kyle indicated that he wanted to pull over and park, which he did before quickly getting out. Tall and wonderfully appealing, he wore dark jeans, a striped button-down shirt, and a black leather jacket. Leaning on the driver's side of the car, he put his hands in his pockets and exhaled a plume of moisture. "It's cold out. Can I drive you somewhere?"

It *was* cold.

"I was headed for the phone shack up the road," she said, still amazed he was here.

Kyle turned, shielding his eyes as he looked into the sun. "May I at least walk with you?" he asked, his dark eyes pleading.

She shrugged, not pleased at the prospect but uncertain what to say. She gestured to his car. "We might as well drive, then."

He broke into a smile, going around with her to open the front passenger door. She got in and was immediately aware of the familiar scent of car leather and the plush surroundings. For a second or two she felt disoriented.

"I hope you don't mind my just showing up." He settled into the driver's seat and started the ignition. "But there wasn't any way to let you know."

There's always the mail.

"So why did you call my mom, anyway?" she asked as he turned the car around and drove slowly up the road.

"It's a long story, Jenny."

"Try me."

He hesitated for a moment; then a look of resignation crossed his face. "I've missed you, okay?"

She was a sitting duck. Here was the man she had adored and loved to laugh with—and oh, how they'd laughed, enjoying every moment together. She'd wanted it to last for a lifetime.

She spotted the crystal praying hands hanging on the rearview mirror, a birthday gift from her. *He kept it. . . .*

"Jenny . . . I was wrong about us. I've been kicking myself for almost two years."

"Kyle, please."

"Is that the phone booth?" he said, pulling the car over in front of the shack.

She turned in her seat. "Why now, after all this time?"

He smiled. "Why not?"

That's his best answer?

Go home, she was tempted to say.

"I'm not asking you to give up your dream, Jenny."

No, she thought. *I'm giving that up on my own.* Her cheek twitched.

"Want to get something to eat?" He touched her arm. "I'd really like to spend some time with you."

Her heart was in her throat. "What then?" It was hard enough seeing him again, but hearing him talk like this threatened to reopen old wounds.

"We can catch up on old times," he suggested.

"Why?"

Kyle looked exasperated. "Fine. You want me to just say it? I thought maybe we could talk about *us.* How things used to be."

She was dumbfounded. "Isn't it too late for that? You left *me,* remember?" She realized her response sounded anything but meek and mild. She was definitely not Rebecca Lapp. "I mean, we were together one minute, and you were gone the next. That quick." She wouldn't tell him how long it took her to recover.

"You were changing so radically, Jenny." He shook his head. "I just flipped out, okay? I don't deny it." He said he'd pondered everything and no longer cared anymore how she dressed. "I respect your Plain yearnings. None of that matters anymore."

She was actually relieved he hadn't made fun of her Amish clothes, though she didn't know why she even cared when she was leaving the People.

Jenny looked over at the phone shed, suddenly feeling claustrophobic. She needed to breathe, to be outside. "I have to make a call before it gets too late."

"I'll wait for you," he said.

Now he'll wait. She bit her lip at the sarcasm.

Nodding, she opened the car door and headed around the brushwood to the phone. Inside, she dialed the number and reached a clerk for the bus company. She asked for their bus schedule to Connecticut and received unfortunate news. Due to weather delays in Philadelphia, the earliest available seat was the day after tomorrow. She exhaled in frustration, and then the thought occurred to her: *What if Kyle drove me back?* He was heading there, anyway.

But would that lead him on?

She thanked the woman and hung up. Returning to the car, she spotted Kyle's expectant face and determined to nip *all* hope in the bud. "Let me say this just for the record."

"Yes?"

"I don't see us getting back together."

He flinched. "I don't blame you—"

"But . . . if you want to do me a really big favor . . ."

Without missing a beat, he nodded. "Say the word."

She asked him where he was staying, and he told her the Bird-in-Hand Family Inn on the Old Philadelphia Pike, not far from here.

Jenny made her request and Kyle seemed pleased. *Too* pleased. Then his eyes squinted nearly shut. "Wait a minute, why are you going home?"

"I'll tell you tomorrow." She directed him back to Samuel and Rebecca's, where they parked on the road near the mailbox at the end of the long driveway. "Tomorrow morning, seven o'clock. Please don't be late."

"I'll be here," he promised.

Jenny saw him wave through the window, and she hurried up the lane to Rebecca. It was time to fulfill her promise to help make the noon meal.

46

WHEN Jenny returned from the phone shanty, she and Rebecca kept busy at their separate work spaces in the kitchen, Jenny glancing every now and then at her friend and hostess. She had no idea how to say what she must.

Once they had the large chicken potpie nearly ready to place in the oven, Rebecca began to talk about the coming snowstorm, going on about how Samuel had complained of his knees aching something awful yesterday from his rheumatism. "He seems to know nearly right on the dot just when a storm'll hit," Rebecca was saying.

Jenny listened, still surprised at Kyle's appearance. Was it a sign from the Lord? After all, he had always been a prayerful man.

Jenny knew she couldn't put off the moment any longer—it was time to tell Rebecca that she was going home. "Rebecca, I want to tell you how much I appreciate everything you've done for me," she said. "You've given me so much." Her voice broke and she paused in dicing apples for a Waldorf salad. "I'll never forget."

Rebecca stopped what she was doing. "Ach, Jenny, what're ya sayin'?"

"I'm leaving Hickory Hollow tomorrow . . . with an old friend of mine." She sighed heavily.

The blood drained from Rebecca's face. "I don't understand."

"I don't see how I can meet the expectations of the Proving . . . not now. Not when I must eventually confess what I know about your visits to Katie." She bowed her head. "And I don't feel good about betraying that, considering all you've done for me."

Rebecca was quiet for a long while, her eyes downcast. When she finally spoke, she merely nodded her head. "If you must, then go with the Good Lord's blessing."

"Denki" was all Jenny could say.

The two of them remained awkwardly silent until they heard the sound of the back door screech open and Samuel tromp in.

··· ➤ ➤ ···

Rebecca looked devastated during the noon meal, and Jenny cringed all through it. *If only things could be different!* she thought miserably. *The last thing I want to do is leave here.*

After dishes were done and there was still no conversation between them, Jenny escaped to her room to write Andrew Lapp a letter, which she gave to him when they met at the springhouse pond that evening. He accepted it but was clearly taken aback by her not wanting to stay and pray as planned.

"When you read the letter, I hope you'll understand," she told him, her voice quivering.

His eyes held hers, his expression concerned. "Wait, Jenny . . . you seem—"

She shook her head. "I'm sorry . . . I really can't talk about it."

He nodded and reached for her hand. "Something's wrong."

She looked down at their entwined fingers. "Jah, everything's wrong, Andrew." Her voice cracked and she reluctantly slipped her hand away.

"I'd like to talk to you," he said. "Will ya stay awhile?"

Tears rolled down her cheeks. "I can never succeed in my Proving. It's not possible."

"Why do you say so?" He moved closer. "I don't understand."

She sniffled. "I just can't . . . not without jeopardizing the peace of someone I care deeply about."

"Is it Rebecca?"

Andrew's words shocked her. How could he possibly know?

She ignored his question. "I'm not the type of person who could—" Her voice broke and she had to pause a moment before continuing. "Please, will you trust me when I say this is for the best?"

"That's what's special about you, Jenny. And I appreciate you not

470

sayin' anything amiss 'bout Rebecca, too." He reached for her hand again. "You're ever so trustworthy."

She was unable to choke down the lump in her throat. *I need to leave now, before I come to care for you even more than I do.*

"Please read my letter, all right? Good-bye, Andrew." And with that, Jenny fled, holding back her tears as she headed back to the farmhouse.

··· ➤ ≺ ···

Jenny could not sleep again that night. She gave up trying to rest at all and instead wrote yet another letter—this one to dearest Marnie. In it, she avoided revealing Rebecca's devastating secret but told her friend she would miss her very much and hoped that she and Roy would be happily married next autumn.

I'd like to stay in touch, she wrote, giving Marnie her parents' phone number and street address. *Your friend always, Jenny Burns.*

Rebecca lay wide-awake, listening to Samuel's irregular snoring, forcing her mind toward happier thoughts: little Sammy's visit. Such an adorable child, sitting like a wee angel on his Dawdi's knee at the table all that while on Christmas Day. It was as if he'd intended to take his meal right there with Samuel. And if she wasn't mistaken, Daniel's blueberry eyes had glistened about then. Samuel's too. And then again tonight, when she told him that Jenny Burns was leaving in the morning. He must've steeled himself, poor man, unbuttoning his shirt without speaking, his actions deliberate and methodical. Then he'd gone to kneel at his bedside and remained there for the longest time, his heart obviously broken.

Like hers.

··· ➤ ≺ ···

Marnie arrived at Uncle Samuel's back door with her handmade wall hanging Thursday morning. She could hardly wait to present this particular gift to her friend and could not believe her ears when Aunt Rebecca told her Jenny was gone. "Left just an hour ago or so," Rebecca said. "She said to give you this."

Marnie stared at the letter her aunt handed to her, biting her lip. *Did Jenny leave because of me?*

She had no right to protest, did she? After all, she, too, was packed and ready to move. But to think her friend hadn't told her in person or bothered to say good-bye. Why?

"Denki," she told Rebecca, deciding to take the wall hanging home with her and wondering if she might simply mail it to Jenny.

"Won't ya come in for some hot cocoa, get warmed up?" Rebecca's eyes pleaded.

Marnie accepted and removed her boots and coat before following Rebecca into the warm, inviting kitchen.

They talked around Jenny's leaving, never addressing it outright, but Marnie could see Aunt Rebecca was greatly troubled.

Jenny was so exhausted she slept for the first two hours while Kyle drove. When she awakened, she was startled at the sight of her own clothing . . . the English outfit she'd worn to Hickory Hollow back in October. In the haze of waking up, she'd nearly erased the last two months.

She wondered if Rebecca would be surprised that she'd packed all of her Amish dresses and aprons. But of course, she'd left Rebecca's black shawl and outer bonnet, and Katie's former things. The room she'd shared with Katie's memory was fast fading in her own mind—or was she simply pushing it aside . . . letting the time in Lancaster County die away to nothing?

"You're tired," Kyle said when she glanced over at him there in his navy blue pants and tennis shoes.

She nodded. "It's been a couple of rough nights."

"Want to talk about it?"

Must I?

"Let's talk about *you*, Kyle."

He smiled, eager to do so. She learned that he'd continued to work as a computer tech at the same company in Hartford but was thinking of buying a large parcel of land near Frankfort, Kentucky. She wondered if this was to impress her. But before she could ask, he volunteered that he'd been thinking of paring down to live a simpler life. "Besides, who wants to live in fear of the national grid going haywire?" He laughed.

"And on that note, let me help out with the gas," she offered as they stopped off to refuel and grab some snacks.

"Don't be silly. The trip's on me."

When they returned to the car and got back on I-95, she asked about her family and was given an ambiguous response. This brought it all back—there wasn't anything to tell, as usual—and she dreaded the thought of going home.

He asked where she would live, since her mother had mentioned she'd left her condo and job. "Well, if my parents haven't disowned me, there's always the guest cottage behind the main house." *Like a detached Dawdi Haus*, she thought, wondering how Ella Mae Zook would take the news that she had left so hastily. *And poor Marnie, too . . .*

She asked Kyle if she could use his cell phone to call the antique shop in Essex. She wanted to see if she might work part-time, perhaps, maybe even eventually get her job back. Not that she expected the owner to agree, but if there was a chance, she preferred to work there. *With old things cushioning me*, she thought, picturing dear Rebecca sitting in her sewing room on her grandmother's cane chair, watching the snow fall.

Does she despise me?

47

THE snow became heavier the farther north Kyle drove, and Jenny prayed silently for God's protection. Kyle brought up the church he was still attending, mentioning a men's prayer breakfast group he enjoyed. He asked her about the Amish church, but she skirted the question. The reality of what she'd done, leaving Hickory Hollow so suddenly and without giving anyone but Rebecca or Andrew a heads-up, became increasingly more painful as the hours passed. And in spite of Kyle's attempt to make her think he wanted to live a tranquil, uncomplicated life, he continued to talk about his job and Hartford. She knew he must care for her a lot to want to give that up to move to a big spread of land in Kentucky. It was sweet and she appreciated him for it, but she needed time to get her head straight.

"I have an idea," he said when they were closing in on the turnoff for Essex. "Let's catch the train in New Haven and go to Manhattan for New Year's Eve."

They'd enjoyed this excitement-charged event once before, and the following month he'd taken her home to meet his parents, close to Valentine's Day.

He looked over at her, beaming. "So . . . what do you say?"

Jenny knew the trip would merely be for old time's sake, because nothing could take her and Kyle back to those days. If anything, he was attempting to reignite something romantic between them, which meant everything would have to be on a brand-new footing. But for him to even suggest a trip to the Big Apple confirmed for her that they were out of sync, and she told him so. "I'd rather not," she said politely. "I'm sure you can understand."

He nodded, but she could tell by his eyes he was disappointed.

Hickory Hollow had altered Jenny forever.

Jenny's mother was astonished to see her, and her dad actually stood up and came over to greet her as Jenny walked in the front entrance. They said absolutely she could stay in the small guesthouse until she got settled elsewhere. And they went with her to the living room and sat there, managing some awkward small talk and getting caught up a little. Jenny asked about each of them—and about her sister and brother—and soon the conversation centered on Mom's various upcoming social events . . . and Cameron's "pretty new girlfriend." No mention of the former one, or the child belonging to the new girl.

After a half hour or so, Dad rose and came over to kiss the top of Jenny's head. "Good to see you again, kiddo." He mentioned having a report to finish and disappeared into his library office.

Her mother lasted somewhat longer, until she remembered she needed to pick out a formal gown from her wardrobe upstairs for her next big function. "Come with me," she said, coaxing with her eyes. "Help me choose it, won't you, dear?"

Seldom had Jenny been invited into the vast walk-in closet—"*the wardrobe paradise*," as Mom had once called it. Shoes and purses were lined up according to color and style—casual, day wear, and evening wear. While staring at the abundant options, Jenny thought of how the old Amish houses didn't even have closets—just a row of wooden wall pegs.

Even though she craved some alone time, overwhelmed by her mother's astonishing passion for opulence and excess, Jenny made herself stay. She wanted to show interest and attempt to connect. And after far longer than Jenny hoped it might take, she confirmed her mother's choice of a gown, which brought a smile from Mom. It was important, Jenny now knew, to demonstrate how much she cared. Had she always held her family at arm's length? Was she partly at fault for the distance between them all these years?

Later, when she'd patiently waited for Mom to choose her accessories, Jenny asked permission to go to the large guest room closet, where she'd left behind a few of her clothes. Then, needing some air, Jenny borrowed one of her mother's casual jackets and walked down to her former workplace to talk with her friend, the owner, who said she'd gotten her voicemail, and yes, she could offer Jenny twenty or so hours a week to start.

Strolling along the lovely main street, Jenny looked forward to getting her bearings in Essex again, needing to put the hapless situation in Lancaster County behind her. She wondered most of all if Andrew had read her letter. Did he think poorly of her? She was actually glad she'd stayed long enough at the springhouse to explain herself so that she hadn't appeared to simply vanish . . . as she had initially from home.

When Jenny returned to her parents', her hair was white with fluffy snowflakes. Mom came into the large entryway to meet her for the second time—and she rather liked the attention. "Your Amish friend Marnie Lapp called a few minutes ago. You just missed her, dear." Evidently Marnie wanted Jenny to call her sometime this weekend and had given the number for the phone shanty. "She said you can leave a voice message if she's not there to pick up."

"Did she say what time I should call?"

Mom smiled brightly. "You know, I believe she did. After supper on Saturday night—yes, that's what it was."

"Denki . . . er, thanks."

"And, dear, sometime when you're ready to talk about it, I'd like to know more about your Amish experience," Mom said, a soft expression on her pretty face.

Jenny caught her breath. "How about now?"

Her mother motioned her toward the kitchen, walking back to an open cookbook. Jenny followed into the grand kitchen and sat on the barstool, observing her. "What would you like to know?"

Mom shook her head. "I have no idea."

"Well, I can tell you that, while I practiced repeatedly, I never managed to make a successful loaf of bread like Rebecca Lapp. Yet it's something Amishwomen do frequently."

Mom raised her eyebrows and pursed her lips.

"Have you ever made bread?" Jenny asked.

"Sure, just not recently. Years ago, I made fresh bread every week."

"Would you teach me how, Mom?"

"Well, why not now?"

Jenny smiled at the sudden sparkle in her mother's eyes.

When she returned to the family's guesthouse, Jenny took time to hang up her Amish clothing, putting the dresses in the far back of the large closet before closing the door. Her time in Hickory Hollow had turned out to be shorter than she'd ever expected, an experiment meant to have a different outcome. "Nothing more," she whispered sadly.

Then, brushing her hair, Jenny was surprised to see that her bangs came all the way down to her nose. She moved to the floor-length mirror and fluffed them a bit. "Well, what do you know . . . one small triumph!"

After a formal dinner the next evening, Jenny made a point of sitting with her father in the den to show him the newly published Pennsylvania Dutch Bible. He thumbed through to various Old Testament passages and into the Psalms. He asked her to read to him, and she did, surprised at how much she'd learned in such a short time. He even asked for the translation of certain words, and she brought up her dictionary. She waited for him to create an excuse to leave, but he didn't, at least not for a solid hour, which pleased her.

He did ask, though, before she headed to the guest cottage, if someone by the name of Andrew Lapp was a friend of hers from Amish country. Curious, she asked where he'd seen the name. "Well, here." He pointed to the second page, the one following her name and the date, which she'd already seen.

The pages had evidently been stuck together when Andrew presented it to her. There, in Andrew's own strong hand, were the words *Delight thyself also in the Lord: and he shall give thee the desires of thine heart. ~ Psalm 37:4*

Andrew had also written a note saying the verse was a favorite and signed his name.

"That's an interesting book—can't say I've ever seen a whole volume in Pennsylvania Dutch before." Dad peered at it more closely.

She nodded and smiled as she looked up Andrew's reference to the Proverb to see the translation, then read it aloud in Deitsch.

"You enjoy studying this language, don't you, Jenny?"

"It wasn't easy for me, despite my classes in German, and I don't have your patience for such detailed work."

Dad chuckled, folding his hands and making eye contact. "Tell me about Amish life. What things stand out most to you?"

She explained how chores were broken up along clear gender lines. "There's a specific hierarchy in Amish culture: Men and women have very defined roles, even from childhood. I was surprised at how much time I spent in the kitchen, for instance—it takes a lot of work to keep up with all those hearty appetites, but Amishmen expect nothing less of their womenfolk."

Dad smiled. "*Womenfolk*, Jenny?"

"That's what we call ourselves. Well, what *they* call themselves." And now Jenny was smiling, too.

--- ➤ ➤ ---

Rebecca looked out when she heard the clatter of a carriage that evening. Her pulse sped up when she saw it was Bishop John—surely he'd heard of their Christmas Day reunion. She'd held her breath, waiting for this dreadful moment, but was in some ways relieved to be confronted at last.

Samuel was sitting near the stove in the kitchen in his stocking feet when the bishop knocked on the back door. "Willkumm, bishop," he said, rising and going to shake John's hand. His expression showed no trace of concern as he pulled up another chair, giving up his rocker for the man of God. "Have a seat," he said.

They exchanged particulars—mostly about the weather and two upcoming farm auctions. Rebecca offered hot coffee and some cookies, and the bishop accepted them, which surprised her a little. Was this not to be a serious visit after all?

At last, though, he began to share what was on his mind. "I heard Katie and her husband were over for Christmas dinner."

Samuel gave a quick nod, his eyes serious. "Was there anything wrong with that, bishop?" he asked respectfully.

The silence grew lengthy as Bishop John studied the coffee cup in his hands. "Well, in my thinkin', there's nothing wrong with a God-fearing man having a visit from his grandchildren. Might be a blessing."

Rebecca thought her heart might stop. "No, but something else is wrong, Bishop," she admitted, wanting—*needing*—to come clean.

Samuel frowned. "Rebecca?"

"I'm talking 'bout what *I've* been doing . . . in secret." She unloaded her burden right then and there, revealing her numerous nighttime visits to see her shunned daughter. "I just couldn't stay away from my grandchildren," she confessed. "My family."

The bishop ran his fingers through his beard, appearing far more flabbergasted at this admission than did her own Samuel. And before the bishop could say a word, Samuel said he wished John had been on hand to see his young grandson Sammy being granted his "dearest Christmas wish." Samuel was as calm yet determined as she'd ever seen him with any of the ministerial brethren, and his composed demeanor made her fall in love with him all over again.

Amazingly, the bishop did not pursue the topic of her breaking the ordinance, though he did not offer to forgive Rebecca, either, just kept his face turned toward Samuel. "Mercy has an important place in our community," John said quietly, his expression serious. "I daresay it's been a long time comin'." This most of all astonished Rebecca. Did John Beiler mean what she thought he was saying?

Rebecca wanted to clap her hands. No, she wanted to give her husband a sweet kiss, and she would do just that the minute the bishop left, which he did much sooner—and more calmly—than she or Samuel might have imagined.

"He didn't condemn my visits to Katie," Rebecca said in wonder as the two of them watched their neighbor head to his waiting horse and carriage.

"Come here, my dear woman," Samuel said, drawing her to himself. "You have nothin' to fear. Jah?"

"Thank the Good Lord," she said, taking the opportunity to lean in and stand on tiptoes. But Samuel kissed her first, before she could even pucker.

48

JENNY never dreamed her sojourn home would amount to such plea-sure on not just her part, but her parents'. And Kiersten, too, had come around a couple days after Jenny's return, wanting to stay longer than just to drop by and say "hey," actually asking questions about Plain life.

To her family's thinking, Jenny hadn't been gone very long. In fact, she assumed they had hardly noticed . . . and here she was back already. Still, Jenny felt almost doted upon by them, and also by Kyle Jackson, who'd taken her to one of her favorite spots—a walk along the Connecticut River in Essex, where Main Street ended at the rushing water's edge.

She asked Kyle if he would purchase the land in Kentucky for himself, if the two of them weren't together as a couple.

"No, probably not," he said, honest as always.

Then why do it? she wondered but didn't want to shoot him down.

"Why do you ask, Jenny?"

"Just curious."

Kyle bypassed that topic and went on to inquire about her stay at the Lapps' farm. Jenny felt more comfortable now and ready to tell Kyle what had transpired there. She even shared about the practice of social avoid-ance called the shunning, explaining that Rebecca's ties to her daughter had seemed to take precedence over the strict church ordinance, although she did not reveal Rebecca's forbidden visits.

Jenny also recounted her time with the Old Wise Woman, and the many hours working together with Rebecca in her kitchen, as well as quilt making and baby-sitting at the bishop's big farmhouse. "Lots of domestic chores," she said, moving on to describe Marnie's and Naomi's plights. Then she described how reserved and soft-spoken Samuel Lapp had been, "until he talked my ear off, showing me how to hitch up the pony to the cart." That had Kyle laughing, saying he'd like to have seen her go flying up Hickory Lane in the pony cart. She did not divulge her calamity with Josie and the pony cart, however. Nor did she say a word about Andrew Lapp.

"Do you know how impossible it is to see the stars here at night?" she suddenly blurted out. Kyle looked bemused, then suggested it was mostly because of the bright city lights. And in that moment, Jenny was glad she'd returned the call to Marnie Lapp, though Marnie had sounded so sad, missing Jenny yet giddy to talk to her again. *We'll stay in touch, like before,* Marnie had promised.

Jenny had quickly agreed, certain things would never be the same but relieved Marnie wanted to remain friends.

She did not permit her mind to wander back to Andrew, though. Dwelling on him was a mistake, knowing as she did the great emptiness she felt—sometimes nearly a lack of air in her chest—when she allowed herself to return to him in her sweet memories. Jenny guessed she might feel that way for a very, very long time.

By leaving Hickory Hollow, she'd lost Andrew Lapp forever. Their precious friendship was a closed book.

··· ⋟ ⋞ ···

The distant sound of firecrackers punctuated Rebecca's dreams, and later, in the wee hours, when she was fully awake and plodded downstairs to the bathroom, she realized she had tears on her face. Had she been dreaming of Jenny Burns again? Or was it Katie?

Samuel had warned her she would miss the daughter figure she'd found in naïve Jenny. Rebecca had indeed begun to mourn this new and unexpected loss, wishing there was a way to let the former seeker know there were no more secrets to be kept. Samuel was now quite sure the bishop would simply turn his head to their visits to Dan and Katie, and vice versa.

Rebecca was compelled to go and look in Jenny's room, thinking how odd it was that she'd lost both girls. *And both to the English world.* So the fancy life won out, when all was said and done, and yet she loved them both. *I put Jenny at risk by going against the Ordnung and hoping she'd turn a blind eye,* she thought. *When I was supposed to be her mentor!* Sorrowfully, Rebecca realized she'd done much the same with Katie by withholding another secret.

"Haven't I learned my lesson yet?" she whispered, remembering how Jenny had flitted from room to room while living here, so taken with the trappings of Amish life: the wringer washer, the smooth bone of the crochet hook, and the comforting livestock in the stable. Yet she was not able to embrace it long enough to make it her own.

Rebecca lifted the heirloom quilts and slipped into the bed where both Katie and Jenny had rested their heads, said their silent prayers, and longed to be accepted. A new year had come on swift wings just hours before, but Rebecca did not care to sleep. No, it was time to pray. "Dear Lord in heaven, be with all of our family this night. Keep them ever in thy loving care. I pray this, too, for Jenny Burns, who is also thy child. In Jesus' name, amen."

··· ➤ ◄ ···

Marnie was shocked to see Roy arrive by van following breakfast New Year's morning. She was helping Mamm redd things up in the kitchen, her younger siblings sitting now at the table, looking at the cute cards they'd made for each other before Christmas.

She went running outside to greet Roy, not bothering with a coat or shawl. "Happy New Year!"

"You, too, Marnie." He was all smiles and she thought he might reach to kiss her cheek, but they did not embrace. "I have *gut* news for you. Had to come in person to tell ya."

"That *gut?*"

He nodded, his eyes alight. "But first, go an' get your coat and scarf so we can walk right quick."

"Let's go to the barn, where it's warmer," she said, liking the thought of being with Roy on this first day of the year. She hurried inside and pulled on her work boots, coat, and scarf, then donned her black candlesnuffer-style outer bonnet. She looked for her mittens and smiled when she found them pushed into her next youngest sister's coat. "I'll be right back, Mamm," she called into the kitchen, not waiting for an answer. Oh, the joy of seeing her beau again!

She listened carefully as she and Roy walked slowly across the back-yard to the barn, where she knew they'd have privacy. Making their way inside to the stable, Marnie could scarcely believe what Roy was saying.

"You're mighty sure?" she said, wanting to be sure she had it right.

"Jah, your bishop and I had a long talk early yesterday morning. He sought me out, said it was all right in his opinion if I take you to gatherings with others who are seeking to understand God's Word."

Marnie found herself shaking her head, amazed.

"I was surprised by John Beiler. I honestly liked him, Marnie. He seems to understand where I'm comin' from—that I love God and want to learn as much as I can from Scripture before I become your husband."

"So he knows that, too?"

Roy reached for her mittened hand. "I'm actually thinkin' of joinin' church over here in Hickory Hollow."

"Wha-at?" Now, this was a surprise! She leaped up and Roy caught her, embracing her and planting a warm kiss on her cheek. "Oh, this is the best news ever!"

"I thought you'd say so." He held her near and removed his black felt hat, then gave her the first-ever kiss on the lips. He explained that he truly thought the bishop was taking a few steps back from the youth who were in Rumschpringe, letting them choose baptism without so much coercion.

This was as astonishing as Roy's tender kiss.

"Can ya stay for dinner?" She looked up at his handsome face. "Perty please?"

He grinned his answer and pulled her close again.

"This has to be the happiest day for us, jah?"

"Well, I can think of a better day yet . . . next fall, ya know."

She smiled. Their wedding day would top this moment, no question on that.

"'Course now there's no need for you to move to Dan and Katie's," he said.

She'd nearly forgotten with all this rush of news. Goodness' sake, was she ever relieved. "Kumme mit—we must talk to my parents, 'specially to Daed."

This will be the best gift ever for my father!

49

I THINK I've learned a tough lesson," Jenny told Pamela and Dorie at the noisy eatery in Hartford days later. "Silly me . . . I have to accept who I am, not what I wish I might've been."

Pamela shook her head. "Sounds philosophical, Jen . . . something your father might say."

"I can't believe you're back," Dorie said. "I mean, you looked so at home in Amishville. We talked about this on the drive back here."

"I agree with Dorie; you seemed really settled there . . . despite your crazy Plain costume." Pamela cringed. "Don't hit me!"

They laughed together, and when their lunch order arrived, Jenny dismissed their remarks, ready to enjoy her salad and crab-cake sandwich. Dorie smiled at her apologetically across the table from behind a mound of fries.

Pamela suggested they pray silently, which they often did when eating out together, but Jenny's mind flew to the dozens of times she'd watched Samuel purposefully bow his head in reverence, with Rebecca doing the same. Jenny still wished she knew what words they prayed—surely it was a learned rote prayer, as was the bedtime prayer. But she'd never asked.

Another regret.

"It's so great to have our little trio together again," Dorie said as she reached for the ketchup.

Jenny took note of the busy place. The walls were lined with posters and other paraphernalia, and it wasn't long before her thoughts were in

Hickory Hollow, where Rebecca's home was anything but frenzied and overdecorated. Tidy, simple . . . that was the Amish approach to interiors.

"A house is a home because of the people who live and love there," Ella Mae had once said.

"Jenny? You look wistful." Pamela leaned near, studying her. "You okay, hon?"

"Of course." Jenny reached for her soda and took a sip, yearning for the unusual taste of Rebecca's homemade root beer.

Later in the week, Kiersten talked Jenny into meeting at an upscale strip mall in Hartford, where they shopped for most of the afternoon, Jenny mostly observing what her sister bought. They capped off the outing with supper. "I'll bet you miss home-cooked Amish food," her sister said, juggling her many purchases as they sat down.

"Well, Mom's the best cook ever."

"So is that a no?" Kiersten probed.

"Food is food, right?"

Kiersten laughed. "You haven't changed at all. I thought you'd return all geared up for our modern ways . . . the ones you looked down on most of your life, remember?"

Jenny listened, trying to get a grasp on Kiersten's perception of her. It was unnatural for sisters who grew up under the same roof to have to go through these kinds of maneuverings. "You must have thought I was checked out, even when I was a little girl. Everyone did."

Kiersten didn't come right out and agree, but it was clear what she thought. "Oh, you know."

"No, really, I'm sorry if I shut you out." She paused. "I must have."

Kiersten waved it off, bringing up Cameron. "Talk about checked out—our brother is crazy in love with Lexi." She explained that he and his new girlfriend saw each other several times a week, and even hauled Lexi's kid along. "Totally surprising."

"So if they marry, he'll be an instant daddy."

"Who knew?"

Jenny smiled. Cameron had been too busy to see her since she'd landed back here. But she could easily overlook that. Things were pretty much the way they had always been between her and her brother—nebulous. *Don't bother me, and I won't bother you.* Still, she hoped to change that, too.

"Do you want to drive up to Mystic with me sometime?" Kiersten said she'd read online about an amazing boutique there. "Or are you still clinging to the pure and simple life?"

Jenny glanced down at her navy blue skirt and cream-colored sweater. "Guess some things never change."

"Why *did* you come home, sis?"

Jenny sighed, not comfortable with the idea of rehearsing the whole excruciating mess. Besides, she was sure her sister was just filling the spaces, uneasy with natural silence. Kiersten wasn't the type to be interested in old souls. She was all about the next cool dress shop or casino restaurant—anything "hoppin' or hot."

"Maybe it's more about why I ever left," Jenny said bravely.

"Okay."

"And sure, I'll go shopping with you in Mystic."

Kiersten squinted her eyes. "You *will*?"

"Name the day," she said, committing to stepping out of her comfort zone. It was about time.

That evening, an unexpected call came in from Rebecca Lapp. Jenny was delighted to hear from her—Rebecca's voice was sweet music to her ears. They exchanged a bit of small talk before Jenny asked about Marnie and Naomi . . . and Ella Mae.

Then Rebecca's voice turned tense. "Things happened so abruptly when ya left, I never had a chance to say a proper good-bye." She wanted to let Jenny know that things had worked themselves out. "Ach, my dear girl, I couldn't bear thinkin' you'd left here because of me." She sounded pitiful. "It wasn't your fault . . . not at all." She paused for a beat. "Honestly, I put you in an awful tough situation, askin' you to keep what you knew from the brethren."

"Rebecca, I—"

"No, listen . . . I failed you in doing so—didn't measure up as your mentor." She continued, explaining that she never should've gone against the Bann. "I've made things right with the bishop; I wanted you to know."

Jenny realized once more how painful this had been for both of them. "I'm so glad you called." She didn't go on to tell her how much she missed talking to her, or any of that. *Best not,* as Rebecca might say. *Besides, what's the point?*

She changed the subject and mentioned how busy she was now with her family, and that she'd started working again while living at her parents' place. "Please tell Marnie hi for me, and Samuel, too."

"I'll be glad to do that. But just so ya know, things ain't the same here without ya. All of us miss you!"

"You're so kind. Thanks for calling, Rebecca. Denki, I mean."

They said good-bye and hung up.

··· ➤ ➤ ···

More than a week later, Jenny received a letter from Andrew Lapp. He wrote that he was still praying for her, and that he understood why she had to leave so quickly. *If you truly believed you wouldn't pass your Proving, you figured you might as well not wait around, jah?*

Reading his considerate words brought her a strange comfort. And she was relieved that, despite his disappointment at her going, he did not seem upset. She knew it was so when she read the last line of his letter: *I pray earnestly that you will be happy in the English world, if that is where God wants you to be, my dear Jenny.* The idea that he still considered her "his" on any level took her by surprise, and she found her thoughts returning to him many times throughout that day and the days that followed. She felt astonished that Andrew was so selfless, releasing her back to the modern world without him. His unexpected letter was a soothing salve for her heart . . . yet she could not help wishing she had not left so much behind in Hickory Hollow.

··· ➤ ➤ ···

The Monday after St. Patrick's Day, a new shipment of antiques arrived at the shop where Jenny had begun working full-time again. Her boss was over in the corner talking to the dealer when Jenny happened to overhear a mention of Lancaster County, and she made a mental note to look through the items, just for fun, before heading home that evening. If she saw anything she liked, she might use her employee discount.

She finished helping several more customers, finding it curious how fashionable the sleek look of the '50s and '60s was to young couples—pole lamps and Danish furniture in particular. It was fun for her to snatch up the occasional find, as well, thinking how nice it might look in a new apartment, since she'd sold everything. She'd had her eye on one residence in particular for the past week or so, but wanted to be frugal rather than impulsive.

Near the closing hour, Jenny took her time to study each of the antiques from Lancaster County—sideboards, corner hutches, and an assortment of unmatched cane chairs. She turned over one of the chairs and saw the name *E. M. Zook,* and for a split second wondered if Ella Mae had perhaps passed away. But there were so many Zooks in Amish country. *"Oodles,"* Rebecca had mentioned early on, also listing some of the other popular surnames—Stoltzfus, King, Fisher, Beiler, and Lapp.

Thinking again of Ella Mae, Jenny was sure Marnie would have said something when they last talked by phone, weeks ago. Surprisingly, her friend had not moved to Katie Fisher's, telling instead of Roy's friendly conversation with Bishop John. *"This changed everything for us,"* Marnie said, sounding so happy. She and Roy were looking forward to taking baptism classes together next summer, prior to their November wedding. *"We're joining church here in Hickory Hollow, of all things!"*

Jenny decided to purchase one of the old chairs, and her dad agreed to pick it up. And all the rest of the evening she wondered what E. M. stood for. *Eli Mathias? Ephraim Marcus?*

In the end, she preferred to think the chair had somehow been linked to the Old Wise Woman. The beautiful chair, along with the wall hanging Marnie had sent her and Andrew Lapp's cards, notes, and gifts were her only keepsakes. *Along with my unforgettable memories.*

50

ANOTHER two weeks passed, and Jenny was happy to keep her hands and mind busy while her heart journeyed here and there. *Well, not really*, she thought. *Only to one place.*

She tried to keep her focus on her present surroundings the Friday after Easter, when her father had planned their first ever father-daughter outing. They settled in at an inviting restaurant, Skipper's Dock on Water Street, in beautiful Stonington Borough. It was an hour before sunset, and Dad must have pulled strings to get a perfect harbor-side view for their leisurely meal.

She felt relaxed enough at this rare event, having taken her mother's suggestion to wear one of her own long, white sleeveless dresses from *the* wardrobe. It was a comfortable yet dressy outfit, complete with a black bolero with white piping. Mom had remarked that she looked like a million bucks. *Oh yes, exactly what I was going for,* Jenny thought, laughing at the paradox.

Her father was impeccable in navy slacks and a white oxford shirt and tie with a tan sports jacket.

"I've been thinking about this evening for quite a while," he said over appetizers of stuffed Stonington clams swimming in butter.

She leaned back in her chair, taking in the waterfront, the piers dotting the fading red sky, and the wail of seabirds. It was hard to imagine being in such a lovely spot, let alone with her dad.

What's gotten into him?

"It's been wonderful having you home," Dad said, his eyes searching her face. "And I think you'll be surprised when I say this, but I'd like to apologize for letting my work crowd out my time with you, Jenny."

"Dad—"

"I'm serious."

He smiled, but there was a hint of something else, something other than joy. Momentarily, he looked toward the wharf, as if second-guessing, then back at her. "I don't think you're all that happy here."

She was surprised he'd picked up on her private reveries. "I'm sorry," she said. "I didn't—"

"Jenny, no . . . don't be. More than anything, I want your happiness, just as your mother does." He paused again. "And you know what, honey? I think you might be right about the Amish . . . the appreciation you've always had for the culture. I really don't think you belong here, in this crazy, modern, stress-filled world."

Jenny considered this as the waiter came to remove their small plates, then left. "You must think I'm still Plain inside."

"Aren't you?"

She didn't want to spoil this special evening. "You must love me a lot, Daddy," she whispered, not fully realizing it until now.

He reached across the table and took her hand. "Enough to let you go, if we must."

Dad's words reminded her of Andrew's first letter after she returned home.

"There's something else," her father said, glancing toward the water. "In many ways, losing you from the family for those two months opened my eyes."

"Dad, I . . ."

He shook his head and reached for his water glass, and she knew he wasn't interested in belaboring the point. He'd said what was on his heart and she appreciated it.

When the main course arrived, Jenny and her father ate heartily, enjoying the scrumptious seafood. And Jenny had much to ponder, realizing again that she had been too impulsive, leaving Lancaster County so quickly. Yet it wasn't as if she could simply return there whenever she wished.

Or could she? Her heart beat faster at the exhilarating thought.

Marnie flew down the stairs to the kitchen, filled with the rich aroma of baking chocolate pies. Her sisters were still playing on the lawn this springtime Saturday, making themselves scarce while Marnie and her mother finished setting a pretty table. Afterward, they chopped onions for the baked ham supper. It wouldn't be long now and all their guests would be arriving.

Feeling like a flibbertigibbet, Marnie dashed back to the sitting room near the large kitchen and ran her fingers over the sideboard's surface for the second time. She smoothed the checkerboard-patterned afghan on the back of the upholstered chair in the corner and glanced out the window.

Her heart leaped and she leaned closer, her nose nearly bumping the windowpane. "Quick, Mamm . . . tell Daed she's just arrived! Ask him to bring Posey along, too, on a leash! Oh, Mamm, she's here!"

Jenny stepped out of the taxi, paid the cabbie, and left her suitcases there on the driveway. She had no idea how well she would be received by the Amish community as a whole, if at all, although Marnie had clearly rejoiced when Jenny had written with her decision.

Presently, she spotted Marnie dashing around the side of the house to come this way, a bright smile on her sweet face. And then Peggy, her mother, appeared, accompanied by brawny Chester and Posey, who barked and wagged her spunky tail.

"Hullo, *liewi Freind!*" Marnie called as she flung her arms around Jenny.

Dear friend . . . Jenny felt the same about Marnie.

Stepping back, Marnie looked her over with delight. "Well, aren't you the cutest Amish girl in Hickory Hollow! All you're missin' is the prayer Kapp, ya know."

Jenny smiled, catching her meaning. "I brought my entire Amish wardrobe back with me."

"Oh, Jenny! Everyone's been fussing 'bout you since we heard you were returning—I mean just *everyone*." Marnie grinned, tilting her head and shielding her eyes from the sun. "But it was my idea to have a gathering here tonight. Hope that's all right."

Chester greeted Jenny warmly, shaking her hand and holding the golden Lab up to show how much Posey had grown. "Seems you've been gone a long while, Jenny. Willkumm back."

Jenny accepted a hug from Marnie's mother, all dressed up in her for-good dress and matching apron.

"I hope you're hungry," Peggy said. "We're havin' Easter dinner all over again, or so says Chester." She laughed and looked up at her husband. "And some of your friends will be here . . . comin' very soon."

Jenny could not believe the warm reception and assumed Marnie's parents had humored their daughter with the plans for a special meal. *Like Ella Mae did for me last Thanksgiving.*

"And someone else is here to see ya," Marnie whispered and grinned, pointing toward the barn, where Andrew Lapp emerged. "Well, I guess I'd better leave ya be . . . for now."

Marnie followed her father, who had picked up Jenny's suitcases and was carrying them up the driveway. Posey scampered along, close behind, and Marnie and her parents hurried toward the house as Andrew came to greet Jenny.

"Quite a nice doin's, jah?" He removed his straw hat and she saw the old mischief in his eyes. "Nearly everything but the fatted calf."

He's right, she thought. *I am a prodigal.*

The earthy fragrance of freshly plowed soil and the feeling of serenity she'd sorely missed swept over her. Once again, she appreciated how very special a place Hickory Hollow was. *And always will be*, she thought, enjoying the bright yellow forsythia bushes in full bloom.

"Not much has changed since you left," Andrew said. "But on the other hand, there *are* some surprising things happening."

She wondered what he meant. When he didn't volunteer more, she let it go. Was he courting someone—was that the reason for the awkwardness between them? Or was he offended by her silence after she'd left? She hadn't replied to his letters because she felt it was unfair and didn't want to lead him to hope she was ever returning. Besides, she hadn't the right to expect he'd wait for her, anyway. The fact that Andrew was even here this evening, welcoming her back as a friend, was a real surprise.

Marnie wasn't kidding. Nearly every Amish friend Jenny had made last fall came to supper that evening. Even Emmalyn Lapp appeared, a blend of beauty and skepticism, while they all milled about in the front room, waiting for the meal to be served. But it wasn't long before Emmalyn came over to talk to Jenny. "I wondered if we'd scared ya off." Emmalyn looked chagrined. "Well, if *I* did."

Jenny assured her otherwise. "I guess I had to return home to see how deeply Plain I really was."

Emmalyn gave her a smile. "Well, you sure weren't here long enough to know for sure, were you . . . *last* time?"

Jenny nodded agreeably. "Things will be different now; you'll see."

Soon, Rebecca Lapp wandered over and gave Jenny a gentle hug. "You have no idea how I hoped and prayed you'd be back again, Jenny. And just so ya know, your room's all redded up and waitin' for you."

Jenny thanked her, grateful for the chance to reconcile their relationship during the rest of her Proving. "It meant so much to me when you called some months ago. And now . . . well, we're on new footing, jah?" she added, and Rebecca nodded and smiled.

Following the meal, the bishop and Mary lingered after everyone left, spending time alone with Jenny in the kitchen while Marnie and her parents and younger siblings scattered about the house. Bishop John read the Bible in English for Jenny's benefit, and later prayed with her and Mary. It was comforting to receive this second welcome, unexpected as it was.

Later, when it was appropriate, Jenny slipped in a comment about Katie Lapp Fisher. "She once told me that she was born fancy, considering her English genetic roots." Jenny paused. "But Katie pointed out that while I was born to Englishers, my heart was naturally Plain, so to speak. I know this might sound strange, but—"

"Not at all." Mary shook her head. "I think I understand what Katie meant. And ya know, I believe she just might be right."

After a while, Marnie came into the kitchen and brought out more cake, but the bishop declined, saying they had to get home to relieve their niece Naomi, who was evidently more settled in the community, too. And Jenny was glad to hear it.

After the Beilers headed home, Marnie offered to walk with Jenny down to Lapps', helping to carry one of the suitcases. Jenny so enjoyed the sound of springtime insects. She smiled when Marnie forgot and slipped into Deitsch occasionally without thinking.

Jenny was very surprised to hear that the bishop had recently permitted Katie Fisher to visit their own home. Not for a meal, but Katie and Mary had sat out on the porch and sipped iced meadow tea together. "I can't tell ya what a turnabout this is," Marnie added. "Nearly a miracle, really."

Jenny realized she'd missed out on quite a lot during a few months. "A very special reunion of true friends, jah?" she said, and Marnie wholeheartedly agreed.

"Oh, Jenny, I'm ever so happy you've returned," Marnie said as they observed the extravagant sunset and the way the clouds reflected the sprays of color.

Slowly, as the brilliance began to fade, Jenny's memory of the touching father-daughter dinner overlooking the harbor, and her father's perceptive remarks, rose up in her mind. She embraced *that* particular sunset, too.

Looking at Marnie, she blinked away tears as they turned into the Lapps' lane. "It's so wunnerbaar-*gut* to be back."

51

A WAKING to darkness, Jenny yawned, and her first conscious thought was of being back at her parents' guest cottage in Connecticut. Sleepily, she ran her hand over the embroidered edging of the pillowcase, wondering if it was the one she'd bought as a girl to surprise her mother. But her awareness kicked in when she heard the wonderful *clip-clop-clip* of a horse and buggy going up the road.

Ah yes . . . jah! She stretched, raising her arms high over her head and bumping the headboard as the handmade quilt slipped away from her. Then she heard stirring in the hallway, and wanting to assist Rebecca with the hot breakfast, she rejected the urge to lie there between the crisp white sheets under the cozy bed coverings. Tossing them aside, she got up and fumbled for her slippers, remembering how chilly the wooden floor planks had been last December. But it was midspring now, and summertime hovered in the wings.

I'm where I belong, Jenny thought, hearing the horse and carriage as it moved up Hickory Lane toward Cattail Road.

Later that morning, Jenny surprised herself by making her first-ever perfect loaf of bread. "Thanks to a few tips from my mother," she told Rebecca, who beamed with happiness when she shared how she'd connected with her family.

"Ach, now, this makes me wonder if you weren't s'posed to return to them for a time."

"I believe you're right." Jenny set aside the loaf to cool.

"Sometimes the Lord leads us to make amends in situations." Tears sprang to Rebecca's eyes. "In His own time . . . and way."

Jenny didn't bring up Katie and Dan, or anything regarding Rebecca's confession to the bishop. There was no need to. But she completely agreed with Rebecca and smiled warmly at the tenderhearted woman.

Later, when their morning chores were finished, Rebecca recited off a list of flowers and other gardening items she wanted to purchase at an Amish greenhouse. "The owner, Maryanna, is expecting me today, and I daresay it's 'bout time you saw her charming place for yourself."

They headed out to greet the balmy day and to hitch up Star. Jenny helped Rebecca, remembering more than she'd expected to, though Rebecca said nothing to point it out. And then they were off.

Jenny was helping to carry flats of fluffy golden marigolds to the back of Rebecca's enclosed buggy when she saw Andrew Lapp coming up the driveway. Not certain she should catch his eye, she wondered if he was headed to the greenhouse, too.

But he came right up to her, made a comment about the wonderful weather, and then asked if she might go for a walk with him later. "Once you're back at Samuel and Rebecca's," he said with a serious look.

She glanced over her shoulder, glad Rebecca was still talking with Maryanna at the entrance to the greenhouse. The two women were obviously unaware of Andrew's presence.

"Sure, I'd like that, Andrew."

His smile was so broad, so endearing, it took Jenny's breath away. "There's the prettiest little springhouse pond just down the road," he said, leaning closer. "I'd like to show ya." He winked at her.

She played along, her heart beating hard. "Sounds nice."

Then, taking her by surprise, he led her around to the other side of the buggy, and when they were completely obscured from view, he reached for both of her hands. "Just so ya know, all that prayin' I was doing back when . . . well, it wasn't just that you'd pass your Proving, Jenny."

She frowned, trying to comprehend what he meant. Then, seeing his familiar twinkle, she smiled. To think he'd waited for her!

496

"You know what I'd really like to do right this minute," he said, his voice soft. "I'd like to take you in my arms and never let ya go."

Jenny knew she must be blushing—even more so when he raised her hand to his lips and tenderly kissed it, his gaze never leaving hers. "I think you stole my heart that very first Preaching service."

"When you admonished me about snitchin' the ministers' food?"

"Ah . . . so you *do* remember?"

Warmed by his sweet admission, Jenny longed to walk and talk with him more privately, as he'd suggested. And soon!

"So, Jenny Burns, how long do ya 'spect to be stayin' with us *this* time?" he asked, still holding her hands.

She smiled up at him. "How's forever sound?"

Epilogue

THE following May, more than a year after my return to the People, the deacon approached me about possibly joining the church. He did so on behalf of all the ministerial brethren. "Do ya feel you're ready?" By now, I was speaking the language fairly fluently and could even hitch up a horse to a buggy—on my own! Even my sock darning improved after Tessie Miller took me under her proverbial wing and taught me a couple tricks.

So, from May to August, I will attend baptismal instruction every other Sunday morning, prior to the September baptismal service. I'm expected to acquaint myself with and understand the *Dordrecht*—the Confession of Faith—as well as meet individually with the ministers on Preaching Sundays.

"Remember," the deacon warned, "it's best never to take this holy vow than to make it and break it later on."

After he left, I thanked God for allowing me to learn and understand the Old Ways. But most of all, I was grateful for the opportunity to live among people with whom I can relate. The topping on the cake is Andrew Lapp, who officially proposed marriage to me the week after the deacon's visit.

We'll wait to marry until after I'm baptized, sometime in the middle of November, Andrew says. My parents and Kiersten and her husband are talking about coming, even though I've informed them of the long service and the hard benches. Dad says he'd like to take another look at my Deitsch Bible, which is heartening. Oh, and he wants to meet Andrew, of course. I'm just glad my family is interested in seeing Hickory Hollow for themselves. Who knows, it might help them understand why I'm so drawn to the place.

At any rate, I've never been so happy, or so settled. What I feel for Andrew Lapp, and he for me, isn't just a special kind of love. Plenty of couples think they have a corner on that sort of thing. We, however, believe God drew us together for a reason, and our love belongs to Him first. Andrew says our love is all wrapped up in a firm and precious faith—*"our foundation's gut,"* he likes to say. And when he winks at me, my heart flutters nearly out of control.

Although Marnie is my first choice for a bridesmaid, I can't choose her to stand up with Andrew and me because she and Roy married last fall, and an Amish bridesmaid is required to be a single young woman. I'm honestly leaning toward Emmalyn, although she doesn't know it yet. It seems like the right thing to do.

Naomi's second on my list, as she and I continue to be close friends. Tessie Miller's a good choice, as well, as are several of Marnie's younger cousins.

All of us get along so beautifully . . . it's like having a dozen or more sisters!

Ella Mae said months ago that she truly suspected—well, no, she was quite positive I would return here, after I left for home. She also insisted that Rebecca's confessing her former secret was the best thing that could've happened. *"Because sometimes when you tell the truth, you can start a fire,"* she said, and I think I understand what she means.

As for Rebecca and Katie, there is even more cause for rejoicing, with another grandson, little Leon Matthew, celebrating his first birthday soon. Samuel declares he's the spitting image of Elam and Annie's son, Daniel—Dan's sister's only child.

Rebecca's confided in me that she still prays for Katie's and her husband's return to the Amish church. But she no longer believes she has thwarted the helpful effects of the Bann on them. If anything, she is more accepting of their earnest faith, as is the bishop. And while the baptized People still aren't permitted to go to the Fishers' to visit, Katie and Dan are sincerely welcomed here in Hickory Hollow.

What Katie once told me is true: A person grows best spiritually when exploring God's Word, letting it get rooted and planted in the soil of the heart. There is no substitute for that for anyone, Plain or not.

And I've discovered that Hickory Hollow is not the ultimate place, no more than any community is perfect. But I *do* know that when the Lord puts a desire in your heart, you'll know it . . . and if you allow Him to nurture it, that yearning will blossom into a *brechdiech Gaarde*—magnificent garden—of blessing and grace.

Author's Note

FOR the very first young woman who wrote to me years ago, pleading to know what it would require to become Amish, I offer a special thank-you for planting the seed of this book in my thinking and in my heart. This story belongs to you! *The Secret Keeper* seeks to bring to life the heart's cry of many thousands of readers who yearn for the Old Ways or who wish to live with an Old Order Amish family somewhere near Hickory Hollow.

I am sincerely blessed with devoted readers, as well as the extraordinary people who edit and publish my novels. Thanks to each of you, especially to David Horton and Rochelle Glöege, ever astute and encouraging—two of my greatest joys.

I also wish to pay tribute to the many unsung heroes of my research, assistants who tirelessly check and double-check my fact gathering, including Amish and Mennonite friends and family, and my own dear Dave and our grown children, Julie, Janie, and Jonathan.

My great appreciation also goes out to the growing number of prayer partners, especially my wonderful friends at Bethany House, who take praying seriously—a real blessing to this author!

For all of you who kept my "secret" (the storyline for this book) while I delved into the journey of Jenny Burns's Proving time, I am truly thankful. And for those who prayed so earnestly when I fell and broke my right wrist just *three short days* before the book's deadline, I am forever grateful.

Hank Hershberger, Pennsylvania Dutch linguist and former Amishman, was always there for me and graciously answered numerous questions regarding *Deitsch*, not to mention how to hitch up horses and ponies to buggies and carts. Thanks so much!

I'm also indebted to the superb writings of John A. Hostetler and Donald Kraybill, the spokesman for the Lancaster County Amish community . . . and to the good folk at the Lancaster Mennonite Historical Society.

It is my ongoing delight to create stories that touch your heartstrings and somehow make a difference in your life or others'.

Soli Deo Gloria!

The
Photograph

To
Carole Billingsley,
whose prayers and love
are twofold blessings.

Now and then, in this workaday world, things do happen in the delightful storybook fashion, and what a comfort that is.

—From *Little Women*, by Louisa May Alcott

Prologue

EDEN VALLEY, 1980

TRUTH be told, I was taught never to feel sorry for myself. *"Nothin' helpful comes from pity,"* Mamma often said, expecting me and my siblings to be grateful and cheerful, no matter what came our way. I confess to missing her and *Dat* terribly as we continue life without them. Yet I've scarcely time to dwell on the past. My youngest sister, Lily, has caused me no small amount of concern since our widowed mother succumbed to pneumonia last winter.

I recall one of those frosty January days when I stepped into Mamma's bedroom and saw her standing with eighteen-year-old Lily near the sunlit window. Our mother was swathed all in white from head to foot and had somehow managed to pull herself up from her sickbed to don her best organdy *Kapp*, matted hair all *strubblich* beneath. She was talking quietly to Lily, her untied bathrobe hanging from her frail shoulders.

"Just look at those critter tracks in the new snow." Mamma pointed out the window, then turned to face Lily, still not noticing me. *"My dear girl, be ever so careful what tracks you make, and where they might lead those who follow."*

It wasn't new, this sort of talk from our mother. But this time, Lily's lower lip quivered, and she looked with sad eyes through the windowpane, saying nary a word.

Little did she or any of us know that precious Mamma would leave this old world behind just three short weeks later. Leaving Lily for me to look after, trying diligently to keep her on the straight and narrow path.

———

Our older sister, Frona, had been fretting over Lily just as I was. She especially worried over what was to become of the three of us, since we were still unmarried and living in the farmhouse where we grew up, here in Lancaster County's Eden Valley. Living there on borrowed time, since our brother Menno had inherited the place from our parents.

"Tonight we'll have some answers," Frona informed me after breakfast this mid-May morning. "I just hope we like what we hear."

The youngest of our four older married brothers, Menno had worked the land there since Dat's passing, helping Mamma and then us to keep things going. While he was often around the farm, he didn't often set foot in the house, other than for the occasional noon meal, but he'd told Frona he was eager to drop by after supper for a talk. By the look of gloom on her face, I felt she needed assurance all would go well. "It's awful *gut* of Menno to check in on us, remember," I replied.

"Ain't sure what's up," Frona said, frowning again. "But I have my suspicions."

"Well, I guess we'll know soon enough." I set about making my delicious peanut butter balls, Menno's favorite, wanting to offer him some when he arrived.

I've learned in my twenty years that a person really has no idea how life's going to play out. Things often start out fine and then take a hard turn. Dat and Mamma, healthy as they seemed, left us in their prime. *Jah*, I knew firsthand that when hard times came, you needed something to cling to. In my parents' case, it was their trust in our heavenly Father. 'Twas the same for me.

Unfortunately, it wasn't true for pretty Lily. Mamma had always been her rock during such times, and without her around, Lily seemed lost. We all were, in our own way, just not nearly as openly, nor as desperately.

At night, when Lily curled her slender body next to mine as we huddled like spoons to keep warm in the bed we'd shared since childhood, I'd hear her talking to herself and crying softly. The words might have been prayers, but if so, they were nothing akin to the ones Mamma had taught us. Sometimes Lily could say the most senseless things, honestly, and I tried my best not to take them to heart.

"*All the fun in life is passin' me by,*" Lily had said soon after Mamma died. "*I work hard from sunup to sundown, and for what? Just to start all over the same way tomorrow.*"

"*But work can be fun,*" I reminded her.

"*Maybe for you and Frona.*"

I let it go, remembering what Mamma's lifelong friend Naomi Mast had once said: "*It's better not to ponder too much what folks say when they're grieving.*"

··· ➤ ≺· ···

"Time to go an' greet your devoted patrons, Eva," said Frona, trying to shoo me out the side door to my candy shop that morning. It was built onto one end of the house—all Dat's doing, although Mamma had been in agreement, back when I was only twelve and already creating the kinds of tasty candies a person couldn't seem to stop thinking about.

"*You've found your calling, Eva,*" my father once said, beaming. "*And we're the happy—and hungry—receivers!*"

Even as a girl, I often lost track of time while creating new recipes, always trying to outdo myself with tantalizing confections to tempt the tongue. Some said my candies were like a riveting series of books—you couldn't wait to get your hands on the next one. And right quick, there were more orders for homemade fudge and crystal sticks than I had room for in our kitchen, large though it was. So my father had taken it on himself to build the sunny and welcoming candy shop, with its attached area for a small work kitchen. The very first time I stepped inside and looked around, I felt like I'd died and gone to Glory.

"*For me, Dat?*" I'd said.

My father kissed my forehead. "*All for you, little Eva.*"

I smiled back at him, one of a thousand happy memories.

"You're daydreaming again." Frona was staring at me, waving in front of my face. "You have customers!"

"Soon as I wash my hands," I told her.

"Be sure to bring back the gossip, ya hear?"

"Why don't ya just come hear it for yourself?" I turned on my heel to head for the sink. "And while you're at it, you could help over there, too."

Frona snapped her long white dish towel into the air. "I've plenty to do here, believe me. Anyway, I saw Dienners' boy out there in line."

"Can't imagine why."

Frona gave me a knowing grin.

I lathered up real good, then rinsed and dried my hands. It wasn't for her to know what was or wasn't in my heart for twenty-year-old Alfred Dienner. After all, he was the first fellow to ask me to go riding, four years ago when I was but sixteen. Alfred was real nice and not bad looking, either, but he planned to farm, and I couldn't bear the thought of being a farmer's wife.

Stuck in a farmer's crowded kitchen . . .

"Best hurry," Frona said, her eyes softening. "We need every cent to pay for new gardening tools." Plain as a plate, my sister was also a worrywart.

I recalled the times Menno and our other brothers—Emmanuel, Stephen, and Rufus—had encouraged Frona to worry less and trust *Gott* more. "For goodness' sake, we'll be fine," I told Frona. "I promise."

"*You* promise?" Frona moved to the back door and looked out the window, dish towel hanging limply over her arm. The sun shone onto her smooth, round cheek. She looked as vexed as ever, despite her pretty green cape dress and matching apron, the hems nearly brushing her ankles.

"We've always managed to pay our bills on time."

Frona blinked her gray-blue eyes at me behind her thick glasses. She'd taken it upon herself to wear Mamma's old pair, saying they helped her see everything she'd been missing. "*Puh!* I've never understood why you're so *hallich*," Frona huffed, like being happy was something to be ashamed of. She leaned her plump self against the windowsill and glowered.

"Mamma loved watchin' the birds, remember? Our heavenly Father looks after even the lowly sparrow."

Frona puffed her cheeks and blew air, then plodded over to the gas-powered fridge. Opening it, she merely stared inside. After a time, she made a sound clear down in the back of her throat and looked back at me. It was as if a gray shadow passed over her.

What's she so worried about?

While Frona was prone to fret, especially over the future, I wasn't exactly immune to that sin. Dat frequently reminded us that problems were designed to strengthen our faith. *"In everything, give thanks,"* he would say.

So, in memory of dear Dat, I was determined to count our blessings—family, friends, and fudge. Then and there, I chose to believe that whatever was on Frona's mind just now, I needn't think twice about. Our Father in heaven would take care of us. Besides, most things a person worries over never come to pass.

1

EVA Esch stood behind the wooden counter greeting each of her candy customers on the warmest morning so far of this budding month of May. Sunlight filled the neat and tidy shop that Friday, and between sale transactions, she happily scurried about, arranging the taffy and the well-formed peanut butter balls in an attractive array. Her father, Vernon Esch, had purposely designed the counter to face the windows, so young Eva could see her customers arrive. *"Not too high and not too low,"* he'd said of it, having her stand just so as he pulled out his measuring tape with a flourish. At her tender age, it was important to take into consideration any growth spurt she might experience; Dat had insisted Eva just might be as tall as Mamma one day.

She realized anew how considerate their father had always been, gone now four long years. With the recollection lingering, she looked up and caught sight of tall, very blond Alfred Dienner. Heavens, he must have been staring at her.

Politely, she smiled back, and Alfred didn't look away as a more timid young man might. His warm hazel eyes held her gaze, and his face brightened, his lips parting.

Has he come to ask me out? Eva wondered.

Alfred stood waiting, turning a slip of paper over and over in his hands. His strapping frame evidenced long hours of hard work at his father's farm on Stony Hill Road. His face was already tan, his manner confident. Whoever ended up married to Alfred would surely be well cared for, raising a brood of future farmers and little dishwashers.

Directly in front of Alfred, two of Eva's kindly neighbors, sixty-year-old Sylvia Lantz and her thirty-year-old daughter-in-law, Josie, talked in *Deitsch* as they made their way up the steps beneath the plain green awning. Above the shop door was the hand-painted sign, *The Sweet Tooth*.

Josie and her husband, Sam, and their school-age children resided in Sylvia's farmhouse, where the senior Lantzes had worked the land and nurtured nine children, eight of whom had survived to adulthood. The youngest Lantz girl had drowned one summer years ago, and two others—Tilly and Ruth—had left the Plain community for the world, living somewhere in Massachusetts near the coast, according to the grapevine. Eva really didn't know all of the details.

What she *did* know was that whenever she tried her best not to look Alfred's way just now, she could still see him out of the corner of her eye. If he offered an invitation, *should* she accept?

As it turned out, both Sylvia and Josie wanted the small white chocolate fingers, as Eva liked to call them. The petite bars melted in your mouth, more than making up for their lack of size with rich flavor.

"Can't resist 'em," Sylvia said with a glance at Josie. "I'll have three dozen, please."

"I sure hope there'll be enough left," Josie said, covering her mouth to smother the laughter.

"You know me better'n that." Sylvia's plump face turned pink. "I'll be happy to share with ya if Eva runs out."

Eva smiled at the banter between them, a bit envious as she watched Josie gently touch her mother-in-law's arm.

"*Mei Mann* will be ever so grateful," Josie replied, a mischievous glint in her pale blue eyes. "Your sweets are truly the best, Eva."

"*Jah*, 'tis a gift, makin' these candies like ya do." Sylvia nodded her head, grinning at Eva. "The most delicious, *wunnerbaar-gut* treats ever, hope ya know."

Josie smiled, too. "*Ach*, I'd give almost anything to be able to make these delicious goodies. My husband would be over the moon."

Eva blushed; it was impossible to ignore Alfred next in line. Even so, she took care to bag up first Sylvia's order, then Josie's, the two women talking about their "perty springtime flowers," and Sylvia marveling aloud about her fifty-year-old rhubarb patch that had once again sprung to life.

Eva wondered if she, too, might someday enjoy a close relationship with a mother-in-law. She certainly yearned for such a connection. Fearing she might betray her private thoughts to Alfred, she purposely looked down at the counter when he stepped up, tall and straight. His voice was confident and clear as he gave his order, then waited politely.

"Will that be all, then?" she asked, noticing his white shirt and black broadfall trousers, like he was going to Preaching and not off to work.

"Oh, and I'd like some hard peppermint candies, too," he said, leaning on the counter as if he might have more to say.

Here it comes, she thought, daring to raise her eyes. She spoke just as he opened his mouth. "Anything else?" She pointed at the glass display case and mentioned the freshly made peanut butter balls. But he shrugged and said maybe another time.

When she went to gather up his order, he followed her over, of all things, and stood watching. Goodness, but Eva was thankful for the steady stream of customers. Anything to keep her busy. Then again, she was afraid someone might suspect her and Alfred of being a courting couple. If not that, then certainly of being sweet on each other. Sure, they'd gone riding together a half-dozen times during the past few years, and they'd played volleyball on the same team, too. She also recalled a picnic in Central Park near downtown Lancaster, where she provided the meal, but none of that meant they were serious. Alfred was quite aware that a handful of other fellows had taken her out, as well. *All of them married now,* Eva thought grimly.

"*Denki,* Alfred, for comin' by—"

"Eva, slow down a minute," he said. "Your customers will wait."

She felt her face warm as Alfred proceeded, in front of everyone, to invite her to play Ping-Pong with him at his cousin's house.

Leaning over the work counter, she lowered her voice and replied, "You're askin' me here. . . ." She glanced behind him.

"*Jah,* 'tis all right." His eyes were smiling as he held her gaze. "So, will ya?"

She noticed their neighbor to the north pretending to study the homemade ribbon candy in the glass display case behind them. Eva felt positively mortified—what was Alfred thinking? The grapevine would have them engaged by day's end.

If I hesitate, will he stay and try to persuade me?

Pleasant and well-mannered as Alfred Dienner was, she wouldn't put that past him. *But, goodness—like a dog on a bone!*

"Um, that'll be fine," she whispered to him.

"*Des gut,* then," Alfred said with a nod.

She placed his order in a large sack and recited the total. "Enjoy the candy. Some very *gut* choices."

Alfred counted out the payment and dropped two quarters in the tip jar. "I hope I can make it last awhile." He gripped the bag of candy and, before turning to go, winked at her. *In front of everyone!*

2

IN Holmes County, Ohio, the maples and oaks were already flourishing against newly mown lawns and countless fields of sprouted corn. Amish farmers welcomed the season. *A time of rebirth.*

From the pinnacle of a hill, Jed Stutzman couldn't help noticing the Amish cemetery, the final resting place for his fiancée, Lydiann Coblentz. The peaceful, leafy green sanctuary of what-might've-beens was located not two miles from his work as an apprentice buggy maker. But today he urged his horse onward, not wanting to ponder what he'd so tragically lost.

Rattling past the three-acre burial ground in his elderly uncle Ervin's buckboard wagon, Jed felt the old, familiar pain, perhaps duller with the passage of a year. He'd spent hours there, contemplating his life without Lydiann, talking to his beloved as if she might hear him, and often as if she hadn't left at all.

He sped up the horse's pace. "You have to keep movin' forward," Jed told himself, drawing a breath, aware of the air's sweet fragrance. The wind had shifted in the past hour, pushing the smell of fertilizer away toward the south.

"The whiff of success," Dat says.

Jed smiled wryly and recalled Lydiann's opinion of what she'd called the *"schtinkich* scent," in spite of the fact that she'd grown up on a farm not far from his own father's. The truth was, his sweetheart had often declared how glad she was the Lord had seen fit to make her a woman, so she could keep house and cook for her future husband and keep him company by the evening fire.

"You would've been a splendid wife," Jed whispered.

Plenty of young men had thought so, too, back before Jed swooped in and began to court Lydiann. Last week at market, an *Englischer* woman who'd known Lydiann for years had declared her an angel on earth.

Lydiann trusted the Lord in a gentle yet mighty way. He considered all the times she'd prayed for God's guidance in their lives as a courting couple—they'd planned to wed this very November. Theirs had been a short-lived yet precious love story, and their mutual friends in the youth group had often remarked about the light in their eyes when they were together.

Heaven had other plans. Jed trusted in the sovereignty of their Lord. For him, as for all the People, there was no other way to approach such a profound loss.

Just ahead, he noticed his cousin Sol Troyer approaching the intersection in the black family carriage. Sol was New Order Amish, so his buggy wheels were solid rubber, which made for a quieter ride on the roads. Jed had always been interested in the difference in buggies around Berlin and surrounding towns, including carriages that were a bit fancier. Not that he'd ever desire anything but what was sanctioned by his Old Order bishop, but because he loved the craft.

"An Amish carriage must be made practically and properly," Uncle Ervin liked to say about his shop. *"Built well enough to last a lifetime."* This was his uncle's motto, and the man was well respected all over Holmes and Wayne counties as a result of his quality work. People came from miles around to order carriages from Ervin Stutzman.

As a lad, Jed had quickly learned that the buggy's framework was made of solid hickory, and that the steel springs and axles were the next thing to permanent if built correctly. Thanks to Uncle Ervin's patient instruction, Jed realized there weren't many ways to build a buggy right, regardless of style and whether they came from Ohio, Indiana, or Pennsylvania, where Uncle Ervin's cousin-in-law built the gray, boxlike carriages so typical of Lancaster County.

Glancing at Cousin Sol again, Jed waved, but Sol didn't see him. Jed thought of trying to get his attention, but he was mighty conscious anymore of all the ways something could go wrong on these narrow roads, especially coming into downtown Berlin with an older horse. The small town was becoming congested with eager tourists, most looking to purchase the fine souvenirs offered at Amish and Mennonite merchants.

Jed directed the horse to turn west onto Main Street. He nodded to a friend waiting for the stoplight near the flea market, where dear Lydiann had worked for a number of years. How many times had she told Jed, her expression glowing, that she could hardly wait to get to work each morning, she enjoyed it so? She'd delighted in the customers and loved attending to the children, thrilled for opportunities to spread kindness and cheer.

Jed pushed the memories aside. *She's with the Lord,* he reminded himself. It was the one and only thing that brought him solace, particularly during the first six months after her sudden death.

A few months ago, his family and closest friends had begun to encourage him to get back "into circulation," so Jed had reluctantly gone to several barn Singings and other youth-related activities, if only to test the waters.

Jed also had Uncle Ervin's retirement heavy on his mind, along with the possibility of taking over the family business. That had once seemed like a sure thing—at least until Perry Hostetler entered the picture.

My own fault, Jed thought. His uncle had always insisted the chosen successor be solidly grounded in the Amish church—a baptized member. Jed had intended to join church with Lydiann this coming September; it was all part of their plan. Now, though, he would be making his kneeling baptismal vow on his own, assuming he was ready. *I'm dragging my feet,* he thought.

Like Jed, Perry was also a buggy-building apprentice, but Uncle Ervin's cousin's son had joined church last fall. And Perry reportedly had a serious girlfriend.

Jed *had* attempted to date a few young women recently. The first, Phoebe Miller, while very nice, struck him as rather self-absorbed. Freida Burkholder, on the other hand, admittedly hadn't cracked open a book since finishing eighth grade. Eye-opening, indeed, considering Jed enjoyed reading as much as his work at the buggy shop. And pretty Mittie Raber, well, she'd chattered nonstop, gossiping like a nosy parrot, which drove Jed *narrish*—crazy.

In all truth, none of the young women had measured up to Lydiann. And he was beginning to wonder if *any* woman alive could make him forget his cherished first love.

Jed spotted the Christian bookstore on the left-hand side of the road and recalled combing through the many shelves there with Lydiann. He, looking for volumes of biblical history, and she, partial to fiction by Mennonite authors.

Continuing up the street, Jed eyed Boyd and Wurthmann Restaurant, their favorite. He and Lydiann had once snuck away to have breakfast together in the back room of the quaint eatery. Lydiann's blue eyes had brightened at her first taste of rich sausage gravy over a breakfast haystack of biscuits and eggs. Even now, Jed relished that recollection, as well as the thank-you note she'd written, starting a chain of correspondence between them, even though they'd lived within a short buggy ride of each other. From the start, she'd made up endearing closures to her letters. In Jed's opinion, Lydiann's creative sign-offs—phrases like *Love till the sea runs dry*—would take the prize for such things.

For me, she *was the prize. . . .*

He made the turn into the hardware store parking lot, glad for the morning sunshine. Then, tying the horse to the hitching rail, he thought of all the times he'd allowed himself to imagine the sequence of moments leading up to Lydiann's accident. He'd sometimes catch himself contemplating the foolhardy buggy race . . . with a speeding train, no less. It was no wonder the terror had managed to bombard his dreams, where he relived the devastating event. For weeks and even months afterward, Jed had privately blamed Lydiann's younger brother, known for recklessness with his fast horse and new black courting carriage. The same boy who'd lost his life as a result.

In that horrid accident, Lydiann's parents had lost two of their children, yet they had expressed acceptance of God's will. Jed had eventually learned he, too, must forgive, or he would be forever haunted by that terrible day.

Only by Gott's grace have I come this far, he thought, tying his horse to the hitching post. He willed his focus back onto the errand for Uncle Ervin.

Just today Ervin had gently prodded Jed to pray about getting baptized.

"And ya might find a good Amish girl to court, too," he'd added with a wink. Jed couldn't blame Uncle Ervin for being eager to retire and wanting to leave his shop to an established Amishman. *If I don't pull it together, I'll lose this golden opportunity*, he thought, tempted to give in to defeat as he proceeded to the hardware store.

3

MANY times since childhood, Eva had heard the charming story of her parents' courtship, Mamma's pretty face alight with the telling.

The Plain People of Eden Valley knew well that Dottie Flaud had married Vernon Esch just one week following her eighteenth birthday. And while it wasn't required by Pennsylvania law to get parental permission at that age, Mamma did so anyway, because she felt compelled to please those in authority. Indeed, Mamma's thoughtful gesture put her fiancé on even better footing with his father-in-law-to-be, if that was possible, considering her parents had set their sights on him as a mate for their daughter back when he was but a schoolboy.

Mamma had said there was an exceptionally large turnout for the Flaud-Esch wedding day, with more than four hundred Amish guests in attendance, including Mamma's lifelong friend, Naomi Mast, like a surrogate mother to Mamma and her older sisters, since their own mother had died when Mamma was in her early teens. Naomi's daughter, Ida Mae, had wed two weeks before Mamma herself, and Ida Mae and her young husband, Joel, set up housekeeping as neighbors to Mamma and Dat on Eden Road. In fact, their dairy farm was situated at the southernmost tip of the Esch property.

But it was Naomi, twenty years older than Mamma, who was Mamma's dearest confidante and closest neighbor. Naomi enjoyed helping Mamma at the drop of a *Kapp*, and the other way around. Some thought the two friends felt duty bound to make certain the other had adequate help gardening and canning and cleaning to host Preaching. It was a remarkably sweet shared conviction.

As a result, when Mamma lost Dat to a farming accident, it was Naomi who immediately took a prominent place in the Esch kitchen, cooking and cleaning, even though Mamma's own sisters were equally sympathetic and supportive.

Then, in the days and weeks after Mamma's own unexpected passing, Naomi began to reach out to Frona, Eva, and Lily, sharing privately that before Mamma passed away, she had asked Naomi to watch over her girls, covering them with prayer and compassion. Naomi especially bonded with Eva, though Naomi was old enough to be her grandmother. It wasn't long before Eva found herself unburdening her sorrow and loss to Naomi . . . and even letting slip a few secrets about some of the fellows she'd gone with, including Alfred Dienner. This was so very out of character for Eva, who'd never shared as much with her Mamma. Yet never before had she needed such consolation, and she was grateful every day that Naomi was always there, especially when Eva felt the world caving in on her, when she needed to just sob and let it all out.

Dearest Naomi. My only motherly source of wisdom now . . .

Eva hurried to dry the supper dishes, working alongside Lily, who'd always preferred to wash. Their immediate goal was to have the kitchen spotless for Menno's arrival. Scanning the large room, Eva noticed the pantry door ajar; bags of sugar and flour inside needed straightening. And the book Lily was reading, still open, spine out, on the kitchen table.

Frona was outdoors sweeping the back porch and steps, giving them a careful once-over. It wasn't as if Menno was coming to inspect, but they'd always tidied up especially well for this rather finicky brother.

"Frona's worryin' herself into a tizzy," Lily said, letting the hot water drip off the plate before she set it in the dish rack. "Like she wants to impress Menno."

"Well, it's not like we don't try."

"He struts around like he's king, ya know."

"You might have something there," Eva replied, wondering why Lily was dawdling with the dishes.

"Yet I daresay Frona's more rattled than we've seen her since Mamma came down sick. Remember?" Lily's blue eyes were solemn. She washed the utensils last before drying her hands on her black apron. "*Nee, ab im Kopp* is what she is."

"Now, Lily. She might worry too much, but she isn't crazy."

"But just look at her." Lily nodded toward the door.

"I honestly think you're the one frettin'."

Lily laughed quietly and shook her head. "You think ya know me, sister, don't ya?"

Eva stopped drying, her dish towel in her hand. "Oh, I know you well enough, Lily. How could I not?"

Lily walked to the table and ran her hands over the back of the chair that had always been their father's. "All I'm sayin' is we oughta be ready for anything."

Eva laughed a little. "You and Frona both . . . what's got into yous?" She laid the dish towel over the rack and left the room.

Why expect the worst?

··· ➤ ◄ ···

Naomi Mast rarely baked so late in the day, but just before supper she'd gotten word one of her English neighbors needed some cheering up. Realizing she would have no time for baking first thing tomorrow, she'd set right to work. Tomorrow, sometime after breakfast, she planned to visit daughter Ida Mae, who'd asked for help with her Lone Star quilt pattern in navy, rust, and tan.

Besides, it was good for them to keep busy, what with Dottie Esch's passing still looming in their minds. *And hearts.* Naomi wasn't one to say much about it, but she could read between the lines when Ida Mae talked about "those poor, dear Esch girls." Fatherless and now motherless, Frona, Eva, and Lily were very much on everyone's mind.

Sighing, Naomi pinched the edges of her rhubarb piecrust just so. Truth be told, she missed Dottie terribly and wanted to live up to the dear woman's faith in her to look out for her unmarried daughters.

I gave her my word.

It hadn't necessarily been easy keeping that promise, what with Lily's head-in-the-clouds attitude and Frona's anxious temperament. *Thank goodness for Eva,* thought Naomi with a twinge of guilt.

526

To the best of her ability, she had lovingly embraced James 1:27: *Pure religion and undefiled before God and the Father is this, To visit the fatherless and widows in their affliction.* . . .

Naomi carried the pie carefully to the counter, privately glad she wasn't the only Plain cook clinging to the old way of doing things. Of course, she'd never think of judging any of the other Amishwomen in Eden Valley who had accepted Bishop Isaac's long-ago nod to permitting gas stoves and other gas-powered kitchen appliances.

Likely the bishop's wife wanted one, thought Naomi, then chided herself.

Pulling small logs out of the kindling box, she stacked them in the belly of the old black cookstove. All the while, she thought of fair-haired Lily, whom she'd seen walking through the wild flowers in the meadow while Naomi washed windows yesterday. The dear girl was often rushing out to Eden Road to check the mailbox. It was beginning to seem that, on any given day, Dottie's youngest was in plain view. It was the oddest thing, considering all the work there was to be done with her Mamma gone.

Here lately, Lily had been wandering up to the shared phone shanty on the property of the next Amish neighbor over from Esches'. Repeatedly so, in fact. Naomi wouldn't have suspected anything amiss, except that personal calls were discouraged, so the frequency made her pause and wonder. A time or two, Naomi had actually spotted her twirling and singing, rare behavior for even Lily.

The way I must've acted when I first started courting. Naomi recalled the rapturous feeling and thought Lily might have herself a secret beau. Naturally, most serious dating relationships were kept quiet around Eden Valley.

Whatever the reason, Lily was running out to the phone shanty quite a lot, the family's snow-white Eskimo spitz, Max, chasing after her. In fact, Naomi had seen Lily with their dog earlier this morning, before Eva's candy shop opened for the day. Lily had practically skipped all the way back from the shanty to the stone wall running along one section of the road, across from Naomi's mailbox. She'd sat there preening like a bluebird beneath the sky.

Not wanting to second-guess why, Naomi placed her pies into the oven and went out to the utility room to put on a lightweight shawl. She opened the side door and stood on the porch for a time, breathing in the fragrance of dogwood and hyacinth. Why did it bother her to see Lily behaving so? Indeed, for a moment Lily had covered her mouth as if to silence laughter. Then, just that quickly, the girl's shoulders slumped and she hung her head, looking for all the world like she'd lost her dearest friend.

Naomi knew the older Esch girls had their hands full, given their household and gardening responsibilities—and that very busy candy store, too. Oh, goodness, Naomi wished her friend Dottie were still alive. If so, she would go straightaway there and talk heart-to-heart with her about Lily. But alas, that wasn't possible, and Naomi hoped and prayed Frona and Eva might be able to rein in their sister as soon as possible.

4

EVA picked up the red plate of peanut butter balls and carried it to the table, placing it smack-dab in the middle, minutes before Menno was expected to arrive. *No more than what a caring younger sister should do,* she thought. Yet she was unable to convince even herself that she was doing it for any other reason than to soften up her brother. *If Menno needs softening.* But certainly both Frona and Lily seemed to think their brother might require several of these yummy candies before they sat down to visit.

"*You have a gift,*" Sylvia Lantz had declared outright to Eva that morning in the shop. To think Sylvia would say such a thing, and then to have Josie agree so wholeheartedly, too—it was both heartening and embarrassing. And yet Eva had been told this back when she first started concocting sweets. Especially by her father, who was always quick to compliment.

Eva loved to get up early in the morning and dream up new recipes, or sometimes she would make her confections for the next day after supper. Often she shivered with excitement as she took the very first bite, curious how her latest effort might turn out.

Eva dashed to the cupboard for Mamma's best white dessert plates, conscious of Menno's horse and carriage clattering into the lane. She stacked them nearest their father's former spot at the table. *Where Menno will likely sit,* she thought, recalling his last visit.

That done, she headed for the back screen door and there spotted

Frona by the rusted-out old pump, no longer in use. Lily was also outside beneath the stable overhang with their dog. "What could be wrong? She looks downright guilty," Eva whispered as she went to rest against the porch banister to await their brother.

Menno waved at Frona, and Eva could hear him suggest they set up a roadside stand once the berries started coming on. Eva wondered why he'd brought that up.

"*Wie geht's*, Eva?" Menno asked, spotting her as he came up the steps. He paused a moment to remove his straw hat.

"*Wunnerbaar-gut*, and you?"

Menno pressed his lips together. "Word's spread clear beyond Eden Valley 'bout your candy sales," he said with a smile. "Heard it again this afternoon."

"Some days I can scarcely keep up."

He nodded. "It's been a *gut* little hobby, I'll say."

Eva noticed his smile had faded, and she couldn't help wondering what he meant by *hobby*. "Frona's real pleased with the extra income. She handles all the money." It wasn't really necessary to say that when Menno was aware Frona held the purse strings. But Eva suddenly felt nervous and wondered if Frona and Lily's worries were inching into her.

Menno waved her into the house with his hat, so she led the way, and Frona followed soon after, tramping up the porch steps and inside. As for Lily, Eva hoped she might oblige and not make them have to seek her out. *Lily knows better than to be standoffish*, Eva thought, watching Menno reach for their father's chair and sit down. She had correctly anticipated his choice. Now it would be a relief if Menno simply relaxed and enjoyed the peanut butter balls, chatting brotherly-like, with no agenda.

Proving my sisters wrong.

··· ➤ ➤ ···

When Naomi was but a girl, she'd stumbled onto crocheting after watching her mother make placemats and sweaters, and was quickly hooked. Now that supper dishes were all put away, she'd gone out to the side porch, taking her crocheting with her to sit and pray while she worked on a set of white booties for one of her grandbabies. And while she prayed silently, she looked up to see if Lily Esch was still out by the stable.

Lord God in heaven, soften dear Lily's heart toward Thee, she prayed, hoping Dottie's youngest would bring honor to her family's name and parents' memory. Dottie's youngest had always seemed more bent on having a good time than on matters of faith.

Naomi watched a patch of thin clouds float past the sinking sun, veiling it for a moment. Across from the barnyard, a row of mature cottonwood trees moved gently with the breeze, their pale trunks fissured from livestock rubbing up against the bark.

Over at the Esch farm, a young Amishwoman clad in a blue dress and matching cape apron practically marched into the lane, barefoot. The girl scurried to Lily, who was leaning against the stable door, arms folded. Naomi watched as the visitor greeted Lily with a brief hug, her back to Naomi, as Max barked and wagged his long, bushy tail. Then the young woman handed Lily what looked like a white envelope, gave her a wave, and turned back toward Eden Road.

Getting a better look now, Naomi recognized Fannie Ebersol, Lily's former school friend and distant relative. "'Tis nice she has such a companion, what with her parents and grandparents all gone to Jesus," Naomi murmured.

Naomi somehow felt better as Lily opened the envelope and peered at whatever was enclosed before clasping the envelope to her heart. With a glance toward the house, Lily spotted Naomi and waved. Feeling a bit sheepish, Naomi waved back.

Lily hurried toward the house and headed inside.

All will be fine, by the looks of it, Naomi assured herself, focusing again on crocheting the booties. "*Ach,* I trust so."

"*Gut* of you to join us, Lily," said Menno when she took her place on the wooden bench next to Eva.

Lily bobbed her head but didn't speak, and Eva inched over to give her some space. "You haven't missed anything a'tall," she reassured her as Frona eyed Lily across the table.

Menno placed his straw hat on the knob of his chair and remarked cheerfully about the tasty goodies while reaching for another peanut butter ball, eyes alight.

The more he eats, thought Eva, *the better.*

A small stack of periodicals caught her eye over on the floor near the pantry, and she wished they'd spent more time redding up. Thankfully Menno hadn't seemed to notice. Not yet anyway.

Her brother drew a long sigh, sat back in the chair, and studied the ceiling. "Has there been any trouble lately with the spring rains seepin' through?" he asked no one in particular.

Frona leaned forward and folded her fleshy hands on the table. "Not once has the roof leaked since Dat had it patched."

"*Des gut.*" Menno got up suddenly and left the kitchen.

Eva and her sisters exchanged glances.

"Told ya this could get thorny," Frona whispered. "Somethin's up."

"Wish he would just say what's on his mind." Lily slumped forward, fingering an envelope.

The day clock *tick-tock*ed the minutes away, and as was her way when she was stewing, Frona abruptly rose to make herself busy, putting some water on the stove to boil.

Eva wished Menno might return. This was no time for mystery, not the way Frona and Lily were fussing.

"Does either of yous want coffee or tea?" Frona asked over her shoulder. She yanked the utensil drawer open, rattling the teaspoons.

"*Kumme, hock dich naah!*" Lily spouted, slapping the bench with her book.

"I can't sit down just now." Frona peered toward the hallway and the front room. She squinted her eyes behind Mamma's spectacles. "Well, for pity's sake."

"What?" Lily practically leapt off the bench.

"Menno's in there measurin' the floor," Frona said.

Eva scarcely knew what to think.

"With his feet or a measuring tape?" Lily said sarcastically.

Frona wrung her hands. "He's walking and counting from one end to the other. Maybe he's planning to build an addition onto the house."

"*Wunnerbaar,*" Lily said, shaking her head as she went to sit again. "Just what we need—more space for the three of us."

Eva caught Lily's eye, but she looked away, evidently as put out with Menno's strange game as Frona, who opened the cupboard and began to remove several coffee mugs.

And there they sat, waiting for Menno, who was taking his sweet time, as far as Eva could tell. Truly, she felt like a caged cat.

5

EVA was relieved when Menno finally returned to the kitchen, yet Frona looked to be holding her breath as their brother took his place at the head of the table.

"Doubtless you're wonderin' why I'm here," Menno said.

Across the table, Frona stirred uneasily.

Menno continued. "Not livin' on the premises is becoming a challenge with all the time I spend working round here, so I plan to take full possession of the farm and the house. I'll be movin' my family in as soon as I can manage it." He paused and sighed. "There might not be room here for all of yous."

Eva's mouth dropped open, but none of them spoke.

Menno cleared his throat and expounded further on his plans. When he was finished, he looked first at Frona, then at Eva. "Why are ya surprised? Surely you knew this time would come."

Eva swallowed. They *were* surprised, thinking since Menno hadn't moved in right after Mamma's passing, maybe he'd wait awhile longer. *At least till some of us marry . . .*

"It'll be a tight fit for all of us," Lily said, bless her heart—she didn't seem to grasp what Menno meant.

Frona turned toward Lily and shook her head. "That's not what Menno's sayin'."

We'll be divided up, Eva thought sadly.

"Well, yous might have to stay with Rufus or Emmanuel instead of here. But it wouldn't be the worst thing," Menno said.

Living with this brother would be! Eva thought dolefully.

"Of course, if only one of you is still single by then, you'll have a place here as a live-in mother's helper for Bena," added Menno. "At least one of you must have a beau."

Surely he'll wait to move here till wedding season, or after, Eva thought.

Lily asked, "What 'bout Eva's candy shop? Dat built it for her."

Menno bowed his head, and for a moment Eva thought he might just come up with something to soften this disappointment. But Menno was true to form. "Eva can't expect she'll spend the rest of her days making candy," he said.

Eva watched Menno closely. *The shop's my last connection to Dat.*

"I can't believe this," Frona said.

Seeing her older sister's burning expression, Eva expected her to press Menno for more information, but she merely rose to offer him some hot tea or coffee.

"Is it instant coffee?" Menno frowned.

Frona nodded. "That's all we have."

"Well then, I'll have one more peanut butter ball and be on my way," he said with a faint smile.

"We might all end up with Great-Aunt Mary Girod clear out in Berne, Indiana," Frona worried aloud. "According to her circle letters, she has plenty of room."

Menno rolled his eyes, but Eva cringed at the thought of living so far from home. *Menno's upset the fruit basket!*

"Honestly, what'd ya think of all that?" Frona asked Eva and Lily once Menno was gone.

"I'm tryin' to get used to the notion of leavin' here." Eva considered Frona's comment about Indiana. "Why'd ya bring up Aunt Mary Girod?"

"Well, she's hinted that one or more of us could go out there, is all. Says she wouldn't mind some company."

Mamma and Frona had kept in close touch with Aunt Mary through the years and learned of the differences between this Plain community and their own.

535

"One thing 'bout living with Aunt Mary, we'd have to learn sign language," Frona added, wrinkling her nose.

Lily looked aghast. "*Aendi* Mary's gone deaf?"

"*Jah*, happened just over the past couple of years," Frona told them.

Eva couldn't imagine being unable to communicate verbally with a woman they'd never met—another rather gloomy thought.

"Aunt Mary's also written that the average age for baptism there is seventeen. So you know what that means." Frona looked Lily's way, but she was staring out the window, seemingly unaware.

Clenching her teeth, Eva felt embarrassed by what Frona had inferred. And her heart went out to their only sibling yet to be baptized. Lily didn't need this added pressure right now. *It won't sit well with her.*

Suddenly Lily announced that she must write a quick letter and rushed upstairs.

Eva stayed put at the kitchen table, feeling numb. "Why do ya think Menno's bringing this up now? I mean, why didn't he take over the farm after Dat died?"

Frona paced the length of the kitchen and back. "Honestly, I'd thought Menno might let us stay put for as long as need be. Guess I was wrong."

Eva found it curious Frona hadn't spoken up to him as other times in the past, particularly over farm-related issues. Not only to Menno, but also to their brother Emmanuel, who helped Menno work Dat's land each day. Frona was never unkind, but she did have a way of expressing what she thought was right and good . . . and what was best for Eva and Lily, too. She thought of herself as the head of this particular house.

Frona stopped in her tracks. "You know, it's been the longest time since I attended a Sunday Singing. I figure you've got a beau, Eva, and I wouldn't be surprised if Lily does, too, considering how secretive she's been lately."

Eva nodded but didn't correct her assumption. It was obvious Frona was thinking ahead to their future. Sadly, she was the least likely to marry, considering her age. And, too, Frona had a way about her that seemed to set some folks on edge.

Forcing a smile, Frona said, "I'm inclined to march over to Menno's place and give him an earful."

"You all right?" Eva asked quietly.

"Well, like Menno said, we weren't gonna live here forever." Trudging to the table, Frona sat in Mamma's former chair and folded her ample arms, like their mother sometimes had at that very spot. "If I didn't know better, I'd think he just wants an excuse to get us out of his hair."

Eva's head hurt. She wished Menno had stayed home with his family tonight, hadn't stirred things up. Truth be told, she felt downright glum and as miserable as Frona looked. "I think one of us should go and check on Lily."

"I have work to do," Frona murmured, then leaned her face into her hands. "Besides, you're closer to her."

Eva had always been able to get through to that sister, and the whole family knew it. She and Lily had shared a room when their brothers were still single and living at home. Yet even after the boys married and there was extra space, Lily disliked the idea of having her own bedroom. Eva didn't mind sharing if it made Lily more comfortable and at peace.

Eva excused herself and headed upstairs. She paused in the open doorway of their bedroom and looked in on Lily sitting at the corner desk, pen in hand. A white envelope was propped against the gas lantern, and Eva couldn't help but see the sad face. *Thanks to Menno.* Yet, in his defense, Menno had given them time together in their parents' house following Mamma's death, and now he'd given them fair warning. *Surely he'll wait till after harvest. . . .*

Eva stepped inside the room. "You're upset, ain't so?"

Lily turned and forced a smile. "Just thinkin'."

Eva went to sit at the foot of the bed.

"For one thing, I kinda feel sorry for Frona." Lily placed her pen on the stationery and moved the chair to face Eva. "It hasn't been easy for her, ya know . . . with fellas, I mean."

Lily's sad over that? Eva realized she evidently hadn't paid close attention to Menno's remarks. "Frona ain't *en alt Maidel* yet."

Lily rose and went to stand in front of the dresser mirror for the longest time. "She's not unattractive, but she does seem to hold a young man at arm's length."

"Frona has her nice qualities, though." Eva disliked saying negative things about anyone.

"You, on the other hand, could have Alfred Dienner," Lily said, moving to sit beside Eva. "Though I doubt you'll marry someone you don't love. Remember what Amy March says in *Little Women?* 'You don't need scores of suitors. You need only one . . . if he's the right one.'"

"But no one has seriously courted me, not even Alfred, though he'd like to."

"*Jah*, well . . ." Lily paused as if lost in thought. Then her voice changed to wistful. "There are always *other* alternatives, Eva."

"Surely ya don't mean someone from the outside?" Eva was startled. "An *Englischer* . . ."

Again, Lily seemed distracted. "If you're determined to marry for the right reason, why would ya even think of settling for Alfred?" Her sister had never spoken so pointedly about a fellow.

Lily rose and went back to the dresser. She opened the lid to the box of hairpins and removed one after another from her bun till her blond hair tumbled over her shoulders and down her slender back.

"*Ach*, Lily, what're ya doin'? We haven't had evening prayers yet."

"I'm goin' to bed early." The mirror reflected Lily's pained expression.

Eva shifted, troubled. They never let their hair down before evening family worship.

Yet Lily began to brush her long tresses, making dramatic sweeps as she went to sit on the opposite side of the bed, away from the door. She hadn't ever slept on the side nearest the hallway. Eva suspected she was afraid of the dark as a child. In the spring and summer, when they kept their door and windows open for ventilation, Lily seemed quite content to sleep on the opposite side of the bed, with Eva as a buffer of sorts.

"Honestly, sister, you're too tired for Scripture reading?"

"I am," Lily admitted. "And for much of anything else round here, too."

Their eyes locked and held for a moment. Lily was the first to look away.

"What's really botherin' ya?" Eva got up and stood near the dresser.

"My heart pains me." Lily continued brushing. "Somethin' terrible."

"Missin' Mamma?"

Lily placed her brush on the dresser. "We keep losing the people we love . . . and now the house where we grew up. Where does it end, Eva?"

"You won't lose *me*," Eva reassured her.

Lily teared up.

"Is something else worrying ya?" Eva asked gently.

Lily was silent for a moment.

"Sister?"

"If only you knew." Lily was staring now at the wooden quilt hanger across the room, where their mother's prettiest quilt was on display, the most beautiful Dahlia pattern Eva had seen in all of Eden Valley, or anywhere in Lancaster County, for that matter. It was the last quilt Lily and Mamma had made together, just the two of them, before Mamma took sick.

"It's Mamma, ain't so?"

"I miss her all the time." Lily leaned her head gently on Eva's shoulder and began to cry like a child.

"I understand. I truly do." Eva slipped her arm around her. "Go ahead, sister. The Lord sees and knows your heart." Such were the very words Naomi used when Eva couldn't keep back her own tears.

"Why'd Dat and Mamma both have to die?" Lily's pitiful sobs filled the room, and Eva guessed there were many more *whys* in her sister's mind, simmering just below the surface.

"I miss them, too," Eva offered, trying to be strong yet sensitive. *Poor, dear Lily.*

"Do ya ever think 'bout what Dat would want ya to do with your future, if he was still alive?" Lily asked.

"Well, we *know*, ain't so?"

Lily pulled a face. "For me to join church and settle in with the People, *jah*?"

"Why sure." She looked at her sister, pretty as a daisy. "Why turn up your nose at that?"

Abruptly, Lily straightened and dried her wet cheeks with a hankie from her dress pocket. "That's just it. I don't know if this is the life I want. Don't you ever wonder what else is out there?"

"My life is here, Lily. But of course I have private moments when I wonder what *Gott* has planned for me, like anyone else." Eva brushed back her own tears. "Losin' our parents might be a test to see what we're made of . . . like Job of old."

Lily's shoulders drooped and she moved to the wooden wall pegs, where their long nightgowns hung on hangers. Lily's were a lovely pale pink, and Eva's plain white. "Like I said, I'm all tuckered out, sister. I'm weary of tests."

Eva returned to sit on the bed, then leaned back and stared at the ceiling. She let the air out and didn't draw another breath for a moment. Tomorrow was their baking day for the week, and while their cousin Rachel tended the candy shop, as she did each Saturday, Frona and Lily were planning to take some pies to several shut-in neighbors, as well as to the deacon's wife. If Lily really *wasn't* feeling well, maybe it was wise for her to turn in early tonight. But in the past, she'd been far sicker and still listened to the reading of the Good Book.

Rolling onto her side, Eva gave Lily some privacy as she undressed. *What would Mamma tell Lily tonight, kind and loving as she always was?*

It was Lily who broke the silence. "Will Frona be miffed if I don't go downstairs?"

"She'll think you're mad at Menno."

"Like *she* is?" Lily sighed audibly. "I'm not goin' down there." She stepped to the dresser mirror and divided her thick hair into thirds and began to braid it, her slender fingers gliding expertly through her smooth locks.

"Aw, Lily, you're not yourself tonight." Eva pushed up against the headboard.

"Well, you're one hundred percent mistaken 'bout that." Lily's firm reply hung like a thick curtain between them. There, in the room where they'd shared every imaginable sisterly secret and confided their hopes and yearnings.

All of our lives.

6

T HE minute supper was over, Jed Stutzman had hurried back to work a mile or so from the family farmhouse. His goal was to finish building another carriage seat by day's end.

Meanwhile, Uncle Ervin sat in the corner of the shop, leaning on his cane with wrinkled hands. Now and then, Ervin scuffed his black work shoes on the cement floor, commenting to Jed about one thing or another, his thread of a voice rising and falling in the glow of the gas lights installed in the ceiling.

A short while later, Perry also showed up and set to work with no prompting from Ervin, who had long since ceased supervising every aspect of both Perry's and Jed's excellent work.

Jed stepped back to survey his handiwork before glancing at his stooped uncle, perhaps the most respected buggy maker in all of Ohio's Amish country. *Oh, to be as shrewd as Uncle Ervin.*

"Say, Jedediah, I've been mullin' something over," Uncle Ervin said. "I thought you might wanna go to Pennsylvania for some input from Jonas Byler, my wife's cousin. He could show ya some tricks to the buggy-making trade."

"Never been there," Jed replied, glad to please his uncle. "Sounds like an interesting opportunity."

"Word has it Jonas may be callin' it quits come fall, so there's no time like the present." Ervin rose with a groan and meandered over, standing

541

close enough for Jed to smell his pipe tobacco. "It would be an honor for you to meet him, Jed. Spend a week or so."

"I'll look forward to it."

"All right, then. I suggest ya purchase a train ticket right away." Then his uncle dropped the other shoe. "I've already arranged for you to stay with Jonas and his wife, Elsie, near Quarryville. They have a right nice granddaughter close to your age, and one a little younger. Both are mighty *perty*." Ervin winked and tapped Jed on the shoulder.

Smiling, Jed played along. He should have known his uncle had more in mind than just getting some wisdom from a master carriage maker!

··· ➤ ◀ ···

"You feelin' all right, love?" Naomi's husband asked when she rolled over in bed for the fourth time that night, trying to find a comfortable spot.

She hadn't wanted to awaken him and felt bad she had. "Just having trouble sleeping."

Abner suggested she drink some warm milk. "Might help."

That used to work, she thought, wondering if her insomnia was the Lord's way of keeping her up to pray for someone. It wouldn't have been the first time.

She slipped from bed, donned her lightweight robe, and reached for the flashlight on the nearby table. She padded downstairs barefoot, holding on to the railing as Abner had urged her to do in recent years. Too many women her age fell and broke a hip. She smiled at her doting husband's suggestion to warm some milk. Ach, *as if for a baby.*

The plank floors felt cool to her feet as she made her way to the kitchen. Naomi shone the flashlight on the day clock above the sink and knew she hadn't slept much, if at all. "What's ailin' me?" she whispered, going to the gas fridge and reaching for the half-gallon bottle, cow-fresh just yesterday. "After midnight, for pity's sake."

She didn't bother to light the gas lamp over the table, instead letting the bright stream from the flashlight guide her movements. She carried the milk to the stove and paused, thinking she'd heard something outside. The Esches' dog barked across the way.

Walking to the side door, she peered out. The sound came again as she opened the inner door to let in some air. That certainly wasn't an animal crying, and the strange sound continued, alarming her for a reason she couldn't put her finger on.

Naomi pushed the screen door open, glad for at least a slice of a moon. Was something amiss out there? She waited, listening. Someone was crying at this hour, and in the direction of the road.

Might be one of the neighbors' teenagers.

The way the side porch was situated, Naomi could see not only the road but across to neighboring farms. Standing near the screen door, she saw someone near Esches' lane as her eyes grew more accustomed to the diminished light. *A trespasser?*

Concerned yet curious, Naomi stepped forward and reached for the porch banister. She held her breath as the slender figure dressed like an *Englischer* moved toward the road.

For a few minutes, the woman stood there as though waiting for someone. Naomi stared, and although her eyes were becoming adjusted to the dark, she was unable to determine exactly who this was. *One of the Esch girls? But if so, why dressed so fancy?*

Just then, an open buggy crept down the road and stopped in front of the neighbors' driveway. The young woman got in, and the horse headed quickly in the direction of May Post Office Road.

"What on earth?" Naomi said, her heart pounding.

··· ➤ ➤ ···

In the wee hours, Eva stretched her hand across the mattress and realized Lily must have gone downstairs for a drink, as she sometimes did in the night. Lying in the darkness, she remembered their troubled conversation following Menno's unexpected declaration. She couldn't forget Lily's strange demeanor—the way she'd sobbed so pitifully.

O Lord in heaven, help dear Lily, she prayed silently before falling back to sleep.

She began to dream of ice-skating with Lily, holding hands and spinning over the ice together as little girls, their woolen scarves flying. They skated till they were breathless, and then Eva shared secrets about the kind of husband she wanted to marry when she grew up, whispering that she much preferred a nice man like their father—*"except not a farmer."* But Lily kept silent and shook her head when Eva asked her and pressed for an answer.

··· ➤ ➤ ···

"Sister, you've overslept. I need your help in the kitchen." It was Frona hovering near.

Eva leaned up momentarily to look at the windup clock on the dresser. "Where's Lily?" she muttered sleepily.

Frona shook her head, her hands on her hips. "Haven't seen hide nor hair of her."

"Must be out for a walk."

"Maybe," Frona agreed, stepping back as Eva emerged from bed. "She sure wasn't herself last evening."

"None of us were." Eva reached for her bathrobe on the footboard.

"A brisk walk might do Lily some *gut*." Frona stared at the floor.

"I'll come down as soon as I'm dressed."

"All right, then." Frona left the room.

Hazily, Eva went to the shared closet and chose a green dress and matching apron for the day. High on the shelf, she noticed the small black overnight case missing. *Did Frona lend it to someone, perhaps?* She thought little of it, but then something compelled her to move to the opposite side of the closet, to Lily's dresses. Everything was as it should be, except for one missing lavender dress and black apron.

She turned and made her way to the dresser and opened the drawer where Lily kept her undergarments. Eva's breath caught in her throat. The drawer was completely empty. "For goodness' sake," she whispered.

Going over to the desk where Lily had sat last evening, Eva looked in each of the small drawers, including the narrow one. But there was no sign of a letter there.

"*I'm goin' to bed early,*" Lily had said. Eva clearly recalled the misery in her sister's face. "*My heart pains me. . . .*"

Eva swiftly dressed around and then also checked the petite chest of drawers across the room. There, atop the white doily, she saw an envelope addressed to her in Lily's hand. She unfolded it and began to read.

Dearest Eva,

I'm sorry if this upsets you, but I've decided to leave Eden Valley. I don't want to hurt you or Frona, or our brothers. Be assured this has nothing to do with any of you.

A friend of a friend has invited me to stay with her, so you mustn't worry over me. I've been pondering this move for months now . . . and I've decided to go fancy. With Menno taking over the farmhouse, the timing seems especially right.

I love you, sister, and Frona, too. I know I'll miss all of my family, but things will be better this way.

Lily Esch

"Better . . . *how?*" Stunned, Eva hurried downstairs.

Frona was busy making bread. When she turned to look, she must have caught the strained look on Eva's face. "Don't tell me . . . it's something 'bout Lily."

"Here, read this." She handed the letter to Frona, who took it warily, then read it, frowning.

"Did she say anything 'bout this last night?" asked Frona, looking up.

"*Nee* . . . but it sounds like Lily's been planning this."

"Still, Menno's visit yesterday had to make things worse."

They sat together at the table, absorbing the shocking turn of events. Any thoughts of breakfast had fled with the discovery of the letter.

"Where would Lily go?" Frona asked.

"I have some ideas, but nothin' certain." Eva sniffed softly. "I can't understand it. There isn't anything in her note 'bout contacting us when she arrives at her destination."

"Lily wasn't thinkin' straight." Frona's face was solemn. "She's been lost in her own world for months."

"Oh, sister."

"I mean it. Think back to how she was after Mamma died. Remember?" Frona shook her head.

"I wonder if she has herself an English beau somewhere." Considering some of Lily's comments, it certainly was plausible.

"Wouldn't she have told somebody?" Frona asked, wearing a worried expression. "At least *you.*"

Eva's heart pumped in her ears, but she rejected the urge to panic. *Lily's not familiar with the outside world.* "Surely we'll hear something from her soon."

"Let's just hope she's not taken advantage of," Frona said, her voice solemn.

The thought gave Eva goose pimples. "Lily is old enough to know her own mind, but I'm honestly concerned," she admitted. "I think I'll take the horse and buggy around the neighborhood right quick while Cousin Rachel looks after my shop. If Lily's had second thoughts and is still nearby, maybe I can help her rethink this ridiculous move."

"Our sister's never been so thoughtless, I daresay."

In that moment, Eva understood that Lily hadn't shown her true colors to Frona. No, Lily had always confided in Eva alone, at least after Mamma died. Even so, one thing was sure: Lily had never once mentioned leaving the People. *And she was writing the letter to me last evening, while I was standing there talking to her!*

Eva tried to remember everything Lily had said.

"I have an idea," Eva told Frona and rushed out the back door. Surely it wasn't too late for *some* clue as to Lily's intentions, something that might relieve their worried hearts. Perhaps Naomi Mast had seen something. . . .

The breeze shuffled the new leaves in the maples overhead as their lane straightened out near the road. Eva stopped in her path, aware of the hard, terrible lump in her throat.

Lily's left us, she realized anew, hugging herself. She took a deep breath.

"Lily's left *me.*" If Eva had been a child, she would have sobbed her heart out right there, sitting on the black iron bench her father had placed over by the tulip beds years ago. Where was Lily going? And who had influenced her to leave?

Eva stared pensively down the long road, recalling the many times she and Lily had walked to school together, meeting up with other scholars, as their teacher called them, along the way. Once she'd even used her lunch bucket to ward off a billy goat to protect young Lily.

"Is my sister in danger now?" she whispered.

7

DESPITE her lack of sleep last night, Naomi felt the need to get outdoors. She swept the entire back porch, then headed toward the steps and the sidewalk, taking in the springtime morning—a time to pray about whatever came to mind.

Earlier at breakfast, Abner had readily summarized his day's chores and mentioned he'd gotten word of an estate auction coming up next week down near the home of the well-known carriage maker, Jonas Byler. Abner talked about that for a while, then asked if anything more had come of their son Omar's flirtation with the world. The last time he'd dropped by, Omar had taken them off guard by announcing he wanted to register to vote in the November general election.

"I haven't heard more than what you've told me." She'd paused. "Is it all right to solicit Ida Mae's help, maybe? She and Omar have always been close siblings."

"Well now, I hadn't thought of that." Abner folded his hands. "I'm not getting anywhere with Omar."

"Hope he's not straddlin' the fence at his age."

"Ya wouldn't think so." Abner shook his head. "Ain't a *gut* role model for his children."

"*Nee*, that's for sure."

"But we're not to judge, remember?" Abner had gone on to compliment Naomi on her "mighty perty" pink rhododendron bushes out front. He frequently brought up such thoughtful things at mealtime.

Now, though, Naomi swept briskly, trying to erase last night's troubling image of the distraught woman waiting to be picked up in the middle of the road. She knew for certain she hadn't dreamed it, because she'd left her flashlight on the counter, along with the milk bottle, after returning indoors and going back upstairs. No, what she'd witnessed had been all too real. The flashlight batteries were kaput, and the milk warm.

Naomi inhaled the fresh air and tried to focus on spring's arrival. Sometimes she just couldn't get over the abruptness of it. One week there'd be mere soil in the barren flower beds, and the next an ocean of green sprouted up from the ground to announce a new season. "I should go over and see if the Esch sisters are all right."

But Ida Mae's expecting me, she thought as she carried the broom to the door. It was then she noticed Eva heading this way.

"*Guder Mariye,*" Naomi called.

Eva turned to wave. "*Gut* morning to you." She looked downright miserable as she crossed the road. "Oh, Naomi . . . I have the worst news ever."

Naomi braced herself.

"Lily's run away."

Startled, Naomi wasn't sure she'd heard correctly. "What'd ya say?"

"It's Lily . . . she's gone."

"*Ach,* gone to one of your cousins, maybe?"

"I hope so, but based on the letter she left, I doubt it."

A *letter?* Naomi motioned for Eva to come sit with her on the side porch, seeing how distressed the girl was.

"I saw someone walkin' outside late last night," Naomi said now, wanting to help.

"What time was that?"

"Oh . . . past midnight." She reached for Eva's hand. "And there's more, my dear." She told what she'd seen—the man in the open carriage stopping by for her.

At this, Eva looked completely *ferhoodled.* "An Amish fella?"

Naomi confirmed it was.

"Tell me everything you saw," Eva pleaded. "What was she wearing . . . did ya notice?"

"Well, it was odd. But whoever it was wore fancy clothes—a white skirt and a dark sweater." Oh, she hated telling poor Eva more to compound her worries, but if this would help to locate Lily, it was worth sharing.

Eva paused as if to let this sink in. At last she said, "Sounds like my sister wouldn't be stayin' with anyone Amish, then."

"But we really don't know."

Groaning, Eva pressed her hands together. "I don't see how we missed seein' this coming." She told how stressed Lily had been last night. "And she seemed distracted when our brother Menno visited."

Naomi noticed Eva said nothing about her brother's reason for visiting.

Eva rose from the porch chair all of a sudden. "I'd planned to help Frona deliver some pies this mornin', but I really must look for Lily. If I could just talk to her, she might not . . ." Eva couldn't continue, apparently, and her eyes filled with tears.

"Would ya want me to go with ya? Help ya search?" Naomi offered, thinking Ida Mae would understand in due time.

"*Denki.* But there's no need for you to put yourself out. I don't even know where to start."

Naomi remembered something more—Fannie Ebersol's brief visit to Lily yesterday evening. Quickly, she told Eva about it and what little she'd observed. "Can't be sure it relates, but I wanted you to know."

"Fannie, ya say?" Eva bowed her head, then whispered, "Fannie's not the best influence, 'tween you and me."

"*Ach,* I'm ever so sorry."

Eva reached toward Naomi, a quiver in her lip. "We'll get through this . . . with God's help."

Naomi wasn't sure Eva was in any frame of mind to handle a road horse alone. Nevertheless, the young woman was clearly determined to find her beloved sister.

Eva rushed back to the house and told Frona what she was going to do. "I need to try an' find Lily. Or at least find someone who might know more."

"Well, is it a *gut* idea to let everyone know our business?"

"I won't sit on my hands and do nothing."

Frona shook her head sorrowfully. "You be careful, ya hear?"

"I'll be home as soon as I can." Truth be told, Eva wasn't sure that even a couple of hours would be enough time to cover all the houses up and down Eden Road and the surrounding area.

"Do ya think she's stayin' round here somewhere?" Frona rubbed her chin nervously. "I mean, considering what she wrote, an' all?"

"I pray she's gotten cold feet and stopped in at one of our relatives'. Who knows what she's thinkin'." Stiffening, Eva continued. "But if Naomi's right about what she saw last night, Lily's more than likely gone. A young man in a courting carriage stopped and picked her up."

"*What?*"

Eva assured her that Naomi was nearly positive it was Lily she had seen climb into the carriage. *Wearing fancy clothes, Naomi said.*

"*Ach*, maybe I should go with you." Frona wrung her hands.

"I'll be all right," Eva replied, preferring to go on her own. Honestly, she didn't think she could handle Frona's company just now, not when her older sister was so out of sorts. Eva hurried out to the stable and chose Prince, their best driving horse.

··· ➤ ⭇ ···

Eva fairly flew down Eden Road in the family carriage, uncertain which direction to take. *Where would Lily go?*

Then, remembering what Naomi had said about Fannie Ebersol, she knew where to head first.

Passing over a small bridge and the stream below, she thought of summer, fast approaching. Eva did not recall a single summertime activity that hadn't involved her closest sister.

How could Lily think of leaving?

On the way to Fannie's, Eva changed her mind. There were closer neighbors who might have seen something amiss. So she chose, instead, to work her way to Fannie's, neighbor by neighbor.

Joel and Ida Mae Yoder's pale yellow clapboard farmhouse came into view. The place had a charm all its own, with distinctive black shutters on all the upper windows. It was with some measure of trepidation that Eva tied her horse to the hitching rail near the kitchen windows and scurried around the side yard to the back door.

"Have ya seen Lily?" she blurted when Ida Mae appeared. "She left in the night."

Ida Mae looked befuddled, then outright dismayed, and Eva felt terrible for barging in like this. "*Ach*, I'm sorry to bother ya."

Ida Mae stared down at the thimble on her pointer finger, and the needle in her other hand, and shook her head. "*Nee*," she said. "Ain't seen her."

"In that case, I'd best be goin' on to the next house." Eva asked if she'd simply keep her eyes and ears open, then turned to leave.

"*Da Herr sei mit du*," Ida Mae called after her.

"The Lord be with you, too." Eva glanced back. "*Denki* for your prayers."

"You can count on them." Ida Mae raised her hand, not waving, just standing there straight and stiff and looking concerned.

Eva headed on toward Lester Lantz's tall farmhouse, feeling worse with each passing moment. *Why didn't Lily give me the chance to talk her out of this?*

She observed the line of lake willows set back on Lester's broad sprawl of a meadow, where as girls she and Lily had often perched themselves on the fence at summer's dusk to watch courting buggies drift by, sharing secrets about fellows at church. The grass there was tall, green, and lush, scattered with wild daisies in late spring and summer. Her heart sank as she remembered those happy days, flown away. She pulled into the Lantzes' lane and clambered out of the family buggy.

When she'd described the predicament, Sylvia Lantz encouraged her to trust in the heavenly Father's care for Lily, "wherever she is." And there in her kitchen, Sylvia promised to pray. "I surely will."

"*Denki*."

"You mustn't lose heart," Sylvia said. "Things may look dismal, but there's always a light flickerin' at tunnel's end."

Eva thanked the thoughtful woman and headed out to the carriage. Time was short, and Frona might soon be fretting if Eva didn't hurry back.

Eva urged the horse on to the Ebersol farm, where she found Fannie outdoors, watering her mother's flowers with a hose. When Eva told her that Lily had left, a peculiar look crossed Fannie's face. *Like she isn't surprised.*

"Do you have any idea where my sister's gone?" Deciding she had nothing to lose, Eva asked it outright before she'd even climbed out of the buggy.

Fannie twiddled with the waistband of her long black apron.

"Ach, Fannie, you know Lily nearly as well as I do."

"I'd best not be sayin'."

"Listen, I think you'd better tell me what ya know!"

"But I promised Lily . . ."

Eva clenched her teeth. "What if she falls into difficulties or danger? What then?"

Fannie looked away. "Lily told me very little . . . only that she was leaving."

"Goin' where?"

"She never said."

"How can that be?" Eva asked.

"I'm tellin' the truth." Fannie blinked back tears. "I warned her 'bout leaving. But she was so determined. She's kept everything so secret."

I'm getting nowhere with this girl. Then she mentioned that Naomi had reported having seen Fannie and Lily together yesterday.

"I was just sayin' good-bye, is all," Fannie explained.

"And it didn't occur to you to warn Frona and me 'bout this?"

"Lily will be fine." Fannie sighed. "She knows what she wants. Just let her be."

"What if you're wrong?"

Fannie glared at her. "Would you want *me* to stand in your way if you were bent on doin' something?"

"If it was something like this, I would. Why not? We're here to help each other." Eva kept her gaze on the accomplice, for surely Fannie was that. "Fannie, if you know anything more . . . anything at all, please tell me."

The young woman's lip trembled, but her expression hardened. "Leave me alone! It's not my fault." With that, Fannie dropped the hose, ran to turn off the spigot, and stormed inside.

Eva blew out her breath at Fannie's stubborn but misguided loyalty. *What now, O Lord?*

8

UNABLE to shake Eva's earlier look of consternation, Naomi headed out on foot to Ida Mae's, having forgotten her sturdy walking stick. It wasn't that she felt old at seventy-three, but some days brought unexpected and painful twinges that were difficult to ignore. Abner encouraged her at times, saying, *"You're still my spring chicken."*

She had to smile, despite her present concerns, knowing the kind, jovial man she'd married—never a lack of laughter around the house, especially first thing in the morning. Marrying Abner Mast had been the best thing she could have ever done for herself.

Once she arrived at Ida Mae's, Naomi felt content to simply sit at the quilting frame and make tiny stitches, not bringing up what had transpired with Lily Esch.

"You're not so chatty today, Mamm." Her daughter's big hazel eyes were intent. "Somethin's bothering ya."

The grapevine would have its way soon enough, but for their time together, Naomi preferred to skirt the tension.

"Are ya worried 'bout Lily?"

Naomi's breath caught in her throat. "You've heard?"

"Eva dropped by just a bit ago, askin' if I knew anything of her sister's whereabouts."

"'Tis a pity. The Esch girls have had more than their share of challenges."

Ida Mae reached inside her gray dress sleeve for a handkerchief and patted her eyes. "I wondered recently if Lily wasn't itchin' to get out and see the world. 'Specially after Dottie passed away—Lily seemed restless to me." She shook her head, sighing. "Guess she finally did it."

"Are ya sayin' she wanted to travel to other places—just to see new sights?" Naomi wondered if Lily wasn't actually interested in *living* in the outside world; maybe she just wanted to experience it during her *Rumschpringe*—the running-around time before joining church. *But where'd she get the money?*

Her daughter rose to make some hot tea. "I s'pose it must be enticing for a curious young woman, wanting to understand fancy ways," Ida Mae said, reaching for two teacups. "All the perty pictures of other states in those geography books, ya know. I remember how it stirred up ideas in me, too, back when."

Sightseeing? thought Naomi. *Is that what Lily is up to?*

"I wouldn't be surprised if her brother Menno didn't play a part in this," Ida Mae was saying as she carried some honey to the table. "Bena told me the other day that her Menno's ready to take over the Esch farm, which might leave the girls scrambling for another place to live."

"Well, now." No wonder Eva mentioned Menno's visit. But she hadn't revealed any of this. *Why not?* Naomi's heart sank. Still, she might've known this would eventually happen, given his parents were both gone now. Naomi supposed Menno was the designated heir to the old homestead.

When the water came to a boil, Ida Mae poured it into the floral cups and offered her mother a variety of teas to choose from. They sat awhile, stirring and sipping, and Naomi's heart went out to all three Esch girls.

Later, when Naomi had drunk her tea and completed a row of stitches, she put down her needle and thimble. "I wanted to mention somethin' else, Ida Mae. Your father and I were talkin' earlier about your brother Omar. Has he said anything about wanting to vote in the presidential election come November?"

Ida Mae's head bobbed up. "*Ach*, why would he want to?"

"Honestly, he's so intrigued by Ronald Reagan and politics in general, makes your father and me a bit concerned."

"Omar's prob'ly itchin' for lower taxes for farmers."

Naomi shook her head. "Who's to say?"

"Well, voting ain't something Joel and I would ever consider doin'. Might be only a handful of Amish who would. Maybe Joel knows more 'bout what Omar's thinkin'."

"*Jah*, talk to your husband and see." Naomi poured a second cup of tea. "Still, I hope Omar's changed his mind. The bishop's not so keen on getting involved with national politics. We're sojourners here, just a-passin' through."

Ida Mae agreed. "There's plenty to do just to keep our churches runnin' smoothly. I say, let the world run the government!"

··· ➤ ➤ ···

Some time later, Alan Yoder, Ida Mae's nephew-in-law, arrived with a baker's dozen of fresh biscuits from his mother. Right away he started talking about Lily. "I heard this morning from Fannie Ebersol's brother Thomas that Lily's left for good."

Word's traveling fast, Naomi thought.

Once people heard the news, likely it would be weeks before some sense of calm returned to Eden Valley. She couldn't help wondering if young Alan had used this delivery as a way to spread gossip.

"Lily asked me to take her to town just last week," Alan said, eyes wide. "She never said what she was doin', but it seemed mighty important."

Ida Mae glanced at Naomi. "What do you mean?"

Alan pushed his fists into his trouser pockets. "Well, she made me wait for her, and when she came out of the mall, she was clutching a small, flat paper sack." He looked up now, singling out Ida Mae. "Didn't think nothin' of it at the time."

Ida Mae stared at him. "What're ya sayin', Alan?"

"*Puh!* My big mouth." He had the good sense to look sheepish.

Naomi's interest was piqued. And because she didn't wish to *renkle*, she bit her lip. Disgusted, she said nicely yet firmly, "It's kind of you to drop by, Alan. Now, don't ya have some other deliveries to make?"

With that, the lad turned and headed outdoors.

Feeling all in, Naomi returned to the front room and sat down at the quilting frame. *Without a doubt, there's more to all of this than poor Eva may ever know,* she realized. *Once young folks leave to become* Englischers, *they're rarely heard from again. . . .*

··· ➤ ➤ ···

Fannie's attitude this morning continued to disturb Eva, and she did not understand why Lily, who'd written of wanting a life away from the People, would arrange for an Amishman to pick her up last night.

Surely, Lily will become disillusioned with the modern world and come back, Eva thought. This hope squeezed her heart, and she tried to take comfort from Sylvia Lantz's wisdom that God's hand was on her dear sister.

Eva slowed the horse and headed back toward home, discouraged. The sun was inching ever higher; Frona was likely cooking the noon meal.

A mere quarter mile from home, she noticed Alfred Dienner pulling out of his father's dirt lane in his buggy. Alfred spotted her, too, and waved politely, his smile enveloping his tan face. She felt a twinge of guilt for having accepted his invitation to play Ping-Pong.

"Alfred's heart turns to sauce when you're around," Lily had once teased, insisting there was nothing wrong with marrying a farmer. *"If you love him enough,"* she'd added.

If anyone took hard work seriously, it was Alfred. He was well respected in the community, too. *"Your love would grow,"* Eva could imagine Mamma saying.

It might, if the Lord wills, Eva thought, putting on a smile for Alfred as she slowed Prince to less than a trot.

She felt a twinge of sadness. A farmer's wife had no time to keep up with a thriving candy store. *Maybe someday in the future, once the children are grown.*

Alfred pulled up beside her, but his smile had faded. In fact, he looked downright somber. "I was just headin' over your way, Eva. Funny runnin' into you."

"Have ya already eaten your stash of candy?"

He gripped the reins and turned slightly in his seat, his manner unusually tentative. "I received an unexpected letter this mornin'," he said. "I'm afraid it changes everything for us, Eva."

She waited for him to continue as his strange phrasing echoed in her head: *"Changes everything for us."* *He's stretching things,* she thought.

"I'm leaving for Kingston, Wisconsin, at first light tomorrow," he said in a quick flow of words. "I wanted you to know."

"You're goin' away?" This was the last thing she'd expected.

"Till sometime this fall."

A long time!

"I need to lend a hand to my father's cousin. He's laid up with a bad back."

"Your family will surely miss ya."

"I didn't want you to think I quit goin' to youth gatherings and whatnot." Alfred seemed to struggle with what to say. "My father thinks it'll be a *gut* change for me." He nodded as though affirming this to himself. "Doing something besides farming, ya know."

She was baffled. "What will you be doin'?" She embarrassed herself with her sudden curiosity.

"Woodworking," he said, but she noticed his expression, like his heart wasn't much in it.

"You might enjoy yourself, *jah?*"

"Hard to imagine," Alfred admitted. "But that's not all I wanted to discuss with you." He leaned across his buggy seat, smiling again. "I know we haven't spent much time together, but I'd like to write to you while I'm away . . . if you're agreeable. Maybe court ya by mail."

She gasped inwardly. It struck Eva as ironic that, after her hesitations about becoming a farmer's wife, Alfred was seemingly being transferred to Wisconsin to learn a trade. And while he hadn't hidden his interest in her, he'd never seemed quite so serious as now.

"Alfred, this is all so sudden."

His countenance dropped. "I'll write more 'bout what I'm thinking, if that suits ya." He paused. "A *gut* way to keep in touch, *jah?*"

She opened her mouth to answer but stopped. Alfred was staring at the floor of his buggy, and she felt just terrible. *What should I say?*

"Eva?" he asked, clearly anxious for her answer.

"Sure, if you'd like to, Alfred," she heard herself reply.

"*Wunnerbaar!*" He clicked his tongue to the horse and waved as it pulled him forward.

During the ride home, Eva felt as if she were at the bottom of a lake, struggling to reach the surface for a gasp of air. By the time she directed Prince into their driveway, she was so flustered she didn't know which she was more worried about: her sister's worldly future or her own.

9

JED awakened in the wee hours the following Monday, anxious to catch the early train to Lancaster, Pennsylvania. He'd jumped at the chance to please Uncle Ervin by going on this trip but was also concerned the shop might fall behind on orders, even though Perry would continue working in Jed's absence. Uncle Ervin had reassured him all would be well. He'd even suggested Jed make sure he took time for socializing while there. *The better for matchmaking?*

As he put on his Sunday best—black broadfall trousers and vest, and a crisp white shirt—his thoughts drifted easily to Lydiann. Bits and pieces of conversation when they were out riding or walking came to his remembrance, and images of her smiling knowingly, reading him the way she did so well. And oh, her wonderful sense of humor!

"Once we're married, I'll have to know how you like your eggs," she'd said once.

"Over easy." He'd played along.

"No omelets, then?"

"I'll eat whatever slides off your skillet."

"Careful now, Jed. You might live to regret that."

They'd shared the heartiest laugh.

Jed pushed the memory from his mind, wondering if his youngest sister would remember to wake up early enough to make breakfast. He hadn't wanted to trouble his mother to do so.

Opening his bedroom door, he immediately smelled the familiar aroma

558

of eggs and sausage and walked to the kitchen, where seventeen-year-old Bettina was already dressed for the day. She looked wide-awake as she carried his plate over from the stove and set it down in front of him before taking a seat herself.

It was still dark outside, and Jed could hear the ticking of insects from the slightly open window behind him. The wide plank floors showed the marks of the years in the soft yellow light of the gas lamp over the oak table.

"How long will ya be gone, *Bruder?*" Bettina asked, thoughtful as always. It was no wonder this tenderhearted, soft-spoken sister already had a serious beau at such a young age. She sat across from him, eyes alert and hair parted straight down the middle. Her face was already sprinkled with freckles from hours spent in the sun planting the family garden with Mamm.

"Only a week." He explained why Uncle Ervin was sending him, leaving off the possibility of meeting Jonas Byler's granddaughters. Bettina would have had too much fun with that little tidbit.

"Might be *gut* to get away for a while." She looked kindly at him.

He nodded. "It's been a while, ain't?"

"Maybe ya won't be so *ferhoodled* when ya come back."

"Somebody's gotta keep you on your toes," he said.

"With brothers like you, I'm gonna need more toes." She left the table and brought back a cup of coffee, setting it down near his plate. "Seriously, I'll be prayin' for ya, Jed. You could use some happiness."

"*Denki.*"

She laughed a little, her spirits high this morning. "I might have something to confide in ya when you're back," she whispered, leaning forward.

"Surely it's not—"

Bettina put her finger to her lips. "Shh, 'tis a secret."

He had a sinking feeling but ignored it. There was plenty of time to deal with whatever it was. Besides, he knew her well enough not to probe further. "Ain't goin' New Order on me, are ya?"

She chuckled and shook her head. "Can you imagine *me* drivin' a car?"

"Well, I've seen ya drive a buggy. . . ."

She frowned with mock annoyance. "Are you pickin' on the sister who woke up early to make breakfast?"

"And it was mighty tasty, let me say."

Sighing, she regarded him with a wistful look, and a long moment passed between them. "*Ach*, Jed. It's so *gut* to see ya smile again. I've missed that."

He took a hesitant sip of coffee and glanced over the top at her. "I know ya wouldn't have gotten up before dawn for just any brother."

"*Jah*, you're the fortunate one."

When he finished, she removed his plate and took it to the sink, and he headed upstairs to close his suitcase. *Go before me today, Lord God, I pray. And make Thy will known to me.*

When Seth Keim, the hired van driver, arrived, Jed was surprised to see other passengers in the second and third seats. He slipped into the passenger side up front with Seth, a slight man in his early forties who had been driving the Amish for at least a decade. They exchanged brief greetings and Jed settled in for the ride, not wanting to add to the talk.

One woman was chattering excitedly about her "little loom room," where she wove different yarns into "the pertiest rugs you ever did see!" Jed didn't glance back, but by the sound of it, she was trying to encourage, even recruit, another woman to do the same. "A room like that's the best place in the house to retreat from *die Kinnerzucht*. A separate place to call your own, for sewing or weaving and whatnot, is a must sometimes."

Jed couldn't imagine his own mother admitting that her children were too noisy or underfoot. In all truth, he doubted his mother would have even wanted a hideaway workroom like the woman behind him. None of Jed's aunts or grandmothers had ever clamored for a separate sewing room, either, that he knew of. *Somehow, they managed. And I think we're better off for the time they took with us.*

He recalled his youngest sister's sweet-spirited temperament. Bettina, being the baby of the family, had been somewhat doted upon—much as his Lydiann had been. Yet neither of them had turned out the least bit spoiled.

Another woman in the van spoke up behind him now. "S'pose I *could* use a quiet place set apart . . . but for my ailin' mother," she said, her voice lowering as she continued. "Mamm's been planning her funeral here lately—every detail, right down to the kind of food she wants served."

"She needs privacy for that?" The first woman sounded shocked.

"Well, she's jittery a lot and needs her rest. Plus, she doesn't want anyone to see what she's writing in her journal. There are days she talks of setting fire to it . . . must be she doesn't want us to see who she's blowing off steam about."

Jed smiled to himself, and if he wasn't mistaken, Seth was over there chuckling behind the wheel. Jed had never heard of someone planning a funeral in advance, but then, it took all types of personalities.

He decided to ignore the frivolous conversation. Alliance was just one hour away. There, he would catch his train to Lancaster.

It was still too dark to read the old classic *The Pilgrim's Progress*. He'd read the book once before but liked to carry reading material wherever he went, even in the buggy. *"You never know when a good book might come in handy,"* his father liked to say, particularly when Mamm or Bettina needed a ride somewhere to shop. *Daed* was of a mind that a book was his "insurance" against waiting idly for his womenfolk in town.

Something else his father had urged Jed and his seven siblings to do was trust in God's provision for the direction of their lives. *"This means believing the Lord will stand strong when you cannot . . . that He will hold you up,"* Daed had said.

This wisdom had been essential for Jed this past year—each time he was tempted to doubt, thinking he couldn't continue on without Lydiann.

"Real *gut* to see ya headin' to Pennsylvania," Seth said, glancing his way. "A change of place is sometimes helpful."

"Just doin' my boss's bidding."

"Well, have yourself a nice time."

"*Denki*," Jed said. And for the first time since Lydiann's death, he realized he was looking forward to something new, if only for a few days.

While waiting in the crowd of passengers to board the eastbound train, Jed overheard an older man telling a young boy about the various train cars they could explore on their trip. "There are dining cars, lounge cars, sleeping cars, and even a dome car where you can look at the sky and all around. You'll see."

"Is there ice cream in the dining car?" the boy asked, his face hopeful.

"We'll find out, won't we?" the older man replied as he ruffled the boy's hair.

Everywhere Jed turned, people were paired up—young couples holding hands, elderly couples assisting each other, families with children. *People in love.*

Once he was on board the train, Jed chose a window seat on the right side of the aisle. As of the first jerk forward, the seat next to him was still vacant. *Like usual.* He turned to gaze out the window and embraced the new day with another silent prayer.

Unknowingly, Jed had drifted off to sleep and was awakened, startled, when someone sneezed. In his groggy state, he bumped something hard wedged between the seat and the coach wall. A brief investigation revealed it was a hardback copy of *Little Women*. He'd seen Bettina reading the classic novel last summer.

Opening the book, Jed saw no name or identification on the front pages. With his own treasured library—accumulated over more than a decade—he'd always printed his full name and address in plain view on the front page.

Thumbing through, he discovered a wrinkled photograph tucked between pages forty-four and forty-five—a pretty Amish girl, possibly in her late teens. He studied the picture more closely, finding it curious that the young woman looked so boldly into the camera while wearing a white prayer *Kapp* shaped like a heart—the characteristic head covering for the Lancaster County Old Order Amish. Though the picture was black and white, it was clear she wore a cape dress and matching apron, as well. The photo looked as though it had been torn from a strip of others, with the bottom of the next picture showing a young woman's folded hands.

Why would a devout girl have her picture taken?

He turned the photograph over and saw penned on the back: *The best and worst day of my life.*

Still more curious, Jed returned the picture to its place between the pages and scanned through the book, quickly noting that the story was focused on four young sisters growing up in New England during the time of the Civil War.

Definitely not my choice of reading material!

Yet, while paging through the book, he came across many notes penciled in the margin—the note writer's own thoughts about family and grief and death, as well as a few tender words about romance and love.

There were also underlined passages, such as *"You are like a chestnut burr, prickly outside, but silky-soft within, and a sweet kernel, if one can only get at it. Love will make you show your heart some day, and then the rough burr will fall off."*

Jed smiled and wondered if the book's owner had been thinking of someone in particular. Certainly he had known a few people who could fit that description!

Two hours later, when the train slowed and then came to a stop in Pittsburgh, a number of passengers got off. By now, Jed had already breezed through a good portion of the book's margin notes and underlined passages, glancing now and then at the photograph to put the words and the note writer together in his mind.

The new passengers boarded and rustled about, taking their places and making conversation with seatmates. Once again no one occupied the seat next to him, leaving him alone for the duration of the journey, but this time the prospect pleased Jed.

He returned to the pages, captivated by the girl's thoughts, sensing a growing connection to her, at times moved by her delicate honesty.

He closed the book, recalling how quickly he and Lydiann had bonded, how rapidly he had known she was the girl for him. *Almost immediately.* That sort of connection came once in a lifetime, or so he presumed. He leaned back in his seat, allowing a gentle sadness to wash over him.

Whatever he'd had with Lydiann was gone forever. There was no point in wishing for it again.

10

TWO days had passed since the unthinkable had happened. In the meantime, Eva and Frona, and their brothers, too, tried to make the best of it. Menno and Rufus had taken it upon themselves to cover nearly all of Eden Valley, the areas beyond Eva's Saturday search, but to no avail. It seemed no one had heard from Lily.

This morning Eva had written in her diary, hoping Lily might simply walk in the door at any moment, having changed her mind. *"I'm sorry I worried you,"* she might say, and whatever agony they'd all felt would be drowned out by sheer relief.

Presently, Eva and Frona were having a dinner of baked chicken and rice, taking their time to plan the week, since they'd gotten the Monday washing hung out much earlier.

Eva suggested, "We might take your tasty jams and my specialty candies down to the Quarryville market come Thursday. What do ya say?" Eva was certain going to market might distract them for a while, at least, from their mutual woes. And, too, perhaps someone might know something about Lily farther south of them.

Frona nodded. "Fine with me." She looked up from her meal. "Word has it a lot of people are comin' into the area for an auction."

"Farm or cattle sale?"

"It's an estate auction takin' place two farms down from the Byler carriage shop," Frona informed her.

"Is that right?"

"Should be quite the all-day event, what with not only the house and everything in it being auctioned off, but the barn equipment and the animals, too."

Eva listened and hoped they might have time to attend.

"I also heard that Jonas Byler may retire come this fall," Frona said. "Might leave a hole in the buggy-making business round here."

Eva wondered how that would be for the highly sought after buggy maker, respected all over Lancaster County. Was Jonas Byler looking forward to the change? "It's hard to hear of older folks having to give up what they've loved doing so long."

"We don't know if it's for his health's sake." Frona reached for the butter dish, a homemade biscuit in her other hand.

"Might just be," Eva said, realizing how much less laundry there had been today. Goodness, but it seemed Lily had nearly as many dresses and aprons as both Eva and Frona combined. *There's something about the sharp smell of our homemade soap that Lily loves,* Eva thought sadly.

In spite of what they did to keep themselves occupied, Lily was in the background of Eva's every thought.

They finished the meal without saying much more to each other, and when dessert was served, Eva made over Frona's chocolate macaroons, still deliciously soft.

"Lily's favorite," Frona remarked. "I'd be willin' to make them every day if she'd just return," she added.

"Maybe she's missing us and already thinkin' of starting home."

Frona nodded slowly, like she wasn't so sure.

Eva reached for another cookie. Not that it helped anything, but the sweet taste couldn't hurt.

Later, while she and Frona were redding up the kitchen, Eva mentioned an upcoming work frolic. The deacon had invited all the young men and women in the church district to help clean up the schoolhouse. "Would ya like to go with me?" she asked. "There'll likely be some nice young men there."

"What on earth. Who are ya thinkin' of—me or you?"

"It's been a while."

"*Puh!*" Frona muttered, the dishes clattering. Another moment passed. "When is it?"

"About two weeks away."

Frona's eyes instantly looked more gray than blue. She stopped washing the dish in her hand and frowned. "You must still be thinking 'bout Menno's announcement."

"His *what?*"

"Well, what would you call it?" Frona said.

Eva shrugged. *She's so dramatic. . . .*

"Well, you were here when he laid it all out." Frona resumed washing the dishes. "I'm thinkin' of going to see him after the clothes are brought in and folded."

"To try an' change his mind?"

"Give him a piece of mine, maybe."

"Oh dear."

"It can't hurt, can it?"

Sure might, Eva thought. She wished Frona would forget about arguing with Menno. What she really wanted was for Frona to commit to going to the work frolic at the schoolhouse. It would get their mind off things. She brought it up again.

"I'll have to think on it." The evasive answer gave Eva little hope of Frona's agreeing.

She knew better than to push too hard with this sister.

Jed was met at the Lancaster train depot that afternoon by Jonas's grandnephew Wallie Byler, who introduced Jed to the short, dark-haired driver, Neil Zimmerman. "It's *gut* of you to come," Jed told them as Neil turned the key in the ignition and backed out of the parking space. A small orange cat with a cheesy grin swung from the rearview mirror—a character Jed had seen once or twice in a cartoon strip.

"Wouldn't have it any other way," Wallie said right next to Jed in the second row.

They made small talk about the weather and tomorrow's auction near Quarryville. During a lull in conversation, Neil switched on the radio and Jed was shocked to hear the news from faraway South Korea—an uprising was following what a reporter called "a massacre" in Gwangju. "These protests against martial law are the necessary crucible of a grass-roots movement to overturn a repressive regime," the reporter said. "More than two hundred students died for freedom."

Wallie glanced at Jed and shook his head. "If folks could just get along, what a better world this would be."

So tragic. Hearing of such mayhem made Jed all the more grateful he had not had to take part in any wars, even to serve overseas as a non-combatant like some of his male relatives had during the war in Vietnam.

Neil turned down the volume and asked if Jed and Wallie wanted to get a quick bite to eat. They were definitely in agreement, and Neil made the turn into a fast-food place.

"It's nearly suppertime round here," Wallie said with a tug on his black suspenders. His light hair showed a distinct dent from his straw hat, which he must have worn earlier. "Did ya have anything to eat on the trip?"

Jed nodded. "My youngest sister sent along ham sandwiches, but I sure could go for a cheeseburger now."

Right quick, Wallie pulled out his wallet while they waited in line at the drive-through. "Uncle Jonas insisted on treating."

"*Ach*, can't let him do that." Jed reached into his pocket.

"*Nee*, better let him have the last word on this, or I'll be in hot water." Wallie laughed. "If you don't know what I mean, you will shortly."

Jed looked forward to meeting Jonas Byler. "Will either of yous be goin' to the neighbors' estate auction, then?" he asked.

"Bright an' early. But I'm just goin' for the food."

Jed chuckled.

Wallie went on to talk about his big dairy operation near Gap. "But I'm happy to help Uncle Jonas out . . . and glad to meet you, too."

When they picked up their burgers and fries and the chocolate milk-shakes Wallie had ordered, they headed south on Route 272 toward Quarryville.

They stopped for additional Amish passengers near an area known as Willow Street, including one younger couple who seemed taken with each other. *Plainly in love.* Jed thought again of the book he'd found on the train, and it crossed his mind: What if he could meet the note writer, the pretty girl in the photograph?

It was a crazy idea. *Besides,* he realized, *whoever wrote in the book might be mortified to know someone else is privy to her thoughts.*

Away from curious and judgmental eyes, he would look again at the forbidden photo later. Maybe he'd missed something about the young woman. *Maybe someone around Quarryville might recognize her . . . if she's from that area.*

He shook his head at the fanciful notion. He couldn't bear to put such a thoughtful soul at risk by showing the picture around, even if it meant he might find her.

11

JONAS Byler's handshake was unexpectedly vigorous for as spindly as he looked—a tall, tanned man in his late seventies. Jonas graciously greeted Jed, then motioned for his wife to come over. "This here's Jedediah from Berlin, Ohio—Ervin Stutzman's nephew, ya know." Jonas introduced him to Elsie before pointing the way into the light and airy kitchen.

Austere in its simplicity, the kitchen reminded Jed of his paternal grandmother's with its low windows along the south side of the room and a considerable freestanding pine hutch, yellowed with age.

"*Willkumm*," Elsie said, her black apron a menu of baking projects—splotches of flour and something sticky, like jam.

"I appreciate your hospitality."

"We hope you'll feel free to stay as long as you'd like." Elsie grinned at Jed and gestured for Jonas to take him upstairs to the spare room. "There's a washroom just down the hallway up there," she added. "We're tryin' to keep up with the times, I guess you could say." She laughed a nervous little laugh.

Jed was surprised she felt it necessary to excuse the indoor plumbing. His parents' home had been updated that way back in the mid-fifties. *Before I was born.*

"We'll have a later supper than usual," Elsie called again up the stairs. "Chust take your time getting settled."

Jed didn't have the heart to say he'd wolfed down a hamburger and fries on the way there.

Leading the way, Jonas opened the door to Jed's room. "My son and family are comin' for the meal tonight—Mose and Bekah and their two youngest daughters . . . both courtin' age." Jonas winked slyly.

Keeping his smile in check, Jed assumed Uncle Ervin must have put a bug in Jonas's ear. *Could be interesting,* he thought and quickly unpacked, then went to freshen up. Strubblich *hair will never do for this meal!*

When Sylvia Lantz stepped into The Sweet Tooth around closing time at four o'clock, Eva smiled. "Happy to see ya," she said, going around the counter to greet her neighbor.

"Came to bring some cheer." Sylvia was all dressed up in a pretty black cape dress and matching apron and wearing her crisp white *Kapp.*

"You couldn't have arrived at a better time." Eva went to the display case and removed the last two bonbons, setting them in a bowl. "Let's go over and sit in the kitchen and have ourselves a little taste of chocolate."

Sylvia was quick to agree, and as they walked through the hall and into the main house, she mentioned receiving a letter from her daughter Tilly Barrows, who lived in Rockport, Massachusetts, with her family. As a youth, Tilly had decided against joining church and had eventually married an outsider after moving to the English world. She and her husband, Kris, had three children—nearly seven-year-old identical twin daughters, Jenya and Tavani, and eighteen-month-old Mel, named for Tilly's brother, Melvin Lantz.

"Will they be comin' for another visit?" Eva hoped so for Sylvia's sake.

"As soon as the twins are out of school for the summer." Sylvia opened the letter once they'd seated themselves at the kitchen table. "Just thought I'd read a little bit of it to you. All right?"

Eva was glad Frona was upstairs—she could hear the footsteps overhead. For her own part, she was all for listening to Tilly's letter, as she'd always liked Sylvia, possibly because Mamma had thought so highly of her.

"I won't tire you with everything Tilly wrote," Sylvia said as she scanned through the lines. "Ah, here we are."

She began to read aloud.

"Our twins have learned to make beautiful little quilting stitches, Mamma—isn't that such happy news? And they can say simple words and phrases in *Deitsch*, even though they haven't grown up with the People, as I did. Seems that Ruth and I let that slip into our conversation more than we know! I thought it might be an encouragement to you and Dat, hearing that some of the Plain culture has found its way to your English grandchildren."

Sylvia looked up from the letter, tears threatening. "Oh, Eva, isn't this the dearest thing? Like a melody to my heart."

Eva hardly knew what to say. Was Sylvia trying to offer her some hope about Lily? But it wasn't hope really; it seemed more like giving Lily up to the world and being satisfied with a letter or two.

"I never dreamed I'd get such letters from our Tilly, tellin' the truth."

Eva knew that Tilly and her younger sister, Ruth, had nearly broken Sylvia's and Lester's hearts. But seeing Sylvia's response to this letter, Eva sensed Sylvia had made peace with losing her dear children to the outside world. Perhaps the years had washed away the worst of the pain.

"Sometimes I wish they'd all relocate to Eden Valley so I could get my fill of seein' them and my grandchildren."

"Ain't likely they'd become Amish, is it?" Eva asked, knowing her own mother had posed the same question to Sylvia after Tilly and Ruth left the People. Against her husband's advice, Sylvia had clung to that hope, even though she'd confided in Eva's mother that she knew in her heart that Tilly and her family would never think of such a move.

"*Nee*, not likely, though I'd like nothing more." Sylvia dried her eyes with a hankie from her pocket. "A mother's heart is never far from her children."

When Frona came downstairs, Eva offered some of her chocolate macaroons to Sylvia, which brought smiles all around. "I do believe I've had my fill of sweets for the week," Sylvia said, thanking them.

Later, Eva walked with her to the end of the lane, aware of the pungent smell of manure in the air. "I'm glad you stopped in." She paused.

"If I know you, you're prayin' for Lily." Sylvia gave her a kiss on the cheek. "Dottie raised you well."

Standing in the road, Eva watched her mother's friend head back down the road, Sylvia's black dress swirling around her bare ankles.

She wondered what had motivated Tilly to leave her family behind and strike out into unfamiliar territory. *Was it frightening for her at first? Or an adventure?*

Thinking again of Lily, she trembled. *Oh, write to me, sister, please write soon!*

Jed was seated to the left of Mose Byler at the long table that evening, with Mose's wife, Bekah, and their daughters Lovina and Orpha across from Jed. *To encourage conversation, no doubt,* he thought.

Elsie sat to the right of Jonas, who presided at the head of the table. She passed the food first to her husband, and then the platters went to the men—pork chops with mashed potatoes and gravy, baked beans, and corn pudding.

Jonas and his son Mose talked for a while, but it wasn't long before Jed, too, was drawn into the conversation. He was mindful of the bashful though pretty blond girls across the table. Orpha, who said she was nineteen, and Lovina, twenty-one, glanced up from their plates every so often. Mose helped things along, mentioning that both young women would be at the auction tomorrow.

"They're helping with the food," Jonas interjected, leaning forward to catch Jed's eye. "*Wunnerbaar-gut* cooking."

"Home cooking's best," Jed replied, smiling back at Orpha, who seemed the more outgoing of the two. "What type of food?"

Orpha replied, "Oh, nearly whatever you have a hankerin' for. Delicious soups: ham and bean, ya know, and chicken corn soup, too. There'll be ham and cheese sandwiches, hot dogs, barbecue, whoopie pies, cream-filled doughnuts, homemade ice cream, and all kinds of pies, including banana cream."

"My mouth's watering already."

"*Des gut,*" Orpha replied, glancing curiously at Lovina.

"Ever been to an auction round here?" Mose Byler asked, eyes intent.

"This is my first visit to the area."

"And you're enjoying working in Ohio with my mother's cousin Ervin Stutzman?" Mose said.

"So far, I'm just an apprentice."

Orpha glanced at Elsie, then at her mother. "That's the best way to start, ain't so?" she said at last.

Jed nodded, smiling back at her. *She's coming out of her shell.*

When it was time for dessert, Elsie's strawberry pie got calls for seconds from Jonas and Mose, but considering Jed's full stomach, he respectfully declined.

Later, Jed found himself alone with Orpha and sitting on the back porch. They weren't by themselves for long. Lovina and her mother wandered outside a few minutes later, heading around the walkway to visit Elsie's older sister living in the *Dawdi Haus*. Then, not so long after, Mose and Jonas appeared and pretended not to see Jed and Orpha there as they made their way over to the carriage shop, full of talk.

When it was just the two of them again, Jed commented on the peacefulness of the hilly countryside around his native Berlin farmland, and Orpha was quick to say how nice it was right there in rural Quarryville. They talked about hobbies and favorite activities—he surmised volleyball was the one commonality between them. The longer they visited, the more he missed the easy style of conversation he'd enjoyed with Lydiann. He wanted to be companionable to Orpha, but everything he said came out awkward and stilted.

Am I trying too hard?

Later, when Mose and Bekah and their daughters left for home, he was invited to join Jonas and Elsie for their Bible reading in the front room. Thankful for this quiet and reflective time, Jed asked again for the Lord's guidance, as he did every night during the prayer time.

When he'd said good-night, Jed headed upstairs, where he spotted *Little Women* on the table near the bed. He hesitated for a moment, feeling more than a little silly as he finally gave in to his whim and turned to the page where he'd left off, marked by the photograph.

Another neatly printed note ran down the side of the page: *How will I know when I find true love?*

Jed closed the book. If he hadn't met Lydiann, he might have wondered this himself. Lydiann hadn't just been his "true love." She herself had been *true*, a young woman of the highest character and noble intention, earnest to do God's will.

That's true love, he thought.

Looking at the photo once more, Jed knew the owner was obviously living too close to the world. It wasn't uncommon for restless Amish girls in *Rumschpringe* to follow their boyfriends right out of the community.

He studied the woman's eyes in the picture. They were kind and bright, but something was amiss.

Again he deliberated the notion of searching for this young woman, who despite her struggles with the ordinance, had written such poignant thoughts about life. By the looks of the delicate *Kapp*, surely the girl lived somewhere in Lancaster County.

But where?

The grandfather clock downstairs chimed ten times, and Jed prepared to retire for the night. Morning would come on cat's paws, sneaking up on him.

12

ARLY the next morning after breakfast, Jed left Jonas's house to peruse the barn equipment up the road, already displayed for the auction. Other men were trickling onto the property, a smattering of Amish and Mennonites and even a handful of English farmers—many of them milling about and surveying the tools and other offerings.

A number of men had gravitated to the stable, talking rapidly in *Deitsch*, a few puffing on pipes, a habit Jed hadn't noticed much in public places back home. *Except for some of the older Amishmen who smoke on their own property, like Uncle Ervin.*

It was certain there would be plenty of competition in the bidding for the barn's and house's contents, all of which were to be sold in separate lots.

Jed observed Mose and his wife riding into the lane, Lovina and Orpha squeezed into the second bench seat with two other younger girls. Right now, though, Jed needed to go over to sign up for his bidding number, in case he saw something that caught his interest.

Several older men were chewing the fat as Jed made his way into the line for the bidding numbers. "Word has it a clinic in Philly has health screening tests for seniors, free of charge," one of the long-bearded men was saying.

"Hadn't heard that," said another.

"How old do ya have to be?" asked a third.

"A senior."

"Well, I've got a few years yet till I hit eighty," the second man said.

"Seems to me that's a super-senior," the first man said with a chuckle.

Jed grinned, and when he'd acquired his number, he moseyed out to the barn to have a look at the animals, eager for the day when he might own more than one road horse and perhaps some goats or chickens.

Later, on his way back toward the yard, he noticed Mose tie his mare to the hitching post, the girls standing in a cluster nearby. The thought of having to talk exclusively with Orpha Byler again felt uncomfortable in light of last evening's porch encounter.

···➤ ➤···

As they lingered at the breakfast table, Naomi Mast pressed Abner about the estate auction down near Quarryville. "Wouldn't it be nice to go for just a little while?"

Paging through *The Budget*, Abner appeared to have other things on his mind. "There's nothin' I'm looking to buy."

"Are ya so sure we wouldn't enjoy ourselves?" she pleaded.

"Fairly sure."

Naomi set her teacup down and added, "We could have some delicious food while we walk around a bit."

Abner inclined his head toward her. "This must mean a lot to ya."

"Well, I've been a-turnin' the idea round and round this morning, is all. We meet such interesting people at these sales, and some of our grandchildren might be there, too. Our son Elam will be, for sure."

Abner set his paper down and came over to the sink to plant a kiss on her lips. "I remember that perty smile of yours, Naomi, and I haven't seen it yet this mornin'. S'pose that means we best be ridin' down to that auction you're so keen on."

"Oh, Abner, ya mean it?" She couldn't keep from smiling as she leaned happily into his strong arms.

"I do indeed."

···➤ ➤···

Their rhubarb was coming on fast now, and from the kitchen window, Eva observed Frona basking in the sunlight like a child. She'd gone out to pick right after breakfast while Eva laid out her candies and other goodies for tomorrow's customers.

Frona was happiest, Eva decided, when she was putting up jam, something she did for the tourists who came to The Sweet Tooth and discovered the preserves for sale alongside Eva's confections. *Sweets upon sweets!*

To keep from going *narrish* over Lily's departure, Eva poured her heart into her own work. And whenever she thought of Lily, she breathed a prayer and ached for whatever pain had propelled her sister away.

A little while later, Ida Mae dropped by with some fresh bread to share. "You two oughta be down at the Quarryville estate auction, selling your jams and homemade candies," she suggested to Eva when Frona came inside. "Might lift your spirits some."

"Oh, there'll be plenty of goodies, I'm sure," Eva replied.

"Your Dat and Mamm are goin'," Frona said, turning from the sink, where she was washing rhubarb. "Naomi said so when I was out mailin' some letters this morning."

Eva brightened. "I'm *sure* Abner's excited."

Ida Mae laughed. "No doubt she had to twist his arm."

"Your Mamm likes to mingle with new folks," Eva told Ida Mae. "She's a social butterfly, my mother always said."

"Well, Dottie would've known," Ida Mae said.

When Ida Mae was gone, Frona returned to the rhubarb. "Are ya lookin' forward to going to market Thursday?" she asked Eva as she took out the cutting board and began to slice the stalks for jam.

"*Jah*, and for the same reason Naomi's goin' to the auction."

"You're itchin' to see some new faces, I 'spect." Frona squinted at her. "Ain't still hoping to meet someone who might know where Lily's gone, are ya?"

"It *would* be helpful to know if she's safe somewhere, ain't so?"

"I 'spect we'll hear something when she runs out of money," Frona spouted.

And the sooner, the better, Eva thought sadly.

··· ➤ ◄ ···

"I got thirty dollars . . . now give me forty," the Amish auctioneer rattled off from where he stood high on a flatbed wagon. "Thirty, thirty . . . give me forty?"

Jed raised his head to the younger man reciting bids while keeping

577

track of indications from the throng of bidders as various items were presented.

"Got a forty-dollar bid—will ya give me fifty?" called the auctioneer.

This was the third item that had caught Jed's eye, but he'd dropped out of the bidding when the price went higher than he felt the particular tool was worth. *I can't see paying these prices.*

By ten-thirty, his stomach was rumbling, and he'd struck out further with each item he'd tried to secure. He wandered over to the buggy shed to have a look at the food selection. The place was crowded with church benches and tables set up on one side. Orpha and two other girls he didn't recognize were helping with the food, and he stepped up to order a barbecue sandwich.

Orpha spotted him and smiled, the roses in her cheeks growing brighter. *I have to admit,* he thought, *she's very friendly. And pretty, too.*

"Anything else you'd like?" Orpha asked, pointing out the soda options.

"There's also plenty of pie and ice cream," another of the girls piped up.

"I'll be back for dessert later," he said, paying for his sandwich and going to sit at one of the only spots available.

While he ate, he wondered if he might have been too quick to judge Orpha. *Should I give it another go?*

After all, he was interested in marrying a level-headed, responsible young woman, and Orpha seemed to be that. She didn't, however, come across as a book reader, though she was smart. His uncle would be pleased if he came home with good news to report.

Still, she's nothing like Lydiann, he thought. And that was the heart of the issue, the answer behind every dating-related question.

The day was mild and sunshine plentiful. The occasional scent of lilacs wafted on the breeze as Naomi walked along with Abner at the auction late that morning. They greeted two other Plain couples, one with young children in tow, and Naomi savored this chance to mingle.

On the other side of the corncrib, Naomi spotted their youngest son, Elam, with his little boy, two-and-a-half-year-old Sammy. The very instant the child laid eyes on his *Mammi* Naomi, he began pulling on his father's sleeve, asking in *Deitsch* if he could walk around with her and *Dawdi*

Abner. Elam agreed and told Naomi he'd catch up with them in a little while.

Sammy's blue eyes sparkled as he looked up at Naomi, who delighted in feeling his small hand tucked into hers. "Such a nice surprise," she said. "Maybe you'd like some ice cream."

Abner tapped their grandson's miniature straw hat, which leaned jauntily toward the back of his little head. "I'm going to amble over to look at the farming equipment," he told Naomi.

Naomi nodded and happily led Sammy to the concessions area, where dozens of folks were lining up. While in the crush of the crowd, Sammy managed to slip away from her.

She turned quickly, calling his name. *How'd he get loose?* she wondered, scurrying about.

Leaving the area, she went in search of the dear child, thinking now that he must have spotted his father and changed his mind, wanting to be with Elam instead. *Like* Kinner *are known to do.*

But she couldn't locate him—it was hard to spot such a tiny boy amidst the throng.

Naomi's heart raced as she headed toward the wagons where the larger tools were laid out. Nearby, she saw one of Abner's cousins talking to another man, but there was no sign of little Sammy. *Help me, Lord!* she prayed, hoping she might find the lad before he became frightened, small as he was.

Jed was pleased to finally have taken the bid on an apparently coveted set of hammers and pliers. He reasoned it was sensible to pay a little more when they were so well made.

He'd brought his prize back to Jonas's house and was eager to return to the jovial atmosphere. When he was on the grounds again, he felt a sudden tug on his pant leg. Looking down, his gaze was met by a small boy staring up at him.

As if embarrassed, the little fellow stepped away and put his hands behind his back.

He thought he recognized me. Jed crouched down. "Hey, there, aren't you the smallest bidder ever?"

The boy swallowed, and a wee smile crept back onto his features.

579

"Are you lost, young man?"

The boy nodded.

"Well, I think it's time to find out who you belong to," Jed replied. "But first, do ya know what might help our search?"

The boy shook his head.

"Some ice cream, maybe with whipped cream and sprinkles."

The boy giggled and all was well. The towheaded child began babbling in *Deitsch*, talking about his Mammi Naomi. A moment later, however, and his smile disappeared again; he rubbed his eyes, his lower lip stuck out.

Jed summed up the situation. "Here, let's get you a better view so you can find your family." Reaching down, he hoisted the boy onto his shoulders. The small straw hat fell off, and Jed caught it, then passed it up to the child. "*Was is dei Naame?*" he asked.

"Sammy," the boy said and clapped his hands with glee perched up there so high.

His Mammi will spot him now. Jed left the bidding area and headed across the field toward the concession table. "Do ya like whoopie pies better than ice cream, maybe?"

More clapping came from above and a pocket-sized "*Jah.*"

"All right, then, let's go."

Jed purchased a whoopie pie, and Sammy's smile returned. Pulling the wrapping off as quickly as he could, Jed handed the treat to the boy. "We need to find your Mammi, young fella. She's gonna worry."

Sammy shook his head, pointing to his treat.

Jed laughed. "Don't worry. You can finish that first."

13

WHAT do ya say we go to the auction now?" Eva suggested to Frona as her sister wiped down the jar rims. "I'll even hitch up for ya."

Frona shrugged casually. "I guess it'd be nice to have the noon meal there. I've been hungry for a nice bowl of ham and bean soup."

"All right, then. I'll hurry." Eva rushed off to the stable, ever so ready for a change of scenery.

······ ⊱ ⊰ ······

When they arrived at the auction, neither was shocked at the size of the crowd—word of mouth never failed to spread such news. Eva recommended they get right in line for something to eat. Frona agreed, and after the ham and bean soup Frona was hankering for, she went for some vanilla ice cream and a large peanut butter cookie.

They weren't poky at the table, since so many families were present. When they'd finished eating, Frona spotted some friends. "I'll catch up with ya later, sister."

"Sure, take your time." The sun felt so good on her back and shoulders. Eva lingered near a cluster of tall oak trees, enjoying the gaiety and observing all the goings-on. At one point, she raised her face to the sky, wishing she might have more opportunities to work outdoors—her little shop kept her inside several days a week.

She remembered the first time she and Lily had gone to a mud sale—

an Amish auction to raise money for local fire departments. They were only young girls, and the mud from spring rains had been so deep that Lily had gotten stuck, her little rubber boots nearly buried in the mushy mess. As Eva called to their Dat for help, she had managed to pull her out partway. She'd never forgotten how their dear father had run over and scooped little Lily into his arms, not caring how terribly soiled his black coat and trousers might get. Dat took Eva by the hand as he carried Lily all the way across the mucky field to their carriage. There, he wiped Lily's tears with his clean white handkerchief.

Eva sighed and turned her attention again to the pleasant drone of the large gathering. Not far away was a tall man with a darling little boy perched on his squared shoulders. Watching them, she noticed the boy's smile; his tiny arm raised high overhead. *He's playing horsey*, she thought, smiling at this from her vantage point.

Then, looking closer, she realized the child was Naomi Mast's grandson. But then, who was the fellow with the strawberry blond hair hauling him around? Eva made note of the young man's hat brim, certainly narrower than those she was accustomed to seeing. Her curiosity got the best of her and she called to Sammy, waving to him.

The man turned toward her, and the youngster grinned, saying her name, "Eva . . . Eva!"

They moved in her direction, the cordial-looking man picking up his pace. But as they approached, his contagious smile suddenly disappeared, and he frowned slightly, his eyes narrowed, almost as if startled by her appearance.

Does he know me? She measured his peculiar expression, but considering his attire, he was certainly not local, and she was quite sure they'd never met.

"I'm Eva Esch," she introduced herself before pointing to Sammy. "And I know this little friend of yours." She reached up to touch the boy's hand, and he laughed.

"He's lost . . . unless you're his Mammi." The handsome fellow's steady gaze was unsettling, but she could see a trace of humor there.

"Well, I do know both of Sammy's grandmothers," Eva said, her neck and face warm in the sunlight. "One is my neighbor, in fact . . . my friend Naomi." Eva astonished herself, talking so freely to a stranger, of all things.

582

The man continued to study her, his head tilted, his expression serious.

"I'll help ya find Naomi Mast," she said, feeling awkward because the young man still hadn't offered his name. "Do I know you, maybe?"

"*Nee,*" he replied softly. "Just never expected to meet you here. . . ."

She felt her forehead crinkle to a frown at the odd response. "Sorry?"

"I . . . I meant," he began, blinking all of a sudden, as though snapping out of a dream or a momentary memory snag. "Forgive me, it's just that—"

"Mammi Naomi!" young Sammy called, jostling up and down, clearly wanting to keep going.

"Jed Stutzman's my name." He gave Eva an engaging smile. "From Berlin, Ohio. I'm in town for the week," he added.

"Lookin' for treasures today like everyone else?"

"Unfortunately, I haven't ended up with many."

Sammy was still bouncing around, trying to get Jed moving again and calling for Naomi.

Jed glanced over his shoulder. "Do you happen to see Sammy's grandmother anywhere?"

Eva scanned the nearest group of people and shook her head. The bidders were clustered around another wagon, and from where she stood, she could see the flat crowns of a sea of straw hats. "Walk with me," she said. "I have an idea where she might be."

"*Wunnerbaar-gut,*" Jed said, clasping Sammy's feet, which dangled near his chest.

They walked so slowly at first, she wondered if Jed might be reluctant to head back into the crowd. It sure seemed that way, considering he kept glancing at her.

"By the way, I'm interested in going to a local market while I'm here," he said unexpectedly. "Do you know of one nearby?"

"Just thataway on Thursdays." She pointed in the direction of Quarryville. "You could prob'ly go on foot; it's quite close." Without thinking, she added, "My sister and I will be tending a table there, actually."

He nodded, eyes brightening all the more. "*Gut,* then, I'll keep an eye out for ya."

"*Denki.*" His winning way made her heart flutter, yet she hardly knew what to think.

They walked farther, Jed telling about his uncle in Ohio arranging for his stay with Jonas Byler and his wife, just two farms over. "They're mighty nice, I'll say. The salt of the earth." He went on to say his uncle was also a carriage maker, and that he and Jonas intended for Jed to spend the whole week learning about Jonas's techniques and perspective on the trade.

"I wonder what the buggy-man, as we call him, will do with his time once he's retired in a few months," she said, falling into step with Jed.

"I, for one, can't imagine not workin'."

She mentioned her little candy shop, just for fun. "It's my pride and joy, but in a *gut* way, if ya know what I mean."

"More womenfolk are opening small shops like this in their homes," Jed replied. "At least out in my area of Ohio."

"Is that right?" She found this interesting. "My father got me all set up back when I was young."

"Hey, maybe *you* blazed the trail." He chuckled.

Just then they heard a woman's voice. "Sammy Mast!"

When they turned, Eva saw Orpha Byler waving, along with two other young women. "Ah, there's one of Jonas's granddaughters with some of her cousins," Eva told him.

Orpha was all a-chatter. "Well, lookee who's got ya, sweetie," she said, reaching to playfully poke Sammy's arm. Then she proceeded to introduce Jed Stutzman to her cousins, Linda and Rebecca, who blushed simultaneously. "That was one delicious supper Mammi Elsie fixed last evening, ain't so?" Orpha declared.

Orpha seemed intent on singling out Jed and making it clear they'd spent time together.

Jed turned respectfully to Eva. "Orpha, have ya met Eva Esch?"

"Oh *jah*. Seen her at market over the years," Orpha said, eyeing her. "But we attend different church districts."

Still more families were arriving now that the house furnishings were going up for bid. Eva looked around for Frona, wondering if she'd decided to spend all of her time with friends.

"It's nice to see you again, Orpha," Eva said, then looked up at little Sammy, who was beginning to pout. "You know what? I'm going to run over and see if Naomi's where I think she is. She's surely worried by now."

Jed nodded agreeably.

"I'll bring her right over, once I find her," Eva assured him.

"I guess we'll be seein' ya later, Jed," Orpha said before leaning closer to whisper in Jed's ear—something about "homemade ice cream, up at the house."

She's carrying a torch for him! thought Eva and wondered if he liked pushy girls.

Orpha and her followers waved at Jed and wandered off.

"Sorry 'bout that," Jed said just as Eva was about to take her own leave.

She shrugged and wondered why he'd apologized.

Just then, from behind them, Naomi came hurrying over, her face as bright as a red beet egg. Then, seeing Eva, too, the dear woman slowed her pace. She looked bewildered as she walked right up to Jed and reached for her grandson. Sammy leaned down and tumbled into her arms. "Where, oh where have ya been, *mei Buwli?*" Naomi kissed his chubby cheeks, hugging the daylights out of him.

"Naomi, this is Jed Stutzman. He's the one who found your Sammy-boy," Eva told her.

"*Denki* for findin' my *Kinskind.*" She smiled and nodded at Jed, then hugged Sammy again.

"He actually found *me.*" Jed explained how the boy had walked up to him and indicated he was lost.

Naomi surveyed Sammy's chubby cheeks again, wiping at them with her fingers. "Looks like someone's been eating sweets, ain't?"

Comically, Sammy pointed an accusing finger at Jed and grinned.

"Mighty glad to help," Jed said, offering a handshake. "Sammy, nice to meet ya!"

The little tyke reached over and shook his hand like a grown-up.

Naomi's eyes widened. "Well, I never."

Eva had to smother her laughter. She was even more aware of the bond between Jed and the boy whom he'd just met.

She and Jed waved good-bye to Sammy; then Naomi took his hand, a look of relief on her face. At Jed's request, Eva lingered, enjoying his company.

··· ➤ ➤ ···

After the auction, and following a light supper of homemade bread and jam, cold cuts, and Jell-O, similar to the shared meal after a Preaching service, Jed and his hosts indulged in some homemade ice cream. Orpha and her parents seemed eager to spend more time with Jed, as well, and Jonas talked about his work-related plans with Jed for the week.

Later, Jonas brought out the cards for Dutch Blitz, and the suppertime gathering was extended. Orpha Byler positioned herself in his group of players, and as the game progressed, she smiled at him frequently, clearly sending a message of interest. For her sake—and for the sake of his wonderful host—Jed did his best to keep an open mind.

Even so, despite all the distraction, it was Eva Esch who lingered on his mind. *The girl in the photograph . . .*

14

EVA and Frona had been tempted to take the long way home after the auction, and they soaked up the lovely evening—mild enough for light shawls in the carriage. The ride brought with it a sense of quiet, ideal for relaxing as the horse pulled them steadily toward Eden Valley. Along the way, they encountered other Amish buggies, everyone waving and calling greetings in *Deitsch* to one another.

"You had yourself a fine time," Frona said, her hands on the driving lines.

"*Jah*, helpin' Sammy Mast find Naomi," Eva said. "He got himself lost somehow."

"That's not what I meant."

"Oh," Eva replied, suddenly feeling a little shy.

"But you certainly did seem to enjoy the search for Naomi. Or, at least, the prospect of it." Frona let out a rare smile. "And you seemed to stick together for a *gut* long time after Sammy went off with Naomi."

Her sister was having fun with this, no question. "Well, Orpha Byler didn't bother hiding her opinion of Jed, now, did she?" Eva volunteered, wondering how long Frona had been observing her.

"Oh, it's just Jed already . . . is it?" Frona's eyes narrowed with mischievous delight.

"*Jah*, Jed Stutzman from Ohio. His boss is related to Jonas Byler by marriage."

"Well, 'just Jed' looks 'bout our age," Frona noted.

Eva didn't know how much more she wanted to divulge. Now, if it were Lily asking, she wouldn't have had any problem with telling all.

"It wonders me how Orpha got so chummy with him, at liberty to march over there with her cousins." Frona was inching into the prying side of things.

Eva began to hum "What a Friend We Have in Jesus" and let the comment be, grateful when Frona didn't weasel for more information. Besides, it was only a single encounter. Who knew if Jed would actually appear at market on Thursday.

You just never know about out-of-towners, she decided, leaning near the window, glad they were nearing the turnoff toward home.

"You ain't listenin', love," Naomi told Abner, who'd admitted he was feeling almost too droopy to drive the carriage after all the pie and ice cream he'd enjoyed at the auction. "I daresay the fella from Ohio seemed awful nice, and a progressive Amishman at that. Did ya notice that right fancy hat brim?"

"You just wanna see Eva happily married, like you?" Abner winked at her. "Is that what you're going to say next?"

"Oh, you!"

He reached for her hand, and she pulled away playfully.

"Come on over here, woman," Abner teased.

"It's still daylight, dear," Naomi cautioned him. "We ain't youngsters no more."

"Well, the fire ain't out yet."

Submitting to her husband's flirtation, she leaned her hand on the seat between them so no one could see as they passed other buggies.

Abner linked his big fingers around hers. "Aw, that's my girl."

"So, what do ya *really* think 'bout the Ohio fella?" she asked.

"No need to think; I've heard all I need to know from Jonas Byler himself."

She held her breath.

"Seems one of Jonas's granddaughters might be interested in him." Abner smiled. "Some competition's always *gut,* of course."

"If I know Eva Esch, she's not one to put herself forward."

"She's one sweet girl, I'll say. But Jed'll only be around till Monday sometime, so it may be a moot point."

Naomi sighed. *Poor Eva.*

They didn't talk much more about it. And eventually, when Naomi felt her husband's hand go limp around hers, she looked over and saw him catching more than just flies while their reliable horse kept trotting, heading homeward.

Much later that evening, once the house was quiet and after the second night of Bible reading with Jonas and Elsie, Jed settled into his room. He'd placed the peculiar photograph next to the bed and glanced over at it occasionally, still puzzled. He was reasonably certain, if not convinced, that Eva Esch and the girl in the photo were one and the same. In which case, Eva, kind and thoughtful as she seemed, must have had a defiant side earlier in her life, defiant enough to flout the Old Order's ban on personal photos. If so, she'd hidden it very well today.

Before meeting Eva, he'd considered privately showing Elsie Byler to see if she recognized the young woman. But he was glad now he hadn't been so foolish. *I might have jeopardized my chance to get to know Eva better. After all, Elsie would surely favor Orpha over Eva.*

After a few minutes of rereading some of the notes in the margins, Jed closed the book and went to outen the gas lamp. He wondered when Eva had taken the train west. Perhaps Thursday at market, if the opportunity presented itself, he would ask her. Nothing pointed or prying, just a simple, casual question.

Lily's done more than leave us; she's made it clear we don't count for much, Eva decided as she wandered out to the stable with the lantern. Max bounded over and sat near her, panting, keeping her company. The air was still, and the katydids and crickets were making a ruckus.

She took down the grooming brush and went to Prince's stall. Poor fellow, he'd trotted ever so hard coming up the incline from the auction hours ago. She would put her angst over Lily to good work on their favorite horse. *Like a pet.*

589

"You miss Lily, too, don't ya?" she whispered, leaning against Prince's velvety nose.

There were times when Lily's absence felt like a stab in her heart, though not as painful as when Dat had died so suddenly.

"Lily sure changed things by goin' away," Eva muttered as she worked on the thick black mane.

How different this moment would be if Lily were still living at home. They might have come to water the horses together, like many other nights. Eva dearly missed the whispering and laughing. How many times had Lily waited up for Eva after a date, and the other way around?

One night, though, when Lily had stayed out longer than usual, Eva had sat up for hours, wondering if she shouldn't just go to bed. It was the evening Lily had finally agreed to go riding with a fellow outside their church district. The nighttime breezes had helped cool the rooms upstairs, and Eva had gone to the open window and leaned on the sill, peering out at the stars.

She'd never planned to eavesdrop or observe Lily with Manny, but there they were walking toward the house in the moonlight. At first, Eva looked away. Then, realizing something seemed amiss, she hurried downstairs and out to the screened-in porch, listening and watching. Manny was telling Lily that he wanted to see her again, and very soon—even before next weekend—in a demanding tone.

Lily backed away, saying she was getting home awful late.

"It'll be even later next time," Manny had said as he reached for Lily, but she brushed him away.

Concerned, Eva opened the screen door and hurried out. "Everything all right over there?" she'd called gently, mindful of their sleeping mother.

Relieved, Lily had come running toward her as Manny turned back down the driveway toward his buggy, his footsteps quick on the gravel.

Upstairs, Lily had been terribly quiet as she dressed for bed. Eva prayed for wisdom all the while. And after they'd turned out the gas lamp and settled into bed, Lily confided that Manny definitely wasn't for her. "No matter how nice he was at the Singing last week." Even though Lily had assured Eva that nothing appalling had taken place, she refused to put herself at risk with such a fellow.

Lily was so careful then. Why was she now so willing to take a risk like running away? Eva wondered.

She finished brushing Prince, then gave him additional water and headed for the house, Max alongside her as the night sounds filled up the darkness.

Inside, Eva said good-night to Frona and took time to wash up, getting ready for bed. Then, sitting at the desk where she'd last seen Lily, Eva took out her journal and began to write.

Tuesday, May 20
  With everything in me, I wish Lily would let us know where she is. It would help so much to know she's safe. Frona would rest easier and so would I. Our brothers seem worried, enough so that all of them have spent time questioning various neighbors and relatives. So Lily's whereabouts are a mystery to us all.
  It wonders me if someday Lily might recognize that she belongs here and not out in the world. Oh, I do hope she will, before she marries outside the church and it's too late.
  At some point, I'm going to have to stop holding my breath. I can't cry for her the rest of my life, even though I would if I thought it might somehow help.
  O, dear Lord above, please watch over our befuddled sister. I do pray this in Thy holy name. Amen.

Then, because Eva hadn't taken time after the auction to make any more candies for tomorrow's customers, she set her windup alarm clock for five. Anxious for some good rest, she blew out the lamp and slipped into the soft bedcovers, reaching for the lightweight quilt Mamma had made. Her mind wandered to the fair-haired young man she'd met today.

Ah, Mamma, what would you think of Jed Stutzman?

Eva couldn't settle down, wondering about the strange but sweet way she and Jed had simply stumbled upon each other. *Thanks to little Sammy.*

But more than that, she couldn't get over the surprisingly tender way she felt about him, even now as she tucked the covers under her chin and watched the moonlight's dance on the wall. She let her mind flit back to all that Jed had said to her, and she to him, and then felt a little ridiculous. *I just met him, for goodness' sake!*

Truth be known, she cherished this day. After the trauma of Lily's departure, such unexpected companionship was the salve her soul craved.

Then, thinking of Naomi and how frantic she had been to find Sammy—*like we are to find Lily*—Eva reconsidered Lily's unreasonable behavior, running off to no one knew where. And while Eva wanted to hold the day's memories close to heart, she began to question the wisdom of entertaining romantic notions about someone from so far away, no matter how kindhearted Jed Stutzman seemed.

15

WEDNESDAY morning before breakfast, but after a stiff cup of black coffee, Jed walked with Jonas Byler out to the carriage shop on Jonas's property. "Your shop looks bigger than Uncle Ervin's," Jed remarked, eager to finally get a good look around.

"I'd say it's pretty typical for a workshop round here—two hundred feet by one hundred—but it's divided into four sections."

"Are ya lookin' forward to retiring soon?" Jed slowed his pace to be respectful to the older man.

"Oh *jah*, I s'pose, but I'll always be workin' somewhere till the Lord calls me home . . . helping one farmer or another, no doubt. Just not the day-to-day business of the carriage shop." Jonas's chest rose and fell. "It's a shame none of my boys wanted to learn the trade. 'Tis mighty important to pass it down through the generations."

Jed agreed.

"That's why I'm seriously thinkin' of selling."

His sons must already be established in their chosen work, Jed assumed.

At Jonas's shop, Jed stepped inside and felt right at home, thanks to a layout similar to Uncle Ervin's. "Real nice and tidy," he said.

"It's fairly well organized today," Jonas said, wiping his beard. "Shoulda seen it last week." He let out a chuckle. "Then again, it's a *gut* thing ya didn't!"

"There are just some days, *jah*?"

Jonas led the way to the impressively orderly back area, where workbenches were set up for building a buggy's wooden base. All across the wall hung hand tools like those Jed was accustomed to using.

Another large room was set aside for storing materials for manufacturing the buggy, including the bench seat in surreys and parts for the hacks or buckboards. The latter were similar to an *Englischer*'s pickup truck, the area behind the seat providing a flat bed for hauling.

"Now, here's something. Ever see a dashboard like this?" Jonas pointed to a panel of inlaid wood with holes drilled for switches for inside and outside buggy lights, as well as turn signals.

Jed ran his hand over its smoothness. "Real fancy compared to some."

Jonas shook his head, amused. "Makes me wonder what the owner's thinkin'—some of the nonsense we put in. *Ach*, the carpet colors, several years back, were downright loud. Just depends on what's allowed in a particular church district . . . how strict the bishop is." Jonas motioned toward the next area. "Say, do your Swartzentruber neighbors still use kerosene lanterns for their buggy lights?"

"They do." Jed was surprised Jonas knew this.

The older man went on to say that the brakes, wheels, and spokes were all made less than ten miles from his shop. "I 'spect it's similar out there, ain't?"

"Probably closer to fifteen miles."

"That far?"

Nodding, Jed found the shoptalk stimulating and was glad Uncle Ervin had suggested the visit with the great buggy maker. *And matchmaker, too.*

Blackbirds pecked at one another in the field near the roadside as Eva and Frona set out for market Thursday morning. The skies were overcast and rain was predicted for later that afternoon.

"Hope we get home before a downpour," Frona said, her attention on the road.

"I guess I don't care one way or the other," Eva said.

"Well, ain't you somethin'?"

"Just glad for any chance of moisture. My garden could really use it."

"*Your* garden?" Frona gave her a look.

Eva wasn't going to remind her that *she* had done the tilling and planting during her days in between working at The Sweet Tooth. *How could Frona forget?* Of course, Frona had single-handedly done all the weeding here lately, so doubtless that's what she meant.

Striving to think pleasant thoughts, Eva peered out at the silvery windmill just ahead as the carriage rumbled along.

"Just because a fella promises something, doesn't mean it'll happen," she remembered Mamma saying, and she wondered if Jed would show up today.

"You sure are deep in thought," Frona said, interrupting her daydream. "Thinking 'bout your young man, maybe?"

Eva sighed. "He's not mine, *Schweschder.*"

"Oh, well, it's just a matter of time." Frona didn't wait for a response. "I saw how he looked at you at the auction—'tis a *gut* thing, too, what with Menno's plans. There's really only room for one of us when they move in, remember."

Eva squelched a smile. Not only did Frona have Eva nearly hitched up with Jed, but poor Frona was still fretting about Menno's move.

The good Lord will see to the future. And that's that, she thought.

The warmth of the morning sun and the strong scent of mown grass heightened Jed's anticipation for the day. He'd slept restlessly, caught up in the hope of seeing Eva Esch again. Truthfully, he hadn't felt such anticipation since Lydiann.

He caught a ride with Mose Byler, who was on his way to the east side of Quarryville to make a delivery for his father—ideal for Jed to get to market around opening time.

"You'll return on foot, then?" Mose asked, sitting tall in the driver's seat.

Jed nodded. "Mighty grateful for the lift."

"Be sure an' take the umbrella," offered Mose, pointing to the back of the buggy. "S'posed to pour cats and dogs later."

Jed went around and opened the back. *"Denki!"*

"Gem gschehne!" Mose lifted the reins and clicked his tongue before heading out of the parking lot.

Inside the market, the place was already busy with folding tables being moved about and set up amidst vendors greeting each other. Jed didn't want to be in the way if he showed up too soon to Eva's table, so he wandered about, heading up the first long aisle. A large glass display case featuring homemade fudge caught his attention, and perusing the options, he considered a purchase. He thought of buying something for Eva but didn't want her to feel awkward.

Even so, he continued searching the fudge counter for a gift, recalling Lydiann's cravings for chocolate.

"Ach, *you spoil me, Jed.*" Lydiann had smiled sweetly that day. *"But, of course, if you really want to buy that chunk of chocolate, I won't refuse."*

He'd whipped out his wallet before she could change her mind. *"It's yours, then."*

And she'd laughed so merrily the sound lingered in his mind for the rest of the week, till he saw her again that Saturday evening.

What if Eva doesn't care much for chocolate? he thought, although he had a hard time imagining it. He recalled what she'd said about her confectionary shop. Was it possible to create sweets and not enjoy them?

"What's your fancy?" asked the large woman behind the counter. Her shoulders slouched as she leaned heavily on the display case.

Jed pointed to the smallest package, covered in a pretty red wrapping. He didn't want to seem stingy, yet a token might actually be better than something too big for a first gift.

"It's buy one, get the second one half off," the smiling clerk told him. "How can ya pass it up?"

He took his time, looking at several other options.

"If ya pick something bigger, well, same deal for that, too," she said.

In the end he stuck with his original order, glad to have the treat for Eva in the little sack the clerk handed to him.

"I think changing the arrangement sometimes *is* wise," Eva was telling Mary Riehl, another market vendor.

Mary had taken it upon herself to stride across the aisle and rearrange Frona's and Eva's wares without their say-so. The middle-aged woman had a mind of her own, but prior to this she'd never demonstrated it in such a radical manner. "Just thought I'd offer a bit of help, is all." Mary gave a flamboyant wave and headed back to her own table.

Frona had cause to frown for sure. And later, when Mary was out of earshot, she told Eva she felt like changing it all back to the way it was. "What do ya say to that?"

"Just let it be. Sometimes it's *gut* to vary things."

Frona stared at their goodies, including her jams and preserves. "Well, if it's already workin' one way, why bother?"

"Honestly, customers don't care 'bout the arrangement, do they?"

"If they're repeat customers, maybe not. But I still like things the way we had them."

Eva could sense there was no compromising with Frona today. "If you put it all back, you can be the one to explain to Mary . . . if she comes marchin' back over here."

"*Puh!*" Frona shook her head. "The woman's got some nerve!"

The whole thing seemed petty to Eva. *Why's Frona so tetchy?*

A half hour or more later, while she was making change and answering questions, Eva noticed Jed standing back near the periphery of a dozen or more customers. *He's here,* she thought, trying not to smile too broadly. But he'd seen her spot him. *Oh, goodness!* And to think there was no way to greet him the way she wanted to, with so many folks there for her candies and Frona's jars of jam and whatnot.

Will he wait around?

Eva disliked feeling so unnerved and torn.

To her great surprise, Jed came around to the side and over to her. "Hullo, Eva. Looks like you're mighty busy."

"It's been this way ever since we opened."

"Ya know what? I'll walk around a bit and come back later." His smile warmed her heart. Once again there was a glint of recognition in his eyes, like he knew her from somewhere.

"All right" was all she could manage, uncomfortable at being observed so, particularly by Frona, who was glancing their way.

Jed left as quickly as he'd come into view.

In a few minutes, Naomi Mast and her daughter Ida Mae arrived carrying shopping baskets. "*Wie bischt?*" Eva asked.

"Just fine . . . you?" Naomi replied.

"Oh, trying to keep the customers smilin'," Eva said.

"Hullo," said Ida Mae, shifting her empty basket. "Looks like you've got your hands full."

"Are ya lookin' to buy some of Frona's delicious rhubarb jam?"

"Ida Mae is," Naomi volunteered and beamed at her daughter. "Ain't ya, dear?"

Ida Mae motioned that she was going to slip into the back of the line.

Meanwhile, Naomi stood with Eva, asking when she'd like to come over again for some dessert. "Just to talk."

Eva was pleased by the thoughtful invitation, especially on the heels of seeing Jed again. "I could come over after supper tonight."

"Suits me fine." Naomi smiled encouragingly. "I'll bake some cookies for us."

"Is Abner along today?"

"One of the cows came down with milk fever, so he's at home getting an IV started."

"Abner's always been conscientious thataway." *Dat was, too.*

"Well, I'd better let you get back to work," Naomi said, giving her shoulder a pat now.

"Glad ya dropped by." Eva watched her go and looked forward to opening her heart to the woman who'd come to understand her so well. *Surely she'll have some advice for me about an out-of-town fella. . . .*

At only twenty-eight, Menno already had a rather arrogant swagger. Eva witnessed this very trait as he moved through the aisle toward them, not making eye contact with a soul.

She was thankful the earlier crowd had thinned out as Menno approached their table. Without even greeting them, he reached down and picked up one of Frona's jars of jam, deliberately turning it in his hand.

"How many have ya sold this mornin'?" he asked.

"More than four dozen," Frona said.

Eva wondered why he'd come. "You needin' some jam?" *Bena's surely got plenty for him at home.*

He waved vaguely. "I've been weighing something and wanted to ask what ya thought." He wandered behind the table, making himself at home, then motioned them into a huddle like the menfolk made before Preaching services. "Bishop Isaac came to see me the other day. He thinks we oughta try and follow Lily's path, so to speak. He wants her back in the fold right away."

Frona nearly gasped. "The bishop, ya say?"

"No need to worry," Menno cautioned. "He's adamant that someone should go lookin' for her. Who knows where she'll end up? Ain't safe for such a girl."

"I tried to get some leads," Eva admitted, "but there was really only one."

It was Menno's turn to be flabbergasted. "Well, let's hear it."

Eva recounted Fannie Ebersol's evasive behavior the morning after Lily had fled. "I've wondered if Fannie knows something she isn't tellin' . . . maybe even where Lily headed." She sighed as she recalled her suspicion and frustration that first day.

"Why have ya kept this to yourself?"

Eva hoped Menno wouldn't cause a scene. "Fannie refused to say. She was convinced that Lily wanted to leave Eden Valley, and there was no stopping her."

Menno looked stricken. "Tell that to the bishop!" He scoffed. "The man of God believes Lily is too young to know what's good for her—and I happen to think he's right."

"Of course ya do," Frona said.

Eva glanced at her sister, who'd turned rather agreeable, as though trying to get on Menno's good side.

Menno nodded emphatically. "I'd hate to think she'd do something to bring more disgrace to the family."

More than just leaving the People, thought Eva. "I'm prayin' for her."

Frona nodded. "In all truth, both of us are."

"What do our other brothers and the bishop think is the best way to handle this?" Eva had to know.

"No one's sayin', really. But Bishop Isaac has urged us to go after her— 'get her home!'"

"Against Lily's will?" Eva asked. "If it comes to that?"

"*Jah,* if she's not thinkin' straight—which she ain't. That's mighty clear." Menno nodded, then abruptly turned and left Eva standing there with Frona.

Eva was shocked he had sought them out at market, of all places. And just that quick, she knew it had been a mistake for Menno to approach them about such a private matter there. Mary Riehl and another woman were eyeing them, wagging their heads, and a short line of customers had formed at their table.

Eva's heart sank with shame. For a fleeting moment, she wished Jed might forget to stop by again. *Not the way I feel right now* . . .

16

O N the ride back from market, Naomi Mast was thankful her daughter insisted on taking the driving lines in hand. Naomi guessed Ida Mae hadn't liked the way she'd handled the horse on the way there. It didn't really matter the excuse; she was glad to relax during the uphill journey home.

"Not sure if you noticed it or not," Ida Mae mentioned when they were about a third of the way. "But Fannie Ebersol was cryin' like her heart might break."

"When was this?"

"Before we left . . . while you were occupied with Mary Riehl." Ida Mae frowned. "What's odd was that Menno Esch was standing nearby, his arms folded and his expression severe. It sure looked like he'd given Fannie a talkin' to."

Naomi groaned. "Anyone else witness this?"

"Only me that I could tell."

"Where was Fannie's sister? Doesn't she usually help tend the market table?"

"That's just it. Fannie was by herself."

"Maybe the rest of the family ain't feelin' well." The spring flu was making its rounds, Naomi thought.

"You know what I think?" Ida Mae said, turning to face her. "I heard Menno say something 'bout Lily Esch. And it sure sounded like he was accusing Fannie of knowin' more than she was telling."

Naomi had known Menno to be a rather bigheaded man when it came to what he thought and how he wanted things done. Nearly proud, especially since his father passed away. "Things must be worrisome if Menno's pressuring Lily's friend for more information."

"All I know is he headed straight for Fannie, talked to her, then waited for her to say something—*'Spit it out, ya hear?'* is what he honestly said. Then, after waiting a while and getting nowhere with her, Menno spun on his heels and left."

Naomi didn't like the sound of this. As dogmatic as Menno Esch had become, she'd never known him to behave so rudely. "I'll admit to feelin' sorry for Fannie," she said softly.

"But what if she is stonewalling and knows something 'bout Lily, Mamm? It might help the family find her."

"'Tis true." Naomi wished she had a cat to put on her lap right this minute. A purring pet could perhaps ease her nerves. Oh, she prayed Lily's disappearance wouldn't disrupt the whole community of the People.

A steady hum filled the marketplace—vendors selling their wares, people stopping by to see what items were new or just to visit and catch up on the previous week. Popcorn was popping one aisle over, behind Eva and Frona's table.

It must have been the Lord's good timing when Jed returned quite a while later. A half-dozen people were milling about near their long table, listening attentively to Frona's method for making her strawberry-rhubarb jam—all *Englischers.*

Eva rose and went to stand near the aisle.

"Here, I bought something for ya." Jed gave her a pretty red package. She couldn't help but smile.

"Hope ya like fudge."

"I surely do!" She was pleased he'd think to do this. "But I won't eat it in front of you, unless you'd like a piece."

He shook his head, blue eyes fixed on her. "It's all for you."

"*Denki.*" She wondered what people were thinking, seeing them like this.

"Would it be wrong to ask if you have time to take a quick walk through the aisles?" He glanced about, undoubtedly surveying the number of customers.

Now that Jed was here and the embarrassment she'd felt over Menno had faded, Eva wished she *could* slip out with Jed. "I shouldn't leave my sister to handle all the customers," she said, smiling up at him. "Hope you understand."

He nodded, respecting her wishes. "How about a buggy ride Saturday afternoon or evening—would that suit ya?"

"Sounds nice," she said in a near whisper. "Evening's better."

Jed's face broke into a satisfied smile. "I'm hopin' we might get better acquainted."

Before he leaves. The realization made her sad. "I'll meet you halfway between my house and our neighbors to the east, all right?" She told him the address of her father's farmhouse on Eden Road.

"Around dusk, then?"

Nodding, she smiled again, suddenly wishing this moment might freeze in time. She was drawn to him, yet she hardly knew him. But what Eva did know, she liked very much.

Jed made his way along the road early that afternoon, pummeled by rain in spite of the borrowed umbrella. Walking in the direction of Jonas Byler's big spread, he was offered numerous rides by Amish farmers. But he wanted to be alone with his thoughts while he could still hear Eva's sweet voice in his mind, so he politely refused the offers.

He pulled the photo from his pocket, hunched over to protect it from the rain, and studied it. The picture was creased in places and soiled a bit, probably taken a few years ago, when Eva was younger. *It's gotta be her,* he thought. *I'm certain of it.*

Perhaps by now Eva was sorry she'd had it taken. If she was a baptized church member, she might even have confessed it to the ministerial brethren.

Replacing the picture, he began to whistle. He was getting drenched but didn't mind. Just having the photo in his wallet gave him an exhilarating feeling, though it was surely against the church *Ordnung.*

Since Jed planned to be in town till Monday afternoon, it crossed his mind to find out where Eva would be attending Preaching. On the other hand, being Jonas and Elsie's guest, he ought to go with them, if it wasn't their off-Sunday. Otherwise, he should accompany them wherever they'd like to go. He just hoped the day might not include their granddaughter Orpha again.

··· ➤ ◄ ···

Thankfully, Eva finished up her chores before scaring up something to eat with Frona that afternoon. She felt like she was walking on a cloud as she recalled Jed's handsome face and blue eyes. And oh, that grin!

Frona had looked at her askance more than once as they made small talk while Frona washed dishes and Eva dried. "Eva, are ya even listenin'?"

Eva apologized, her mind whirling with the day's events—Jed's seeking her out at market, his confident smile, that look in his eyes, as if he'd known her for years.

"You're daydreamin' again," Frona said.

"Prob'ly so."

Eva dried faster, wondering if Frona had ever had special feelings for a young man. "Naomi's expectin' me over there soon."

Frona made a small groan. "Don't mind me. I'll be workin' on the pile of mending."

Eva instantly felt sorry. "S'pose I could go another day. We *did* miss out on a few tasks, bein' at market and all."

"What? And miss the chance to share your heart with Naomi? You mustn't keep her waiting."

She's upset. Eva wished she'd done a better job of keeping her giddiness to herself. "Frona, I—"

Her sister waved as if to silence any further discussion, then continued with the dishes, her head bowed.

Pursing her lips, Eva continued drying. Sometimes it was easy to forget that Frona, for all her anxious prickliness, was sensitive, too.

I need to be more forgiving, Eva thought. *And more aware.*

They finished redding up, working silently for a time. Then, out of the blue, Frona mentioned Menno's surprising visit at market and his determination to confront Fannie.

"I can't help wondering how that'll go," Eva said. "Menno can be . . . a little harsh."

"Well, I don't feel sorry for Fannie. I mean, what's she thinkin'?"

"*Jah*," Eva replied sadly. How had everything gotten so *verkehrt*—topsy-turvy?

When the table and counters were wiped clean, Frona leaned against the sink and gazed out the window, her eyes misty and expression grim.

"I'll be back right quick," Eva said as she hung up the tea towel. "In time for evening prayers."

Seemingly lost in her own worries again, Frona shook her head, working her lips. "Everything's a-changin', Eva." Frona shifted her weight, and the floor creaked.

She's afraid, Eva thought. "Remember, we can count on our Lord . . . for today and for tomorrow."

"Now you sound like Mamma."

Eva gave her a smile. "Besides, no matter what happens, you're still stuck with me."

"Don't make promises you can't keep, Eva. You'll end up leavin' like Lily. You'll be marryin' Alfred—that is, if the fella from Ohio who was makin' googly eyes at ya doesn't win your heart."

Eva's mouth dropped open. "What kind of eyes?"

"Oh dear," Frona muttered, setting her chin.

The kitchen was hushed, tension evident between them, until Eva could hold it in no longer. One giggle was followed by another, and then they were both laughing.

"You'd better get goin'," Frona finally said. "I can't handle all this fun."

Ain't that the truth, Eva thought, grinning as she headed out the door. "See ya later, sister!"

··· ➤ ➤ ···

Eva waited on this side of the road while Abner Mast pulled his open wagon out of his driveway. She had checked for mail this late, thinking surely Lily would realize she must get in touch with her family. But there was nothing from Lily or anyone.

Eva thought again of how she'd left Frona with the unfinished mending. *I'll sew a new dress and apron for her,* she decided, wanting to do something nice for her.

Once Abner was out on the road and ready to head on, he waved his hand over his head. "Naomi just took the cookies fresh out of the oven for ya," he called in his deep voice, a grin on his pleasant ruddy face.

"*Denki!*" She crossed narrow Eden Road after the horse pulled forward. Inside Naomi's sparkling kitchen, the place smelled of cinnamon and vanilla. "Let me guess. You made snickerdoodles, *jah?*"

"That's a right *gut* smeller." Naomi motioned for her. "*Kumme,* sit at the table with me."

Eva hugged her friend and got settled at the table. She began to share her private hope that her brothers might not be so caught up with their own families and focus more on finding Lily.

"Well, they love Lily just as you and Frona do," Naomi said. "Just 'cause you don't see them all too often doesn't mean they don't care. You know what's in their hearts."

"*Jah,* s'pose."

"No s'posin' about it." Naomi folded her plump arms. "Listen, my dear. I bumped into Bena at market, and she said Menno's been worried sick over Lily. It keeps him up at night."

"Menno himself stopped by to see Frona and me today about her." Eva felt she should own up to that much.

"So, see there?" Naomi smiled, her round face rosy.

Eva took a second warm cookie from the pretty plate. "These are so delicious," she said, changing the subject.

Thankfully, Naomi seemed to understand and let it drop. She had that way about her.

Then they got to talking about ways Eva could help direct her worries to praying whenever Lily came to mind. "Prayin' while you make your delicious candies, too," Naomi suggested.

Sighing, Eva thought of her wonderful little shop. "I guess my whole world can't just be making sweets and selling them."

"'Tis true, and I, for one, know it ain't."

Eva wondered what, if anything, to say about Jed Stutzman. Unsure of herself, she ate more cookies than necessary and let Naomi talk gently about how the best exercise for one's heart was to practice reaching out to pick someone up—"and carryin' them, if need be."

"I certainly would reach out to Lily if I knew where she was."

"I know ya would." Naomi's eyes shone with sympathy.

Eva held her breath, refusing tears.

Naomi got up and poured some homemade meadow tea and set it down in front of Eva. "Now, I've been doin' my share of talking. Is there anything you'd like to bring up that we haven't already discussed?"

"Well . . . you remember meeting Jed Stutzman, the fella who took care of little Sammy at the auction?" She paused. "He invited me to go riding come Saturday."

Naomi's eyes sparkled. "*Ach*, isn't that nice?"

No words of caution?

"It'll be fun," Eva agreed.

"And something to look forward to during this sad time." Naomi tilted her head toward her. "Jed's his name?"

"*Jah*. And not a very common name round here."

Naomi looked away, her chest rising and falling. "I daresay if you two fall in love, he'll take you away from us."

Just like Frona said, Eva thought.

"And I'd have to say selfishly that I'd miss you something awful."

"It's just a carriage ride," Eva said, but it sounded empty even to her. Buggy rides could lead to courtship, even marriage, and she recognized that the interest she was feeling from Jed was unlike anything she'd experienced before.

At that precise moment, someone knocked at the back door, and Eva was relieved at the interruption. But then she saw who it was—Fannie Ebersol, who looked sheepish when she noticed Eva sitting there.

"Goodness, Eva, never expected to see *you* here."

What on earth? Eva thought.

Fannie's firm jaw—the way she cast her gaze at first Eva, then Naomi—gave Eva a twinge of misgiving.

17

W HAT do ya mean you pledged on your honor?" Eva asked Fannie when she was seated at Naomi's table.

"Your sister was determined," Fannie answered. "She didn't want anyone to keep her from leavin', or even to go lookin' for her. That's why I didn't tell you where she went."

Naomi's face fell. "You've known all along?"

Fannie nodded her head, eyes lowered. "I wanted to keep my word to Lily, since she . . . well, kept all *my* secrets."

"Oh dear," Naomi whispered.

Eva felt she might burst. "So where's Lily now?"

"Do ya promise you'll never say where ya heard this?" Fannie looked pale.

Eva glanced at Naomi. "If it saves Lily from ruin, what's it matter?"

There was a long and painful silence. At last Fannie said, "I'll only tell you what Lily told me 'cause she hasn't written like she said she would . . . and I'm worried."

Eva held her breath.

Fannie began to share more. "Lily's staying somewhere in Ohio."

"Where in Ohio?" Eva asked.

"I'm not sure, really," Fannie said. "Lily talked 'bout different places over several weeks' time, but I don't remember now."

How could she forget? Eva wondered. "Please try," she urged. "If you

608

could just remember the city or town . . . that would help us ever so much." She felt frantic.

"Well, if it helps any, Lily was supposedly gonna stay with her boyfriend's married sister and family for a while."

Eva's mouth dropped open. "A boyfriend? That's why she left?"

Fannie bit her lip. "I hate bein' the one to say. . . ."

Hearing it helped in some ways but also raised so many questions that both Eva and Naomi started talking at the same time. "Go ahead," Eva said, motioning for Naomi to continue.

"*Nee* . . . you first, she's your sister." Naomi eased back into her chair.

"Since Lily's gone fancy," Eva said, scarcely able to get it all out, "then her beau must surely be English."

"*Jah.*" Fannie continued, seemingly eager now to reveal that the young man in Lily's life was twenty-one and a mighty *gut* horse trainer. "He's from somewhere over near Canton, if I remember correctly. Lily met him a year ago when she went with my family and me to Kidron to visit relatives. She hit it off with this *Englischer* fella and said that he hardly noticed she was Amish, which kinda had me surprised."

She ran off to be with a worldly beau. Eva tried to let this sink in.

"He must've been writing to her all this time to influence her so," Naomi said, looking thoughtfully at Eva.

"That's where I came in—the go-between," Fannie confessed, sounding somewhat embarrassed. "Lily gave her boyfriend my address, which meant the envelope was always addressed to me, but with no return address. My mother actually thought *I* had a beau in Ohio."

Eva struggled to remain calm. "How'd Lily get out there?"

"My brother Thomas picked her up that night and took her to Strasburg, where she met a van driver. She wouldn't tell me much else. And Lily kept other things secret, too," Fannie admitted. "It was the oddest thing—she was open 'bout certain things but not others."

"And you haven't heard from her to know if she got there in one piece?" Naomi asked, looking concerned.

Fannie shook her head. "I can't understand it for the life of me. She promised to keep in close touch."

A tremor ran down Eva's back. "Is it possible Lily changed her mind about where she wanted to end up? Maybe she didn't go to Ohio, after all."

Fannie sighed loudly and leaned her face into her hands. Then, after a time, she looked out the window. "Makes no sense why she hasn't written to me . . . or to *you*, Eva."

Fannie's emotions and her obvious concern for Lily seemed to point to the fact that she was finally telling the truth. Or so Eva believed.

Jed's pulse raced as he drove toward Eden Valley that evening in Jonas's buggy, thinking it wise to chart his course to the spot where Eva had suggested meeting on Saturday. He'd made a mistake, having failed to ask her out for tonight, since he planned to leave for home next Monday afternoon.

Even now, he could not erase Eva's guileless expression when he'd first seen her at the auction and her surprise when she'd spotted Sammy riding on his shoulders. And her pretty face—the delightful yet unexpected connection to the photograph in his pocket.

Providential, he thought. *And yet . . .*

The fly in the ointment was the forbidden photo itself, lingering proof of Eva's disobedience. On the other hand, if she *hadn't* had her photo taken, Jed might never have sought her out.

Can anything good come of something so wrong?

Hidden beneath his struggle was the biggest question of all. Why had Eva had her picture taken? *Do I dare ask?*

The prospect was both exciting and alarming.

On Eden Road, he got stuck behind a slow-moving buggy—*probably an older horse*—and decided not to attempt to pass, but slowed up and sat back in his seat. Passing by a large farmhouse, he saw three little Amish girls jumping rope while their older brothers hung back near the stable, heads together. *They're up to something, guaranteed.* He smiled and remembered when he was their age, always looking for a way to make mischief with his brothers after chores were done or on lazy Sunday afternoons. And some evenings, too, when the older youth were busy at Singings and other gatherings.

Finally the pokey horse and carriage turned off, and Jed urged the horse onward, noticing a young woman walking this way, her head down. He slowed again, staying well inside the right lane.

It was still light enough that as he came closer to the woman, he saw that it was Eva, deep in thought. Goodness, if he didn't keep running into her, although it was less surprising when he was traipsing around her neck of the woods.

Pulling over, he waved to her, leaning out the right side of the enclosed carriage. "Eva . . . it's Jed. Would ya like a ride somewhere?"

She looked startled, so he quickly reassured her. "I was just out here double-checking where we're going to meet Saturday evening."

She smiled at his explanation. "'Tis a welcome surprise."

Jed got out and stood near the horse, holding the driving lines. "We could ride a little while now, if you'd like."

She didn't say at first if she would or not but glanced over her shoulder, presumably toward her house. "My sister's expecting me home."

"Of course. I didn't mean to interrupt. Need some time alone, maybe?"

She shook her head and crossed the road, then got right into the buggy. "I don't mean to be standoffish. It's just a nice evening for a walk," she added.

Something's bothering her, he thought as he returned to the carriage. He could sense it, and not because she was reluctant to talk. Eva was completely different than she'd been today at market. Her exuberance had vanished.

She folded her arms and turned to look out the window on her side. For a good minute or longer she was silent.

"Everything okay?" he asked.

Eva took a breath and let it out slowly. Another moment passed before she turned to him. "My younger sister's run off. It's that simple, really, and it's ever so hard on my family . . . and embarrassing, too. But most everyone here knows, so I guess you might as well hear it, too."

Jed was at a loss for words.

"I think I've shocked ya," Eva added.

"You're obviously worried for her."

"Putting it mildly, *jah*." Eva hung her head again. Then, sighing, she sat up straighter and said, "I just learned Lily's gone to live in Ohio."

"A long way off," he said, then added feebly, "Stayin' with relatives?"

Eva shook her head, visibly upset. "You don't understand, Jed. She left without tellin' us where she was going—not a word, not a clue."

He wondered if this sister was sowing her wild oats as some did before joining church. Eva shared more of her concerns, admitting she didn't think Lily was capable of handling herself among strangers. "We've all been through a sad time with my mother's recent passing," she added. "My candy shop has made the biggest difference for me, keeping me busy. Lily didn't have anything like that." She stopped talking and peered at him. "Listen to me, rambling on."

He felt so drawn to her, pulled into her heart and her life, and deeply touched by her compassion for her missing sister.

"I really need to get home," she said abruptly. "I don't want Frona to worry that I've jumped the fence, too."

He didn't know how to respond.

Eva sat without speaking as Jed drove to the spot where she'd said they should meet Saturday evening. On the way, they passed a makeshift sign, *Homemade Soaps for Sale*, and Eva explained that when these neighbors had first started selling soaps, Lily had insisted her mother and sisters go over and buy several as an encouragement.

"Sounds like Lily's a very caring person."

"*Jah*, she is." Eva bit her lip. "She's just mixed up right now."

A curtain of silence fell between them once more; then Jed decided to speak up. "I really want to get to know *you*, Eva." By this, he hoped to assure her that Lily's issues would not interfere with that.

Yet Eva remained quiet until she got out of the buggy. "I'll see ya Saturday, Jed."

He watched her hurry up the road and wondered if she might have preferred to cancel their upcoming date. *I'm glad she didn't*, he thought and hoped he wasn't being selfish. As it was, he had little time to win her heart.

Jed slapped the reins and considered Eva's rebellious sister, who'd apparently escaped to his home state, of all places. Indeed, he felt sorry for Eva and her family. *Surely Eva has moved past the mistake of having her photo taken—a youthful indiscretion.* He presumed she'd be mortified if he brought it up, particularly now, with Lily's disappearance on her mind. He preferred not to risk doing anything to break the connection he felt with the sensitive young woman.

Eva's been through a lot.

On her way back to the house, Eva's eyes caught sight of the large bushes alongside the house, where the back sidewalk met the driveway. She and Lily had often tossed their scooters into the shade of those bushes when they were little. Oh, she wished Lily were around so she could share her thoughts of Jed. Talking with Frona about such things just wasn't the same.

"Frona!" she called as she rounded the house and stepped into the empty kitchen. "I have to talk to you!" She darted from room to room, looking for her sister. "Fro-na!"

Just about the time she was beginning to think her sister had gone somewhere, Eva found her out in the stable pouring grain into a feeding trough. "I've been lookin' all over for ya," she said breathlessly.

"I thought you were over at Naomi's."

"I was." Oh, she felt so *ferhoodled.*

"What's the matter, Eva? Your face looks all red." Frona came forward. "*Ach,* you've been cryin'."

"Fannie Ebersol finally talked about Lily. She thinks Lily's somewhere in Ohio."

"It's 'bout time Fannie coughed up what she's been keepin' to herself."

"And there's more. Lily's got herself a worldly boyfriend." Telling Frona this made Eva feel all the worse.

"Well now. We should've expected as much."

"I guess Fannie felt persuaded to tell because she's worried 'bout Lily, too, since she hasn't heard from her. This time I'm sure she wasn't makin' it all up."

Frona's face softened. "Slow down now. Start at the beginning."

Eva recounted what Fannie had said about Lily's *Englischer* boyfriend and where she'd met him.

Frona shook her head, dismayed but also determined. "I know just what to do. I'll send out word to our Ohio relatives. If Lily has shown up in a small town, maybe, how could she keep this sort of thing quiet?"

"You wouldn't think it's possible."

"Someone will surely know and make the connection, the Lord willing," Frona continued, stooping to pet Max. "Well, Lily went to that there town—Kidron—last summer with Ebersols!"

"Why didn't we go with her?" Eva shook her head. "We should've!"

"You and I didn't accept the Ebersols' invitation because Mamma needed help with gardening, and you couldn't leave the candy shop untended during tourist season." Frona hung the feed scoop on the designated nail and wiped her brow. "Remember?"

"After Lily returned from that trip, I found some fashion magazines and dress catalogues under our bed—a few love stories, too, especially contemporary novels like Mamma's always discouraged," Eva said. Lily had always loved to read and had once declared to Eva and all of their girl cousins that she was going to read a book every single day for the rest of her life. But up till last summer, her interest had only been in the classics.

Lily's words when confronted came back now. *"Books can't be the only way to experience the rest of the world,"* her sister had said. *"As much as I love to read, I don't want to just* imagine *what's out there!"*

At the time, Eva had hoped this wasn't going to turn into a phase, like the curiosity of a handful of other youth in the community. *Lily must have given in to her inquisitiveness,* she thought as Frona headed to the house.

"Would she still be here if I'd said something?" Eva wondered aloud, giving their Eskimo spitz a gentle pat. She recalled the look of surprise on Jed's face when she'd told him about Lily. *He must think little of our family now. He's probably glad to return home soon.*

But that wasn't her biggest concern. Right now Eva couldn't understand why Lily hadn't kept her word to Fannie. *Why didn't Lily contact her? Or us?*

18

THAT evening, after a late dessert of lemon sponge pie, Naomi Mast lingered at the table with Abner. She listened as he talked of his long day spreading fertilizer on their alfalfa field and of having some troubles with one of the mules, causing the whole team difficulties.

When Abner paused for more coffee, she mentioned her unexpected visitor that afternoon. "Evidently, someone thinks she knows where Lily Esch ran off to."

"Really now?" Abner blew on his coffee.

"*Jah*, Fannie Ebersol says she didn't feel at liberty to tell till now, wanting to keep her promise to Lily."

"What's different now?"

"She has some concerns about Lily, too . . . and it didn't hurt that Menno confronted Fannie at market, putting pressure on her to tell what she knows." Naomi paused. "I'm not sure how certain Fannie is 'bout any of it, honestly."

"Well, I ran into Menno just this morning. He's been appointed by the bishop to find Lily and bring her home."

"Who better than her brother?" Naomi revealed that Lily was supposedly living in Ohio with her English boyfriend's sister.

Abner muttered under his breath.

"What're ya sayin', dear?"

"*Puh!* I'm gonna say it right out, right now." Abner shook his head. "I partly blame those battery-operated boom boxes and whatnot for so much of the *Druwwel* with our youth. There's a general fascination with the world, and those just feed into it. "

Naomi scratched her head. "The radios young people are listening to in their courting carriages are causin' them to run away?"

"Trust me on this: It's just one more temptation tuggin' on them," Abner said, picking up his coffee cup and holding it in front of his beard. "Worldly music is a trick of the devil . . . and it's infiltrating the Plain community faster than you can say *Sis en Sin un e Schand*."

"A sin and a shame," Naomi whispered. "So do the other menfolk also blame radios for our youth's troubles?"

"Oh *jah*. You should hear what they're sayin'."

Since the arrival of warmer weather, Naomi had been awakened by some of those boom boxes in the dead of Saturday nights. "Well, I know one thing: Spring is in the air . . . and with it, notions of romance."

He rose with a smile on his face. "That, my dear, ain't no foolin'." And he leaned over and kissed her soundly.

··· ➤ ◄ ···

"'The best and worst day of my life.'" Jed recited the words on the back of the photograph as he drove toward Eden Valley for his date with Eva Saturday evening. He'd spent a beneficial day with Jonas Byler, even though by late afternoon Jed was anxious to get cleaned up and out the door. Yesterday had been equally interesting, meeting a number of Jonas's loyal customers and suppliers, as well as learning a few new techniques for buggy making that Jed was eager to pass along to Uncle Ervin.

One of the leisure stops this morning, however, had been to Mose Byler's place, where Orpha had been sitting out on the porch, as though expecting him, wearing her ever-present smile. While the others remained in the kitchen to eat their three-berry pie, Jed had taken the opportunity to thank her for being so welcoming. Along with casual talk, she had shared her concern over one of their ailing ministers.

Jed was touched by her empathy for the man of God, and knowing it wasn't fair or right to encourage Orpha to believe that they might further their friendship, he had tried to gently let her down. Surprisingly, Orpha took it well, although her unchanged demeanor made him uncertain she'd accepted the message. At least he had been forthright with her, difficult as it was.

Presently, Jed slowed the horse as he topped the hill before the turnoff from the highway. If he was a good judge of how things were developing with Eva, the potential for a relationship seemed good. Consequently, showing her the photograph tonight could prove disastrous. Besides, he wouldn't think of putting her on the spot.

"But I *can* test the waters." He began to formulate a plan while directing Jonas's black gelding onto Eden Road.

··· ➤ ➤ ···

Jed saw Eva waiting near some underbrush and slowed the horse with a "Whoa." He pulled back on the reins as the carriage rolled to a stop. "Hope ya don't mind ridin' in Jonas's old family buggy again," he said as he got out to meet her, waiting till she was settled in on the left side of the seat.

"That's fine," she said. "*Denki.*"

Then, hurrying around to climb back in, he jokingly added, "Of course, we can be sure this carriage is well built, *jah?*"

She smiled in the fading light.

He picked up the reins and signaled the horse to move forward, relieved Eva was in better spirits this evening. "Jonas gave me *gut* directions to a place for dessert later."

She nodded, her hands in her lap.

"I like chocolate cake. Do you?" he asked.

She said she did, and he was pleased Eva wasn't as bashful as one of the girls he'd taken out riding in recent months. He was relieved, too, that she didn't seem nervous about being alone with him. Had that been part of the reason for her reticence Thursday evening?

Jed was conscious of her nearness, aware of the lightly scented perfume she must have dabbed behind her ears, like his youngest sister did before going out with her beau. The scent reminded him of lilacs or honeysuckle, and he wished he might transport Eva to Berlin for the summer, so they could take their time getting to know each other.

"My younger sister, Bettina, likes to wear a similar fragrance," he said. "She's just seventeen and is very active in her buddy group." Jed brought up the rest of his siblings and then mentioned Eva's older sister, reminding her that he'd seen Frona at market. But he purposely didn't refer to Lily.

Eva was quiet now, and akin to last time, they rode in a haze of silence.

Suddenly she faced him. "You might like to know more about my family."

"I would indeed."

"Well, my mother isn't the only one who's deceased," she told him softly. "My father is, too."

The words jarred him, and he carefully weighed his response. "I'm very sorry."

"My parents were much too young," she added. "Dat died in a farming accident, and Mamma got sick and just couldn't get well. She passed away last winter."

Not so long ago . . .

"Do you and Frona live with a married brother and his family, perhaps?" he asked, diverting the topic.

"It's the preferred way round here, but because Frona's older and able to run the house—and likes doin' so—our brother Menno has been letting us live there alone since Mamma's death. He and Bena will be moving in soon enough, though."

"Ah, so he must be the youngest of the sons?"

"*Jah*, that too."

He looked at her, unsure what she meant. "Sorry?"

"Menno can be severe at times."

Jed didn't press for an explanation. He let Eva talk about whatever was on her mind. And there was plenty, beginning with her seeming interest in his hometown of Berlin—what sort of carriages he built, his daily life, and if the Plain community there catered much to the tourist trade, like in Lancaster County.

Is she curious because Lily's gone there? he wondered.

The more Eva talked, the more he found himself comparing the way she spoke to the words she'd written in the margins of *Little Women*, down to the similar phrases she used to describe her feelings.

I know her better than she thinks, he thought, feeling a little guilty. After all, her notes had given him a window into how she expressed herself, an idea of what things were important to her. *Would she forgive me if she knew?*

In spite of his distraction, he attempted to answer her questions, still uncertain if she was making polite small talk or if she was actually curious about his life and work. And Jed considered when he should slip in the question that weighed on his mind. Could he do that without interrupting the easy flow of their conversation?

"How do you like Lancaster County?" she asked.

"I'm very glad my uncle Ervin suggested I glean some knowledge from Jonas Byler. Jonas is a cousin to Ervin's wife," he added.

"Oh, so that's why you stayed with them."

He waited for her to mention Orpha, perhaps, but Eva was already on to another subject.

"What sorts of quilt patterns do your sisters make out in Ohio?"

"You'd have to ask them." Jed chuckled.

Now she, too, was laughing. "I guess men don't pay much attention to such things."

"Well, we have our own ideas about what's important."

"Like what's for supper?"

He smiled, enjoying her all the more for her spunkiness.

"You don't have open surreys out there, do ya?" she asked.

"Only the courting carriages are open. Why do you ask?"

She mentioned an elderly aunt who lived in Berne, Indiana, where all the carriages, even the family ones, were open, no matter the season. "It's surprising, the differences between church districts, 'specially between states."

Jed agreed.

"Yet some things don't change. The cloistered life can be stifling for some young folks."

"You must be thinkin' of Lily," he said.

"S'pose I am."

Quickly, Eva moved from Lily and their Indiana aunt to how nice the weather was for the ride.

"The sky's clear," he agreed. "And in a little while, we should be able to see Venus, the evening star." He pointed toward the west, and she leaned forward to look.

"I wonder if Lily can see it where she is," Eva whispered.

"She can if she's searchin' for it." He sensed Eva's great affection for her sister—and apprehension. Curious, Jed dared another glance at her, pleased they had this time together.

Eva watched for the golden glow of gas lamps in each Amish home as they rode, speculating how far toward May Post Office Road Jed would take the horse and carriage. She enjoyed that he was more talkative than most fellows she'd dated, even Alfred, especially when the topic of conversation surrounded family, either Jed's or hers. It wasn't odd for Jed to bring up Lily, considering all Eva had told him. Still, she felt *naerfich*—nervous—and protective of her strong-willed sister. *Or am I simply overreacting?* This respectable young man certainly wasn't nosey.

"How 'bout if we ride up to White Oak Road?" Jed asked, breaking the silence. "Jonas Byler suggested it."

"Sure." She was glad she didn't have to propose their route.

Jed smiled at her, though she could scarcely see his features now that the sun was down and the shooting rays of light had vanished from the sky.

"Are ya lookin' forward to getting back to work?" She was anxious to start the conversation again.

"We do have a backlog of orders. Besides that, Bettina might have some news for me when I return."

"What sort of news?"

"She loves a *gut* mystery, so she's makin' me wait . . . and wonder. But I do have an inkling. Best not to say more till she confirms it, though." Jed also mentioned their recent celebration of Ascension Day, which he said most Ohio Amish communities observed. "I do know of Amish in Indiana who treat it like any other day, however."

"*Ach*, our bishop wouldn't hear of that."

Jed nodded. "The businesses in Berlin close, and *die Youngie* team up to play softball or volleyball. What 'bout here—what did you do?"

"Mostly just played games and went visiting, like a no-Preaching Sunday. Frona encouraged us to spend time thinking 'bout how the day commemorates the Lord's physical ascension into heaven." She paused a moment. "Some districts have church; it just depends on the bishop, I guess . . . and the standard custom."

Jed shifted on the seat beside her. "Would ya say your bishop is traditionally strict, then? 'Specially with the youth?"

"Oh, prob'ly as strict as most older bishops. He's in his midseventies, same as Abner Mast across the road. Abner is my friend Naomi's husband."

"It sounds like Jonas's bishop is also firm on the *Ordnung*," Jed said.

"Well, that's because his bishop and ours happen to be one and the same."

"I would've guessed the two church districts might be closer in proximity, then."

"Actually, it's been that way since I was little."

He glanced at her. "May I be so bold as to ask why Naomi is such a close friend?"

"Honestly, Lily was when we were growin' up. She was my best sounding board, too, but that changed after Mamma died. Naomi became more of a confidante then. She was so close to my mother . . . really wanted me to know I wasn't alone." Eva had stuck her neck out and hoped to goodness he wouldn't probe further. She wasn't sure she was up to talking more about either Lily or Mamma tonight.

Jed's voice grew softer. "Life throws us curve balls sometimes."

"Still, I like to remember that the heart of love is always kindness, even with a difficult family member."

Jed was mum.

"*Ach*, sorry. I didn't mean to talk out of turn," she said.

"Sometimes the ones closest to us are the real test." Jed seemed to understand. "In fact, my Dawdi Stutzman has often said that 'familiarity breeds contempt.'"

"He must've read Aesop's fables, then."

"As a matter of fact, he has. What about your family—are they big readers?"

"We all are. It's a *gut* way to experience new things without ever leavin' home." She also told him she liked to read the Bible to start the day.

"Then you must know Psalm 50? Maybe from memory: 'And call upon me in the day of trouble: I will deliver thee, and thou shalt glorify me,'" he recited, smiling when Eva joined him for the last phrase.

"That's such a comfort," she said, considering it. "We're taught to regularly read *die Biewel* in both *Deitsch* and King James English, but we don't purposely memorize Scripture. I s'pose after reading passages often enough, though, they become part of our thoughts. And that's certainly one of them."

"Our bishop actually encourages us to study and memorize passages from Scripture."

She found this interesting but didn't care to debate the differences between their church districts. Not on their first and possibly only date.

After some time, a half-moon rose, and Eva was able to see Jed better as they made their way along the two-lane road toward the small junction at Nickel Mines. She looked forward to being able to see his expressions as they talked across the table during dessert.

Jed directed the horse into a small café parking lot, where newly painted white lines marked individual spots. "Are you hungry yet?"

"Mostly thirsty . . . maybe for a root beer float."

Jed grinned, looking quite dapper in his straw hat with its narrow brim. "Whatever you'd like."

She waited for him to tie the horse to the hitching post, then come around and open her side of the carriage. When he offered his hand, she took it and felt her heart skip a beat.

19

THE Nickel Mines café's dining room was a narrow space with windows on both sides. The soda fountain sat at the far north end, where, from Eva's vantage point, its counter shone with a glossy finish. A lone yellow rose adorned each of a handful of tables, the one in the middle of their particular table having lost its vitality. Eva reached out to touch its pretty petals and tried to prop up the blossom with the stem's leaves. "Looks like we might be the last customers today," she whispered.

Jed glanced around. "Are you all right here, or would ya like to move to a different spot?"

"One with a perkier flower, maybe?" she joked, surprising herself. Now that she could see his face better, she felt more comfortable. The waning light of the ride over had felt a bit distancing.

He grinned. "So, are ya sure it's just a root beer float for you?"

The waitress was heading their way, a pencil pushed into her hair above one ear.

"Sounds *gut.*" Eva leaned back in her chair, letting him order.

Once the waitress retreated to put in their requests, Eva brought up his apprenticeship, and they settled into another interesting conversation. And later, she enjoyed seeing him become even more talkative after a few bites of carrot cake. *Must be the sugar,* she thought.

"I'd like to see you again before I leave Monday afternoon," Jed said, appealing to her with his engaging eyes. The way he looked at her, so inquisitively at times, made her wonder what he was thinking. "Is there a place we could go walkin' tomorrow afternoon following your Preaching service?" he asked.

"I know a spot." She felt pleased. "Naomi and her husband have a large property with a big pond—I'll bring some bread crusts to feed the ducks."

Jed nodded. "I haven't done that in years. Are ya sure your neighbors won't mind?"

"Not in the least," she said most assuredly, her heart already beating more quickly at the prospect of seeing him again.

Why don't I feel like this with Alfred?

··· ➤ ➤ ···

Jed did his best to keep the horse trotting steadily as they headed back toward Eden Valley. He wished the night would slow down. Eva was not only fun to be with; she seemed to be warming up to him.

"What if I wrote you a letter when I get home to Ohio?" He didn't think it was too soon to ask.

"Well, I'd read it, of course."

He laughed. "And if you read it, would you write back?"

"Depends on what you write."

He delighted in her bantering. "I'll be careful what I say," he promised.

"*Gut*, then."

And they left it right there as their time together drew to a close.

He glanced at her, and she was smiling. Her eyes caught his, and her pretty face brightened all the more. The moment passed between them, and within it was an understanding that neither wanted to let it go.

When they pulled up to the end of her driveway, Jed tied the horse to the nearby fence post and went to help Eva down from the buggy, happy to offer his hand again, wishing he could keep hers in his. *Too soon for such affection*, he reminded himself as he walked with her to the back door and said good-night.

He returned to the carriage and untied the horse, and it was all he could do to keep from leaping into the driver's side. Not delaying, he urged the horse back out to the highway, and up and down the hills toward the Bylers'.

A glance at his watch with the help of a flashlight showed that it was much later than he'd planned, and he hoped Eva's older sister hadn't waited up. And what might Jonas and Elsie Byler think of his borrowing their buggy and returning it so late? *Especially since I'm not out with their granddaughter Orpha!*

He remembered something Eva had said earlier tonight, when they were talking. *"The heart of love is always kindness."*

He'd read that before, but where? *In her book, perhaps?*

Pulling into the Bylers' long lane, Jed wondered what Lydiann might have thought of Eva. Would she have liked her, too? What a peculiar thought, yet considering how much he'd loved his fiancée, he realized it wasn't strange after all.

Jah, thought Jed, *she would definitely approve.*

20

B Y the time they arrived at Bishop Isaac's farm a little before eight
o'clock Sunday morning, Eva felt somewhat settled, enough to
attend worship. But as soon as she and Frona stepped into line with the
other womenfolk, one after another began to whisper concerns about
Lily. Some even had questions.

Everyone knows, Eva thought, stiffening.

"Have ya heard from your dear sister?" Sylvia Lantz's grandmother
Suzanne asked, blinking her milky blue eyes, her cane dangling off her
arm.

"*Ach,* you mustn't worry," Frona said. "Not at your age!" and then added
something Eva could not hear in a reassuring tone.

Others, just as well meaning, asked how she and Frona were getting
along. Although Eva knew it was all in a spirit of compassion, it nevertheless was beginning to wear thin.

When Menno's wife, Bena, arrived, Eva observed her walk across the
backyard with little Katie Ann in tow. Their matching blue mother-
daughter dresses moved gracefully around their calves, and they had on
new black shoes.

"We'll sit with ya," Bena said with a sweet smile when she approached.
This sister-in-law had always been one to exhibit the utmost reverence for
the Lord's Day. It was one of the reasons Eva's mother had liked her so
well for Menno when they were first dating. Mamma had shared this with
Eva when she also reached courting age, wanting to note a good example.

"*Denki*," Eva whispered and lowered her head, hoping not to attract any more attention to Frona and herself.

During Preaching, Eva fought to keep her mind on the ministers' sermons—the first one an hour long—and also during the second, lengthier sermon. Their pointed words were a clear warning to young people not to entertain foolish notions. *Like Lily's*, thought Eva.

When it was time for the final silent prayer, they all turned to kneel at their wooden benches, and Eva beseeched almighty God to lead Lily home according to His loving and sovereign will. *I trust Thy wisdom, heavenly Father. Be our compassionate guide, and strength and comfort. May Thy protecting hand cover my wayward sister, Lily, and grant all of us divine peace.*

After the announcements, Eva made her way outside with the other young women her age while the benches were converted into tables for the shared meal. She noticed Alfred Dienner's mother, Miriam, talking with Naomi Mast on the back porch. Miriam and her sister had been assisting the bishop's wife with serving cold cuts and pie, but Miriam made a real show of smiling and waving at Eva.

For goodness' sake, thought Eva. *What has Alfred told her?*

With a bag of bread crusts in hand, Eva waited for Jed beneath two sheltering oaks that balmy Lord's Day afternoon. Since her first unexpected meeting with him, Eva believed she'd crossed an imaginary line in her mind, and perhaps in her heart. *My sister leaves . . . and Jed arrives*, she thought, torn between sadness and exuberance.

She recalled Naomi's endearing smile after the common meal, when Eva asked if it was all right to go walking with Jed around the Masts' pond. Not only had Naomi said repeatedly that it was fine, but she offered to leave some treats and cold lemonade in the backyard gazebo, "*if you won't think I'm interfering.*"

Now, spotting the Bylers' gray carriage coming into view, Eva's heart thrilled to see Jed wave out the window. His enthusiasm delighted her, and she waved back.

The sun dazzled everything in sight—suddenly the meadow looked greener and Naomi's climbing roses a brighter pink, as if Eva's surroundings were tinged by her own happiness.

"I'm glad to see you again, Eva." Jed's voice was warm as he offered her a hand up, then went around the buggy to get into the driver's side.

"It's all right if you want to pull into Abner's lane," she suggested with a smile. "He won't mind."

"What if we just ride for a while first? All right with you?"

Eva was perfectly content to sit there next to him and asked about his morning, knowing the Bylers' church district had an off-Sunday, since their shared bishop had held the Preaching service for Eden Valley at his own house. Jed mentioned a quiet breakfast with Jonas and his wife, then family worship, followed by a long walk around their property.

"How was your Preaching service today?" he inquired.

"The house was packed," she said softly. "I don't think anyone was missing, come to think of it." She caught herself. "Except for Lily. And I almost wonder if that wasn't the reason for the larger than usual attendance." She mentioned a good number of people had offered to pray for Lily.

"Reminds me of our church." Jed tilted his head thoughtfully. "It's God's way—the People lookin' after each other."

She nodded in full agreement. "It does help, but it doesn't always ease the pain."

"I understand," he said quietly, taking his time. At last he met her gaze. "You see, I lost my fiancée to an accident a year ago."

"Oh, Jed." Her heart broke for him.

He inhaled deeply. "Lydiann died instantly, I was told . . . a blessing for her, but . . ." He paused, clearly uncomfortable with the recollection. "Not for the rest of us. At the time, I didn't think I could bear it."

"I'm so sorry." Eva didn't ask about the accident. *Some things are just too painful.*

"It was shocking, sure, but no more than your father's death was for you and your family."

"There's no time to say good-bye with a sudden loss, but it's quick and over with for the person," she said. "A lingering illness gives time for the family to accept the death, but the patient suffers more—like Mamma did."

Jed glanced at her, his expression caring. "Afterward, I remember feeling exhausted all the time. I couldn't seem to get enough sleep."

"Oh, and ya feel so alone," she admitted, swallowing the lump in her throat. "At Mamma's burial service, I kept wonderin' if anyone could see how forlorn I felt . . . ever so lost." She glanced at Jed. "Like the orphan I am."

Jed was nodding his head. "For me, it seemed like my hopes and plans dried up. It took days, even weeks, for the truth to sink in. I kept wakin' up and thinking it was a horrible dream."

"I felt that way for months, too, but not so much about my future hopes as for the giant hole in our family."

"Did you find yourself wishing you'd done something different the day of your father's death?" he asked.

"For sure. To this day, I wish I had cut one more piece of my birthday cake for him."

Jed's eyebrows rose. "Your father died on your birthday?"

She bowed her head. "My sixteenth—four years ago. It was terrible."

They talked further, more slowly now. Then Eva asked, "What about you? Did ya wish you could change anything 'bout the day Lydiann died?"

"Over and over, I wish I'd offered to take her to visit her aunt, instead of letting her go with her younger brother—as if *I* had the power to change God's will."

He turned to face her again, and in his eyes she saw the pain he carried, the enormous loss.

"I'm learning a lot about faith through grieving—trusting that our sovereign Lord knows what is best for each of us . . . about everything," Eva whispered, blinking away tears. "To be honest, it's a difficult journey."

"*Jah*, for certain." Jed reached for her hand, and despite her sadness at what she had lost, Eva felt an irrepressible joy.

After the ride, Jed pulled into the Masts' lane and tied up the horse under a shade tree. They set off walking toward the pond, where there was a grove of willows along one side, nourished by the water. Jed set an easy pace as they enjoyed soothing breezes beneath the graceful branches. The place was peaceful, hidden by dozens of green tendrils.

"My father cautioned me against bitterness in the early days after the accident," Jed admitted. "I was sorely tempted to fall into that pit. *Ach,* there were days . . ."

She purposely didn't look at him, lest he was struggling. "I can't imagine your loss, Jed."

"And I can't know *yours.* I have a feeling that each loss is different . . . and unique, too, in how a person grieves."

"With my father's death, I mostly fought the disbelief—the shock of it—and with Mamma's illness, I felt so helpless. Oh, the sorrow, the ache in my heart for them both once they were gone."

Jed glanced at the sky, then back at her. He mentioned someone had indicated he'd taken Lydiann's loss too hard, that he should have gotten over his sadness sooner, since they hadn't married yet. "But no one can really say how another person should grieve, or for how long."

Eva fully understood. *Oh, do I ever!*

A cloud concealed the sun from their view as they emerged from the willow grove. Eva spotted several ducks gliding through the water toward them. "I think they must know somethin'," she whispered, opening the bag and breaking off a long piece of crust for Jed. "Lookee there."

She pinched off a small piece and tossed it, and then another, and Jed did the same. He looked so handsome in his Sunday clothes—black trousers, white shirt, and black suspenders, and his narrow-brimmed straw hat, too. She had to remind herself to feed the ducks instead of watching Jed squat to toss the crumbs into the pond.

Soon, two larger ducks waddled out of the water and came right up to Jed, quacking for more. He held his hand flat, and the first duck ate off of his palm.

"They're not afraid of you." Eva was intrigued. "Lily can do that, too. The ducks and Canada geese come right up to her."

Jed looked at her. "You've suffered a third loss," he said so tenderly she thought she might cry. "Lily's leaving an' all."

"A frustrating kind of loss, *jah.*" *Because no one knows how it'll end.*

He rose and brushed off his hands, but the two ducks stood there quacking for more.

"Here, why don't you take the rest." She was amused by his interaction with the more persistent birds.

Jed pinched off a few more pieces and moved closer to the water. Now many more ducks were swimming this way, some flapping their dark wings and splashing as they came.

Once the crumbs were gone, Jed and Eva walked twice around the pond's perimeter, and each time, when they wandered beneath the willows, Jed took her hand.

"I'd like to see your candy shop before I leave town," he said. "Might I drop by tomorrow?"

"Well, I open later on Mondays to help with the washing. If ya stop in after the noon meal, that'd be best."

"Fewer customers then?"

"Possibly." She couldn't help but smile.

"Do you have a Closed sign?" He winked at her.

She blushed. "I do, actually."

"So maybe we could slip away for another walk."

She liked the idea. Then, second-guessing it, she said, "Honestly, it might be better to stay put in the shop to visit.'"

He seemed to acquiesce. "I don't want to leave without sayin' so long, ya know?"

She encouraged him to come by The Sweet Tooth around twelve-thirty, after dishes were done.

"Will it be all right with Frona?" he asked.

"I don't plan to tell her," Eva replied with a little laugh. "Hopefully, if anyone spots you, they'll assume you're there to purchase sweets."

One last visit with Jed . . .

21

THE wonderful smell of bread dough filled the kitchen as Eva made her way down the cellar steps on washday morning. Frona was fretting about coming that close to getting her fingers stuck in the wringer. "*Ach*, I'm glad ya didn't!" Eva said, hurrying to help lift the heavy, wet clothes out of the washer and carefully feeding them through the wringer with her sister's assistance.

Later, once the first load was out on the line and they'd loaded the second batch, they stopped to have a cup of tea. And after the breakfast dishes were washed and put away, Eva rushed to the mailbox and found a letter from Alfred Dienner. Truth be known, she wasn't very excited to hear from him, especially since meeting Jed.

Nevertheless, she slipped away to her room to read Alfred's letter.

Dear Eva,

How are you? Are you keeping busy with your candy making and your customers?

I've been doing quite a lot in the woodworking shop here, more than I realized would be necessary. That's why I haven't written sooner, even though I do think of you every day.

Have you given any thought to our last conversation? Ach, I sometimes wish I could hear your voice. Maybe I'll call you at the phone shanty sometime, even though it might be frowned on if we talk too often that way.

There are some fine places to eat here in Wisconsin, but I haven't found a shoofly pie like my Mamm's. I will say, though, that the cheese is very tasty!

As for learning the woodworking trade, I enjoy the creativity involved more than I ever expected.

Alfred's letter continued by describing some of the folks he'd met since first arriving there, and even though he seemed happy enough, sharing his activities with her, Eva could tell he must be homesick. It was odd, because she didn't know how she should think about Alfred, uncertain how her new friendship with Jed Stutzman would play out once he returned to Ohio.

It's unusual to have the attention of two young men at the same time, and for both to be out of state, she thought as she pushed Alfred's letter into her dresser drawer.

Two buggies rolled into the driveway, and she figured they were candy customers. Happily, she hurried downstairs and into The Sweet Tooth just as they pulled into the parking spaces.

As planned, Naomi stopped at Ida Mae's after the washing was on the line. She'd noticed Frona and Eva outdoors exceptionally early getting theirs up, too. Not that she was in competition, but her neighbor to the west certainly made a valiant attempt to be first on *Weschdaag* mornings. After years of this nonsense, Naomi just let her win. What was the point? She'd once told this to Abner, who'd chortled.

"Your father went to see Bishop Isaac first thing today," Naomi informed Ida Mae on their ride to the General Store for sewing notions. "I know you'll keep it to yourself, but it was 'bout Lily Esch's possible whereabouts in Ohio. He's mighty worried, as are the Esch boys."

Ida Mae gasped. "Lily's made it all the way there?"

"Evidently, there's a young fella involved . . . an *Englischer.*"

"Lily's always been such a *gut* girl. What's gotten into her?"

Naomi nodded. "Poor thing, losing her mother threw her, I gather. We all know Dottie raised her girls right."

"*Ach,* Dottie would weep if she knew."

Naomi tried to relax her grip on the reins. "Have ya thought any more 'bout traveling to Paradise with me the end of this week to help with some sewin' for your second cousin?"

"Poor Connie must be really bad off if she can't even hold a needle."

"She can't thread one either, her wrist's so painful," Naomi added.

"Honestly, I don't see why she doesn't have it put in a cast."

"Well, you and I both know why."

Ida Mae looked away, pulling on her shawl. "It wonders me why some people are timid 'bout getting medical help and others ain't. It's just odd."

"The community's split down the middle on that." Naomi waited for Ida Mae to say whether she would go or not.

"I s'pose I could take one of my impatiens plants to Cousin Connie. Cheer her up, maybe."

"I think she'd like that, I surely do." Naomi was relieved, since she hadn't wanted to travel alone all the way south, though she'd made the trip by herself before.

Naomi tapped on the carriage brake when they reached a steep decline. There was something else she thought Ida Mae should know. "Your brother Omar also went to speak with Bishop Isaac today. Sounds like your father bumped into him on the way in. Anyway, Omar asked outright what Bishop thought of him going ahead and registering to vote in the election."

Ida Mae's eyes popped. "*Ach*, really?"

"Know what the bishop said? He told Omar that if he fasted and prayed 'bout it for three days, the Lord God would show him what to do."

Ida Mae clapped her hands. "Well, ain't that the best answer ya ever did hear?"

"Your Dat completely agreed."

"And what did Omar say?"

"Knowin' Omar's penchant for food, I would've thought he would say he'd keel over with starvation in three days." Naomi shook her head. "But he's considerin' it." She went on to say that when she'd tried to talk sense to him, he was as closed as a book. "The bishop was mighty prudent, if ya think about it, putting the decision right back in Omar's hands."

"I do hope my brother is willing to fast and pray like the man of God asked."

"If he refuses, the voting issue will be the least of our fears."

They talked about other things for a while. Then, as they neared the store, Naomi asked, "By the way, how early did ya get your washing hung out today?"

"Before breakfast. Why?"

Naomi grinned at her. "Just curious."

··· ➤ ➤ ···

At 12:42 that afternoon, Eva saw Jed pull into the parking area in front of The Sweet Tooth. She knew the exact time because she'd been watching the clock since the last few customers left, hoping Frona was busy writing to a couple of Ohio relatives about Lily's whereabouts, as she'd volunteered to do.

Eva put the last few triple chocolate–nut clusters onto wax paper to cool, so delighted at seeing him again, she did spontaneous little steps in place. Not a dance but nearly. "What if we *did* slip away for another walk?" she murmured, recalling yesterday and how they'd shared their hearts. She'd felt sad for his loss of his first love.

Eva could hear Jed whistling as he tied the horse to the hitching rail out back. Shaking out the lower part of her black apron, she wanted to look as neat and presentable as she could once Jed came up the walkway and opened the shop door. Watching him from afar, she felt almost dazed at her good fortune—this especially handsome and kind young man seemed so eager to see her again.

He wants to write to me, she reminded herself, aware of her own widening smile.

Jed's stride was long and even, and his hair shone in the sunlight as he approached the shop. His black suspenders were stark against his long-sleeved white shirt, its sleeves rolled up.

"Hullo again." He came inside and turned to quietly close the door.

"You're nearly on time," she teased. It occurred to her how very comfortable she already felt with him.

"I might've been earlier if there hadn't been an accident out yonder."

"Oh dear. Hope no one was hurt."

"It looked like just a fender bender. Might've been a tourist who'd lost his way—the driver gawking about and not paying attention."

She'd seen plenty of automobiles racing around buggies, but she had never run across two cars in such a mishap. "Well, I'm glad *you're* in one piece, Jed."

He brightened as he met her gaze, then looked around the place. "So this is where you spend much of your time?"

"The shop is only open four days a week—Monday, Wednesday, Friday, and Saturday—and never for more than a few hours. I do spend a fair amount of time makin' goodies, though! Would ya like a tour of this small corner of my world?" She showed him the little kitchen, where she pointed out the chocolate-nut clusters cooling on the counter. Then she brought him back to the display case to show him other favorite offerings, including the Butterfinger truffles made with semisweet chocolate, fresh cream, and Butterfinger candy bars.

"Choose a sample or two, if you'd like."

"They all look *wunnerbaar-gut*," Jed said with a grin.

She even led him behind the counter so he could see all the cubbyholes for storing paper bags and boxes, string, tape, and the like.

"You're very organized." He moved closer to the display case, eyeing the truffles. "I'll purchase a few of these," he said, his nose practically touching the glass.

"They were flyin' off the shelf earlier."

Jed reached for his wallet and set it on the counter.

She shook her head. "*Ach*, you treated me at the café . . . won't ya let me treat you?"

"That was our *date*, Eva. And if I lived round here, this would be just the first of many purchases."

She smiled and felt her face flush, surely as pink as the geraniums on Naomi's porch. "I'd like to send some sweets along for your trip, all right?"

Jed reluctantly gave in, and it took no time for her to gather up a half-dozen truffles and wrap them. "I've hired a van driver, since there are a few tools and other items to take back," he explained. "Couldn't see storin' any of that in the luggage hold of a train, not when there's a driver already going that direction."

"Sounds like you've got everything planned." Oh, she wished he didn't have to leave.

He walked around the counter while she pulled out a small sack. A glance out the window reassured Eva that no other customers had arrived, and they still had a moment or two to themselves.

"I meant what I said the other night 'bout writing, Eva," Jed said as she handed him the truffles.

"It'll be real nice to hear from ya."

"That you will." He picked up his wallet and a small picture fell out, landing facedown on the counter.

She leaned forward to retrieve it, but just as quickly, Jed reached for it. The photo slipped from his grasp and fluttered away. *"Nee!"* he muttered, trying to seize it.

His obvious nervousness startled her.

"I've got it," he said, finally getting a grasp on it, but not before she'd caught a glimpse.

Her heart stopped, then sank. *What on earth?*

"Jed . . . who *is* that?" Eva asked, though she was certain she knew.

He reddened. "I found this photo on the train," he said, looking at the picture before reluctantly offering it to her.

Tears sprang to Eva's eyes as she gazed upon the face of the last person she would have expected to see. *Lily.* "It's my dear missing sister."

After a moment, she raised her gaze to his own befuddled expression.

"Did *you* take this picture?" she asked at last.

"Of course not," he stammered. "Like I said . . . I found it on the train." He frowned. "But wait . . . did you say *Lily?*"

"Jah, this is a photo of my sister." She stared at him, still wondering why this photo was in his possession but now equally perplexed by his present confusion.

He must not have known it was Lily. . . .

And then it came to her: Jed had thought *she* was the girl in the picture.

"Go ahead and keep it," Jed said, attempting a smile.

"Lily and I do look quite a bit alike," she said, taking a deep breath. "Or at least people say we do."

Jed removed his straw hat and stared down at it. "I don't know what to say. . . . I honestly thought . . ."

That I was the girl, Eva thought again, stunned. "I don't know anything 'bout this photo or where it was taken. What could have prompted Lily to do this?" She slid it into one of the cubbyholes beneath her cash register, wishing it might vanish just as her sister had.

It was evident now why Jed had looked so inquisitively at her when they'd first met at the auction. *Like he'd seen me before.*

The awkwardness was strewn before them like broken glass, and every bit as painful to step on. *Was he looking to meet Lily?* she wondered. *Is that why we met?*

"I hope I haven't offended you, Eva." Jed stepped toward her, then, as if out of bounds, he inched back.

Her head was spinning.

"Listen, I don't care about the photograph," he began again before hesitating, but the way he said it wasn't very convincing.

I feel like crying. How on earth had everything gone so wrong so suddenly?

"Eva . . . I thought about telling you, but then I wasn't sure what you'd think."

They heard the sound of the doorknob turning and the door whisking open. Eva spotted Bishop Isaac smiling at them beneath his formidable-looking black hat. Except for his long-sleeved white shirt, he was dressed all in black.

"I'd best be goin'," Jed said abruptly. "You have another customer."

"Ain't necessary to go," she heard herself say. But it was apparently pointless for him to remain to pursue the young woman he'd assumed Eva to be. She managed to nod her head. "*Jah*, maybe 'tis best." She sighed. "So long, Jed."

He turned slowly and then glanced back at her, as if still trying to reconcile her face with the photograph. He reached for the door as the bishop stepped up to the counter. Once again, Jed looked back at her and nodded politely.

The worst timing! she thought.

"*Willkumm*, Bishop," she said. "What sweets might ya be interested in?"

Her heart sank anew as through the window she saw Jed hurrying to his buggy.

"Nothing today." The bishop kept on his black felt hat. "But I'd like you to follow me into the main house, where Frona's waiting."

638

What else can go wrong?

"Let me just hang up my Closed sign," she said, thankful now that she and Jed hadn't set out for a walk. But then Lily's forbidden photo might still be safely tucked away in Jed's wallet.

All this time, Jed thought I was the girl in the photograph.

22

EVA sat respectfully at the table while Frona informed the bishop that Menno had stopped by earlier. It was surprising to hear that Menno had contacted their cousin Jeptha King in Apple Creek, Ohio. "Jeptha's agreed to nose around some of the surrounding towns . . . see what he can find out about Lily," Frona said with a glance at Eva.

After what had just transpired in the candy shop, it was hard to keep her mind on what the bishop was saying in response. Eva was still so baffled Lily had dared to have a picture made of herself . . . and that Jed had found it on the very train he'd taken here. The whole thing was mind-boggling.

"Menno's a conscientious farmer," Bishop Isaac was telling Frona. "I understand why he can't just up and leave, 'specially with cultivating filling his hours."

"I'm doin' my part to help," Frona chimed in, explaining she'd written to some Ohio relatives. "It shouldn't take long to find out something, I wouldn't think."

"But what will happen if Lily refuses to come home?" Eva asked softly.

Bishop Isaac folded his big, callused hands on the table where their father had always sat. "*Gott* has a sovereign plan for your sister, and I believe it's right here with the People. No doubt in my mind."

Eva hoped with all of her heart he was right. After all, he was the man chosen by God to shepherd the flock here.

"In the long run, though, it'll be up to Lily to surrender her prideful independence," Bishop Isaac said.

All the same, Eva fought against the idea of someone forcing Lily to return against her will. *If she's even still single,* she thought. That was the only way it could possibly work, because if Lily had already eloped . . . Oh, she didn't want to think about that. They must find her, and soon!

"We'll put our complete trust in our heavenly Father." The bishop rose and made his way toward the door. "I'll leave you sisters to your work now."

"*Denki* for comin', bishop," Frona said right quick.

But Eva said nothing.

… ≻ ≺ …

Jed tortured himself on the ride to Quarryville, where he was scheduled to meet the van driver for the trip home. "How could I have made such a fool of myself?" He could not escape the memory of Eva's utter disappointment. And the way she'd wanted him to stay, then changed her mind and agreed he should take his leave. *What a time for the bishop to appear. . . .*

Lily certainly resembled Eva. But now Jed's disappointment was less over the girl in the photo than the realization that Eva wasn't the author of the notes in the book's margins. To think he didn't know her as well as he'd imagined! That was the most disappointing fact of all.

"Just when I was beginning to think God had brought us together in the most unlikely way," he muttered miserably.

… ≻ ≺ …

Eva waited until the bishop backed out of the driveway before she dashed over to the candy shop. There, she found Lily's picture and brought it into the kitchen to show Frona, who was busy slicing the fresh bread.

"Where do ya think Lily had this taken?" She pushed it in front of Frona, who leaned forward for a better look.

"Where'd ya get this?" she demanded.

Eva hesitated, unwilling to say. "I just came across it . . . and want to know what you think."

"I think you'd better burn it, that's what."

Eva nodded and studied it again. "*Ach,* I wonder if Fannie has an

641

opinion 'bout it. She seems to know more than I would've guessed 'bout our sister."

"True. You could ask her." Frona glanced out the window. "Right now, though, it looks like you're getting a customer."

Eva could see the carriage pulling in. "Come to think of it, maybe this photo might help Cousin Jeptha locate Lily."

"Well now, ain't that a thought?"

"It would help a lot if they could narrow things down—Ohio's an awful big state," Eva said, picking up the photograph. "Cousin Jeptha can't just run around all over, ya know."

"*Nee*, that's for certain." Frona bobbed her head toward the shop. "Hurry up, now."

"I'm goin'," Eva exclaimed, leaving Lily's photo there on the counter.

Jed loaded his tools into the back of the van to make room for five other paying passengers. The driver, Arnie Strout, informed him it wasn't necessary to skimp on space since none of the other passengers had much luggage.

Sitting in the front passenger seat, Jed was plagued by Eva's disillusionment. *What a mess*, he thought. *It was ridiculous of me to carry that photo around in the first place!*

And he had made a terrible mistake in assuming Eva was the girl in the picture. *I should have known she wouldn't do such a thing.*

Jed recalled everything Eva had said about her younger sister. She had been pretty tight-lipped, perhaps to protect Lily. He didn't know and wasn't sure he was supposed to know.

Now he felt convinced that finding the book on the train had been purely coincidental. *Anyone could've picked it up. . . .*

"Was there a crowd at the auction?" Arnie asked, interrupting Jed's thoughts.

"It was well attended."

"I wonder if the sellers will spend winters in Florida like other Amish retirees are starting to do."

"Is that so?" Jed hadn't heard this.

"Oh yes, and Pinecraft's the place for Plain snowbirds. At least that's what I'm told."

"I don't know of any Amish who go there." Jed was truly interested. "Is it a set-apart community?"

"I guess it's somewhat isolated from the more modern surrounding neighborhoods. Some of the cottages have electricity, though, but since these are mostly rentals and most folks are only there for a few months out of the year, the bishops are looking the other way." Arnie added, "Once a person experiences the warmer temperatures, it's doubly hard to endure another Pennsylvania winter."

The conversation lulled, and Jed found himself contemplating the way he'd left things with Orpha Byler. Had she finally accepted the fact that Jed was only interested in a casual friendship and nothing more? Indeed, yesterday he'd almost thought Orpha and her family might come again for dessert after supper, but he was relieved when the meal rolled around and it was just him and his hosts seated at the table.

He hoped his uncle wouldn't be frustrated to learn that things had gone nowhere with Jonas's granddaughters. Jed simply hadn't been able to think of anyone but Eva once he'd encountered her at the auction.

And now I've ruined that.

23

JED'S youngest sister met him in the kitchen that night, sporting a big smile.

"I want you to hear this from me first," Bettina said, eyes dancing as she told him of her wedding plans come November.

He knew she was hoping for his brotherly blessing. "I'd be happier if you were a little older. What's the big hurry, sis?"

"Aw, Jed . . ."

"Well now, think about it. You've only been goin' to Singings a year."

"Levi and I *love* each other," she said, wringing her hands. "Why should we wait?"

She was far from ready to be a wife, young as she was. "Have ya thought of talkin' to Dat and Mamm?"

She ignored his question. "I forgot to tell you—Levi wants you to be one of his side sitters at our wedding."

"Shouldn't *he* be askin'? That's traditionally the way it's done."

"Oh, Jed, I'm just so thrilled! I can hardly think straight."

Thinking straight should come first. . . .

"Remember, Lord willing, you'll be married to Levi for a long time— might be sixty years or more," he offered kindly. "Besides, isn't Levi the only fella you've ever gone with?"

She nodded. "And he's the one for me, so there's no point in arguing that." Bettina sighed. "*Ach*, you're too tired to be happy for me, I daresay."

644

He *was* tired. Evidently undaunted, Bettina left the kitchen to go upstairs.

Jed recalled Eva's interest in Bettina's possible news, but he pushed the thought away. What did it matter now?

He headed back to his bedroom, adjacent to the front room, and noticed Lily's book lying on the dresser. There hadn't been time to give it another look during the trip from Lancaster County, what with all the conversation in the van. Jed had wanted to be considerate of his driver and fellow passengers.

I could mail it to Lily, he thought. *If I knew where she was.*

He heard voices drifting down the stairs now and assumed Bettina had taken his suggestion to heart, although Jed supposed their parents might have guessed something was up. *The way she's prancing about like a young filly.*

Their father might also caution about Bettina's young age, although Daed had married Mamm the year they each turned eighteen.

Flipping through the book's pages, Jed zeroed in on a note: *Love gladly sacrifices itself for the beloved.*

He closed the book, still aware of the muffled conversation. *Bettina's arguing for her own beloved,* he thought as he leaned back onto the bed, his hands behind his head.

I have no right to discourage her.

··· ➤ ◄ ···

The next morning, Jed rose an hour before the alarm clock went off, anxious to turn up at work before Uncle Ervin arrived. Considering the raucous birds outside his window, he'd needed no further incentive.

O Lord, pave the way for me today with Uncle Ervin, he prayed, on edge about whether his absence might have proved a boon to Perry.

Bettina met him in the kitchen, looking like she hadn't slept much. "Well, I did your bidding," she said conspiratorially.

He nodded. "How'd it go?"

"Not the way I expected. And Mamma's not feelin' so well this morning because of it." She groaned and went to the fridge and reached for some orange juice and milk. "I hate causin' her worry," she said as she opened the cupboard and brought over two choices of cold cereal.

Jed picked up the cereal box. "This is all I get?" He rose to get a clean bowl from the shelf and returned to help himself to a large amount of Wheaties without saying more. He was dismayed by his sister's apparent mind-set. It wasn't *his* doing she'd gotten herself engaged too young.

"Mamma was cryin' by the end of our talk," Bettina volunteered.

He kept his mouth shut, except to eat, believing anything he might say could make things worse.

"So now you're not talkin' to me?" Bettina poured orange juice into a tall glass and set it down in front of him.

He thanked her with a nod, but she ignored him and left with a sad face. A *dramatic start to the day*, Jed thought.

Ervin Stutzman wasn't the easiest boss to please, despite the fact that Jed was related to him. He was known to expect perfection, or close to it, and he wanted his employees to work long hours when necessary. Now that he'd had two apprentices for some time, Uncle Ervin's exceedingly high standards were even higher than before, although here lately he was nearly too frail to bark orders.

These thoughts were running through Jed's mind as he walked up the familiar lane to the shop and pushed the door open.

Surprisingly, there sat Ervin, smoking his pipe, surrounded by stacked plywood for seats and the main box of the buggy, as well as lumber for the canopy frames. He sputtered when he spotted Jed. "Didn't expect ya this early."

"Mornin', *Onkel*. Just thought I'd get a head start since I've been gone."

His uncle gave him a nod and returned to puffing away. "*Willkumm* back."

Jed proceeded to tell him about Jonas Byler's carriage shop—the equipment, the setup, and the various techniques he'd learned there. "Found it takes Jonas and his employees about a hundred and fifty hours to make a buggy, same as here."

Ervin smiled and slowly nodded his head. "It's never right to cut corners, *niemols*."

"Jonas has quite the big operation," Jed said, catching his uncle up on all that he'd seen and heard.

"And how was your visit with Lovina and Orpha Byler?" Ervin asked with a quirk of his eyebrow.

Jed might have guessed this would be next. "The Byler sisters were pleasant enough," he replied. *But that's where it stops.* His uncle didn't need to know the rest of the story.

Uncle Ervin got up and leaned heavily on his cane. "They were pleasant, ya say? Just pleasant?"

Jed smiled. "Orpha seems like a real *schmaert* and helpful young woman, too," he added.

"Helpful is *gut*, but ya don't sound like a would-be beau. She chust ain't for you?"

"'Fraid not."

Quickly, Jed changed the subject. "I'm wondering if Perry finished makin' the seat for the surrey he's been building."

"*Jah*, and one of the curtained doors and the hinged door in back, too. Perry's a fine welder and painter and mechanic, but he needs to work on his upholstering and painting. Ain't nearly as *sarchsam*—painstaking—as you in all areas of work."

Rare affirmation.

Jed set to measuring the vinyl-covered black cloth for the new buggy tops, sides, and back and decided the day was turning out better than it started.

24

EVA heard one of Abner Mast's heifers bellowing across the road as she emptied the trash early Tuesday afternoon. Frona was finishing up the ironing, and Eva had felt restless, going from room to room to gather up the wastepaper baskets. She felt she needed to get away from her sister, who had nothing good to say today. *She's out of sorts, stewing over Lily.*

Returning from behind the barn, Eva saw Sylvia Lantz pull into the driveway in her family carriage, waving. Eva hurried her step, then set the empty trash can down near the old hand pump. "Nice to see ya," she called to their neighbor.

Sylvia got out and went around to the opposite side of the buggy, where she removed a large casserole dish nestled in her handmade quilted carry-all. "I decided to bring some supper over as a surprise," she said. "Since it's your day off from the candy shop, I thought I'd catch ya before you start cookin'."

"Perfect timing." Eva was especially pleased because it was her day to cook. She walked with Sylvia into the house. "Heard from Naomi that you're expectin' company this weekend."

Sylvia nodded. "*Jah*, Tilly's girls attend a private Christian school that lets out earlier for the summer than most public schools in Rockport, so the family's comin' for a nice long visit. Oh, I can't wait to get my hands on their youngest! Tilly wrote in her last letter that he's growin' as fast as kudzu. It's past due for them to come see us." Sylvia set the dish on

648

the counter. "Hope ya like homemade noodles and turkey with carrots and onions."

"*Wunderbaar*," Eva said. "*Denki*." She asked if Sylvia could visit awhile.

"For a little bit, I guess."

Frona was still ironing in the next room, but she came around to poke her head in to see who was there. "Did I hear something 'bout a turkey casserole?"

"I made a double batch." Sylvia sat down at the table and smiled at Frona, then Eva.

"Well, it ain't like we're in mourning," Frona said, startling Eva and obviously Sylvia, too.

"That is, we're putting on our bravest faces, waiting to hear—" Eva started to say, hoping to soften the blow of Frona's bad temper.

"It must be awful hard," Sylvia interrupted.

Frona frowned. "We're struggling . . . that's for sure." She sighed. "Eva and I are grateful for your thoughtfulness, Sylvia." Then she withdrew to the next room.

Sylvia motioned for Eva to join her at the table. "None of us knows what we'd say or do if we were put in the same circumstance as you and your family."

Eva smiled. "You're always so kind."

They talked about Menno's contact in Apple Creek, Ohio. "Let's pray he'll be able to find Lily and bring her home," Eva said, not surprised when Sylvia admitted she'd already heard a little about this from Menno's wife, Bena, just up the road.

"Something *gut* has to come of this." Sylvia touched the back of Eva's hand. "You believe it, too, don't ya?"

"I certainly try." She asked if Sylvia would like something to drink. "We have plenty of meadow tea in the fridge."

"I'll have a small glass," Sylvia replied. "What about you, Frona? Can you hear me . . . would you like something, too?"

Eva was pleased Sylvia had reached out to Frona, but Frona merely said she wasn't thirsty from the other side of the wall. *She must be embarrassed.*

While they sipped their cold tea, Eva asked if Sylvia might reintroduce her to Tilly. "If ya think it might suit sometime while they're visiting."

"I'll ask once they arrive," Sylvia assured her.

She didn't mind that Frona had probably heard what she was saying; Eva could just imagine her perpetual frown. "I'll look forward to meeting your daughter," she added.

"And Tilly will enjoy getting to know you, Eva."

Eva hoped she could manage without being too bashful. Oh, she wanted to pick Tilly's brain about ever so many things.

That evening, after they enjoyed Sylvia's hearty casserole meal, Eva and Frona each indulged in one of the delectable leftover truffles. Eva asked Frona's advice about letting Naomi see Lily's photograph. "I know she'll keep mum, if I ask her to."

"Show it to anyone you like," Frona said, wearing her oldest blue kerchief over her thick hair bun. She looked tired and was apparently still distressed over her rude response to Sylvia earlier. "It might be the last we see of Lily."

Eva sighed at Frona's dispirited remark. "Let's keep prayin'."

"Well, the bishop and I talked briefly yesterday before he went over to get you from your shop," Frona said. "According to him, the world can be more appealing than the Kingdom of God, 'specially to younger folks."

"That's one of the reasons we're praying."

Frona seemed to ignore this. "By the way, you never said how you ran across that photo."

Eva shrugged, not willing to admit to the sad affair. "You surely remember how Lily started backing away from the church after Mamma died."

"*Jah*, I do." Frona set her fork down. "But where'd you find the photo?"

I'll have to say eventually, Eva thought, not wanting to be impudent but still reluctant to talk about her final visit with Jed. *Not just yet.*

"Eva, ain't ya listenin' to me?"

"I don't think it matters, Frona. Honestly, I doubt Lily meant for us to see it."

"You and Lily, fully of secrets." Frona grimaced. "Guess I can't squeeze blood out of a turnip."

After the dishes were washed and put away, Eva headed across the road and straight to Naomi's side door. *How many times did we girls come over with Mamma for homemade ice cream?* she recalled. *Naomi's heart and home have always been open to us. . . .*

Inside, Naomi rose immediately from the table and led Eva into the front room while Abner stayed put with the coconut cream pie.

"Poor Abner," said Eva. "I've interrupted your dessert."

"*Ach,* I can tell by the looks of ya, you need to bend my ear, ain't so? Abner will understand."

"You know me well," Eva admitted and began to share about the surprising photograph of Lily. "Have a look if you want." She pulled it out of her pocket and showed Naomi.

For the longest time, Naomi held it out a ways from her face, her chin up as she stared at it. "Well, I've never seen Lily so dolled up before," she said softly, glancing now toward the doorway to the sitting room.

"What do ya mean?"

"Well, it looks to me like she's done something to make her eyes stand out." Naomi pointed to the photo, and Eva leaned closer to look. "See there?"

"I haven't the slightest idea where she would've gotten makeup," Eva said. "I never saw her wear it. And I can't figure out when she would've had this taken."

"Wait just a minute." Naomi put her hand to her mouth. "I was over at Ida Mae's the mornin' after Lily left, and Alan Yoder stopped by to deliver some biscuits from his mother. Evidently, a few weeks ago Lily asked him to take her to the mall—she was adamant that he wait for her in the parking lot."

"Wha-at?"

"*Jah,* he said Lily came out later clutching a flat paper sack."

"Maybe that was the day she had the picture taken." Eva was flummoxed. "Did ya read what's on the back?"

Naomi turned it over, and her lips moved as she read Lily's writing. "I wonder what was goin' through her mind. 'The best and worst day . . .'"

"It's awful peculiar."

"You haven't said how ya came across this." Naomi gave the photo back to her.

Eva leaned back in the chair, trying to relax—she felt too wound up. "You remember Jed Stutzman? He found it on the train comin' here."

"Well, I'll be. Must've been the same train Lily took to Ohio."

"I thought of that, but it also might've been that another traveler found it in a van or a cab and carried it onto the train. Without being able to ask Lily, how can we ever know for sure?"

Naomi reached for the settee pillow and pushed it behind her back. "We can't always know why things come our way. But we know this: 'All things work together for *gut* to them that love God, to them who are the called according to his purpose.' Remember?"

Eva was anxious to tell her more about Jed. "It was so nice of him to take me riding and walking. We had a wonderful time feeding the ducks at your pond, too. And then, before he left town, he stopped by The Sweet Tooth to see me."

Naomi was trying not to smile. "You're fond of him, and there's no doubt in my mind he likes you, Eva. Anyone who saw the two of you together would have to agree."

Eva felt confident enough now to reveal everything—how the minute Lily's picture had fallen out of his wallet, Jed's attitude had changed before her very eyes. "I can't explain it, but I know there's a link between that photograph and him seeking me out after we met by accident at the auction."

"Are ya sayin' you think he's enamored with the picture?" Naomi asked, eyes wide.

"I wondered at first, but I don't think it's that." She went on to tell Naomi about Jed's former fiancée. "It could be that he's just not ready to move on."

"Well, for pity's sake." Naomi put her hand on her chest. "Will you hear from him by letter, perhaps?"

"He said he'd write, but that was before I found out about the photo. Now I have my doubts." Eva thought of Alfred Dienner just then and told Naomi of the letter she'd received from him. "It surprised me, really."

"Why's that, my dear?"

Eva lowered her head.

"Listen here, these young fellas know a perty face when they see one." Naomi leaned forward. "And you've got a beautiful heart inside."

"Tellin' the truth, I've never been so confused." Eva poured out her angst over her uncertain future. "Menno's determined to take over the house as soon as possible, and there's really only room for one of us to stay. He seems to think—well, he *hopes*—we girls will be married by then." She sighed. "But now, with Lily gone, it just doesn't feel right to me. First Lily . . . and now Frona and I won't be able to stay together, either." She went on to tell Naomi that if things didn't work out for them to live with one of their other brothers, Frona supposed they might end up living in Berne, Indiana, with a great-aunt.

"So far away?" Naomi exclaimed.

Eva rose and went to stand next to the large window. "I'd miss ya something terrible."

"And I'd miss you, too. Yet when ya think 'bout it," Naomi said, coming over to stand beside her, "when you do marry, things will definitely change anyway—you won't be over here as often, of course."

"Even so, I don't want to rush into something with Alfred or anyone else just for the sake of stayin' put here."

"You don't have to cross that bridge yet." Naomi slipped her arm around Eva's waist. "I believe you have too many thoughts pushing round in your head for one evening, child."

Eva turned to clasp Naomi's hand. "You're prayin' for me, aren't ya? And Lily, too?"

"You know I am."

"Mamma always said prayer was ever so important."

Naomi nodded sweetly, and if Eva wasn't mistaken, there were tears in her eyes.

When Eva walked through the kitchen toward the back door, Abner was still sitting at the table, his old German *Biewel* open. His pointer finger was on the page, following the lines.

"Have yourself a restful night," he said, looking up at her.

"*Denki* for lendin' your wife's ear."

"Well, let's see once," he said, getting up to look at Naomi's ear. "Ah, it's still attached. *Des gut.*"

"I do love talkin' to her." Eva smiled at Naomi.

"Now, that's better. We like seein' our Eva smilin' again," Abner said before he returned to his reading.

"*Our Eva.*" The words were so dear and more comforting than the two of them could ever know. Best of all, Eva was grateful for Naomi's ongoing prayers for Lily . . . and for herself. *Only heaven knows what we're up against!*

25

B EFORE Naomi and Abner finished breakfast the next morning, Lester Lantz dropped by. Abner waved him inside to join them, and Naomi greeted him, quickly excusing herself to pour Abner's brother-in-law some hot black coffee.

"Been hearin' some rumblings 'bout Omar," said Lester as he rested one elbow on the table. "Anything I might do to help?"

"Ain't sure what ya might've heard," Abner said, then went on to mention Omar's interest in voting.

"Wonder where he came up with that," Lester said. "Sure isn't like there's any leaning toward politics round here. That's the world's business."

Abner raised his coffee mug to take a sip. "'Tis the truth."

Naomi returned to the table, bringing some fresh fruit and another plate of sticky buns, which both men reached for the second she set it down. Taking a seat herself, she decided not to have anything more to eat, just slowly drink the rest of her apple juice, surprised and heartened that Sylvia's husband was this concerned for their Omar.

"We've tried to steer Omar in the right direction, but ultimately it's up to him to make his own decisions." Abner glanced at Naomi as though to cue her to say something.

"*Des gut*, really," Lester agreed. "I'll admit that I regret the way I pushed our Tilly away, when all was said and done. Honestly, if I could do it over, I'd be gentler with her." He drank some coffee; then, setting it down, he looked at first Naomi, then Abner. "I would caution you against using the same approach I did. It made Tilly even more determined to go her own way."

The room was still for a moment. Knowing Lester as she did, Naomi was glad to witness the softening in his face when he spoke of his daughter—many were the times young Tilly had sought comfort from her and Abner.

Lester continued. "Omar's mighty fortunate to have a father . . . and a mother who know how to talk to him 'bout something that other parents might take a hard line against. Some might even turn away from him, considerin' the controversy."

Naomi nodded as she listened. "We're hopin' he'll submit to the bishop's authority and consider fasting and praying 'bout his decision."

They talked further about the hardship of having Tilly and her younger sister, Ruth, out of the fold, yet wanting them to know they were welcome to visit anytime. "Sylvia and I wish the girls had made a different choice, but being they were never baptized into the church, we don't see any wisdom in shunning them. It's not going to bring them back."

Naomi voiced her agreement before going down to the cold cellar for some stewed tomatoes for the noon meal as the men settled in to talk of crops and livestock.

"I'll keep Omar in my thoughts," Lester said once he got up and made his way to their side door.

"*Denki*, means so much," Naomi said. Abner rose, as well, and walked with her out to the backyard as Lester headed to his waiting horse and carriage.

"Well, wasn't that nice?" Naomi said, wiggling her bare toes in the grass.

"He's been through more than we can imagine with Tilly and Ruth," Abner said. "A right *gut* man."

Eva was pleased when Bena dropped by with two-year-old Katie Ann to provide Cousin Jeptha's mailing address for Lily's photograph. Bena hemmed and hawed, acting altogether curious to see the picture yet not coming right out to ask.

Frona's lips parted in a slight smile when Eva offered to show it to Bena, who quickly accepted.

Bena stared at it and shook her head. "I can't imagine what Lily was thinkin', can you?"

"Well, if nothin' else, this might help someone find her," Eva replied.

"Oh, an' before I forget, Menno mentioned that your brother Stephen thought you should have a copy made, in case this gets lost," Bena said, stroking Katie Ann's blond braids.

Frona spoke up from where she had returned to chopping carrots at the kitchen counter. "If it turns up missin', then so be it."

"Guess we'll take the chance and just mail it as is," Eva said, glancing at Frona, who clearly wanted to have the last say.

Bena seemed to accept that. She went to the pantry and got a box of blocks out for Katie Ann to play with. "I'm sorry I haven't been able to spend much time helping. What can I do?"

"There's always the mending," Frona grumbled, moving to the sink to wash her hands.

So Bena sat right down and helped mend for a good hour before she and little Katie Ann left for home.

"That was kind of her," Eva remarked to Frona. "'Specially when she has plenty to do at her place."

Frona smiled faintly. "I still can hardly believe she'll soon be in charge of this kitchen."

Eva went upstairs to address an envelope at her desk. She slipped the photograph carefully inside, wishing she were writing to Jed. *If he writes, what would I say?* she wondered, recalling their pleasant conversation while walking with him at the pond. But that sense of ease had come to an abrupt halt the moment Lily's photo fluttered to the candy counter.

"As open as Jed was about his fiancée and all he's suffered emotionally, why couldn't he be open with me about the picture?" she murmured, trying to suppress her feelings of missing him.

The more Eva contemplated this, the more she felt it signaled a lack of trust on his part. *Would Jed have withheld the truth from Lydiann, had she been in the same circumstance?*

Somehow, Eva doubted it.

Discouraged, she headed outdoors to mail Lily's photo. Back inside, she went to the small sewing area in the corner of the sitting room and stitched on the facing, then set in the sleeves for Frona's new dress. All the while, she prayed for Lily.

That night, after supper, Eva was determined to finish writing her letter to Alfred. She'd taken time to read through the few sentences of greeting she'd already penned, still wondering how she could be anything more than his friend. Truly, she wished she might hold on to her dream for a very special kind of love.

In light of what had happened with Jed, she wondered if it was wise to cling so tenaciously to her desire. Wasn't it time to abandon that hope and focus on her friendship with Alfred? *After all,* she thought, *he's the one pursuing me.*

Slowly, she began to write.

> *Honestly, Alfred, I'd feel better about all of this if we could talk directly. Letters can sometimes be confusing, so if you'd like to wait till you return this fall, that's all right with me.*

Groaning inwardly, Eva hoped he wouldn't think she was impolite or putting him off. She really needed more time. Regardless of what it might mean for her immediate future, now wasn't the time to agree to court—at least not by mail. She folded her letter and placed it in the envelope, then picked up her Bible and read the first five chapters of Job before heading downstairs to hem Frona's dress.

"You really didn't have to do that," Frona said when Eva mentioned the dress was for her.

"I wanted to surprise ya, since you're feeling blue these days."

"Who's blue?" Frona looked about her comically.

"I just thought—"

"We're on pins and needles here. The whole family is." Frona sat down at the table and pressed her thick fingers into her neck. "Menno's tryin' to think of how else we can hunt for Lily."

"Well, that's why we sent the picture off to Ohio."

"*Jah,* but if nothin' comes of it, what then?" Frona's head covering drooped to one side, but she didn't seem to mind. "The bishop wants our brothers to take action—not let any grass grow under their feet. He says he'll be checking up from time to time."

Eva realized how difficult it must be for Frona to simply bide her time while they awaited word of Lily. Frona had always been somewhat in charge; Eva suddenly grasped that their parents had looked to her as a mother's helper since Frona was only eight or nine years old. *They molded her into being a fussy hen,* Eva thought. And in that moment, she wished with all of her heart she might lift the burdens poor Frona was expected to carry even now.

Admiring the newly sewn dress, even though it still needed pressing, Eva sighed—she had really hoped this gesture might go a little way toward cheering up Frona. Clearly, it would take far more than a new dress to do so.

Early Saturday morning, Naomi hurried out the door to thank Abner for hitching up the horse and carriage. "You're always so helpful, dear," she said, patting his shoulder.

"It's the least I can do for ya," he said, then offered to drive her and Ida Mae down to Paradise and drop them off for the day.

"*Denki,* but I don't see us bein' there all day." Naomi laughed, adding, "Let's just say I'd rather not."

"Cousin Connie's not bothersome, is she?"

"Ain't that. But I can just imagine the grapevine's trailed down there by now, and who knows what she'll say 'bout Lily."

"Now, you can't expect the worse." Abner sounded like he was scolding.

Naomi headed for the carriage, and he helped her in. When she was seated on the right side and ready for the driving lines, she turned to him. "*Ach,* I forgot my walkin' stick."

"You gonna bop your cousin Connie to keep her in line?" Abner was chuckling as he went back into the house. A moment later, he returned and handed the stick to her. "Here ya be, my love. Now, watch yourself," he teased.

"I'll be home well before supper." She waved to him.

"Lord willin' and the creek don't rise." Abner grinned as she left.

··· ➤ ◄ ···

Cousin Connie had two one-gallon jars of meadow tea brewing out on the back step when Naomi arrived with Ida Mae. Glad for her walking stick, Naomi hobbled up the stairs and was greeted warmly by Connie, whose plump cheeks were pink and moist with perspiration. "We've come to help with your sewin' projects," Naomi announced, to which Connie nodded and grinned.

After a refreshment of fruit and banana bread, Naomi and her daughter set to work, with Connie "directing traffic," as Abner might have said. Naomi smiled at the thought, glad to be sitting with the light from the window coming over her shoulder. *Best for my eyes.*

Ida Mae began to pin on the pattern for Connie's husband's new white shirt while Naomi worked on his black vest.

"Jacob will be mighty thankful," Cousin Connie told them. "He ripped his old Sunday clothes not long ago while out chasing down two of our mules after church."

"What's he been wearing to Preachin' since?" Ida Mae asked.

"*Ach*, he borrowed a shirt from his brother and is nearly swimmin' in it," Connie said, taking another sip of the tea. "And the vest he borrowed from his nephew is three sizes too small, so he has to keep it unbuttoned." She started to giggle, then covered her mouth. "Oh, if Jacob wasn't a sight last service!"

This got Ida Mae laughing, too. "Now, that's quite a picture, ain't?"

"And ya wouldn't believe how the mules escaped. Our watch dog let 'em out," Connie told them.

"Wha-at?" Naomi thought for sure she'd heard wrong.

"*Jah*, Buster jumped up and knocked the gate latch loose." Connie shook her head and laughed. "Have ya ever heard such a thing?"

"That's quite a story," Ida Mae agreed. "*Dat* would enjoy that one."

"Abner's had his fair share of *gut* stories, seems to me," Naomi said. "He's got a whole river of 'em, including one about the wintry day a snowbird spooked his driving horse and put the buggy into quite a spin. Round and round they went." Naomi bobbed her head. "Goodness, ain't?"

Connie's eyes widened. "Well, that *is* somethin'!"

Naomi nodded. "It would've been one rousing gathering today if Abner were here." She didn't reveal that he'd offered to bring them, and now she almost wished he had.

Later, when Naomi had finished sewing the vest seams and was hand stitching the facing, Connie said outright that she feared Lily Esch was setting a poor example for other young girls in the area.

"That story's not over yet," Naomi said softly yet firmly.

"But she's left the Plain life behind."

Ida Mae spoke up. "What Mamma means is we're all beseeching God for the outcome."

This quieted Connie down some, although it wasn't long before she brought up Jacob's encounter with Omar at the recent auction. "I'm tellin' ya, my husband got himself an earful from your Omar. He thinks it's important to vote for the next president of the United States, of all things. Makes me wonder where he's getting these ideas."

Naomi felt her face redden, and she wished Connie would calm her tongue. Ida Mae also looked embarrassed.

"You'd think Omar would listen to your head minister up there. Bishop Isaac, ain't? Such a wise man of God."

"That he is," Naomi said. "And he often preaches against the sin of gossiping."

This must have caught Connie off guard, because now *she* was red-faced. Right quick, she made an excuse that she needed to go and check on something upstairs.

"Is this what we get for comin' to help?" Ida Mae whispered.

"Now, don't fall into the same trap Connie's in."

"It's obvious she's upset with our family—and Lily Esch."

Naomi pursed her lips. "I believe she means well, I truly do." Privately, though, it was troubling that news of both Lily and Omar had traveled this far from Eden Valley—though the latter was Omar's own doing, speaking out as he had. And right then, Naomi was glad Abner had allowed her to come here on her own.

The minute the sewing's done, we'll head home.

26

EVA and Frona finished washing windows at the schoolhouse frolic with the help of other Amish youth who were also involved with sweeping and scrubbing walls and floors, as well as doing repairs on swings and other playground equipment. The sisters had started at eight-thirty that Saturday morning as partners—Frona had practically refused to go unless Eva agreed to this. And stick together they had, scrubbing side by side until Eva's knuckles were pink and peeling.

But when it came time to break for a sack lunch, Sol Peachey came over to the two of them and sat down in a desk next to Frona, who looked so startled she practically bristled. Sol was an eligible young man from one of the Big Valley Amish communities nestled in the central Pennsylvania mountains. Eva knew he was a year younger than Frona and quite the cutup, too.

"Say, I noticed streaks on some of them windows," Sol mentioned offhandedly. "Saw 'em when I was tightening up the seesaw out yonder." He gestured in the direction of the playground, a humorous glint in his blue eyes.

"*Puh!* Couldn't have been the windows I washed," Frona said, reaching for her ham and cheese sandwich.

"Well, if you'd like, I could walk you around the building and show ya."

The brave fella wants to get her alone for a few minutes. Eva attempted to squash a smile.

Frona's eyes were wide. "And while we're at it, would ya like me to check on that seesaw you tightened?" she spouted back.

Sol's head went back with his laughter, but evidently he wasn't amused enough to stay put. Rather, he took his lunch and went over to sit near his cousins, in another aisle of desks.

Frona glanced at Eva and smiled mischievously. "That'll teach him, *jah*?" she whispered.

Sighing, Eva wondered if there was ever going to be *anyone* for Frona, for pity's sake!

Later, as they rode toward home, Eva talked of the fun she'd had seeing many of their own relatives at the frolic, as well as a few unfamiliar young men, although most of them were likely younger than Eva and Frona. *We're inching ourselves right out of the running,* Eva thought but said nothing about that to her decidedly prickly sister.

"No one breathed a word 'bout Lily's absence," Frona said as Prince turned into the driveway.

"Thankfully. 'Twas a relief."

"Well, I expected someone might." Frona shrugged and got out near the barn.

Max came running, wagging his furry white tail, begging for some attention.

Eva reached down to give him a nice hard rub around his neck. "*Gut* boy . . . glad we're home?"

She and Frona set to work unhitching the horse, quickly doing the task they'd learned as children, knowing who would accomplish what. After they had unhooked the tugs and pushed them into the *Hinnergscharr*— the harness on both sides around the back—they held the shafts and led out the horse. Eva volunteered to take their sleek black gelding to the stable, Max nipping at her heels. This was the graceful, swift horse their father had always doted upon, taking apples out to him in the stable, and sugar cubes, too.

"You want something to eat, don't ya?" She reached up and tousled Prince's shiny mane.

In the distance, she spotted the narrow path that led all the way out to a small patch of woods where Eva and Lily had, years ago, stumbled onto a tiny hut concealed by trees and brushwood. At the time, Eva had just started attending school, and Lily had followed her every step that late autumn day. Mamma had been busy with other womenfolk back at the house, making knotted comforters for a sunshine linen shower for two widows and a *Maidel* in need. The three elderly sisters shared a house up the road.

It had been Eva's idea to go exploring, and they'd followed a squirrel down the dirt trail while birds cried overhead, flashing from tree to tree.

The little wooden shack was locked that first day, but Eva managed to pry off the rickety catch and push open the door. The place was bare of furniture, too small for anything more than a table and a chair, if that . . . maybe a spot to count to one hundred while playing hide-and-seek. But Lily had insisted it was a playhouse, and it turned out she was right.

Eventually, they told Dat and Mamma about the enchanting discovery. Dat had forgotten about the cozy little place his own grandfather had built for his three young girls.

Eva recalled taking storybooks Mamma bought and pretending to be the characters, sometimes making up plays from *Little Women*, their favorite. *It was the most fun when only Lily and I knew about it,* Eva thought.

With a flash, it occurred to Eva that Lily might feel the same way about her beau in Ohio. Now that she'd gone to pursue him and he was no longer secret, maybe it didn't seem so fun anymore. Eva dearly hoped so. *Does she miss us at all?*

"Eva!" Frona called, pulling her out of her reminiscing. "Sylvia Lantz is coming up the road, headin' this way. Are you expectin' her?"

Tilly and her family must be arriving. "I'll come right back to the house soon as I stable Prince," Eva told her.

By the time Eva was finished watering the horse and putting more feed into his trough, Sylvia was walking barefoot through the side yard, waving.

"*Wie geht's,* Sylvia?" Eva hurried her step.

Sylvia was beaming. "We'd like to invite you and Frona to come for dessert this evening. Tilly and Kris will be arrivin' in a couple more hours. Would ya like that?"

"If you're sure it won't put you out," Eva said and invited her inside for something to drink.

Sylvia shook her head, saying she had just a few things to do yet. "It's no trouble at all, and I know you'll enjoy meeting Tilly. Oh, and I'll remember to put a bug in her ear 'bout taking some time to talk with you, all right? Maybe a nice walk?"

"She might be tired from travelin'. So whatever works out is fine."

"Tilly's on the go a lot, and she'll be ready to stretch her legs." Sylvia smiled, then hurried down the driveway toward the road.

Sylvia's so thoughtful. Eva was curious to interact with the woman's *Englischer* daughter. She recalled hearing from Mamma that the former Amishwoman had been quite outgoing, and with a mind of her own even before leaving the community instead of joining church. But being thirteen years younger, Eva had never had reason to encounter Tilly one-on-one.

Eva headed into her quiet little shop and began to wipe down the counters and the empty display case. She swept the floor and got down on her hands and knees to scrub the wide planks till they gleamed.

Then she went around to the cupboard and found her favorite candy dish, a gift from Mamma on her sixteenth birthday. "The day Dat died," she whispered, carefully turning the pink bowl-like dish in her hands. She still remembered the delicious roast beef dinner Mamma had made for the noon meal that day. Dat had been smiling as he often did as he sat down to eat; then his kindly face turned solemn when he reverently bowed for the silent blessing.

If only they'd known he would not return to them alive, she would have asked him to linger long after the midnight chocolate cake was served and Lily had started up the birthday song, leading out in her pretty soprano voice. Eva would never have let him leave the house.

All was well with our family then. . . .

Gently sliding the lovely dish back into its spot, she turned and looked around her. She tried not to think of having to say good-bye to this special place when she married the man her heart yearned for, or if she was the one to go and live elsewhere. "It's in Thy hands, O Lord," she whispered into the air that usually held such an inviting aroma.

She moved to stand near the window, thankful for dear parents who had taught her and her siblings to love and revere their heavenly Father. And to trust always.

"Surely Lily hasn't forgotten so quickly. . . ."

··· ❯ ❮ ···

"We prob'ly shouldn't rush the Lantzes' suppertime," Frona cautioned when she heard about Sylvia's invitation.

"*Jah*, we'll give Tilly and her family time to settle in and have a nice hot meal with Lester and Sylvia." Eva dried the plates carefully, remembering how Mamma loved to talk with them while cleaning up the kitchen, asking about their school day and what they'd learned. "Mamma really liked people, didn't she?" Eva asked, the question popping out.

"Like Lily, ya mean?"

"Well, not sure I meant that, but maybe."

"Mamm was a talker, for sure."

Eva nodded. "And Lily used to be."

"Wonder what made her change so."

Eva felt she knew, and if Frona thought more about it, she would, too. Lily had been just fifteen when their father died, and now she'd lost Mamma. And their younger sister was surely feeling pressured to join church, from Menno, especially. "Did Lily ever talk with Mamma 'bout taking baptismal instruction, do ya know?" Eva asked.

"Never heard."

Eva put away the dried dishes and tumblers. "Think what would've happened if she *had* been baptized and then ran off." She shuddered.

"Knowin' Bishop Isaac, she'd be under the temporary *Bann* already unless she came back and repented."

The shun, Eva thought. "Lily has a soft heart. Truly she does."

Frona reached for the soiled pans and slid one into the sudsy water. "But if a body's not careful, a heart can turn to stone."

"Mamma once said the Lord sometimes lets things happen to break the hardness . . . to make a heart pliable again."

Frona handed the clean pan to her to dry. "To be honest, I'm afraid to pray 'whatever it takes' for the Lord God to bring Lily home," Frona admitted.

Eva shivered again.

··· ➤ ≺ ···

On the long walk over to Lester Lantz's farm, Eva noticed a possum lying dead off to the side of the road. "I sure didn't see it on the way home earlier."

"A car must've got him," Frona said, scrunching up her face.

"Makes me wonder 'bout Lily. Do ya think she'd try driving? Not that she would be reckless."

Frona looked at her. "Driving already?"

"What'll stop her if she wants to be fancy? The longer she's gone, the more likely she'll fall into the world's grasp." Eva sighed. "I'd like to ask Tilly 'bout how long it took before she felt settled on the outside."

"I hope you're prepared to pry it out of her." Frona sounded adamant.

"Sylvia thinks Tilly will welcome my questions."

"Might depend on how nosy ya get."

Eva laughed nervously.

"I'd like someone to interview *me*," Frona said, then chortled.

"Oh, so you can say why you'll never leave the People and are very happy to just stay put here, *jah*?"

"How'd ya guess?"

They shared a laugh. Feeling relaxed with Frona for a change, since she was in such a pleasant mood, Eva decided now was as good a time as any to tell her about Jed's visit to the candy shop. "I know you're interested, so I'll just say it was Jed Stutzman who gave me Lily's photograph."

"*He* had it?" Frona's eyebrows rose suddenly. "Why?"

"He found it on the train, of all places." Eva admitted to not telling Frona this earlier because she wanted to keep mum that Jed had stopped by to see her. "Things were going so well till Lily's picture dropped out of his wallet. After that, things ended oddly between us. He seemed awfully uncomfortable."

Frona began to swing her arms. "So things with this Jed fella are kaput?"

"We didn't get to say much to each other. Bishop Isaac arrived and interrupted our conversation, so it's hard to know. Even so, I haven't heard from him since." *He hasn't bothered to write.*

Frona looked thoughtful. "Did ya load Jed up with plenty of sweets before he went?" she asked.

"I sent half a dozen Butterfinger truffles with him."

Frona clapped her hands. "Then I say there's a *gut* chance he'll come around."

Frona was doing her best to cheer Eva up, but no matter how addictive those truffles, Eva doubted she'd be seeing handsome Jed Stutzman again.

27

THE livestock rustled about, chomping on feed at the troughs as Jed helped his father sweep out the barn that evening. He worked quickly with the push broom, leaning into each long stride, thinking of Eva Esch all the while and wondering how she was doing. He recalled Perry asking yesterday if he felt ill, and Uncle Ervin mentioning that Jed hadn't been himself since returning from Lancaster County. Apparently Uncle Ervin was disappointed, because he'd meant the Pennsylvania trip for Jed's benefit.

If I could just talk to Eva, Jed thought. He'd started a letter several times but felt too embarrassed to finish. One thing was certain: He couldn't stop thinking about her. He finished sweeping and headed to the well pump to wash before making his way to the house.

Walking through the Lantzes' side yard, Eva noticed the white car parked in the drive alongside the main farmhouse where Sam and Josie lived with their children. A small black teddy bear peeked out the rear car window. *One of Tilly's children must have left it there,* Eva assumed, wanting to rescue it and carry it over to the *Dawdi Haus,* where Lester and Sylvia had moved two and a half years ago, when Sam took over the farm. "Should I?" she asked Frona, who immediately shook her head and encouraged Eva to stay focused on why they'd come.

In the kitchen, Lester and Sylvia warmly welcomed Eva and Frona

668

and offered places at the table while Tilly's son played on the floor with wooden building blocks. In his colorful striped outfit, Baby Mel looked out of place to Eva—little Old Order boys wore black broadfall trousers and blue, green, violet, or white shirts. Even tiny Mel's golden blond hair had been cut to reveal his ears. She didn't know why, but it struck Eva as odd, and she realized she'd been hoping Tilly might have adopted something of the Plain way of dressing her children. Even Jenya and Tavani, Tilly's look-alike twin girls, seemed just like any other English children, except perhaps for their braided blond hair. The twins were taller than Eva had expected, and when Tilly's husband, Kris, came over to introduce himself, Eva saw where the girls must have gotten their genes for height. Kris was not only tall but also congenial, and Eva understood why Tilly had fallen for him.

They all sat down to enjoy some butterscotch pie, and Eva was impressed with the children's polite behavior at the table. They were as mild mannered as any Amish children she'd helped care for, including her young Esch nieces and nephews.

Tilly seemed eager to talk about the girls' interest in hand sewing, kindly including Frona and Eva in the conversation. "Jenya's making a quilted wall hanging right now—I have a snapshot of that and Tavani's embroidered pillowcases, too." Tilly went to get her purse and brought back two photos, which were passed around amidst quite a lot of oohing and appreciative remarks. "I hope they'll be fine seamstresses one day," Tilly added.

Both twins blushed and glanced shyly at each other, and Sylvia's sweet face shone.

She's gotten her Tilly back, Eva thought. *But what is it like to see her grandchildren only a few times a year?* This was so foreign to the way of the People, whose very lives revolved around work frolics, neighborhood gatherings, and worshiping together at house church every other Sunday.

When all but a few crumbs of the delicious dessert had been devoured, Frona offered to help Sylvia with the dishes, and as if on cue, Tilly asked Kris if he'd get the stroller out, glancing at Eva. "Would ya like to walk with me?" she asked quietly while the twins headed into the front room with their Dawdi Lester.

"Sure," Eva said, feeling self-conscious and wondering what Sylvia had revealed to Tilly. *I can't be shy,* Eva thought. *This might be my only chance to talk to an Amishwoman turned Englischer.*

Frona glanced her way with a smile, and Eva hoped it was all right to leave her and Sylvia with all the dishes. *Won't Jenya and Tavani help dry?*

Outdoors, Tilly put little Mel into the stroller while Kris held it steady. He kissed her cheek before heading into the house.

"It's nice of you to make time for me," Eva said right away. "I wondered if ya might be tired after traveling."

"Actually, this is the best way for me to unwind." Tilly raised her face to the sky briefly as they headed down the lane, past the flower beds surrounding the birdbath. "Walking has always been my favorite way to relax." Tilly looked about them. "Especially back here at home . . . on a blue-sky day."

"Do ya miss Eden Valley?" Eva asked hesitantly.

"All the time."

Eva was a little surprised but glad Tilly seemed to feel comfortable telling her so.

"My mother says your younger sister has left the family," Tilly said softly.

"Seems like years already, but it's only been a couple weeks."

"This has to be hard for all of you."

Eva said it was. "Not to be snoopy, but was it during your *Rumschpringe* that you began to wonder 'bout the modern world? Was that when you first became curious?"

"There were other issues, personal ones . . . unresolved circumstances that compelled me to leave." Tilly stopped walking to check on her son, leaning down to talk gently to him in the stroller. "To be blunt, Eva, I never felt like I fit in with my family." She paused, then straightened. "Particularly with my father."

Eva chose not to reveal that it had been the exact opposite for her; she'd been exceptionally close to both her parents.

"I became bitter over time, and that led to my departure," Tilly added. "Thankfully, all of that has been talked through now."

Eva realized Tilly's reasons for leaving had to be much different than her sister's. "What are the chances of Lily changin' her mind and coming home, do ya think?"

Tilly pushed her shoulder-length hair over her shoulder. "I don't want to discourage you, but once I flipped on a light switch and experienced the other conveniences—and freedoms—of life on the outside, there was no turning back." She paused before continuing. "I eagerly embraced all of that. Even the different style of worship appealed to me. I discovered so many new opportunities . . . things I wouldn't have experienced here in Eden Valley."

Eva felt like the wind had been knocked out of her. "Quite a few here are prayin' for our Lily, though," she said softly.

Tilly nodded.

"So if the Lord God wants Lily back with the People, He'll lead her home, *jah?*"

Tilly agreed. "He can change her mind, of course. God is all powerful in every way, and we can trust Him with our hearts."

They talked more about Tilly's church, and Eva asked if she missed anything about the Amish way of worship. Tilly was surprisingly forthright, saying later that what she missed most was seeing her Amish family, including her aunt Naomi Mast. "And Uncle Abner, isn't he the most fun ever? And wise as King Solomon, too."

Eva felt a semblance of relief as the conversation changed direction. And the farther they walked, the more she enjoyed being with Tilly.

"Do you know if your sister has an English boyfriend?" Tilly asked.

"Supposedly so, but what little I know comes from her friend Fannie. But how long will the fella be interested?"

"Well, in my own experience, it's been a challenge to mesh my husband's and my backgrounds. I think it's hard enough when a couple has different church affiliations, let alone the enormous clash between the Plain and fancy ways of life. There are some pretty significant cultural differences to work through."

"I can only imagine," Eva said. "I have a few ideas of what my sister is up against."

They walked all the way down to Stoney Hill Road, then turned back onto Eden Road. The air was a bit chilly as they headed north, and Tilly stopped again to check on little Mel, saying he was "all tuckered out."

A buggy rumbled toward them from the opposite direction, and the two young Amish fellows inside gawked as they went by, focusing especially on Tilly. Their stares weren't as pronounced as those of *Englischers* might have been had an Amishwoman been in the reverse setting. Eva couldn't help but wonder how Lily was managing out there in the world. Did she stick out like a sore thumb?

"I can't tell ya how *gut* it is to talk so openly," Eva said as the Lantz farm loomed into view.

"Hopefully it gives you a glimpse from the other side of the fence." Tilly looked at her and smiled. "Honestly, it's nearly impossible to remove the Plain life from a person's awareness. There were times I wept over my decision to leave, feeling constantly pulled back to my upbringing by strong cords. And it wasn't just missing the familiar life I'd abandoned. The Old Ways were ingrained in me, everything I'd come to know and understand. I was an odd puzzle piece in a world where my piece simply did not fit."

Yet she didn't feel like she fit in at home either, poor thing.

"For a while I leaned one way and then the other, even though I knew I'd closed the door on being Amish ever again when I married Kris." Tilly stopped pushing the stroller and turned toward Eva. "I know a number of former Amish who describe their leaving the same way. The Plain life doesn't just get under the skin; it runs deep into the soul. Being Amish isn't just what you do; it's who you are." Tilly wiped her eyes. "Lily will feel she's being ripped down the middle of her heart, wanting to live in both worlds. It could be excruciating for her."

If this proved true for Lily, Eva didn't see how her sister could stay fancy . . . unless she married her *Englischer* beau before she took time to think all of this through.

"Are *you* happy now?" Eva had to know.

"Very." Tilly said it convincingly enough. "Always remember: Embracing the Plain life is a choice."

Tilly's words played over in Eva's mind as they headed into the house, and later when Lester Lantz gave Eva and Frona a ride home after dark, following more fellowship and food. And Eva realized how unlikely it would be for Lily to return home, apart from divine help.

28

As the days progressed and Lily was still missing, Eva sensed Frona was walking on eggshells, wondering when or if Menno or the bishop might come rushing over to say Lily had been found. But at the end of each day, when still no word came, both sisters prayed all the more fervently. Eva promised herself—and God—that she would never give up on Lily.

Candy sales were climbing ever higher, and Eva feared it was somehow tied to Lily's disappearance. Her loyal customers were anything but snoopy, yet nearly all offered their concern.

Ida Mae was one of them. "Lily must be markin' the days off on her calendar, figuring out a way to get home," she said with a heartwarming smile.

Others who were waiting in line overheard and glanced at each other, some nodding. One longtime English customer said she'd requested prayer for Lily at her ladies' Bible study group, and another mentioned asking for prayer for Lily at her monthly book club.

Naomi Mast was a frequent visitor, as well, although she was more focused on Frona and Eva, helping out with whatever they agreed to let her do in the house, given she had her own kitchen—and Abner—to look after.

"Word's getting out beyond Eden Valley's borders," Eva told Frona the evening of the first Saturday in June. "It's remarkable, the folks who care 'bout Lily."

"Can't believe we haven't heard a peep from my appeals to Ohio relatives," Frona said, putting a small basket with golden biscuits, nice and flaky, on the table. There was also raw honey straight from the bee-keeping neighbors up the road.

Eva tried to take what Frona said in stride. How was it possible that *none* of their Ohio cousins—and anyone they'd surely talked with by now—had heard anything about Lily?

Outdoors, the farmhands were heading for home. *If I married Alfred,* Eva thought, *I'd have a full table of workers to feed twice or more a day, like Mamma always did.* After their father died, Menno had stepped in and brought in new help. Now with Mamma gone, too, Frona only occasionally invited all of the menfolk to stay around for the noon meal—any more would have put a strain on the monthly budget. Several times a month, Bena cooked for the whole crew, since she and Menno lived only a short distance away.

Eva considered Alfred again and wondered what he'd thought of her letter. Not hearing back right away gave her some breathing room—time to ponder being courted by a man who was more like a friend than a possible mate. If it came to it, could she marry him and be content?

"Supper's ready," Frona said, and they sat down to a yellow tureen of corn chowder that had simmered all day.

Once Frona concluded the time of silent blessing, Eva chose a biscuit and waited for her sister to reach for the long ladle and dish up her own serving. The sight of Mamma's tureen brought back happy memories of days with many sets of feet under this big table, and dear Mamma dishing up Dat's bowl.

"Have ya heard anything from Jed Stutzman?" Frona said, reaching for the honey.

"I don't expect to."

"You had such a nice time while he was here. I'm really sorry for ya, sister."

Eva looked up, surprised at this from Frona, who rarely seemed so sympathetic. "Awful nice of you. *Denki.*"

Frona's cheeks reddened. "We need each other," she said softly. For a moment, Eva thought there might be a tear in her eye. "I did something today . . . something I never thought I'd do."

"Oh?"

"This morning I overheard Emmanuel talkin' with Rufus, and I spoke up," Frona admitted. "Evidently Menno had plans to knock down the playhouse out yonder, where you and Lily used to take your dollies and books."

Eva was horrified. "Why would he do that?"

"For firewood, Emmanuel said. Menno thinks the place has seen better days."

"Lily once told me she felt closest to God in that sweet little place. She could pray better there than kneeling at her bedside."

Frona grimaced. "You wanna know what I told our brothers? I interrupted and said they were *not* tearin' it down unless both you and Lily gave the say-so."

"You said that?"

"I've had it up to here." Frona tapped her forehead. "I'm beginning to feel like I might burst, all this fussin' over Lily, and no one able to find her."

"*Gut* for you, makin' a stand."

"I even went to see if Lily might have decided to hole up out there."

Eva hadn't thought of that.

"I didn't find her, of course, but I did see one of your shared books." Frona motioned to the sitting room. "I put it in there—a child's poetry book. Robert Louis Stevenson, remember?"

"Aw . . . Lily loved that book. I didn't know it was missin'."

"Maybe Bena's youngsters will enjoy it."

When they move in here and everything changes, Eva thought, looking pensively at Frona.

Naomi was out tending her flower beds and had just stood up to rest her aching back, thankful for the late-day sunshine. The first cutting of hay was at hand, and the air felt warmer. A breeze came up, cooling her brow, and with it the hush of the leaves high in the old trees that made up the northern windbreak.

She remembered being a little girl and pretending she could fly by riding on the crest of the wind, though she'd never told anyone. Not even her closest sister. Naomi wondered if Eva and Lily had ever shared those kinds of childish secrets. If so, wouldn't Lily feel like a lost soul wherever she'd taken herself off to?

The sun was sinking quickly now, and as Naomi made her way toward the house, stopping at the potting shed to put her hoe and trowel away, she noticed the bishop's horse and carriage coming up the road. Menno was riding inside with the man of God.

Oh, her heart leapt up, and she hoped this might be the good news they were all waiting for. Even though Lily had been gone for less than a month, it seemed like a long time coming.

Bishop Isaac stared at Menno as he sat across from him with Eva and her sister. "You'd think something would come of all the searching."

Eva sighed. Should she speak up . . . say what she was thinking?

Menno removed his straw hat and put it on the bench. "From what I was told, Cousin Jeptha King solicited help from a half-dozen other men and some women, too. They've gone to a good many small towns—rural, mostly—and talked to nearly all the local merchants, restaurant managers, and the like in each location, but not a soul has seen Lily or even heard of her."

"What if she's somewhere else?" the bishop asked. "Has anyone considered that?"

"Anything's possible," Menno said. "Which makes me wonder if we need to do more."

The bishop inhaled deeply. "You're not thinkin' of getting the authorities involved, are ya?"

"She can't really be classified as missing," Menno said, his eyes serious.

"*Nee* . . . since there's a note in her handwriting." Bishop Isaac glanced over at Eva. "Do you still have it?"

Eva nodded. "Would you like to see it?"

"If ya don't mind."

She was actually glad for the opportunity to leave the kitchen, tense as the atmosphere was. How was Frona managing? If she knew her sister, she would soon have coffee made and poured, and produce a plate of cookies, too.

Upstairs, Eva found the note, and while she didn't mind showing the bishop, she almost wished she hadn't offered it. Lily had written this only to Eva. "On this very desk." She ran her hand over the smooth surface—some of Dat's best handiwork.

How many times had their father sanded down this desk to make it extra smooth? She and Lily had watched him that day, years ago. Dat was perspiring and covered with sawdust from his work, yet he never would have considered stopping till the finished product was ready to be stained. She had been so delighted when he'd eventually placed it in this bedroom.

Drawing a sigh, Eva hoped the bishop wouldn't keep the note.

Naomi wasn't expecting their son Omar that evening, but all the same, he walked right into her kitchen without so much as a knock on the side door. Unlike their other grown children, who knocked or rang the bell, he had never been one to do so, even once he'd left home to marry. Evidently Omar felt the most comfortable here. His light brown hair looked darker than usual tonight. *Oily from working in the fields all day,* Naomi thought, wishing he might have respected his father enough to clean up.

Abner invited him to sit at the table, where he and Naomi had been enjoying each other's company over a slice of snitz pie.

Naomi offered both men a cup of coffee, and Omar a piece of pie, which he politely declined, saying he'd already had dessert at home. Omar jokingly made a point of reminding her that he took his coffee black.

"Did ya think I'd forgotten?" she chuckled and opened the cupboard for one of her new coffee mugs.

Omar smiled as she poured him a cup before joining him on the wood bench. "I'd like to talk over my political leanings with ya, Daed."

"*Ach,* son." Naomi turned quickly, speaking out of turn.

Abner waved his hand and sent her a message with his eyes: *Let him get this out.*

Omar began again. "I know the Scripture verse from Romans the brethren like to quote: 'And be not conformed to this world . . .'"

"I read that one aloud quite a lot to you and your brothers and sisters while you were growin' up," Abner said.

Omar nodded. "That you did. And just so ya know where I stand on this, I don't believe that verse has anything to do with voting or perform-ing jury duty, neither one."

"Jury duty?" Abner grimaced and took a slow sip of his coffee.

"*Jah*, I could be asked to serve once I'm a registered voter," Omar said, fiddling with the spoon near his coffee mug.

"Have ya talked this over with one of the ministerial brethren?" Naomi asked.

"I followed the bishop's urging and spent time fasting and prayin'," Omar said. "I really believe the Lord is directing me to vote."

Naomi was pleased to hear he had gone ahead and done this, but she was surprised, even disappointed, that he was still moving forward with registering. *We're citizens of heaven*, she thought.

Abner glanced at Naomi.

"For this election, at least," Omar continued, "I plan to vote on local ballot issues . . . and possibly in the presidential election."

Abner set down his coffee mug. "The outcome's not a'tall what I'd hoped for, but I'm glad you've taken time to consider this, Omar. It's important not to let the world direct our behavior . . . or the way we think. You've always been such an upstandin' church member."

Omar pushed his fingers through his bushy beard. "I know you and Mamm want me to be a *gut* testimony. Ya don't have to worry whatsoever. My wife and nine children are on my mind, as well as my baptismal vow."

Abner gave him a nod, and Naomi sighed.

"I'll be prayin' for ya," Naomi said gently. "Like always." She still didn't understand Omar's fascination with voting, but she was relieved that it seemed to be where his interest in the world ended. *If only the same were true for Lily Esch . . .*

29

PRIOR to the shared meal after Preaching, Jed encountered Bettina's young fiancé, Levi Hershberger, out near the stable while the courting-age men waited to be called indoors.

"My cousin Marilyn Halverston might show up ridin' with Bettina and me tonight after Singing, if you're interested," Levi said, his hands stuffed deep in his trouser pockets.

Marilyn Halverston? Jed was surprised. Marilyn was an exceptionally pretty girl, sweet spirited and soft-spoken, but her beau had gotten into some trouble, left the church, and been shunned.

"Marilyn doesn't have any expectations at all—she knows you've been through a rough patch, too," Levi continued. "It'd strictly be a favor to me and Bettina."

"A favor, you say?" Reluctantly, Jed agreed to the double date. "Just this once, though." He laughed a little. "Guess it's one way for me to keep an eye on you and my spunky sister."

Levi's eyes narrowed, and then he chuckled as he seemed to realize Jed was joking. "Tell Bettina for me, okay?"

Jed said he would. It wasn't long before *die Youngie* were called in to eat, and as Jed moved toward the house, he noticed Marilyn and three of her sisters walking together, all wearing pastel blue dresses with white organdy aprons. He caught Marilyn's eye. She gave him a demure smile before looking away.

I hope I haven't made a mistake, Jed thought.

A month ago he would have thought nothing of her innocent flirtation, but ever since his visit to Eden Valley, things were different. There was only one smile he longed to see now, and it wasn't Marilyn's.

Jed appreciated the thick shelter of trees as he and Bettina talked after the light meal that Sunday afternoon. They strolled through the well-manicured backyard, heading through the field lanes, where their father's six-mule team moved from one field to the next. Across the way, the neighbor's windmill turned slowly, creaking as the sun poured down on tall meadow grass.

"Daed talked to Levi first, then to his father," Bettina said with a glance back at the house. "He's convinced Levi is a *gut* man, Jed."

You're still too young, Jed thought, not wanting to lose his closest sister.

She poked his elbow. "So ya really don't have to worry 'bout me."

"Just sayin' it doesn't make it true." He watched the play of emotions on her face; Bettina wore her feelings on her sleeve. All the same, he was determined not to point out that just because Dat thought Levi Hershberger was a good man didn't mean she was ready to be a wife in charge of a farmhouse and, in time, a mother.

Bettina tugged on her white Sunday apron as they walked in the heat of the day. "Both Daed and Mamm are leanin' my way little by little."

"Like all parents, they want to see you happily married," he said, knowing she was thoroughly caught up in her love for Levi.

"I *am* happy! Why can't *you* be happy for me?"

They walked without speaking for a moment, and Jed picked up a brittle twig and tossed it.

Bettina folded her hands, keeping up with his pace. "Are you worried maybe because of Lydiann's passing?"

Her expression was soft and respectful. She'd loved Lydiann, too. Everyone had.

"Ain't fair for me to hold you back," he replied, "just because I've found it hard to move forward."

"Well, you are, though, whether you like it or not. Levi and I are prayin' for you."

He smiled. "Maybe it's working."

"What do ya mean?"

He hesitated. "Well . . ."

"Well?"

He plunged ahead. "If ya must know, I met a girl in Lancaster County."

"Honestly?" Bettina stopped walking, her face beaming. "What's her name?"

"Eva Esch."

"And you like her?"

He breathed deeply of the warm air. "I think so."

"You're not *sure*?"

"Well . . . she's compassionate and expressive, but not *too* chatty. She's really smart and—"

"And is she perty?"

He paused, embarrassed. *"Jah."*

"You have to think about it?"

"Nee. Ain't that."

Her eyes were wide. "Jed, this is great news. And you know why, too."

"I s'pose it means I'm ready to let go of the past."

"So," she said, "I have to ask: Why'd you agree to double-date with Levi and me tonight? Aren't you goin' to court this Eva from afar . . . write to her?"

"I doubt she'd agree to it." He shook his head. "Things went sour between us right before I left to come home."

"Sour? What happened?"

"A misunderstanding." Jed shrugged.

"But still, if she's someone special . . ."

"Jah, she was."

"Was?" Bettina shook her head and turned to fall into step with him as they began walking again. "You can't just ignore this, can ya, Jed?"

He thought of the book and the photo, and of meeting Eva, who had been understandably distracted with Lily's disappearance. Even now, he recalled the look of heartache when Eva had realized the truth—when *he* had realized it—that he'd been carrying around a picture of her missing sister all along. Things had been so muddled up in his mind.

"Trust me, it's not fixable. Eva doesn't have a very high opinion of me anymore."

"Everything's fixable!" Bettina blew out a breath. "Honestly, sometimes it wonders me if some men are just *Dummkopps!*"

Jed laughed. "But you still love me, ain't?"

"You're my brother. I *have* to, according to Scripture."

"That's the only reason?"

"*Jah.*"

He folded his arms and puffed out his cheeks, and she giggled. He reached for a branch overhead and pulled off a leaf, tossing it at her.

"Seriously, Jed, is there anything I can do?"

"Prob'ly not."

"Well, you know that I'm here for ya. Besides, my prayers are like God's little arrows aimed right at your heart!"

He grinned.

"Maybe I could write to your Eva and beg her to forgive you."

Jed chuckled. "Don't you dare!"

"Well, try to have some fun tonight with us," Bettina said. "Who knows, maybe Marilyn will be the perfect match."

I had that once. . . .

Jed contemplated the evening ahead. *I can at least be friendly.*

Jed's pent-up tension on the walk to the barn Singing dissolved as soon as he entered the upper level, where a long line of well-scrubbed young men in white shirts and black suspenders sat on one side of the long table. The young women, ages sixteen through about nineteen, sat on the opposite side, still wearing their best dresses and crisp white aprons from Preaching earlier.

He lifted his voice in unison with the other men. Catching Bettina's eye, he smiled. He envied her rosy glow—surely she looked forward to spending time with Levi, who was as polite to Jed tonight as he was admiring of Bettina.

Jed didn't dare look Marilyn's way, not wanting to make her feel self-conscious. *No pressure,* he thought while waiting for Perry's younger brother Abe to blow the pitch pipe and lead out in the next song, "Nearer My God to Thee."

··· ≻ ≺ ···

Eva hadn't planned to wander out to the old playhouse at dusk. It wasn't a place she and Lily had typically gone after daylight hours, but Eva needed some time alone. There were many thoughts in her head, and the steady chirp of crickets soothed her, as did the pretty pink still in the sky.

"Lily hasn't come home, dear Lord," she whispered, not accustomed to saying her prayers aloud. "Yet Thou art with her always. . . . I believe this with all my heart."

The truth was Lily's return home looked hopeless, apart from a miracle.

She noticed several white birch trees had been toppled by windstorms last winter. Seeing them felled made her even sadder, and she quickened her pace, carrying her father's large lantern. She had gone to check on the livestock after supper, especially the new calves. She recalled Dat's gentle way with the newborn animals. All her years growing up, she had witnessed his expert help and gentle care during difficult births for not only their cows, but also for one of their horses.

He was nurturing with us, too.

When Eva reached the little shack, she opened the door and stepped inside, having to duck now that she was all grown-up. It struck her as comical that their great-grandfather hadn't considered that his grown daughters might someday want to show their own little girls this place. No doubt they would have had to stoop just as Eva was now.

Looking around, she set down the lantern and felt the urge to sweep out the cobwebs and make the small window shiny and spotless. *In memory of Lily.*

"That's silly," she said right out. "My sister's not dead."

Just ferhoodled . . .

Eva leaned against the wall, still crouched lest her head bump the low ceiling. There was no need for tears. Even so, she was having one of those moments Dat used to talk about—when something sweet comes to mind, and you want to cherish it for as long as possible. *Till daily chores and other things push in, and you forget why your heart was so tender.*

She appreciated that her father's passing was a gift in a sense. His dying first had spared him the terrible pain of losing Mamma. *He loved her that much,* she thought. *Though poor Mamma had to bear the sting of Dat's passing.*

Moving toward the east-facing window, she slid her fingers along its frame, where she and Lily had long ago discovered a small piece of paper— a note their great-grandfather's little girls must have written and pressed into the wood frame, concealing it for posterity. Eva eyed the spot where she was sure the note had always been. The last time she and Lily played there, Lily had pulled it out and waved it around, chanting the quote from *Little Women:* *"Take some books and read; that's an immense help, and books are always good company if you have the right sort."*

Wondering if the note had fallen, perhaps, Eva brought the lantern closer and searched around the floor near the window, then carried it all around the small square of a room, bending low to look.

But the note seemed to be gone.

"At least I have my memories of it," Eva whispered, blue that the age-old paper was missing.

After the actual Singing, couples began to pair up—some were prearranged double dates, like Jed and Marilyn with Levi and Bettina, while others were known courting couples. The youth in their church district were not as secretive about their dating partners as were other districts in both Ohio and Pennsylvania. *A wise thing,* Jed thought, especially because it had given his parents the opportunity to discuss things sensibly with Bettina, airing their concerns about her marrying so young.

"Are ya comfortable?" he asked Marilyn as they got settled in the second bench seat, behind Levi and Bettina in the enclosed surrey. The details of the carriage interior weren't clear in the starlight, and Jed wondered who'd built it, then chastised himself for not paying attention to his date. *"Once a buggy maker, always a buggy maker,"* Uncle Ervin often said.

"It's a nice night for ridin'," Marilyn commented as she put on her black outer bonnet. Levi had mentioned there were several warm blankets in the back if they got chilly.

Levi and Bettina visited quietly up front, and Jed wished Bettina would turn around and address either him or Marilyn. But for the moment, her sister and fiancé were too caught up in each other.

"Which schoolhouse did you attend?" he asked Marilyn to break the ice.

She described the location, a few blocks north of the railroad tracks, evidently not realizing that had been the scene of Lydiann's fatal accident. It was all Jed could do not to visibly wince.

"You must've gone to the school close to your father's house," Marilyn said.

He told her where and quickly changed the subject, asking now if she was busy with the family garden, which got her talking about the many types of vegetables she and her sister had planted.

"We're out waterin' by hand a lot since we haven't gotten as much rain as usual for June."

"Not as *gut* as water from the sky."

"*Nee* . . . and hand carryin' water isn't the best use of my time, either. Though I'm not complainin', really."

A cloud passed over the moon, and suddenly the buggy was cloaked in shadows. He remembered taking Eva in Jonas Byler's carriage and feeling frustrated because he couldn't see her face in the darkness.

Marilyn continued to talk about her day, and Jed could detect his sister's soft giggles in front of him, but his mind was hundreds of miles away.

He had told Eva he would write but hadn't. The truth was, while he doubted she'd want to hear from him, he *was* curious if Lily had returned home, or if they'd gotten word of her whereabouts. Jed regretted again his final visit in Eva's beloved candy shop.

"*It won't be mine much longer*," she'd told him while showing him the shop, her eyes glistening with sadness, as if her whole purpose was about to be taken from her.

"Jed?"

He jerked to attention. Marilyn was talking to him, and he hadn't heard a word.

"Sorry?"

She smiled and repeated it. "What's your favorite ice cream?"

"Chocolate."

"Mine too," she replied. "And I say dark chocolate's best."

"Well, it's certainly much richer tasting than milk chocolate."

"For sure." She added that she also liked to make chocolate chip ice cream and chocolate-covered cherries. "And have you ever eaten chocolate bread custard?"

"Did I hear something 'bout chocolate back there?" Levi asked, turning his head toward them.

"It's chocolate everything," Marilyn answered, laughing softly.

"Since we're talkin' food, are we ready for sundaes?"

"Whenever you're hungry," Jed said, ready for a break from the confines of the buggy. *I shouldn't even be here. . . .*

Levi directed the horse to a trot, and as they drew closer to the ice cream shop, Jed knew without a doubt he must try to get in touch with Eva. And as far as he could see, there was only one way she might be willing to give him another chance. *Only one.*

30

THAT Tuesday, Eva ironed all the pillowcases and top sheets, too, like Mamma had always done. Eva mentioned to Frona that she had gone out to the old playhouse to reminisce on Sunday evening. "I think maybe we're both tryin' to hang on to what's left of Lily," Eva said.

Frona looked up from her embroidery, eyes soft. "Sometimes I do that with Mamma." She sighed and laid the hoop on the table. "After the washing was out on the line yesterday, I went into the big bedroom while you were sellin' candy next door. I felt downright blue, so I headed upstairs and opened the door to our parents' bedroom and just stood there."

"I haven't looked in there for months."

"Prob'ly *schmaert*, really."

Eva folded the pillowcases on the warm ironing board. "I'd actually thought you should move in up there and make that room your own, but that was before Menno told us his plans."

"I'd feel out of place havin' Mamm and Dat's room."

"Well, since you're the oldest of us girls," Eva replied.

Frona's face broke into a sweet smile. "Awful nice of you."

Eva had noticed that Frona seemed different lately. Gentler, in some ways; less abrupt, too. It was such a lovely change, she wanted to go over and throw her arms around her, the way Lily used to do with Eva, but she didn't want to upset the fruit basket and scare Frona back into her grouchy shell.

When she'd put away the ironing, Eva walked out to the barnyard and groomed Prince, taking her time with him. She slipped him a sugar cube when she was done, then strolled out to the road to check the mail, breathing in the familiar farm smells. Across the road, back near his stable, Abner Mast took off his straw hat and waved it at her.

The day's as perfect a June day as they come, she thought, opening the mailbox. There, along with three circle letters for Frona, and one for her, was a thick envelope from Alfred Dienner.

She drew a quick breath and held the letter tentatively, like a soiled dishrag. Just then, a middle-aged *Englischer* came riding down the road on his bicycle, nodding as he passed. She'd never seen him around the area before and guessed he must be fit enough to pedal quite a long way. What must it feel like to ride so fast and free? She tried to imagine it as she watched the man disappear from view.

Turning toward the house, Eva decided to read Alfred's letter right away, instead of waiting till after chores were done. This way she could mull over whatever was on his mind.

··· ➤ ➤ ···

The early robin's robust song had awakened Naomi around four o'clock that morning, making it difficult to return to sleep.

Thankfully, she'd felt reenergized after two cups of coffee and a hearty breakfast—three eggs for Abner and two for her, plus a half grapefruit each, and a generous portion of scrapple.

Omar had stopped in an hour or so later before going to work with Abner, telling them that he'd registered to vote. Why, oh why, couldn't Omar just settle down like the rest of their grown children?

Is this how Dottie Esch felt about Lily? she wondered.

Abner came inside looking for something to nibble on, hungry again. "Eva was out getting her mail just now," he said, making small talk. "She didn't seem her usual cheerful self."

"Well, no wonder," Naomi said. "They still haven't heard from Lily." She sliced two thick pieces of homemade wheat bread and slapped a good amount of peanut butter and strawberry jam on it to make a sandwich. "Maybe this will stick to your ribs till the noon meal."

"What'll it be today, love?"

She smiled. "Aren't you the bottomless pit?"

"Must seem like it to you." He grinned. "But I'm mighty blessed to be married to such a *gut* cook."

Naomi eyed his snack, nearly devoured already. "Want another?"

"Better not. I have to start liftin' hay bales with Omar and Elam right quick."

"Well, ain't you somethin'," she teased, waving him back out to the barn.

Eva ran her thumbnail along the edge of Alfred's envelope. She'd excused herself to the barn, to Dat's former office, where Menno had set up file cabinets and altered the place to suit his needs. She closed the door and settled into the swivel desk chair.

Bracing herself, she began to read and quickly noticed that most of Alfred's letter was comprised of his daily schedule at the woodworking shop and of learning to use various saws and other hydraulic tools. He'd also mentioned finding a candy store, but it didn't have offerings nearly as delectable as Eva's candies. *And I sampled quite a few,* he'd written.

In the final paragraph, he said he wanted to call her a week from today. *Will you be able to get away to the phone shanty at three o'clock in the afternoon?*

Eva knew talking had always been easier for him than writing. He'd admitted this some time ago, when he went with his family on vacation and hadn't bothered to send her even a postcard. She sighed. If he was more comfortable by phone, then so be it.

Eva had to decide how to reply; if she didn't hurry and do so, he'd have to postpone his anticipated phone call. Yet if she *did* agree, what would he say to her?

"What should my answer be, O Lord?"

She glanced at Tuesday, June 17, on the large farm seed calendar on the wall and found herself wishing Jed Stutzman had written instead.

31

EVA hurried out to the strawberry patch to help Frona pick the fresh crop, enjoying the warm day. There seemed to be less humidity than yesterday, and the birds were chirping merrily, competing with Max, who was barking as he raced through the meadow with the pony.

"I wonder what Lily's doin' today," Eva said, setting her large tin bucket down on the dirt near her bare feet.

Frona looked over at her, her blue bandanna keeping her hair bun secure. "Whatever she's doin' certainly doesn't include us."

"I'm sure she misses us as much as we miss her, though."

Frona moved to the next plant and stopped to get out a hankie to wipe her forehead. "I seriously doubt that."

Frona's old mood had made a reappearance, and Eva didn't think now was the time to share Alfred's request to call. Sure as the sunrise, when next Tuesday afternoon came, she'd have to explain why she was leaving to head across the field.

"*Gut* thing we're out here before the birds decided to make a *Fescht* of the strawberries," Frona said, then muttered something about nasty creatures.

When her pail was close to overflowing, Eva carried it to the house, careful not to spill a single berry. She drew some cold water and gently took handfuls of the bright red fruit and placed them in the sink, washing each one carefully before cutting out the stem.

690

By the time Frona came inside with her full pail, Eva was ready for that batch. They planned to make jam right away to lock in the freshness.

Later, as they were washing canning jars, Bena and little Katie Ann arrived with a casserole dish of tuna and noodles. Then, not ten minutes later, Naomi showed up with some pulled pork and scalloped potatoes.

"Well, isn't this somethin'?" said Frona, who thanked both women and invited them to stay for cold meadow tea.

"I thought you'd enjoy not having to cook with all those strawberries comin' on fast," Bena said, setting Katie Ann on her lap at the table. "But I had no idea Naomi was thinkin' the selfsame way."

This brought a round of laughter.

"It does get busy round here," Eva said, realizing how much Lily had helped in the past. She took babbling Katie Ann from Bena and walked straight to the cookie jar to let Katie nibble on a treat.

"Not too many," Bena warned, looking like she could use a few minutes to sit and rest.

"*Ach*, we got caught," Eva whispered to her tiny niece. "Better just eat half, all right?"

Little Katie Ann frowned her disapproval, and Eva knew she was in a pickle, so she brought her niece back to Bena, who broke the cookie in half. The tot accepted the smaller portion and leaned her head on Eva's shoulder.

"She's such a dear," Eva said.

"What do ya expect? You offered her a sweet," Bena teased.

Eva asked Naomi, "Would ya like some more cold tea?"

"*Ach*, maybe so." Naomi fanned herself with the hem of her apron.

Eva gave Katie Ann back to her mother. "I'll pour some milk for her," Eva said, going to the fridge.

"As you can see, we're about to put up some strawberry jam," Frona was saying while Eva poured the milk. "Can hardly keep up with that berry patch!"

Bena mentioned they were trying to eat at least some of their fresh pickings. "We've plenty of little mouths to feed."

Katie Ann babbled in *Deitsch*, telling Bena she was ready for the other half of her cookie, and they all laughed about it.

"Sounds like she's got herself a mighty sweet tooth," Naomi said.

"Like her Mamma," Bena said, squeezing Katie Ann. "Ain't so, *Bobbli?*"

Katie Ann reached up a chubby hand, and Bena kissed it.

They talked of other things—an upcoming work frolic at the deacon's house, and another auction, too, this one a farm sale.

After a while, Bena said, as though she had been waiting for the right moment, "I have some news. Menno received another letter from Cousin Jeptha."

Eva swung around, all ears.

"He's heard rumors 'bout a runaway Amish teenager livin' somewhere outside of Kidron," Bena told them. "We're still lookin' into it. Not much to go on, really."

Eva took a seat next to Naomi. "*Jah*, not very reliable at all. But hopeful."

Bena nodded. "Jeptha assured Menno he's keepin' his eyes and ears open." She held the milk glass up to her little daughter's mouth, and Katie Ann put her dimpled hands on top of Bena's.

"Makes ya wonder how many *Youngie* run off lookin' for greener pastures," Frona said.

Or pastures that aren't so green, Eva thought.

Naomi's eyes welled up. "Perhaps this is the beginning of the miracle we've all been hopin' for."

Eva stared at Bena, not sure what to make of this news. Oh, she hoped Naomi was right.

It was unbearably warm and sticky in the buggy shop; the battery-powered fans hardly made a dent in the oppressiveness. Jed had been working all morning on the wooden dashboard for the two-seater surrey he was constructing.

His mind was occupied with several futile attempts to explore various leads about Lily Esch via the Amish grapevine, which could sometimes be so undependable. And he'd also placed phone calls from the carriage shop to Mennonite churches in the area, as well as to relatives. He even found the number for a halfway house for Amish runaways in Sugarcreek, and planned to call there, too.

Wouldn't someone, somewhere, have heard of a former Amish girl trying to go fancy? Perhaps one of the many scribes for The Budget *might write about it this coming week.* The thought spurred him on.

Needing something cold to drink, Jed walked the length of the shop to Uncle Ervin's office area, where there was a small refrigerator with chilled drinks. He reached for an orange soda and saw his uncle heading this way. "Say, I'm glad I caught ya." Jed stepped aside at the doorway.

"Something on your mind?"

Jed waited for him to lower himself into his comfortable chair near the handcrafted credenza. "I've been thinkin' a lot about joining church come September."

"Well, I'll be turkey feathers," his uncle declared, crossing his arms. "That-a boy. Mighty glad to hear it."

Jed smiled and nodded. "Ain't something I wanted to rush into, considering everything."

"You're wise to take your time—to know for certain this is the life you want. The baptismal vow is the most serious promise you'll ever make."

To God and to the church. "Later this summer, I'll begin my instruction with the deacon."

Uncle Ervin leaned back, his gnarled hands gripping the arms of the chair, and closed his eyes. He was silent for some time; then suddenly his eyelids fluttered open. "Such *gut* news . . . truly 'tis."

Due to the high humidity, the office room seemed cramped with the two of them, despite its being a decent-sized space. Jed took another long swig of his soda and said, "I'll get back to work now."

Uncle Ervin eyed him solemnly before Jed turned to exit. Over in Perry's work area, Jed strode past the partially built buggy and nodded cordially, then made his way to his own space.

As he worked, Jed recalled the latter part of his date with Marilyn Halverston. In all truth, Marilyn was just as pleasant as he'd expected, and things might have gone differently had Eva not been so heavily on his mind. He had felt so distracted that he wondered why he'd ever agreed to Levi's suggestion to double-date. Of course, the sundaes had been exceptionally tasty, given there were more than a dozen choices of toppings—various sliced nuts, miniature marshmallows, and chopped hard candies. Jed had chosen chocolate crumbles and walnut pieces, and

Bettina had giggled as she pointed out the instability of the high mound atop his double dips, insisting it was all going to come rolling off.

Later that night, after returning home, he'd wandered out to the large pond overlooking the old ice house on his father's land, juggling his conflicted thoughts. He relived the long Sunday walk with Eva, when they'd fed the ducks. *When I held her hand . . .*

One thing was readily apparent: Not once since leaving Lancaster County had Jed longed for Lydiann, the woman he'd mourned a full year.

32

EVA worked side by side with Frona at Thursday market, where they'd put out dozens of pint jars of strawberry jam for sale, along with a selection of nut brittles, almond bark, and other candy—taffy, caramels, and toffee. She had written the labels with her best printing, something Lily had always enjoyed doing for Mamma, and then Frona. Presently, Eva cordially engaged their customers, all the while holding her breath for Cousin Jeptha's contact to discover more so that a trail might begin to open and lead them to Lily. This was Eva's constant hope and prayer. Since hearing from Bena two days ago, she had awakened in the night several times after dreaming about her sister.

Jed Stutzman had also shown up in one of her dreams. It was strangely vivid, and Jed and Lily had been walking through a large milking parlor in an Amish barn, smiling as they strolled along. Eva had awakened with a start, feeling dreadfully annoyed, as if they'd both abandoned their affections for her. *How odd*, thought Eva, wondering how her longing for Jed had become tangled up in thoughts of Lily.

Later, when there were fewer customers gathered about their table, Eva walked to the fudge display where Jed had purchased her surprise gift. She stared down at the colorful wrappings and remembered how her heart had fluttered at the sight of the box.

Jed felt something for me, she soothed herself.

"Can I help ya make your choice?" asked the clerk.

"Just lookin'."

"*Ach*, well, lookin's not tasting."

"Believe me, I know." She moved along the display case and admired how these candies were arranged, thinking of her own display.

She remembered again the last time she'd seen Jed. The tour she'd given him of her shop, his eyes so earnest, his smile infectious. "I'll have one of those," she said suddenly, pointing to the same type of fudge Jed had given her.

To relive that happy memory, she told herself as she reached for her purse.

It was Frona who noticed the flag down on the mailbox when they neared the turnoff to their driveway. "Looks like the mail's come."

"Are you expecting something?" Eva asked.

Frona shook her head and guided the horse to make the right-hand turn. "We're all caught up on circle letters, ain't?"

Eva said she was. "Your idea to spread the word to our Ohio cousins might be partly why Cousin Jeptha found out what he did. Have ya thought of that?"

"Like you, I'm leavin' it up to the Good Lord. Worryin' causes me an upset stomach anymore."

Frona said it so seriously, Eva's heart went out to her. "Aw, sister."

Then, halting Prince, Frona suggested Eva go and check the mail while Frona started to unhitch.

Eva hurried to the mailbox, since Frona could certainly use her help. It was no easy chore unhitching alone, and besides, it was beginning to rain.

She looked over at Masts' to see if either Abner or Naomi was in view. Abner was surely around someplace, given the work dairymen were required to do—sterilizing the milk house equipment, including scrubbing the bulk tank, and cleaning out the barn. All of it needed to pass muster with the milk inspector.

Eva opened the mailbox and pulled out a single letter with her name on the envelope. "Lily's handwriting," she whispered.

"Oh, praise be!" she said again and again, running now up the long driveway toward Frona, clutching the letter to her chest to protect it from what was now a downpour. "It's from Lily! Oh, Frona . . ."

Frona brightened but stated, "First things first," blinking through the deluge. The horse was still half in and half out of the harness and needed to be stabled and rubbed down and watered. Both girls were getting drenched as Eva returned from quickly putting the letter in the house for safekeeping.

Eva worked as fast and as efficiently as she could. With Frona's good help, they finally finished—the longest and soggiest twenty-five minutes ever.

Once Prince was settled in his stall and Dat's fine carriage was parked, Eva scurried into the house and washed her hands, waiting for Frona to do the same. "I'm soaked clear through to the skin," she said, shivering.

They took time to change into dry clothes before sitting down at the table. There, Eva opened Lily's letter with trembling hands and began to read aloud.

"June 9

Dear Frona and Eva,

If I know you, you're probably both very concerned about me.

But happily, I am safe and staying with a large family who runs a dairy farm, helping out as I can to earn my room and board. In my free time, I often get to see my boyfriend—an *Englischer*. He's one of the reasons I came here to live, and oh, it's been wonderful to have so much time with him!

I should have told you what I was planning, except I feared you'd try to stop me. It was wrong, and I pray you forgive me.

It's taking some real courage to be accepted by English folks, but I'm doing my best, and you mustn't worry about me. Promise?

I love you, sisters . . . and my whole family back there in Eden Valley.

Yours always,
Lily Esch"

"She sounds quite settled," Frona said, eyes misting. "Is there a return address?"

Eva showed her the front of the envelope. "The postmark is Wooster, for goodness' sake!"

"You don't see dairy farms in cities, so is she really where she says?"

Eva scanned the letter once more. "It's odd. I mean, if Lily was gonna write and tell us she's safe and happy, then why not reveal exactly where she is? I don't understand."

"She sounds too happy 'bout her beau, if ya ask me."

Eva nodded. "I hope she doesn't forget us."

Frona slipped her arm around Eva, and they sat that way for a moment, the letter before them.

At last they rose, and Frona laid out their money on the table and began to count it quietly. Eva set to work making a light supper, since they'd snacked here and there at market, what with the many vendors offering free samples.

Lily's letter stirred up a feeling of helplessness in Eva that she found hard to endure. How could she feel good knowing Lily was struggling? *"It's taking some real courage to be accepted."*

According to what she'd written, Lily might actually be living with Plain folks, Eva thought, considering the reference to a dairy farm. This was heartening, but it didn't line up with what Fannie had told them about Lily's plan to stay with her boyfriend's married sister.

Eva set to work chopping cabbage for slaw.

Frona looked up. "Still thinking 'bout Lily's letter?"

Eva admitted she was and set the knife down on the cutting board. "She's not interested in being found, is she?"

Frona shook her head. "She's made that clear."

Hearing Frona's opinion out in the open like that made it seem all the more certain.

During evening Bible reading and prayers, Eva sat quietly, respectfully, noting Lily's regular spot. Eva's emotions were emerging in a new way, and while on one hand she sensed a burden roll from her shoulders in relief at finally hearing something, she was equally troubled—even angry—over Lily's apparent apathy toward her and Frona. *And everyone else in our family, too.* Eva had expected more from the sister she'd known her whole life.

Is this what happens—the world changes who you are?

Her talk with Tilly had addressed numerous things but nothing like this, and Eva hardly knew what to make of Lily's letter as a whole. Still, she refused to doubt there was hope Lily might find her wits and come home.

33

THE next few days were dreary with rain, the thunder waking Eva in the night, then the steady downpour on the roof lulling her back to sleep.

Each morning, when Menno and Emmanuel came into the utility room to fill their thermoses with cold water at the sink, they seemed thankful to be in out of the rain, even taking a few minutes to visit with Frona and Eva. Emmanuel, especially, was interested in sampling Eva's new concoctions for The Sweet Tooth, more than happy to taste test.

Once the worst of the heavy rains had passed, Eva inspected the flower beds and saw that the delicate petunias had been beaten to the ground, and there were deep ruts in the soil of the vegetable garden.

At the designated time for Alfred's phone call Tuesday afternoon, Eva was pleased when Frona left the house for Ida Mae's to help make strawberry pies for several families, including the two preachers'. *She'll be gone long enough for me to talk to Alfred and return home,* Eva thought, calling for Max as she hurried across the backyard.

The grass was soggy, and she was glad they'd kept Mamma's old work boots so she could tromp through the meadow. Max kept running circles around her, looping forward, then back—the finest dog ever, and most companionable, too.

Glancing over her shoulder, Eva could see Menno and the other workers moving from the stable to the barn, where grain and hay were stored. She realized then how peculiar it would be to experience whatever adjustments might come once Menno and Bena moved in. *For whoever ends up staying on here as a mother's helper.*

Naomi Mast had once said that change was inevitable. *"It's one of the things you can always count on,"* she'd said. The observation had made Eva think.

She crossed a rise covered with wet maidenhair ferns; these volunteers had taken over the place since Dat's passing. Their roots were solidly placed, and unless they were mowed down or intentionally dug up, they were there to stay.

Transplants, like Lily? Oh, I hope not.

The old wooden telephone shed came into view, but because the preachers had deliberately placed it in the middle of a stand of fast-growing silver maples, a person had to know where it was positioned in order to find it.

Moving down the muddy path that led to the narrow shanty, Eva breathed in the thick scent of damp earth and bark. The meadow grass looked taller and deeper in hue because of recent rains.

Eva checked her wristwatch. *Six minutes before Alfred's call.*

For as long as she'd known him, Alfred had been prompt and a person of his word. But what he wanted to discuss today, she couldn't be sure, and she curled her toes in her Mamma's boots, shaky as a newborn calf.

Eva remained just outside the door of the phone shed. She disliked standing inside, too aware of the cobwebs she often batted down with her hand in an attempt to dismantle any evidence of spiders—her least favorite insect in God's collection of bugs.

The last time Eva had come here was cloaked with sadness, for it was the day she'd run headlong through the deep snow to dial 9-1-1. Mamma was near death's door, and the ambulance had arrived too late for the paramedics to revive her.

Max wagged his tail and panted as he looked up at Eva. A butterfly caught his attention, and he turned and bolted after it. *Saturday is Naomi's surprise birthday party,* Eva thought, looking forward to making a pretty card to take to Ida Mae's when the rest of the womenfolk arrived after noon with cake and ice cream. *We'll have us a nice time. . . .*

The phone rang loudly, and she stepped inside the shed. "Hullo?" she answered, suddenly feeling bashful.

"Eva, it's Alfred. *Wie bischt?*"

"Fine . . . and you?" Truthfully, she wasn't feeling altogether fine just then. He sounded different to her, or maybe it was the long-distance connection.

"I've been looking forward to callin'," Alfred said, then went on to mention the weather, one of his favorite topics. "Heard it's been raining quite a lot there."

"The fields are like sponges."

He laughed a little. "Hope ya wore your boots."

She told him she had. "Is it nice out there?"

"Not too hot, which is always helpful when you're workin' inside a woodshop."

She let him talk about his work, noting his obvious enthusiasm.

"The more I learn, the more I believe I'm cut out for woodworking."

She smiled at the clever quip and wondered if he was aware of what he'd said.

"I really enjoy handling different types of woods and such, Eva—each job brings something new. It's far more creative than farming, of course. Less reliant on the elements, too."

This was a surprise. Never had she expected to hear Alfred say a word against farming.

"There's plenty to learn, of course, but it seems I've got a knack for it, or so my boss tells me."

"I'm happy for ya," she said.

"But that's not the only reason I called. I have a terrific idea, and I hope you'll agree."

She listened, unsure what was on his mind.

"You might have noticed I've written about the young people here and some of the places I enjoy. The countryside is beautiful, too. It's a growing area for *gut* reason."

Where's he going with this? Eva wondered.

"It's happened awful fast, but I've been offered a job as a shop assistant. I'll continue to learn the trade as I go, like an apprentice, but with decent pay." He stopped for a second. "Enough for me to settle here."

Alfred's not coming back?

He went on. "So I got to thinkin', instead of waiting till we marry, I'd like for you to come here for our courtship."

She was stunned.

"What would ya think of that, Eva? I've already found a nice place for you to stay."

Well, she didn't think much of it at all. No, she could just envision poor Frona living all alone, bouncing around in their parents' large house until Menno and his family moved in. Or maybe he'd move in all the sooner, Eva didn't know.

"This is so sudden," she said. "I hardly know what to say."

"I miss seein' you, Eva. It'd be *wunnerbaar-gut* to have ya out here with me."

How could she say she'd think about it when she just wanted to hang up the phone?

"*Ach*, Alfred, I didn't envision our courtship progressing quite this fast . . . 'specially with Lily gone an' all." Feeling cornered, she wanted to still her racing heart.

"*Jah*, I wondered how you were holding up when Mamm said there'd been no news."

Eva nodded into the phone. "It's one of the worst things to happen to my family."

"I wish I could comfort you in person, Eva," he said softly. Then, going on, he said, "I could easily arrange for you to be here within a few weeks."

She considered his remarkable offer, but things were moving much too quickly. "If you're willing to wait, Alfred, I'd like to think about it. And meanwhile, we could discuss this further by mail, all right?"

"I'll wait, *jah*." His voice brightened considerably. "I'll be glad to."

After they said good-bye and hung up, she walked back over the water-logged pasture toward home. "'Tis unbelievable," she whispered.

Their spitz sprinted up behind her, then slowed to walk alongside. "I'd miss *you*, dear Max," she said, running her hand across the length of his white back. "And everyone here in Eden Valley." Just then Eva realized how happy she might be feeling about such an unusual proposal if it were coming from Jed.

But that door appears to be closed, she thought regretfully.

··· ⋟ ⋞ ···

During a short break that afternoon, Jed slipped away to Uncle Ervin's office area to use the phone. Searching the yellow pages, he found the number for the Ohio Chamber of Commerce.

Immediately, Jed was encouraged when he spoke with a woman who seemed eager to help. "I live here in Ohio," he explained, "but I'd like to request a listing for tourist accommodations in Plain communities." He told her that he'd heard there was such a list, which included Mennonite and Amish guest housing.

"I can mail it to you, sir." The woman asked for his name and address.

Jed gave her the information, then thanked her and said good-bye, his spirits rising.

34

FRIDAYS were typically frenzied at the carriage shop, and this one was no different as Jed worked on his assigned surrey. He and Perry had to have their six-day workweek wrapped up before the Lord's Day—from the earliest time of their apprenticeship, Uncle Ervin had nudged them to be as productive as possible.

Jed was meticulous while finishing the flooring of the large family carriage. All the while, he could hear Uncle Ervin making small talk with Perry, who was building a two-wheeled cart, the simplest type of buggy.

Perry was describing a recent visit to Charm, where he'd run into some old school chums, one of whom was leaving the Amish life behind. Uncle Ervin wagged his head at that, then said something that caught Jed's attention.

"Speaking of Amish going to the world, I ran into a farmer friend, Abram Kurtz, who grew up in Lancaster County but now lives in Kidron," Uncle Ervin was saying. "Abram was in line at Lehman's Hardware behind an *Englischer* girl, who was all dolled up in earrings and makeup, short skirt, fancy hairdo, but—get this—she had an Amish accent a mile wide and kept mixin' up her Dutch with English."

"Not fancy a'tall, I'm thinkin'," Perry interjected. "You can take the girl out of the Amish, but you can't take the *Amish* out of the girl!"

Ervin nodded. "Abram was convinced she wasn't from anywhere in Ohio!"

"Why's that?"

"He could tell by her accent she was from his old stompin' grounds back in Pennsylvania."

Jed turned to get a better listen, very curious.

Perry slapped his knee, fully engaged, and Ervin kept going. "So Abram decided to have some fun with her and said right out loud, 'What part of Lancaster County are you from?'"

Ervin continued his story. "Well, I guess the young woman turned as white as a sheet in the wind. And Abram took it even further and said he had some friends who lived south of Strasburg—asked if she knew 'em."

Perry howled with laughter.

"Her mouth dropped, and right quick, he offered a handshake and introduced himself all proper-like. She played along, it seemed, told her name, but it wasn't *Amish*, let me tell you. Then suddenly, she excused herself like she'd forgotten something, and rushed out of the store, leaving her things behind."

Perry shook his head. "Guess it ain't funny after all."

Ervin agreed. "If ya leave the People, son, you'll spend the rest of your life pretending to be what you're not."

Perry nodded and glanced at Jed.

Unable to keep quiet any longer, Jed asked, "So, what was the young woman's name?"

Ervin thought for a moment. "Well now, I don't recall." He was frowning, apparently still trying to remember. "Wait a minute. *Jah*, I believe 'twas something like . . . Lillian."

Perry harrumphed and stepped back to use the level on the buggy box he was constructing. "Doesn't sound very Amish, does it?"

Ervin agreed. "But the Pennsylvania Amish do use some different first names than round here."

Lillian? An Amish girl from Lancaster County?

"What're the chances?" Jed murmured, going over to Perry's fine-looking two-wheeler. He commented on the well-built base, hoping his uncle might say more about the conversation with his friend. Finally Jed asked, "So this was at Lehman's Hardware, ya say?"

Ervin gave him a quizzical look. "*Jah*, in Kidron."

"Small town," Jed added casually.

"Sure is," Ervin said.

Too small to hide in, Jed thought. A sudden idea presented itself, and Jed knew right where he was going to be tomorrow—if he could work fast enough. *And if I can hire a driver, too.*

⸺ ➤ ⭇ ⸺

After supper that evening, while his father and the neighboring farmer were nailing together beehive frames, Jed offered to help Bettina groom the horses. The stable smelled of fresh bedding straw, and he drank in the scent—he missed some aspects of daily farm life after spending nearly all of his daylight hours at the carriage shop.

"I need to pick your brain," he told his sister with a glance over the horse's mane.

"Sounds painful." She smirked in the horse stall next to Jed.

"I'm serious."

"What's on your mind?" she asked, grooming brush in hand.

"It might sound peculiar, but let's say you decided to go fancy and wanted to hide from your family in the outside world—"

"What on earth?" Bettina blinked, her eyebrows rising. "Somethin' you're not telling me, Jed?"

He shook his head. "It's not about me, *Simbel*—silly."

"Who, then?"

"Just put your thinkin' cap on for a minute and help me out."

"Well, I wouldn't dress Plain, that's for sure."

Obviously, Jed thought. "So how would I spot you if you looked like every other *Englischer?*"

"Oh, I see." Bettina stopped her brushing and placed her hand on the chestnut mare. "You must be lookin' for a girl who's gone a little overboard. She wouldn't have a very *gut* fashion sense—for an *Englischer,* that is. She'd look fancy but a little off."

"How do ya mean?"

"If it was me, I'd be the one trying too hard to fit in. First, I'd cut my hair real short and maybe color it, too." Bettina touched her auburn hair where it was visible outside the white bandanna. "How would I look as a brunette?"

Jed pondered her response.

"Most of all, I wouldn't *sound* Amish, if I could help it," she continued.

Jed nodded. According to Uncle Ervin's friend, it was the woman's accent that gave her away.

"I'd also spend nearly all my time with Amish folk, since I'd be awfully homesick," Bettina said, clinching his plan.

Of course! Jed thought. *There are oodles of Amish at Lehman's Hardware.* "I guess I just need to check with the locals . . . ask if there are any fancy folk hanging round Amish."

"*Ach*, Jed." She stared at him, frowning. "Is this a *real* girl we're talkin' about?"

"She's very real, and she's a runaway."

"Well then, I'm sure someone will know *exactly* who you're looking for. But, Jed . . . most likely, even if ya could track down a girl like this, she might not have a thing to do with you. Runaways are fed up with bein' told what to do and how to be."

Lillian, he thought. *If Lily's changed her name, what else has she changed?*

"Tell me more." His sister stepped out of the horse stall and came to the door where Jed was working. Leaning on the door, she was clearly curious. "This doesn't have anything to do with the girl you liked in Lancaster County, does it?"

"There's nothin' to tell, frankly."

Bettina gave him a look. "I'll keep mum, I promise."

He thought of Eva's sisterly concern for Lily, and of Uncle Ervin's comments—if they panned out. "I'll let you know when or if I find out. How's that?"

Turning back, she slipped inside the other stall again and picked up the grooming brush once more. "It'll be your fault if I don't sleep tonight, ya know, wonderin' what you're up to."

"I'm just spinning my wheels. Prob'ly nothin' will come of it." He fluffed the bedding straw with a pitchfork. If Lily wanted to be fancy, that was her right, since she was old enough to make her own decisions. Even so, it was Eva he was concerned about, and he couldn't help but wonder if she had heard from Lily by now.

And if not . . .

What if I could bring Eva at least some measure of relief? But do I dare interfere in her life after messing up so badly?

Yet Jed felt he had little hope of another chance with Eva if he did nothing about Lily. It wasn't a perfect plan, but it was *something.*

Later, when he and Bettina had finished with the horses, his sister headed to the house to help their mother with some hemming, and Jed made his way to the woodshed to split a pile of dry logs with his father.

Right away, Jed brought up the idea of an Old Order Amish person trying to go English. Typically, he and Daed didn't talk much when they worked together, but he wanted to hear what insight his father might have.

"What's this about going fancy?" His poor father looked *ferhoodled*.

"Ain't me, so don't worry."

"'Tis *gut*. Thought I heard from the deacon you were planning to take baptismal classes this summer."

"Right." Jed knew he'd better come up with something to shed a bit of light on what he was planning. "Someone I met in Pennsylvania has a relative who left the Amish community back there."

"And you'd like to locate him?"

"Well, it's a young woman, actually."

"I see."

Jed didn't feel obliged to tell more. "I just thought you might've heard accounts of some Amish youth tryin' to fit in with the outside world . . . and if they're ever persuaded to return to their families. What helps them want to stay put once they're back home?"

Daed leaned his axe against the woodpile and scratched his neck. "You don't hear of this a lot round here. Does the girl have a good church family to keep her from backsliding? Because none of us is immune to temptation, son."

"I know very little about her or the church district."

"Well, given the right—or wrong—circumstance, any of us is capable of sin." His father quoted 1 Corinthians 10, verse 12. "'Wherefore let him that thinketh he standeth take heed lest he fall.'"

Jed had heard that very verse during Sunday sermons.

"The Lord gives us the responsibility to keep track of each other." Daed stopped to wipe his brow with the back of his shirt sleeve. "Makes me wonder where the young woman's family is in all this."

"Sadly, her parents are deceased—her mother passed just recently."

"So then someone else needed to come alongside the girl to encourage her in the faith, ain't so?"

Jed wondered, now that his father had said this, if Lily's brothers had been too caught up with their own families, perhaps, or if they weren't even aware of Lily's struggles. Surely the latter was true. Yet with a loving, caring sister like Eva, how could Lily have been enticed by the world?

Daed had more to say. "The Deceiver of souls looks for discouraged and disconnected believers—'specially those isolated because of grief or disappointment. Such folks are cut off from the church body as a whole by their own doin'." Daed looked off in the distance like he was remembering someone in particular. "You've known people like this, Jed. They tend to drift away like chaff in the wind."

Jed nodded, keenly listening. "I'd like to help this young woman, if I can find her."

"Be careful, son. You might not like what you discover. Satan's trickery abounds." Daed picked up his axe and began chopping again, and Jed worked, too, glad to help his wise father.

May the Lord be with me, Jed prayed, wanting to do this for the right reason . . . though he could almost imagine Eva's lovely face when she learned that Lily had been found.

35

A T the breakfast table the next morning, Jed's father opened his big Bible to the book of Proverbs. Mamm and Bettina were scrambling eggs and making waffles when Daed slid the Good Book under Jed's nose. "Here's another helpful verse to consider, son, concerning our conversation last night."

Jed read it silently. *Where no counsel is, the people fall: but in the multitude of counselors there is safety.*

He thanked Daed, and during the silent table grace, Jed asked God for direction in his search. *Please let me find some answers, O Lord.*

Following family worship after the meal, Bettina caught up with Jed as he was hitching up for work extra early so he could take off for Kidron at three o'clock that afternoon. "You must've talked to Daed 'bout what you told me," she said as she held the horse steady for him.

"It's always a *gut* thing to get our father's perspective."

Bettina agreed, smiling. "You said you'd let me know, remember?"

He assured her he wouldn't forget, if he even had anything to relay once all was said and done. The more he thought about Lily Esch, the more saddened he was that she'd allowed herself to become disconnected from her church . . . and, obviously, from her family. It just didn't make sense—how could a wayward girl have such profound thoughts and ideas about life . . . and love?

··· ❯ ❮ ···

After a noon meal in which Menno, Emmanuel, and three farmhands had enjoyed Frona and Eva's cooking, Eva slipped her homemade card for Naomi into an envelope she'd found in Mamma's old writing desk. Eva and Frona then headed down Eden Road to Ida Mae's house for Naomi's birthday gathering. "Do ya think she'll be surprised?" she asked.

"Don't know why not," Frona replied. Like Eva, she wore her best blue dress and matching long apron.

"I'd thought of giving Naomi something from Mamma's dresser drawer—a pretty embroidered hankie or something like that, as a keepsake."

"Ain't a normal sort of birthday gift, is it?"

Eva glanced at Frona, who was apparently in a blue mood. "Would it be all right with you . . . when the time is right?"

"Don't we have more important things to think about today, Eva?"

Without saying more, she matched her pace with Frona's and kept quiet for the duration.

When they turned into Ida Mae's lane, several neighbors had already arrived, including Sylvia and Josie, as well as Naomi's daughters-in-law, Marian and Laura.

"*Ach*, I never thought my birthday was somethin' to celebrate much," Naomi said, cheeks pink as she sat in the kitchen. "Not at my age, anyway."

"You ain't that old, Mamma," Ida Mae said, taking a dish of nuts to the table.

Eva noticed the beautiful two-layer chocolate cake with two dishes of mints on either side. There was also a large glass pitcher of fruit punch. *She deserves a nice celebration*, Eva thought, glad Sylvia and Ida Mae had put their heads together and managed to get Naomi here without suspecting anything.

The party commenced with a fast game of Dutch Blitz, which got as loud and lively as Eva had ever experienced. When things calmed down a bit, Ida Mae wanted Naomi to open her cards and small gifts—a stationery set and a large-print leather New Testament several of the women had gone together to purchase.

Later, while they were enjoying birthday cake and ice cream, Naomi's older daughter-in-law, Marian, began to share about a young Amish couple from New Holland who'd purchased the farm next to them. "I'm not sure if they're kidding or not," Marian said, "but they said they'd removed the fire alarms, sayin' alls they need is a big bag of popcorn taped outside their bedroom door."

Marian had everyone's attention round the table. "According to her, if the house catches fire while they're asleep, the poppin' corn will wake them up."

Eva was amused and looked over at Frona, who muttered under her breath and shook her head.

"'Tis a joke, right?" Sylvia asked, her face reddening as soon as she'd spoken. "Surely that wouldn't work."

Eva kept waiting to see if Marian's expression changed, making it clear it was just a funny tale. But Marian took a bite of her cake and denied the other women's comments that this must have been something she'd read in *The Budget*.

"I wouldn't lie," Marian insisted. "You know well enough there are conservative Plain groups that prohibit fire alarms."

Naomi acknowledged this with a nod. "It's comforting to know you can wholly trust our heavenly Father no matter what you do—install a fire alarm or not, or put slow-movin' vehicle signs on your buggy. The Lord's will is highest and best."

We can depend on God's sovereign will, Eva agreed silently.

———

Afterward, while Frona and Ida Mae cleaned up the kitchen, Eva and Naomi went to sit in the front room, the sunlight pouring in around them. "Are ya sayin' that Alfred's declared himself to you?" Naomi asked.

Eva decided to tell her about the letters, the phone call, and the surprising invitation to move to Wisconsin. "The thing is, I'm not ready to take the serious step of relocating to allow him to court me."

"Did you let him know this?"

"I've been praying 'bout it, just as I told him I would. Honestly, though, I'm not leaning in that direction a'tall."

"If your heart's clearly against it, then you must say so." Naomi crossed her legs at the ankles, her feet bare. She studied Eva. "But can ya live with that decision?"

Eva sighed. "Maybe someday I might have feelings for him. Shouldn't I just be patient? Give things more time?" She looked toward the window, still feeling Naomi's gaze.

"Are ya concerned you'll end up a *Maidel*? Is that it, my dear?"

"Maybe so." Eva sighed. "I do want a loving husband and a family of my own someday."

Naomi rose and walked the length of the room, her hands clutched behind her back. Then, turning, she went to the tall, ornate grandfather clock and pulled the chain, watching first one weight rise, then the other. "You know what I believe?" She ambled back to sit again. "If the Good Lord wanted you married to Alfred, you'd find that kind of love in your heart right here and now, not hope it would blossom someday."

The wise, gentle words sounded like something Mamma might have said—Naomi cared so deeply about Eva's future.

"I daresay you can trust that your feelings aren't there for this young man. Nor your commitment."

Eva's mind was racing. "*Denki* for takin' time to chat, 'specially on your birthday."

Naomi laughed a little and folded her hands in her ample lap. "I'm doin' what I enjoy . . . spending time with one of Dottie's dear girls."

Eva began to feel better as she clung to Naomi's words on the way back to the house, where she and Frona set to shining their black church shoes for tomorrow's visiting Sunday.

"Did Naomi get you all straightened out?" Frona said, not looking up from where they were working out on the back porch. She dabbed more polish on one shoe at a time.

"*Jah* . . . guess I have a letter to write," Eva said.

"Poor Alfred."

Eva ignored her. "Naomi was so pleased over the party. Makes me think we oughta do this more often."

"Well, not on *my* birthday."

Eva disregarded that comment, as well. When she'd buffed her shoes to a shine and left them to dry, Eva excused herself and went upstairs, feeling all in.

Sitting on her bed with a sigh, she began to pray in earnest. When she was spent, Eva gave in to her mental exhaustion and leaned back on a pillow, promptly falling asleep.

The sound of a horse neighing woke her, and Eva discovered she'd rolled over onto her side during her nap. She stretched and yawned. The small clock on the bedside table showed that a half hour had already passed, and so deep her sleep had been, she must have dreamed, although she didn't recall the details. Even so, she was all the more certain that she could *not* marry Alfred. She'd had a taste of how it felt to really connect with someone, and even if she never heard from Jed again, it would not change the truth.

I won't settle for less than what God's put in my heart. A lasting and meaningful love.

Getting up, Eva walked to the writing desk and sat down with renewed resolve. She opened the narrow middle drawer and removed a single piece of stationery, then began to write.

Saturday, June 21

Dear Alfred,
    I hope you are doing well.
    I've given your invitation some thought, and after praying about it, I know I cannot accept.
    From what you've told me, it sounds like you're enjoying your work in Wisconsin, and the church district there, too. I don't doubt you'll make many new friends and sooner or later meet someone who loves you the way you deserve to be loved.
    Thank you for being so kind to me. You're a very fine man.

                        Your friend,
                        Eva Esch

36

ONCE noontime came and went, Jed had caught himself glancing at the black wall clock every half hour at work. He had paced himself so that at three o'clock, he would be ready to meet his driver out front. Since Kidron was only twenty miles or so away, Jed knew he'd have ample time to look around there, pick up the items on his mother's shopping list, and nose around for information about the young woman named Lillian. Even so, he really had no game plan. *I'm looking to the Lord for that*, he thought as he hung up his work apron and called good-bye to Perry and his uncle, then hurried out the door.

"If you've never been to Lehman's Hardware, you'll be astonished at all there is to look at," the driver, George Garver, told him. George had been driving the Amish for decades, according to Uncle Ervin, and came highly recommended.

"I've been there a good number of times," Jed said, opening his mother's list. "I have a few things to locate while I'm there."

"Well, you'll have no trouble, believe me. They've got just about everything."

"High on my mother's priorities is an antique brass shopkeeper's bell."

"Oh? Is she setting up shop out back?"

"Hard to say." Jed chuckled. "But she's real eager for some of Troyer's trail bologna. Daed'll like that, too."

"Ah, smoked over hickory wood—nothin' like it," George said, smacking his lips. "It really pays to buy in bulk, ya know. I'll bet she wants

716

some canning dome lids, too, and sugar. My wife gets all of her canning supplies at Lehman's."

Nodding, Jed tuned out the driver, becoming lost in his own thoughts. Was it even conceivable to think he could find Eva's younger sister? And if so, could he talk Lily, a girl he'd never met, into returning home to Eden Valley?

··· ➤ ⩤ ···

Just as Jed remembered, Lehman's Hardware was flawlessly organized into sections—hardware, kitchen wares, canning supplies, handcrafted items, wicker baskets of all shapes and sizes, and large appliances, such as wood-burning cookstoves and gas-powered ranges, too. There were clocks, radios, and batteries of all manner of type and voltage, and books such as *Baer's Almanac*, *The Foxfire Books*, and a book demonstrating how to build your own root cellar. He was drawn to the home and farming tools and spent several minutes perusing the shelves.

Then he wandered over to the maple-sugaring supplies, vegetable and herb seed packets, and old-timey poplar fruit baskets, fruit harvesters, and food grinders.

I sure could lose track of time here, he thought, going to get some help from a nearby clerk, a Mennonite woman around his mother's age who welcomed him, then proceeded to share that she'd worked at many different retail outlets, and Lehman's was the best of all. With her assistance, in short order, he managed to gather up all of the items for his mother.

At the checkout, when Jed finally asked his question, the cheery woman said she'd never heard of a Lillian from Lancaster County or anywhere else. "Are ya sure that's the name?" the clerk asked as she searched for the price on the brass shopkeeper's bell.

"It's quite possible she goes by Lily." It was a long shot, but it was all he had.

"If she's going English, maybe she's gone south, where there's a non-denominational ministry for runaway Plain youth . . . helps them get acclimated to the outside."

Jed drew a deep breath. "Are there other Amish folk I might talk to 'bout this?"

"Well, there's ol' Joseph over yonder." She pointed behind Jed as she rang up the total. "If anyone has an ear for that sort of news, it's him or his wife."

Jed hadn't seen the older gentleman whom he now spotted sitting near the cookstoves, arms crossed, a piece of straw between his teeth.

Cautiously hopeful, Jed took his purchases and went to dillydally by the barrels, kegs, and crocks, feeling a bit awkward as he moseyed over to the aforementioned Joseph.

"May I help ya?" the friendly Amishman asked, leaning forward as Jed approached.

Jed glanced down at his large bag. "I found what I came for, but I'm wonderin' if you might've heard tell of a young newly fancy gal by the name of Lillian."

Joseph pinched up his round face and removed the piece of straw. "*Newly* fancy, ya say?"

"Within a month or so," Jed added quickly, then recounted the snippet of information he'd overheard his uncle telling Perry. "Have you heard anything along those lines?"

The old man paused a moment, then nodded. "Honestly, I don't miss much of anything. And *jah*, I have seen a newly minted gal in here quite a bit, and it looks a little strange 'cause she's not the kind of young woman you see in a hardware store." He paused again. "At least not dressed like she was. Lillian, you say?"

Jed nodded, hopes rising again.

"Hmm." The older man gestured toward the door. "Can't place the name, but I've seen a fancy girl walkin' down the street, usually by herself, so I'm gonna say she lives no more than a few blocks or so from here."

"Which direction?"

"East," Joseph said, pointing. "Likely right off Emerson." Then he cleared his throat. "Well, I can't rule out Jericho." He shuffled a bit. "Well, no, prob'ly Emerson."

Jed sighed. *A lot of homes along Emerson.* But it was a place to start, if only he had more time. He thanked Joseph, then was headed for the main entrance when he heard the old man bellowing across the store, "Why don't ya try the machine auction over yonder? Somebody there might help ya get closer."

Jed thanked him again and headed out the door, making his way to the van parked in front of the store. There, he unloaded his purchases and told George he was going to wander about the auction. "Would ya mind waitin', say an hour or so?"

"Take your time." George smiled and waved his hand. He'd gotten himself a Coke somewhere and had the radio going.

Jed walked across Kidron Road, where town workers were applying a patch of asphalt. A few black carriages were coming this way, and on his side of the street, a fatherly looking Amishman was pulling a small red wagon with two young boys inside. The bearded man nodded and said, "Hullo," pulling off to the side of the road. *Probably headed to the auction, too.*

More Amish, two teen boys and a girl, came strolling along, the boys wearing black Preaching clothes and the girl in a pale violet dress and black apron. The girl ceased talking when she spotted Jed. Then, as they passed, she let out a hushed giggle.

Like Bettina might.

Jed decided to head to the auction, too, and started asking a few folks outside the building. Once inside, feeling nervous, he approached the first Amishwoman he saw and explained his mission, but she only shook her head, so Jed went on to the next woman. For the next forty minutes, and feeling increasingly foolish, Jed asked one person after another, but no one could recall an Amish teenager recently turned English living in the vicinity. "Could be anyone, really," one woman said. "There's a bunch of former Amish living round here."

And Jed began to wonder if Joseph was imagining things.

It wasn't long before the hour was up, and Jed had nothing to show for it. He headed across the street, ready to throw in the towel for today.

Deep in thought, he glanced up and saw a young couple, both *Englischers*, heading this way. The woman was especially pretty in navy walking shorts and a white sleeveless top, her short blond hair in soft waves as she talked to the man in jeans and a black T-shirt.

Jed nodded as they approached, then passed. He lifted his gaze toward the sky, taking in the warm air and wondering if he'd done the right thing, coming here.

He felt frustrated that he didn't know where to turn, or what to do next, so he prayed for God's help as the late afternoon sun played on the trees, dappling the leaves and casting shadows on the ground as he walked. Was the gate slamming shut on his hope of finding Eva's sister?

When he'd gone clear to the outskirts of town, Jed hurried back to the van, not wanting to keep his driver any longer. "Thanks for your patience," he said as he got back into the front passenger seat, realizing he'd met his dead end. On top of that, he'd missed supper back home. *I'll be eating warmed-up leftovers tonight.*

37

JED'S driver turned cautiously onto Kidron Road, mindful of the many cars and buggies. And as they crept along, Jed felt reluctant to leave the area for home, though he couldn't put a finger on why.

A few blocks up, Jed noticed the same blond girl he'd seen earlier walking alone wearing sunglasses, barefoot now as she dangled her white sandals. Oddly, her young man was hurrying down the street in the opposite direction with a determined gait, as if angry.

Wait a minute, Jed thought.

"Could ya pull over and park here, George?" he blurted.

The driver looked askance at him.

"This shouldn't take long." Jed opened the van door and got out. He waved to the young woman, feeling mighty awkward as he tried to catch her attention.

She glanced toward him and then turned away, heading up the sidewalk.

Jed continued briskly and did the only thing that made sense. He called her name, hoping she'd respond. "Lily!"

The young woman stopped walking and turned to face him, clearly startled.

Jed was a few yards away, hoping not to spook her any more than he already had, when she removed her sunglasses and squinted. "Lily Esch?" he called to her. He suppressed his smile, having stared at her photograph long enough to know this was, in fact, Eva's sister. "It *is* you."

Her mouth dropped open. "How do ya know me?"

Jed was close enough to smell her perfume. Her face was made up, her lips bright red. Jed had already mentally rehearsed what to say to her, aware that he had only so long to win her over. "I know your sister Eva," he said hastily.

A worried look crossed her countenance. "Did something happen to her? Is that why you're—"

Jed shook his head. "Eva's fine."

Lily seemed relieved, then scowled again. "Did she send you here to look for me?"

"*Nee,* but she's very worried."

Lily's eyes suddenly clouded.

"Can we talk?" Jed asked.

She glanced back at the retreating man, now more than a block away. "I'm not sure, I . . ." Fidgeting with the hem of her top, she stared at her feet.

Jed sensed his moment slipping away. "It's not too late to go home, Lily, if that's what you want."

Her head came up at the suggestion, and for a moment, he expected her to laugh at the notion, or to become angry at his presumption that she would *want* to return home.

He waited for her reply as she stared back at him, as though debating her reply. Once again, she glanced up the street, then back at Jed, her expression riddled with indecision.

I spoke too soon. "Listen, you don't have to decide this minute," he said now. "You can think about it."

"*Ach,* what a dumb thing I've done." Tears began to roll down her cheeks.

"Are you okay?"

"Not at all." She brushed away her tears, smearing her makeup so that she had dark smudges under her eyes. She looked at him curiously. "I'm sorry . . . who did ya say you are?" she asked in *Deitsch.*

"Jed Stutzman, from Berlin . . . not far from here."

"And you know Eva?"

She's not convinced.

"Eva gave me a look around her candy shop after we met at an auction near Quarryville a few weeks ago." He described the glass case filled with candies, naming some of Eva's favorites. "She loaded me up with her famous truffles for my trip home."

"How are they doin'—my sisters?" Lily struggled to ask.

"They're terribly concerned. Eva was distracted the whole time we were together, frettin' over you."

"And I'm stuck out here, trying to be something I'm not." She groaned as she fiddled with a heart-shaped necklace. "I could kick myself."

"There's only one way to fix a mistake," Jed said gently, looking back at George in the van. "Just don't keep goin' forward with it."

"Poor, dear Eva, what I've put her through! How can my family forgive me?"

The sight of this fragile yet beautiful girl crying right there on the street made him want to take care of her somehow. *But I'm a stranger to her. . . .*

"I guarantee they'll welcome you with open arms," he said quickly.

Lily shook her head. "I can't just go home as if nothin' happened."

"They love you. You're their sister."

"But I have no money, not even to make a phone call."

He saw his chance and took it. "Leave that to me. I'll get ya home, Lily."

At first, Lily was hesitant to get into the van with two men she didn't know.

George saved the day when Lily gave him the address of the Mennonite family with whom she had been staying. He lit up, saying they were his relatives. "That's one of my father's many brothers. You can call him if you want to double-check," he offered Lily.

Everyone's related round here, Jed thought, grateful for another divinely ordered facet to his search. *And to think I nearly gave up looking!*

Clearly reassured by this happenstance, Lily wasted no time in getting into the van. George drove them directly to the redbrick farmhouse surrounded by cornfields, where Lily quickly gathered up the few articles of clothing she'd brought, as well as thanked her kind host and hostess. It was time to say good-bye.

··· ➤ ➤ ···

As they neared Jed's parents' farmhouse in Berlin, George pointed out the neighbors, who were putting on a new roof. A half-dozen Amishmen were crawling around high on the pitch of the roof, nailing down shingles. "A fine day for such a big chore," George said.

It was so quiet behind Jed that he wondered if Lily had fallen asleep. She'd said very little once they'd left Hank Garver's place.

By the time they were turning into the familiar lane, Jed had decided how he would tell his family about Lily's need to spend the night. He hoped to leave for Lancaster before dawn tomorrow, a visiting day for Jed's church district. *We'll arrive in Eden Valley a little after noon, perfect for a surprise reunion with the Esch girls.*

Jed hadn't thought much farther ahead than that. The whole thing was in God's hands—He alone had arranged Jed's every step thus far.

George had already consented to drive Jed and Lily to Lancaster County. *I'll run up quite the bill with this driver,* he thought.

He paid George in cash, then helped carry Lily's small suitcase to the back porch, where he asked if she'd mind waiting in one of the hickory chairs there. "Don't worry," he assured her. "You'll like my family."

This is a first, he thought. *I've never brought home a fancy-looking girl before!*

"I'm sorry to put you out like this, Jed," said Lily, sounding chagrined.

"Believe me, no bother."

His mother was kindly accommodating when he mentioned he was helping a young woman return to her Amish community.

"Your father mentioned this to me last evening," Mamm said, her dish towel slung over her left arm. "I'll warm up some supper for the two of yous, all right?"

Just then, Bettina walked downstairs and into the kitchen. "There's a girl in shorts sittin' out on the porch," she said quietly. "Is this—"

"*Jah,* her name's Lily Esch," Jed said. "I'm taking her home to Pennsylvania tomorrow."

"You found her that quick?"

"It's a long story, and it all started with finding a photo of her in a book on the train. She's a sister of the girl I met back in Lancaster," Jed explained. "And I don't know what happened to change Lily's mind, but something definitely has. I guess I was in the right place at the right time— glory be." He wondered how ridiculous this must sound. "Honestly, I was ready to give up and head home when I felt prompted to stay the course."

724

"Kinda like a miracle?" Bettina asked.

"*Jah*, I'd say so." *Beginning with the book and the photograph.*

Bettina grinned at Jed. "Surely George can get Lily home without you tagging along, ain't so?"

"Why, sure, but . . ." Jed stammered. "I just want to make sure . . ."

Bettina's face shone with delight. "And you say she's the *sister* of the girl back in Lancaster?"

Jed sighed. Bettina was going to have fun with this. "*Jah*," he confirmed, crossing his arms, waiting for further grilling.

"You're gonna look like quite the hero, I'll say."

Jed nodded. "That's the goal."

"Plus, you'll see your friend again . . . uh . . . what's her name?"

Mamm spoke up at last, eyeing Bettina. "All right, young lady. Leave your brother be."

She laughed, and Jed couldn't help laughing with her.

Eyes dancing with humor, Mamm snapped her fingers at Bettina. "Hurry now. Go up an' make sure there's fresh bedding on the spare bed, won't ya, and stop being such a troublemaker!"

Bettina nodded, but before she left, she grabbed her mother's tea towel and snapped Jed's knee.

"Daughter!" Mamm exclaimed. "Behave yourself!"

But Bettina was already gone, scampering upstairs to finish her chore, leaving an echo of giggles trailing behind her.

Jed smiled at Mamm and headed outside to get Lily, who looked quite relaxed in her chair.

Lily glanced up and smiled. "I'll need to do something 'bout these clothes."

Jed pulled up another chair and sat, appreciating her concern. "Did ya bring along a change?" he asked, thinking also about tomorrow. Her attire would disappoint her sisters.

"Unfortunately, I got rid of everything Plain." Lily pulled on her hair and looked glum. "And this curly mop." She moaned. "How will I ever get it under a *Kapp*?" She confided in him, saying that the first thing she'd done upon arriving in Kidron was to get her waist-length hair cut. "Got a permanent wave in it, too, but it turned out too curly."

Jed smiled encouragingly. She looked beautiful to him, but he could see how it would be mighty tricky to get her hair into a bun. *Nee*, he thought, *impossible for many months. She must've been determined to be English.*

"Why am I tellin' you all this?" she laughed, blushing.

"It's okay, really. I have a sister who tells me strange things. Well, a few sisters, actually."

She smiled and covered her legs with her hands. "I wonder if one of your sisters might have a dress I could borrow. I look so, um, worldly."

To her credit, her shorts weren't short shorts like some fancy women strutted around in, but Daed wouldn't know what to think. Such attire simply wasn't respectful.

"It's just Mamm and my youngest sister inside, so now's a *gut* time to meet them and find out if Bettina has something for you."

Lily offered a relieved smile and gushed her thanks.

He picked up her suitcase and held the screen door for her. Tomorrow was another day, and hopefully it, too, would prove to be providential.

38

BETTINA joined Jed and Lily when they sat down to the reheated leftovers, something Jed assumed Mamm had privately asked his sister to do. Bettina had managed to work wonders with Lily upstairs. With the help of many bobby pins, Bettina had plastered Lily's hair down on both sides around her middle part. Bettina's lavender dress and black apron were equally transforming on Lily, who'd washed the makeup from her face, as well scrubbed as any rosy-cheeked Amish teenager.

While they enjoyed Mamm's leftover pork chops and onions, and mashed potatoes and gravy, Bettina kept the conversation going, and it appeared that Lily liked her rather well. *She spared Lily further embarrassment,* Jed thought, watching the two of them interact so comfortably across the table.

Lily glanced over her shoulder and must have noticed that Jed's mother had slipped outdoors. Leaning forward, Lily lowered her voice. "I've never known any fella to be so *ferhoodled* as my boyfriend," she said, eyes sad.

Bettina covered Lily's hand, her manner warm and gentle. "How did you meet him, Lily?"

Lily took a small breath and sighed. "I met him a year ago, when I was in Kidron with my friend Fannie Ebersol and her family. Mark was at the Thursday hay and cattle auction, where Fannie and I had gone for fun. Mark came right over while I was looking at some of the craftware. He said he was a horse trainer, and a very *gut* one. I guess I should've picked up on his bluster even then." She went on, reliving the relationship aloud, explaining how Mark had been eager to seek her out despite her Plain appearance. He'd even urged her to give a mailing address where he could write to her. "With Fannie's permission, I gave him her address, and he began writing to me there twice a week. For nearly a year, he never missed."

Jed couldn't get over how trusting Lily had been of an outsider, and as she described their quickly developing romance, she admitted that reading Mark's expressive letters had made her yearn for modern life.

"I mistakenly believed that if I could just live closer to Mark, I'd learn how to put my Plainness behind me," Lily told them. "But as it turned out, he became upset, even angry—that's what happened again earlier today, when he stormed away—and denied that I was givin' my all to be English, like him. 'You're more Amish than you know!' he hollered at me." Her chin trembled, and she bowed her head.

Bettina put her arm around Lily's shoulders. "Aw, Lily, it seems to me it was a *gut* thing he lost control of his temper and left ya. Don't you?"

"I never dreamed things would go downhill so quick." Lily was crying now.

Hearing Eva's sister talk about the futile relationship, Jed recalled her notes in the book. *More than anything, I long for a love that makes my heart sing,* she'd written on one of its final pages. He felt truly sorry for Lily. Her dreams and romantic wishes, all thought to have been found in Mark, had not been fulfilled in the least. *A young woman who was sadly misguided in looking for true love—enough to give up her family and faith.*

Jed made a call to Uncle Ervin's shop phone and left a message on the answering machine about his sudden trip to Lancaster County tomorrow. "Depending on how it goes, I may not be back till sometime Monday."

Later, alone in his room, Jed reread one of the highlighted passages that had popped out at him earlier in *Little Women: "Love will make you show your heart someday. . . ."*

He let the words flow through his mind, knowing he must return the novel to Lily tomorrow. It had been an enlightening journey in many ways, but it was winding down and coming to an end.

··· ⊱ ⊰ ···

That Lord's Day morning, Eva read aloud the first half of Psalm 139. "'O Lord, thou hast searched me, and known me. Thou knowest my downsitting and mine uprising; thou understandest my thought afar off.'" She continued through verse twelve, then passed the Bible to Frona, after which they had their silent prayers. Following their family worship, they discussed which relatives to visit today, an off-Sunday from Preaching service.

Frona mentioned two aunts they hadn't seen in some time. "But I'd like to be home for the noon meal, even if it's a bit later than usual," she said. "Honestly, I'm tired, and some peace and quiet might be in order."

Eva agreed, thinking Frona looked a bit peaked. *Being apart from Lily makes us both feel off beam.*

"I wouldn't mind if we just stayed put at home resting and reading," she said, her heart going out to Frona.

"Well, what if we made just one stop to Mamm's aunt Rose Anna down on Groff Road? In fact," Frona said, rising from her spot on the front room settee, "what if we took our time and walked over there?"

Eva liked the idea, considering the amount of time it would take to hitch up the horse and all. The sunshine and fresh air would feel ever so good.

"We'll leave midmornin', then," Frona said.

"And I'll take along some candies to spread cheer."

⋯ ⋗ ⋖ ⋯

Naomi sat outside with Abner on the front porch that late June Lord's Day, rocking on their chairs and enjoying each other's company. As was sometimes the case, neither said much, content as they were.

They'd had their devotions together after breakfast, and presently Naomi took her rest in the words of their Lord in the Gospel of Luke. *Take heed to yourselves: If thy brother trespass against thee, rebuke him; and if he repent, forgive him. And if he trespass against thee seven times in a day, and seven times in a day turn again to thee, saying, I repent; thou shalt forgive him.*

Closing her eyes, she prayed again for Omar. *May he find his peace in Thee, O Lord.*

She breathed the fragrance of nearby honeysuckle blossoms. *Sweet as Eva's candies.* And, lo and behold, across the way, Frona and Eva herself were strolling down their driveway toward the road. Eva was carrying a small white box with a pretty pink bow perched on top. *Must be some of her delicious concoctions,* Naomi assumed, waving to them.

Abner called, "A blessed Lord's Day to ya both!"

Frona merely nodded, but Eva smiled. "Same to you," she answered.

"Such a thorny road they must walk," said Naomi. "I pray the Lord God comforts their dear hearts."

Abner reached for her hand. "'Tis my constant prayer."

"Just look at them," she said.

"Last year at this time, they seemed so happy, remember?" Abner remarked. "All of them . . ."

Naomi refrained from saying what was on her mind. Seeing the Esch girls, just two of them now, made her heart ache so.

"Ain't possible to put a price tag on the love of family, *jah?*" Abner raised her hand to his lips and kissed it.

The van was heading into the populated retail and restaurant sector of Route 30, approaching the turnoff onto Route 896 to Strasburg. Jed's pulse beat a little faster as he recalled his first trip there by train. He reached behind him for the novel packed in his duffel bag on the seat opposite Lily but couldn't quite get it.

"Would ya mind handing that bag to me?" he asked, leaning around the front seat. "There's something I've been meaning to return."

Lily lifted the bag forward.

"I found this book on the train to Lancaster." He removed it from the bag and handed it to her. "It was stuck between the wall and the seat."

She accepted it with a puzzled frown. "You *found* this?"

"I was on the same train you must've taken to Ohio."

Lily's eyes widened.

"You left your picture in it," he added.

"*Ach* no," she muttered.

"Far as I know, Eva has the photograph now."

Lily shook her head, clearly embarrassed. "I'm sure she destroyed it, which is all right with me."

Jed recalled the words on the back of the picture but didn't want to open old wounds, considering all she'd been through. But his curiosity got the best of him. "Lily, I couldn't help noticing what you wrote: 'The best and worst day . . .'"

Lily smiled wistfully. She was quiet for a moment, as if gathering courage. "*Jah*, I was giddy with happiness, eager to please Mark. . . . I thought I loved him," Lily said softly, glancing at their driver, who didn't flinch. "I had a strip of pictures made for my boyfriend and kept one for myself. It was an impulsive thing to do . . . and terribly wrong."

Jed waited for her to say something about what she meant by the worst day, but he guessed it meant all that she was giving up for Mark in Ohio—her Amish life, her family, too. Besides, he didn't want to make her feel any more self-conscious than she already was.

"You must've thought I was shameless to have a picture made while wearing my *Kapp*."

"It was a bold move."

She reclined against her seat with a sigh. "I have so much to make up for."

They were deep into farmland now, whizzing past bank barns and giant silos and herds of grazing cattle. Often, Amishmen waved to them at the yield signs on the road. *Everyone waves*, Jed thought.

He was about to turn back in his seat when Lily spoke again. "So now *I'm* curious. How'd ya happen to meet Eva?" She was thumbing through the front pages of the novel. "There's certainly no address in here."

Jed considered that and told his story, leaving out the part about his fascination with the margin notes and underlined passages. "It was while I was in town to meet Jonas Byler that I ran into Eva at an auction. I thought she was *you*."

Lily laughed a little. "Honestly? So you and Eva obviously became friends in a very short time. Have you kept in touch . . . written, perhaps?"

He hesitated, then figured she'd eventually hear the full account from Eva anyway. "Unfortunately things ended on a sour note between us. You see, I didn't tell her about the photograph right away like I should have." He shook his head at the memory of Eva's shocked and befuddled expression that day. "Guess maybe she thought I was a little too taken with your photograph."

"That's silly." Lily laughed again.

Jed shifted in his seat, wishing he'd sat back there so they could talk more privately. This had become a very open conversation, considering George was hearing everything. "Actually, I was impressed . . . but not by your picture, Lily."

She placed her hand on her chin. "What do ya mean?"

"I paged through your book."

"Not exactly male reading material, *jah?*" she said.

Jed chuckled. "You've got that right. But honestly, I was taken with your notes and what you chose to underline."

She grimaced. "Jed—"

"What I'm sayin' is . . ." He paused. "Okay, I understand how foolish this might sound to you."

"You felt a connection with the person who wrote the notes?" Lily interrupted.

"Like minds, I guess you could say."

Lily smiled and looked at *Little Women*. "My sister Eva is the dearest person to me, so I'm not surprised you would be impressed with her notes. Her thoughts are all over these pages."

Jed frowned. "What?"

Lily's smile widened. "It's not my book, Jed. I only brought it along so I'd have something to remind me of Eva."

The book isn't Lily's? Jed could not have imagined this.

Their driver, George, burst out with a chuckle. "Well, Jed, ain't that something?"

Jed and Lily joined in laughing at his unexpected interjection.

Moments later, Lily's smile disappeared as she glanced out the window, wringing her hands. "Thanks for takin' me home, Jed. But I'm so nervous."

"They'll be excited to see you, so don't be," Jed said.

Lily sighed again. "I hope so."

Still amazed at Lily's revelation, Jed turned to watch for the turnoff to Eden Road as they headed south through rolling hills and pastureland. "Is this the quickest way?" he asked George.

"You seem anxious, too, Jed," said Lily with a titter.

He glanced over his shoulder. There was a mischievous glint in her eyes now that they'd shared each other's secrets. "Do I, now?"

"After what you've told me, I'm not sure which of us is more keyed up."

He chuckled. She was right. "Will ya put in a *gut* word for me with Eva?"

"I think you'll do fine without my help, honestly."

He asked to see the book again one last time. Opening at random, Jed noticed one of his favorite notes: *Yearning for true love points us to the all-lovely one—the great Lover of our hearts, the Lord Jesus.*

He wholeheartedly agreed. *To think it was Eva all along . . . from the very start,* he thought, closing the book.

The driver slowed to heed the speed limit on Eden Road, and as they gradually moved west, Jed spotted a line of lake willows set back beside a broad meadow covered in wild daisies—and then his eye caught something more. *Can it be?*

"Let's stop here," he instructed George. "Look there, Lily," he said, opening his door, then getting out and opening Lily's. "Your sisters are sittin' over on a fence. See them?"

"I can't believe this. It's Eva's and my spot," Lily said, her eyes dancing. Then, just as suddenly, she shrank back. "What if . . ."

"Follow me," Jed said, leading her.

Eva must have seen them; she was already running this way, her skirt tail flying. Frona was hurrying behind her, waving.

"Lily!" Eva called. "Oh, Lily, you've come home!"

Jed didn't have to look to know there were happy tears; he could hear Lily's sniffles. And then she took off toward her sisters.

Observing the heartwarming scene unfold, Jed hung back, letting Lily have the promised reunion in the grassy meadow.

"I don't have to introduce you to Jed, do I?" he heard Lily say.

Grinning, he reached down to pick one of the daisies.

Eva hugged Lily repeatedly—this was so unbelievable. Yet she'd longed for this moment every single day of Lily's absence. "God answered our prayers," she said, reaching for Lily's hand. "He obviously wanted you home, where you belong."

Frona started to laugh, though she was trying to smother it as she stared at Lily. "Your hair is, well, very different, sister."

Another curl sprung loose as Lily reached up to touch it. "It's the worst thing I've ever done to myself."

"*Ach,* it'll grow back," Eva said with a tug on Lily's hand.

Lily glanced back at Jed, standing yards away. "Someone came a long way . . . and not just to accompany me home," she whispered.

Eva's glance followed her sister's, and she was struck again by how handsome Jed was. But she wasn't surprised to see him with Lily. "I'm so glad Jed finally found you." The thought was bittersweet, but she was too happy to see Lily again to let anything interfere with her joy. "He must've been awfully determined to manage to track ya down once he got back to Ohio."

Lily broke free, her eyes alight with mischief. "*Jah*, I'll say he's determined. But the girl he was searchin' for was right here all along."

Eva was confused. "I don't understand."

Lily gazed earnestly into her face and gently held her by the shoulders. "Jed only came back with me to see you, Eva."

"Are ya ever so sure?" she whispered, guarding her heart.

"Come, Frona, let's head for the van," Lily said with a grin back at Eva. "We should leave the two lovebirds alone."

Looking toward Jed, Eva walked to him, her heart in her throat. *Does Lily know what she's talking about?*

"Hullo again," Jed said, offering a yellow daisy.

"*Denki* for bringin' my sister back to us. I don't know how to thank you."

"It was the Lord's doing, but I have to admit I asked Him for a hand. S'pose you didn't expect to see me again so soon."

She sniffed the flower, then looked up—his eyes were fixed on hers. "Seein' you is sure a welcome surprise, Jed." She couldn't help but recall the times she'd prayed for peace in the midst of her bewilderment. And to think Lily was home again, and here Jed was, standing before her, too.

Frona said he'd be back for more of my truffles, she thought, letting a smile take over her face.

They went to the van, where Jed asked George to take Frona and Lily home. "We're going to walk awhile."

George nodded. "At your service."

Lily let out a little giggle, and Frona shushed her before Jed closed their door.

"I want to tell you a little story," Jed said as he fell into step with Eva on the dirt shoulder.

"Sounds nice. I like a *gut* story." *Especially love stories*, she thought, wondering what was up his sleeve.

"This one's about a fella who was a little sweet on a girl he'd never met," Jed began. "And then when he naïvely thought he'd met her, he knew he was a goner—she was better than he'd imagined." He stooped to pick another flower and gave it to Eva. "Of course, he really confused things by not being straightforward with the girl—a mistake he's regretted ever since," he added. "But then there was a twist he wasn't expecting."

"Sounds like a mystery." Eva liked this.

"One with a startling surprise at the end."

"*Jah?*"

Jed nodded. "When the fella finally figures it all out."

"And does the story end happily?"

"Well, that part's unfinished," Jed said, catching her eye.

"Maybe we could finish it together," Eva suggested.

They walked along slowly, the breeze warm on their faces. Birds twittered high overhead, flapping their wings as they soared against the wind. Eva noticed the run-in shed the neighbors had recently built for their horses, and the way the trees moved gracefully, as if somehow swaying to a heavenly melody.

At last Jed said, "I was wondering if I could borrow your copy of *Little Women*."

Startled, Eva turned her head quickly but saw the twinkle in his eye. She played along. "I'm afraid that book's just for women, Jed."

He chuckled. "Well, I've already read a good portion of it. Besides, it's where I found Lily's photograph."

Jed told her the full story, and her eyes widened.

"So you've been reading my secrets, have ya?"

Jed slowed his stride. "Can you forgive me?"

"Absolutely not." Then she began to laugh.

He was grinning now and stopped walking to face her. "I said it before: I want to get to know you, Eva."

She smiled. "Honestly, I think you already do."

Eva couldn't help it—her heart sang as Jed reached for her hand and raised it slowly to his lips this shining Lord's Day afternoon.

Epilogue

IF someone had said even a month ago that I'd be courted long-distance by a serious beau, I wouldn't have believed it. In addition to Jed's frequent letters, he visits me every other weekend. Abner and Naomi have opened their home to him when he's here, welcoming him as warmly as Dat and Mamma would have—they're sure Jed Stutzman was hand-picked by God for me. It's hard not to blush when Naomi privately tells me such things.

As for Lily, her longing for the fancy world is a thing of the past, and she has been cheerfully received back by the People. Our neighbors have gone out of their way to drop by to visit, some bearing red and pink bleeding hearts picked from their flower beds. Lily has fully embraced the Old Ways and even plans to join church come mid-September. She revealed this recently when we wandered out to our old playhouse together, where she confessed to having taken the *Little Women* quote jotted down decades ago.

"When I left home, I needed something of my early roots," Lily explained. *"That's why I took your book, too."* While we were there, Lily also made a point of explaining why she hadn't written for so long after her disappearance. *"And even then, I had someone mail my one and only letter from Wooster, in case ya noticed the postmark. I was awful selfish, not wanting you to come lookin' for me."*

Together, we slipped the quote back into its narrow quarters along the window frame. It was a meaningful moment, and we decided that, perhaps in the future, one of our own little girls might discover the words hidden in the playhouse, since Menno has promised not to turn it into firewood. Thanks to Frona!

When I think of leaving Eden Valley behind someday, I know how much I'll miss my family, and our dear neighbors, too. But being Jed's bride will be worth the parting many times over—should he ask me.

I'm so thankful to have met a man who shares my heart. Nice as Alfred is, I could never have settled for him. Here lately Miriam Dienner told Naomi Mast that Alfred has met someone in Wisconsin. It's comforting to know, because Alfred deserves someone to love him, too.

During blistering August, when the cornstalks towered high over us and the humid days stretched longer than the nights, Jed came to Eden Valley for another visit and borrowed Abner's family carriage to take me riding.

He eased back in the seat and slipped his arm around me. "I've been talkin' with Jonas Byler about renting his carriage shop, and all the tools and equipment, too, just till I can afford to officially take over his business. My time with him and his many connections will be awful handy once I relocate to Lancaster County."

"Oh, Jed." Happy tears welled up. "You're movin' *here*."

We talked further about his plans, including Perry Hostetler's eagerness to run Uncle Ervin's buggy shop. Jed also wanted me to attend his sister Bettina's wedding in Ohio. "My family can meet you at last."

"Are ya sure you want to move away from them?"

"Why wouldn't I?" He cupped my face with his hands and looked deep into my eyes. "My heart's right here, Eva . . . with you."

The following May, when the lily-flowered tulips painted the beds yellow along my parents' former front porch, Jed dropped by to see me at Abner Masts'. I had accepted their kind offer to stay with them once Menno and his family settled into my childhood home last October.

Jed wanted to walk around "our" pond, and I felt sure something was up. The willow grove behind the Masts' house was bursting with new foliage, and there beneath the heavenly green canopy, Jed bent down and kissed my cheek. "I've been thinking 'bout something," he said furtively. "But everything hinges on one thing." He paused and smiled tenderly. "Only one."

I felt nearly breathless. "What is it?"

He rubbed his smooth chin. "I'm wonderin' if ya still have that recipe for those tasty truffles," he said solemnly.

"Believe me, I would never think of losin' that top-secret recipe!"

"*Des gut,* 'cause if you'll have me as your husband this wedding season, those truffles would be perfect at the feast."

I started laughing so hard I could hardly stop.

"Well, I hope *that's* not your answer," he said, feigning horror. "I mean, a hearty laugh instead of: '*Jah, Jed, I'll be happy to marry ya.*'"

"Oh, you!" I tried to regain my poise, taking a deep breath. "I would be honored to make irresistible sweets for ya all the days of your life."

Jed made a big show of wiping his brow. "*Ach,* you had me worried."

"Don't be silly." I rose up on my tiptoes to kiss his chin.

"My whole family will want to come for our wedding," Jed said. "That is, once I inform them that you've agreed to marry me."

"And I surely have." My heart was as full as a cream-filled bonbon.

"By the way, I've got an idea. My uncle, a few years older than Frona, might be her ideal match."

"Really? Surely not a *perfect* match?"

"Considering he's nearly as tetchy as Frona can be, they might be cheerfully prickly together."

I smiled. "And just when do ya plan to introduce this relative of yours?"

"At our wedding, of course."

"If it's a match," I said, the wheels turning in my mind, "Frona won't have much reason to worry anymore."

"And Lily?"

"Oh, I assume she'll continue being a mother's helper for Bena, at least for the time being. Or do you have more unmarried kin up your sleeve?"

Jed's laughter rang out. "I'll see what I can do."

Later, the sun beat hard on the gray vinyl roof of Jonas's buggy as we rode, coming upon Ida Mae's roadside vegetable stand down the way. We waved and she motioned for us to stop and have some ice-cold lemonade. "Freshly made," she said, bringing two tumblers to the buggy.

"What do ya know? A lemonade drive-in," Jed joked as he reached into his pocket.

Ida Mae refused his payment. "It's the least I can do for you two."

The word's out. I glanced lovingly at Jed.

Thanking her, we headed onward, and it was a joy to see this verdant area through his eyes, especially when he stopped in front of a modest clapboard house on the east end of Eden Road and pointed to the *For Sale* sign out front.

"Lookee there." He leaned forward. "I wonder how hard it would be for someone to build a candy shop in back." Jed turned to wink at me.

"Are you kiddin'?" I whispered, searching his dear face.

He admired the house again. "Seems solidly built—perfect, too, for tourists comin' in and out of the lane."

My smile was so big, I could feel it stretch clear across my face. "When can we see it?" I paused, realizing I was jumping ahead of Jed. "I mean . . ."

He pulled into the lane and checked his wristwatch. "The real estate agent should be arriving right about now."

My heart was beating wildly. To think I'd worried about having to someday leave my family and Eden Valley!

Later, after seeing every inch of the lovely house, we took our time while driving back toward Abner Mast's place. And as we turned into the drive, I noticed the front porch swing moving in the breeze.

"I know my parents would've liked you," I said when Jed came around to offer a hand.

"Somehow, I hope they know how happy you are, Eva."

"Oh, I trust so." I could hear Abner calling his lead cow in his down-to-earth way, ready to bring the herd home for afternoon milking.

"I'll water the horse," Jed told me. "You go in and talk to Naomi. I'm sure you want to."

With all of my heart, I did. I hurried across the yard, past Naomi's rainbow of peonies in mature bloom, a gift from Mamma years ago. Standing on the side porch, I took in the rich array of pinks, whites, and crimsons. *Gifts of love live on and on.* I thought of these flowers appearing every springtime . . . and of Dat and Mamma's sweet love for each other and for all of us.

Jah, they would rejoice in my love for Jed. *The man I was born to love.*

Author's Note

THIS particular story is sweet to my writer-heart for many reasons. I admit to being drawn to the Amish farmland around which I grew up, and the return to the setting of Eden Valley from *The River*—and the glimpses of Tilly Lantz Barrows and her growing family—are a result of my desire to step back into this rural area not far from my own childhood home. It was there that my sister and I read *Little Women* and acted out plays, just as the four celebrated March sisters did. I share Eva's love for that classic novel, as well as her yearning for a love that makes her heart sing.

Speaking of love, I am grateful to my own dear husband for his superb help with the first edit of the initial manuscript, as well as the appetizing breakfasts and lunches he so cheerfully makes when I'm on deadline. A thousand thanks and more, Dave!

To my faithful prayer partners—Jim and Ann Parrish, David and Janet Buchwalter, Aleta Hirschberg, Iris Jones, Donna DeFor, Judy Verhage, Amy Green, and my immediate family: God bless you abundantly for your care and faithfulness.

To my astute and very supportive editors—David Horton, Rochelle Glöege, Ann Parrish, and Helen Motter: I am in awe of your expertise, encouragement, and the way you seek to enhance my work.

To my research assistants, fact-checkers, and proofreaders—Hank and Ruth Hershberger, Fred Jones, Barbara Birch, Dave Lewis, Rhonda Abbott, Teresa Lang-Tsingine, Jolene Steffer, Cheri Hanson, and dozens of Amish and Mennonite readers and consultants: You continue to play such a vital role. Thank you!

To my lovely readers: Thanks for your cheery cards, gifts, emails, snail mail, and Facebook posts and messages. You are the dearest reader-friends ever!

Also, I am indebted to the writings of Louisa May Alcott, whose endearing letters and journals I have read and relished for decades, along with her renowned novel *Little Women*.

Researching my stories is part of the fun of writing, and while I strive for accuracy, sometimes it is necessary to fictionalize certain details. For the sake of this story, I devised a common passenger coach between Alliance, Ohio, and Lancaster, Pennsylvania. After all, Jed needed somewhere to discover that intriguing photograph!

My magnificent Eskimo spitz, Maxie, makes his debut in this story, brought to life again on the page as a reminder of happy childhood days in Lancaster County. And one of my favorite sweets is here too—peanut butter balls like Eva's own.

As I close this note, I think again of Dottie Esch's instruction to young Lily. May we all remember that the footprints made on life's journey can either lead others astray or lead them aright. Thankfully God is ever near to guide when we ask.

Soli Deo Gloria!

Beverly Lewis, born in the heart of Pennsylvania Dutch country, is the *New York Times* bestselling author of more than ninety books. Her stories have been published in twelve languages worldwide. A keen interest in her mother's Plain heritage has inspired Beverly to write many Amish-related novels, beginning with *The Shunning*, which has sold more than one million copies and is an Original Hallmark Channel movie. In 2007 *The Brethren* was honored with a Christy Award.

Beverly has been interviewed by both national and international media, including *Time* magazine, the Associated Press, and the BBC. She lives with her husband, David, in Colorado.

Visit her website at www.beverlylewis.com or www.facebook.com/officialbeverlylewis for more information.

More from Beverly Lewis

Visit beverlylewis.com for a full list of her books.

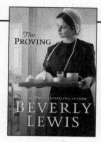

Having left the Amish life for the English world, Mandy Dienner is shocked when she learns she has inherited Lancaster County's most popular Amish bed-and-breakfast. The catch is she has to run it herself for one year—and coming home to the people she left behind won't be easy.

The Proving

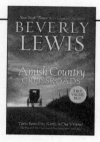

Three wonderful novels for the price of one! *Amish Country Crossroads* takes you deep into the fascinating world of the Amish with tales of family drama you won't soon forget. Includes *The Postcard, The Crossroad,* and *Sanctuary* (with David Lewis).

Amish Country Crossroads

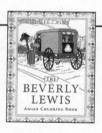

Experience the tranquil, homespun world of the Amish of Lancaster County, the setting of Beverly Lewis's many bestselling novels. This inspiring coloring book is filled with artful depictions of Amish life, including quilting bees, buggy rides, farm scenes, and more. As you color the charming images, you'll be blessed by gems of Amish wisdom and Scripture.

The Beverly Lewis Amish Coloring Book

⬦ BETHANYHOUSE

 Stay up to date on your favorite books and authors with our free e-newsletters. Sign up today at bethanyhouse.com.

 Find us on Facebook. facebook.com/bethanyhousepublishers

 Free exclusive resources for your book group! bethanyhouse.com/anopenbook

More from Beverly Lewis

Visit beverlylewis.com for a full list of her books.

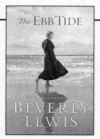

When Sallie Riehl takes a summer job as a nanny in beautiful Cape May, she forms an unexpected bond with a handsome Mennonite. Has she been too hasty with her promises, or will she only find what her heart is longing for back home?

The Ebb Tide

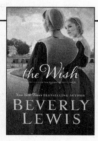

When Leona Speicher sets out on a mission to persuade a friend to return to the Amish church, will her dearest wish lead to her own undoing?

The Wish

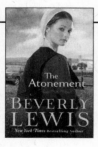

Troubled by past transgressions, Lucy Flaud rejects courtship by her longtime friend. Is it too late to embrace redemption . . . and the power of love?

The Atonement

◆ BETHANY HOUSE

More from Beverly Lewis

Visit beverlylewis.com for a full list of her books.

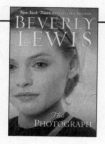

Old Order Amishwoman Eva Esch feels powerfully drawn to the charming stranger from Ohio. Will the forbidden photograph he carries lead to love or heartache?

The Photograph

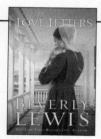

When Marlena Wenger is faced with a difficult decision—raising her sister's baby or marrying her longtime beau—which will she choose?

The Love Letters

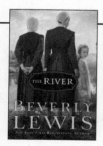

When two formerly Amish sisters return home for their parents' landmark anniversary, both are troubled by the past and the unresolved relationships they left behind.

The River

◆BETHANYHOUSE